CITY OF KEYS

NIGHTMARKED
BOOK III

KAT ROSS

For my family at Silk City Coffee

Isles of the Eastern Witchdom

Chapter One

Malach hefted the pickaxe, sweat plastering the linen shirt to his back.

Which witch would it be today?

Which witch?

Time blurred in the pit, each day bleeding into the next, but if it was Luansday, that meant Darya.

He pictured her cool pewter eyes and plump mouth. Shards of rock exploded as the pick bit into the canyon wall. A seam of jaxite glimmered in the sunlight. He attacked the surrounding sandstone, chiseling a furrow. Six more blows and a sizable chunk of the mineral broke off. Malach tossed it into a bucket. He tipped his last waterskin back, draining it, then resumed hacking. The dull black seam widened as he gouged deeper. Jaxite tended to shatter, but the bigger the pieces, the faster the bucket filled.

Experience had taught him to seek out the nearly imperceptible flaws that would liberate the most jaxite in a single blow. He traced a calloused fingertip along the fine striations, then raised the pick, bringing it down at a precise point the size of his thumbnail.

Crack!

Malach leapt back as a head-sized chunk broke free. He hefted it in one practiced motion and thunked it into the bucket. Then he lugged the bucket to the winch site, grabbed an empty one, and returned to the seam. A shimmery, sweltering haze rose from the canyon floor as he picked up the last bucket and hiked out, passing dozens of other dusty men. He buckled into a harness and signaled to a foreman above. The straps creaked tight. He was winched to the surface of the pit, crab-walking along the slanted walls.

A young witch with long russet hair waited for him at the top. She wore a complicated dress made from a single narrow length of silver-threaded cloth. It wrapped around hips and bosom and then all the way down one arm to the wrist, leaving the other arm and shoulder bare.

He found the garment erotic—a single tug and it would all come apart—though not on her. Stacked rings adorned her fingers, each set with a different jewel. More shone in her hair and on a gold chain at her throat.

"Hello, Darya," he said with an easy smile, unstrapping his helmet and tossing it on a pile.

The witch smiled back. "You look well, Malach."

All his minders spoke fluent Osterlish, with the quick, lilting accent of Dur-Athaara. They fell into step together, heading toward the barracks.

"The foreman praised you," Darya remarked. "He says you are tireless."

"I find hard work satisfying."

Her fey eyes met his. "Do you? I am glad." Darya fanned herself with a straw hat. "I heard six men collapsed from heatstroke today. It's been a brutal summer."

Lithomancy demanded a steady supply of raw ore, gemstones and crystals. The Mahadeva Sahevis, the witch-queen, had kept her promise of sweating the arrogance out of him, setting him to work at the pit mines that honeycombed the island.

The men were well-fed and well-paid—even Malach. He'd started with four days on, three off, six-hour shifts. When it became clear that there was no way off the island, he'd asked them to double his hours. The foreman had raised an eyebrow, clearly expecting him to crumble, but Malach threw himself into the labor, punishing himself until he fell into his bunk like a dead man each day. Gradually, his body hardened to steel. Now he worked five dawn-to-dusk shifts in a row. It was mind-numbing, but at least he had something to vent his frustration on.

When the witches caught him on the beach and brought him to Dur-Athaara, Malach had been confident he'd find a way to escape. But they'd burned every ship and severed contact with the outside world. Three times, he'd run away and stolen fishing dinghies. They all floated straight into the witch-queen's grotto, no matter which way the currents ran. The Mahadeva seemed to find his escape attempts amusing. Like a child allowing an ant to scurry away before scooping it up with a leaf and returning it to the habitat.

"There's shade in the canyons," he said. "Except at midday. But I'm used to it."

Darya nodded, looking pleased. "It is well you have found a useful occupation, *aingeal dian*."

His jaw tightened. Fallen angel, the witches called him. It only reminded him of everything he'd lost. Nikola Thorn was the reason he worked himself to the brink every day. The worry for her was a rat gnawing at his gut. It never stopped. If anything, it worsened with every passing day.

"The Mahadeva is wise. Has she asked about me?"

"She does not need to," Darya replied. "The Crone sees all."

A lie. The witch-queen was powerful—but not a god. She'd admitted that she didn't know where Nikola was or what had become of her. Only that she had borne his child and the two of them lived.

That was months ago. Anything could have happened in the meantime.

"Tell the Mahadeva that I wish to speak with her," Malach said. "Please."

He said the same thing every day. And every day, the witches gave the same reply.

"I will convey your request." Darya laid a hand on his arm. He tried not to flinch at her touch. "But when she wants to see you, she will let you know. Be at ease, Malach."

He turned away before she could glimpse the loathing in his eyes and joined a line of men at the outdoor showers. Dur-Athaarans had no modesty about naked bodies. The showers were wide open to public view. He stripped down and let the lukewarm water beat against his skin. Within seconds, the spray sluiced away the dull coating of rock dust. Colors bloomed on the Marks across his chest and arms—bloody red, golden amber, deep greens and blues. All worthless.

He lathered twice with a cake of soap, fingers probing the ridged muscles of his abdomen. A scar above his hip marked the spot where the priest had stabbed him. Malach didn't care about that. It was what the witches had put inside him that made him want to strangle Darya with her own dress. He poked and prodded, but the kaldurite stone was lodged too deep to feel. It didn't hurt, or interfere with anything but his ability to touch the ley.

The only thing that mattered.

Malach grabbed a towel from a stack next to the showers and dried off. He kept his back to the witch, but he felt her eyes on him. A tingling, itchy sensation that started at the nape of his neck and worked its way down his spine. Somehow, he always knew when a witch was near and watching. Was Darya attracted? Repulsed? Or did she feel nothing for him?

He wore long sleeves and buttoned his shirt to the neck, but the other men knew he was a mage. They shunned him, which suited Malach just fine. Many were former slaves who'd been given sanctuary in Dur-Athaara. For all Malach knew, he might have sold some of them to the witches himself.

He kept to himself, eating alone in the barracks and going into the city every second Luansday to see Tashtemir. A witch always accompanied him on these expeditions, usually Darya, but sometimes one of her sisters. They treated him with condescension—like a naughty boy capable of mischief but who could learn correct behavior with a little discipline. Since his last failed escape attempt several months ago, Malach had been unfailingly polite and obedient. Let them think he'd given up.

Darya had no clue that she was about to learn a lesson herself.

"I was thinking of paying a visit to the temple," he said, drying his hair with the towel. He gave her a wry smile. "Would you care to join me?"

"Ah, let me think about it." The witch pretended to mull it over. It was a joke he'd started with her a while back. As if they would ever allow him to roam loose unattended. But the small intimacy was another thread he'd tied to her.

"Why, yes, Malach, I would be happy to make a devotion to Valmitra." Darya stuck the straw hat on her head and moved to the shade of a date palm. "I will wait for you here."

Malach tossed the wet towel in a bin. He went inside to his bunk, donned a fresh shirt, and knotted a Rahai around his waist. It was one of the few aspects of life here he'd come to appreciate. The simple skirt-like garment was loose and comfortable, much more so than his heavy cardinal's robe. It had no pockets, but he had no belongings, so it made little difference.

He joined the witch at her ancient automobile. It had been sitting in the sun and the leather seat burned his ass straight through the Rahai. Malach rolled the window down and stuck an elbow out as she pressed the starter button. The engine coughed and sputtered to life. They started down the winding road from the highlands at the center of Tenethe. Low, rugged mountains ringed the Pit, but the scenery grew lush as they drove south. Colorful flowers bloomed everywhere, filling the air with heavy perfume.

"How old is this thing?" Malach studied the array of knobs on the dashboard. Few functioned for their original purpose anymore—definitely not the one that promised climate control.

Darya laughed. "Not Second Dark Age, but close."

"How do you keep it running?"

"We have a guild of mechanics that goes back hundreds of years." Her lips quirked. "Why, do you wish to learn?"

"How's the pay?"

"More than you're making now. But I'm afraid the trade is hereditary. Passed from mother to daughter."

"No men?"

"A few. Not many."

"Why?"

She swept an errant lock of hair from her eyes, then took the hat off and tossed it into the back seat. "That's just how it is, Malach."

He was still trying to get a handle on how the witches viewed men. The culture was matriarchal, yet he sensed no resentment at the camp. The witches who came for him were greeted respectfully and he'd never heard a word against them —not even after they were gone.

"Do you think we're too stupid to be mechanics?" he wondered.

Darya frowned. "I do not think you're stupid at all. Obviously, your physique is suited to heavy labor. But men also work in the markets, as you have seen. They are potters and weavers. And they care for the children, of course. It takes great stamina and patience to work in the creches."

"Uh-huh."

"You are skeptical, Malach, because you've been taught

different ideas of what it means to be a man. That is all. The people who founded this land—men and women both—decided to build a society that would not repeat the mistakes of the past. Men are the more emotional sex. It makes little sense for them to hold positions of authority." She glanced at him. "You cannot argue with the fact that while the Via Sancta tears itself apart, we are at peace."

The knot in his chest tightened. "Have you heard anything?"

The car crested a rise and the azure sweep of the sea came into view. An offshore wind farm stood sentinel over the waves, white blades spinning slowly.

"I don't mean to mislead you. I have no news from outside." The witch gave him a *chin-up* smile. "But you're much better off here, I am certain of it. Try to be patient and trust in the Mahadeva's guidance. When you are ready, she will let you return."

How many times had Malach heard the same refrain? Each time, it sounded more hollow.

"Are you a mother, Darya?"

She shook her head.

"Then you can't know what it's like to be a parent yet never to have seen your own child."

"No," she agreed. "I do not know." A sharp glance. "But nor do I pity you. There are those among us who would see you under lock and key. Be grateful for the indulgence you have been given."

Malach bit back a sarcastic retort. "I am. But I cannot help pining for those I left behind."

He lurched forward, bracing a palm on the dashboard as the witch braked for a herd of spotted goats. Her crappy car lacked seatbelts, too.

"I didn't expect a nihilim to be so sentimental." Darya tapped the horn. The curly-haired boy herding the goats shooed them to the grassy verge and the car crept past. "Isn't self-interest your central belief?"

Malach ignored the jab. "If you refer to the Via Libertas, its central tenet is freedom," he said in a mild tone. "Personally, I have no belief in anything."

"You wear the Mark of the Broken Chain around your neck."

"It's given to every mage from Bal Kirith."

"So you have no faith of any kind? I pity you."

Malach eyed her slender neck. If he could snap it before she found a way to retaliate . . . but every stone on her fingers held protective power. And killing Darya, however satisfying, would only gain him an extended stay in a cell.

"You can pray for me at the temple," he said.

Her face darkened. "Do not blaspheme, aingeal. It was your kind who—" She cut off, hands tightening around the wheel.

"Who did what? Why do you hate us so?"

"I do not hate you," she ground out. "You cannot help the sins of your forebears. But I will not pray for you!" She stared straight ahead. "Be silent now."

A tiny smile curled the corner of his mouth. "As you wish, Darya."

Chapter Two

The dirt road widened and the crowds thickened as they approached the capital of Dur-Athaara. It was a backwater compared to Novostopol, the only other city Malach knew, and lacked the frenzied hustle of that great metropolis. People moved at a leisurely pace, pausing to chat with food vendors or rest in the botanical gardens that wound through the landscape like green arteries.

None of the stone buildings had square corners. Every street and wall curved in serpentine fashion, following the canals that allowed the sea to flow in and out according to the tides. The odor of spiced fish mingled with smoke from the pyres along the esplanade, where Athaarans brought the bodies of the dead to be burned.

The practice had seemed grim the first time he saw it, but as they drove past the wide blossom-strewn steps leading down to the water, Malach sensed the peaceful solemnity of the people gathered there. He turned his head to watch as a corpse wound in bright saffron cloth was set alight and the bier gently pushed into the waves. Voices raised in song. Not a dirge but a joyful celebration of life.

They drove across an arching bridge and the massive

Temple of Valmitra came into view. It was circular, the walls carved with overlapping scales, each inlaid with precious metals and glittering jewels. A glass dome capped the structure, bathing the interior in light. Darya parked in the lot reserved for witches and they entered through a side door, pausing to take their shoes off.

The temple looked more like a menagerie than a place of worship. Lizards clung to the vine-covered walls and skittered through the shadows. Serpents of varying sizes slithered freely across the cracked stone floor. Malach counted sixteen witches, along with twelve acolytes whose eyes had not yet turned gray. They all turned to stare at him. Darya smiled, though her gaze was cool.

"You may go visit your friend, Malach," she said. "Find me here when you are done."

She broke off to join a group at the main stone altar, which was fashioned in the image of a serpent with three necks but only two heads. Scented smoke drifted from a pair of fanged mouths. A garland of white flowers draped the severed stump of the third. Dead mice lay on the stone slab. Malach watched in queasy fascination as a cobra emerged from a narrow crevice, spread its jaws, and devoured one of the rodents whole.

The temple was open to all. Besides the witches, devotees of Valmitra came and went, leaving offerings of fruit or bowls of milk. They formed a line, each bowing three times, foreheads lightly touching the floor, a whispered prayer on their lips. The men wore Rahais, the women dresses or loose trousers. A heap of straw sandals sat near the main doors.

Malach made his way through the crowd, eyes locked on the ground. Some of the serpents were harmless. Others less so. The witches kept a supply of antivenin on hand, but he had no desire to test its effectiveness. Tissue-thin wisps of shedded skin rustled beneath his bare feet as he took a flight of winding stone stairs behind the altar down to a warren of rooms below the temple. Malach's steps slowed as he reached the open door of the caretaker's consulting room. He muttered an oath under his breath.

Tashtemir Kelevan knelt next to a python that stretched from one end of the room to the other. Its skin was patterned in gold and black whorls that would blend perfectly with the dappled sunlight of a forest. Malach had run across constrictors that big in the Morho. They weren't fast, but once they got hold of you, it was over.

"Cardinal!" A smile of delight lit the vet's long, mournful face.

Malach returned the smile but kept well back. "What's wrong with it?"

"Fungal infection," Tashtemir explained, moving a damp cloth in gentle strokes along the side of its massive head, where patches of white discolored the skin. "Poor darling. But with repeat treatments, she'll be fine." He laughed at Malach's hesitation. "She won't harm you."

"How do you know?"

"Because she's already eaten." He patted a lump in the center of the snake. Malach didn't ask what the python had dined on, but he mastered his fear enough to enter the chamber.

Tash wrung out the cloth over a bowl and stood. The Rahai was a versatile garment that could be worn in different ways. Tash's draped over one shoulder and fell just above his knees, covering part of a hairy chest.

"The treatment is my own recipe. I found an excellent apothecary at the market, though he's starting to run low on everything because of the embargo." He sighed. "I'll just have to make do somehow. How are you?"

"Eager to be gone," Malach said. He stepped back as the snake lifted its head and slowly slithered out the door. "Did you get the name?"

"I might have." Tash started replacing an array of glass

bottles on their shelves. "But I still urge you to reconsider this plan."

"Just give it to me."

Tash turned. His wavy dark hair had grown long, but that wasn't why he looked different. There was a softness to his face. A light in his eyes. It took Malach a moment to realize that the southerner was happy here.

"If it was a matter of simply cutting it from your skin . . . but the stone is deep inside you. I have no idea if this doctor is skilled." Tash glanced at the door, lowering his voice. "A lot of shady people are desperate for money right now, Cardinal. The black market dried up when the Mahadeva banned trade with the Curia. Everyone comes to pay respects to Valmitra and I've gotten to know a few of them, but that doesn't mean they're trustworthy."

"Then you do it."

Tash gave him a weary look. "As I've already told you a dozen times, I don't have the instruments to attempt it. Nor would I even if I did. I can sew up a wound and cure a case of indigestion, but I'm not a surgeon."

"How much will it cost?"

"A lot."

Malach stared at him in silence. Tashtemir finally shook his head. "Six major gems or the equivalent in lesser stones."

Malach did a swift calculation. The most prized gems were diamonds, rubies, sapphires and emeralds. He was paid in lesser stones and had saved all his wages, but the price was staggering.

"I don't quite have it. Can you lend me the rest?"

Tash made a dour face, then nodded reluctantly. "There's a commission for the middle-woman. I suppose I can cover that, too."

"What did you tell them about me?"

"Nothing. These people don't ask questions, Malach." He took a folded piece of paper from the waist of his Rahai but didn't hand it over. "If the place looks dirty, promise me you'll call it off."

"I'm not a fool."

"That's debatable." He eyed the scar along Malach's hip. "You just healed from the last impromptu surgery."

Malach gave him a desperate look. "It's worth the risk. I have to find Nikola. And my child. I have to."

Tash's face softened. "I know. Just wait here, I'll get the stones."

Malach leaned against the wall while Tash went to his rooms in an adjacent building. The cloying smell of incense churned his stomach. Or maybe it was the prospect of being cut into again. Unlike his cousin Dantarion, Malach did not enjoy pain. But there was no other way. Once he had the ley back, he could compel one of the witches to help him escape. If the Mahadeva caught him, he'd use it against her. Never again would he allow them to get close enough to force one of those cursed kaldurite stones into his mouth.

Tashtemir returned with a small pouch. Malach tucked it into his boot.

"You look like a wild man, Cardinal," Tash said. "Don't they let you shave?"

Malach scrubbed a hand through his beard. "I'm too tired to shave," he admitted. "And there are no mirrors. I'd likely cut my own throat."

"Well, I would be quite alarmed if I encountered you in a dark alley." He clucked his tongue. "And you used to be so fussy about your appearance."

"Me?" Malach laughed. "You were the dandy. Do you miss your silks and lace cuffs?"

"Not really. The Rahai is sensible for this climate. Do you wear it in the pit?"

"They give us trousers and shirts, but no one except me wears a shirt. Too hot."

"It is a ghastly penance the witch-queen has set you."

"No worse than yours," Malach replied. "I would take the pit over a python any day."

Tash grinned. "Just be glad there are no crocodilians in the isles. They, too, are considered the children of Valmitra."

"How long do you plan to stay here?"

"The Imperator's term expires in one year. Then I shall decide—if the ban on travel is ever lifted."

Malach frowned. "Could they maintain it indefinitely?"

"No one knows. But with the Void broken, the mages must be waging open war against the Curia. I expect the witches will keep their distance until the dust settles." He looked at Malach seriously. "Who do you think will win this contest?"

Malach shrugged. "If I've learned anything, it's that winning is a subjective concept. They have greater numbers. We have greater control of the ley. A conflict like that can drag on for decades. One wonders what will be left at the end."

"Have you become a pacifist?" Tash asked with a laugh. "What happened to the ruthless, bloodthirsty beast I know and love?"

"Oh, he's still here." Malach smiled. "Older, yet seemingly no wiser."

Tashtemir nodded. "Only two things are infinite, my friend. The ley and human stupidity." A rueful grin. "And I am unsure about the first. Come, make yourself useful and refill these jars."

Malach spent the next hour helping Tash in the examining room. He was permitted to treat a cut on a tiny salamander. It was a pretty creature, not slimy but cool and dry. He let it sit on his wrist afterwards, marveling at the vivid orange hue and delicate spots.

"She likes you," Tash said.

"How do you know?"

"Because she hasn't run away." He saw Malach's expression and swallowed. "I didn't mean—"

"It's all right," Malach said dryly. "Nikola was right to leave. And I've no idea if she wants to see me again. But I won't know until I find her, will I?"

Tash nodded. "I think she only did what she thought she had to. But I saw the way she looked at you. She tried to conceal her feelings, but my time at court taught me to read volumes in the smallest gesture. And hers were obvious."

That pleased him. Malach sat very still, communing with the newt, while Tashtemir mixed his elixirs and tidied the examining room.

They'd met three years before when Tash was caught at the docks in Novostopol by three Masdari mercenaries hoping to claim the bounty on his head. Sensing an opportunity, Malach had fought them off, striking a bargain to bring Tash back to Bal Kirith, where even a veterinarian was better than no doctor at all. After some prodding, Malach learned that Tashtemir had bedded the Golden Imperator's wife. Not being the forgiving sort, the Imperator had vowed to see him sorely punished for it. Tash was hiding out abroad until her seven-year term ended, at which point he hoped to return and secure a pardon from her successor. Tash always seemed sad when he spoke of his distant homeland. For the first time, Malach understood the bitter longing of an exile.

"The surgeon is expecting you tonight." Tashtemir laid a hand on his shoulder. "I suppose we may not see each other again so . . . good luck, Cardinal."

Malach had few friends in the world, but the southerner was one of them. He clasped Tash's hand, then pulled him into an embrace.

"I know what you're risking for me. I won't forget it."

He found Darya at the altar feeding crickets to a blue-tailed skink. The creature was comically fat, with tiny hind legs that could barely support its weight.

"How was your visit, Malach?" she asked cheerfully.

"Tashtemir is content here. It lifts my spirits to see him."

"You see? It is not as bad as you make out." She seemed to have forgotten their spat. "We are lucky to have you both. My sisters tell me Tashtemir is the best caretaker they've ever had. His experience in the bestiary of the Imperator was invaluable. Now, is there anywhere else you wish to go? The bazaar?"

"No." He covered a yawn. "I'm exhausted."

"Have you eaten?"

He shook his head. Darya made a sound of reproach. "You must take better care of yourself, Malach."

The witch bought him two chicken kabobs from a vendor in front of the temple. Malach ate them in the car as they drove back to the pit.

"You have tomorrow off," she said as they pulled up at the barracks. "Would you like to see some sights? The north end of the island has orange groves with walking paths. Or perhaps an afternoon at the beach?"

"I prefer to sleep."

For four months, since his last escape attempt, Malach had not deviated from a rigid schedule; work like a maniac for five days straight, visit Tash, then stay in his bunk sleeping for two.

A notch creased Darya's forehead. "Are you depressed, Malach?"

The concern in her voice made him want to laugh. "Why would I be depressed?"

She gave him a flat look. "I know you're unhappy. But the sooner you accept your situation the swifter the time will pass."

He smiled. "I thank you for the offer. Perhaps next time. But as you said, the heat takes a toll. Goodnight, Darya."

He walked to the barracks, skin crawling the entire way. As he reached the door, the engine started. He heard gravel crunch under the tires as she drove away.

Malach found his bunk and lay down, lacing his hands behind his head. The fog of male bodies was potent, but he hardly noticed it anymore. On either side, men snored and sighed in their sleep. He watched the moon rise beyond the line of windows. When it was high and full, he lifted his mattress and took out a fat leather purse. He added Tash's gems to it and stuffed the purse in his boot. Then he crept between the bunks and out the door.

Torches burned in the pit, casting a reddish glow on the rocky ground. The mining never stopped. Night shifts were coveted since they were cooler, but Malach had never asked for one. If he was on shift, there would be no way out of the pit until it ended.

And night was the time for running.

The witches didn't set a full-time guard on the barracks. They were confident he couldn't get off the island, but whatever magic they'd worked left him the leeway to move around Tenethe—for a brief time at least. He steered clear of the pit's rim where most of the activity took place and followed the road toward the city. Driving, the trip was about twenty minutes. On foot, it took him the better part of two hours. But Tash had drawn a crude map and Malach found the address with no trouble.

It was in a quiet area fronting one of the canals. Dr. Fithen lived in a round two-story house with blue and white flowers blooming on the windowsills. Lamplight gleamed on the still, dark water. He studied the house for a moment. Well-kept and respectable with a small plaque on the door bearing the words *Medical Clinic*.

His nerves hummed, but nothing about the place tripped the danger wire in his brain. Malach knocked. The door was answered by a small birdlike woman with a sharp nose and short graying hair. He gave Tash's name and she nodded, admitting him into a reception area with three wooden chairs. A younger woman in spotless whites emerged from a hall. Neither had the eyes of a witch.

"This is Surena," Dr. Fithen said. "My assistant. Did you bring the fee?"

"I'd like to ask some questions first."

"Of course."

"How long have you been practicing medicine?"

She looked amused. "Thirty years. I started as a midwife but received my full training when I was twenty-six. I've performed dozens of surgeries."

"How many were successful?"

"All but one. The patient had a seizure on the operating table. But that was due to a preexisting condition." She looked him over. "You're a healthy-looking man. Unless there's a history I don't know about?"

Malach shook his head. "How long will I be out?"

"A few hours. Then you'll be moved to recovery upstairs. I'll allow you to stay in the room for three days. After that, you must leave."

"How big of an incision are we talking about?"

"With luck, quite small. I'll have to cut through the abdominal wall, but no more than half an inch in diameter. Then I'll use forceps to remove the stone and suture you up."

That seemed acceptable. "May I see the surgery?"

"Naturally." She nodded at her assistant. "I'll go wash up."

Surena took him to a room down the hall. She flipped on a bright overhead light. It held a gurney and IV stand with a bag of clear fluid. There wasn't a speck of dust anywhere. Malach took the purse from his boot and handed it over.

"Wait here," Surena said. She withdrew, presumably to count the gems. He sat down on the edge of the gurney. Steel instruments gleamed on a white cloth. The room smelled of antiseptic. Malach pressed a sweaty palm to his stomach.

He had lied when he told Darya he believed in nothing. The twin comets he'd seen at the Mahadeva's cavern were a sign from the ley. He still didn't know what it meant, but he was not the same man who had first met Nikola. She had changed him—or simply introduced him to an essential part of himself that he'd never met before.

Malach knew his shortcomings were not magically gone. He had too many for that. But he would protect her to the death. Be loyal to his last breath. She befuddled him and set him aflame in the same moment. She made him laugh. She terrified him.

Love, he understood now, was greater than the sum of its parts. He could tally up all of these things and they still fell short of the depth of the whole. She didn't feel the same way about him, but it didn't matter. Finding her was worth any price.

He looked up as Dr. Fithen entered the room, now wearing crisp whites. A cloth cap covered her graying hair.

"Where exactly is the stone?" he asked as Surena took a needle from a tray and filled it with liquid.

This made all the difference in how much damage he sustained.

"I'll find it through external palpation, don't you worry," Dr. Fithen said. "Undress, please."

He unbuttoned his shirt and took it off. Then he tugged the Rahai loose and handed that over, too. Fithen's gaze swept across his Marks.

"Lie back." She winked at him. "You won't feel a thing, I promise."

Malach levered himself onto the gurney, a chill sweeping his bare skin. Surena approached with the needle. Her bland expression unnerved him. Tash had told them nothing, yet neither woman seemed surprised at the Marks. His gut tightened. Something felt wrong.

"Wait," he said.

In one quick motion, she jabbed his biceps and depressed the plunger. Malach slapped her hand away. The needle fell to the floor.

"I told you to wait!" he snapped.

The two women stepped back, regarding him warily. "Are you changing your mind, aingeal?" Dr. Fithen asked.

"I . . . ." He raised a hand to his head. Her face blurred, then doubled. "What did you call me?"

Fithen turned away, checking the instruments laid out on the tray. Malach tried to stand, but his legs didn't work. Surena laid a hand on his chest and pushed him flat. Her face swam above him. "Just relax."

Straps cinched around his wrists and ankles. Surena stuffed a cloth into his mouth.

"Shouldn't we kill him now?" she asked.

"No." Dr. Fithen walked over. Her face was a blur, but her voice held a new coldness. "Let him suffer while I cut it out."

"I know he is aingeal, but—"

"If you prefer, you can keep the fee. I'll sell the kaldurite. But you must help me throw him in the sea after. He's too heavy to carry alone."

A sigh. "Yes, doctor."

Malach's eyes slid shut. He dragged them open and managed to raise his head a centimeter from the table. The glint of a scalpel hovered above his abdomen. In an instant, he was back at a stone chamber in the Arx of Novostopol, Falke's priests pinning his arms and legs as the blade bit into his wrist. A muffled scream filtered through the gag.

"I told you we should cut his throat. Someone might hear."

He felt weak as a newborn, yet every muscle tensed as cold steel touched his navel. He forced his body to relax. Minimize the blood loss. If he survived the cutting long enough for them to extract the stone, he'd have the ley. It flowed all around him, right there. When he died, he'd make sure they went with him.

Malach fixed his bleary gaze on the circle of light over-head, panting through his nose. Whatever drug they'd given him, it didn't dull sensation. A sharp sting—not too bad. The gentle clink of the scalpel striking the steel tray. A pause as Dr. Fithen chose another instrument. Then pain greater than he'd ever known. It burrowed to his roots. Mist devoured the edges of the room, but he refused to pass out.

Please please please please find it.

The instrument finally withdrew.

"It's deeper than I thought," Dr. Fithen said. "Lodged in the lower intestine. I'll need to widen the incision. Get the probe ready."

Malach's heartbeat thundered in his ears. So loud it almost sounded like running feet—

A force rocked the gurney on its wheels. The ceiling spun as he careened across the operating room. The IV stand crashed over. A woman screamed. Malach's head flopped to one side. Dr. Fithen cowered in a corner. Two blurry figures stood over her.

The pain drained away. He could hear it leaving, a steady drip-drip. The quiet embrace waited to enfold him. Very near now.

Then Darya's fingers curled in his hair, lifting his head. Her rings gouged into his scalp. Pewter eyes stared down at him.

"Ah, aingeal," she whispered, cheeks pale with rage. "I think you'll get your audience with the Mahadeva now."

Chapter Three

Malach's eyes opened to the sting of salt water. A heavy weight crushed his chest. He sucked in a panicked breath. The sea poured in. Fingers scrabbled over the flat stone pinning him. It was brutally heavy.

Long shifts toiling in the pit—and sheer panic—finally shifted it aside. He sat with a gasp. Water rattled in his throat. A long minute elapsed before he managed to speak.

"If you intend to murder me, go ahead," he rasped. "But I thought you'd be more creative than drowning." He glanced around. "In a pool less than a meter deep."

The Mahadeva Sahevis started to laugh—all three of them. The Crone had the rusty screech of a gull. The Mother chuckled quietly. But the Maid flailed in helpless mirth, her giggles echoing through the grotto.

"He thinks we're trying to drown him." She eyed Malach fondly. "Silly aingeal!"

"Be silent," the Crone snapped, her own cackles fading. "Valmitra has seen fit to heal you, feckless boy. A little gratitude is in order."

Malach pressed a hand to his stomach. The skin was smooth and unbroken. Even his other scar had vanished. Yet the agony was seared into his memory. He recalled only a fraction of the ordeal at Fithen's house—but that was enough. The woman had gutted him.

"It's not possible," he whispered, staring at them each in turn. "Even the ley cannot heal!"

The Crone shook her head. "How little you nihilim understand." White cauls covered her eyes, but her blind gaze pierced him nonetheless. "Count yourself fortunate that the Great Serpent took pity on you. It is a thing rarely done."

Not for a single moment had Malach believed in their god. The concept was ludicrous. A serpent that coiled around the core of the earth, breathing out ley? But he couldn't deny that an apparent miracle had occurred. He rose from the pool and strode to the rock shelf. A clean Rahai sat there. He unfolded the garment and knotted it around his waist. His stomach growled loudly.

"How long was I down there?" he asked.

"A week," the Mother replied.

"A *week?*"

She dragged a jade comb through her hair. "That butcher you went to inflicted mortal wounds. So we gave you to Valmitra. If you lived, you would surface. If not . . . . We did check on you periodically."

"What happened to Dr. Fithen?" He hoped it was something terrible.

"Her medical license has been revoked. She will atone for her offense."

Malach nodded thoughtfully. "Tell her I want my money back."

The Maid leapt to her feet, scowling. "Do not jest! You have made us very angry!"

"Have I?" He gave her a cold stare. "And what did you expect? I am not a dog to be leashed and brought to heel. You show me signs and portents. Declare that I am dangerous but not why or to whom. You refuse to tell me how long I must remain here or anything that is happening in my homeland. Where I have not one but *two* newborn children! So yes, I tried to remove the kaldurite. You left me no other choice!"

The three women—he still thought of them as three, although they shared a single mind—regarded him with quicksilver eyes. They resembled each other, more so the Maid and the Mother. Bold nose, thin lips, and high, angular cheekbones. The Maid's hair was a rich mahogany, threaded with silver in the Mother and fading to pure white in the Crone. They wore no clothing, only dozens of jeweled bracelets, anklets, rings and overlapping necklaces that gleamed in the dim light of the grotto.

"If Valmitra saved your life," the Mother said at last, "it is because we were right. You have importance in the scheme of things."

"Then let me meet my destiny, whatever it is!"

The Crone shook a leather dicing cup and tossed the contents between her bony legs. They were not gems, merely rough pebbles that looked like every other rock in the grotto. The Maid and Mother crowded close. They whispered to each other for a minute.

The Crone gave a satisfied grunt. "Valmitra has confirmed our choice."

The Maid grinned impishly. "He will not like it."

"It does not matter what he does and does not like," the Crone said. "He will submit."

Her voice held total assurance. For the first time in his life, Malach felt utterly outmatched.

"Submit to what?" he asked wearily.

"The mines were a poor choice," the Mother said. "They stoked your aggression and failed to stimulate your mind."

"I like the pit," he said, jaw setting stubbornly. "If I must be here, that is my preference."

"And therein lies the problem," the Crone said. "Your judgment is poor, aingeal. We would lock you up before sending you to the pit again. But we do not desire to punish you more than you already have been."

He leaned back on his palms, crossing his ankles. "What are you offering?"

The Maid's eyes glittered. "A challenge, aingeal. If you succeed, we will consider setting you loose."

There were too many conditions in that sentence to take it seriously, yet Malach felt a glimmer of hope.

"Then I will rise to the occasion." His lips quirked. "Shall I slay a monster for you? Seek out a magical sword?"

"You will join a creche," the Mother said. "Rear children."

Malach laughed. "No, really, what is it?"

The Maid scampered over and stroked his hair, toying with the damp locks. "Why do you doubt?"

He opened his mouth, then closed it again. She gave his beard a playful tug, then kissed his cheek and returned to her elders.

"You would trust me around your children?" he asked in disbelief. "Me?"

"Would you harm them, Malach?" the Mother asked.

"No, but—"

"Then it is done."

"I haven't agreed yet!" Unsettled by the swift turn of events, Malach cast about for another excuse. "With all respect, Mahadeva, I don't speak the language. Menial labor is more suitable."

The Crone's thin lips twitched. "*A bheil thu a' creidsinn gu bheil sinn gòrach?*"

He gazed at her, all innocence. "Your pardon, Mahadeva?"

"I say again, do you believe us to be stupid?" She swept the stones up. "Very well. *Glasaidh sinn suas thu.*"

"No!" He frowned. "Do not cage me again."

The Maid tossed a pebble at him. "Liar," she growled.

After four months immersed in the speech of Dur-

25

Athaara, Malach had picked up a good deal. In that way, the witch was right. He'd been so bored at the pit, learning their tongue was the only real challenge. And he'd thought he might need it to escape.

"*Dè cho fada 'sa dh'fheumas mi seo a dhèanamh?*" he asked.

"You will remain at the creche for as long as it takes." The Mother's bracelets jangled as she rose to her feet. "Maybe you'll come to like it."

"That's not the point."

She smiled. "The Great Serpent will tell us when you are ready."

"How? Do you speak with it?"

"The pronoun is *them*. And Valmitra will send a sign."

"But if you cause any trouble," the Crone continued, "you *will* be locked away. Consider this a last chance, aingeal dian."

Malach swept an arm across his waist and gave them a bow. "I will take it to heart, Mahadeva. If the Great Serpent has blessed me with their mercy, I shall do my utmost to merit it."

The Crone snorted. "Pretty words mean little. We'll see what you are made of, Malach. If you are a boy who beats his head against granite and wonders why he keeps getting hurt, or a man who faces his responsibilities."

The irony of *that* was too much. He stalked from the cavern. The rhythmic splash of waves grew louder as the passage widened. A dinghy rested on the crescent of black sand. Paarjini, his old nemesis, waited at the oars. Malach gave her a brusque nod and pushed it out, wading to his knees. When the craft floated free, he climbed into the stern. Her arms were slender but strong. She pulled hard on the oars and the boat cut through the swells, turning to take a parallel route along the shore.

"Aren't ye goin' to jump out?" she asked after they'd been rowing for several minutes. Paarjini's accent was very thick, her speech clipped but soft on the vowels. "Make a swim for

it? The continent's only a few hundred leagues west. O'
course, 'tis against the current. But who knows? Maybe ye'll
make it."

The witch's bruises had faded, but Malach doubted she'd
forgotten the feel of his chains around her throat. "Are you so
eager to see me imprisoned again?"

"Not at all." She tugged on the oars. "In fact, we have
wagers on how long you'll last in your new task. My sisters say
a week. But I put ten rubies on a year." White teeth flashed.
"I'll be a rich woman if I win."

A year? He eyed her sourly. "How did Darya find me?"

"An informant saw ye enter the house. We've been
watchin' Dr. Fithen. She's unscrupulous. There are very few
people who'd cut kaldurite from a man's belly, but Fithen is
one. You're lucky the sisters arrived in time."

"Twenty minutes sooner would have been even nicer."

Sunlight scattered on the sapphire net binding her hair as
Paarjini shook her head with a look of disgust. "They dinna
stand outside listenin' to ye scream if that's what you're
implyin'."

"I never said they did."

"But ye wondered."

He forced himself to hold her gaze. "Yes."

She stopped rowing. "I know I treated ye roughly when I
took ye on the beach, Malach," she said. "Ye fought like a
devil. But I saw ye when they brought ye out o' Fithen's abba-
toir. I would never allow such a thing t' be done to anyone, not
even ye."

When he didn't answer, she took the oars again. "If you're
wonderin' about your friend, he's too skilled t' be removed
from his position at the temple. But ye will not be seein' him
again."

Malach had expected this, though he felt relief that Tash
wasn't being punished for his own mistakes.

A creche. Did the Mahadeva think that caring for other

people's offspring would be sufficient to soothe his anguish? If so, she was a fool. But after Sydonie and Tristhus, the hellion orphans of Bal Kirith, Malach felt sure he would have no trouble managing normal children.

"Why did you wager so many gems on me, Paarjini?"

Her gaze flicked across his Marks, lingering on the two-headed snake at his hip. Her brow notched. Then she met his eyes with a musical laugh.

"Because ye don't break easily, aingeal."

Chapter Four

Paarjini rowed along the shore for a while, then steered the dinghy into a cove. The sea was clear as green glass and schools of bright fish darted through the boat's shadow. When the oars scraped bottom, she turned to Malach.

"Hop out and pull us in, aingeal," she said.

Malach clambered out, feet hitting soft white sand. He grabbed the rope at the bow and hauled the dinghy up past the high tide line.

"We drive from here," Paarjini said, leading him up a narrow path through the dunes to a dirt road. A car was parked on the verge, this one in even worse shape than Darya's. Half the body was rusted, the other half patched with clumsily welded sheets of metal. Stuffing poked from seams in the seats. It didn't even have a windshield. Paarjini rummaged in the glove box and handed him a pair of sunglasses.

"They'll keep the bugs from yer eyes," she said.

Malach put the glasses on. Someone had shoved the passenger seat all the way forward. He tried to slide the seat back, but the lever seemed to be locked in place. He sighed and stuffed himself into the car, knees wedged against the dashboard.

Paarjini drove for about two hours along sun-baked dirt roads. Malach had no idea where they were, except that it was somewhere up in the hilly highlands of the interior. He dozed off, waking to find that they'd stopped at a tiny settlement.

"We'll grab a bite to eat first," Paarjini said. "You'll need your strength to meet the wee ones."

"How young are we talking about?" Malach asked, stretching his legs with a silent groan.

"At this creche? Four to eleven, I believe."

"What are we expected to do with them?"

"Ach, do I look like I work there? Save your questions for after lunch."

"I need a shirt, Paarjini," he said. "People will stare."

"Well, I dinna have one." She grinned. "Ye'll just have to give 'em a show."

Malach shook his head. "What about the creche?"

"They already know all about ye."

"And they don't care? I find that hard to believe."

"If the Mahadeva trusts ye, Malach, that's good enough for the rest of us." A laugh. "I think ye'll find it's the least of your problems."

The village had a small market and cafe that served food at outdoor tables. He chose the farthest one, ignoring the other patrons' curious looks, while Paarjini placed their order at a window. The fare was brutally spicy, but Malach's palate had hardened along with the rest of him. He devoured two plates of pepper chicken and rice, followed by a cooling yoghurt drink called maatha. Other than hunger, he felt no ill effects from his week-long submersion in the pool. The Mahadeva could have been lying about that. But why would she? He hardly required another demonstration of the witches' power.

As they ate, Paarjini kept stealing glances at the two-headed snake on his hip. "Tha' looks like Valmitra," she said at last. "Did ye choose it, aingeal?"

He shook his head, scraping up the last bit of sauce with a piece of flatbread. "The ley chooses the Mark. But it's drawn from my mind."

"Tha's interesting. I know little about your kind."

"What do you know?"

Paarjini's gaze became guarded. "Tha' your tribe and mine dinna get along."

"Tribe?" He stared at her in puzzlement.

"T'was a very long time ago, aingeal." She rose. "Perhaps you'll learn more at the creche. But I've no time for a history lesson."

She returned her dirty plate to the window of the cafe and strode back to the car. Malach followed suit, feeling drowsy after the heavy meal. Insects buzzed in the undergrowth and a cool breeze kept the gnats at bay. In Bal Kirith, it was the sort of afternoon for lying in the tall grass and watching the clouds drift overhead. He had a sudden memory of Nikola riding her horse around the field, silver tooth winking as she passed him. A surge of longing hit him like a mailed fist. He slid into the car, slamming the door so hard the lever to roll the window up broke off, landing in his lap. Malach picked it up, looked at it in mute rage, then tossed it into the backseat. Paarjini arched a brow.

"Did I offend ye, aingeal?"

He stared straight ahead. "Just drive."

She shrugged and started the car. They went a short distance and turned up a narrow, rutted drive that ended at a dirt yard with a swing set and seesaw. Chickens scattered as Paarjini parked next to a covered pavilion, where two men and ten children in red shirts sat at picnic tables. It was such a bizarre sight, Malach froze with one hand on the door handle.

In the Via Sancta, crimson held dire connotations. It was strictly banned for its connection to the mages and abyssal ley.

"Ye comin'?" Paarjini said impatiently.

He nodded and stepped out of the car. One of the men jogged over. He was tall with light brown skin and sun-streaked hair coiled into a messy topknot. He wore a dark blue Rahai and sleeveless tunic. There was nothing soft about him except for his eyes, which crinkled in a welcoming smile.

"You must be Malach," he said, touching his chest in the Athaaran manner of greeting.

Malach returned the greeting, slipping easily into the local tongue.

"I am Finlo." He didn't even glance at Malach's Marks. "The children are eager to meet you, so we can make quick introductions and then I'll show you around." He turned to Paarjini, head dipping just enough to convey respect. "Sister. Have you had lunch? You're welcome to join us."

"We just ate, brother. But I thank you for the offer."

They eyed each other a few seconds longer than seemed appropriate. Paarjini grinned and looked away. "I'm afraid I must be goin'," she said, switching back to Osterlish. "But I'll be back to see how ye fare." The witch turned, pitching her voice for Malach's ears only. "Don't fail me, aingeal."

Finlo watched her walk to the car with a lazy grin, his gaze openly appreciative. Every day brought new lessons about the balance between the sexes here. Malach had expected men to be treated as little more than beasts of burden, but it wasn't the case. They were only barred from using lithomancy. The art fascinated him. If he only had the ley, he might learn to wield it himself—

"Shall we?" Finlo asked, breaking his train of thought.

Malach smiled. "Of course."

He trailed Finlo to the pavilion. The other minder was a stout, bearded man who introduced himself as Yvar. The children studied Malach with frank interest. At Finlo's prompting, they each gave their names, none of which Malach remembered.

"Ready for a tour?" Finlo asked.

"Sure." Malach waved at the kids and they strolled toward the house. It had an air of cheerful decrepitude that reminded him of Bal Kirith. The foundation was stone, the walls curving timbers of age-dark wood half hidden by ivy. Yellow birds darted from hidden nests in the eaves. Like most of the buildings in Dur-Athaara, it was round and had two stories with large windows that could be sealed with shutters if a storm blew through.

"So you all live here together?" Malach asked.

"One big family," Finlo agreed, stepping inside.

It was tidier than Malach expected given the number of children. The ground floor held the kitchen, two schoolrooms with blackboards, and a living area with battered, comfortable-looking furniture and boxes of toys. Childish drawings were pinned to the walls, along with maps of the islands and posters identifying different stones and minerals. His gaze slid down the list, pausing at the rainbow-hued stone halfway through the alphabet. *K is for . . . Kaldurite!*

Malach wrenched his eyes away.

"Laundry's in a building out back," Finlo explained. "Three washers and dryers. Thank the goddess we're on the solar grid. In the old days, they had to do it all by hand. I can't even imagine."

Malach grasped the concept of a washing machine, though he'd never actually seen one. "You'll have to show me how to use them," he said.

"Of course." Finlo gave him a wry smile. "Don't worry, you'll get plenty of practice."

A flight of stairs led up to the bedrooms. Four belonged to the children, who slept three to a room. The walls were painted in bright murals of fish and other sea creatures. At the end of the circular hall, Finlo showed him a larger room with one double bed. The mattress had been stripped and clean sheets sat on a wooden chair. A vase with fresh flowers sat on the dresser. After the barracks, it looked like a palace.

"The children picked those for you," Finlo said, nodding at the vase. "I understand you don't have many belongings. There's a few Rahais in the dresser, and some shirts. They ought to fit."

"I'd like to shave," Malach said, rubbing his beard.

"Fresh from the mines, eh?" Finlo grinned. "You can borrow my razor. Then we'll buy you one of your own in town." He nodded at the bedroom across the hall. "That's mine. Just knock if you need anything."

"Where does Yvor sleep?"

"Oh, he'll be leaving now that you're here."

"So it's just the two of us?"

Finlo nodded. "Some creches are larger, with one minder to ten kids." He smiled. "That can get a little rowdy. But you'll only have five under your care."

"Great." Malach nodded confidently, as if he had any clue what he was doing.

"You'll get a feel for it as you go," Finlo said. "There's a pretty strict routine. Breakfast, then lessons until midday. Afternoon is free time. Gardening, games in the yard, that sort of thing. The little ones still take naps. Then story time, supper, baths and bed."

"Sounds simple enough."

"Good. You can watch them while I clean up from lunch."

Malach felt a mild jolt of alarm. "What, now?"

"Do you mind? You can take the dishes, if you prefer."

Malach did, but he wouldn't admit it. "No, I should get to know them. Which are the troublemakers?"

Finlo laughed. "A good question. Cristory and Roseen like to tease Ealish. Lonan gets upset easily, but he's also easily distracted. Inry eats anything he can get his hands on. Dirt's okay, but if he eats a worm, Ealish freaks out, so try to stop him. Now, Bretan—"

Malach paid little attention to the litany, well-meaning though it was, since he had no idea which of them was which. They headed back downstairs and went out to the pavilion. The children had already run to the playground.

"Any advice for me?" Malach asked Yvor, as Finlo started stacking the dirty plates.

"First time at a creche?"

He nodded.

"If you need help, don't be ashamed to ask for it."

Malach nodded sagely. "Got it."

He touched his chest. "Goddess bless you."

Yvor made the rounds, giving each of the children a quick hug. Then he went into the house. Malach saw him chatting with Finlo through the kitchen window. Yvor came out with a backpack, waved, and set off down the drive.

Malach was about to relax at one of the tables when shrieks erupted near the swings. He walked over, thinking one of the children had fallen down. The others stopped playing to watch. A chubby dark-haired boy was standing over one of the girls. As Malach approached, he balled his hands into fists, snatching at something invisible.

"Mine!" he shouted.

The girl, a tiny thing with blond hair in two messy pigtails, sobbed hysterically.

"He's stealing my air!" she screamed.

Malach stood for a moment in mute wonder.

"Mine!" the boy yelled again, grabbing at nothing. "It's mine!"

"Hey," Malach said. "Quit that."

His words had no effect. The girl was bright red, face scrunched in rage.

"What's your name?" he asked the boy.

The kid snatched at Malach's air. "Inry!"

"Okay, Inry." He put some snap into his voice. "I'm ordering you to stop."

"No!" More frantic snatching.

Malach reached for him and the boy darted away. Inry sat down and peeled something grayish-black from the asphalt, then popped it into his mouth and started chewing. It looked like old gum.

"Can't breathe!" the girl shrieked.

She threw herself to the ground, screaming and kicking. The other children looked at her, then at Malach. He saw Finlo watching through the kitchen window while he washed dishes.

The only discipline Malach had known growing up was of the extreme corporal variety. He felt fairly certain that would be frowned upon here.

He considered the rules of engagement. Two strategies came to mind. One, knock the enemy off balance. Do something unexpected that leaves them stunned and confused. Second, the inner front strategy. Infiltrate their ranks, pretend to be one of them, and stage a brutal coup d'etat.

He regarded the screaming child. "No, no," he said calmly. "You're not doing it right. You have to really throw your arms and legs into it. Here, I'll show you."

He lay down on the ground and let out a bloodcurdling scream. If felt great. He could see why they liked it. Malach shouted himself hoarse, jerking around in paroxysms of wrathful abandon. After a couple of minutes, he realized that the children had gone quiet. He lay there panting, then brushed himself off and sat up.

"*That's* how it's done," he said.

The girl had stopped crying. She stared at him in wonder.

"What's your name?" he asked.

"Cristory," she whispered.

"Well, carry on," he said, getting to his feet.

She swallowed. "I'm okay now."

He smiled. "Good! Want me to push you on the swings?"

She nodded cautiously. He plopped her onto the swing and gave it a shove. After a moment, the rest of them shrugged and went back to what they'd been doing before. The next hour passed with no major incidents. Malach was proud of himself for noticing when Inry started digging up worms and managed to prevent the boy from ingesting any. But then he made the mistake of giving one of them a horseback ride, which meant he had to do it for all of them.

He didn't realize Ealish had peed her pants until the others started to point and laugh. The girl was blank-faced, unable to meet his eye.

"It's not funny!" Malach told them sternly. "Come on, we're going inside."

It took some nagging, but he managed to herd them into the playroom. "Just wait here," he whispered to Ealish, ducking into the spotless kitchen.

Finlo stood at the butcher block counter, chopping vegetables. "I'll take the older ones for lessons in a minute," he said. "Let me just finish prepping dinner."

"One of the kids had an accident," Malach said quietly.

Finlo didn't seem surprised. "Ealish, right? She's scared of the toilet. The noise of the flushing, I think. So she holds it and holds it, until . . . whoosh. Yvor was trying to work with her, but you don't want to traumatize the kid, either."

"Isn't she old for that?" Malach wondered.

"Yeah, but we can't keep her in diapers. She has to learn sometime. Can you take her to change?"

"Sure." Malach went back to the playroom. In the two minutes he'd been gone, a hurricane had swept through. Every toybox was upended and the contents strewn across the rug. The volume of noise was ear-splitting.

"Come on," he said, taking Ealish's hand. "Let's go upstairs."

She led him to one of the rooms and was about to sit on

the bed. Malach tugged her hand. "Not until you change your clothes." He started for the door.

"Can't!" she wailed.

He turned back. "What do you mean, *can't?* How old are you?"

"Three and a half."

"So?"

She stared at him. "Yvor helps me."

"Don't you want to learn how to do it yourself?"

Her face started to crumple. "Okay, okay," he muttered. "Don't cry."

Malach undressed the child and rooted through her dresser, grabbing a clean pair of shorts.

"Don't want that one!" she said firmly.

He stared at the garment in his hand. "Why not?"

"I want *that* one." She pointed to a pair that looked exactly the same.

"Fine," he growled. Malach stooped down and held out the shorts. She clumsily stepped into them. Her shirt looked more or less okay so he didn't bother with it. He took her hand to go back downstairs. She frowned at him.

"Can't leave those." She pointed to the floor.

"Eh?"

"They're wet."

He glanced at the soaked shorts.

"Put it in there." She pointed to a hamper.

"Why me?" he asked.

Ealish gave him a look of disdain. Malach tossed the wet shorts in the hamper.

"I need a bath," she declared.

"But you just changed."

"It itches!"

"Bath time is later."

Ealish squirmed. "Itchy!" she whined.

"Fine. Where's the tub?"

She dragged him to a bathroom with a large clawfoot bathtub. "I can do it!" Chubby hands twisted the faucet. She pulled her clothes off—no trouble with that, he noticed—and threw them on the floor. He was about to leave when he noticed steam rising from the tub. Malach took her arm as she was about to jump in. "Wait."

Ealish watched with interest as he stuck a finger in the water. It was burning hot. He turned it to cold, let the temperature adjust, then switched it back to warm. He remembered to find her a towel and left it on the toilet seat.

"Be back in a while," he said. "Have fun."

Ealish clambered into the tub. He heard her singing as he went back downstairs. The rest of the children were gathered in the playroom. Finlo sat on the floor reading a story to the older ones, who listened quietly. Malach caught Lonan and Inry fighting over a doll and settled the dispute by taking it away, but by then Roseen had pinched her finger in the hinged lid of one of the chests and was wailing loudly. The others watched wide-eyed as Malach examined it. He pressed the finger to the dagger Mark on his forearm and declared it healed, which worked, but then Cristory—who had been picking her nose not thirty seconds before—poked the Lady of Masks on his chest and shouted, "Healed!" The others swarmed him, giggling and shouting until Finlo stopped reading and glanced over.

Malach hissed at them to pipe down. "Let's build a tower," he said, crawling to the pile of blocks. The girls joined him, carefully stacking the blocks, but the boys resumed their fight over the doll. Malach snatched it away again, earning dark looks. Inry's lip began to tremble.

"Where's Ealish?"

Malach looked up, the doll in his fist. Finlo stood over him with a slight frown.

"Uh, taking a bath."

"Alone?"

39

Finlo didn't look happy. "I'll go check," Malach said, jumping to his feet.

His pulse slowed at the sounds of splashing and singing. But the tub had overflowed and water soaked the bathroom floor. He twisted the faucet in exasperation. "Why didn't you turn it off?"

A blank stare. Malach handed her the doll. He pulled the plug and let it drain to half full.

"Are you mad?" Ealish whispered, one hand anxiously stroking the doll's yarn hair.

He drew a deep breath and smiled. "I'm not mad."

Malach ran to his bedroom and grabbed the clean sheets, throwing them on the floor to soak up the mess. "Don't touch the faucet," he warned her.

She slapped her hands against the water, sending a spray into his face. "I won't! Promise!"

He left a trail of drips as he went back downstairs. "Everything's fine!" he declared.

Finlo eyed his soaked Rahai with a grin. "They're supposed to take naps now, but I think they're too excited. Maybe you can just play with them for a while. I'll keep an eye on Ealish."

The next hours passed in a blur of sticky hands, loud voices and incessant demands. By the time they'd served supper, bathed the rest of the children, tidied the playroom, read more stories, cleaned up the kitchen, and tucked them all into bed, Malach was beyond exhaustion. He staggered to his room. The bed was made up with fresh sheets.

When had Finlo found the time? He'd done all the cooking and most of the storytelling, managed a hysterical freakout after Roseen bit Cristory, and supervised the older children's homework without breaking a sweat.

Malach woke at dawn the next day with a glob of formless dread in his stomach that wasn't the kaldurite. But his promise to the witch-queen drove him to his feet, determined to make it through the day without accidentally killing anyone.

Finlo had left a pair of scissors and a razor on top of the tall dresser—well out of reach for small fingers, Malach realized. It wasn't something that would have occurred to him yesterday. But he had a hazy recollection of Finlo showing him where the kitchen knives were kept and warning him to never, ever leave them sitting out.

Malach took the potential weapons to the bathroom, locked the door, and showered, then filled the sink with hot water. He wiped steam from the mirror. It was the first time he'd taken a good look at himself in months. His face was deeply tanned, the faint lines at the corners of his eyes deeper. Tash was right. With the scraggly, unkempt beard, he was the picture of a deranged hermit. He wondered what he'd looked like throwing a temper tantrum in the dirt. Too bad Darya wasn't there to see it.

Malach attacked his beard, exposing paler skin beneath. His hair had been very short when he first arrived. Now it curled around his ears, but he lacked the energy or motivation to tidy it up. He dressed and went downstairs, tiptoeing past the children's doors so as not to wake them.

He was halfway down the stairs when he stepped on something hard and pointy. Malach swore softly, rubbing his bare foot. It was a fucking triangular block, left point-up on the riser like a booby trap. He kicked it down the stairs and limped to the kitchen. Finlo was already there, cooking a vat of porridge. He looked over with a smile.

"There's tea in the pot."

Malach started banging through the cabinets in search of a mug.

"Third on the left," Finlo said. "I make it strong, hope that's okay."

"The stronger the better," Malach muttered, finding the right shelf.

"I used to work in the mines, too. For many years. It got boring. I chose this and I don't regret it. But my first day was worse than yours." He blew on his tea. "By far."

Malach sank into a chair at the long table, intrigued. "What happened?"

Finlo set his mug down. He twisted his hair into a topknot and pinned it with a colored pencil. "I was doing laundry. One of the kids started crying and I left the dryer door open to check on him. While I was gone, Lonan pushed Cristory inside, closed it, and hit the button."

"Oh, shit," Malach said with a laugh.

It wasn't really funny, but he knew the child was fine.

"Oh shit is right," Lonan agreed. "By Valmitra's grace, Lonan hit fluff instead of dry so there was no heat. But Cristory had lumps on her head for two weeks."

"They didn't fire you?"

Finlo shook his head. "I was only gone for a moment. How do you foresee something like that? But that's the thing. They're capable of anything. Anything at all. If you remember nothing else, remember that."

"What happened to Lonan?"

Beleth would have beaten the child. Malach had earned countless whippings for much less.

"He was four. Cris was three. He had no idea what he was doing." Finlo laughed. "Think of it as an asylum with small, adorable inmates. But they won't always be that way. They'll grow up, and that's the hardest part of our job. To make them into adults we'd like to know."

Malach considered this. "Where are their parents?"

"I don't know. The creches are optional. Some people choose to rear their own children. But we have a one-child policy and a lot of people want their kids to have the experience of siblings. It socializes them." He shrugged. "Or they both work and don't have the time."

"Do they visit?"

"No, it's too confusing. And it would undermine our authority."

"So they just give them up?"

"Pretty much. If the children want to find them when they get older, and the parents agree, we share the names. It might seem strange to you, but that's how we've always done it."

"Are there babies, too?" Malach couldn't begin to imagine that.

Finlo nodded. "We have other creches for infants up to three. More minders, less kids. But I prefer the older ones. They're more fun."

Malach started to lay the table with a dozen bowls and spoons.

"Are you good with taking the three to fives? When Yvor was here, I supervised the six to nines. There's different challenges with the older kids and I'm pretty comfortable with the academic curriculum. The little ones are easy, just basic numbers and letters."

"I don't mind." He wondered what happened as they grew older, but Malach didn't aim to be there long enough to find out.

Finlo glanced at the door. "Can you get them dressed? Keeping to the routine is reassuring."

Malach completed this task with minimal fuss, his first victory of the day. When Lonan held his arms out, Malach picked him up. A sleepy head rested on his shoulder. The child smelled sweet, his hair soft as thistledown.

"Ready for breakfast?" he asked.

A nod. He set the boy on his feet and they trailed him like a line of ducklings to the breakfast table.

It was the last moment of peace. Ealish wet her pants twice, for which the child was teased mercilessly. Malach decided that honesty might be the best policy and asked her if she planned to piss herself for the rest of her life, which made her cry and him feel guilty. To make up for it, he offered to take them all into town for maathi shakes at the cafe. Finlo reluctantly gave him the use of the creche's car, but that too turned into a disaster when Lonan had a nosebleed all over the upholstery. He did manage to teach a literacy class without incident, but then he fell asleep on the floor while they were coloring and woke up to find they'd unbuttoned his shirt and covered themselves in "Marks" that imitated his own, some quite inappropriate. The waxy crayons had to be scrubbed off in the bath, which elicited more tears and howls.

Finlo left him to solve the various messes he'd created. When Malach finally toppled into bed that night, after staying up well past the monsters' bedtime to clean blood from the car, he wondered if Paarjini might lose that bet after all.

Oddly enough, he felt no desire to beat them senseless, as he'd been raised. Only to run—swiftly and without looking back. The Mahadeva Sahevis, Malach reflected, was cunning in her retribution. The pit hadn't broken him because it played to his strong points, whereas the creche brought out every weakness. Lack of empathy first and foremost, but also a basic ignorance of how to care for another person who lacked even a modicum of common sense.

If it was meant to show him that he'd make a terrible father, it was working like a charm. Yet he'd survived his first full day. Perhaps he'd survive another. He stared at the ceiling, resolving not to quit until he'd left some legacy behind. Something of value that changed their lives forever.

"I will toilet train that kid," he muttered, "if it kills me."

Chapter Five

A sea of umbrellas jammed the plaza before the Pontifex's Palace. It had rained on and off all morning. Dark, low clouds blanketed Novostopol and although the drizzle had paused, no one was falling for it.

Nikola Thorn watched from the roof of the Castel Saint Agathe as Beleth was led out to a balcony and displayed to the faithful. Stripped of the elaborate tiered wig and face powder, she might have been any woman in late middle age. Perhaps that was Falke's intent. Unmask the monster and it loses its power.

Of course, the heretic Pontifex of Bal Kirith was too far to clearly see her face. Nikola remembered the frosty blue gaze and uncompromising slash of a mouth. The pitiless voice as she ordered a thirteen-year-old Malach to approach the stelae and read out the inscription. He'd been spitting blood by the end of that so-called *lesson*.

Still, Nikola felt pity for Beleth. It was hard not to considering the palpable hostility of the crowd. She would always root for the underdog—even if it was a little bit rabid.

Beleth recited her crimes into a microphone, pausing now and again to wait for a squeal of feedback to subside. The litany was not short. By the time it ended and Falke roused the crowd with a speech trumpeting his supposed victories in the Morho, Nikola was bored to tears.

"Do you think half of that was true?" she asked the knight sharing an umbrella at her shoulder.

Captain Vasily Komenko cast her a sharp look. "You doubt the confession, Domina Thorn?"

"Oh, no," she replied innocently. "I'm sure they would never coerce her into saying things that weren't a hundred percent accurate. Like all the skirmishes we're winning with the mages at Bal Agnar."

He shifted. "It would not help public morale if they knew the truth."

"No," she agreed dryly. "I'm sure it wouldn't."

"Beleth gave us many names. Cooperated fully. That's why she still has her left hand. The Via Sancta shows mercy to its enemies if they are willing to repent."

"I don't believe you."

The captain laughed, though there was scant amusement in it. "All right, Domina Thorn. I suspect Falke is using her as bait to draw Malach."

A doomed plan, she thought, since he's halfway across the sea.

Nikola looked at the thin gold band on the knight's finger. "Congratulations, by the way. Will they give you leave for a honeymoon?"

Komenko's jaw tightened. "He's already back in the field."

"Saints, I'm sorry."

He met her eye with a brief smile. "I'm being deployed again tomorrow. But I'm more afraid for Lev than myself."

"Will you be together, at least?"

"I don't know. He's cavalry. We've applied for a joint spousal assignment. I submitted the paperwork last week. So maybe."

Nikola sighed. "I will miss you, farm boy."

Komenko was the only one who treated her well. Once she'd physically recovered from the birth, she'd begged to be put back to work. Anything to break the tedium. Falke had refused, of course. She couldn't be trusted.

Nikola had seen her daughter only once, through the window of her cell. A small girl was crossing the plaza with four vestals. At first she didn't believe it. The child was already walking. It couldn't be hers.

But a mother knows. As Nikola studied the springy black curls, the golden-brown skin and rounded arms, she knew it in every fiber of her being.

And she felt nothing.

Only frustration that the child was free while she sat locked up in a room.

Proof positive, if any was needed, that she would make a terrible parent.

She clasped Komenko's hand. "The Saints watch over you both."

"And you, Domina Thorn."

They joined the flow of chars and vestals heading for the staircase from the roof. Everyone had been required to watch Beleth's performance—even Nikola, though she was apparently unredeemable. Komenko paused at the door to her room. He lowered his voice. "How long will they keep you here?"

"Forever, I expect."

He rubbed his jaw. The shrapnel wound had healed, leaving a white scar in his thick blonde hair. Lev Stepanchikov was a lucky fellow. The captain had shown her a picture of his boyfriend once, the day he planned to propose and was pacing up and down in her room. They were both pretty hot.

"That's a violation of the civil code," he said. "They haven't charged you with a crime?"

She shook her head. "I'm not sure I've committed one.

47

Well, you know, getting knocked up by a mage. Quitting my job without notice. I guess that earns a life term around here." She said it lightly, but Komenko was a true believer in the Via Sancta. One of the *good* zealots, if such a thing existed. He took her arm and guided her past the door, his face blank.

"Where are we going?" Nikola whispered.

Women moved through the corridors, but the pair of them were a common sight and no one gave them a second glance.

"I might not come back," Komenko replied quietly. "If I die, I want a clean conscience."

Her pulse quickened. "But you just got married."

Why she said that, of all things, Nikola didn't know.

"Lev agrees. I told him about you."

They stepped outside. He unfurled the umbrella and pulled her close. Hundreds of people were steaming towards the gates of the Arx. Komenko merged with the jostling crowd, Nikola at his side.

"I can't take you all the way. The guards might recognize me. But I won't raise the alarm until I think you're through."

"What will you say?"

"That you broke away from me and ran. I lost you."

She studied his long legs and broad shoulders. "No one will buy that."

The cynical smile broke her heart a little. He was always so earnest. But the war had stripped even Komenko of his illusions.

"What will they do?" he asked dryly. "Send me to the front?"

Nikola rose up on tiptoes and kissed his cheek. "Thank you, captain."

He nodded and gave her the umbrella. "*Skol*," he said, striding off into the rain.

Good health.

Nikola shuffled along, willing the crowd to move faster. She kept the umbrella low, covering her face, though it meant she couldn't see anything except the feet in front of her. In the last four months, she'd hatched a dozen schemes to escape the Arx. Overpowering a char and stealing her uniform. Faking illness so she'd be brought to the infirmary. Even the old classic, tying bedsheets together and shimmying down from the window. All her plans ended at the gates. She knew she'd never make it through.

The only viable possibility was to climb into the trunk of a car without anyone seeing her, and Nikola hadn't figured out how the hell she might accomplish that.

But today, in the midst of a thousand people, she just might pass unnoticed.

Nikola stole a quick peek from beneath the dripping brim. The Dacian Gate was a hundred meters ahead. Oprichniki in yellow slickers were waving everyone through. She pressed behind two women who were gossiping about Beleth.

". . . gave me a copy of one of her books," one said.

Her friend gasped in mock outrage. "He didn't!"

"I burned it, of course." A laugh. "After reading it cover to cover. You wouldn't believe the woman's lurid imagination. I have to admit, I was impressed."

"You're awful."

"Just curious. Honestly, Sasha, I didn't understand half of it—"

The two women stopped abruptly. The crowd tightened up to clear a path. Nikola found herself trapped at the front as a line of black cars moved slowly toward the gates, each with a gleaming chrome raven on the hood. Six knights jogged ahead of the motorcade.

"Umbrellas down," they shouted, eyes sweeping the crowd.

She furled her umbrella, silently cursing. People cheered and pushed, craning for a better look. The first car rolled past. Nikola looked up just as the next went by. Rain streaked the windows. She glimpsed the familiar hawkish profile of Dmitry

Falke. His head turned. She could have sworn he met her eyes, though the glass was tinted. Then the motorcade disappeared through the Dacian Gates.

Nikola let out a slow breath. Was it possible he hadn't seen her?

Or had Falke *ordered* Komenko to let her go?

Nikola's head spun. Then she was shuffling forward again. Just before the gates, she stumbled, jostling one of the women, who wore a stylish belted raincoat and chunky rings over her gloves.

"I'm so sorry," Nikola said quickly.

Kohl-lined eyes took in her drab dress. Pity unfolded across the woman's face. "It's fine," she said, already turning back to her friend, the one who'd read Beleth's book.

Nikola followed them through the stone arch. Radios squawked in the guardhouse, but no one tried to stop her. The Oprichniki didn't even look at her. Komenko had kept his word—or it was all a pretense to get rid of an embarrassing burden Falke had no use for anymore.

She walked swiftly around the traffic circle. There was no sign of the motorcade. After months of confinement, the lights and noise of the city left her lightheaded. When Nikola looked up and found herself at the very spot where Malach had waited for her to pass by, she stopped, the rush hour commuters swirling around her.

She'd instinctively taken the route home from work. For ten years, since the day she turned sixteen and found a job at the Arx, she'd walked past that same alley, thinking only of reaching her flat so she could change her clothes and go out again.

She'd spent as little time as possible at home. It was too quiet. Too empty. She preferred the buzz of conversation in a bar or cafe, though she usually went by herself. Just to sit and watch people. Try to figure out what made the Marked different from herself.

She'd never found the answer to that.

Now a strange sensation came over her, as if she stood in a gallery of mirrors with versions of herself stretching out to a vanishing point. A thousand Nikola Thorns. Most of them died young. Others clung on, faces puffy from drink, hands and knees chapped raw from scrubbing floors. Five or six ran away and met unknown fates in the Morho Sarpanitum.

Only one took a different path.

She saw herself, cloak wrapped tight, another umbrella in her hand, and Malach in his shabby overcoat and horn-rimmed glasses, fogged by the rain. The briefcase sitting at his feet.

They'd shared a bottle of wine at a bar months before. Nikola had both longed to see him again and dreaded it. As if part of her knew all along the kind of trouble he'd be.

The last time we met, she'd said, *you asked me what my heart's desire was.*

And you never answered me, Malach replied.

He'd been smiling at first, the impudent grin of a man with a winning hand, but his expression had grown serious then. As if he genuinely wanted to know.

Nikola knew her heart's desire now. Freedom—and him. Luckily, both were in the same place.

She hurried past the alley, away from the army of Nikola ghosts, and headed downhill for Novoport. Dusk was falling by the time she reached a dockside tavern and pulled out the wallet she'd lifted from the woman in the crowd. She used the wad of *fides* to buy some crisps and as much water as she could carry, then left the wallet sitting atop a piling where someone might find it and return it to its owner. There were pictures of kids inside she'd want back.

Two warships sat in the harbor. It was a moonless night. Nikola surveyed her options. Sailboats floated at anchor in the private marina, but she had no clue how to rig them. The large ferryboats were out, obviously. Her gaze lit on a wooden dinghy tied up at one of the long piers.

She waited for full dark, then crept down the ladder, juggling the heavy flat of glass bottles in one arm. All they had was the fizzy kind, but it would do. She untied the rope from the mooring and set the oars in the locks. The man in the tavern said the currents flowed east. He'd eyed her strangely when she asked, and more so when she bought the water, but then a crowd of students from the Lyceum had breasted through the doors and he'd moved off to pull a pitcher of beer.

There was an reasonable chance she would die. More than reasonable. But at least she would die beyond the borders of the Via Sancta.

Nikola used an oar to push off from the dock. She rowed out past the marina and the red and green buoys marking the channel. At the harbor mouth, the steel hull of a warship loomed above her, the glow from its bridge reflecting in the smooth water. It was a moonless night. She drifted quietly past.

Open ocean lay beyond. A swell lifted the boat, tugging it away from the lights of Novoport. Perhaps she should have been afraid, alone in the dark in a small boat, but she felt only a great sense of adventure, as though she had turned a corner and found the road wide open before her.

Nikola tugged her gloves off and threw them overboard—a defiant gesture she would come to regret—and pulled hard at the oars.

Chapter Six

Nikola rowed until weeping blisters rose on her palms. Then she curled up in the bottom of the boat, drank a bottle of water, and slept. When she woke, the land was gone. She'd known solitude before, but this was a new world. The indifferent stars shone down on an expanse of black so vast there seemed no end to it. She resumed her seat at the bench. The first strokes were the worst. She settled into the pain, fell into a rhythm with the oars. With no point of reference, the boat seemed to remain stationary, yet every stroke drew her further from the Via Sancta and that was all that mattered.

A brisk wind rose. The exertion kept her warm, though every time she paused, gooseflesh rose on her arms. Then something bumped the hull. Just a gentle nudge, but her heart clawed at her chest. A reminder that she was not, in fact, alone. Nikola shipped the oars and drifted, but whatever it was did not return.

Her lips cracked, but she didn't dare drink more water yet. If she could make a hundred kilometers a day and stay on course, she might reach the isles of the witches in less than a week. Food she could do without, but running out of water would be miserable.

The ocean grew rougher. The rolling motion made it impossible to keep both oars in the sea. Her shoulders and back burned. So did her bottom. Nikola had planned to row for hours, but she would have to take regular breaks if she didn't want to pull a muscle.

The sun rose during one of her rest times, painting the eastern horizon with streaks of rose and yellow. By noon, it beat down full force. She wetted her headscarf in the sea. Shed the dress and used it as a cushion for her aching bum. Her body looked painfully thin, the ribs poking through. She touched the stretch marks on her belly.

"I couldn't take you," she muttered. "How could I? You're theirs now."

She ate the last of the crisps, wishing she hadn't bought something so salty. Eyed the last five bottles of water but saved them for later. At sunset, a pod of whales appeared in the distance. Nikola stopped rowing to watch. One swam closer and a great intelligent eye met hers as it breached. Wordless awe filled her heart.

The whales followed the boat at a distance, curious. That night, she heard one blowing in the dark.

"Hello!" she shouted hoarsely. "I am here!"

The next morning broke overcast and windy. She searched for the pod, but it was gone. Choppy seas made rowing difficult. Water kept swamping the boat, forcing her to bail with an empty bottle.

"Ten strokes on one oar, then the other," she muttered.

Her hands were in a very bad state, but there was nothing to be done for that. She counted strokes, resting at a thousand. Everything was drenched, but the sea had grown warmer. She stood to stretch her back just as a rogue swell slapped the boat. Her feet slid on the slick planks. She woke at the bottom of the boat, face sticky with blood. Nikola touched her forehead with a wince. Dark clouds mounded on the horizon.

"Good," she said, fighting a wave of dizziness. "Rain is good."

She drank the last of the water, guzzling it with abandon. There would be more soon. She attacked the oars. Cream and black dolphins passed, at least a hundred. She envied their swiftness. Night fell, but the storm never came. By morning, the thirst was excruciating. She rowed and slept, rowed and slept. The handles of the oars were rusty with flecks of dried blood. No sign of life. Only the restless waves.

The fourth day broke with sunny skies and a strong breeze from the south. Would it push her off course? Or was she already off course? The sense of being a speck at the mercy of the sea was humbling. Nikola began to accept the fact that she would die out here. She started to row, muscles screaming with each stroke. Sometimes she heard distant voices on the wind. Saw dark shadows moving beneath the surface, though she couldn't say if they were real.

She kept at the oars, letting the pain distract from the thirst. When dark fell, she broke down and tried to drink salt-water, but quickly retched it up. Her eyes felt strange. Like hot stones. She curled up in the bottom of the boat.

Nikola woke to a gentle patter on her face. She opened her mouth, shivering with relief as the rain hit her parched tongue. Presently, the rain grew harder. Lightning forked on the horizon. The waves turned violent, rocking the boat so hard it almost capsized. Her bleeding fingers clung to the gunwale. It was like riding on the back of some huge beast determined to throw her off. The skies were black, the surface churned to a white froth. For long hours, she crouched in the bottom, slapped by waves that spun the craft in circles and dashed it headlong into the deep, surging troughs.

It was only a matter of time before a big enough wave came, and come it finally did. Nikola held fast to one of the oars as she was lifted and thrown over the side. She wrapped her arms around the length of wood, choking on saltwater. Within seconds, the overturned boat sank into the deep.

Easier to let go. Face the inevitable without a fuss. Yet Nikola clung on tighter. She shouted defiance at sky and sea. If they wanted her dead, they could send something along to eat her up. Stupid, but when had she ever been smart?

The storm raged all around, whipping the surface to a salt-laden mist. Naked and adrift, Nikola surrendered to the rough caress of the gale. Her hands went numb, but they must be holding on for the blade of the oar pressed into her cheek. Gradually, the wind's fury abated. Through a grey veil, the faint outline of wave crests appeared. Dawn was breaking.

The swells turned long and rolling, moving with incredible speed. She floated on her back, more than half-stunned to be still alive, when a thin wail broke the monotony.

My baby! They took my baby!

Her eyes opened. A gull hovered high above, head tilted into the wind. After a moment, it flapped away. Gulls flew hundreds of miles from land. It meant nothing.

But she made herself look around. A line of darker shadow broke the horizon. She coasted down the spine of a wave and it disappeared. The sea lifted her up again, neck craning. Land! Either the witches' or someplace else. Yet her trajectory was wrong. The island would pass by and nothing lay beyond but endless leagues of open ocean.

Before she could question the wisdom of her decision, Nikola let go of the oar and tried to swim. Her arms refused to obey.

One stroke. Just one, then you can drown.

The oar drifted away. She dog-paddled, floated on her back, then paddled again.

Just one more. Only one more. Then you can drown.

The current didn't fight her. If it had, she wouldn't have stood a chance. But she caught one last glimpse of the oar and knew from its position that if she'd clung to it, she would have journeyed onward to realms unknown. As it was, she cut a diagonal course. The land remained steady.

One more. One more. One more.

The isle grew bigger. With the last of her reserves, she clawed her way forward. A wave pushed her to the shallows. Toes brushed sand. She staggered along, finally dropping to her knees and crawling the rest of the way. How strange to touch something solid and unmoving. The sand was black and fine like pepper.

With a croak of triumph, Nikola passed out.

SHE WOKE ON A LEDGE. Fangs of rock descended from the roof of a cavern. She rolled to one side, pain flaring in a dozen places. Her groan cut short as she realized she was not alone. Three women watched her from across a luminous green pool. Two were obviously mother and daughter, with matching slate gray eyes. The third was blind. She was the oldest person Nikola had ever seen.

"You have a strong will," the blind woman said.

"Where am I?" Nikola studied her palms. They were so shredded, she wondered if she would ever regain the full use of her hands.

"Tenethe. We expected you might turn up." A rusty laugh. "But not like this."

Nikola looked up. "You are witches."

"We are Valmitra's daughter." The blind one touched her breast. "We are the Crone." Her head turned to the others, who spoke in unison. "We are also Mother and Maid."

The youngest witch stared at her intently. "You are the consort of the aingeal."

"I'm no man's *consort*," Nikola replied. "Do you mean the mage? What have you done with him?"

"You made this journey for the aingeal?"

"I came because there is nowhere else for me."

The women beckoned her over. Nikola did not trust them, but they were cooking food. The smell set her mouth watering.

"Sit and eat with us," the Mother said, patting the ledge.

The girl used a stick to poke a leaf-wrapped package from the coals. Nikola juggled chunks of steaming fish. They burned her tender fingers, but her stomach could not wait. She wolfed the fish down and ate another.

"Why did you take him?" she asked warily. "Where is he now?"

"We took him because Valmitra willed it." Lines of sorrow bracketed the Mother's mouth. "But he is beyond your reach now."

"What?" The meal roiled in her stomach. "Why?"

"The aingeal went overboard," the old woman said. "He desired death and they could not stop him."

A fierce throbbing closed her throat. Nikola lunged at them, only to be thrown headlong into the pool by an invisible force. She surfaced, sputtering.

"You lie!" she shouted.

"We will show you if you don't believe." The Crone held up a gemstone. "This holds a sweven that was taken from one of the sisters who was there. I swear on the Great Serpent it is a true memory. Do you wish to see it?"

"No!" She tore her gaze from the stone. "No, I do not."

"You will not believe until you do," the Mother said gently.

"Why do you care what I believe?" Nikola spat.

"Because your journey was not wasted. You can start a new life here. A place will be found for you."

She backed away, chest heaving. "Do not speak to me, witch!"

The youngest moved to follow her and was restrained by

the blind woman. Nikola stumbled down a narrow crevice, tears blinding her eyes. It led to a hole in the cliff face. No way out except to swim and she was not ready to face the sea again. A slow, twisting agony unfurled. She'd convinced herself he was alive because she wanted to believe it. But she could easily imagine Malach choosing death over captivity.

An immense rage made her tremble. Why had she opened her heart even the tiniest crack to him? He would do nothing but break it again and again.

"I hate you," she whispered. "And I will always hate you until the day I die."

She dredged up every trial he had put her through, hoping it might dull the pain, yet one image kept forcing its way unwanted into her mind. Malach, weals on his cupped fingers, offering her freshly picked blackberries. A stripe of sunlight fell across his eyes, picking out a single strand of silver in his dark hair. Mouth unsmiling but soft as he watched her eat them.

Once she'd thought him cold, but he had deep reserves of passion. When they weren't directed only at fulfilling his own desires, they shone bright and warm like the sun.

He could have run the instant he saw the witch. But he had warned her and stayed to fight so Nikola could escape. Funny, how she had been so bent on getting away from him. She hadn't wanted the child, either. She still didn't. Yet now that both of them were gone forever . . . .

She sank to her knees and wept bitter tears. At length, the storm passed, leaving a hollow calm in its wake. When she trusted herself again, Nikola returned to the cavern.

"Give it to me," she said tightly, holding out a hand.

The Mother pressed the stone into her bloody, calloused palm. Such a small thing to feel so heavy. Nikola bit her lip. "How does it work?"

"Every gift of the earth contains a small amount of ley.

This one has been altered to hold a sweven. We will release it when you are ready."

The witches could be lying. They probably expected her to refuse.

But if it *were* true . . . once she had the memory, she would never be able to unsee it. His death would live inside her mind, to be replayed over and over. Blood rushed in her ears like the tidal flux of the ocean as the Mother reached for her.

"Wait!" she cried.

Light flowed outward from the stone, curling in tendrils around her wrist. She tried to cast the stone away, but her fingers only clenched tighter. The ground tilted beneath her feet—

THE CREAK of rigging and snap of sails billowing in a steady wind. It tugs at your skirts as you study the prisoner in chains on the deck. A well-made man, handsome despite the nightmarish images that cover his naked body. It's unfortunate he is so tainted.

"You are aingeal," Cairness spits angrily. "Never to be trusted!"

Paarjini scowls. "Enough, Cairness."

"Then why bring me here?" he asks, jaw tight.

"Because you are a thorn in the foot of the ley," your sister hisses. "The flaw that breaks the alloy. You should be—"

Cairness never could leash her temper. You warned Paarjini not to bring her along. She's always hated them with a passion. Nursing the old grudges like a babe at her breast. Now the prisoner looks panicked. He doubles over, spitting blood on the deck. "Ah, please. It hurts! Like a knife twisting in my guts!"

An obvious ruse, but two of the sailors run up. He is lying

in a tight ball now, eyes closed, broad shoulders wracked with shivers.

"Help him!" the Masdari shouts.

Before you can stop her, Paarjini bends down. "This should not be happening. I imbued the stone with a spell of protection—"

In an instant, his chains are around her throat. The prisoner drags her to the rail.

"Drop a longboat," he yells. "Or I snap her neck!"

Paarjini's eyes bulge. She claws at the chain.

"Do it!" he snarls.

You tamp down irritation. Paarjini was a fool to come within his reach, but it is done. At least one of you can remain calm and try to salvage the situation. Captain Aemyn swears as you slide a hand into the pouch at your waist, groping for the chunk of turquoise. The stone is cool against your skin. You open your inner eye to the ley and it surges forth, even as you realize that it is already too late. He planned this from the start.

He looks directly at you with a small smile. Then he tumbles overboard into the clear green water. You rush to the rail and lean over, but he has already vanished beneath the waves. Only a pale blur now, the chains dragging him swiftly into the depths—

———

THE STONE FELL from her hand. Nikola stumbled to the edge of the cavern. The meal burned like acid as she retched it up. She braced a palm against the rock wall, letting the pain of her injured hand wash over her. They'd given her no warning. Not a word that the sweven was drawn from the woman who sent Malach to his death.

In that instant, it was as though Nikola had done it herself. She felt soiled beyond redemption. There was no question of the sweven's veracity. It wasn't just Malach's Marks or the various scars on his body, each one of which she knew intimately. She recognized every fleeting emotion that crossed his face. Fear, determination—and, at the last, acceptance. Yet there was one thing she couldn't understand.

She drew a deep breath through her nose and walked back to them.

"Why didn't he use the ley to defend himself?" she asked tightly.

"He had the kaldurite in his belly," the Mother replied.

"My kaldurite?" As if it couldn't get any worse.

The witch nodded. "He would have killed Paarjini. The sisters could not allow that."

Nikola clenched her jaw against angry tears. "I told you to wait!"

"*We* did," the Crone rasped. "You took the sweven yourself before we could stop you."

"I . . . ." Nikola blinked. "That's not possible."

The Maid stalked over, a jeweled braid coiled over one bare shoulder. "It should not be. Yet it is."

Nikola kicked the stone, sending it skipping into the pool with a splash. "How do I leave this place? I am done with all of you!"

The Crone's blind eyes fixed on her. "But we are not done with you, Nikola Thorn."

"What does that mean?"

"It means," said the Mother, "that you are already a witch —and a powerful one."

"I . . . No." She shook her head. "You're mistaken."

"You instinctively drew the sweven, untrained. Now that your ability has awoken, it won't go away. And we will not have you running about with no knowledge of how to control it."

The weight of her words sunk in. Nikola gave a hollow

laugh. "You think I'd become one of *you*? After you murdered the father—" She cut off, cursing her loose tongue.

"Of your child?" the Mother finished.

"We know more than you think," the girl added haughtily.

"I want nothing to do with the ley," Nikola said. "If I did touch it somehow, it was by accident. I will never do it again."

She'd been raised among people who worshipped the ley like a god—a god who'd rejected her as unworthy. The power meant nothing to her. Yet it was true that the witch had not been touching the stone when the sweven unspooled in her mind. And she had *seen* the ley herself, for the first time. An unearthly blue light.

"You are Unmarked," the Crone said with an edge of disdain. "A pathetic castoff in the eyes of the Via Sancta. Is that the life you choose for yourself? Is running all you are fit for?"

"Yes," Nikola growled. "It's suited me fine so far."

"Has it? We do not believe you."

Her hatred swelled beyond all reason. She was about to tell the witches that they could go fog themselves sideways when a thought occurred to her. There might be hope of redemption yet. As much as she still hated Malach for leaving her, it was partly her fault. He had come to the beach for *her*. It was *her* stone that stole his power away.

She already knew the name of the witch who had caught him. Paarjini. Nikola recognized her as the one on the beach disguised as a sailor. She had only to find out which of them the sweven belonged to. She had one hint already. A glimpse of the woman's hand as she raised the stone, palm open in a deadly offering. The skin was blue-black, several shades darker than Nikola's. She wore distinctive rings. And she was much taller than the plump red-haired witch at her side. Taller even than Captain Aemlyn. That should narrow it down considerably.

Nikola would discover her name. Then she'd make her pay, however long it took.

"Perhaps you're right," she said. "If I have this talent, at least I should learn more about it."

The girl's storm-cloud eyes narrowed at her abrupt change of heart, but the Mother smiled. "A wise choice."

The blind one sniffed. "Your hands must heal first. Then we will see what can be done with you."

Her ordeal finally caught up. Nikola swayed on her feet, eyes swollen and heavy-lidded. Now that her course was decided, she wanted only oblivion.

"Go lie down, child," the Mother said.

Nikola did as bade, stretching out on the damp stone. The ledge might have been a goosedown mattress for all the difference it made. When her eyes closed, she saw Malach, gathered into the sea's embrace with a faint smile on his lips.

I'm coming, she thought, following him down, down into the warm dark. Just wait for me. Wait—

Chapter Seven

Malach stood at the sink as the children lined up to hand him their dirty bowls.

"Finish that," he said to Inry, pointing at the half-empty bowl of porridge. "If you don't, you'll be begging for a snack in an hour."

The boy threw his head back with a theatrical groan but sat at the table and shoveled in another mouthful.

"Cristory, go fetch your raincoat. And get Roseen's, too."

"Yes, Malach." She skipped off, braids swinging. He eyed the smoothness of the weave with satisfaction. He'd added coconut oil while it was still wet from the bath. Then it wasn't snarled when she woke up and it made pretty waves when he combed it out later.

"Where are your boots?" he asked Lonan.

"Don't know."

"Go find them."

"Already looked. One's gone."

Malach thought for a moment. "You were wearing them when we came inside yesterday. Check under the couch."

The boy dawdled.

"Now," he said firmly, making eye contact.

He rarely yelled, but he'd learned that if you didn't look at them when you spoke, they'd ignore you.

"'Kay." Lonan ran off. A long pause. "Found it!"

"Then put it on!" He turned to Ealish. They were alone in the kitchen. Malach wiped his hands on the apron. "Remember what we talked about?"

She gave a sullen nod.

"Finish your orange juice."

Her chin stuck out. "It's got pulp."

The girl had taken to not drinking so she could avoid the bathroom. Malach wasn't having it.

"I believe in you," he said quietly. "You're going to show them that you're a big girl." An evil grin. "And I can't wait to see the looks on their stupid faces."

Ealish's lips twitched.

"So finish the juice. Then you'll give me the secret sign later. We're going to make it this time. I can feel it."

After weeks of coaxing, he had her at the point where she'd at least attempt to use the bathroom. They'd started with just sitting on the toilet when she didn't have to go. For some reason that was easy. But she balked at actually using it. They'd made it inside the bathroom several times, but she always peed on the floor.

Ealish slumped down at the table. She drank the juice, complaining about the pulp the entire time. He rinsed the cup and set it on the drainboard. Then he crouched down so they were eye to eye.

"I'm proud of you no matter what, okay?"

She nodded, not meeting his eye.

"But if you do it once, just once, that'll be it. No more itches." He stood. "Get your boots."

"It's raining."

"Playing in the rain is fun."

"Yvor always made us stay in."

"Do I look like Yvor?"

She took his hand and stroked the dagger. "No, you're bigger. But we like you better."

He blinked in surprise. "Why?"

Ealish looked at him shrewdly. "'Cause you don't lie like other grownups."

"Oh."

"Is it because you're aingeal?"

He stiffened. "Where did you hear that?"

Finlo never used the word. Malach had told the children his Marks were made from ink.

"Bretan says so."

He was one of the older boys in Finlo's charge.

"I am aingeal," he admitted. "But my people lie, too."

She absorbed this with a thoughtful expression. "Why don't you?"

"I do sometimes." He smiled. "Just not to you."

She threw her arms around his waist. Poor Ealish. She was so desperate for affection. Roseen was the harshest, but all the kids thought she was weird. Malach picked her up and set her on his hip. At three and a half, she already had long legs.

"Be brave for me today," he said. "Now get your stuff."

He set her down and took off the apron, watching as she scampered from the kitchen.

They'd be muddy as hell when they came back inside, but he already had four loads of laundry to do. What did one more matter? And some form of exercise was crucial. If they stayed in, they'd trash the playroom and then refuse to nap, which was the worst possible outcome. Without that hour of quiet, he'd never get his other chores done.

"Form up!" he bellowed, grabbing a slicker from the hook by the front door.

There was the inevitable delay as he tied shoes, zipped jackets and located the stuffed snake with a red cloth tongue that Cristory couldn't live without. If she took it outside, he'd have to pry it from her hands to wash it later, but he couldn't face the battle it would require to leave it behind, so he delayed that fight until afternoon. Maybe he could sneak it away while she napped.

Finlo had taken the older ones on a field trip to visit one of the smaller temples to Valmitra. The house was pleasantly quiet.

They went out to the yard. It wasn't raining too hard. Inry and Lonan beelined to the swings, immediately fighting over who got the one on the left. Both swings were identical. Unless it came to blows, he wouldn't intervene. Then Cristory and Roseen discovered the deep puddle beneath the other swing where the children's feet had eroded the ground. After jumping in it, they sat down to make mud pies.

"Take turns!" Malach called over when the boys' dispute escalated. Each of them had hold of the swing, jerking it back and forth. They paused to stare at him.

"Inry went first yesterday. Today it's Lonan's turn."

Inry scowled, but the solution complied with the children's moral code. He backed away and let Lonan have the swing. "When do I get a turn?"

"Practice your numbers. Start counting to fifty."

Finlo had given him that trick. Two birds with one stone. He'd be too busy counting to cause trouble and it satisfied the need for a definite end to the turn. Plus, Lonan needed the practice. Instead of writing numbers like all the others, he drew pictures of rainbows.

Inry backed up and let the swing fly. His feet hit the puddle as he passed over it, splattering the girls. Malach waited for a scream, but they seemed to like it.

"Do it again!" Cristory laughed.

The swing was passing dangerously close to the girls. Malach performed a rapid calculus. Tell them to move and they'd be mad. It was clearly the best puddle around. Sure, someone might get hit, but it wouldn't be the first time. He used to be terrified of the swings. What if they fell off? Or crashed into another kid? As it turned out, they never fell off unless they were actively trying to. And the collision, while hard, wasn't bone-shattering. The kid would get knocked over, cry, and then go on with whatever they were doing.

Malach chose to let fate take its course.

Raising children, he had learned, required *some* degree of forethought—if only to the next fifteen minutes. Who will get hungry and do I have a snack? If I have a snack, is a food item they'll eat, or is that particular food on a taboo list? If I allow one child to do something, am I truly prepared to let *all* of them do it? And the most important of all: Never, ever make threats you don't mean to carry out.

They were like the nihilim. If they wanted something, it was all they thought about. All they lived for. To get that one thing. Children were smart. They knew your attention was divided in a million places. If they just kept at you and kept at you, they'd eventually find a weak spot in the defenses. Yet with Malach they met a stone wall. It took weeks, but the children finally understood that he meant what he said.

And he never lied.

After that, things got a little easier. He learned the fine art of compromise. He was generous with praise when it was deserved. They obeyed his orders, mostly, though they didn't warm to him.

That changed with the vomit soup.

It was another rainy day. He was exhausted by noon—a seemingly permanent state of affairs. The children were bored and cranky. So, in a fit of madness, he'd brought them all into the kitchen, yanked a huge bowl out of the cabinet, and told them to make soup.

The stove had safety latches. Through a fog of harassed distraction, he made sure they were all set and no sharp implements were lying around. Then he wandered into the playroom to straighten up the horrific mess before Finlo returned and passed out on the rug, having failed to learn his lesson from the last time.

He woke to Ealish shaking his arm. "Wake up, Malach! *Wake up!*"

He cracked his eyes.

"Come see what we made!"

Malach rolled to his back, filling with dread.

She tugged at his hand. "Come see!"

"Is everyone alive?" he asked blearily.

She ignored the question, but he thought screaming would have woken him. Probably.

"Come see, come see!"

The rest were crowding around now. All five. That was good. He moved to stand, Lonan hanging from his shoulders, and hoisted the boy higher. Piggyback rides were what had destroyed him after breakfast, but he felt better for the nap. Ready to face whatever fresh horror lurked in the kitchen.

It was about as bad as he'd expected. Every cabinet door standing wide open. Every drawer rifled as though the place had been robbed. Chairs were dragged to the cabinets so they could access the upper shelves. Flour coated the floor and table, along with various spices and condiments. A brimming bowl rested on the table.

"We made lunch!" Cristory announced, running to set out teacups as Lonan stirred the mess with a crusted wooden spoon.

Malach put on an expression of astonishment. "How did you know my favorite dish? It's an old family recipe."

They exchanged looks. "What's it called?" Inry asked.

Broken chunks of carrot and other nameless things floated in a milky, speckled liquid.

"Vomit soup," Malach said.

This was met with screams of delight. He pretended to eat some, then told them to clean it all up. That didn't go so well, but at least he'd made a token gesture at teaching them responsibility. He poured the liquid down the sink and sent Roseen, who could generally be trusted, to give the scraps to the chickens.

He didn't realize Ealish had laughed so hard she peed her pants until she sat on his lap.

Once, Malach would have felt private disgust, but he'd lost even that capacity. He simply said, "Whoops," picked her up, stuck her in a bath, changed his Rahai, put on a clean one, and threw a load of the laundry into the washer without another thought. Personal dignity had no meaning down in the trenches with four-year-olds.

Now he watched Ealish closely. She'd drunk quite a lot of juice at breakfast. It was almost magic time.

"Fuck," he muttered.

A car crept up the drive. Malach ran over and bent to the open window, rain coursing from the hood of his slicker. "Not a good time, Paarjini."

He could have spoken in Athaaran, but he liked to make her use Osterlish. A petty inconvenience, but satisfying nonetheless.

The witch smiled. "Happened to be passin' by, aingeal. Thought I'd see how you're faring with the wee ones."

"Fine," he said, glancing over at the children.

"Finlo says they've taken to ye. And you're not half bad at it."

"What do you want?"

"Only to say ye've done me proud." Her gaze moved to the house. "Where's Finlo?"

"Field trip."

She looked disappointed. "Tell him I say hello."

"Yeah, I will. Look, I really have to get back."

Her occasional visits were a reminder that they were watching. But he knew the witch also had something going on with Finlo. It would have been amusing if she wasn't about to ruin weeks of hard work.

"So eager to be rid o' me?" Parrjini laughed. "All right then." She raised a hand in farewell, rolled up the window, and threw the car into reverse, backing down the drive.

Malach turned to Ealish. The girl crouched at the puddle, patting at her mud pie. Cris and Roseen played nearby but didn't include her in their games, as usual. When Ealish suddenly stood up, knees pressed together, Malach leapt in for the kill. She was supposed to give him a secret sign, but she never did.

"Let's go inside," he said, loud enough for the others to hear. "Help me grab the snacks."

She gave a shaky nod. They hurried to the door. She was covered in mud. Did he dare take a few extra seconds to get her boots off?

Malach glanced down at her tense face.

No.

No, he did not.

They ran into the half-bath next to the kitchen, leaving a trail of muddy footprints. He'd left the light on. She wouldn't pee in a dark bathroom. Nor would she let him close the door. Like some superstitious primitive of yore, Ealish insisted that the stars had to align perfectly, in every way, if the monster that lurked in the toilet wouldn't get her.

"Almost there," he said calmly.

They'd made it to the doorway countless times, only to fail at the last instant. The child stared straight ahead with a fixed, determined look in her eye. She was already yanking down her shorts. The toilet loomed ahead. Malach felt a surge of wonder as her butt hit the seat.

She held it in. She actually held it—

Ealish let out a stream of urine so hard it hit the doorknob. Malach leapt back. Hysterical laughter bubbled in his throat, but he held it inside. Laughing at her would ruin everything.

"Can you try to lean forward?" he wondered.

She clung to the seat, back rigid. At last, it ended. Ealish looked up at him with a glow of triumph. "I did it, Malach! I did it!"

"You sure did," he said, grinning back. "Don't forget to wipe. And wash your hands."

She complied, then ran off without flushing. That would be another battle. He stood for a moment, confounded. He didn't know little girls could even *do* that.

The kids played in the yard for a while more, then ate lunch and went down for naps. Malach dealt with the mess. When Finlo returned, they sat for a cup of tea in the kitchen. It was a daily ritual that Malach looked forward to with pathetic eagerness. They mostly talked about the kids, but just speaking to another adult kept him sane. He heard about the field trip, then proudly announced that Ealish had made it all the way that afternoon.

Finlo clapped him on the arm. "Nice work! I can't believe she peed in the toilet."

Malach looked at him seriously. "Well, she sat on it. And she peed. But she didn't pee *in* it."

Finlo looked puzzled.

"Not a single drop went in," he explained. "Not one. She peed straight out." He pointed to give a visual aid. "It went *everywhere*—except in the toilet."

Finlo choked on his tea.

"I didn't know what to do. I actually ran into the kitchen and grabbed a pot lid," Malach explained, laughing so hard he could barely get the words out. "To . . . deflect it . . . . But it just made it worse."

"Oh, goddess." Finlo slumped at the counter, wiping his eyes. "Uh, which lid?"

Malach doubled over.

WHEN HE TUCKED them in that night, Ealish said she had to go, and this time she managed it in normal fashion. The child seemed peaceful as she burrowed beneath the covers. He kissed her brow, smoothing the dark hair back.

Is someone doing the same to my daughter?

The thought came out of nowhere. He'd been so consumed with getting through the days, his own grief had receded into the lightless depths—and Malach did everything he could to keep it there. But it was always waiting to bite if he came too close.

He switched off the lights, chest aching with a devouring emptiness.

Chapter Eight

Nikola faced the plump, flame-haired witch. "I don't understand what you're saying," she repeated, more slowly this time.

She'd woken in another cave, but the rough-hewn chamber was furnished with a bed, table and two chairs. Someone had dressed her in a white gown and bandaged her hands. They felt stiff. No sooner had she sat up than the witch appeared, yammering at her in a foreign tongue. It was guttural in parts, musical in others.

And altogether incomprehensible.

The witch eyed her impassively. "You must learn our tongue while you recover," she said in a thick accent. "The task has fallen to me. We have little time, so I hope you are a quick study." She touched her chest. "Es ain dom Cairness."

The other witch from the ship. Nikola schooled her face to a bland expression. She could not let them know much she despised them. Not until it was too late.

"Es ain dom Nikola Thorn," she replied.

There was no hint of approval in her gray eyes. "This is the last thing I will say to you in Osterlish, Nikola. If you want something, you will ask for it in *my* tongue. If you have a question or complaint, it will be spoken in Athaaran. You will do nothing else but practice the language until you *dream* in it. Do you understand?"

Nikola gave her a sour nod. "What's the word for *yes?*"

"Ta. I expect to hear it from you frequently."

Cairness handed her a battered primer made for children. It had pictures of everyday objects and people doing things, with words beneath.

"*Sgrùdadh*," she said. "Study. *Ionnsachadh*. Learn."

Nikola set the book aside. "I have to pee."

Cairness stared at her. She said something that sounded like *thigib* and strode out the door. Nikola hurried to follow. A network of caves burrowed into the rock, some for sleeping, others for gathering. None had doors. A few women in the same wrapped dresses as Cairness glanced over as they passed. The steady, rumbling wash of the sea was not far off. Yet the rooms were dry and snug, with thick carpets covering the stone. The witch led her down a passage to a small alcove. It had a hole in the floor. A roll of toilet paper rested on a narrow ledge. Nikola peered into the hole. Waves surged below.

"This is it?" she asked.

The witch pretended not to hear. She left Nikola to it.

Sitting on the hole with her sore bum was unappealing, so Nikola braced a leg on either side and peed straight down. A metal bin seemed meant for the used paper. It wasn't so bad. Men peed that way. Though she didn't look forward to the other.

She found her own way back to her chamber and studied the book until Cairness returned and brought her to a larger chamber overlooking the water. Six witches sat at a long wooden table, with two other women in the plain white dress Nikola wore. The girls were younger, one dark, one fair. They chattered to each other, sneaking glances her way. Cairness made no attempt at introductions.

Since Nikola was forbidden to speak Osterlish and understood nothing of the conversation, she ate in silence. More fish, very spicy, and yellow rice. Water was the only beverage, but it was fresh and cool and tasted like ambrosia. After, Cairness showed her the bathing chamber. A pool like the one in the Mahadeva's grotto, deeper and so hot she had to ease into it by inches. The soak did wonders for her stiff muscles.

Back at her own room, Nikola unwrapped the sodden bandages. Her palms were cracked and raw but didn't look infected. She sniffed the skin with a grimace. They'd applied some sticky ointment. It smelled foul. She lay back, staring at the rough ceiling. It wasn't as bad as the Arx in Novostopol, though she seemed fated to always be the outsider, hovering at the edges.

"I'm not here to make friends anyway," she muttered.

Could she really learn lithomancy? Be a powerful witch in her own right? The idea stirred feelings she didn't care to examine too closely. With a sigh, she blew out the candle and went to sleep.

AT HOME, Nikola rarely bothered with books. When she did pick one up, she'd be daydreaming by the third page. Absorbing an entire language at the ripe age of twenty-seven proved torturous. When she finally mastered the first primer, Cairness brought her two more. There were regular verbs to memorize, present, past and future. Then all the *irregular* verbs. Then the genders of the nouns—a stupid, pointless complication that Osterlish lacked. She attempted halting conversations, though deciphering the witch's rapid, clipped speech was far more difficult than reading the books. Sometimes she caught words here and there when she eavesdropped on the others, but not the meaning of the sentence. It was maddening.

Cairness had not lied when she said Nikola would do nothing else until she grasped the basics of the Athaaran tongue. Only the knowledge that her revenge depended on it kept Nikola from hurling the primers straight down the piss-hole. That vow burned like a quiet, steady flame inside her. She threw herself into her studies, often skipping meals because she had her nose stuck in a book. Even Cairness, who had never once expressed any interest in Nikola's welfare, began to chastise her for working too hard. She insisted that Nikola walk along the beach each day to stretch her legs. The other acolytes were assigned to accompany her, which is how she learned their names. Bethen was the fair one, with spun gold hair and long, gangly limbs. She had a sunny innocence that made her hard to hate.

"I like your silver tooth," she said with a grin, speaking slowly and pointing to her own white canine.

Nikola tried to explain how she'd lost the tooth riding a bicycle and saved up her salary for weeks to buy a fancier replacement. The tale required a combination of pantomime and creative use of her meager word list, but Bethen seemed eager to help, teaching her the correct terms and covering a sympathetic gasp of laughter as Nikola pretended to fall off the bike. *Oh shit* was apparently a universal expression.

Jenifry was more reserved, but not exactly unfriendly. They were already well into practicing simple spells and hadn't been forbidden to talk about it in general terms. Thus Nikola learned that lithomancy had to do with something the witches called the "inner eye." One used this intuitive capacity to tap the ley inside the stones.

There were different types of witches. Some served at the temples. Others helped the crops grow. Still others were warriors, defending the isles from invaders. This much they admitted, but when she pressed them about how lithomancy actually worked, they clammed up.

"Your time will come, Nikola," Bethany said gently.

"Do they ever speak of me?"

The blond novice shook her head. "No, but they never speak of others' progress." A sigh. "It is very difficult to master. Most are years in training. Trust me, I am not much ahead of you."

Nikola returned to the vat of laundry she was scrubbing. "I did not come all this way to be a char again," she muttered.

"Why did you come?"

Nikola turned her face away. The grief came and went in waves. She'd be fine for days and then it would strike over the stupidest thing. Rain made her think of their last night together. The yarrow blossoms growing near the sea reminded her of his scarlet robes, the chunks of dark amber on Paarjini's bracelet of his eyes.

"To escape," she said simply, which was true. But the chains of memory were not so easily broken.

One night, six weeks into her language studies, Cairness came to summon her for supper. Dark had fallen. Stacks of primers covered the table, along with the stubs of used candles.

"You must eat," the witch said, hands on her hips. "Your mind will not function properly if you deny the body it is attached to."

Nikola looked up, bleary-eyed, and covered a yawn. "I'm almost done with this chapter. There in a minute."

"Now."

Nikola's lips thinned. Curse the woman! She pushes me relentlessly, and now she complains when I do as I'm told. I ought to—

Nikola blinked. She realized that not only had they been speaking easily in Athaaran, but she had just *thought* in Athaaran. She leapt to her feet.

"When can I begin my real training?" she asked, holding out her hands. "They are healed. And you must admit I speak well enough to understand."

Cairness arched a brow. "I will discuss it with the Mahadeva."

Two more days went by, during which Nikola awaited their decision in an agony of impatience. She was rinsing out her headscarf when her shoulder-blades began to tingle. Nikola turned. A statuesque woman with short-cropped kinky hair was watching her. She had a full mouth, wide-spaced eyes and broad, flat nose between chiseled cheekbones. Nikola's gaze dropped to the rings on the witch's hands. Her heart beat rapidly in her chest.

"I am Heshima," the woman said. Her voice was rich and husky. "I will be your tutor."

Nikola wrung out the scarf and stood. "I am eager to learn," she said.

"Good. Come to me after supper."

Heshima turned and walked away. Nikola watched her, fighting the urge to race after and drag her to the ground. It could be no accident that they had given her the very witch who cast the spell against Malach. Or did they think her too stupid to realize? If it was a test, she intended to pass. Bide her time. Extract every drop of knowledge—then decide on a suitable punishment. Something to make her hair and teeth fall out, perhaps.

And that would be just the beginning.

She barely tasted the meal. It took some searching, but she finally found the witch in an empty chamber with one wall open to the sea. Dozens of beeswax candles burned on the floor. Nikola sat down cross-legged across from her. To her vast relief, there were no books. Just a large leather pouch.

"All magic is change," Heshima said. "Transformation. It is through the grace of the goddess that we have the ley and the means to use it. What do you know of Valmitra?"

"Very little," Nikola admitted.

"Then I will tell you. She takes various shapes. Serpent. Wyrm. Dragon. Like those creatures, her form is in constant flux." Heshima held up a gemstone. "Every scale contains a fragment of her power. When she sheds her skin, it works its way to the surface. This is why the mines never run dry. They are constantly replenished from below."

Nikola nodded, tamping down her impatience. She had no interest in their religion.

"To tap this power, there are three requirements. First is the need. The emptiness that cannot be filled by any other means. The wish and the will. Second, the emotion associated with the need. Without passion, need has no force or meaning. Lastly, the knowledge. The rituals known only to the witch."

Again, Nikola nodded, hanging on every word now. At last she was learning something useful!

"Explain what I just said in your own words," Heshima ordered.

She swallowed, sifting through her still limited vocabulary. "The mind tells the hand to move, but the hand must hold the proper tool to do the work."

Heshima gave her a considering look. "Yes, that is one way of looking at it. But there is a fourth thing of great importance. The moral standpoint. Magic is used to protect. To restore harmony. It is performed out of love, not hate. "

Nikola held her steady gaze.

"Some are drawn to magic because they think to use it as a weapon. This is wrong. Attempt to wield manipulative magic and it will rebound on you tenfold."

The hypocrisy of this statement made her blood simmer, but Nikola would not rise to the bait. "I understand."

"I hope you do. Now, I will explain the basics. When a stone holds ley, it is *charged*. That means it has the potential to create change. The spell discharges the energy from the stone. Most can only be used once. There are two types of energy: projective and receptive. The first projects power outward. It connects to the subconscious mind. Receptive stones are the natural complement. They direct the ley inward. They are soothing and calming. Protective. They attract good. With practice, you will know just from looking at a stone which type it is. That is where we will begin."

She took a gem from her pouch and handed it to Nikola. "Feel the weight. The size and color. Which do you think this is?"

The gem was dark red and heavy. "Projective," Nikola guessed after a moment.

Heshima's face gave nothing away. "Why?"

"The color."

"What about the color?"

She looked away. "It made me think of giving birth. Blood and pain. But also creation."

Nikola sensed the witch's surprise in a slight widening of her eyes. "Yes, garnet is projective. What about this one?"

She set the garnet aside and examined an oval, pearly-looking stone. "Receptive."

"Why?"

"It looks like a pool on a still night with the moon shining down overhead."

"And?"

"The image is peaceful. Sleepy." She set it next to the garnet. "Was I right?"

"In every respect." The witch eyed her warily now. "Moonstone is both receptive and strongly associated with water." She opened her pouch and spilled an array of stones across the floor. "One by one, Nikola."

She chose a black stone. "Projective," she said immediately. "It makes me think of a mirror. Reflecting back another spell."

"Onyx. It is defensive."

"This one . . . . " She cupped the smooth blue stone. "I see a falcon high in the sky, hunting."

"Lapis. It enhances eyesight. Which makes it what?"

"Receptive."

Nikola worked her way through the pile. Not all were gemstones. There were chunks of marble, coins, lumps of ore. She didn't know the names, but she unerringly named their properties. By the end, she no longer needed to touch them. Just the color and shape were enough. Heshima grew quiet, affirming each choice with a slight nod.

"There are so many to remember," Nikola said, flushed with her triumph. "But I will set myself to learn the names. Do you have any more?"

Heshima swept the pile back into the pouch. "We have been working for three hours. I think it is enough."

Nikola felt surprised. The time had passed quickly. "Can we resume in the morning?"

"No."

Nikola scowled. "Why? Haven't I pleased you?"

The witch barked a deep laugh. "I have never seen talent like yours before. I think you are ready for the first initiation. It comes much later for most acolytes, but you are an unusual case." Her pewter eyes flickered. "In more ways than one."

"What's the initiation?" Nikola wondered.

Heshima smiled.

She tossed and turned that night, brain whirling with disconnected thoughts. The next day, Cairness led her down the beach. The tide was going out, leaving clumps of black seaweed. Little crabs burrowed into the sand. Nikola walked in the shallows, letting the waves wash her feet. Her nerves sang, but she wouldn't let the red-haired witch see it.

She expected a bunch of them to be waiting, some ritual prayer followed by a demonstration of ability, but Cairness led her inside another cave and down a long passage. It ended at a vertical shaft leading down into darkness. Iron rungs were attached to the sides of the shaft.

"To commune with Valmitra, you must enter her domain," Cairness said.

Nikola peered into the hole. "How far down does it go?"

"Far enough."

She listened, but there was no sound of waves splashing below. "What am I supposed to do?"

"You will remain at the bottom until she names you."

"How long does that take?"

"It depends. Sometimes hours, sometimes days. I will wait here. But if you come out before Valmitra makes her will known, you will learn no more."

Nikola considered this. "What happens to acolytes who fail the test?"

"They go home. Since you have no home, nor skills, you will be given a job in the fields."

And lose all hope of getting back at them.

"I will not fail."

Cairness said nothing. She sat down on the floor and started reading a book.

Nikola climbed down the rungs. Gradually, the shaft around her faded until she moved purely by feel. At last her feet touched bottom. She groped along the walls. The chamber was barely larger than the shaft itself.

What did "naming" mean? How would she know when it was done?

Boredom set in immediately. She passed the time reviewing the lesson with Heshima. *Nicomar*. Receptive. Used for protection and success in an endeavor. *Kunzite*. Also receptive, with strong earth properties. *Fairy-shot*. Projective. Used for divination. *Black amber*. Receptive and a ward against nightmares. *Cat's Eye*. Projective. An aid for youth and beauty, but also to make a cloak of invisibility. Heshima had not told her that, but she'd sensed its potential for illusion.

When she finished with stones, she turned to metals. Gold, brass and antimony. Rulers of fire. Aluminum, mercury and tin. Rulers of air. They must be part of the blasting spells. Definitely projective. Copper, lodestone, and silver ruled water. She wondered what would happen if you mixed fire and water with the proper focus. Could she make a person's blood boil in their veins? Yet she had taken the witch's warning to heart. Nikola would not attempt magic with malicious intent until she felt certain she had complete mastery.

The hours unspooled. She paced in circles. Just the brief taste had opened a whole new world of possibility. The endless combinations of stone and metal. It was far beyond what Marks could do! Lithomancy was the first thing she could claim any talent whatsoever for, though why it was so, she had no idea.

Nikola had feared it would be like learning their language. Rote memorization that made her head pound. Yet lithomancy felt more akin to remembering something she had forgotten. In every other way, her instincts were terrible. Striking a bargain with Malach was merely the *coup de grace* in a lifetime of dubious choices. But this! It came as naturally as great sex—without the regrets.

She basked in the glow for a while, but eventually tedium set in again. She sat and dozed. Woke and paced. The temptation to climb the ladder and invent a story for Cairness was strong, but Nikola resisted. The craving for knowledge outweighed everything else. Her natural skill would only get her so far. She wanted all their tricks. Every scrap they possessed. If she had to sit in a hole for a month to get it, she would.

Hunger and thirst were minor annoyances. She discovered new reserves of stubborn patience. She would wait them out. Wait wait wait. Surely something will occur!

Interesting, what happens to a mind left in darkness. Memories surfaced—of Bal Kirith, but also her childhood and life at the Arx. The people she had known. Old grievances. Then the future. Will this happen? Or will that happen? What if I get what I want? What if I *don't* get what I want? Will anything make me truly happy?

Then, the remorse. Does the child hate me? Does she know my name? Does she look more like him or like me?

On and on.

And at last, when the machine broke down and the war was lost, a strange quiet.

Her own heartbeat. The slow movement of air. Nothing else. Time ceased to have meaning.

Pain brought her back. Just a twinge at first. She coughed, pressing a hand to her chest. Her eyes opened, though in the black it made no difference. Hunger gnawed at her stomach. Nikola swallowed, the discomfort increasing. Something scraped at her womb.

Saints, not her monthly blood. *Not now.*

The pain ceased. She exhaled slowly, then reached for a rung of the ladder and hauled herself up. Weak. How long had she been down there? Wait too long and she wouldn't have the strength to climb out. Would Cairness come looking? Nikola wasn't sure.

"Not yet," she whispered. "I will stay a little bit longer—"

Her larynx closed. She let go of the ladder, dropping to hands and knees. Sweat erupted at the edge of her headscarf. Something was very wrong.

She coughed hard, throat burning. Coughed again. Violently. A hard object slid past her tongue. She heard it strike the ground. Nikola spat, wincing at the taste.

"You've got to be kidding me," she muttered thickly.

She felt along the ground until she found it, slippery with saliva.

"Oh, you bitches," she whispered with a shaky laugh.

A thrill of excitement coursed through her. It was only the size of her thumbnail, but the edges had sharp facets. She cleared her throat. Spat again. She had no pockets. With a sigh, she stowed the stone between her teeth and climbed the ladder on watery legs. When she got to the top, she spit it into her palm and held it out for Cairness's inspection.

"That's what I got," she said. "It looks like kaldurite, but it can't be. There's ley inside. So what is it?"

Her voice sounded as raspy as the blind crone.

Cairness examined it with a frown. The light in the cavern was dim. "I don't know."

"How can you not know?"

"I have never seen this before. Give it to me."

Nikola closed her fist. "It's mine."

Cairness blinked at the fierceness of her tone. "Very well. But you must show it to Heshima."

The bright sunlight of the beach stabbed her eyes. When they reached the main cavern, Bethen ran up. "You have been gone three days, Nikola! I was only one and a half, and that seemed very long." Her gaze went to Nikola's closed fist. "I see you were successful. We knew you would be." Her voice lowered. "Everyone heard what you did with Heshima. They talk of nothing else."

Nikola allowed the girl to take her hand and draw her to the dining chamber, where food and drink awaited. She gulped down some water, clutching her prize beneath the table. Bethen was clearly burning with curiosity.

"I got agate," she said, holding up the gem that now hung from her neck on a silver chain. "It's—"

"Both projective and receptive," Nikola muttered through a mouthful of rice. "Elements of both earth and fire. Used for courage, fertility, healing. A sovereign charm against the mages' sorcery."

Bethen's eyes widened. "Yes!" She leaned forward. "Though I did not know the last."

"Nor did I until a moment ago." Nikola let her fork fall. She felt peculiar. Both sluggish and hyper-alert. Too many thoughts crowded her mind. "I wish to sleep. But not until I know how I have been named. Where is Heshima?"

"I am here."

Nikola turned. The tall witch stood in the doorway.

"The Mahadeva will see you," she said.

Bethen clasped Nikola's free hand and gave it a squeeze. "Blessings to you, Nikola," she said.

A fragment of her hate died at the girl's lack of envy. Nikola smiled. "And to you, Bethen."

The walk through interlocking caverns was a blur. She could not determine exactly how they reached the grotto. It didn't seem right because she knew that the only passage led out to the sea. But minutes later she knelt before the witch-queen. The three of them stood shoulder to shoulder, wild chestnut curls fading to gray at the temples and at last, to pure snow.

"Show us!" the Maid said impatiently, sticking out a hand.

This time, Nikola deemed it unwise to refuse. She pressed the stone into the child's eager palm.

It was shaped like a teardrop with bands of vibrant color that fractured the light. The center was the deep, smoldering red of banked coals. This faded to velvety black, then blue like the depths of a northern ocean. And, at the very fringe, akin to the outer ring of an iris, violet. It pulsed light and dark like a beating heart.

"What is it?" Nikola asked, transfixed by the stone.

"Serpent's eye," the Crone said. "The rarest of all gemstones."

"A close cousin of kaldurite," the Mother added. "But instead of repelling magic, it contains every layer of energy in equal measure. As such, it has elements of fire, water, air, earth and spirit."

"We should keep it," the Maid muttered. "She cannot be trusted with it."

Nikola stiffened. "The stone was a gift from your god. For me!"

"She is right," the Mother said sternly. "Give it back."

The Maid's mouth twisted, but she relinquished the stone. Nikola clutched it tight.

"Cairness said it would name me. What does that mean?"

"That you are strong enough to be a *laoch*," the Crone replied. "A shield against the dark. Heshima will explain. But know this. You must not use the power in your name-stone for anything but the final defense of your life. And even then, not all of it. If you do, there will be a steep price."

"What price?"

The wrinkled lips pursed. "Let us hope you never discover it."

"We must tell her," the Mother said. "Else she will use it anyway."

The Maid skipped in a circle around her. "You will die, Nikola Thorn," she whispered with a glint in her eye.

The Mother tsked in disapproval. "Go comb our hair!" she snapped.

The Maid skulked away. Nikola paid her little attention. She sensed some of the stone's properties, but it was far more complex than any she'd encountered before. Almost like several different stones melded together.

"We spoke truly," the Mother said. "The ley inside that stone is bound to you. Sisters have died drawing too much. It is a weapon of final resort." She smiled. "But you needn't think of that now. You are safe here. And this should be a joyous occasion."

Only the Mother seemed pleased. Heshima was regal and expressionless. And the Crone looked *angry*. The last gave Nikola no small degree of satisfaction. They didn't expect her to get such a rare and powerful stone.

Nikola bobbed her head. "Thank you, Mother," she said.

They left the cavern through a crevice. When Nikola glanced back, the wall behind looked solid again.

"We will begin tomorrow," Heshima said. "Now, give me the stone so I can have it set for you."

Nikola eyed her warily. The witch laughed. "No one wants

to part with their namestone. But it will be safe with me. Or will you carry it around in your fist forever?"

She unfurled her palm, gazing down at the serpent's eye. "I want it set in gold, with a silver chain. And tin for the backing."

"It will be done."

It took every ounce of Nikola's will to hand the gem to Heshima. The witch she hated above all others. But she would play the part of an obedient novice until she had what she wanted.

Then she would destroy them.

Chapter Nine

The witches let Nikola sleep for a full day after the naming, but then her studies commenced again in earnest. The other two acolytes were given to Paarjini, but she had Heshima to herself. Nikola welcomed the chance to learn her enemy's weaknesses—though so far she'd found none. Bethen said she was one of the most powerful witches on the island.

Heshima looked somewhere in her thirties, though it was hard to tell. She used the words *magic* and *ley* interchangeably—another stark difference from the Via Sancta, which viewed the power in strictly scientific terms. Oh, there was religion mixed in, but it was all for the betterment of humanity. How like them to take the fun out of it!

Nikola much preferred thinking of the ley as magic.

"Lithomancy has four primary branches," Heshima explained. "Abjuration, illusion, divination, and conjuration. The first concerns protective spells, which will be your focus."

"What's conjuration?" she asked hopefully.

"It encompasses the most powerful—and dangerous—projective magic," the witch replied. "That is not your concern at the moment. First you must learn to recognize and balance both types of energy. Which is your dominant hand?"

"Left."

"Then that is the projective hand. For you, right will be receptive."

"What would happen if I used the wrong hand?"

"The spell would not work. Or worse, it might backfire on you." A dry look. "So try to remember."

She gave Nikola two stones. One chalcedony, the other carnelian.

"Hold them. What do you feel?"

"The chalcedony is receptive. The carnelian projective."

"What else?"

Nikola closed her eyes. "The first is ruled by water. The moon."

"And the other?"

"Fire. The sun."

"Which is stronger?"

"The carnelian," she said immediately.

"Why do you think so?"

"Because it's projective." She opened her eyes.

Heshima smiled. "Yet if you were under attack, which would you want to have?"

"The chalcedony."

"Just so. Neither is stronger than the other, they simply have different purposes. Now, can you sense the ley inside?"

Nikola gripped the stones, one warm, one cool. She saw other layers of power, for luck, eloquence, courage, yet in an abstract way. She had no idea how to actually use those properties. "I don't think so," she admitted.

"Because it is dormant. You have the tool, but it holds no purpose. That must come from your will. How do the stones make you feel? What emotions arise?"

Nikola tried to sort it out. "The chalcedony is peaceful. It makes me feel calm." She shifted her focus to the other hand. "The carnelian . . ."

"What?"

Heshima's deep voice stoked the embers of her hatred. "It feels . . . ." Nikola gasped in pain and dropped the reddish gemstone, shaking her hand. A blister rose on the palm.

"It is dangerous to seek in the ley inside a stone when your emotions run wild," Heshima said, her face unreadable. "You have just learned your first lesson."

"But you told me to do it!"

"And now we know that you are a hothead." She sounded amused. "But that is your problem, not mine. Pick it up."

Nikola held her gaze, then picked up the stone. "Is the power expended?"

"I don't know. You tell me."

"I thought they only worked once."

"For some spells. Not others. Each stone or metal holds a finite amount of ley, but it depends on how much you used. Does it still hold ley?"

After being burned, Nikola felt wary, but she closed her eyes and relaxed. "How do I know?"

"Do you sense its properties?"

"Yes."

"Then the stone still holds ley. Give it to me." Heshima set the carnelian aside. She rooted in one of her pouches and gave Nikola another stone, nearly identical. "What can you tell me about this one?"

Nikola took the stone. She frowned. "Nothing at all except what I can see with my eyes."

A nod of approval. "That is what a stone feels like fully discharged. It is dead and may never be used again. Now, I am going to use what is left in this one"—she held up the first piece of carnelian—"to set your dress on fire. I want you to use the chalcedony to stop me."

Nikola blinked. "Now?"

"Why not?"

"Because you have not taught me how to do it!"

"Unfortunate, yes? But it gives you a strong incentive to

learn." She eyed the stone in her palm. Heshima's eyes darkened to silver shadows.

Nikola gripped her chalcedony in a sweaty fist, heart hammering. Water . . . and calm. Protection—

She yelped as a flame erupted from the hem of her dress. She snuffed it with a handful of sand.

Heshima eyed her serenely. "What happened?"

"It didn't work," Nikola muttered.

"What didn't work?"

"I tried to think of the stone's properties. But they didn't manifest."

"Why not?"

Nikola itched to slap her. "Just tell me, witch!"

Heshima shook her head. "Do you remember nothing of what I taught you? What are the three principles of lithomancy?"

"Will, emotion, and technique."

"So you do remember. Technique comes to you naturally. It is the others you lack. Let us try again."

She lit Nikola's dress on fire six more times. At last, Nikola tore the singed garment off and threw it down, enraged. After her initial smashing success, she'd expected to be *good* at this. But she was terrible.

"I suppose it will have to be your hair next time," Heshima remarked. "Sit down."

Nikola balled her fists and complied, simmering with resentment.

"When I was an acolyte," the witch said, "I had the same problem. You doubt yourself."

She shook her head. "It is the opposite. I am overconfident."

"So you say. But you do not truly believe it." Her gaze raked Nikola's bare skin. "You have been treated poorly all your life because those fools in the Via Sancta had no idea who you are. They made you believe their lies." Her gaze burned fiercely now. "But you have worth, Nikola Thorn. And I *will* set your hair on fire if that's what it takes to convince you!"

A strange welter of emotions overcame her. *I must hate her. I must.*

Yet the witch's words rang true. She'd left Malach because she knew with certainty that he would tire of her. And she secretly felt relieved that someone else had the child—even if it was Falke. She could never be a mother.

But perhaps she could be a witch.

"You are in control of the ley," Heshima said. "You, and no one else. It *will* do as you command. Do you understand?"

She nodded, jaw tight. "Yes."

"Then stop me, Nikola!"

This time, she *saw* the spell coming. A shockwave of red ley bursting from the heart of the carnelian. She sensed the witch's will, giving it purpose like an arrow fired from a bow. The chalcedony went cold in her fist. A spark of power glimmered inside, ripe with potential. Nikola had time for a single urgent command. Save me!

The two energies met in a sizzling crackle. Calm and fury, ice and fire. She smelled burning hair and drew deeper, scrabbling for every speck of power. The contest was settled an instant later when an enormous wave reared from the shallows and soaked them both. Heshima gasped in shock, then let out a hoot of laughter.

Nikola was too startled not to join her. The slap of saltwater had severed her connection to the ley, but the stone was almost dead anyway. Only a residue remained.

"I think you drew from the quartz in the sand, as well," Heshima said ruefully, shaking water from the stack of bracelets running up her forearms. "It holds projective power. But *that* is what happens when there is an imbalance in the energies."

Nikola looked away. Their shared triumph felt too inti-
mate. "I see how it is done now," she said quietly.

"You see a tiny fraction," Heshima corrected. "Is that
what you intended to occur?"

"No," she admitted.

"Then you have a long way to go. But you have taken the
first step. That is often the hardest." She stood. "It took me
two months to block a spell." A dry chuckle. "I was singed
bald by the time Anaji finished with me."

"I would like to keep practicing," Nikola said.

"And I have other duties besides you," came the crisp
reply. "It is enough for today."

"Then leave me some stones. I will try them on my own."

Heshima snorted. "You will not touch the ley without a
sister present. I am willing to set you aflame, but I will not
have your doing it yourself."

Nikola frowned. "What will I learn next?"

"Simple illusions, perhaps. I will discuss it with Paarjini."
She regarded Nikola gravely. "When you are a full witch, you
will carry a pouch with many different types of stones mingled
together. You will wear stones in your hair, on your fingers.
Carry coins in your pocket, forged from varying alloys." A
pause. "What would happen if you had no control over which
ones you drew from? Or if you drew from them all simultaneously?"

Nikola blinked. "I cannot imagine."

"Nor I. But a disaster it would be for certain. Do not allow
your impatience to be your undoing." Her voice hardened. "If
you are caught practicing on your own, you will be cast out.
There is no appeal. No second chances."

"I understand."

"Good. Now go do your chores."

Nikola sighed and followed her back to the caverns. She
was used to hard work and didn't mind it—but that was
before, when she had no other interests besides drinking alone

in pubs. Acolytes were expected to earn their keep doing laundry and helping in the kitchens. She had learned that there were many caverns like this one, with other novices in training. Witches seemed to come and go. Only Paarjini, Cairness and Heshima lived there, along with Bethen and Jenifry.

She spent the next days blocking spells with different stones. Then metals and crystals. Her confidence grew. Yet she wasn't always sure what would happen. Once, she accidentally melted the sand into obsidian glass when she focused the wrong power from a ruby, drawing on the fire element rather than its protective quality. Heshima made her practice visualization techniques, imagining specifically what she wished to do with the ley. The witch would not allow her to touch *anything* when she practiced that.

It was days before Heshima trusted her with a stone again.

They turned to illusions, which Nikola found boring. She longed to go further, to delve into conjuration on her own, but fear of getting caught always stopped her. That and the fact that they guarded all the gemstones. After several weeks, she could form a passable illusion of almost anything, even herself, though it dissipated to mist when Heshima attacked it. Maintaining the illusion's form required the use of several stones at once, and one of her weaknesses was a tendency to be distracted.

"Why must we learn to protect against other witches?" she wondered one day as they walked down the beach, gathering sea stones. "Aren't you the only ones in the world?"

Heshima gave her the amused look Nikola despised. "What are the aingeals," she replied, "but another kind of witch?"

"They don't use lithomancy."

"If one lays hands on you, you will find the difference to be very small, Nikola." A cool smile. "Your eyes have not changed yet, but they will. Once that happens, you will be named as a witch by any aingeal who sees you. Not even illusion can veil your eyes."

Nikola thought of the witch who had attacked Malach. Paarjini. She realized with a jolt how he had recognized her. "Why not?"

"No one knows for certain. Perhaps they are like the aingeals' Marks. Once the magic brands you, you will never be rid of it."

She suppressed a shudder. She didn't want to look like them. Only to have their power. But one did not come without the other.

"That is what it means to be *laoch*," Heshima continued. "A warrior-witch, dedicated to preserving our land against external threats. Your namestone, the serpent's eye, is the symbol of a guardian. It is a grave responsibility."

Nikola avoided her gaze by bending to pick up a smooth seastone. They held power, too, though only a tiny spark.

"Why do you hate the nihilim?" she asked.

She'd never mentioned Malach, afraid it would put the witch on her guard, but the question ate away at her.

"The aingeals are our age-old enemies," Heshima replied. "The Isles of the Blessed were founded to get away from them."

"What did they do to you?"

"They betrayed Valmitra." Her lips tightened. "And that will never be forgiven."

She refused to say more. Nikola put it out of her mind. What did it matter? Old stories meant nothing to her. What she *wanted* was to hurl someone across a room.

But acolytes didn't get to learn that.

So she bided her time, taking only the baby steps Heshima permitted and dreaming of the day when she would be given a pouch of her own. At one year, acolytes were granted more liberties. Nikola hoped to earn them sooner. When Jenifry and Bethen asked her to join them in walks, she declined, sitting on her bed to practice the visualizations over and over. Never the things she truly wanted. Just the mundane tasks she'd been assigned.

In her spare time, she studied the serpent's eye. It had both receptive and projective qualities. The red heart simmered with heat and pulsing blood. It stirred a restlessness in her when her mind touched it. The blue layer was different. Touching that part was like drifting on a twilight sea. Serene and eternal, with the cold stars overhead. But the outer ring of violet puzzled her. Its power was thin and ethereal. Spirit? Certainly not anything to do with the tangible elements.

She couldn't learn more without tapping the power it held. As Nikola had no wish to die, she kept her explorations superficial. But she wore the stone at all times, hanging from a gold chain just tight enough to nestle in the notch between her collarbones. Every witch did the same. She thought often of what she might do with Heshima's, if the sister ever took it off.

They practiced day and night, inside the caverns and outside on the beach. Certain stones behaved differently in moonlight, sunlight, starlight or firelight. They were too far south to see the Aurora, but Heshima told her that it, too, changed the resonance of the ley. The setting of a stone affected its energy, as did the type of jewelry. The more Nikola learned about lithomancy, the more she realized how fantastically complex it was. One could study for years and still not grasp half its potential.

That only fueled her hunger. She'd always accepted what the Curia said about sociopaths. Their short attention span and low threshold for frustration. But Nikola found that she could, in fact, apply herself to something with single-minded discipline. It was a revelation. Her progress was swift. Heshima seemed pleased. She gave Nikola her first bracelet. No stone, but still she wore it with pride.

"All magic must be in harmony with nature," Heshima

said to her, for the thousandth time, as Nikola wove the illusion of a warship floating just beyond the breakers.

It was a complex illusion and she felt rather pleased with it.

"That is not natural," she pointed out, frowning as Heshima dissipated it with a wave of her right hand.

The witch was right-side dominant and it held all her projective power. The only weakness Nikola had discovered thus far.

"Illusions are simply lightwaves, woven and bent to reflect in a certain way to the eye. Nothing more."

"Divination?" Nikola persisted.

They'd hadn't even gotten to that yet.

"Changes nothing tangible," Heshima replied. "It is a simply of reading of what *might* be. Not always what will be."

"So what kind of magic is in disharmony with nature?"

The witch blew out a breath. "There is a thing called forcing. Making something happen that should be impossible, under any circumstance. Few can do it." A sharp look. "But you might be one such. So consider your actions carefully. Even if a thing is very unlikely—" Light flared from Heshima's closed fist. Nikola bellowed in outrage as a sudden gale tore her dress over her head and sent it flying down the beach "—it must always be possible."

Nikola chased after her dress. She yanked the sandy garment back on a scowl.

"You are too fond of object lessons, Heshima," she said.

"But you will not forget this particular one, I think. Now, make me a swan. A black swan with a golden beak."

Nikola took the proffered stones with ill humor. She made the swan, and then its mate, giving them both sapphires for eyes.

"Pretty," Heshima remarked. "Now make them fly."

Nikola learned to judge how much ley a stone held. Then to practice drawing only a specific amount. A very few stones,

Heshima said, *could* be recharged, though it required a witch's own energy and immersion in fresh running water.

Slowly, her determination to punish them all faded into the background and the thirst to learn took center stage. The sisters treated her the same as any other acolyte. They allowed her to take walks down the beach when she wished to be alone, but if it was company she sought, there was always someone to sit with and share a cup of tea, as she used to do with the other chars. For the first time, Nikola felt a sense of belonging.

That all changed the day she overheard Paarjini talking about Malach.

Chapter Ten

Nikola had just finished scrubbing the pots in the kitchen and was making her way back to her room when she heard voices. The caverns carried sound in strange ways. Sometimes one could hear what was spoken in a distant chamber quite clearly. But these voices were faint. If it hadn't been so late, and so quiet, she would not have heard them at all.

A burst of laughter. Then more soft talk. She recognized Heshima's husky baritone and Paarjini's clipped lilt. Nikola hoped they might speak of her and when she would be permitted to practice on her own. After a quick glance around, she crept closer. None of the chambers had doors. She paused outside one of the comfortable nooks where the sisters often gathered.

"Do you think it's wise to get involved with the other minder?" Heshima asked.

"It's just a bit o' fun." A soft chuckle. "If ye saw him, you'd understand. Finlo's easy on the eyes. And discreet. What more could a woman ask?"

Nikola grinned. So the witches weren't above a dalliance. But Heshima's next words trapped the breath in her throat.

"What of the aingeal?"

"I told ye he was cunning." Paarjini sounded satisfied. "He figured those kids out right quick."

A snort of disbelief from Heshima. "From what I saw, the man was spectacularly ill-suited for a creche. Violent and short-tempered."

"Yer not wrong. But that's the thing about him. He'll do whatever he has to. If it's breaking rocks, he'll do that. If it's wiping a snotty nose, he'll do that, too. He doesn't care. Just give him a scrap o' hope and he won't quit."

"But it was the aingeals' pride that—"

"*Was*, sister. He might be descended from their line, but it's been nigh on a thousand years now. I'm not saying they don't all carry the traits. The man does have pride. *And* arrogance. But his neck is not so stiff as Gavriel and the rest. He will bend it if he must."

Nikola shook her head. It couldn't be. They'd caught another nihilim. Though by all the Saints and Martyrs, the description did fit Malach to a T.

"In truth, I think it's doing him good. Just as the Mahadeva predicted. He did not seem half as angry when I saw him yesterday." A laugh. "I suspect he is too tired to be angry."

Heshima grunted. "Are you sure you did not *divine* this outcome?"

"Pah. You know how poor I am at scrying. No, I merely see Malach for what he is. A survivor—above all else. And that's why I'm about to win our little wager."

The women continued to talk, but Nikola heard little after Paarjini spoke his name.

Malach was alive.

And . . . minding children?

Her head spun. The sweven still haunted her dreams. It was so vividly real. But the Mahadeva had tricked her. Let her mourn a man who was not dead at all.

Bitch!

Or was it *bitches?*

The reason was obvious. She did not want Nikola looking for him. Had they told Malach the same about her?

Nikola forced herself to listen again, hoping they'd let something useful slip. But if anyone mentioned the name of a village or city, she'd missed it. The talk had turned to larger matters.

". . . and now the remnants of the aingeals tear each other apart," Paarjini said. "We must be ready for them."

"It was inevitable."

"Yes, but it is worse than we imagined. The Black Sun rises again, stronger than ever. Of course I respect the Mahadeva's decision. Yet we cannot sit here doin' nothing forever—"

The voices drew closer. The women were walking toward the door! Nikola sprinted down the tunnel, rounding the curve just in time. Yet she couldn't help pausing to catch the end of the conversation.

"—must do as the stones command," Heshima said. "They are the will of Valmitra."

"I know. Yet I worry, sister. Can't you feel it? A storm gathers on the continent. In time, it will spill over—"

The voices faded away in the opposite direction. Nikola returned to her chamber and sat on the bed. All her plans crumbled to ash. Heshima had not, in fact, killed him. Malach was here, somewhere on this island. But did they have any future together? She wasn't the same person she had been. She had purpose now. Her *own* purpose.

During her captivity at the Arx, Nikola had imagined him dangling in chains from the wall of a witchy dungeon, or flinching under the lash as a galley slave. But for some unfathomable reason, the Mahadeva had made Malach a *babysitter.*

Nikola almost wished she had not eavesdropped, but there was no going back now. The only question was what she would do with the knowledge.

If she could just see him, once, that would help her decide. *But how?*

NIKOLA GREETED Heshima with a smile the next day. "When will I learn divination?" she asked.

The witch studied her. "Not all are suited for it. That is why you were given to me instead of Cairness. It requires a very sensitive inner eye. That is not your strength, Nikola."

"What is my strength?"

Heshima laughed. "You don't know yet? Projective power, of course. Your illusions are passable. But you have the fire for conjuration."

"Still," she said stubbornly. "I wish to learn the theory of divination, at least. To round out my knowledge."

Heshima arched a brow. "All right. There are several kinds. The tossing of stones in a pattern. The Mahadeva has a strong talent for this. Then the choosing of stones at random from a pouch. Lastly, scrying."

"What's that?"

"Staring into a reflective surface. If you have the talent, you might see images. But we will not bother with that one. I cannot do it at all and could teach you nothing."

"What of the first two?"

"The key element is chance. You let the magic guide the stones. If it wishes to tell you something, it will." She smiled. "That's the brief version. The witches who have mastered it fully could lecture you for days."

"Do any stones work?"

"Again, very briefly, yes. The properties matter less than the choice."

"Can I try?"

"If you wish. There is not much danger in it. We will start with something simple." Heshima eyed the sky. It was overcast, with high, drifting clouds. Some were tinged gray at the edges. "Tell me if it will rain in the next hour."

"What do I do?"

The witch shrugged. "Choose five stones from my pouch. Then ask the ley and tell me if you see anything."

Nikola shook out five stones at random. Agate, smoky quartz, red jasper, topaz and citrine. They were a mix of colors and textures. Nikola laid them out on the sand, then sat cross-legged, forming the question in her mind. She had practiced visualization techniques so many times, the quiet focus came instantly.

Will it rain today?

She felt the push and pull of the opposing energies. The reservoirs of ley. Many other qualities, overlapping in a symphony of meaning. The smoky quartz made her think of thunderclouds, but the citrine and amber were warm and dry. She tamped down impatience.

Will it rain today?

There was no sudden vision. She tried stirring the ley, but it only made her nauseous. Nikola opened her eyes. "I don't know," she admitted.

"Keep trying," Heshima said. "Do not seek the answer. Let it come to you."

Nikola nodded. She unclenched her jaw and cleared her mind. Tried to drift without actually doing anything. Long minutes passed. She tried focusing on each of the stones in turn. The citrine drew her the most.

"No," Nikola said decisively. "It will not—" She cut off as a drop of rain struck her face.

Heshima laughed. She didn't seem surprised. "It is a gift of intuition that requires surrender. You are too strong-willed."

Nikola frowned.

"That is not a bad thing." Her tone turned wry. "You must

accept that while you have great talent, it isn't limitless. Focus on what you can do."

Nikola nodded, but she meant to practice in her spare time. If she didn't use the ley, they couldn't catch her at it. And she could use any old stones—even ones cast up by the sea.

"Let us practice summoning," Heshima said, setting two black pebbles in the sand ten meters away. "Draw the stones to your hand."

Nikola used her right to grasp a piece of lapis and weave a thin current of air. The pebbles trembled and jumped, then rocketed into her right palm.

"Give them to me," Heshima said.

She walked away and set them down again at double the distance. Nikola still had a little power left in the lapis. She couldn't see the pebbles, but she sensed their unique qualities like tiny beacons in the sand.

"Can it be done at any distance?" she called out.

"In theory," Heshima replied. "Though the farthest I have ever seen is two leagues."

Summoning fell under conjuration, which she had no trouble with. Nikola thought she probably *could* throw someone across a room if she wanted to. But that required one of the greater stones—diamond, ruby, sapphire or emerald—and it would be months before Heshima gave her any of those.

———

AFTER SUPPER, Nikola set off on a long walk down the beach, gathering smooth stones at random. When the cavern had fallen far behind, she sat down next to a boulder and let the stones tumble into the lap of her dress. She laid her hands on them, feeling the slight resonance of ley within.

Where is he? Show me a picture.

The wind sighed. The waves curled and smashed against the rocks. She tried to relax and let the answer come.

Nothing.

She swept up the stones and hurled them down the beach. The answer was right there, if she could only grasp it. Heshima said divination required surrender, but clearly that didn't work. Perhaps the witch had lied. Of course she had! Heshima wouldn't want Nikola learning the truth. In a blind fury, she focused her will to a white-hot pinprick, fueling it with single-minded, all-consuming need.

Where is Malach? Where?! SHOW ME.

The ground lurched. A sickening sensation of vertigo. A clap of bone-rattling thunder. Her ears popped. Then she was tumbling through the air. Nikola landed on her back in a shower of sand. The afterimage of a jagged bolt shimmered in the air above her.

"Saints," she muttered, raising a trembling hand to her eyes.

Her body felt bruised but not burnt. Had she called down lightning? If so, she should be dead.

Rain pattered against her face. Insects chirped in the undergrowth. There was no sound of waves. Where was the sea?

She'd felt a surge of lithomantic power. The sudden weaving together of opposing forces. But how? She didn't have any stones—

Nikola's eyes went wide. A hand shot to the serpent's eye at her throat.

"Oh no," she whispered. "Oh, *shit.*"

The gemstone felt warm against her skin. It still brimmed with ley. Nikola gripped it tight, fingers trembling. Perhaps she'd only used a little bit. But for what?

She brushed sand from her face and sat up. The after-image had faded, but sparkling motes still danced in the corners of her vision. She was in a small wood. Several bucketloads of beach had come along with her. Some of it was fused into branching tubes that resembled coral. Or bolts of lightning. She picked up one. It was brittle, flaking apart in her hand.

"What did I do?" she whispered in a panic.

A round house peeked through the trees. Lights shone in the windows. Nikola's breath caught as the door opened. She heard voices, a child crying, and then Malach stepped outside. His hair had grown long enough to tuck behind his ears. He strode to the middle of the yard, scanning the dirt. Then he smiled and jogged over to the swings. He picked something up —a stuffed snake?—and strode back to the door. A sniffling child stood there. He hoisted her to one hip and gave her the snake. The child clutched the toy with one hand, throwing the other arm around his neck. The door closed.

Nikola pressed a hand to her mouth, covering a burst of shocked laughter. Tears stood in her eyes.

Just walk up to the door and knock.

Yet she couldn't move.

He'd ask where his own child was. And how she found him.

Nikola tore her eyes from the house. She gripped her namestone. Focused her will to a single urgent command.

Take me back to the beach.

Nothing happened. A flutter of true panic now. Much longer and they'd come looking for her. She tried to remember how she'd done it. A joining of the opposing powers in the stone? The red and blue layers repelled each other. They fought like living animals, tooth and claw. Receptive and projective magic were not meant to be used in a single spell. Sweat beaded the edge of her headscarf as she forced them into a tight ball, binding it with chains of violet ley. She imagined herself inside a box, and the box existing in another place simultaneously.

Again, the gut-twisting vertigo. The clap of silent thunder

and sudden pressure in her ears. She landed on her lonesome spit of beach, this time bringing the dirt beneath her feet and branches from nearby shrubs, charred to lumps of coal. Nikola frantically buried the evidence in the sand.

There, she chided herself. You've seen him. And it cost you dearly. They warned you not to use your own stone. Twice is more than enough. You're lucky it didn't kill you!

Popping from one place to another was definitely against the laws of nature. It must be what the witches called forcing. Heshima had warned her about that, too. She hadn't said what the penalty was, but exile would probably be the least of it.

Yet . . . the possibilities!

Nikola rejected that train of thought. She walked slowly back to the cavern, letting the rain cool her burning cheeks. By the time she got there, her face was calm. But a her heart was a razor shard in her breast.

Chapter Eleven

Nikola waited for a summons from the Mahadeva. Days passed and it never came. Slowly, the knot in her belly unwound. *They didn't know.* She was burning to ask Heshima more about forcing but didn't dare.

"Bethen," she asked, as they swept sand from one of the caverns. "I was wondering about something. Does a witch know if another witch uses lithomancy nearby?"

The golden-haired acolyte glanced over. "Only if they are in sight of it."

"Ah."

Bethen lowered her voice. "I hope you aren't thinking of trying spells on your own. I know it's hard to be patient, especially when you have such a strong natural gift, but they're very strict about it. There was another woman here before you came. Cairness caught her practicing illusions and she was cast out."

Nikola smiled. "No, I was just curious. It fits with what I've noticed myself. If Heshima shows me something, I can learn it. But I couldn't tell you if a sister is casting the ley in another part of the caverns."

"There *are* spells that can reveal such a thing," Bethen

added. "It falls under protective magic. But they're complex. We haven't begun to learn them yet."

Nikola left her feeling relieved, but the brief glimpse of Malach did not give her the solace she'd hoped for. When she'd believed him dead, she'd had a purpose—revenge. Now doubts crowded her mind. She still wanted to be a full witch; there was no turning back from it. Yet the feelings she'd managed to bury spilled over into every waking moment.

"You've been working too hard," Heshima said, when she failed to produce even a simple illusion of an orange tree.

"But—"

"You will take the rest of the day off. And tomorrow, as well. I will not waste my time with you in this state."

"Fine," Nikola grumbled. "Then what am I to do with myself?"

"Perhaps you should go meditate in the hole."

"No," she replied quickly. "But some exercise might do me good. I will take long walks."

"As you wish." Pewter eyes regarded her. "Go, then. Do not return to me until your mind is clear."

She set off down the beach, the witch's eyes on her back. Restless, reckless energy burned in her veins. The same Nikola who had set out in a rowboat across five hundred kilometers of open ocean. The one who'd struck a bargain with a Night-mage one rainy night in Novo, and floored the accelerator through the roadblocks on Liberation Bridge.

She had suppressed that part of herself since arriving here, but it would never be gone. The Curia called her a sociopath. A risk-taker with an impaired sense of right and wrong. Malach had recognized the quality, too. It was why he had chosen *her* out of thousands of people. They were alike.

In a sudden rush of understanding, Nikola knew what she needed to do.

See him once more. Just once. Then she'd be cured.

She went farther this time, all the way to the end of the

spit of land at the northernmost tip of the island. It was a good two-hour walk from the caverns. No one came out here save for the colonies of nesting gulls. She stood for a moment, watching the ocean crash against the rocks. The swells were much bigger on the windward side.

A smile touched her lips. *If I do this, I need a name for it. So . . . I will call it forcing the box.*

She joined her mind to the reservoir of ley in her name-stone, melding the attractive and repulsive forces.

Take me to him.

This time, she tried to place the box closer to the ground. Knowing the terrain in advance helped. She bent her knees and landed with a jolt but didn't fall—though again, a fair amount of sand came along for the ride, fused by the magic into fantastic shapes of quartz and silica. Some were glassy, hollow tubes. Others were delicate lattices, stark white and branching outward into ever finer filaments. She swept it all into a pile and sat down to wait.

Dusk fell. It started to rain. One by one, the lights in the house came on. She heard young voices laughing and singing. Watched Malach silhouetted against the window as he washed dishes at the kitchen sink. And then, one by one, the lights went out again. It was early still. They must rise at the crack of dawn.

She half expected to see him sneak out in search of some amusement after the children went to sleep, but the house remained quiet. She crept up to the front door and tried the knob. Unlocked. Nikola moved through the dark house. All seemed tidy, though she nearly tripped over a low child-sized table in the shadows. She crept up the stairs. The bathroom light had been left burning, the door ajar, casting a stripe of yellow across the hall carpet. In the room beyond, moonlight illuminated three small humps in the beds. The next three rooms also belonged to children.

Nikola reached the end of the hall and opened another

door. An adult's room with a single bed. A form lay under the covers, one arm flung wide. The Mark of a long, slender dagger, its blade inscribed with elaborate runes, stretched from knuckles to elbow.

Nikola's heart thumped faster as she studied him, fast asleep.

Leave now. No good will come of this. You know that—

She silenced the warning, overcome with a desire to touch him. To prove he was real and not some fever dream. She slipped into the room, easing the door shut behind her. Thought ceased as she crossed the room. A floorboard creaked. Malach shifted in his sleep, head turning her way. His eyes started to open and she pressed a hand to his mouth.

"Shhhh. Don't speak."

Instant alertness. He grabbed her wrist, dragging her hand from his lips. "Nikola," he said hoarsely.

"Shhhh," she whispered again, sliding under the sheet. He pulled her close with a heavy sigh, lips finding her neck. There was a hint of something sweet and soapy in his hair. Bubble-bath? She groped under the covers. He seemed to be wearing a . . . skirt? She tugged at the knot against his hip. The cloth slid away.

"What are you doing here?" he murmured, pulling her head scarf loose and tangling his fingers in her hair. A choked laugh. "I can't believe it. I—"

"Later," she whispered urgently, wrapping her thighs around him.

Malach's breath hitched. His body was already responding and she felt him lose control, just as she'd hoped. He rolled her to her back, yanking her dress up. A warm hand stroked her inner thigh. He kissed her again, deeper, fingers stoking her desire. Malach made a small sound of satisfaction. An instant later, their bodies joined. She shivered in mindless pleasure, still disbelieving that she'd done this.

"Nikola, Nikola," he whispered. "I knew you'd come back to me."

She bit her lip against a moan.

"Quiet now." His voice was thick. "We mustn't wake them."

She pressed her face to his shoulder, tasting the faint tang of salt on his skin. He moved with infinite slowness, though she felt him trembling. How perfectly they fit together. She curled her toes along his calf and the tender hollow behind his knee. His body felt leaner. Harder. But his skin was just as silky as she remembered, and his voice was the same, a low, wicked tease in her ear. Nikola tried to make it last, but didn't manage to hold out very long. She clung to his neck, back arching, and felt him go rigid. A snort of stifled laughter puffed from her nose as he bit down hard on the pillow.

When the last tremors faded, he eased himself down to one side, searching her face. How she had missed lying with him, so close their lashes almost touched and she could see the flecks of gold and green in his irises, like the scales of a dragon. She wished they could stay like this. Not speak. Just be together for a little while, with the world far away and meaningless.

"Tell me everything," Malach said, one hand idly stroking her arm. "How did you find me? Is our daughter with you?"

Nikola's heart shattered at the mingled fear and hope in his eyes. The weight of her mistake came crashing down. She cupped his cheek and drew a tiny spark from the blue layer of her stone, potent with receptive magic. It conjured a raft on a glassy, stormless sea. A man adrift and slumbering beneath a full orange moon, dark hair fanned against a bower of blood-red roses.

"Sleep," she whispered, power coursing through her fingertips. "Just a dream."

His eyes narrowed. They slid down to the gem at her neck with sudden wariness. "What are you doing?"

Nikola drew deeper. The magic was there, strong and pure. But the ley vanished where she touched his face. A knot of panic formed. The kaldurite! The stone cut both ways. It blocked him from using the ley, but it also gave him immunity to witchcraft. How could she have forgotten?

Nikola scrambled away, leaping from the bed. Malach caught her wrist. She yanked it free and ran for the door. A muffled curse behind, but she didn't look back. She flew down the stairs three at a time, breath rasping in her throat. Seconds later, she was out the front door and crossing the playground, bare feet splashing through the puddles.

"Nikola!"

The confused anguish in his voice almost made her turn back. But if she told him the truth, he'd find a way to go back for their child. Nothing would stop him. And he would die in the attempt. She couldn't face that. Not again.

She would rather flee like a coward.

But transporting a body in motion seemed like a bad idea. Nikola spun around at the edge of the woods, chest heaving. Malach sprinted towards her. His mouth was tight, his eyes raw.

"Stop!" she cried. "Don't come any closer!"

She formed the box in her mind. Wrestled the oppositional forces into a knot, binding them with strands of violet. He slowed to a jog but kept coming. Rain plastered strands of black hair to his forehead. Nikola dropped to a crouch. "Get back!"

"Wait!" He flung a hand out. "Don't—"

The ground shifted. A percussive blast rang in her ears. She spilled to the sand, hatred burning like acid on her tongue. Hatred for the witches *and* the Via Sancta.

MALACH STOOD in the pouring rain, staring at the spot where Nikola had vanished.

"How?" he muttered. "*How?*"

Her bracelet was still in his hand. It had slid from her wrist when she fled. Plain gold. But she'd worn something around her neck. A gemstone that felt chilly against his skin. He'd been too preoccupied to notice until afterwards.

His mind reeled. Perhaps the witches *had* caught her. But why would they teach her their secrets? And what had he done to make her run away from him again?

He let out a mirthless laugh. "Well, she's alive. That much I can vouch for."

The memory of her in his arms brought an unwelcome stirring. Malach realized he was standing in the yard with nothing on and hurried back to the house. He streaked up the stairs, terrified he'd bump into one of the kids using the bathroom, but the house was quiet.

Thus far, he'd managed a weird sort of calm. But the sight of the rumpled bed, and the scent of her that lingered in the air, ignited a bonfire of fury. He'd done nothing but worry and fret for months. And she wouldn't even speak to him! Worse, she'd tried to use the ley. He'd sensed it. That same itchy crawl down his spine he got when a witch stared at him. With a sudden revelation that stoked his anger to new heights, Malach knew that they'd been trying to work spells on him. Testing the kaldurite's defenses.

He sank heavily to the bed.

A witch. She's a bloody witch.

He fell back, too wound up to sleep, but the next thing he knew someone was banging on his door.

"Hey!" A laugh. "Are you ever coming down?"

Malach's eyes opened. Bright sunlight flooded the room. He swallowed, his throat as parched as if he'd been drinking cheap wine all night.

"What time is it?" he muttered.

"Late, my friend," Finlo replied through the door. "Are you feeling well?"

"Yep." Malach rolled to his side. "Down in a minute!"

There was no time to dwell on the insanity of it all. He dressed, brushed his teeth, and hurried downstairs. The kids had already eaten and were dying to get outside. Cris and Inry jumped up and down on the couch, narrowly missing Lonan, who rolled around between their feet. Roseen and Ealish stood at the door, holding their shoes.

"Come ON, Malach!" Roseen whined.

"Fuck it, just give me a second!" he snapped.

The girls blinked.

"Fuck it!" Inry shouted gleefully from the living room.

Malach sighed. "I'm sorry."

It was one of the few words Athaaran and Osterlish had in common.

"Manners!" Finlo hollered at Inry.

"*He* said it!"

Malach gripped his head.

"Bad night?" Finlo asked, handing him a cup of tea.

"Not exactly," he replied slowly. "Bizarre is more like it."

Malach felt like he was losing his mind. He had a sudden urge to tell him everything. He remembered Yvor's advice that first day. *When you need help, don't be ashamed to ask for it.*

"Can you come outside with us?" he asked.

Finlo picked up on his desperation. He gave a quick nod. "Sure. I'll just get my gang settled with some coloring books."

Malach gulped the tea, scalding his tongue. He bent to tie five pairs of shoes, then unleashed his charges on the playground and slumped at one of the picnic tables. A minute later, Finlo joined him. He waited patiently as Malach gathered his courage.

"You've never asked anything about me," Malach said at last.

"Not my business," Finlo replied evenly.

"So they told you nothing?"

"Just that you're from the continent. An aingeal dian."

"And that doesn't bother you?"

"If the witches think you should be here, I trust their judgment." He held Malach's gaze. "I like you. So do the kids. And believe me, I've seen men lose it. Not everyone is cut out for this. It's fucking hard. So, yeah, I wondered if you'd make it." He smiled. "But you have."

Malach picked a splinter from the wood. "I left my own child behind. Not willingly. She wasn't even born yet."

It was too complicated to explain *both* kids. And he'd never let himself feel attached to Dantarion's. She'd made it clear the infant belonged to her, and her alone. But Nikola's daughter . . . she was meant to be *his*. A sealed bargain.

"I'm sorry," Finlo said with a frown.

"Yeah." Malach let out a sigh. "I thought the mother was back there, too. But she turned up last night."

"Here?"

"Yep. She tried to use lithomancy on me. Then she ran off." He looked up. "She vanished into thin air, Finlo."

The Athaaran blinked. "Is she dangerous?"

"Not to you or the kids. I'm sure of that."

Finlo nodded slowly. "I can see how that would shake you up," he said wryly. "But I'm confused. You had a child with a *witch*?"

"She didn't used to be. I don't know what the hell she is now."

"That's strange."

"To say the fucking least."

"You want me to ask Paarjini about it?"

Malach shook his head. "Don't mention it."

"Okay."

The answer sounded glib. He gave Finlo a sharp look. "Do you really mean that?"

The Athaaran studied him. "I enjoy Paarjini's company. I

have nothing against any of them and only the greatest respect for the Mahadeva." His eyes hardened a fraction. "But men need to stick together here."

Malach nodded. "Yes, we do," he said with feeling.

"As long as it doesn't affect the kids, your secret's safe with me."

A howl of outrage snapped their heads around.

"Did you leave the toolbox out?" Finlo asked.

Malach swore softly. "Yeah, I was up on the roof yesterday fixing one of the loose solar panels."

He stood up from the table. "Put that screwdriver down!" he shouted. "Or you're all getting haircuts! Really short ones!"

As soon as the words came out, he knew he didn't want to follow through on the threat. He loved brushing Cristory's waist-long hair. They'd probably both cry if he had to lop it off. But the kids were so used to his ruthless promise-keeping that Lonan stopped poking Ealish immediately.

"That's not fair!" Inry yelled indignantly, glaring at Lonan. "*He* did it! I *told* him we'd get in trouble!"

Malach thrust out a hand. "Bring it here."

Lonan trotted over and handed him the screwdriver, face pale. He had a terror of haircuts.

"See?" Finlo said with a grin after the boy darted off. "You were born for this, brother."

Chapter Twelve

It wasn't until she was washing dishes that Nikola realized she'd lost her bracelet. She always took it off before plunging her hands into the soapy water.

Why, oh why, hadn't she just left him alone?

She clung to the hope that it had fallen off while she was forcing. But she had to find it before Heshima noticed it was gone.

"I'll say I lost it swimming," she whispered, frantic. "No, that won't work. She'll make me practice a summoning to bring it back. And she'll watch where it comes from."

Summoning spells did not make things magically appear. That would be against the laws of nature. The spells drew the object directly through physical space, usually a short distance. They were never, ever to be done with a living creature. Misjudge the force and it could rupture internal organs.

Nikola searched the beach on hands and knees, combing her fingers through the sand. No bracelet. She waited for dark to fall. Waited some more. In the small hours, when the moon had retired and the only light was the cold gleam of stars, she slipped out of the caverns and hurried to her secret spot behind the boulder. The ley in her namestone seemed a little weaker than before, which made her nervous. But she couldn't force without both projective and receptive power, which meant stealing multiple gems, and there was no hope of that. The storerooms were all girded with powerful spells.

Nikola's jaw set as she prepared to transport herself back to the woods behind the creche. She landed like a cat, sand spraying outward at her feet. This time, the disorientation faded quickly.

"So you're one of them now."

Her head turned. Malach was sitting beneath a date palm. He held up one of the peculiar branches, then crumbled it with his fingers. "I showed it to Finlo. This is what happens when lightning strikes sand. Except we're thirty kilometers from the beach."

"I'm so sorry," she said, pulse pounding with guilt and surprise.

"Sorry for which part?" He gazed at her coldly. "Fucking me? Or trying to hex me afterwards?"

"It wasn't a hex."

"No? What's the proper witchy term, Nikola?"

"A spell of serenity. Of sleep. I wouldn't hex you."

He tossed her the bracelet. "I guess you came back for that."

She caught it and slipped it around her wrist.

"There are no ships from the continent. How did you get to Tenethe?" He glanced at the fused sand. "Like that? I'm really confused here."

"I rowed."

He was silent for a moment. "You *rowed?*"

"Yeah." She stared back, her own temper rising. "In a piece-of-shit dinghy. To find you!"

Malach rose to his feet. His face was blank, but she knew how deeply she'd wounded him.

"They told me you were dead," she said. "The Mahadeva

gave me a sweven. I saw you attack Paarjini and go overboard. In chains!"

He blinked. "They pulled me out again."

Nikola shook her head. "Well, I never saw that part. But I drew the sweven from the stone all on my own. By accident. They told me I had a natural talent for lithomancy. That I could learn. I only agreed to get back at them, Malach."

He swallowed. "Why?"

"Because I care about you, idiot!" she exclaimed.

"Then prove it," he said tightly.

Nikola walked over. Malach looked different. Older and younger at the same time. "I overheard Paarjini talking about the creche. When she said your name, I . . . I had to see you. I didn't know where you were." She shrugged. "So I found a way."

Malach stared at her. "Your eyes haven't changed."

"Not yet. But they will."

He sighed and pulled her into his arms. She rested her cheek on his shoulder.

"When did you arrive?" he asked.

"Couple months ago."

He stepped back, meeting her eyes. "Where's our child, Nikola? Do the witches have her?"

She shook her head. "I gave her up."

"To whom?"

She swallowed. "A nice couple—"

"Don't." The edge in his voice made her tense. "Don't you lie to me."

As much as she wanted to, Nikola found she couldn't. "Falke has her."

Malach went very still. He shook his head in denial.

"I was caught by knights. They're occupying the whole Morho. They took me back to the Arx. I gave birth there." Every word struck another blow. "Falke is Pontifex now."

"What?"

"Feizah is dead. Everyone thinks you killed her, Malach."

He exhaled a long, unsteady breath. "Is the Void truly broken?"

Nikola nodded. "It's civil war back there."

He was quiet for a long time. "What's her name?"

"I don't know. Falke wouldn't let me see her."

Malach paced a few steps away. His fists clenched. He dragged his hands through his hair, tugging at it hard.

"The child is gone," Nikola said gently. "She belongs to them now—"

"Don't say that!" He spun around. "She will never, *ever* be theirs!"

The possessive fury in his voice sparked an ugly feeling. Jealousy of her own daughter? Nikola pushed it away, but her heart beat fast.

"You promised, Malach. You said that if it came down to it, you would choose me!"

A flash of pain. "And I meant it. But tell me something first. Do I even have that choice anymore?"

She said nothing. He nodded slowly. "I thought so. I offered you power once and you rejected it—"

"Your power!" she cried. "I don't want someone else's *Mark*, Malach. This is completely different! It belongs to me. And no, I won't give it up! But that doesn't mean we can't find a way." She turned to the creche. "When I saw you in the playground, you seemed happy—"

"Saw me? So you were here *twice* before?"

"By accident!"

He growled something under his breath.

"I couldn't stay that first time. Heshima might have caught me. But I wanted to see you again, so I came back. And then . . . ." She looked away.

The anger dissipated. "Couldn't resist me, hmmm?"

"I must have been mad," she muttered.

Malach took her hand. "Come talk in my room."

She laughed. "Talk? I don't think so."

"Why not?"

"You know why not."

He raised a brow. "Is your self-control so fragile?"

"No."

Malach's face darkened. "Or do you plan to run from me again?"

"Not that either."

He regarded her seriously. "Please."

She felt her resolve crumbling. "What about the kids?"

"They're sleeping."

"What if we're caught?"

"I already told Finlo about you. He's the other minder."

"*You told him?* Are you insane?"

"He'll keep quiet."

She bit her lip. "I thought you'd be the silent, stoic type."

He barked a laugh. "Then you don't know me as well as you think you do."

"I don't think I know you at all," she grumbled.

He gave her a slow smile. "I'm an open book. You just need the patience to read to the end."

She laughed. They did need to talk. And the mosquitoes were starting to gather. She slapped an arm. "Very well. Let's return to the scene of the crime, shall we?"

They crept through the darkened house. She felt like a teenager sneaking into her boyfriend's room. Inside his bedroom, Malach flipped on a table lamp. "Did you seriously row here?"

She showed him her hands. They still had scars. Malach kissed each palm.

"You're crazy," he said.

"I saw whales."

He laughed. "Where's the boat now?"

"You won't be rowing home," she said dryly. "It sank in a storm."

He frowned.

"I held onto an oar."

"Let me guess. The current swept you into a cavern with three weird women."

She nodded. "What do they want with you, Malach?"

"I don't know. But they won't let me leave." He studied her face. "I'm sorry for what happened to you. It was never my intention to put you through all that."

"If I hadn't met you, I'd still be scrubbing floors and drinking too much. I'd probably have ended a suicide—"

"Don't say that!" he said sharply. "Not even as a joke."

"I wasn't joking." She smiled. "So let's call it even."

"Did Falke mistreat you?"

"Not really. He just kept me locked in a room until the baby came."

"What does she look like?"

"Now? I only saw her once. She would have been about three months old." Nikola paused. "She was already walking."

"We grow swiftly the first year. Then it slows down." Malach sat on the edge of the bed. "I'll call her Rachel. That was my mother's name."

The longing in his voice ignited a spark of fear.

"I didn't know that." She paused. "What was your father's name?"

"Devorion. I barely remember either of them. They died when I was very young." Malach eyed the necklace at her throat. "I've never seen a stone like that. What is it?"

"Serpent's eye."

"The witches gave it to you?"

"In a way," she hedged. "They say it's the rarest of all gems."

"Then it suits you." He took her hand, tugging her closer. Warm hands circled her waist. He started to ease her hem up.

Nikola pushed it down again, feeling exposed in the lamplight.

"Don't," she said.

"Why not?" He stroked her knee.

"Because I'm ugly now."

Malach frowned. "Why would you say that?"

"I have stretch marks."

He regarded her through his lashes. "I want to see," he murmured.

Before she could stop him, her dress was above her hips. She covered the scarred seams on her belly with a hand. Malach gently drew it away.

"I like them," he said, tracing one with a feather-light brush of his lips. "They give you character."

Nikola snorted. "Stop! It tickles!"

"Not so loud . . . Does this tickle?"

Curse him! Curse her twice! Before Nikola quite knew what was happening, they were rolling around on the bed, frantically shedding clothing. Afterwards, Malach lay on his back, gaze sweeping restlessly across the ceiling. She'd tried hard to wear him out, but he still burned with a fierce energy.

"Help me, Nikola. Help me get her back. Then I'll never ask anything of you again."

She propped herself up on one elbow. "Even if I put you inside the Arx, you'd never get her out again."

"Unless you brought us both back." He rolled over, face intent. "I'd raise her with the other children."

She blinked in surprise. "You'd come back here?"

"Yes," he replied without hesitation. "I would. It's the safest place for her."

"What about the other nihilim?" She regarded him skeptically. "Would you really walk away from this war?"

He held her eyes. "I'll admit, that used to be all I cared about. But there's more to life than some endless struggle for dominance. *You* taught me that." He shook his head. "I was obsessed with leaving, but only because I wanted to find you. Now that I have. . . ." He stroked her cheekbone with a thumb. "I understand that you want something else. But if I had our daughter, I would be at peace."

The words rang with simple sincerity. Yet what he was asking . . . .

"And if they kill you?" she demanded.

"They won't." He eyed the stone at her neck. "Can you remove the kaldurite?"

"Where is it?"

"Inside me." He patted his abdomen. "Somewhere thereabouts."

She shook her head. "I have no idea how to do that."

"Try."

Nikola laid a hand on his stomach. The stone itself was a void, a black hole the ley could not touch. But she sensed complex charms of protection winding around it, binding the kaldurite to his essence. She couldn't fathom how the witches had accomplished it. She withdrew her hand.

"You're asking me to draw a warded stone from living flesh. I've only just mastered the basics!"

Malach's eyes narrowed. "Transporting yourself from one place to another doesn't sound like the basics, Nikola."

"That's different. I stumbled over it. Frankly, I'm amazed I haven't killed myself. But if I attempted to summon that stone, it might kill *you*."

He sat up. "Fine. Then I'll go like this."

"With no ability to use the ley?" she asked in disbelief.

"Falke doesn't know that."

"I'm not even sure I could move someone else."

"I bet you can."

Privately, Nikola thought so, too. The box was the box. Whatever was inside it got forced. All the debris that came along for the ride was evidence of that. But she wasn't going to admit it.

"No," she said flatly.

"Then I'll cut the stone out myself."

She stared at him. "You wouldn't."

Malach gazed back. "You doubt me?"

His face was deadly earnest. A bluff? Impossible to know for sure. He had a streak of madness. She'd seen it the night he nearly killed himself crossing the Wards at the Arx. Nikola cursed herself again for coming back. How neatly he'd set the trap.

"Why?" she snapped. "Why can't you just let her go?"

He was silent for a long moment. "If my daughter was dead, I could accept that. If *anyone* else had her, I might be able to live with that, too. But not Dmitry Falke." His jaw tightened. "He's the one who led the campaign against Bal Kirith. He murdered my sister in her cradle."

Nikola felt a jolt of shock. "You did have a sister."

"A newborn. Scarcely a week old." His eyes grew distant. "When the knights breached the walls, my father told me to watch over her. I was in her nursery when a shell hit. Falke came. I thought he'd kill me, but he told me to run." Malach swallowed. "I . . . I did. I left her there."

She took his hand. "I'm so sorry. How old were you?"

"Four."

"Saints."

"Both my parents died that day. I scavenged in the Morho until Beleth found me, half-starved and burning with fever. Another mage would have left me to fend for myself. I was a burden. But she kept me. Taught me to survive. In the end, I abandoned her, too." He lifted his head. "Do you understand now? I have no choice in this, Nikola. If I let her go, if I let *Falke* raise her as his own, it'll devour me."

Nikola wanted to deny it, but she saw the truth in his eyes. "Won't the witches know she's here?"

"If I explain it to Finlo, he'll keep his mouth shut. Paarjini barely notices the kids. One more won't make a difference."

"You won't fool the Mahadeva."

"Perhaps not," he conceded. "But at least Rachel would be here. That's all I want. It's what the witches want, too."

"They'll know I did it."

"Please, Nikola." His voice was raw. "I'm begging you. Help me get my daughter back. You're the only one who can."

She thought of the tiny Raven Mark on the infant's neck. "You don't know anything about her, Malach. And she doesn't know about you. You said she'd be powerful. What if she fights us?"

"She can't use the ley on me. I know it's not too late! But the longer I wait, the harder it'll be for her. Please."

She looked away, full of misgivings. "I'll take you, Malach. And I'll bring you both back. But I can't be involved in raising her. You must agree to that."

"I have no objection."

She steeled her voice. "This is a formal bargain, mage."

He smiled faintly. "Done and done, Domina Thorn."

"I'll need gems." She touched her necklace. "I can't keep using this."

"Why not?"

She didn't want him to know the price she'd paid. "I just can't."

"I have stones. They pay me for my work here."

He strode to the dresser, opened one of the drawers, and tossed her a drawstring pouch. "Will those work?" he asked.

Nikola surveyed the contents. It was a decent mix of both projective and receptive stones. "I think so. When do you want to do it?"

"Right now."

She muttered an oath.

"It's the middle of the night," he said reasonably. "Always the best time for an ambush."

"I don't even know where she is!"

"Falke does. And I'll wager he keeps her close. We take him hostage—quietly—make him bring us to Rachel, and get out."

She stared at him, heart thumping. It was mad.

Yet not impossible.

And Malach was right. If they were going to do it, why not right now?

She pictured the look on Falke's face when he opened his eyes to find them both standing over him.

"All right," she said. "Let's go get the kid."

Malach grinned. "No mercy. If we meet any knights, I'm killing them." His eyes glinted. "And I'll fucking enjoy it."

She pulled her dress on. "I don't want to be part of a bloodbath, Malach."

He scowled. "How can it be avoided?"

"I know a few tricks."

"Fine. But I won't let them take us."

She tied her head scarf on. "Agreed. I just hope you're right about Falke keeping her close. I should be able to bring us into his bedchamber. I know the Pontifex's Palace."

Malach pulled on a pair of boots. He tied a length of cloth around his waist and donned a long-sleeved linen shirt.

"No pants?" she asked with a tense smile.

"It's called a Rahai. Haven't you seen them before?"

She shook her head. "There are no men where the witches train their acolytes."

"So you've never even been to the temple in Dur-Athaara?"

"No. What's it like?"

"Full of snakes. Tash is there. He takes care of them." A grimace. "I used to visit him, but I haven't seen him in months."

"Is he well?"

"He seemed happy the last time I was there." A pause. "I'm glad for him."

Malach paused in the curving hall, eying the children's bedroom doors. "I won't say goodbye," he muttered. "It's bad luck."

No one woke as they slunk back down the stairs. Outside, Malach asked her to wait and ducked into a shed next to the garden.

"*That's* your weapon of choice?" Nikola asked, when he emerged with a rusty shovel.

"We don't keep swords lying around," he said dryly. "And we only have one good chopping knife. Finlo'll kill me if I lose it."

Nikola eyed the shovel. "I feel like we're about to dig our own graves."

Malach tried out a fancy quarterstaff move. The shovel flew from his hands. "Whoops," he muttered, jogging to retrieve it from a puddle.

She shook her head. "Come over here."

Malach stepped up.

"Closer."

He smiled and wrapped an arm around her waist. "Do you believe in me?"

She studied his face. "Oddly enough, I do."

"Do you think the spell will work with the kaldurite inside me?"

"I hope so," she muttered. "But I haven't a clue. This is unnatural magic. If my theory is right, I'm not doing anything to you directly. Just changing the space around you."

She took two gems from the pouch, gripping one in each hand. Left for projective, right for receptive. "The landings aren't smooth, so brace yourself."

He nodded, muscles tensing.

Nikola joined her mind with the stones, tapping the opposing forces of ley inside them. Threads of power snapped and crackled. Her will sharpened to a single blazing point. Nikola fed it with the kindling of her need. Her anger at

Falke. She wove the threads together, picturing two tall bronze doors and the lavish room that lay beyond. At the same time, she built a box large enough for two. Walls of shimmering ley formed around them.

Nikola forced the box.

Chapter Thirteen

A spear of ice stabbed Malach's gut. The breath evaporated from his lungs in a burst of searing heat. He clung to Nikola with one hand, gripping the shovel in the other. The world blurred into a dizzying kaleidoscope. He closed his eyes and fought the urge to retch. The pressure in his head built to a buzzing ache. Then blessed relief as his ears popped. He sucked in a startled breath as the ground fell away beneath his feet.

It lasted only a moment. Malach landed with a jolt, squinting in sudden torchlight. A high-ceilinged stone corridor swam into focus. Three knights in mail stared in shock. A fourth lay on the ground in a pile of charred sand, smoke drifting from his open mouth. Malach swung the shovel at the first knight within range. It met his skull with a crunch.

Blades scraped from scabbards. He ducked blindly. A sword whistled above his head. He kicked a kneecap and leaned away from a wild slash as the man staggered to regain balance. Malach whacked him across the face. He dropped the shovel and was scrabbling for the fallen blade when the knight flew backwards, slamming into the stone wall.

Malach turned, panting. Nikola stood with her left palm

open. She tossed the stone aside and rummaged through the pouch. The last knight stood behind her, his sword raised for a killing stroke. Malach lunged, dragging him to the ground. An elbow smashed his nose, sending a lance of pain through the top of his head. He managed to pin the knight's blade arm. Then Nikola was crouching down, fingers twined in the knight's hair as she pressed a bluish stone to his forehead.

"Sleep," she whispered.

The man writhed, his eyes going even wider. Nikola frowned, then quickly switched the stone to her other hand. "Sleep, dammit!"

This time he fell limp. Malach rolled away. She threw the stone away, muttering something about her dominant hand.

Nikola looked up and down the corridor. "I missed the bedchamber. Not by much, though. We're just on the wrong side of the door. Saints, you're bleeding."

He wiped his face with a sleeve, climbing to his feet. "I'm good."

They were in an alcove outside a pair of tall, heavy doors. The wood and hinges looked brand new. She gave a push and shook her head.

"Bolted from the inside. But that's why I got it wrong," she said. "They must have replaced them after Feizah was killed."

"The doors were ripped off?" Malach wondered, his heart still stuttering with adrenaline.

"Guess so." She drew another stone from the pouch. "Stand back."

He picked up a sword, adjusting his grip. The words *Virtus, Veritas, Lux* were embossed along the blade. Courage. Truth. Light.

The fucking hypocrites.

"Here goes," she muttered.

Nikola's fingers folded around the gem with a look of intense concentration. Her hand sprang open. The doors splintered and blew back, sagging on their brand-new hinges.

"Shit," she whispered. "It actually worked!"

Malach stalked into the dim chamber beyond, thick carpets whispering beneath his feet.

Dmitry Falke sat up in an enormous four-poster bed, a single candle on the table illuminating a face hard with fury. Malach reached him in four strides. He laid the edge of the blade to Falke's throat, just below the Raven Mark. "Where's my daughter?"

Falke stared at him with contempt. "How did you get in here?"

Malach pressed the steel deeper, drawing a bead of blood. "*Where is she?*"

The dark, hooded eyes showed no fear. Malach nodded, flexing his free hand. "Fine. I won't kill you. I'll just invert every single one of your Marks. You can have a nice long stay at the Batavia Institute like Lezarius."

A muscle twitched in Falke's jaw. "Listen to me, Malach. The child is safe here. Loved and cherished. If you truly care about her—"

"Shut up! She's nearby, isn't she?"

Falke said nothing, but Malach knew he was right. "Get up."

The pontifex's gaze slid past him to Nikola. "I should never have let you go," he muttered.

"Quiet your Marks," Nikola said coldly. "They won't do you any good."

Malach couldn't see the ley, but he realized that Nikola could. She was telling him that Falke was trying—unsuccessfully—to use the power against him. Malach felt grim satisfaction at the flash of surprise on Falke's face.

"Get up!" he snapped.

Falke threw the blankets aside. He wore purple silk pajamas. The gold ring of the pontifex glittered on his right hand. The man still had a certain regal dignity, but he seemed *old* now. It was strange to see the enemy he'd hated above all others, the Curia's greatest general, move so stiffly. Yet Malach knew better than to underestimate him again.

Falke's mouth tightened as they walked him past the fallen guards. "You'll never get her out," he said. "There's five hundred knights between you and the Dacian Gate."

Malach prodded Falke with the blade. "That's my problem, isn't it? Yours is to do what you're told so I don't take your head off."

Nikola prowled ahead down the corridor. When they reached the first juncture, she looked back and raised a hand in warning. Falke opened his mouth to yell. Malach grabbed him by the hair, pressing the blade to his throat. "Hush."

Nikola jogged back, moving silently on the balls of her feet. "Two knights are guarding a door," she whispered. "Just around the corner."

Malach twisted Falke's head around. "It's her, isn't it?"

The look in his eyes confirmed it.

"Follow my lead," Malach told Nikola.

He dragged Falke to the juncture, then swiftly stepped around the corner.

"Hey!"

The knights lounged against the wall. They spun to attention. Malach gripped Falke's hair tighter, yanking his head back, the blade skimming his jugular. "On your knees!"

They froze, eyes locked on Falke. One dropped a hand to his sword.

"Toss those away or I cut his throat right in front of you."

The men exchanged a look.

"I killed the last pontifex." Malach smiled. "Do you really want to test me?"

The men sank to their knees and laid the swords down. Nikola strode up and kicked them away. She dug into the pouch again with a frown. "That's not what I need," she muttered, poking through the remaining stones. "Where are you?"

The knights looked at each other.

"Uh, Nikola," Malach muttered. "Can you hurry it up?"

"I know there's a moonstone *somewhere*—"

One made a grab for the pouch. Gems spilled across the floor. She fell to her knees, snatched one up, and fisted it with a yelp. A huge black swan waddled down the corridor, wings beating, beak opened in a hiss. The knight reared back in surprise. His companion leapt for one of the swords. Nikola swept up more gems, juggling them between her hands. "Be still!" she shouted, an edge of panic in her voice.

The knight holding the blade went rigid and slowly toppled over, his eyes rolling wildly. Nikola stared at him in astonishment. "Damn," she muttered.

The swan disappeared. The second knight locked eyes with her. Nikola's palm sprang open. Malach saw the glitter of a blue gemstone. "Sleep," she hissed.

He yawned and shook his head like a dog with mites. Tried in a lumbering fashion to stand up. With a grunt of frustration, Nikola seized one of the fallen swords and whacked him over the head with the hilt. The knight slumped down next to his frozen comrade.

"Witchcraft," Falke rasped. "Where did you learn—"

"Be quiet or she'll turn you into a toad." Malach eased the blade from Falke's throat, using the tip to nudge him to the door. Nikola tried the handle. It opened freely.

She cast an anxious look at Malach and pushed the door wide. His heart drummed as he stepped inside. Faint light spilled through a tall, arched window. His could make out the dark shapes of furniture along the walls. He forced Falke deeper into the room. A small bed sat next to the window. It was empty, the sheets rumpled.

"Where is she?" he hissed.

Falke turned to shoot him a silent glare.

Malach pressed a palm to the bed. Still warm. He shoved Falke to the ground and looked underneath. Candlelight bloomed behind him. Enough to see the space was empty. Malach stood.

Nikola held a candle in her hand. She had a taut expression he couldn't quite read. But it *was* Rachel's room. He knew it. Everything was child-sized except for a rocking chair. A copy of the *Meliora* rested on the chair. The Via Sancta's foundational text. A sudden image of Falke rocking in the chair while his daughter played on the floor brought a wave of furious heat to his face.

"She used to be here," Falke said hoarsely. "But I moved her. You'll never find—"

"That's why you posted knights outside? To guard an empty room?"

"To trick you," Falke spat. "And it worked!"

"If he moves a muscle," Malach said to Nikola, "hit him with something nasty."

His gaze lit on the tall wardrobe. Malach walked over, mouth dry. He set the sword on top of the wardrobe. Then he opened the door.

A child crouched inside. She had a heart-shaped face and large hazel eyes with thick lashes. Curly dark hair that puffed out in a cloud around her head. She wore a tiny white nightgown that brushed her feet. Her skin was a dusky caramel. She looked just as he'd imagined, only even more beautiful. A current of love swept through him, tempered with remorse that they should meet this way.

"I won't hurt you," he said softly. "Come on out."

She clutched a book to her chest. It was small, made for little hands. Was she reading already? The thought of all he'd missed cut him like a knife. But he had her now. Nothing else mattered. In time, she would learn to love him.

"Do as he says, Lessa." Falke's voice was calm.

Her head turned. "Papa?" she whispered.

A red blossom of rage unfurled in Malach's chest. He tamped it down. None of it was her fault.

"Everything's fine," he said. "Please come out."

The child eyed him warily. He stepped back. After a moment, she climbed down from the wardrobe. Barely six months old and she was a head taller than Roseen. Falke spread his arms. She tried to run to him. Malach snagged her around the waist. The child gave a cry of alarm.

"Don't scream," he whispered. "It's okay, it's okay."

"Papa!" she screamed at Falke.

Malach heard distant shouts in the corridor.

"Stop," he pleaded, as she writhed against him. "I'm not going to hurt you."

She bit his hand, drawing blood. He swore under his breath.

"Maybe we *should* leave her," Nikola said tightly. "I warned you this would happen."

"No!"

"It's too late, Malach," Falke said, an edge of satisfaction in his voice. "You cannot corrupt her. She's been raised in the light."

Malach managed to wrap his arms around her, though she still fought like a cornered badger. "They lied to you," he said firmly. "Just listen to me, Rachel. Falke is not your father!"

Her struggles grew more violent. Boots rang in the corridor.

"Bar the door!" he shouted.

Nikola delved into the pouch. She raised her hand. Wood creaked and swelled in the frame just as a resounding blow came from the other side.

"Take us back!" Malach urged her.

Nikola hurried over, her face grim. Rachel thrashed wildly. A small foot caught her shin, eliciting a grunt of pain.

"Hurry," he snapped.

Nikola shot him a dark look. "I need the right ones." Her jaw tightened as she sorted through the pouch, finally choosing two stones. The kaldurite ignited like a lump of ice in his belly as power swelled around them.

"Hold on to me, Malach," she muttered. "Can't you keep her still?"

Falke rose to his feet. "Stop! You cannot—"

Malach's skin crawled as invisible walls formed around them. He shifted his grip on the flailing child to take Nikola's arm. In that instant of distraction, Rachel wrenched free. She flung herself at Falke. Nikola let out a string of oaths as Malach leapt after her.

"Wait!" he cried. "Just wait!"

He felt like a monster prying her fingers free from Falke's shoulders. Their eyes locked. Malach saw the disgust in his face. Then he had Rachel back in his arms, howling like a banshee. He turned to run to Nikola. A deep clap of pressure rattled his ribcage. Sheet lightning flickered. A burst of intense heat seared his skin. Malach flung an arm up, stumbling backwards. He crashed against the door. It shuddered under a series of heavy blows from the other side.

Malach blinked, half-blind. His vision slowly cleared. Falke was staring in astonishment at the empty square of melted stone where Nikola had stood a moment before.

"She'll come back," Malach whispered. "It was a mistake. She'll come."

But she didn't. And he finally understood that it was no accident.

She'd left him there.

Rachel stopped her frenzied struggles. Her body was still in his arms as he ran to the window. A four-story drop to a courtyard below.

No way out.

Another resounding blow. They had axes. The edge of one bit through the wood, pulled back, struck again.

If the knights took him, they'd sever both his hands for sure this time.

Sweat slicked his palms. He had no ley to defend himself. He had nothing.

Nothing but his daughter.

He set her on her feet and crouched down to look her in the eye. Malach forced his voice to calm. "Listen to me carefully. I know you can do something special. Every half-blood has unique power. Tell me what it is."

She shook her head in a swift denial. And Malach saw it.

The Raven Mark on her neck.

The last rational piece of him withered like a seedling in a sudden blizzard. He passed beyond rage to a frozen wasteland where nothing mattered except survival.

"Tell me," he growled, "or I'll break your father's neck. Do you believe me?"

The look in her eyes would have ripped his heart out if it wasn't already in shreds.

"Yes," she whispered.

The bitter irony was that he couldn't kill Falke now, no matter how badly he wanted to. If he did, Rachel would die, too. The Curia called it Mark sickness. It started with hallucinations, then bone-rattling chills, and eventually, a miserable, screaming end. If Falke had given her the Mark—and Malach knew he had—their lives were entangled forever.

But that didn't mean he couldn't make Falke suffer. Tear down everything he'd built, leaving him as empty and ruined as Malach felt at that moment.

"Tell me what your special talent is," he said.

She swallowed. "I talk to the sky."

"What does that mean?" He turned to Falke. "What the hell does that mean?"

"I don't know! She's too young. I haven't even tried to find out." Falke's heavy jowls were mottled with anger. "You would use her in this way? Have you not a single drop of compassion—"

Malach shut him out. He barely heard the thud of the

axes falling, the wood splintering into pieces. There was only Rachel and her frightened gaze.

"If you want him to live, you'll make us a way out of here," he said. "Tear down the whole Arx if you have to!"

"No," Falke cried. "Don't listen to him!"

She cast an agonized look at the man who had stolen her. Lied to her. Imprisoned her own pregnant mother and then discarded Nikola like a piece of trash once he had the infant. The man who had murdered her grandparents. Who had vowed to see her entire race eradicated.

Malach swept the child up and strode to the window. "Do it now," he snapped. "*Break them!*"

Her rosebud lips tightened to a line. She tilted her face to the heavens. It was an unusually clear night for Novostopol. With the Wards dead, the Arx was dark except for a few faint lights burning across the plaza. The sky was thick with stars.

If she refused, Malach would jump. Part of him wanted to keep her in his arms. Shatter them both on the stones below rather than give her back. But even in his madness, he couldn't do it.

He studied her profile. She had her mother's mouth, but there was something of him, too. Whoever did her hair was careless. It looked dry and unkempt. She should be sleeping in braids.

He wondered what her smile looked like. The sound of her laughter.

Why had the ley brought him here if not to save her? Or were the witches right? Did he ruin everything he touched?

Behind them, the door gave way with a mighty crack.

He opened the window and slid a leg over the sill.

"My name is Malach," he said quietly. "Know that I loved you. Always."

He exhaled slowly, eyeing the courtyard below. When he looked up, the stars were moving.

Malach watched, transfixed, as the flares of light grew

brighter. A dozen fireballs streaked at a low angle across the sky, trailing long white jets. They made a whistling roar like incoming shells, the sound high and low at the same time.

There was no time to react. He dropped to a crouch, shielding the child with his body as the windows exploded. Glass rained down. A rapid series of booms rocked the Arx. Dust choked the air. He curled tighter around his daughter. The ground shook. Shards of stone blistered his back.

It sounded like the end of the world.

After an eternity, the barrage stopped. Silence rushed in, punctured by the groans of wounded men. He coughed. Black smoke filled the air. Malach examined Rachel with trembling fingers. She seemed unhurt, but her face was blank.

Meteors still streaked across the sky. He heard distant explosions as they landed. Malach lifted her to his hip and staggered over to Falke. The Pontifex lay on his back. Blood trickled down his cheek, but Malach saw no other injury. He kicked him in the ribs.

"Get up," he growled.

Falke's eyes fluttered. Malach nudged him again. "Get up! You're coming along."

Falke sat, bracing a palm on the bed. Blood and dust matted his hair. "What have you done?" he whispered hoarsely.

The old general's nerve was fractured at last. His gaze swept over the damage in stunned disbelief. Half the ceiling had come down, exposing fragments of hellish red-tinged sky above.

Malach picked a path to the door, Rachel's cheek limp against his neck. Rubble clogged the corridor beyond. Mailed limbs stuck out, unmoving. The rest of the knights must have fled. Booms shook the night, both near and far.

"Move!" Malach glanced back. "Before the building comes down on our heads!"

Falke gave a faint nod and limped to the door, his skin

ashen. They found a staircase that had survived the impact and took it to the bottom, skirting heaps of crumbled wall. The exterior of the Pontifex's Palace lay open to the air. The plaza was a deep crater scattered with chunks of burning rock. Everywhere, knights and Curia officials ran for their lives. Headlights pierced the gloom, revealing a scene of devastation.

An eerie glow lit the sky above. Two more fireballs streaked toward the earth as Malach watched. They hit the eastern edge of the citadel with ear-shattering bursts.

His head jerked around at the roar of an engine. A transport came careening down the Via Fortuna. Malach gently set Rachel down. He tore his shirt off and used it to pick up a chunk of rock. Even through the cloth, it was so hot he almost dropped it. He stepped into the headlights and hurled it at the windshield. Glass spiderwebbed. The transport skidded, brakes squealing. He ran up and yanked the driver's side door open. The knight inside took one look at the Nightmarks on his chest and scrambled out, fleeing into the dark.

Malach caught Falke's arm as he tried to stagger away. A fist to the jaw and he slumped into oblivion. Malach threw him into the back of the transport, then returned for his daughter. She blinked once when he took her hand, but hardly seemed to see him. She didn't resist as he led her to the armored vehicle.

"It's okay," he murmured. "You're going home now."

Malach sat her in the passenger seat, buckled her harness, and slid behind the wheel. He'd never driven a Centurion and didn't recognize half the dashboard instruments, but the engine was running. He floored the accelerator. They skirted more craters and heaps of rubble where buildings had stood. The vehicle had four-wheel drive and he ended up gunning it straight through a wooded park, swerving to avoid knights who frantically waved their arms for a lift.

There were no checkpoints anymore. Those lucky enough

to have found a vehicle were driving full speed for the Dacian Gate. Others stumbled in desperation for an exit. Half the outer curtain wall was down and tiny figures poured through the gaps. A grim smile touched Malach's lips.

They sped through the Dacian Gate and out of the Arx into the city of Novostopol. Lights shone in every window. Crowds were gathering outside their apartment buildings, pointing to the glow in the sky. Malach blew through the red lights, only pulling to the side when emergency vehicles screamed past in the direction of the Arx, sirens wailing. The damage seemed mostly confined to the inner citadel. It was still the middle of the night. No one knew what was happening yet. Other than the ambulances and Oprichniki squads, the streets were relatively clear.

He hit Liberation Bridge doing a hundred and twenty, the waters of the Traiana surging below. Malach changed lanes to pass a slower car and glanced in the rearview, wincing in the glow of high beams.

The side mirror showed nothing behind him.

Nothing but a blinding, white-hot glow.

Bitter adrenaline flooded his mouth. He flipped up the mirror and stomped the pedal to the floor. The Centurion surged forward, engine roaring. They shot off the ramp just as an explosion rocked the roadway. The transport fishtailed in the shockwave. Malach yanked the wheel, narrowly missing the guide rail. They came within a whisper of rolling. The wheels lifted up, then slammed back down. Heavy tires gripped with a screech of rubber. His eyes flicked to the side mirror.

Liberation Bridge was gone. A dense cloud mushroomed above the river.

His knee shook as he eased back on the accelerator. Bile rose in his throat. Five seconds slower . . . .

"Enough!" he said. "It's enough. Make it stop!"

Rachel gave no sign of hearing him. Malach swore.

They sped through wealthy, manicured suburbs, then rice paddies and farmland. Rows of stelae came and went, standing like tombs to the ideals of the Via Sancta. Their Raven Wards were dead stone now that the Void was gone. Scattered trees appeared in the headlight beams. The southern edge of the Morho. Malach pulled to the verge. He raked his hands through his hair and slumped back against the seat. The adrenaline rush ebbed. Pain filled the vacuum. His back was on fire. The seat felt sticky with blood.

He turned to Rachel. "I'm sorry."

She stared straight ahead with glassy eyes.

The engine ticked in the cool night air. He rolled a window down. Crickets sang in the undergrowth. His ears buzzed in the quiet.

"I'm not going to hurt you. I . . . ." Malach trailed off.

The mindless rage was gone. Shouldn't he feel triumph now? He'd won. Taken his daughter back and delivered retribution beyond his wildest dreams.

He'd promised to bring her home.

But where was that?

"I understand," he said wearily. "We don't have to talk right now."

Malach peered into the back. Falke was still out cold. He threw the vehicle into gear and drove on. After a few kilometers, he veered into a rutted track that would eventually join the overgrown network of roads that ran through the Morho all the way to Bal Agnar. When the trees crowded thick, he pulled over and studied the dashboard until he found the button to raise the soundproof barrier between the front and rear. It whirred upward, obscuring Falke behind a thick layer of tinted shatterproof glass.

"Stay here," he told Rachel.

He walked around to the back and opened the hatch. It held a large empty space with built-in storage along the sides. Falke sprawled across the panels. Malach opened one of the compartments. A stack of ready-to-eat meals was stowed inside, along with jugs of water. He took a long swig, clearing the dust from his throat. The next held a field radio and manual with the knights' radio codes. *That* could be useful. He switched the radio on. Nothing but static. A third compartment had a small knife in a leather sheath and four sets of manacles. He snapped a pair around Falke's wrists, then fixed them to steel rings above his head.

"Time to wake up," he said, lightly slapping Falke's jowls.

The Pontifex moaned. His eyes fluttered open. When he saw Malach, he jerked away, gaze sharpening to defiance.

"I've read all your books," Malach said. "Did you know that?"

Falke jerked at the handcuffs. "Where's Lessa?"

"I have her. And I won't bother threatening you with death again. We both know I can't since you . . . ." He bit off the words. Remarkable how quickly the anger came surging back when he thought of the little Raven on her neck. "But I do know *you* intimately, Dmitry Falke. I've spent my life studying every campaign. Every tactic and strategy. Not to mention our personal chats during the Cold Truce. And you do have a weakness. *Pride*."

Malach curled a hand around Falke's forearm. "It would give me the greatest pleasure to invert your Marks right now. Watch you slide into gibbering madness. What would Lessa think of you then, hmmm? The condition can't be reversed. But you're tough. I bet you could live for longer than most. Sitting senseless in your own filth—"

"What do you want?" Falke demanded.

"Information. Do you still occupy Bal Kirith?"

A brusque nod. Malach had expected as much. He must have deployed a huge force there. It wouldn't be easy to rout.

"What about Bal Agnar?"

The ruined city was the only place Malach could think of

that might be safe for him now. His kin must be gathering somewhere.

"We took it last month," Falke said calmly, though a tic fluttered at the corner of his eye. "A joint force of Nantwich and Novostopol—"

"You're lying. I know you too well. So: One more chance. Then you'll be tumbling down the rabbit hole." Malach leaned forward, letting Falke see the madness in his own eyes. "And I promise you, it's deeper and darker than you can begin to imagine."

He held up the knife. Falke's eyes flicked to the white scar along his wrist.

"Or I could sever your hands. Just as you tried to do to me." He pressed the edge to Falke's left wrist, then moved it to the right. "Which one should I take first?"

Falke held his gaze steadily. The old bastard might not have any scruples, but he did have courage. "Don't bring her there, Malach. I beg you—"

Malach turned away. He slammed the hatch shut.

"Bal Agnar it is," he muttered.

He slid into the driver's seat. Rachel had fallen asleep. Her features were soft, one thumb stuck into her mouth. He eased it out, stroking her hair.

"I'll protect you," he whispered. "Don't worry. Everything's fine now."

He started the engine and flicked on the high beams. With a rumble, the transport lurched into the dark forest.

Chapter Fourteen

Nikola knelt on rough stone, spewing her guts out. When she managed to lift her head, she counted nine witches arrayed in a semicircle around her. Paarjini stood with hands on hips, dark brows drawn down in a scowl. Torvelle whispered in Heshima's ear. Her tutor's black eyes simmered with anger. Nikola didn't know the others' names, though their faces were familiar.

Mother, Maid and Crone regarded her with identical expressions of disappointment.

"Nikola Thorn!" The Crone's voice was a whipcrack. "You have broken every law. Violated every rule of your training. Worse, you aided the aingeal dian—"

Nikola managed to gain her feet, temples throbbing with pain. She reached for her namestone to force a way out, but Heshima was too quick. Her hand lashed out and ripped the gold chain from Nikola's neck.

"Give it back!" she screamed. "You must let me return!"

"Where is he?" the Crone thundered. "Where did you take him?"

"The Arx in Novostopol. We had the child!" Nikola's

panicked gaze sought out the Mother. "Please, bring them both here! Do what you did to me!"

"We cannot. The serpent's eye drew you to us, but he cannot be forced at a distance with the kaldurite inside him."

Forced at a distance. She'd never even considered the possibility.

"I may have broken your rules," she said heatedly, "but you lied to me!"

The Crone made a sharp gesture. The other witches retreated from the grotto. Hashima gave her a final hard stare before disappearing down the narrow passage.

"Be grateful we did not summon you through the air all the way from Novostopol!" the Maid growled. "You'd be picking bugs from your teeth for a week!"

Nikola had a brief image of herself flying over the waves at high speed.

Yes, that would be worse. But still . . . .

She sank to her knees again and held out a beseeching hand. "Please, I beg you. Let me go back. He promised to return here. I wouldn't have done it otherwise. They'll kill him!"

The Maid frowned and ran for the dicing cup. She handed it to the Crone, who quickly cast her gems. Scattered motes of light danced on the ceiling of the cavern.

"He is not dead," the Mother said. "Nor is the child."

"But many others are," the Crone added. Her white-cauled eyes lifted. Nikola felt the piercing stare in her bones. "You have brought disaster down."

"We should have told her," the Mother muttered. "All of it."

The Maid skipped over. "We did not lie *exactly*," she said, her cheeks flushing. "We only showed you part of the truth. Allowed you to make your own assumptions."

"You said he was dead!"

"No, we did not," the Mother replied. "We said he desired

death and the sisters could not stop him. All that was true. He *did* throw himself overboard."

"And they fished him out," Nikola said bitterly. "But you neglected to mention that part."

"You are not meant for each other." The Crone's voice gentled. "I do not deny that this was partly our doing." She shook her head, white hair swaying. "But we didn't imagine it would go so far, so quickly. What were you thinking?"

"He threatened to cut the kaldurite from his own belly if I didn't help him get the child. I feared he would do it."

The Mother rolled her eyes. "Did he tell you how he tried that once already and nearly died?"

Nikola shook her head, sickened.

"He is determined to meet his fate," the Crone said. "The pull of it is too strong. We tried to turn his rudder. The ley would not allow it. But that doesn't change the fact that we have foreseen an even worse disaster than the one that just occurred."

Her gut sank. "What has he done?"

"A starfall," the Mother said. "Called down by the child at Malach's behest."

"Your daughter is powerful," the Maid said, bringing a foot to her mouth and chewing thoughtfully on the toenail. "They are still together."

Nikola sagged with relief. "But he must think I abandoned them. Why won't you let me go back? I swear to return."

"It is too late now. But there will be no more forcing today," the Crone said sternly. "Or *ever.* Didn't Heshima explain the dangers to you?"

"Not exactly."

The Mother clucked her tongue. "She did not expect you to do it. Not yet, at least. What do you know?"

"It requires two stones, one projective and one receptive." Nikola knit her hands together. "But instead of using them in opposition, I meld their forces together. Then I tie a knot of spirit to hold the whole mess together. It doesn't last long, but it gets me where I want to go."

The Crone gave a heavy sigh. "This is what happens when the strongest novice in generations is unleashed," she remarked to the air, "half-trained and with delusions of her own competence."

The Maid spit out a piece of toenail. "Every time you force, you create a hairline fracture in the universe. A tiny singularity where the laws of space and time cease to have meaning."

"Do it enough times," the Mother finished, "and the world will shatter. Perhaps all worlds."

"It nearly did in the last Dark Age," the Crone muttered.

"And that is why we try not to force." The Maid smiled without a trace of humor. "There are already thousands of fractures. They all add up."

Nikola swallowed. "I see."

"It might not be the next one. Or the next. Perhaps you could force a million times before the whole structure gives way. But we do not know for sure, you understand?"

She nodded. "I do, Mahadeva. I am sorry." A pause. "But you did it. Just now."

"It was a last resort and required nine sisters working in tandem," the Mother said. "We hoped Malach might appear in the box, too."

"How did you know we were together?"

"Paarjini can track the kaldurite. She left a spell around it that tells us his whereabouts."

"So we can still find him?" Nikola asked hopefully.

"Yes." The Crone's lips pursed. "And I think we must. The course is set now, but there is still a slim chance he can be turned." She swept the stones up and returned them to the cup. "He will go to Balaur," she said quietly. "Just as we saw."

Nikola thought she misheard. "Balaur? He's been dead for thirty years!"

A rasping laugh. "If only it were so. He gathers power in the Morho Sarpanitum. Drawing those who are weak of will and bending them to his purpose. It is his corruption we sensed in the north, but now that the Void is broken there seems little to stop him." She tilted her head. "He will come here eventually."

When Nikola was a child, she used to chant a ditty when she played hopscotch in the schoolyard. It was before she'd failed the Probatio tests, when she still had friends. She couldn't remember where she'd learned the rhyme. Every kid just knew it.

The lady in red
Met the man in red
They joined their hands
Said I thee wed

I'll build you an Arx
Said the lady in red
With walls so high
They flay the sky

I'll give you silks
And furs and skins
And knucklebones
To rap their shins

But the man in red
Made no reply
For the man in red
Had lost his head

Yes, the man in red was . . . DEAD!

Scrawny, pigtailed Nikola would shout the last word, leap

into the end square on one foot, and collapse with her eyes rolled back and tongue stuck out. It was only a decade or more later when she was at a rooftop party on Savior's Eve that someone drunkenly explained who it was really about. Beleth and Balaur. She'd felt silly for not figuring it out sooner, but it was just a ghoulish little song.

Now Nikola's legs, still unsteady from being forced, gave out. She sat down hard on the ledge of the pool.

"Saints," she whispered. Then a thought occurred that made her angry again. "Why didn't you warn him? Tell him what you saw? I can promise you, Malach isn't evil. Not like Balaur! I wouldn't—" She cut off, heat rising to her face. "I wouldn't care for him if I believed that."

"He would have denied it," the Mother said. "In every casting of the stones, telling him changed nothing. The only hope was to keep him here, away from the chaos." A hard look. "We did not expect you to learn the truth, let alone find him."

"More fools us," the Crone muttered. "They are pearls of the same oyster."

"Feckless and rash," the Maid hissed.

Nikola cast her eyes down, pretending to be chastened, though she was still angry. "What will you do now?"

The Mother rose. "Despite your disobedience, we cannot afford to throw you away. The Great Serpent named you *laoch*. Few are strong enough in projective power to join their ranks, but the guardians are needed now more than ever."

"I didn't mean me," she said—though she did wonder how severe her punishment would be. "I mean about Malach and Balaur."

"The gems have spoken," they intoned as one, lifting the hair on her arms. "The Third Dark Age looms. The Deir Fiuracha must rise against it. The three nations broken must be made whole again. This is the will of Valmitra!"

The olivine namestones around their necks glowed blindingly bright, then subsided.

The Crone raised a trembling hand. "We will sail to the continent. Fetch the child ourselves. And the aingeal, if it is not already too late."

The Maid hopped on one foot. "You will come with us, Nikola Thorn!"

"And the Masdari," said the Mother.

"We will gather the strongest among us and bail this leaky skiff before it sinks," the Crone rasped.

Nikola suppressed a grin. A whole *boatload* of badass bitches! She almost pitied Balaur. They'd eat him alive.

Her good humor died at the Crone's next words.

"However, since it will take some time to make the preparations, I think you would benefit from meditating on the importance of keeping your emotions in check."

"The hole?" Nikola asked in a small voice.

The Crone gave a toothless smile.

NIKOLA CLIMBED down the long ladder and sat cross-legged with her back against the wall. It was pitch dark down there. *Suffocating.*

She wondered how long her penance was supposed to last.

Well, it was a miracle they hadn't kicked her out. She ought to be grateful.

But if they hadn't lied to her, none of it would have happened in the first place!

Malach must hate her.

He had his daughter. Maybe he was happy now.

Rachel. She sounded *scary.*

Starfall?

Nikola smiled grimly. She'd warned Falke. *The child will destroy you someday.*

Was he among the dead? She'd forgotten to ask.

Saints, a third Dark Age?

Would she ever be a full witch now? Maybe they just planned to use her as bait. To trick him again.

No, they meant well. She had to believe that.

It was all some crazy shit, wasn't it?

Hashima had her serpent's eye. Would she ever give it back? It was so unfair!

Her thoughts whirled for some time. Then the stillness came.

It settled over her shoulders like a heavy, warm blanket.

She dreamt that she was held in the coils of a giant snake, but she wasn't afraid. The snake was wise and good. She saw a sword, with runes along the blade, that made her spine tingle. Such power.

Not the benevolent kind.

She saw a city of gold and she saw a mountain, covered in snow.

She saw many other things she didn't understand.

But when the serpent hissed in her ear, she knew what it said, though the words were in language she had never heard before.

Free me, daughter.

Chapter Fifteen

Malach gave Bal Kirith a wide berth, driving east to the coast and then looping back north and west. The radio started picking up chatter and he managed to avoid the patrols. From what he gathered, the knights were hunkered down at Bal Kirith, trying to hold the enemy territory they'd already seized. He took grim pleasure in the reports of damage at the Arx in Novo until he realized his daughter was listening. Then he shut the radio off.

Rachel refused to speak, though she ate when he gave her food and drank when he offered her water. A dozen times he almost told her who he was. But after what he'd made her do, he couldn't face the look in her eyes when she learned the truth—if she even believed him. He would tell her everything later. After they were safe.

He stopped at a river and washed the blood from his back. He rooted through the first aid kit and found some antiseptic ointment. With luck, it would stave off infection.

Malach hardly dared to sleep for fear she'd run away. If Nikola had only waited, Rachel would be with the other children in Dur-Athaara, not fleeing through a war zone. After two days, his hopes faded that she would find them. He was alone and his wits were the only thing that might keep them alive.

Malach's jaw tightened every time they drove past a Wardstone. The Void was broken at long last, the forest flooded with abyssal ley, yet he still couldn't touch a single drop.

He worried about what awaited them at Bal Agnar. If the nihilim found out about Rachel's power, they would seek to use her, just as he had. And he couldn't let them discover his own weakness.

Then there was the problem of what to do about Falke.

When the humid jungle gave way to conifer forest, and night brought a pine-scented chill, Malach pulled over. He wrapped Rachel in blankets from one of the compartments. The Rahai was poor insulation against the cold, but he made do. If she got sick, he'd never forgive himself.

"Would you like to hear a bedtime story?" he asked.

No response.

Malach told her one anyway. It was from one of the books at the creche. He'd read it aloud to the kids so many times he knew it by heart.

"Once upon a time, there was a garden where all creatures lived in harmony. Their mother was a great serpent, who could also take the form of a beautiful woman with eyes like jewels and scales for skin. She lived in a mountain holdfast where the earth met the clouds. All was well until one day, her seventh son came to her and begged for a boon. His name was Gavriel."

The story was a long one, full of twists and love and blood and betrayal, like all the best fairytales. Rachel pretended to be asleep, though he could tell she was listening At length, her breath grew deep and even, her hands curled softly, and he knew she slumbered. He went around back and opened the hatch.

"Please," Falke croaked. "Water."

Malach took the last jug from one of the compartments

and unlocked the manacles from the ring. Falke gulped the water. His cheeks were hollow and fuzzed with a gray beard. After a moment, Malach snatched the jug back.

"That's enough."

Falke wiped his mouth with the back of his hand. "How is she?"

"Rachel's welfare is my concern now," Malach replied. "Which means I have to keep you alive too. But if my kin learn who you are, they'll execute you on the spot—if you're lucky. They might just sever your hands and hang you up for the crows."

"Then let me go."

He laughed. "There's small chance of that. But I have an idea. Play along and you stand a chance. Refuse and I can't be responsible for what happens to you."

Falke regarded him stonily. "Go on."

"I doubt any of them know what you look like now. I'm the only mage who's ever been inside Novostopol." He eyed Falke's filthy, torn pajamas. "There's nothing we can do about your Raven Mark, but without the ring you look like any retired priest. I'll tell them you're one of mine—"

Falke recoiled. "I'm not taking your Nightmark!"

"And I wouldn't give it to you even if you begged me. But there's no reason for them to search you for it. My word is enough." He smiled. "I'm a cardinal in the shadow church. I still have authority."

"Above Balaur?" Falke spat. "Would you truly put your own daughter at his mercy?"

Malach stared at him, uncomprehending. "What are you talking about?"

"You don't know?" Now Falke looked surprised.

Malach covered his shock. "How could Balaur be alive after all this time?"

"Who do you think deposed Lezarius?" Falke replied. "Inverted his Marks and sent him to the Batavia Institute?

Who posed as the Lion of Jalghuth for the last four years, corrupting all he touched?"

"Who told you this?"

"The Reverend Mother Clavis."

"And how does she know?"

"She heard it from one who has seen him in dreams."

"In dreams," Malach repeated flatly.

"It was one of Balaur's talents. To enter the dreams of others. Surely you know that."

Malach shook his head. "He was executed at Jalghuth."

"Apparently not." Falke's mouth thinned. "That must be why Lezarius shut himself away for thirty years. He was guarding a terrible secret. In the end, his mistake caught up with him. Balaur escaped somehow. Forced Lezarius to break the stelae. He might still be in Jalghuth. Or he might be at Bal Agnar. In which case, you will be taking your child to a den of depravity. Is that what you want for her?"

Malach knew the stories about Balaur. He doubted a third were true. "You have no proof."

"I trust the Reverend Mother."

"Well, I'll find out when we get there." He hardened his voice. "Dmitry Falke is dead. Your name is Severin Kula. A retired priest from a wealthy family. I was holed up in your manor house for the last few months. Rachel is your granddaughter."

Falke put up a struggle when he reached for the cuffs, but he was weak. Malach had no trouble securing him again. He gripped Falke's right hand and pulled the gold signet ring off.

"You follow the Via Libertas. I brought you along as my personal servant."

"The others may not know what I look like, but Balaur does," Falke said. "Please, do not do this—"

Malach slammed the hatch shut. Balaur? He was the scarecrow the Curia used to terrify disobedient children. If he was alive, he'd be even older than Falke by now. But at least he was nihilim. One of Malach's kin. They would be welcomed. And where else could he go? The Morho was crawling with knights. He couldn't hide there forever.

His fist clenched around the ring. Malach drew his arm back to hurl it into the trees, but thought better of it. His palm opened. He stared down at the ring.

What if he could use Falke as a bargaining chip to demand that the Curia knights evacuate Bal Kirith? If Malach got his own city back, that might solve everything.

The plan had too many *ifs* and *mights*, but it was the best he could improvise. He stowed the ring in his boot. Then he tilted the seat back and slept for a few hours, driving again at first light. The radio went silent. The jungle gave way to pines and spruce. It grew colder and he cranked the heat to full blast. They were getting close to Bal Agnar.

Malach stopped in a wooded hollow and went around to the back. "I'm unchaining you now," he said to Falke. "Try to run and I'll break your legs."

Falke gave a sour nod. Malach unlocked the handcuffs and ordered him into one of the rear seats. Rachel twisted around to cast Falke a searching look. He nodded. "I'm fine, Lessa."

"Her name is Rachel." Malach turned to his daughter. "No one needs to know about what you did. You're not special in any way. Just a little girl. His name is Severin and he's your grandfather. Do you understand?"

She stared straight ahead.

He was being shunned. Lonan did the same when he was mad about something.

Malach threw the transport into gear and rolled down the rutted track. The land rose steadily into the rugged foothills of the mountain range variously called the Torquemites or the Sundar Kush, depending on which part of the Via Sancta you hailed from. White-breasted hawks perched on high branches. Little streams trickled across the road. Malach stopped to splash icy water on his face. He felt bleary when he needed to be sharp and alert. The first patrols would see a Curia transport. He hoped they didn't blow him to smithereens.

One moment, the woods looked empty. The next, air hissed from the tires and the transport fishtailed as they bumped over a line of iron spikes. A green-cloaked shadow materialized from the trees. A crossbow leveled at his head. Malach rolled the window down.

"Now, Lexa," he said with a cocky grin. "I expected a warmer welcome."

The mage drew closer. Hard eyes stared at him from a nut-brown face. Her hair had been shaved to the scalp on the sides, leaving a narrow strip that was dyed bright purple.

"Cardinal!" She lowered the crossbow with a startled laugh. "Everyone thinks you're dead. Where have you been?"

Caralexa's cousin Jessiel strode up behind her. They looked like sisters, except Jess had blue-gray eyes and a mass of unruly brown curls. She peered past him at the passenger seat. "Who's the kid?"

"Her name is Rachel."

The girl regarded the mages in watchful silence.

"She looks a bit like you, Malach." Jess smirked. "You do get around, don't you?"

"She's not my natural daughter," he said, hating the lie. "But I've adopted her." Malach got out, glancing through the window at Falke, who slumped in the back seat, face averted. "That's her grandfather. He's loyal to us."

"You're a mess." Jessiel touched his shoulder with a wince. "Are those shrapnel wounds?" She eyed the Rahai around his hips. "And what are you wearing? Looks like a skirt."

"It's the fashion down south these days," he replied lightly. "I was in Novo when disaster befell the Arx. We fled in a car, but knights caught us in the Morho." Malach smiled. "To their eternal regret. After I killed them, I figured it made sense to switch vehicles."

"What disaster?" Caralexa demanded. "We've heard nothing of this."

Malach frowned. "Two days ago. A starfall. I assumed one of us did it."

The cousins shared an incredulous look. "Do you know anyone capable of that, Malach?" Lexa wondered. "'Cause I sure as shit don't."

"Manners," he said without thinking.

Jessiel laughed. Caralexa looked puzzled. "What the fuck are you talking about?"

"Never mind," he said hastily. "What's the situation? I hear you're holding the city now."

Lexa nodded. "Everyone's gathering. Mages, Perditae. Some of the Ravens came over to us, too. And contingents from Nantwich and Jalghuth."

"You have knights in the city?"

"Former knights. Now they're all Nightmarked. The abyssal ley flows strong again." Her eyes gleamed. "Don't you feel it?"

He smiled and nodded, crushing his frustration. "Of course."

"They're seeing things our way, Malach. It's only a matter of time until we get Bal Kirith back." She eyed him. "What of Beleth?"

"Dead." He looked away. "They hit us hard. We were outnumbered fifty to one. I barely got away."

"We heard the tale from Sydonie and Tristhus," Jessiel said.

"They escaped?" He shook his head with a grin. "Of course they did. Those brats are indestructible."

"A few others, too. Not many."

"Where have you been, Malach?" Caralexa asked. "Why didn't you come straight here like the rest of us?"

He shrugged. "After Bal Kirith fell, I went back to Novo. I

have Marked there who gave me sanctuary. I tried to gather intelligence, but the city was locked down tight."

"Didn't you dream of him?"

"Dream of who?"

Caralexa gave him an odd look. "Balaur."

Shit. "No, I didn't." Malach glanced at the transport. "Look, I'm exhausted. I've been driving for two days. How far is the city?"

"Not far." She whistled. Malach grinned as Valdrian trotted out of the woods. They were both orphans and had been best friends growing up. When they were sixteen, they'd been ambushed by knights during a hunting trip. Valdrian was taken prisoner. Malach had snuck into the camp and gotten him back, but not before they'd severed his right hand. Valdrian covered the stump with a leather cap and spring-loaded blade. If Malach trusted anyone, it was Valdrian.

The mage's blond-bearded face split into a wide grin. They embraced, laughing. Malach repeated his story, embellishing here and there. None of them questioned it. They glanced at Falke without interest. Just another servant.

"You drove all the way from Novostopol like this?" Valdrian asked, looking at his back. "Brother, it's nasty."

"I put some stuff on it," Malach said. "From the first aid kit. But we left in a hurry. It was crazy."

Valdrian shook his head. "I'll ride into the city with you," he offered. "Take my cloak."

He slung the green cloak around Malach's shoulders. Rachel moved into the back with Falke and Malach slid behind the wheel. They passed a dozen more patrols. Malach knew most of the mages by sight, though not well. Twenty minutes later, they reached the outskirts of Bal Agnar.

It had been sacked by Lezarius's army thirty years before, then shelled by Falke and Clavis in the campaigns that followed. The jungle devoured the remains, though people were hard at work with machetes hacking at the vines strangling the partly demolished buildings. The clang of hammers rang out, and the rasp of saws as carpenters trimmed branches from a pile of felled trees.

Thousands of campfires glowed in the night. As he drove slowly over the buckled asphalt of the main road to the Arx, Malach glimpsed Raven Marks from Novostopol, the Crossed Keys of Nantwich and the Blue Flame of Jalghuth. He saw Perditae, thin and ragged, with feral faces and the slitted pupils of goats. The four groups each stuck to their own, leaving space between the various encampments. Red-robed nihilim strode through the neutral zones, every eye warily following them.

His kin were keeping order, but Malach sensed an undercurrent of repressed violence that made his skin crawl.

Both Bal Kirith and Bal Agnar had fallen when he was a little boy. Malach had never seen them at their height, though Beleth spoke of that time often. She'd made it sound wonderful. A garden of earthly delights where everyone was free to do as they pleased, unrestrained by the moral strictures of the Curia.

He'd expected some degree of chaos, but this felt like a zoo full of half-starved animals waiting for the keepers to let their guard slip. The first serious misgivings crept in. He should never have brought Rachel here.

They passed through the towering gates of the Arx. A dozen nihilim stood watch. Some were armed with bows, others with swords, but their true power stemmed from the ability to wield abyssal ley. A single touch and any attacker would be rendered senseless—or compelled to take their own life.

Red ley tapped the most primal impulses, beyond rationality and conscious choice. The knights wore armor to protect against that deadly touch, though judging by the number who had willingly come over to Balaur, it did little to defend against the currents of abyssal ley that saturated the forest.

Malach was relieved to find that only mages occupied the inner citadel. He couldn't imagine closing his eyes for an instant among Balaur's human followers.

"The Reverend Father will want to see you," Valdrian said as they passed the Pontifex's Palace.

It gleamed in the failing light like the carcass of some fossilized beast. The walls were green with lichen, the windows smashed. Headless statues stood in a grim line atop the roof. The frail beams of light coming from within only deepened the enshrouding darkness.

"I'd like to get settled first," Malach said. "Where can we stay?"

Valdrian shrugged. "It's up to you. There aren't many amenities yet. I can offer a roof. Hot food. We're working on the water supply, though it's not running yet."

"That's fine." *Anywhere but the palace.* His gaze lit on a limestone building at the end of the plaza. It had grand pillars in front and wide steps leading to the entrance. The facade was scorched, but the roof looked sound. "How about that?"

"The old archives? Be my guest. There's a few of us in there but plenty of room."

Malach drove to the entrance and killed the engine. The needle sat deep in the red.

"Any power?" Malach asked. If they did have to run, he'd need to recharge the battery first.

Valdrian laughed. "Someday. But we're still dealing with basic repairs. Go find a spot. I'll bring some pallets."

Malach got out and opened Rachel's door, taking her limp hand. Falke looked shaken.

"Bring the first aid kit," Malach snapped. "Blankets, radio, all of it."

The pontifex just stood there, his face ashen.

"*Move,*" Malach hissed at him as Valdrian strode away.

Falke snapped out of his trance. He loaded his arms with supplies from the transport and they climbed the stairs. The bronze doors had been torn from their hinges. A cavernous room lay beyond, three tiers with balconies running the length of the walls. Most of the shelves were bare. Mounds of ash and charred paper dotted the marble floor.

"You do love a good book burning, don't you?" Malach muttered.

"If the writings are heretical and violate common decency," Falke retorted.

"Keep your voice down." Malach shot him a warning look. "*Severin.*"

Falke subsided, though his face was grim.

They took circular metal stairs up to the next level. The outer balcony had nooks that looked down on the main reading room, but Malach found a warren of closed chambers behind that must have been used by the archivists. They smelled of damp, but some still had furniture.

Most of the latter showed signs of recent occupancy and Malach left them alone. Finally, he found one that looked unclaimed. Crumbling sheets of yellow parchment lay in drifts across the bare floor. Thick gray spiderwebs festooned the corners. It had a desk, two armchairs, and a small hearth. A narrow window gave a view of Pontifex's Palace. The paint was flaking, but the ornate moldings and lighter spots on the walls where tapestries had hung hinted at former grandeur.

"It'll do for now," Malach said. "Wait here."

"This is madness," Falke muttered.

"Perhaps, but you'll never get past those gates. And if you try I'll be forced to tell them who you really are." He turned his back on Falke and crouched down to Rachel's level. "I know that none of this makes sense to you. You just have to trust me. I promise we won't stay here long. Don't try to run away. Please." He swallowed. "I'm doing my best, but I need you to listen. Do you understand?"

She nodded. The barest movement, but he felt a surge of triumph. It was the first response he'd gotten in two days.

"Don't leave this room," Malach told them both. "For your own safety."

He went back outside and sat down on the steps. Torchlight glimmered in the shells of the decrepit structures ringing the plaza. Here and there, mages strode through the Arx, some trailing servants who walked two paces behind with their eyes to the ground. A few called a greeting. Most eyed him coldly. Malach had made plenty of enemies in his time; mages who opposed the Cold Truce he'd struck with Falke or resented the favor he was shown by Beleth. He'd have to tread carefully.

At last, Valdrian returned with a covered basket. Malach cracked the lid. It held a stringy-looking haunch and some burnt tubers.

"All I could find," Valdrian said. "We're short of everything."

"How does Balaur intend to feed all these people?" Malach wondered.

"He says we'll be marching soon."

"On Bal Kirith?" Malach hoped it was so.

"Maybe. But this is just the beginning, Malach. The Void is gone. If Lezarius hasn't made it again, that means he can't. They won't hold out against us for long."

"Lezarius is alive?"

"Balaur left him in Jalghuth. But the north will fall again when the time is right."

Malach reached for the basket, but Valdrian smiled. "I'll carry it in for you. I expected you'd send your servant to do it."

He silently cursed the oversight. Valdrian was a friend, but another mage would be suspicious. Malach tensed as they neared the chamber, but his prisoners were still there. Rachel sniffed the meat, then made a face and built a little nest for herself with the blankets. She crawled inside with her thumb jammed into her mouth. From the way Falke frowned, Malach got the feeling it was an old habit he'd tried to break her of.

"Gather some wood and light a fire, Severin," he said brusquely. "Then tidy the room and fetch some water." He pointed to the filthiest corner. "You may sleep over there."

Falke bobbed his head. "Yes, master."

The old bastard was trying, Malach could see that. But his voice still had the ring of authority and he met Valdrian's gaze far too directly.

"When I return, I expect this room to be spotless," he said. "Or I'll have you whipped."

This time, Falke flushed and averted his gaze. "As you say," he grunted.

Malach walked Valdrian back outside. "I plan to Mark the child. She means something to me. But I'd prefer it if the others don't know that."

"Understood." He searched Malach's face. "I thought you might be with Dantarion."

"I don't know where she is." That much was true. "The last I heard, she had Lezarius in her custody. Is there no word of her?"

"None. We have scouts looking."

"She's resourceful."

"I pity any knights that cross her path. She's alive, I'm sure of it. Perhaps she'll turn up like you did."

Dantarion was the last person he wanted to see right now. She'd take one look at Rachel and know the child was Nikola's. He hoped Dante and their son or daughter were somewhere safe—just not *here*.

"What of the girl?" Valdrian asked. "I must admit, I'm confused at your choice of traveling companions. Severin is old for a servant. And this is hardly the place for a child."

Malach shrugged. "The idea of fatherhood appeals to me."

"You? I wouldn't have expected it." He smiled. "But I haven't seen you in a while. I'm glad you're here."

Malach gazed at the palace. "Tell me about Balaur. What's he like?"

"The Reverend Father is unwell." Valdrian's voice lowered. "Truthfully, I'm not sure how much longer he'll last."

"Then who's in charge?"

"He is. The orders come down and we carry them out. I only saw him once." A shadow crossed Valdrian's face as though the memory was an unpleasant one.

"Is he sane?"

Valdrian shrugged. "He's winning. Does it matter?"

"It matters to me."

"Then, yes, I think the Reverend Father is sane, despite his long captivity at Jalghuth. You can judge for yourself. He is eager to meet you."

Malach frowned. "He already knows I'm here?"

"Word spread quickly." He handed Malach a bundle. "I would suggest you change first, Cardinal."

Malach gave Valdrian his green cloak back. He shook out the robe and pulled it over his head. The wool was a fine, soft weave, falling in crimson folds to his boots. As it settled over his shoulders, some of his old confidence returned. Kaldurite or no, he was still a mage of Bal Kirith.

One of the last.

But his city could be rebuilt, greater than before. With the ley flowing freely, anything was possible. Perhaps someday Rachel would wear the Pontifex's ring.

"Take me to him," Malach said.

———

NIHILIM GUARDED the main entrance to the Pontifex's Palace, but beyond the great doors all was silent and dim. The chill deepened as Malach walked with Valdrian through stark stone halls, past sputtering torches in brackets that only enhanced the icy darkness.

"The Reverend Father is a student of alchemy," Valdrian said. "Don't be alarmed by his personal guard."

Malach shot him a quizzical look. "Alchemy? So Balaur is a mystic?"

"He uses the ley through elemental materials. I don't pretend to understand it, but I've heard rumors of a laboratory where he conducts his experiments."

So he *was* mad. "What kind of experiments?"

Valdrian looked uneasy. "Physical enhancements. He uses Perditae."

Malach didn't like the sound of that. "The normal ones are bad enough."

"If they can help us defeat the Via Sancta, we must use every weapon at our disposal." Valdrian stared straight ahead. "They can be destroyed later. The Reverend Father also brought clergy from Jalghuth. The cardinals who betrayed Lezarius and helped to free him. They are . . . well, you will see for yourself."

Malach's unease grew as they ascended to the uppermost level and followed a long corridor to the heart of the palace. The torches were few and far between here. Then two figures appeared in the gloom. Silhouettes at first, oddly-shaped. He thought the protuberances above their shoulders were the hilts of swords, but as Malach drew closer, he saw that they were in fact leathery wings. The creatures wore blood-red robes like his own. Taloned feet emerged from the hems, gripping the stone floor. Monstrosities, yet their faces and hands were human.

Distaste churned Malach's gut, though he concealed it with a bland expression.

Valdrian gave a respectful nod. "Cardinal Vinaya, Cardinal Sabitri. I have brought the mage from Bal Kirith."

Dark eyes studied him. The female stepped aside. "You may enter. Alone."

Malach shot a quick look at Valdrian, then stepped through.

A blaze roared in the enormous hearth, casting flickering shadows across the chamber. The room was stifling yet the man lying in bed had thick blankets drawn to his chin. He was blonde with sharp blue eyes and a face that might have been handsome once but now bore the ravages of long illness.

A young woman in a black robe and turban perched on a stool at the foot of the bed. Teetering stacks of books occupied every surface. She held one in her lap, idly flipping the pages. A quick, incurious glance at Malach and she returned to the book. He glimpsed the sinuous lettering of the Masdaris on the spine.

"Come in, cousin, come in," Balaur said, hoisting himself to sit with a wince.

It smelled like a sickroom. Unwashed skin and stale breath.

Gnarled hands gripped the coverlet as Balaur adjusted himself. He lacked three fingers on his left hand. It was a well-known tale. Falke chopped them off in single combat. The last lingering doubt that this was indeed the infamous Pontifex of Bal Agnar faded.

"Reverend Father," he said, bending a knee.

"And you are Malach!" A warm smile. "I remember dandling you on my lap when you were just a babe. Come closer, let me see you."

Malach approached, sweat beading his brow. How did Balaur stand it? The Masdari seemed unaffected, as well. Their land was a waste of burning sands. She must be used to the oppressive heat.

"I see much of your mother in you," Balaur said. "A shame you never knew her as I did. She was a fine woman. Your father, too. So many we have lost. Yet a new generation must carry the torch of the nihilim now. I will see us restored to our rightful place. And I have need of mages I can trust." A rattling cough. "My health is poor, as you can see."

"What ails you?" Malach ventured. "If I may ask, Reverend Father."

Balaur fluttered the stumps of his fingers. "I'm past eighty. If there is an elixir of youth, I am yet to find it. But I still have my wits." He noticed Malach eying the gold signet ring on his left hand. "You wonder where I got this. Well, it belonged to Lezarius." A chuckle. "I hear Falke keeps mine encased in glass on his desk. He uses it as a paperweight."

Malach was unsure how to reply so he kept his mouth shut.

"But these symbols mean little, don't you agree? You've seen the city. You know our numbers. Soon we will overrun the continent."

Balaur studied him in silence. His skin was waxy as a corpse, his breath rasping, yet there was something horribly *alive* at the same time, as though his frail body struggled to contain a blazing will to live.

"You came from Novostopol?" he asked at last.

"Yes, Reverend Father."

"There was a surge in the ley. What happened there?"

"I'm not sure. Stars fell from the sky. I thought perhaps you had done it."

Balaur stared at him. "Not I," he said softly. "It is most peculiar."

"The Arx sustained great damage." Malach met his gaze. "I heard Falke is dead."

A dry laugh. "*Caput corvi*. The Raven is headless again. Oh, they will replace him, but the rule of the new pontifex will not last long." He reached for a cup of water and took a trembling sip.

With any luck, Malach thought, you won't either.

"I've heard the stories," Balaur said. "You are bold. The

only mage ever to enter the mighty Arx itself when the Wards were still active! Is it true you killed Feizah in her own bedroom?"

Malach smiled modestly, though he had no idea who'd actually done the deed. "It is, Reverend Father. A lucky chance. I took it."

"You still have the passion and energy of youth running in your blood. I would raise you high, Malach."

That surprised him, though likely Balaur had made the same promise to others.

"Thank you, Reverend Father."

"To begin, I would make you my Nuncio in Nantwich. Until my health has improved."

"Nuncio?" Malach blinked. "Since when does Clavis have diplomatic channels with you?"

"She will not hold the city much longer. It will be ours in a matter of days."

"How?"

"I have allies in many places. The Order of the Black Sun rises everywhere. Leave the details to me. You would serve as both regent and ambassador, ruling in my stead until I am fit to travel. Do you agree?"

Malach had never been to Nantwich, but at least it was a real city. He was desperate to get Rachel out of there as soon as possible. "If you can take Nantwich, then I will gladly serve. What about Bal Kirith?"

"Once we've established a foothold, we'll sever the supply lines from Novostopol, dividing their force in half. If the Ravens are broken, the Kvens will fall into line." His fist clenched. "And we will annihilate what remains of the Via Sancta."

Malach considered the plan. It seemed sound. "What of Jalghuth?"

"It's a frozen backwater. We will take it at our leisure."

The tone was dismissive, yet Malach sensed something in

his eyes. Fear? Lezarius might not be as toothless as Balaur claimed. Yet he didn't really care what happened to Jalghuth. Malach wanted only two things.

A place to call home.

And to see Falke's dream extinguished and the man himself bear witness to his final defeat.

"Empires collapse a piece at a time," Balaur continued. "If we stretch ourselves thin, we will be making the same mistake as Falke. He relied on the Nants to pen us in. They are the key, if you'll excuse the pun. But once they're removed from the equation . . . ."

"Nantwich is a port city," Malach said consideringly. "We could use their ships to sail south. Attack from both land and sea."

"Precisely." A pleased smile. "I see I've chosen my new Nuncio well."

Malach glanced at the Masdari woman in the corner. She was still flipping through the book, though he got the impression she listened to every word.

"What's your involvement with the League?" Malach asked.

"As I told you, I have friends in many places. You must learn to think beyond the borders of this continent. But we get ahead of ourselves. One move at a time."

Malach dipped his chin. "Of course, Reverend Father."

"Now, when you arrive in Nantwich, you will find a woman at the Arx. A cartomancer. Securing her is your highest priority."

First alchemy, now cartomancy? The man *seemed* sane, but he had strange obsessions.

"What's her name?" Malach asked.

"Kasia Novak. Also Katarzynka Nowakowski."

A jolt of surprise. He remembered the young woman on the rooftop. The same one he went after in the Arx. "I met her once. In Novostopol."

Balaur leaned forward, intense fascination on his gaunt face. "Tell me," he hissed.

"She had something I wanted. I tried to compel her, but she broke through it."

"Ah." A soft sigh. "Because she is one of us, Malach."

He swallowed a laugh. "I don't think so, Reverend Father."

"But she is. I have spoken with her in dreams. You must find her."

"Why do you want this woman?"

"She has knowledge I desire."

"Of what?"

"Kasia has the power of foretelling through cards. A unique talent. And she may hold the solution to a special project of mine." Balaur's gaze flicked to the Masdari emissary. "That is all you need to know."

"When do I leave?"

"In two days. I've sent a force to lure Clavis out of the city. Once she's in the Morho, my plans will proceed." He smiled. "The city already rots from within. Her house is made of straw and we are the whirlwind that will sweep it away."

"What about Bal Kirith?"

"The city will be restored to you, Malach. It is yours by blood. Beleth was your aunt. If we cannot find Dantarion, you are next in line."

"Thank you, Reverend Father."

"I expect great things from you, Malach. Loyalty first and foremost." He gazed at his mangled fingers with a chuckle, but the amusement didn't reach his blue eyes. "The hand that giveth can also taketh away. Remember that, cousin."

Malach wanted to press him about what exactly his plans entailed, but he sensed a dismissal.

"I will serve to the best of my abilities, Reverend Father," he said with a bow.

"I'm sure you will." Balaur leaned back against the

pillows. "Let me now. I will summon you again when it is time to depart."

He backed out of the stifling chamber. The Masdari briefly caught his eye, then returned to her book. He heard Balaur give another ghastly, rattling cough and then he was striding past the pair of weird cardinals. Valdrian hadn't waited. Malach didn't blame him.

He made his way through the palace lighter of heart despite the oddity of the encounter. Balaur couldn't live much longer. When he died, there would be a power struggle to claim his place, but Malach would be in Nantwich by then. And the city was the keystone to both north and south. It would tip the balance solidly in the nihilim's favor.

Once the dust settled, he would seize Bal Kirith, rebuild it, and keep Falke locked safely away. If Lezarius hid Balaur from the world for thirty years, Malach could do the same. Rachel would come to see how much he loved her. She'd realize that he'd done everything for her own good. He would give her his Mark and find a way to remove the Raven from her neck.

Malach whistled a jaunty tune as he strode through the frigid halls, boots ringing on the marble floors. The pall hanging over the palace seemed to lift a fraction as he contemplated this new turn of fate. This morning, he'd been another stateless refugee. Now he was Balaur's Nuncio! To Nantwich, of all places. Clavis was rumored to be stern and unyielding, but he'd wager she had a bedchamber with soft sheets and a gilded bathtub with steaming hot water on tap.

Two more days and he'd be soaking in it.

Back at the archives, he found Rachel curled up under a blanket and Falke staring morosely into the fire. The floor had been swept and the furniture wiped clean of dust.

"Where'd you find the clothes?" Malach asked.

The Pontifex of Novostopol wore a baggy shirt spun from rough cloth and seamed with patches. His once immaculate silver hair stood up in tufts. He sat with knees drawn to his chest, one hand rubbing the third finger of his right hand where his ring used to be. From the distant look in his eye, he wasn't aware he was doing it.

How far the mighty had fallen.

"I begged another servant for these rags," Falke muttered. "The man took pity on me."

Malach sat at the desk. He opened the basket and started eating what remained of the supper.

"I met your monster," he said, tearing a shred of tough meat from the bone.

Falke glanced over.

"He seemed like a pleasant old man."

"That's what he would have you believe," Falke replied. "He always wore a mask of civility. Until the day he takes it off and you see his true face."

Malach yawned. "I told him you were dead. He didn't seem to care one way or another."

"Balaur is a dangerous madman. You'll learn that in time." Falke rubbed his arms. "The ley here turns my stomach. It is vile!"

"Your knights seem to like it," Malach said.

Falke turned to him with haunted eyes. "You've never known true evil, Malach. Beleth was a libertine, but Balaur is a butcher. Why do you think he ordered his clergy to wear red?"

"Because it's the color of abyssal ley. Everyone knows that."

"No. It was to hide the blood when they——"

"Enough," Malach said curtly. "Rachel might hear you." He tossed a stick of wood on the fire. "We won't stay here long. In the meantime, you must play the part of my servant."

"And if I'm recognized?"

"Keep your hood up. Speak to no one. Act frightened. My cousins will see what they expect to see. But if you never leave this room it will draw suspicion. What use would I have in a servant who did no work?"

Falke nodded grudgingly.

"You will keep the fire going and fetch water. Line up for rations."

"What of Rachel?"

"I would keep her away from you if I could," Malach said bitterly. "But I can't leave her alone. Nor can I bring her with me to the palace. No one can know about her."

"So you won't use her again?"

Malach eyed him with loathing. "I never wanted to *use* her at all. That is the difference between us."

He took one of the blankets and spread it out in front of the door.

Two days.

Two days to hide them both from Balaur.

Two days to hide his own inability to touch the ley.

If he failed, his fall from grace would be even swifter and deeper than Falke's.

Chapter Sixteen

Malach woke to furtive rustling. He cracked an eye. Sydonie was rummaging through the first aid kit. Looking for something to steal, most likely. In his sleep, he must have rolled away from the door.

A second later, he realized they were alone.

The girl jumped as Malach's hand shot out and gripped her arm. "Where is she?" he demanded.

"Cardinal!" Her face lit up. "We thought you'd never come!"

Her bone-straight dark hair was shoulder length now. She was missing a front tooth. It made her look waifish and adorable, if you didn't know better.

"Where's my servant?" His heart raced. "And his granddaughter?"

"The old man went to fetch water. The girl's with my brother."

Malach leapt to his feet and ran barefoot into the archives. Early morning sunlight filtered down through holes in the roof.

"Rachel!" he shouted.

A dove took flight from a nest in the ceiling. He'd murder Falke for leaving her alone.

"Trist! Where are you?"

Malach heard laughter, quickly smothered, and the patter of feet on the main level. He galloped down a spiral staircase. The place still smelled of old fire.

"Gotcha!"

Tristhus leapt out from between two shelves, brandishing a bone dagger in his chubby hand. Malach checked it for blood.

"We're playing mages and leeches," the boy declared.

Malach knew that game. The "leeches" were Perditae. If you found one, they got "killed." The children had never actually murdered each other, but they were both armed to the teeth. The thought of Rachel playing with them made his blood run cold.

"She's not supposed to leave the room," Malach snapped.

"Why not?

"It's dangerous."

Trist stared at him, befuddled. He'd lived all his short life in the ruins of Bal Kirith. The jungle was haunted by both rabid humans and saw-toothed crocodilians. Beleth and the other nihilim were almost as bad.

"Don't worry, I'll find her!" Syd said cheerfully, running up behind. She had the radio in her hand. The batteries were dead, but she pretended to talk into it anyway. "Rachel, Rachel, come in, Rachel! Yeah, copy that—"

"Let me try!" Trist yelled, grabbing it away. He was smaller than his sister, but the kid had grit. He clung to his prize as Syd howled in outrage, shaking him like a terrier with a rat.

Malach left them fighting over the dead radio. He finally found Rachel under a desk in one of the abandoned rooms. He brushed cobwebs from her hair as she climbed out, trying hard to keep calm. It wasn't her fault.

A moment later, the hellspawn came pelting in, Syd

holding the radio up over her head. Rachel had shunning down to an art form. It was as if Malach didn't exist. She ran to Tristhus and threw her arms around him. To Malach's amazement, the boy hugged her back and patted her head.

"She was playing a leech," Trist explained in a condescending tone. "You're supposed to stay quiet."

"Come on, beasties," he said wearily. "Time for breakfast."

Falke had returned by the time they reached the chamber. A bucket of water and three chunks of bread sat on the desk. Malach picked one up and knocked it against the wood. Hard as stone. He tamped down the urge to berate Falke in front of the children.

"That's it?" he asked.

Rachel snatched up a piece of bread and started gnawing on it. The poor kid must be starving.

"It's all I could find," Falke muttered.

"You'll address him by his proper title," Sydonie snapped.

Malach smiled at her, softening. The child did have her good points.

A flush crept up Falke's neck. "My apologies. It was all they had left at the canteen, Cardinal Malach."

He looked at the two siblings and offered them the rest of the bread. "Here, you must be hungry."

"We already ate a big breakfast," Syd said. "Want us to get you some real food?"

"Sure. Where do you go?"

They exchanged a quick look. "The palace kitchens," Syd admitted. "They have all kinds of good stuff in there. Balaur hogs it all."

"I don't want you to get into trouble."

She laughed. "They never catch us. They're stupid."

"Can we take Rachel?" Trist asked.

"No!"

The boy scowled.

"You can play more later," Malach promised. "But I want you to help me with something first." He turned to Falke. "Stay here, Severin." A meaningful look. "Don't leave her alone again."

"I didn't, Cardinal. She was still sleeping when I went out—"

"No excuses," Malach snapped. "We'll be back with food."

"Yes, master," Falke replied smoothly, though his cheeks burned.

Malach hated to leave Rachel under his influence, but he couldn't stay in the archives all day. He left with the two young mages. Syd had grown since last he saw her, reaching his shoulder now.

"We killed six knights at Bal Kirith," she said. "How many did you kill, Malach?"

"Uh, two."

"That's all?"

"I'm not a bloody idiot. I took off."

She nodded. "We dreamed about Balaur and then we had to meet him, but I don't like him. He smells bad."

Malach glanced down at her. "Don't let anyone else hear you say that."

"I'm not a bloody idiot."

He grinned. "I missed you two."

"Really?" Trist flicked a lock of hair from his eyes. They had purple shadows underneath. He'd always been a weak, pale, sickly-looking child. As much he squabbled with his sister, she was protective of him.

"Really. What happened to your eyebrows?"

"Shaved them off."

"Why?"

Trist shrugged. "Dunno."

"You look like a mannequin."

The boy smiled. "Vicious."

"Huh?"

Syd eyed Malach with condescension. "That's what we say now. Why does Rachel have a Raven Mark?"

She looked at him without guile, but he heard the gears ticking away in her clever brain.

"She didn't want it. The Curia made her take it. I'll give her my own soon enough."

"Can we have more, too?" She yanked a sleeve up and studied the Mark on her forearm. It was a creepy-looking doll with a shock of red hair. One of the eyes was half-closed, the other staring with a fixed gleam. "Mirabelle wants a friend."

"If you do what you're told." He led them to a secluded spot behind one of the tumble-down buildings. "How would you like to be my spies?"

"What do we get?" Syd demanded.

"I told you. I'll give you more Marks."

That bribe always worked—not that he could deliver on it without the ley. To his surprise, Trist shook his head.

"We want to play with Rachel. We never get to play with other kids."

"Yeah," Syd said, folding her skinny arms. "That's what we want."

Malach hesitated. "She's really little. You have to promise to be nice to her."

"We're always nice!" Sydonie protested.

It was time to communicate in the language they understood. "I'm not fucking with you, Syd," he said in a low voice, holding her gaze. "If she comes to harm, I'll invert you both. Every single Mark. Are we clear?"

She swallowed. "Yes, Cardinal."

"Trist?"

"Yes, Cardinal."

He nodded. "She's your cousin now. You have to protect her. Be her bodyguards."

They liked that idea, he could tell. Syd gave him a gap-toothed grin.

"Anyone messes with Rachel, we'll fuck them right up, Cardinal! Won't we, Trist?"

Part of him couldn't quite believe he was doing this. Look up "rotten apple" in the dictionary and you'd find their mug shots. But there were no good decisions anymore.

Just bad and worse.

He couldn't watch Rachel every minute of the day. Playing with them was the first time he'd seen her come out of her shell. The first time he'd heard her laugh. They *were* cousins by blood. The generation that would rule the Arx at Bal Kirith someday. Maybe they would grow to be like him and Valdrian, loyal to the end. Plus it would cut the ties Rachel had to Falke.

"It's a bargain," he said.

"Done and done," Syd replied seriously. "Who do you want us to spy on?"

"Everybody. Just report back to me what you see and hear. I don't care about the camp, just the Arx. In fact, you should stay out of the camp."

He looked past the wall. Smoke rose from thousands of campfires beyond, painting the sky a dirty red.

"We don't go there," Syd said. "They're fucking crazy."

"Good. No cursing in front of Rachel."

"You curse."

"Because I'm a Cardinal."

Syd rolled her eyes.

"Now, Balaur has a Masdari advisor. What do you know about her?"

"She's called Jamila al-Jabban."

"Do you know why she's here?"

Syd shook her head. A sly smile curved her mouth. "But we can show you where to find her."

MALACH STOOD in the shadows of the columned loggia in the east wing of the palace. Dust filtered down in the beams of sunlight that pierced broken stained glass windows. When the bells rang out for sext, the Masdari appeared with a small rug rolled up under one arm. She cast a furtive look around, then unrolled it facing south and knelt to make obeisances to the Alsakhan. He had seen Tashtemir do it a thousand times.

Three swift bows, forehead touching the ground, followed by a prayer that was sung rather than chanted. He waited for her to finish her ritual, then stepped into view.

"Ehlah," he said. *Hello.*

Her head whipped around. She rose quickly to her feet. "Ehlah, Cardinal. You speak our tongue?"

"That's all I know," he said apologetically. "I hoped to ask you some questions."

She rolled up the rug. "I am at your service."

His first impression had been right. She *was* young, no more than mid-twenties. She had large brown eyes and a delicate face, olive-hued. She wore seven small silver hoops in her right ear and a black robe sewn with beads at the bottom.

"Why are you here?" he asked bluntly.

"Merely as an advisor." Her Osterlish was perfect, with only the faintest accent. An educated woman. "I represent certain parties in the Masdar League who have an interest in the outcome of this conflict."

"So you expect us to win?"

A faint smile. "It seems likely."

"Did the Golden Imperator send you?"

"I'm not at liberty to disclose my patron."

"Of course." He smiled back. "What matters are you advising us on?"

She shrugged. "Your Reverend Father is interested in the political situation in my homeland."

"Which is?"

"There will be a change of government soon. The seven-year term of the Imperator, may the Alsakhan bless her, is expiring. A new Golden Imperator will take her place. Naturally, Balaur would prefer to see power transferred to a faction with favorable views toward the mages."

"Naturally. But what does your patron get out of it?"

She regarded him with amusement. "If it's details you're after, Cardinal, I think it best you ask your Reverend Father directly."

Malach inclined his head. "I was merely curious."

She made a flowery gesture. "It has pleased me to make your acquaintance, but I fear I am wanted elsewhere. *El am salaam*, Cardinal."

"*El am salaam*," he echoed, watching her walk away.

She must be wearing silken slippers for her feet made not a sound.

———

WHEN HE RETURNED to the archives, he discovered two things.

First, Sydonie and Tristhus had made good on their promise to bring "real food." A feast awaited. Fresh, soft bread and creamy yellow butter, apples and pears, a hearty vegetable stew and even a plate of small honey tarts with raspberries, most of which had been devoured already.

The other thing was that Syd had given Rachel a haircut.

"Do you like it?" Syd asked, jumping up and down with the scissors in her hand. "She looks just like Bishop Caralexa!"

Malach snatched the scissors away. She'd shorn the sides of Rachel's head, leaving a strip from front to back, and dressed her in a green cloak, raggedly cut off at the bottom.

"Doesn't she look pretty?" Syd demanded, anxious now. "It didn't hurt! She *likes* it, don't you, Rachel?"

Rachel grinned and nodded—at Syd, not him.

Malach drew a deep breath. "Yes, it suits her very well. But ask next time."

He sat in one of the chairs and devoured a plate of stew, ignoring Falke's grim stare. If anything, the disapproval made him more determined to let Rachel spend time with her cousins. Yes, they seemed to regard her as a life-sized doll they could dress up at whim, but that's what older kids *did* to younger kids. As long as Rachel didn't mind, what did it matter?

After the meal, he let them go play on the main floor. Screams and shouts drifted up from above, but they were the happy kind. It occurred to him that Syd and Trist were starved for company too. He just prayed he could manage them.

"You see?" Falke said in a low voice as Malach sopped up the last of the stew. "Balaur hoards all this for himself while the rest of us starve!"

"I'm not starving," Malach mumbled through a mouthful of bread.

"Because those creatures stole food from the kitchen—"

"They're not *creatures*," he said warningly. "They're children. And cousins of mine. I suggest you guard your tongue lest you lose it."

Falke huffed. "How much longer must we remain here?"

"Until I say so."

A crash resounded from below. It sounded like a bookcase toppling over. Malach froze with the bread halfway to his mouth. Then he heard Rachel's distinctive giggle, a neighing snort that reminded him so much of her mother it hurt. He finished the bread.

Falke scowled. "You cannot seriously mean to allow them—"

"What did I just say?"

Falke fell silent.

"She's mine now. She may not be speaking to me yet, but I'll win her over. In time, I will. You know it. So for your own sake, it's better you stop fighting the inevitable." He leaned forward. "You are nothing but a warm body keeping my daughter alive. You have no will of your own. No purpose other than to draw your next breath. And soon enough, your empire will be in ashes."

Falke's eyes narrowed. "What did Balaur tell you?"

Malach smiled. "Mox nox, Severin."

Soon, nightfall.

Chapter Seventeen

Sydonie and Tristhus proved to be invaluable allies. They not only told him the names of every mage at Bal Agnar, but they knew where everyone slept, who they conspired with and who they hated.

Malach found Valdrian and confirmed most of it. His cousin readily agreed to be part of the advance party to Nantwich, as did Caralexa and Jessiel. They seemed as eager as Malach to be gone.

He wondered if it was true what Falke claimed, that the ley was tainted here. He had no way of knowing for certain—the children seemed immune—but Jess told him stories from the camp that made him ill.

He wondered how much longer the mages would keep control.

One by one, he sought out those whom he respected for their level heads and independence from the scheming of the old guard. By the end of the second day, Malach had a list of two dozen men and women he meant to bring with him when they rode out.

He was walking back to the archives at dusk, feeling pleased with himself, when Syd came sprinting up.

"They took him away, Malach! Your servant!"

His heart stopped. "What about Rachel?"

"She's with Trist." Syd paused to catch her breath. "They're okay."

He was relieved, but this was still bad. *Very bad.*

"Who did it?"

"Two of the nasty old cardinals." She adjusted the bow across her back. "I've been looking for you everywhere!"

If Falke had been brought to Balaur, they were both done for.

"Shit," he muttered. "Shit!"

"I know where they went," she said, tugging his hand. "I'll show you."

A sudden wave of paranoia swept over him. "Are you lying to me, Syd?"

"No! I like you. I don't like them." She pulled harder. "Come *on*! Before they kill him!"

Malach followed her at a run to an abandoned ruin near the outer wall of the Arx. It was half buried in thick vegetation. As they neared, she pressed a finger to her lips. He heard voices inside. Malach crept up to the crumbling edge of a wall and peered inside.

A wiry old woman in a red robe paced up and down. Cardinal Mandrake. One of Beleth's cronies and a prize-winning bitch. Falke lay on the ground. His hands were bound behind his back with rusty wire. Two more figures stood in the shadows.

"We must bring him to the Reverend Father," one rasped.

Malach recognized the voice. Bishop Aarin. The scar on his sagging face was from Tristhus. Aarin had made the mistake of trying to fondle the boy. By the time Malach had heard about the incident, the fucker was long gone from Bal Kirith or he would have killed him himself.

"Not until I've had some fun. I watched him murder my husband!"

Mandrake had to be Falke's age. Early seventies. But her step was lithe as she strode up and delivered a kick to his ribs.

The third laughed, a nasal bray that named him as Mandrake's youngest son, Valoel. A shifty-eyed shit who was, unfortunately, also huge.

We have to kill them all, Malach mouthed at Sydonie.

She nodded and silently drew an arrow from her quiver.

"Why are you here masquerading as a servant?" Mandrake demanded, delivering another vicious kick. "How did you get inside?"

Falke stared at her through a swollen eye.

"We'll cut the truth out." Valoel came forward. A blade gleamed in his hand. "I could compel you, but my mother wants entertainment."

"Go ahead," Falke said, spitting at his feet. "You'll get nothing."

Malach almost admired his courage. He must know how bad this would get, but he hid his fear.

"Your father deserved to die," he said. "My only regret is that the rest of you escaped justice."

Valoel crouched down, pressing the tip of the knife to Falke's eyelid. "I'll try to save a piece of you for Balaur, but I can't make any promises—"

The mage made a gurgling noise as Syd's arrow pierced his throat. The force knocked him back. The blade slid from his hand. Malach leapt though the gap in the wall. Mandrake spun around, teeth bared. She lunged at him, her hands curling into claws. The kaldurite went cold in his belly.

Aarin dove behind a pile of rubble. Another arrow whizzed over his head. Syd calmly nocked another.

"Take the blade and kill the girl," Mandrake hissed at Malach, her nails sinking into his flesh. "Now!"

He sank down and picked up Valoel's knife with wide, blank eyes.

"Cut her ears off first. Then cut out her heart and kill yourself—"

Malach flipped the blade up and caught the hilt. "How about this? I kill *you* first." He glanced at the cowering bishop. "And then I kill *him?*"

Her mouth worked but no sound came out. Malach buried the knife right where her heart would be, if she had one. Astonishment flashed across her face. Then the cardinal collapsed.

"Please!" Aarin pleaded, licking his lips, as Syd walked toward him. "I never meant to . . . . All a misunderstanding!"

"I don't like you." She frowned. "My brother doesn't like you either."

He whimpered as she aimed the bow at his groin.

"Finish it, Syd," Malach said. "We don't have time for this."

"Yes, Cardinal." The arrow took Aarin right at the juncture of the Broken Chain Mark around his neck. He gasped, shuddered, and lay still.

Malach turned to Falke. "Can you walk?"

He nodded. Syd took out a knife and cut the wires around his wrists. He rose with a grimace.

"How were you found out?"

"I'm not sure. I was on the ration line. I took my share and started back. They must have followed."

"Did anyone else recognize you?"

"How should I know?" Falke managed a haughty glare through his slitted, blackened eye. "I warned you this would happen."

Malach regarded the dead mages. "We have to hide the bodies."

Syd retrieved the arrows, yanking them unceremoniously from her victims, and shouldered her bow. She glanced at Falke. "Who is he, Cardinal?"

He pulled her aside, trying to remember if any of them

had spoken Falke's name. He didn't think they had. "That's my secret."

"I can keep a secret."

"I doubt that."

Her lips pinched. "Tell me."

Malach said nothing.

"Ooooh. I bet I know." Syd fished in a pocket and held up Falke's heavy gold ring. "He's a pontifex!"

She'd lifted it from Malach's own pocket. When, he had no idea.

"Give me that, you little thief!"

She danced away. "Only if you tell me everything!"

He knew when he was defeated. "Listen, Syd. Rachel's my daughter. Falke stole her. I took her back. But I have to keep him safe."

"Because of the Raven Mark?"

Why, Malach wondered wryly, did he ever imagine he could fool this child?

"Yes. No one can know about him."

She poked her tongue through the missing front tooth. The one next to it looked loose. She gave it an experimental wiggle. "I wish we could kill him."

"Me too." Falke was watching them both. "But it's not happening, so put it from your blood-soaked little mind."

"I won't tell."

"Good girl." He looked at her dirty cloak. The holes in her shoes. He thought of her quick intelligence and sunny smile that hadn't yet soured. "Do you want to come to Nantwich with me? Stay in a palace with a real bed and nice things?"

"Is Rachel going?"

"Of course."

"Can Trist go, too?"

"Obviously."

"Can I drive a car when we get there?" She mimed jerking a steering wheel. "A super fast one!"

He shuddered inwardly. "Sure, why not?"

She threw her arms around his waist.

Falke cleared his throat. "Did you say Nantwich?"

Malach almost laughed. The poor bastard sounded so hopeful.

BACK AT THE ARCHIVES, he found Tristhus and Rachel trying to set fire to a pile of paper in the room next door. Happily, it was too damp to catch. The stern lecture that followed would probably last as long as an ice cube in the Masdari desert, but Rachel was down for a nap now. He'd told her "Severin" walked into a door. She looked at him like she knew better. She probably assumed he'd done it.

So much for detente.

Malach sent Tristhus to make sure no one else saw Falke hauled away. He broke out the first aid kit and pulled his robe off. Valdrian had loaned him a pair of pants. They'd felt strange at first, but he wasn't sorry to be rid of the Rahai.

"Would you have a look, Syd?" he asked, straddling the back of the chair and leaning forward.

She rolled her sleeves up. "Want me to do surgery?"

"No, thank you. Just put some of that on." He pointed to a half-empty tube of ointment.

"Were you near a shell blast?" she asked, squeezing an enormous glob into one palm and messily smearing it over his back.

He winced. "Is that what it looks like?"

"Yeah."

"No, but I got hit by lots of little rocks."

"How?"

"Meteors."

He braced himself for another barrage of questions he didn't care to answer, but all she said was, "Oh, right."

As if that was an everyday occurrence.

———

THE SUMMONS from Balaur came the next morning. Malach went to the palace unsure if he was about to be killed or formally anointed Nuncio.

Tristhus hadn't heard any whispers about Falke, but that meant nothing. If Balaur knew, he'd probably just lure him there, snuff him like a candle, and dump the body where it would never be found.

He entered the stifling room already sweating. The Masdari woman was not present, though he caught a whiff of her sandalwood perfume. Balaur was sitting up in bed. He looked marginally improved.

"Malach! I have news to please us both. A Markhawk arrived. All is in place. You will ride out tomorrow. I hope to join you in a few days, once I complete my course of treatment."

He decided not to ask what that entailed. "I would like to choose the mages I bring with me. It pains me to say it, Reverend Father, but there are some here I do not trust."

Balaur made a wry face. "They are likely the ones who say the same about you, Malach. Ah, do not frown so! I have been told that you are too young to be given such responsibility. They also wonder how you managed to escape when others shed their last drop of blood in defense of Bal Kirith."

"We were overrun!"

He waved a hand. "I know. Petty jealousy, no doubt. Ambition runs in our blood, does it not? But I am certain you will prove them all wrong." A slight frown. "It is curious, though. Cardinal Mandrake—one of those critics whom we speak of—has not been seen since yesterday. We seem to be missing Bishop Aarin, as well. And Mandrake's son. Have you seen them?"

"No, Reverend Father." Malach smiled. "But I say good riddance."

Balaur regarded him for a long moment. Then he laughed. "Ah, it reminds me of the old days. If one dabbles in intrigues and conspiracy, one must take care not to be ensnared oneself, yes? Well, we shall pray for their safe return. In the meantime, you may commence preparations for the journey. When you arrive, the first priority is to secure the cartomancer. I have already made my own advance arrangements so you should have no trouble with that."

"She's at the Arx?"

Blue eyes twinkled. "She is indeed. Kasia is most valuable to me, Malach. She must not come to harm."

"I will ensure it."

"Very good." He tilted his head. "Jamila tells me you approached her."

"Only to be certain of her intentions. She is very close to you, Reverend Father."

"Your concern is admirable. Well, I can assure you that Jamila is working toward our success. I would tell you more, but the negotiations are at a delicate juncture. I can't risk jeopardizing them. Not even for my new Nuncio! But all will be clear in time."

We both have our secrets, Malach thought. As long as you never discover mine, they can crown you the new Golden Imperator for all I care.

"This starfall," Balaur said. "Did you witness it?"

"Yes, Reverend Father. I was staying up in Arbot Hills. I had a clear view of the city."

"Did it *target* the Arx?"

"Truthfully, I'm not sure. It was chaos. I fled."

"Just as you fled Bal Kirith?" he asked softly.

Malach stiffened. "Should I have stayed in Novostopol as the city blew apart around me, Reverend Father?"

"No, no. Though I wish I knew how this came about." Balaur gave a windy sigh. "I imagine the cartomancer will be able to tell us. She is quite extraordinary."

Playing cards! Had it been a witch, he'd be worried. But Kasia Novak was obviously a charlatan. If she was nihilim, he was a Praefator.

Malach nodded solemnly. "I look forward to meeting her."

"Yes." Balaur rubbed the stumps of his fingers, his gaze distant. "As do I, my son."

Chapter Eighteen

Sleet stung Alexei's eyes as he strode through the tangle of alleyways, shoulders hunched against the cold. The Mark-hound was a dark shadow ahead, trotting along with her nose pressed to the ground.

She'd caught his brother's scent again.

He could tell from the alert set of her ears. But Alice knew better than to make a sound. One bark and Misha would know he was being followed.

Alexei reached the mouth of the alley just as his brother emerged from a nondescript house half a block down. He slipped back into the shadows, snapping his fingers. The Markhound's slender body blurred into the darkness and vanished.

A minute later, Misha strode past, whistling a cheerful tune. He wore the Blue Flame tabard of the knights of Jalghuth. A sword rode at his hip.

Lezarius had made him captain of his personal guard. Misha's knights loved him. Everyone did. Alexei's brother was handsome, charming, intelligent, decisive. A skilled leader who had honed Lezarius's dispirited army into a tightly-organized, professional fighting force.

He'd designed the new garrisons on Khotang Lake, fortifying the natural barrier against Bal Agnar. Recruited and trained civil militias to patrol the northern reaches of the Morho. Lezarius trusted him completely. Mikhail had saved him from the assassins at the Batavia Institute, then from Falke's hunters in the Morho, and finally from Balaur himself.

No one but Alexei, Lezarius and the Reborn knew about his brother's Nightmark.

Mikhail laughed and smiled as he always had, equally quick with a joke or some cunning strategy to keep the mages from their throats. He'd gained weight and no longer bore any resemblance to the half-starved wraith at the Batavia Institute. His blue eyes gleamed, his teeth were white and strong. He wore a scruffy dark beard as he had when they fought in the Void together. It suited him.

Yet Misha was *off*.

Alexei noticed it in brief, unguarded moments. A tightness in his eyes. Eruptions of temper over nothing. He always found some excuse when Alexei tried to spend time with him, as if he feared what his brother might see. Unlike the others, Alexei knew him too well to be deceived.

One morning, he'd walked in on his brother while Mikhail was pulling a tunic over his head. Alexei caught a glimpse of the Mark on his chest—a blindfolded man with a knife at his throat—but it was the yellowing bruises along his ribs that ignited a spark of worry. Mikhail had yanked the garment down with a flash of annoyance. When Alexei asked, he claimed he'd gotten them sparring with his knights.

But no one ever landed a blow against his brother. Misha was too quick.

Their rooms were in the same wing of the palace. Alexei still had trouble sleeping. When he heard a soft tread in the corridor late one night, he'd known it was Mikhail. He'd followed and discovered that Misha was leaving the Arx at night to prowl the city. Wine sinks and brothels. Bare-knuckle boxing matches.

He'd watched his brother beat a local favorite so badly, the loser was carried in a bloody heap from the ring. It had taken six men—all thick-necked giants—to pull Misha off. Alexei had told Lezarius about it. The pontifex sent knights to shut the place down, though he wouldn't hear a word against Mikhail. *Blowing off steam*, Lezarius called it.

The willful blindness to his brother's condition frustrated Alexei no end. He still believed Lezarius to be the best of the bunch—better than Falke, certainly—but where Mikhail Bryce was concerned, the pontifex simply refused to face the truth.

On the surface, life in Jalghuth was back to normal. But Balaur's occupation had left permanent scars. The city had a dark underbelly that drew his brother like a moth to a flame.

Misha must have suspected something because he grew more careful. Alexei had only managed to catch his trail tonight because he'd used Alice. Now she sat at his feet, lips pulled back in a silent snarl. The Markhound knew something was wrong, too. She'd known since the day Misha's Nightmark was restored to its original purpose.

A slow decay of the soul.

Alexei scratched her behind the ears.

"*Mane*, little sister," he told her. *Stay*.

Alice's rump obediently hit the snow. He walked to the house and knocked on the door, mouth dry. Over the last month, two women had been found murdered in their beds, both on nights Mikhail had been roaming the city.

Relief flooded him as footsteps approached. The door was opened by a petite woman in a blue silk robe. An exotic beauty with a river of shining black hair and large almond eyes with thick lashes. A startled expression crossed her face as she took in his clean-shaven face and plain brown cassock. Then she gathered her composure with a smile.

"How can I help you, Father?"

"May I come in?"

She inclined her head and stood aside. He stepped past her, inhaling a whiff of musky perfume. "You thought I was my brother."

She cocked a thinly plucked brow. "Who?"

"I saw him leave just a moment ago."

The woman tucked her hands into embroidered sleeves. "You have the same eyes. Like the ice on Khumbu Massif. Did he send you here?"

"He doesn't know. I . . . I followed him."

"My clients pay well for privacy. If you seek information, you should ask him yourself."

Alexei took out a wad of folded bills. "I'd rather ask you."

She counted the money. "So much for a question? All right. You've bought one."

"What does he do here?" Alexei asked bluntly.

Her dark eyes regarded him without shame. "I provide a specialty service, Father. For some, pleasure and pain are the same."

Alexei's heart sank. "So he hurts you?"

She laughed. "You misunderstand. Men come here for punishment."

"So *you* hurt *him*?"

"At his request."

"How often does he come?"

She shrugged. "It used to be once a week. Lately, every night." A playful smile. "That's two questions you've asked me now." She looked him up and down. "Perhaps you are alike, hmmm? Craving a taste of the lash?"

Alexei's cheeks warmed. "A kind offer, but no. That is not my fetish."

"A pity." She drew the robe tighter, her voice turning cool. "I'm afraid I have other appointments. If you'll excuse me."

He left the house and stood for a minute in the quiet street, both relieved and unsettled.

They were both consenting adults. Alexei felt slightly ashamed for sticking his nose in.

It doesn't mean he isn't doing other things, a voice whispered. *Things you know nothing about.*

Alexei's gaze moved past the Arx, following the ice road to the octagonal spire of Sinjali's Lance. A construction of the ancient Praefators who founded his faith, the tower sat atop a wellspring of the ley and acted like a prism, dividing it into three layers.

Blue for the logical mind. Violet for the unconscious. And red for the deepest, most unruly power.

He wished he understood Nightmarks better. How they worked exactly.

Sanctified Marks were given by the clergy. They tamed the red ley.

Nightmarks fed it. They were invented by Balaur when he was the young pontifex of Bal Agnar. Expressions of the subconscious in its purest form, with no filter of rationality.

The ley interacted with each individual mind. Ferran Massot had abused his patients. Tried to attack Kasia. As soon as Alexei heard about the two murders of women, he'd been terrified it was Misha.

But the demons lurking in his brother's mind seemed to have their own unique hungers. That Misha was dangerous Alexei had no doubt. But now he wondered if the threat was really to *others*, as he'd assumed.

And why Mikhail Semyon Bryce, the most decorated captain of his generation, a paragon of virtue in every other respect, despised himself so much?

IT WAS STILL DARK when Alexei left his rooms and walked through the clusters of jaunty, tilt-roofed buildings down to Lake Khotang. The snow had stopped. In the distance, the jagged teeth of the Sundar Kush seemed to scrape the stars.

Torches glowed in the slits of new-built towers along the shore. It had been Mikhail's idea to use the stone from the stelae field to construct a ring of defensive forts.

Beyond lay the dark mass of the Morho Sarpanitum. The forest had been quiet so far, but Bal Agnar was less than a day's march. The lake was the only thing standing between them and Balaur's army.

And the Sundar Kush. The rugged mountains guarded Jalghuth's eastern flank.

He waited in a stand of pines until he heard the rhythm of pounding feet. Alexei stepped into the path just as Misha came around a bend. His brother drew up short, breath coming in puffs of white fog. He wore sneakers and sweats with a small Blue Flame embroidered on the breast.

A guarded expression crossed his face. "Alyosha."

"Oh, hey." He smiled, feigning surprise, and performed a few casual stretches that made various body parts creak in protest.

While Misha was training knights and building forts, Alexei had been shut up with Lezarius, going over all the administrative tasks of the Arx that Balaur had neglected to deal with, like ensuring an adequate supply of crops from the lowland valleys. Proper care for the sick and infirm. The reopening of schools. A million other essential aspects of a functioning city.

"I thought I might run the circuit with you," he said.

"It's 20k."

Alexei concealed his dismay. "I can handle that."

"There are hills."

"You think I'm out of shape?"

Misha's teeth gleamed in the dark. He took off at a sprint. Alexei cursed and ran after him.

The first kilometer was brutal. By the third, he wished for death—and doubted it would be far off. His heart felt like it might explode. But the old competitive instinct refused to let him concede defeat.

Alexei still remembered the first time he'd managed to beat his brother in a foot race. It had taken a whole summer of obsessive training behind his back. The expression on Misha's face when his little brother overtook him in the last ten meters had been priceless.

Their father encouraged the rivalry. He made a big deal about Alexei's victory, ribbing Mikhail for weeks until even Alexei grew weary of it. But his brother never seemed bothered. Once he got over the surprise of losing, he'd looked relieved. As if he were tired of being perfect all the time.

By the time they crossed the bridge over the lake's inlet, somewhere around the 7k mark, Alexei could feel his blood starting to oxygenate. Every muscle burned. It would be worse —far, far worse—tomorrow. But the frigid air swept the cobwebs from his mind. He felt the euphoria that came from pushing through agony into a clean, pure state of forward motion.

Dawn broke as they passed through the foothills on the northern shore, the flank of the mountain rising to the left, and then down a long wooded incline. When they neared the road back up to the Arx, Alexei sprinted ahead. He heard a muffled curse.

Something thumped against his back. Icy water trickled down his neck.

Alexei shouted in outrage and gathered his own snowball, packing it tight. Mikhail ducked and it splattered against a tree.

Within seconds, the battle was raging. When they were kids, his brother's strategy was to endure bombardment while he assembled an arsenal, then unleash them all in a rapid-fire barrage. He hadn't changed. Alexei managed to nail him four times before brutal retaliation came.

He collapsed into the snow and curled into a ball as Misha unloaded a series of missiles perfectly aimed at the gap in his sweats. By the time it was over, they were both soaked and shivering and laughing harder than they had in years.

His brother pulled him to his feet. "I won," he said, grinning through the frost on his beard.

"How do you figure that?"

"Whoever throws the last one wins."

It was an ancient argument.

"But I hit you more times!"

"Doesn't matter." He backed away as Alexei started packing a fresh snowball. "Last one standing!" He tore off.

Alexei hurled the snowball and missed. "Shit!" he cried, running to catch up.

He was cooling off and everything was starting to hurt now. Misha left him in the dust, only pausing to wait when they were past the snow line halfway up the ice road.

"We should do this again," Mikhail said. "Tomorrow?"

He didn't seem winded at all.

"I'll think about it," Alexei panted.

They walked the rest of the way without speaking, but it wasn't the brittle silence that had stretched between them before. Back at his rooms, Alexei took a hot shower. He'd needed the exercise. If nothing was torn, he'd stick with the routine. The first week would be the worst.

But it wasn't just the run that left him with a warm glow. He knew now that his brother was still there. The one he respected and loved and looked up to. All he had to do was help him remember.

He'd just pulled a fresh cassock over his head when a knock came at the door. Mikhail poked his head in. He'd changed into a Blue Flame tabard.

"The Reverend Father wants us both," he said.

"What about?" Alexei fell into step with him in the corridor.

Misha shook his head with a sigh. "I'm not sure, but I have a feeling it isn't good."

Chapter Nineteen

They found Lezarius in the council chamber with a small group of cardinals and bishops. It was a pleasant room that smelled of old parchment and beeswax candles. Arched windows looked out over the white expanse of Lake Khotang.

The assembled men and women murmured greetings as they took seats at the long table. Lezarius studied a map of the continent.

"A Markhawk arrived this morning," he said. "From Luk. Novostopol was attacked two days ago."

Alexei stared in shock. The city's location at the southern end of the continent left it far from the fighting in the Morho Sarpanitum.

"I thought the mages were penned up in Bal Agnar," he said.

"Not that kind of attack. It was a starfall."

"Starfall? You mean *meteorites?*"

Lezarius nodded. "It caused great devastation. The fact that it mainly damaged the Arx suggests the mages had a hand in it. Balaur is the obvious culprit, but it makes little sense. If he commands such power, why hasn't he done the same to Nantwich? Or to us?"

Alexei exchanged a worried look with his brother. All their preparations had been for a traditional siege.

"Luk says there will be a meeting of the pontifices in Nantwich," Lezarius said. "He urges me to come."

"Will Falke be there?" Mikhail looked around the table. "I hardly need to remind you that he sent assassins for both of us at the Batavia Institute. The man is a viper."

"Peace, Captain," Lezarius said gently. "Falke is missing. Presumed dead, though they haven't yet found his body."

"Saints," Alexei murmured. "How many casualties?"

"They're still digging out. Half the Pontifex's Palace was destroyed, and many other buildings. I don't know the final numbers."

There was a grim silence.

"Nonetheless," he added, "Novostopol is committed to sending a representative to this council."

"Who is it?" Mikhail asked.

"Bishop Maria Karolo," Lezarius replied. "What do you know about her?"

"She's the head of the Order of Saint Marcius," Mikhail said. "An arch conservative."

"Ah. And how does she view her authority?"

"Without limit," Alexei said dryly. "But Feizah reined her in."

The Order of Saint Marcius enforced the *Meliora* in cultural matters—meaning it acted as the Curia's censors. Depictions of sex and violence, in particular, were frowned upon. But Novostopol was a free-thinking city. The trends waxed and waned depending on who ran the Order. Karolo's predecessor had been notoriously tolerant of almost anything. A collective groan went up among the liberals when she was appointed.

"She and Falke despise each other," Alexei said. "So there's little chance she knew about the conspiracy to kill you, Reverend Father."

"Well, *that's* encouraging," Lezarius said with a mordant smile. "The question is, should I meet with them?"

"Absolutely not," Misha said.

"I'm for it," Alexei said after a moment, ignoring his brother's scowl. "The Curia must face this threat together."

"I agree," Bishop Panday said, studying each of them with keen brown eyes lined heavily with kohl. She was the youngest member of the council—and also, in Alexei's opinion, the smartest. His brother thought so, too, seeking her opinion on most of his plans. Misha looked unhappy that she wasn't taking his side.

"It's tempting to fortify our position and dig in," Panday said. "But despite all Captain Bryce has done, I fear that Balaur could take this city if he tried hard enough. Without the Wards and stelae, they will sweep over us. The fight must be brought to them. A joint offensive in the Morho is the best option."

Cardinal Jagat frowned. He was the only one present who had remained at the Arx during Balaur's occupation. He'd believed he was being loyal to Lezarius. The shock of learning that he had served a false pontifex left him deeply distrustful, bordering on paranoid.

"If we make it until spring, the ice on the lake will soften," Jagat said. "Should Balaur's forces try to cross in boats, the archers will set them alight." He tapped the map. "There are passes in the Sundar Kush, but a hundred knights could hold them against an army."

Alexei shook his head. "A regular army. Not nihilim with full access to the abyssal ley. If any of them broke through the lines, they would turn our soldiers against each other. I've seen it happen."

Misha leaned forward, voice soft. "Am I the only one who remembers that Clavis also wanted our Reverend Father dead?"

"I remember," Panday replied. "But she is still the lesser evil."

All eyes turned to Alexei, who now had a Crossed Keys Mark on his neck, given by the Reverend Mother when she sent him to Jalghuth four months before.

"The Void is gone," Alexei said to Lezarius. "The worst has already happened. She has no reason to fear you anymore. Nantwich sits on our southern border. If our cities don't forge a strong alliance, Balaur will pick us off, one by one. Regardless of how you feel about her, you both face an enemy that is far worse. At least find out what the others intend."

One by one, Lezarius's aides spoke up. Some were for it, some against. Mikhail was firmly in opposition. Lezarius listened to each of them. Then he rose to his feet.

"I will consult the Reborn," he said. "Then I will give you my decision." His gaze settled on Mikhail, then slid to Alexei. "Come with me, eh?"

His brother never went up to the Lance. Not since the children had taken over occupancy.

Mikhail stayed at the table with the others, reviewing various scenarios. When they stepped outside the palace, Alexei gave a sharp whistle and Alice bounded up. He felt bad for not taking her on the run, but her hostility towards Misha made it impossible.

"I've never met Clavis," Lezarius said. "What is she like?"

He blew out a frosty breath. "Militant. She wears a sword."

"I'd heard that," Lezarius said with disapproval.

"But I think she means well. And her skills in the field are legendary. Perhaps she is not the pontifex you would choose during a time of peace, but in a time of war . . . I would rather have her on my side than not, Reverend Father."

Lezarius grunted. "Well, what you say is true. We are sister cities. The only ones to hold the north. And we cannot lose the Lance again. The very thought is terrifying."

As they took a sledge up the winding ice road to the black tower, Alexei could feel the purity of the ley, newly risen from the depths of the earth. A pale figure in blue sneakers stepped from the shadow of the great doors. Alice ran to greet him, tail wagging. Will sank down to ruffle her fur, then looked up with a smile. The child's skin was bloodless, his hair and lashes white as sea foam. One eye gleamed ebony, the other a kaleidoscope of swirling color.

Even after many months at Jalghuth, it was still unnerving.

"Lezarius, Father Bryce. It is good to see you."

"And you, Will," Lezarius said warmly. "May we enter the Lance?"

"Of course." He stepped back. "There is something I must show you."

He led them through an antechamber and down a cramped flight of windowless spiral stairs to a labyrinth of corridors below. There was an almost imperceptible downward slant to the stone floor. Alice raced ahead, doubling back to snuffle at Will's hand.

"She smells Greylight," the boy said. "I was petting her earlier."

"Traitorous creature," Lezarius said fondly. "She abandoned me for the children."

"I gave her a fish from the lake, but she prefers to catch mice."

"Wild at heart. All cats are, aren't they?" Lezarius tweaked Alice's tail as she loped past. "Not like you, faithful girl."

"We've been exploring together." Will looked back over his shoulder. "Sinjali's Lance is very old, but it was built atop something even older."

Alexei and Lezarius exchanged a glance. "I didn't know that," Lezarius admitted. "I never came down here much."

"It's unlikely you would have found it," Will said. "The entrance was hidden."

The chill deepened as they wended their way down. At

last he stopped before a partly demolished brick wall. They climbed through the hole. The floor of the chamber beyond was riven by a deep fissure down the center. Alexei glimpsed the remnants of a Black Sun mosaic.

A ladder had been lowered into the crack. Cold air wafted out. Alice trotted along the edge, nosing at the gap. She let out a puzzled whimper and sat.

"Can you manage it, Lezarius?" Will asked.

"Most certainly," the pontifex replied. "But what is down there?"

"I think you must see it for yourself," Will said. "My brothers and sisters are waiting."

He scrambled down the ladder. Alexei eyed the fissure, unsure why he felt hesitant. The ley flowed cleanly here. Even more so than above. Lezarius moved to follow and he shook it off.

"Meet us down there, *da*?" he said to Alice.

She cocked a brow, then faded to shadow and vanished. Alexei trusted her instincts. If the hound was willing to go, he would, too.

It was a long way down, longer than he expected. Will steadied the bottom of the ladder as they descended the rungs into a vast circular room that must have been as wide as the Lance itself. When he reached the bottom, Alexei stood still, struck dumb by amazement.

The walls were carved in runes that blazed with white light. Archways at regular intervals led to more galleries, each similarly decorated. Three of the children stood at distant points in the chamber. They held notepads on which they were presumably copying the patterns. Alice raced around the perimeter in a frenzy of excitement, her barks echoing against the high ceiling.

"Wards," Lezarius exclaimed. "And they are still working!"

"Have you ever seen these symbols before?" Will asked.

They were sharp and angular, straight lines joined by

small circles in a dizzying array of combinations. From the spacing, they seemed to form words.

"Never," Alexei said.

Lezarius shook his head. "They must have been put here by the Praefators."

"No." Will walked up to the nearest wall and traced one with a fingertip. The light brightened at his touch, fading when his hand fell. "These predate the Praefators by thousands of years."

"How do you know?" Alexei wondered.

A shrug. "We just know." He pointed. "Look, this stone is different."

Alexei studied it. Sinjali's Lance was forged from some dark substance, but the chamber had a pearly sheen.

"You cannot read the runes?" Lezarius asked.

"Not yet. But they are a binding spell of some kind. To keep something out." He tilted his head. "Or perhaps to keep something *in*."

The hair on Alexei's neck prickled. "But they don't affect the flow of the ley?"

"No. Their purpose is different."

"How far does this place extend?" he asked.

The other children had given no greeting, but they abandoned their task to crowd around Alice, who endured the clumsy petting with a long-suffering expression.

"There are deeper levels, all with runes like this." Will regarded them both impassively. "I hoped you might know more."

Lezarius looked troubled. "The histories all date from the Dark Ages. We have no idea what came before. But whoever put these here must have had a reason. I think it would be unwise to tamper with them."

Will said nothing. His eyes moved across the runes. Tracing them, then flicking back and tracing them again.

"Willem?" Lezarius prompted. "Do you agree?"

The boy turned his head. "We study them only, Lezarius. But it might be of importance. We will continue."

The tone was mild, but Alexei wondered what Will would do if Lezarius tried to forbid him. The children were, for all purposes, immortal. The extent of their other powers was unknown. They exercised dominion over the Lance and so far, Lezarius had seen no reason to challenge their authority. The Reborn had done nothing but good.

If that ever changed, they'd be in a world of trouble.

"You will not break these Wards?" Lezarius pressed, holding the boy's gaze.

"We do not know how," Will said.

Which, Alexei thought, wasn't an answer.

"Tell me if you learn anything more," Lezarius said. "But we've come for another reason." He chafed his hands. "It's freezing down here. May we speak somewhere else?"

"Of course. You must warm your bodies." Will smiled—a sweet, guileless smile that made Alexei ashamed for thinking ill of him. The boy wore a thin t-shirt bearing the logo of one of the ice-fishing companies. He neither ate nor slept as far as Alexei knew. None of them did.

He'd wondered what the children got up to at the Lance all day and night. They never left. Now he knew why.

They had a new project.

But Lezarius seemed to trust them and there was little Alexei could do about it. They had other more immediate problems to deal with. He climbed the rickety ladder behind Lezarius in case the pontifex lost his footing, Will coming last, and they walked back toward the upper reaches of the tower. Presently, Alice reappeared to trot at Alexei's heels. Will lit a fire in a small room that Lezarius had furnished as a study during his time as Balaur's warden.

"I've been invited to a meeting of the pontifices," Lezarius said. "In Nantwich. I am inclined to go, but I would have your advice before I decide."

Will sat on the floor, knees drawn to his chest. "We don't see the future. I cannot tell you what to do."

"Can't you read minds?" Alexei asked.

"Not so far away, thank the ley. I cannot imagine being privy to the thoughts of every living being on this continent. It is one reason we prefer to stay in the Lance. For the quiet." A pointed look at Alexei. "So the answer is no."

Lezarius eyed them both with bemusement. "What was the question?"

"I was wondering if perhaps Will might come along to advise you," Alexei admitted.

"Ah. To tell me if the others had ulterior motives, perhaps? Or intended treachery?"

He nodded.

"It would be helpful." Lezarius stroked his chin. "But I would not use them for my own benefit even if they agreed."

"I know. I didn't even say it aloud!"

"Never mind. Is there nothing you can tell me, Willem?"

"Only this. We felt the surge of ley in Novostopol. It was not abyssal."

Alexei felt a jolt of surprise. "So the mages didn't cause the starfall?"

Will looked puzzled. "I cannot tell you *who*. It wasn't natural. A mind guided the phenomena. But it did not touch the red ley."

Alexei and Lezarius shared a glance. "That's important to know," Lezarius said at last. "I must tell the others."

"So you will go?" Will asked.

He nodded. "I think I have to."

Alice heaved a deep sigh, flopping down before the fire to rest chin on paws.

Will's mismatched gaze fixed on Alexei. "Take your brother. He must depart Jalghuth."

Must. It was the first time the Reborn had issued a direct order. The children were changing, Alexei thought uneasily.

Lezarius frowned. "I meant to leave Mikhail in charge."

"That would be a disaster. His very presence taints the ley."

Alexei wasn't surprised, but Lezarius seemed shocked. "Is it so bad?"

"Nothing like the Red King, but bad enough."

"Can you hear my brother's thoughts?" Alexei asked.

Will shook his head. "He has learned to shut us out."

"Won't you help him?" Lezarius asked in despairing tones. "Stop the corruption?"

"We preserve the source," Will said. "Our presence here has slowed his condition, but even we are not strong enough to halt the progress of the Nightmark."

A thought occurred to Alexei. "Could you dam the abyssal ley? It feeds the Mark."

"What you're asking is impossible. Like trying to block one current of a river. It's all or none and the ley must flow." He frowned. "Not even the Red King attempted to sever it completely."

"And the Mark cannot be removed?" Lezarius persisted.

Alexei knew the answer. He'd already asked more than once.

"If you cut the skin away, it would return when he heals," Will said. "If the cutting itself didn't kill him."

A bleak silence fell.

"How long do we have before it consumes him?" Alexei asked at length.

"Your brother is fighting it as he did before. He keeps himself on a tight rein."

Alexei swallowed. "Yes, I know."

"For this reason, his descent appears gradual. But it is an illusion. When his control slips, as it eventually must, there will be a sudden turn for the worse." The child moved forward. Icy fingers closed around his own. "We wish you both well, Father Bryce."

Alexei held on, though the touch chilled him to the bone. "I know you do."

Lezarius rose to his feet. "I will return within the week. But . . . what am I to do with Mikhail?" He looked lost.

"Come, Reverend Father," Alexei said, putting an arm around his shoulders. "We will discuss it on the way back to the Arx."

They settled into the waiting sledge and the driver shook the reins. Leather harnesses creaked as four of the shaggy, horned beasts called *gauru* hauled the sledge back down the ice road. Alexei settled a blanket over Lezarius's knees.

"What do we tell him?" Lezarius wondered. "He's worked so hard to fortify the defenses. To train my knights. Mikhail has devoted every waking moment to preserving us from the darkness. I cannot believe it is truly so bad."

Alexei was forced to squeeze against the pontifex as Alice materialized at his side. She hogged the lefthand seat, hanging over the edge with her snout pointed into the wind.

"Do you know what my father used to say?" Alexei asked.

Lezarius arched a shaggy white brow.

"That when you run out of courage, hope and luck, you still have one thing left. Stubbornness." He smiled. "And then my mother would point out that it was often the twin of stupidity."

"Which are we?" Lezarius asked glumly.

"A little of both, I imagine."

He sat back, listening to the runners hiss across the ice, the soft snorts of the galloping gauru. Behind them, purple shadows cratered the steep valleys of the Sundar Kush.

"We will find a way to save him," Alexei said. "We *will*."

Lezarius gazed down at the lights of the city below. "Yes," he said, forcing a smile. "I am sure you're right. But we must not tell him what the boy said, Alexei. He cannot know."

"It would do no one any good," Alexei agreed. "So you

will tell him that he must lead your honor guard. I don't think he'll argue. He's leery of this council."

"He is my protector," Lezarius said softly. "I trust him with my life, whatever Willem says."

The sledge drew up before the Pontifex's Palace. Alexei helped Lezarius climb out. They were about to enter when Alice's sharp, agitated barks drew their attention. A group of six knights approached from the main gate. A shackled prisoner walked in their midst.

"*Sileo*," Alexei commanded, stroking the hound's flank.

She subsided but stared hard at the prisoner, hackles raised. He was a tall, heavyset man with greasy black hair and a scowling face.

"What's he done?" Lezarius called out.

Their lieutenant jogged over and gave a quick bow.

"We caught the murderer, Reverend Father," he said with a grim smile. "A local carpenter. He tried to assault a woman in her home. The neighbors heard her screams and summoned a patrol."

Alexei eyed the prisoner. He gazed back coldly.

"Is the woman all right?" Lezarius asked.

"She managed to escape and lock herself in an upstairs bedroom. He ran off, but the witnesses recognized him. We arrested him at his workshop. There were bloodstained clothes. Items stolen from the two other victims. There's no doubt, Reverend Father."

Alexei had never uttered his fears aloud. The wave of relief weakened his knees.

"A monster," Lezarius muttered. "Thank the Saints he was found." He shook his head. "We never had crimes like this before. Let us hope they are the last."

The lieutenant bowed again and returned to his men, who dragged the prisoner toward the holding cells.

"What will you do with him?" Alexei asked.

"Keep him locked away forever," Lezarius replied. "What else?"

"He could be Nightmarked. Balaur held the city for three years." He paused. "There might be others."

In fact, he knew there were almost certainly others.

"So we examine every man, woman and child?"

Alexei gave him a level look. "It might make people feel safer. If they have nothing to hide."

"Perhaps when I return," Lezarius agreed. "But for now, we must lay our plans for Nantwich."

Alexei lightly slapped Alice's rump. "Off to the kennels with you, little sister. It's past your suppertime anyway."

She knew the word *kennels*. And *supper*. Alice was an uncommonly smart hound. He watched her streak away, dark form merging with the lengthening shadows. Lezarius was already striding past the knights guarding the palace. Alexei hurried to catch up. Two more guards stood stiffly at the doors beyond the antechamber.

"Find Captain Bryce and send him to my study," Lezarius said.

One gave a smart salute and left to carry out the order.

In a short time, the pontifex was ensconced behind his rosewood desk, poring over maps while Alexei sat in an armchair, jotting down thoughts for the meeting to come.

"I want you to attend as my Nuncio," Lezarius said. "As I recall, you asked for the post when you arrived."

Alexei glanced up. "With pleasure, Reverend Father."

He smiled. "There. The appointment is formal now. I imagine whatever agreement we come to will be a thicket of legal jargon." Lezarius made a face. "I expect you to untangle it for me."

"Oh, I'll scrutinize every word."

Alexei was surprised to find he felt eager at the prospect. He never dwelt on his years as a defense attorney. They seemed like another lifetime. Another person entirely. But he missed the intellectual combat of a jury trial. Poring over witness statements and police reports in search of a discrepancy that could undermine the case against his client. The hours in the law library searching for precedents and favorable rulings.

But his specialty was appeals.

Reviewing the entire court transcript, every aspect of the investigation and subsequent trial, and then conducting his own inquiry. He'd managed to overturn many convictions by unearthing new evidence or exposing prosecutorial misconduct.

Treaty law was not quite as exciting, but the stakes of this one were high enough to whet his appetite. Then an unpleasant thought occurred.

Alexei cleared his throat. "I should disclose something, Reverend Father."

Lezarius looked up. "Yes?"

"A possible conflict of interest. Luk's Nuncio is a bishop named Morvana Zeigler. She holds my Marks. Almost all of them."

The pontifex blinked. "Does she?"

"Yes, she does. And I left Kvengard without a word. I don't think she'll be pleased to see me."

"Luk's Nuncio, eh? Well, he is our steadfast ally. I see no reason to withdraw your appointment. It's my business who my Nuncio is, don't you agree?"

"Are you sure? I don't wish to cause friction with the Kvens."

"No, no." Lezarius waved the suggestion away. "I want you, Alexei. Your loyalty is unquestioned. Let us put this behind us."

"Thank you, Reverend Father."

"Come here." He beckoned. Alexei walked around the desk, peering over Lezarius's shoulder. The pontifex pushed the map aside and unfurled another, this one showing the region's topography in more detail.

"I used to study these for hours," he said. "Much can be read in the skin of the earth. It shapes us as much as we shape it. Perhaps more." A gnarled finger traced the outlines of Jalghuth. "Our language is distinct, while the others have a common root in the Old Tongue. This is because the Kindu culture evolved in isolation." He pinched his lower lip in thought. "Did the Praefators intend it to be so? Or was it an accident of geography?"

"What does the word *Kindu* mean?"

"People of the serpent," Lezarius replied.

Alexei frowned.

"It is the shape of the mountain range," Lezarius explained. "Do you see?"

He tapped the sinuous spine of the Sundar Kush.

"I see. Mount Ogo is the head."

Lezarius looked pleased. "I made this map myself."

"It's beautiful," Alexei murmured.

Every contour line had been drawn in a precise hand. The Morho Sarpanitum was rendered in shades of green, the seas in vivid blue. Elegant calligraphic lettering identified the six major cities of the Via Sancta. A tiny version of each Arx sat below the names. Lezarius had even added fanciful sea monsters off the coasts.

Alexei met his gaze. "Do you ever wish you had stayed a geographer, Reverend Father?"

"Often." A rueful smile. "But that is not what the ley intended for me." He looked up as the door opened, face splitting in a grin. "Mikhail!"

Alexei's brother came inside and joined them at the desk. He regarded Lezarius warily.

"I tried to go to the Lance," he said. "They barred the door to me."

"Did they?" Lezarius rolled up the map, avoiding Misha's

eyes. "Do not make too much of it. The children discovered something beneath the tower. They are protective of it."

A glint of curiosity. "What?"

"A chamber engraved with runes. They say it is very old."

"You saw it?" This was directed at Alexei, who nodded.

"The runes were active," Alexei said. "They didn't break with the stelae."

"That's . . . weird," his brother said.

"Very. The children are studying them. I've never seen the like."

"Do you think Balaur knew about them?"

"No way of knowing. But they were walled away, so perhaps not."

Mikhail grunted. "Let us hope." He seemed to gird himself. "I take it you've reached a decision, Lezarius?"

"I'm going."

Misha sank into a chair, long legs splayed out. "I expected as much," he said unhappily.

"And I want you to come as captain of my personal guard. It would mean much to me. Bishop Panday can oversee the defense of the city. She's more than capable."

"Of course," Misha replied without hesitation. "If you must go through with this folly, I will stand at your side."

Lezarius looked both relieved and irritated. "Do you truly believe Clavis will try to murder me in her own city before every senior member of the Church?"

"No. I expect it will be a knife in the dark or a poisoned chalice."

Alexei sighed. "Surely you can grasp that there's no point in assassinating him now! The damage is already done—"

"Peace, brother." Misha smiled. "I was joking. But we will travel by ship. *That* I insist on."

"Agreed," Alexei said. "I'll make the arrangements."

"Father Bryce is my new Nuncio," Lezarius said.

Misha leapt to his feet and clapped Alexei on the back.

"Thank the Saints," he declared. "Let him argue with other people for a change."

"That's what I thought," Lezarius said with a twinkle in his eye.

"Well, I am glad," Misha said soberly. "Your talents were wasted in the field, Alyosha. It is time for higher pursuits."

Alexei winced. "Now you sound like our father."

"He wasn't always wrong." Misha cleared his throat. "How many knights will you let me have, Lezarius?"

The pontifex tipped his chair back, regarding them down his broad nose. "Enough for a visible presence but not so many it looks like an invasion. Two dozen will suffice."

"That's all?" Misha frowned.

"It is the standard number for a visiting Pontifex."

"In times of peace. This is war."

"Yes, but we are *not* at war with Nantwich. Two dozen, no more."

"Very well. But I get to choose them."

"Do it quickly. We leave tomorrow morning."

"So soon?"

"It was my Nuncio's advice."

"There's a psychological advantage to arriving early," Alexei explained. "In a multiparty negotiation, the first at the table has a tacit position of strength. It makes the others wonder what deals might have already been cut behind their backs."

"Not that I intend to," Lezarius said hastily. "We must not lose sight of the goal, which is unity against Balaur."

"Of course not," Mikhail murmured. A quick, humorless smile. "But I like the way your new Nuncio thinks. I don't doubt that Maria Karolo is scheming for any edge she can find."

They talked long into the evening. Servants brought a covered platter of chatar, an aromatic blend of rice and chickpeas that was the city's staple dish. They ate it with flatbread and bottles of strong beer, though Mikhail opted for water. He seemed more himself than he'd been in a long while. Perfectly at ease and in a good humor. Not at all like a man who was dangling by a thread. Yet Alexei hadn't forgotten Will's warning.

When they finally retired, Misha surprised him by following Alexei into his room. He sat on the bed, then rose and paced to the window. Sinjali's Lance wasn't visible, it was too high above the Arx, but Misha's gaze turned in the direction of the black tower.

"You saw Willem Danziger," he said quietly.

Alexei nodded.

"We were friends once. Willem helped me wake from the drugs they gave me in Kvengard."

"He doesn't wish you harm," Alexei said carefully. "He's only concerned for your welfare."

Misha banged a fist on the stone sill. He spun around, face tight. "My welfare? What does *that* mean?"

Alexei said nothing.

"Have I done you some wrong, brother? Speak!"

Alexei sank into a chair, weary beyond belief. "No."

"I know you watch my every move. I see it in your eyes every time you look at me! The doubt." He gripped his hair, yanking it so hard tears sprang to his eyes. "Yes, I've sought diversions. A release from the pressure . . . you've no idea what it's like."

"Then tell me."

Misha exhaled a hitching breath. "Do you really want to know?"

He nodded.

The fight seemed to go out of him. His brother slumped against the window.

"Like a stranger walks behind me," he said in a low, toneless voice. "A shadow. I can hear his footsteps. Growing closer. It's maddening."

"So you run."

A brief nod.

"Don't stop," Alexei said. "And know that I'm at your side for every step of the way."

Misha shook his head. "That's not what I want."

"I don't care. That's how it is."

His brother smiled suddenly. "You've changed. I used to be able to boss you around with no problem."

"That's not how I remember it."

"No, no, you were clay in my hands," Misha teased. "I suppose you rank above me now. Nuncio! Mamushka would be bragging to all the aunties." He sank down to the edge of the bed. "Do you remember the stories she told about Feizah's old Nuncio? What was his name?"

"Ah, Gregorin?"

"That's the one!" Misha chuckled. "He could barely manage a single encounter without some dire diplomatic misstep. He once mistook the Kven legate's wife for his daughter—"

"And then spilled a bowl of borscht on the poor woman in his haste to backtrack." Alexei shook his head. "Gregorin was a legend."

"The rabbits?"

"Oh Saints, the rabbits!"

"Mother said he was so traumatized, he wouldn't leave his quarters for a week. He had a phobia after that—"

"Okay, how about the champagne cork that nearly took out Karolo's eye? She tried to ban spirits entirely after that—"

"And Gregorin went on a hunger strike in protest." Mikhail wiped his eyes. "He won, too. It saved his career."

"Big shoes to fill," Alexei said.

"The biggest," Misha agreed. "When we get to Nantwich . . . " He tried and failed to keep a straight face. "When you get there, just make sure . . . one of them doesn't squeak . . . ."

They both lost it then.

Alexei could hear his mother's dry voice as she related the many tales about Fra Fyodor Gregorin. She never even cracked a smile, which made them even more hilarious. Eva Copeland-Bryce was a true raconteur. Juries loved her. She was the sort of person who could charm anyone within five minutes, usually by making them laugh. But she also was a passionate advocate for justice, not just for the rich and well-connected. There was nothing she despised more than hypocrisy.

How on earth she had married their father, Alexei didn't know. Yet they'd loved each other completely. One of the great mysteries of his childhood.

They talked for a while more and then Misha said goodnight. Alexei could tell he was anxious to start hand-picking the knights he planned to bring. Alexei dragged out a travel bag. After a moment's hesitation, he opened a carved chest that held extra blankets and fished out the book he'd hidden at the bottom.

Der Cherubinischer Wandersmann by Angelus Silesius.

The Wandering Cherubs. Another name for the Reborn children.

He'd taken it from the archives in Kvengard. An ancient tome on alchemy that had led him to the Danzigers. He knew much of it by heart now, though he didn't understand even half of the meaning.

He carefully turned the brittle pages to the end. The book had painted illustrations, fantastical beasts and arcane symbols, but none resembled the runes he'd seen below Sinjali's Lance. Whatever they meant, it didn't seem connected to alchemy.

Alexei paused at the last page. He'd studied this picture many times. It drew him; he couldn't say why exactly.

A golden city of tall spires. The border had a sun and moon, and six keys, each of a different shape and size. The title at the bottom said *Die Stadt der Morgenröte. The City of Dawn.*

Alexei closed the book. He would give it to Kasia. She could read layers of meaning in images. Assuming she wasn't still angry with him.

The thought of seeing her again made him hopeful, nervous and excited in equal measure. Alexei finished packing and sat in the armchair, knowing he'd never fall asleep if he lay down in bed.

There had been no way to send a letter through the Morho. Clavis would intercept any hawk sent to Nantwich, and Lezarius had forbidden communication until he knew what her intentions were.

Alexei hoped he'd made the right choice in supporting this journey. He wanted desperately to go back. Had that colored his judgment? What if his brother was right and they were walking into a trap?

But why would Clavis—

"Stop," he muttered. "The decision is made."

He leaned back and closed his eyes. *Please, just let me sleep for an hour or two. That's all. Just an hour.*

He tried to meditate. To still the incessant, whirling thoughts.

He named the saints and the martyrs. His breath slowed. His eyes slipped shut. And at the instant when he was no longer fully awake but not asleep either, he saw the city again. Saw a dark sun rising above it, saw the light go flat and queer, like dusk but with no shadows. Saw it spread across the land.

Not day nor night, came the drowsy thought. Not here nor there.

And then, with a soft sigh, Alexei slipped across the threshold.

Chapter Twenty

The Pontifex's Palace in Nantwich was a hive of activity. Gray-clad chars bustled through the hallways, carrying piles of clean linens and fresh flowers. For the first time since the end of the war, delegations from the three other cities would be coming for a council.

Kasia nursed a cup of black coffee in the commissary, stifling a yawn with one gloved hand. For four months, she had gone to parties and private clubs. Given hundreds of readings. Struggled to decipher meaning in the cards.

And she was no closer to digging out the Order of the Black Sun.

If only she was allowed to use her power, Kasia felt certain she'd make progress, but the Reverend Mother Clavis had forbidden it. She believed the alchemists had fled the city to join Balaur at Bal Agnar. But Kasia felt sure they were still here.

Waiting for something.

Sometimes when she came back to her rooms, small items were out of place. A vase of flowers moved from a table to a windowsill. Shoes taken from the closet and set neatly on the floor.

The Order was sending a message.

We're watching you.

When she told Patryk Spassov, he'd staked out her room for two days. He swore no one came in or out. Yet the strange moving of objects continued. She'd taken to obsessively searching her bedding each night to make sure no one had planted lithomancy stones.

"Do you think Alexei will be with the delegation from Jalghuth?" Natalya asked.

"I hope so." Kasia gave a wan smile. "It would be good to see him again."

"He could have sent a Markhawk to tell us he's alive." She'd pulled her hair into a bushy ponytail and wore a tight beige turtleneck and slacks that emphasized her long, slender limbs. Natalya caught a young vestal staring at her and smiled flirtatiously, eliciting a blush.

"Maybe they don't have them at Jalghuth," Kasia said.

"I wonder what happened to his brother. And the children."

"If Lezarius is there, they must be all right. What time is it?"

"Almost terce."

Kasia leapt up. "Saints, I'm late to meet Cardinal Gray."

"Find me later?"

Kasia nodded and hurried from the commissary. Autumn had come to Nantwich and dead leaves skirled around her feet as she walked through the bailey and followed a path through the wooded ground of the Arx to the Chapel of Saint Edvard. She rarely met with Clavis anymore. The Reverend Mother was too busy—and Kasia had nothing to report. The failure stung.

She'd hoped that the Order would come after her if she presented an appealing target. But either Balaur had lost interest in her abilities or they weren't willing to risk it.

She slipped into the chapel, eyes adjusting to the dim light that filtered through the stained glass windows. Cardinal Gray knelt before the altar, head bowed. At the sound of her footsteps, he rose with a smile.

Like most of the clergy, Clavis's chief aide was young. Middle thirties, she guessed, with spectacles and a scholarly air. He had a thin nose and short-cropped hair that was just starting to go white at the temples.

"Kasia," he said, brown eyes crinkling behind the steel-rimmed glasses.

"I'm sorry I'm late, Lucas."

He insisted she call him by his first name. At first it had felt strange—the customs of Novostopol were much more formal—but over the last months they'd gotten to know each other. He was her liaison with the Reverend Mother, giving her assignments and reporting back. Understandably, Clavis could not be seen as taking a particular interest in Kasia. It would raise too many questions about her presence here.

"How are the preparations coming along?" she asked, sinking down next to him on one of the pews.

He made a wry face. "The Reverend Father Luk arrived early this morning. It's no secret that relations with the Kvens have been cool these last years. But the reception went off without a hitch. We've just grateful he agreed to come. It's a positive sign."

"Will he fight?" Kasia asked bluntly.

Gray spread his hands. "That remains to be seen. But he convinced Lezarius to leave Jalghuth and join us. After what happened in the north, I think there's little doubt the Lion will want to vanquish Balaur once and for all. So an alliance is promising. But any formal treaty will be agreed at the summit tomorrow."

"What of Falke?"

"That's one of the reasons I asked you to meet with me, Kasia. His body has not yet been found."

"Then how can they be sure he's dead?"

Whatever his flaws, Falke seemed indestructible. He'd survived dozens of campaigns against the mages. That he would be killed in some freakish meteor shower seemed surreal.

"It's been almost a week now. Hope is fading.'" Gray paused. "The Eastern Curia has elected to send Bishop Maria Karolo in his place."

Kasia suppressed a groan. "Karolo?"

"I'm afraid so." He picked at the hem of his sleeve, not meeting her eye. "Which presents us with a rather awkward situation."

"To say the least," Kasia muttered. "She thinks I had something to do with Feizah's death."

"Which is nonsense, of course," he replied stoutly. "Clavis doesn't believe that for an instant. Obviously, or you wouldn't be sitting here. She fully intends to honor her agreement with Falke and keep you safe. But the Reverend Mother thinks it advisable for you to stay in your rooms for the duration of the summit."

"Of course." Kasia hesitated. "Did they already name her Pontifex?"

"No, no. Merely the designated emissary. But if Karolo learned we had given you shelter, it could derail the talks. She's a ... testy woman. Quick to take offense and slow to forgive."

Kasia grimaced. "Oh, I've seen it firsthand."

A smile tickled the corner of his mouth. "Did you really throw her off the dock?"

"Spassov did. And Natalya was there, too. So I guess we're all personae non gratae."

Gray nodded briskly. "As long as you keep out of sight, it shouldn't be a problem."

"I suppose we won't be attending tonight's reception?" She grinned at him. "I had my dress all picked out."

"Er, I'm afraid not."

Kasia sobered. "When does the delegation from Jalghuth arrive?"

"They're expected in the morning."

"Is…?"

His eyes sparkled. "Fra Bryce coming? Yes, his name is on the list. As the Reverend Father's new nuncio."

Kasia feigned indifference, though her pulse picked up a notch. "How does the Reverend Mother feel about that?"

"I'm not entirely sure. She Marked him herself, you know. I think she hoped he would return. But we are all loyal to the Via Sancta first, yes?" He gazed at her earnestly. "In recent years, the Curia has become more like a collection of independent city-states than a united theocracy. But it was the Praefators' intention for us to stand as one. To uphold the ideals of the *Meliora* together. Perhaps this war will have a silver lining and return us to our original altruism."

She impulsively reached out and clasped his hand. "I hope you're right, Lucas."

His cheeks flushed. "Thank you for understanding. I'll see that meals are sent to your room. The delegation from Novostopol is staying at the Palace on the opposite side of the Arx."

"No chance encounters."

He gave a mock shudder. "Can you imagine the look on the bishop's face?"

Kasia laughed. "All too well."

He let go of her hand. "I don't suppose you've learned anything new regarding the *other matter?*"

They were alone in the chapel, but Gray still lowered his voice.

"No," she admitted. "But I worry, Lucas. Especially with three pontifices gathered in one place. I can't shake the feeling that the Order has been waiting for something. It's likely this is it."

His brows drew together. "I share your concerns, of

course. But security will be very tight. All the delivery trucks are being stopped at the gates and searched."

"And the drivers, too?"

"Naturally." His face softened. "We'd never underestimate our foes, I assure you. But if the Order were still active here, wouldn't you have seen some sign by now?"

"But I have!"

"Your rooms, you mean? No char has entered in weeks. Per *your* request. Not to doubt, but could the stress be getting to you, Kasia? It is no easy task the Reverend Mother set you. She holds no blame for . . . ." He trailed off.

"My failure?" She tried to keep the bitterness from her voice. "I know. Yet it still burns me, Lucas."

He patted her shoulder. "I'm sorry, I must be getting back. There are so many things to attend to. But if the summit is successful, we will move on Bal Agnar in force. One way or another, the Order will be crushed."

She nodded and forced a smile. "I hope it goes smoothly."

"As do I." He stood. "Karolo arrives tonight. If you want to have a last beer at the commissary, now's the time."

Gray bade her farewell and strode from the chamber, purple robe sweeping the floor behind him.

———

"So we're stuck in our rooms for how long?" Natalya demanded when Kasia broke the news.

"I don't know. A couple of days, I imagine. Until the delegations leave."

"Maria Karolo," she muttered. "Why did it have to be *her*?"

"She was second in line to be elected Pontifex," Spassov pointed out, blowing a stream of smoke through the cracked window. "Makes sense."

They were in his room at the Villa of Saint Margrit, which

overlooked the clumps of trees at the far end of the plaza. Natalya claimed the afternoon light was better than *her* room, so she'd commandeered half of it for an easel and sketching supplies.

"What if they make her the next pontifex?" Natalya slashed a charcoal across a blank sheet of paper. "Then I can never go home."

"Do you want to?" Kasia asked.

She lounged on Patryk's rumpled bed, flipping through one of his romance novels.

"Of course I do! Someday, I mean. I miss everyone." Nashka glanced up. "Don't you?"

Kasia hardly thought about her old life in Novostopol. She was too consumed with the Order of the Black Sun.

"Oh yeah, sure," she said. "All the time."

"Liar." Another savage sweep of the charcoal. "Tell me one person you miss."

"Uh…"

"You don't even remember their names, do you?"

Kasia frowned, rummaging through a dusty compartment of her brain where she stashed Natalya's old lovers. "Peter!"

"I broke up with him nine months ago."

"Olga then."

"*She* broke up with *me*. When we were still teenagers."

"Really?"

Nashka bent to the paper, charcoal dusting her blonde spiral curls. "You're antisocial, Kiska."

"Now, now," Spassov said mildly.

"Ah, I'm just kidding. I meant obsessive."

"One of us has to be," Kasia retorted.

Natalya studied the drawing. "What's that supposed to mean?" she asked in a distracted tone.

"Nothing."

She smudged a line with her thumb. "Means something."

"Saints," Spassov grunted, rubbing a palm across his bald

spot. "It's been less than an hour and you're already bickering. I planned to drink my way through this quarantine in peace and quiet."

"We're not bickering," Natalya protested, attacking the drawing with a flurry of rapid motions. She unpinned it and held it up. "What do you think?"

"Looks exactly like her," Spassov said.

A monstrous version of Maria Karolo stared back at them. Her razor-angled chin-length bob framed a snarling slash of a mouth. Natalya had captured the Raven Mark on her neck with four quick strokes, the beak open in an indignant screech.

"They should present it to her when she arrives," Kasia chuckled. "An official portrait."

Nashka crumpled the drawing in a fist and tossed it to the floor. "Harpy," she muttered.

"Hey!" Patryk dove for the sketch, cigarette dangling from the corner of his mouth. "I want to keep that."

Natalya grinned as he smoothed it out and propped it on the dresser. "Read to us, Kasia," she said. "Find a dirty bit."

Kasia leafed through the pages, squinting. "It's all dirty bits."

"Not true," Patryk protested. "There's plenty of character development at the beginning."

Kasia cleared her throat. "Page four. We rolled to the floor and she led my hand to her moist grot, thrusting her chrysanthemum wildly in my general direction. My big stamen trawled the tender petals, chafing chafing chafing—"

"Ouch," Natalya remarked.

"Hush. Chafing chafing chafing—no commas—"

"That's a literary technique," Patryk explained.

"Astride into the malleable maw, panting like a lion, unfolding in her folds—"

"Oh, I like *that.*"

"The vaginal lips darting and parting like a school of tropical fish—"

"Yes!" Natalya threw her head back.

"Sight abandoned me. I whined the cry of a mole delving its burrow through the damp and welcoming earth, quakes of sweat-pleasure gripping my—"

"Give me that." Patryk snatched the book away and dug a pair of reading glasses from the pocket of his cassock. He leafed through the pages while Nasha rummaged around for a drink.

"Here's the best part," he said. "It's later, after they've both been arrested and thrown naked in a jail cell." Spassov cleaned his glasses and propped them on his nose. "Ready for pure gold?"

Natalya swigged from a pint bottle of vodka. "Amaze me."

"The mage's testicles reminded Sasha of a small monkey with supplicating paws, begging for—"

A brisk knock came at the door.

Patryk slammed the book shut and sat down on it. "Hello?"

"It's Lucas," came the muffled response.

Natalya froze with the bottle tipped heavenward. She glugged a mouthful and ran to the easel, pinning a fresh sheet of paper in place. Kasia lurched to her feet and stood at her shoulder as Spassov answered the door.

"Hope I'm not disturbing you?" Gray said in his crisp Nant accent, peering over Spassov's broad shoulder.

"Not at all," Patryk said. "We were just . . . ."

"Passing the time," Natalya said brightly. "Do come in."

Gray came inside. His gaze slid to the sketch on Patryk's dresser. "She's here," he said. "Early."

"Oh." Natalya's face fell. "So it's lockdown, then?"

"I'm afraid so." He seemed genuinely regretful. "I'm sorry. I heard laughing in the corridor—"

Patryk sat down on the book again. "Just having a lark."

"Are occasional visits allowed?" Natalya asked hopefully.

Gray hesitated. "As I told Kasia, the delegation is in another wing. Just don't tempt fate too often."

"Understood," Kasia said. "We'll nestle right down in our dark little caves."

She almost added the word *throbbing*, but caught herself.

Gray gazed at her in puzzlement. "Er, yes. That'll do."

BACK IN HER OWN ROOM, Kasia perused several books of a very different nature. They were by the authors she had glimpsed in the laboratory at Kvengard. Trismegistus and Al-Farabi. Magnus and Llull. Other names from the distant past. Most of the ancient works on alchemy had been burned by the Church, but the pontifices of Nantwich believed in preserving knowledge, whether or not they agreed with it. The archives in Nantwich were vast.

Kasia now knew a great deal about the Magnum Opus. A supposed formula for eternal life. It was hardly surprising that Balaur would seek such a thing. If he'd already achieved it, they were doomed.

But she didn't think he had.

The books were all written in an archaic, mystical style that she found hard to decipher. None were for beginners. They assumed prior knowledge on the part on the reader and omitted crucial details like the exact formulae, while still managing to be dryly technical. What exactly did a solution of "sulphur in white light" mean? Or calcination in elixir? Multiplication in virtue?

Nor did they seem to agree about what was required. Some said four stages. Other twelve, or even fourteen. They used cryptic symbols to refer to different processes, neglecting to provide any key.

But Kasia was determined to understand all she could about what manner of foe they faced. She'd spent weeks studying the books late into the night, often waking in the mornings with one cheek pressed to the fragile pages. After a while, she began to see patterns, to grasp the edges of it, though much of the philosophy remained slippery.

The Magnum Opus was not an evil undertaking in itself. It merely sought a state of enlightenment.

She traced a finger beneath a passage from Trismegistus. "Thus thou wilt possess the glory of the brightness of the whole world, and all obscurity will fly far from thee. This thing is the strong fortitude of all strength, for it overcometh every subtle thing and doth penetrate every solid substance."

That sounded very much like the ley.

"The Sun is its father," she whispered aloud, "the moon its mother. The wind hath carried it in its belly, the earth is its nurse. The father of all perfection in the whole world is here."

The children had achieved the Magnum Opus because their souls were unblemished. Their *prima materia*, the base starting point of all alchemy, could be shaped into something new. Something pure.

But Balaur was already corrupted beyond redemption. He might enter the Nigredo, the long darkness, but Kasia suspected he would become trapped there, never to emerge into the light.

She closed the book and pushed it away. Of course, she could be wrong. He must know far more than she did. But why else try it on the children first? The Magnum Opus was the most powerful—and dangerous—undertaking in alchemy. Perhaps he wished to see what it would produce before he attempted it himself.

Kasia still didn't know exactly what had happened in Jalghuth. Only that the children had driven Balaur out. Clearly, they weren't what he had expected.

It was time to try another reading. She chose four cards with her non-dominant hand and turned them over.

The Fool. The Hierophant. The Star. The Tower.

It was the fifth time she'd drawn this same cluster.

The Fool was Malach and The Hierophant was Falke. Clearly, the reading was connected to what had happened in Novostopol. It was all anyone had talked about for days. But the Star meant hope, enlightenment, courage. An end to a dark period in one's life.

Not disaster.

She examined the card. A naked child stood on a twilit shore, arms stretched to the heavens. One foot stood in the sea, the other on the beach, representing the union of earth, sky and water. The ocean of the collective unconscious meeting the solid land of the individual psyche.

Above her, a single star shone bright, surrounded by seven planets.

Kasia recalled a verse from one of the alchemical texts. *The Necessity of the Art of the Elixir* by Abu Nasr Al-Farabi.

Heaven above
Heaven below
Stars above
Stars below
All that is above
Also is below
Grasp this
And rejoice!

The Star was the twentieth trump, coming just after the Tower of Destruction, which showed stunned, wide-eyed figures plummeting from a lightning-struck spire. It ushered in a time of contemplation after catastrophic events. A return to the divine order and the larger tapestry of one's destiny.

The cluster implied that Falke and Malach were together. Was Malach behind it all somehow? And if so, why a message of hope?

Kasia didn't like to think about her biological brother. She hoped never to lay eyes on him again. Yet she couldn't help feeling curious about their parents. Falke viewed them as war criminals. *High-priority targets* was the phrase she'd gleaned from the sweven. Kasia didn't even know their names, let alone what their crimes were. Tess might have known.

But Tess was dead.

Malach was the only person who could tell her the truth about them now.

But he was her enemy. He'd Marked Alexei's brother. Ruined both of their lives.

He'd also tried to defend her from Falke. Just a little boy, but he'd thrown a rock at an armored knight, teeth bared in a snarl.

Kasia pushed the memory away.

The reading troubled her. She wished Gray would return so she could tell him about it, but she'd been forbidden to leave her chamber.

Kasia shuffled the cards and laid out a three-card spread.

The Knight of Storms, a bold adventurer who journeyed places others feared to tread. She strode down a narrow, vaguely sinister alley, umbrella in one hand, map in the other.

The Nine of Keys for secrets revealed.

And The Sun, inverted.

When a card was drawn from the deck upside-down, it had a different meaning. In this case, The Sun did not give light. It devoured light. The Black Sun.

That meant the Order.

The card had popped up here and there in spreads before. Every time, she had given the name of the client to Gray. He investigated them, but nothing ever came of it.

She bit her lip. What was she to do now?

Without the ley, her readings were muddied. If only she could use a trickle of power, the message might come clear.

Would Clavis really know if she did?

Kasia had sworn never to touch abyssal ley again. It was

too dangerous. But the blue surface layer was harmless. People used it all the time to soothe violent emotions and enhance their natural talents. Natalya, for example. She was a gifted artist, but the ley made her a genius.

Even liminal ley, the thin middle layer where the blue and red mingled, was deemed acceptable by the Church. It was the most subtle and governed the boundaries of things. The shadowy edges where land bled into sea, day into night. Beginnings and endings. Twists of fate. Doorways from one place to another.

It ran strong in Nantwich. That's why the city had two crossed keys for its emblem.

The Arx was bursting at the seams with foreign delegations, all of them channeling power through their Marks. Would Clavis notice one tiny ripple in the ocean of ley?

Kasia peeled a glove off and ran a fingertip across the Nine of Keys, letting her mind open. A line of blue fire traced the image.

She waited for the echo of boots in the corridor. The crash of a mailed fist against her door.

Open up in the name of the Pontifex!

Ten minutes passed. When nothing happened, she vented a quick breath and laid her palms across the three cards. They flickered with ley. Blue shifting to purple at the edges.

Kasia closed her eyes. She saw a Black Sun, radiating dark power. A river coursing through endless night.

And a doorway.

Her eyes opened.

A rectangle outlined in violet ley shimmered on the wall. It was no longer blank stone but a dull, cloudy silver.

Her breath caught as she stood and hesitantly reached out a hand. Her fingertips pushed straight through.

A liminal door.

In a flash, she understood. This is how the Order came into her rooms unseen.

Her skin crawled. Had they watched her as she slept?

She swept the cards into a pile, keeping the Nine of Keys in her palm. It flickered with violet ley, feeding the doorway.

"I've got you now," she whispered.

Kasia drew a slow, deep breath and stepped through.

Chapter Twenty-One

The liminal doorway parted around her like mist. Kasia found herself in a stone passage.

The Nine of Keys flickered and died. So did the doorway.

She felt a moment of worry, but ley still flowed around her feet. When she reignited the card, the doorway appeared again.

Reassured, Kasia let go of the power and took her bearings. The passage was as wide as a city street and lined with columns that rose to a coffered ceiling far above. A low, dense mist hovered above the floor, swirling around her bare feet. There was no visible source of light, yet she could see well enough.

When she spun around, she cast no shadow.

The passage extended in both directions. After a moment's hesitation, Kasia turned left and started to walk.

Every now and then, she passed an alcove containing a statue. People carved with lifelike precision, their faces kind and wise. Smaller niches held fantastical creatures. Fish with beaks and birds with the feet of hounds. They struck her as beautiful but lonely. Who had made them? And for what purpose? It must have been the Praefators. The great architects of long ago. Did every Arx have a secret world?

But the Order had access to these passageways—which meant no one was safe.

The farther she went, the stranger her surroundings became. Doors upon doors marched into the gloom. She crept through a classroom, each desk arranged at a precise distance from the next, the blackboard wiped clean and a box of chalk on the teacher's desk. The hands of a round clock on the wall had stopped at five minutes to three.

After that, a vast gymnasium with a concrete pool half filled with black water. Not a ripple stirred the surface, but she kept well away from the edge.

She glimpsed staircases that twisted at impossible angles. Furniture draped with dusty sheets. Then the waiting room of a hospital, with tattered magazines on a table and a sign forbidding smoking. She knew it was a hospital because there was another sign that said ADMITTING and painted arrows pointing to TRIAGE and SURGERY, but they both led to blank walls.

Kasia stepped through an accordion door marked *Public Telephones* and found herself in a bland, carpeted passage with numbered doors that looked exactly like the hallway of a mid-priced hotel. There was a lift at the end, with a brass arrow pointing to the lobby, and a black call button.

She didn't try to summon it. If she got in, she had a feeling she might never step out again.

She saw no one. Not a single soul. The silence and emptiness were absolute, like the instant between an inhale and exhale. She crouched down and fanned a hand, parting the thin layer of mist. She was unsurprised to find the vibrant purple of liminal power flowing beneath it.

What a peculiar place, she thought. It is nothing but moments between one thing and the next—both familiar and eerie at the same time.

She took a door labeled "Fire Exit" and was relieved to enter one of the wide stone thoroughfares again. Kasia was about to turn back and find Cardinal Gray, Maria Karolo be damned, when a symbol scratched into the wall made her stop cold.

She took her cards out and found The Emperor. A hooded man sat on a throne with ram's heads carved into the arms. *Balaur.* He held a ring of keys and a sword. And on his right hand, a Mark of nested geometrical figures. Circle, square, triangle, circle.

They were identical to the ugly gouges on the wall.

Someone had made it recently. Someone who didn't mind marring the elegant beauty of the secret city. Perhaps someone who hated it.

Another door?

Kasia pressed the Nine of Keys to the symbol, feeding it with liminal ley.

Lines of violet traced a rectangle.

Her pulse thundered in her ears.

She should turn back now. Find Gray and return with two dozen knights.

But the Order had slipped through her fingers before. And Gray would be furious that she had used liminal ley against the Reverend Mother's orders. They'd never trust her again.

"Oh, fog it," she muttered. "I'm not defenseless. I'll use my cards if I must."

The wall turned to mist. Before she could entertain second thoughts, Kasia stepped through.

Music thumped in her ribcage. She stood in a luxurious room lined with deep red velvet. It smelled like the clove cigarettes Natalya smoked when she'd had too much to drink. The heavy, dark furniture was carved with faces, all with the eyes closed. Sleeping—or dead.

A door stood against the opposite wall. Oak with a brass knob in the shape of a hand. Kasia crossed the room and pulled it open. The music rose to a deafening wall of sound. Someone gripped her arm and she let out a startled scream— though it was barely audible over the din.

She spun around. A blonde woman in a skimpy dress stood behind her, though the room had been empty just a moment ago. She wore a black lace demi-masque. Her lips moved, but Kasia couldn't hear what she was saying.

The woman tipped her head back in laughter, revealing a slender white neck. She grasped Kasia's hand and pulled her back through the door.

The music quieted. Kasia tugged her hand free, eyeing the woman warily.

"Welcome to the Lethe Club." She walked on stiletto heels to a sideboard and poured herself a drink. "Do you have an invitation? We're exclusive here."

Kasia met her gaze. "I fear I've misplaced it."

The woman drank deeply, then set the glass down. "You must wear a masque. Those are the rules."

Games.

"Can I borrow one?" she asked.

"You may have mine." The woman slid the demi-masque free and handed it to Kasia. Her face was blandly attractive. Anywhere from late twenties to a well-maintained forty.

"You are the cartomancer." Her smile was cool and knowing. "I have heard of you."

"From who?"

"Word gets around."

Kasia put the masque on. "I offer you my services."

"How generous. But we have other entertainments here."

"Such as?"

"Take a look for yourself."

Her feral gaze followed Kasia to the door. The hall beyond led to a cavernous dance floor. A hundred bodies writhed and gyrated to the pulsing strobe of black lights. Kasia skirted the press of bodies and found another hall, this one leading to a room with leather banquettes. A haze of cigar smoke hung in the air. Masked faces turned to watch as she approached a long mirrored bar. Kasia's nape prickled as she sat down on an empty stool.

The bartender placed a small crystal goblet brimming with dark red liquid before her.

"On the house," he said with a wink.

The man's head was shaved to white-blond stubble, his face hidden behind a silver masque, but something about him seemed familiar. And the accent . . . thick and guttural.

She nodded thanks but didn't touch it. He moved away to pour drinks for a party at the end of the bar.

The music was quieter here, just a distant thump. She slid a hand into her pocket and gripped the cards.

The Lethe Club. It had the surreal quality of a nightmare, but this was no dream. She felt sure she'd walked straight into the dark heart of the Order.

A man in crisp black-and-white evening attire and the masque of a fox slid onto the next stool. Dark hair swept back from a pale brow. He glanced over at her.

"First time here? I'm sure I would have remembered you."

She tamped her hatred down to smoldering embers.

"Even with this?" Kasia touched her own masque.

"Even with that." His voice was amused, with a cultured accent.

"I'm looking for friends."

She sensed a smile behind the masque. "Then you came to the right place. Do these friends have names? Perhaps I know them."

"That's the funny thing. I don't know their real names."

He signaled the bartender with a gloved finger. "How mysterious."

"But I do know a few things about them."

He tilted his head. "Go on."

"They think they're very clever."

Kasia took a tube of lipstick from her pocket. It was the last thing she had of Tess. Her reflection swam in the glass behind the bar as she carefully applied it. Kasia blotted her mouth with a cocktail napkin. "And they're a little bit afraid of me."

"Do you bite?" He glanced down at the perfect scarlet oval on the napkin.

"Sometimes I do."

He laughed. "Then they're right to be wary."

"We've been looking for each other for a while now. Every time I'm close to finding them, they vanish like smoke."

"It sounds like you're chasing specters."

"They want me to believe so. But they're real enough."

His drink arrived, two fingers of amber liquid on ice. The man raised his glass. "Well, I wish you luck."

"My friends are waiting for something. But I don't know what it is."

He took a swallow, eyes gleaming through the masque. "Do you think they're here now?"

"I'm certain of it."

"Then why don't we look for them together?"

How relaxed and confident he sounded. She wondered what he'd do if she set his masque alight.

Of course, if she drew too much ley, the whole place might go up in flames, with her inside. She hadn't touched her power in months. It might not work the way she expected. It might not work *at all*. And then they would descend on her like a pack of hungry jackals.

"I'd rather dance," she said.

That caught him by surprise. He opened his mouth, then closed it again.

"Excuse me." Kasia walked away, pulse racing.

They *were* waiting for something. She could feel it in the air. A crackle of anticipation.

No children had gone missing in Nantwich. Whatever the

Order was up to, it wasn't a repeat of what they'd done in Kvengard, thank the Saints. But they were plotting something. That was certain.

Cold eyes followed her progress across the lounge. Whispers rose, like the skitter of dry leaves. She gripped the cards in her pocket with white knuckles, fighting the urge to lash out.

But if she used abyssal ley, Clavis would know. The punishment was death for anyone who wielded red ley within the walls of Nantwich.

Would she be merciful if it was wielded in service of the Via Sancta?

The Reverend Mother was a hard-liner. Kasia didn't care to test her. And once she started she might not be able to stop. Now that she knew her own nature, she had to be vigilant not to feed the worst of it.

You can choose, Tess had told her.

It was one of the last things she'd said. Kasia understood that it wasn't a single choice, but the same one, again and again. Never to give the darkness a single inch.

It was time to get reinforcements.

The trick now would be leaving.

She merged with the sweaty whirl on the dance floor, seeking a path to the hall that led back to the entrance. Strobes flashed, freezing the dancers in postures of wild abandon. Revulsion twisted her stomach every time one of them brushed against her. The ebb and flow drew her nearer the exit, then farther away. There was no sign of the man in the fox masque.

Abyssal ley surged around her feet, fueling the frenzy. A woman raked black-painted nails down her own cheek, then laughed as her partner leaned in to lick the blood.

Kasia struggled through the humid jungle of bodies. She only saw the other dancers in dizzying flashes, but some looked . . . wrong. Arms jointing the wrong way. Teeth too long and sharp for a human mouth.

She gained the edge of the dance floor and stumbled into the corridor. It felt smaller. Tighter. Like the walls were closing around her. She'd kill the blonde woman if she had to. Anything to get out of here—

A tall figure lounged against the wall ahead. He stood in shadow, but then the strobe flashed, catching his profile.

Thick, wavy blonde hair. One bright blue eye.

Kasia drew up short, mouth dry. He turned to face her, pulling his masque off.

"Domina Novak." Lips curved in a smirk. "You look like you need some air."

Disbelief washed over her. It couldn't be.

His gaze flicked past her shoulder. Kasia glanced back.

The music still pounded, but the dancers stood perfectly still. Staring at her.

She tore a card from the deck and tossed it at his feet.

The Jack of Wolves.

Lines of bright violet light radiated outward like spokes from a wheel. She stomped on the card. Jule Danziger winced. He threw an arm across his face. Then he turned and darted through the doorway.

Kasia bolted after him. The blonde stepped into her path. Kasia balled a fist, punching her in the nose. She screeched and teetered back on her heels. Jule was disappearing into the liminal door. Kasia leapt through.

The corridor was empty.

No sound of running feet.

She swore and spun back to the liminal door. The mist was darkening. Ice touched her skin as tendrils of black ley snaked outward, creeping across the stone like ink.

Kasia backed away, hands shaking.

Jule Danziger was dead. She'd watched his body decay.

"Saints," she breathed. "Saints!"

Kasia ran. Her mind raced, but her memory didn't fail her. Left, then right, then through the hospital waiting room, the abandoned gymnasium with its swampy pool, and other echoing, empty places betwixt the known and unknown. The threshold between *what was* and *what will be.*

At last she reached a broad stone avenue, turning again at the statue of a scaled lion. Minutes later, she was back in her room.

The alchemists hadn't given chase. Why not?

Were they truly afraid of her? Or did they no longer care about secrecy? A thrill of dread ran through her. What if they were planning to attack the Arx this very night?

Kasia released the ley. The violet rectangle faded to blank stone. She strode to the door—the regular one—and threw open the bolt. She'd get Patryk and Natalya. Tell them everything. Then she'd go straight to Clavis and suffer the consequences.

Kasia turned the knob, but the door didn't budge.

She kicked the wood in renewed fury.

Someone had locked her inside.

Chapter Twenty-Two

Flurries of snow sifted down from a slate sky as the ship departed Jalghuth from the outlet of Khotang Lake. Alice refused to cross the gangplank, choosing to simply materialize on board. Alexei joined Misha at the rail as the oarsmen rowed it out into the current.

"Do you remember Patryk Spassov?" he asked.

Misha stared at the far bank of the river, where smoke rose from the chimneys of a small village. "Vaguely."

"He was my partner. He used to come to the Institute with me."

"That time is a blur. They had me on heavy meds, Alyosha."

"I only mention it because he's in Nantwich. I want you to meet him."

Misha scrubbed a hand through his beard. "A priest with the Interfectorem? Sounds awkward."

"Spassov isn't like that. He served, too. Cavalry, '67 to '69. He knows what it was like. The choices we had to make, each one worse than the last. Patryk's been a good friend to me. He tried to help when Falke locked me up."

Misha shook his head. "Falke," he muttered. "I trusted him completely." A bitter laugh. "What a fool I was."

"You were in his Praesidia ex Divina Sanguis."

Protectors of the Divine Blood. A secret order within the Church that answered only to Dmitry Falke.

"He told you about that?" Misha asked in surprise.

Alexei nodded. "He tried to recruit me himself. Gave me the whole spiel about how only the nihilim can give Marks and we need them or our faith will be destroyed."

"It's true," Mikhail said quietly.

"I don't deny that. It's Falke's methods I have a problem with."

A gull flapped past, white wings against a white sky. Alexei could smell the sea on the wind. They weren't far from the channel.

"I would have done anything for him," Misha said. "When he proposed that I take Malach's Mark—"

Alexei gripped his arm. "Wait. That was Falke's idea? He told me you volunteered!"

"At his urging, yes. What does it matter now?"

"It matters to me."

His brother looked over. "I wouldn't take it back."

Alexei knew he meant the Nightmark. "How can you say that?"

"I never wanted you to join the knights."

"Well, it's what I wanted."

"Why? You were happy practicing law. I always envied you."

"You envied *me?*"

"Of course I did. Top of your class. Carrying on the family tradition. I wish mamushka could have seen you graduate."

Alexei realized that his brother was now the same age their mother had been when she died. Thirty-five.

"She was proud of you, too," he said.

A crooked smile. "She thought I was weird."

"She did not!"

"Come on, I *was* weird." He laughed softly. "I thought joining the Church would make me better. Make me something other than myself. But you know what I discovered?" The tone was light, but his blue eyes had a hard gleam. "I'm a seriously fucked up human being, Alyosha. And there's not much the sutras can do to fix that."

Even as a boy, Mikhail had their father's supreme confidence. He'd never been afraid of anything. Was it the Nightmark talking now? Or had he always felt this way? Alexei had the sudden unsettling feeling that the person he thought he knew best in the world might be someone else entirely.

"That's bullshit," he muttered. "Would you please stop?"

"All I'm saying is that I should have known it, and Falke should definitely have known it. But at the time, I believed I was incorruptible. That I'd convince Malach to spill all his secrets." A hand stole to his chest. "That this would be another Mark like all the rest. But it didn't quite work out that way."

"What was the bargain with Malach?"

"Yes." He gave a faint smile. "There's always a quid pro quo, isn't there?"

Misha fell silent. They reached deeper water. Alexei felt the vibration through the soles of his boots as the steamer's engines rumbled to life. The great screws began to churn. The ship picked up speed, plowing through the river mouth and turning south.

You did it for me, he thought. Blood for blood. That's what Falke said. The real reason Misha took the Mark was so the nihilim wouldn't kill his brother. Yet he didn't say any of that aloud.

"There's something I have to tell you," he said. "About Kasia Novak."

He'd already told Misha about the flight from Kvengard

after he took the Reborn on the ship. Their arrival in Nantwich. Mikhail had met Kasia once before, in Feizah's chamber the night he went to the Arx. But he didn't know everything.

"I'm in love with her," Alexei said.

Misha blinked in surprise. "Okay. Where is she now?"

"Nantwich." He swallowed. "There's more. It's bad."

His brother's smile faded. "How bad?"

"Pretty fucking bad," Alexei said.

BY AFTERNOON, the ramparts of the Arx appeared atop a white cliff. They sailed into Nantwich harbor and dropped anchor, waiting for the arrival of a pilot boat to guide them into the slip. Lezarius waited on the deck with his honor guard.

"It's still strange not to see the Wards," he said, gazing up at the ramparts of the Arx.

"They weren't needed for more than seven hundred years," Mikhail replied. "We'll manage."

He'd donned armor for their arrival, polished to a high gleam. His beard was neatly trimmed, though he'd refused to cut his hair, twisting it into a topknot in Kindu fashion.

"Yes, of course. It will be good to see Luk. The last time was, oh . . . years ago now. He was always a friend to Jalghuth."

The weather was warmer in the south, though it held an edge of autumn. The leaves were starting to turn, dotting the ancient city with splashes of yellow and red. Alexei felt more at peace than he had in a long while. Mikhail had listened to Alexei's long, convoluted explanation of Kasia's birth with little reaction other than to agree that Falke had done the right thing in sparing her life. If anything, he seemed surprised Alexei hadn't told him before.

"She has nothing to do with it," he'd said.

"I know."

"I am happy for you both, brother. I hope you'll let me meet her again." His cheeks flushed a little. "Under better circumstances."

And that was it. The moment he'd been dreading was a total anticlimax.

A pilot boat flying the Crossed Keys flag drew up alongside and briefly conferred with the captain. Within minutes, they were snug against a long pier, the crew tossing mooring ropes to waiting dockhands.

A motorcade of black cars snaked down from the Arx. Alexei disembarked with his bag, Alice trotting at his heels. Lezarius and his honor guard of twenty knights came next. They flanked him as the driver of the first car got out and opened the rear door. A young woman with short, dark curls, wearing a chainmail byrnie and white cloak, stepped lightly from the automobile and approached.

"Reverend Father," she said.

To Alexei's astonishment, Clavis bent a knee and kissed Lezarius's ring.

"I am honored to meet you at last," she said, rising to her feet. "These are dark days. Thank you for agreeing to come. You have my personal pledge that the Arx is secure."

Lezarius looked nonplussed. "Reverend Mother," he said. "It's been a long time since I came to Nantwich. It is a fair city. Perhaps one day I can host you at Jalghuth."

She grinned. "I will pack my warmest furs."

"You already know my Nuncio," Lezarius said, gesturing for Alexei to join them.

"Nuncio?" she repeated. "Does he wear the Blue Flame now?"

"My loyalty remains to the Curia," Alexei said. "But I will advise the Reverend Father Lezarius in these talks."

She looked irritated, but gave a nod. "Luk is already here. Bishop Karolo arrived this morning."

"So I am the last," Lezarius said with a frown.

"And you all came early," Clavis said wryly. "Then we need not delay. Unless you are weary from the journey?"

"Not in the least," Lezarius said. "The sooner the better."

"Would you ride to the Arx with me, Reverend Father?"

Mikhail's eyes narrowed. He bowed his head to Clavis just enough to convey respect. "As Captain of the Reverend Father's honor guard, I hope you will permit me to join you."

"I have no objection." Clavis looked at him closely, then at Alexei. "Are you . . . ?"

"They are brothers," Lezarius said. "My closest aides."

"Ah." It was Clavis's turn to look disconcerted. "I didn't know Fra Bryce had a brother, let alone that he was in Jalghuth. He neglected to share that information when last we spoke."

So she wasn't aware of Falke's various plots, Alexei thought, nor of his secret order. It made him trust the young pontifex more.

"Well, now you know," Lezarius said cheerfully. "Shall we?"

They piled into the cars and bounced through a series of narrow cobblestoned streets, past working warehouses and into a bohemian district of cafes and galleries that occupied large buildings Alexei guessed had once been part of the docks. Graffiti-covered brick facades kept the gritty feel of the waterfront, but the young people sipping coffee and signs advertising loft-style flats signaled a shift toward gentrification.

Of all the cities he'd seen so far, Nantwich was most like Novostopol. A blend of old and new, eternally reinventing itself. He felt a pang of homesickness.

"How long since we've had a cheese blini?" he asked Alice, who was drooling all over the leather seats. Her tail thumped at the word *blini*.

They drove through the thick outer wall and into the bailey. Alice knew where the kennels were and vanished before the car had even stopped, apparently eager to visit her old friends. Half the knights from Jalghuth went off to quarters in the barracks. The other half, including Alexei and Mikhail, followed Clavis and Lezarius up the broad steps to the Pontifex's Palace. Normally, such a visit would be the occasion for great fanfare, but the mood at the Arx was subdued. Clavis herself escorted them to their rooms in the west wing. She promised to send refreshments and inform the others of their arrival.

Once she was gone, Mikhail insisted on searching Lezarius's suite before he was permitted to enter. Two knights stood in the hall, guarding the pontifex, while Misha and the others opened chests and closets, drew the curtains and locked the windows, shook out the bedding, and poked into every crevice.

"Is this really necessary?" Lezarius asked.

"Yes," Misha replied. He picked up a table lamp and examined the base, then set it down.

"Do you think she installed listening devices?" Alexei asked in a low voice.

"You never know." He turned to one of his women. "Check the toilet tank. And the ventilator."

She nodded and trotted into the bathroom. Alexei heard her banging around.

"Saints," Lezarius muttered.

"Clear," she called out a minute later.

"Clear," the others echoed.

Misha was kneeling by the bed, running his hands beneath.

"I'm going to my room," Alexei said.

It was right next door, two adjoining rooms overlooking the plaza. He unpacked his bag, stowing *Der Cherubinischer Wandersmann* under the mattress. Mikhail was paranoid, but maybe he was right to be. And it wasn't the sort of book one left lying out for all to see. He washed his face and hands and returned to Lezarius's chambers.

A light meal had been brought. Alexei reviewed his notes while he ate, listening with half an ear as Misha and Lezarius set up a chess board and launched into a cutthroat game. When a knock came at the door, he was surprised to find two hours had passed.

It was Cardinal Gray, Clavis's aide.

"Reverend Father," he said with a solemn bow, pushing his spectacles up on his nose. "And Fra Bryce! How good to see you again." He turned to Misha. "You must be Captain Bryce?"

"I am. Will I be permitted to wait outside the council chamber?"

"Of course." A dry smile. "You will not be alone. Bishop Karolo brought a delegation from the Order of Saint Marcius. And the Kvens, naturally."

"Then let us join them," Lezarius said. He grimaced at the board. "You have saved me from yet another defeat, Cardinal Gray."

They followed the Cardinal to a room on the second floor of the palace. To Alexei's irritation, they were the last to arrive. A deliberate slight? If so, he would extract payback one way or another. He paused in the doorway as the assembled dignitaries rose from their places at a large round table.

Luk looked even more gaunt than the last time Alexei saw him. Bishop Morvana Zeigler stood next to him. Her green eyes were cool, but she gave them both a polite nod. Luk smiled at Lezarius, ignoring Alexei completely.

Maria Karolo and an aide occupied the side nearest the window. Her severe bob swayed as she turned to regard them.

Clavis waited until Lezarius sat down, with Alexei to his left. Gray closed the door and joined her.

"Thank you all for coming," she said. "I will open this

council with what I know, and then you may add your own intelligence. First, I may as well state the obvious. The Void is broken." Her gaze fell on Lezarius. "But we are not here to cast blame. The fault is Balaur's. We are all grateful that your health has been restored. The question facing us now is how to contain him. Bishop Karolo?"

"We still hold Bal Kirith," Karolo said. "But we sustained massive casualties in the last attempt to take Bal Agnar. Falke deemed it seemed unwise to mount any further offensives."

"A stalemate," Luk said.

Clavis nodded. "I sent a thousand knights into the field, but desertion remains a problem."

"They're going over to the mages?" Lezarius asked.

"Some. The abyssal ley burns like wildfire around Bal Agnar. It pollutes their minds. If not for that, our superior numbers would have routed the mages long ago."

"What about the Order of the Black Sun?" Alexei put in. "We cannot forget the threat from within."

"Those who were found in Kvengard were arrested," Luk said.

He eyed Morvana, who nodded confirmation. "There were not many left alive," she said. "We have them under lock and key."

"I am appalled at what they did," Luk said, his thin brows drawing down. "But Lezarius says the children are safe in Jalghuth now."

"They are in my custody," Lezarius said carefully.

"What about the other cities?" Alexei asked.

"The Order is not here," Clavis said firmly. "I've conducted a thorough investigation. They have no reason to hide in the shadows anymore. I expect those who sympathized with Balaur have left to join him in Bal Agnar."

"And Novostopol?"

Maria Karolo hesitated. "It's possible they staged the attack," she conceded, "but an investigation will have to wait until we've repaired the damage." She looked shaken at the memory. "I was asleep when it happened. I woke to explosions on all sides. I feared we were being shelled. It is only by the grace of the ley that I managed to escape. But the Reverend Father Dmitry . . . ." She paused to wipe an eye, though they both looked perfectly dry to Alexei. "Well, he has not yet been found, but he was in his chamber when the ceiling came down. Rescue workers are still sifting through the rubble."

Of all of them, only Clavis appeared truly distressed at Falke's death.

"You have our deepest sympathies," she said, her voice hoarse.

The sentiments were echoed by the others.

"I have something important to add," Lezarius said. "The children say it was not abyssal ley that caused the starfall, yet it *was* guided by someone's hand. They could not tell me more than that."

Clavis frowned. Gray leaned over and whispered in her ear.

"You speak of these children," she said. "Who . . . *what* are they?"

A reasonable question, Alexei thought. He wished he knew himself. They saw themselves as guardians of the Lance, the great prism that divided a powerful source of ley into three parts, but he knew Lezarius intended to keep that a secret for now.

"They call themselves the Reborn," Lezarius said. "They have a deep connection to the ley. And they don't lie. They are not capable of it."

There was silence for a moment.

"Well, let us take that as a piece of good news," Clavis said at last. "If it had been Balaur or those who serve him, we can be sure they would have used abyssal ley." Her finger tapped the table. "I dislike mysteries, especially at a time like this, but perhaps we will solve it in time."

She drew a breath, looking at each of them in turn. "Now to the heart of the matter. Do we all agree that it is necessary to commit violence in the name of saving everything that we believe in? I am ready to deploy my forces for an over-whelming assault on Bal Agnar."

Maria Karolo nodded. "We already have two thousand knights in Bal Kirith. Half will march north."

"And we will march south to meet them," Lezarius said. "I spent nearly thirty years trying to reach Balaur. To find some spark of reason. It does not exist. Then I was betrayed, inverted, hidden away at the Batavia Institute while he ruled in my place. If you had seen the state of Jalghuth when I returned, you would understand that there is no choice. It would be a greater crime to leave him unchecked."

All eyes swiveled to Luk.

The Pontifex of Kvengard studied the gold ring on his finger. "The thought of war turns my stomach," he said slowly. "I will not pretend otherwise. How can we uphold the ideals of nonviolence through violent means?"

Clavis stared at him in silence. Karolo's lips tightened. Without Kvengard, their chances of victory would be fifty-fifty at best. Luk had to know it.

"It is a dilemma," Luk continued, "and one that must be taken seriously."

Alexei looked at Morvana. Her expression was bland, giving nothing away, but her hands were clasped so tightly, the knuckles had gone white. How would she have advised her pontifex? She was a staunch opponent of force, Alexei knew, but she had presumably seen the alchemical laboratory. She knew what their foes were capable of.

He's showboating, Alexei thought. Making us sweat a little, but he's going to agree. Saints, let him agree—

"I am not blind," Luk said. "I fear what will become of us either way." He looked at Lezarius. "You tried to do right. To exemplify the ideals of the Via Sancta. But the evil you faced was stronger. Now it would destroy us all. So Kvengard will stand with you. Four thousand knights and all the Markhounds in the kennels." A wry smile. "They, at least, cannot be corrupted. They will fight the mages to the death."

There was a collective exhalation of relief.

"However," he raised a gloved finger, "you must agree to take prisoners whenever possible. Not the mages, but our own brothers and sisters who have been seduced by the abyssal ley. Perhaps those who succumbed can be rehabilitated and brought back into the fold. I am certain the ley will cleanse itself in time, once Balaur is eliminated."

Murmurs of agreement went around the table. No one liked the thought of massacring their own knights.

Cardinal Gray began scribbling on a piece of parchment as they hashed out the details. Alexei reviewed each clause carefully, suggesting minor amendments here and there. But it was a remarkably simple document with none of the jockeying for advantage he'd expected. It gave him hope that they all genuinely wanted peace.

When it was done, Gray rewrote the treaty in an elegant hand and passed it around the table. A single page, pledging unity, with all future decisions to be taken collectively. The three Pontifices signed it and pressed their rings into hot wax, marking it with their seals. Since Novostopol's ring was lost with Falke, Bishop Maria Karolo used her own.

"I will have copies made and distributed," Clavis said. "We will formally announce the treaty at the reception tonight."

They were gathering their papers when a Markhawk flew through the window, landing hard on the table. Blood speckled its breast. Luk gently took the creature in his hands, prising loose the message around its foot. His face darkened as he read it.

"It comes from the knights at the Fort of Saint Ludolf," he said. "The Fort of Saint Agnes is besieged."

"What?" Clavis exclaimed.

"They are holding for now, but they won't last long. My knights tried to fight through and free them. Rademacher lost many men and was forced to retreat."

He handed Clavis the message. She studied the tiny script.

"Two hundred nihilim. How did they slip past our scouts?" Clavis muttered. Her fist tightened, crushing the paper into a ball. "Saint Agnes is only a few hours' ride from the city. We cannot allow them to establish a foothold. I will take to the field myself at dawn."

Luk frowned. "Do you think that's wise, Reverend Mother? Perhaps the mages mean to lure you out from the walls."

"Then they shall get their wish," she said angrily.

"I can send some of the Ravens with you, Reverend Mother," Karolo offered.

Clavis nodded. "We'll hit them hard." She looked around the table. "If anything, this confirms what I expected. Balaur has no intention of remaining at Bal Agnar. He means to march. If it is a test of our resolve, let us show him that he has no chance of extending his reach through the Morho."

The young Pontifex looked eager to ride out, but Alexei felt uneasy as she strode from the chamber, Gray hurrying behind her with the treaty in hand, the ink barely dry.

"Could Balaur have known about this council?" Luk wondered. "The timing could not be worse. There is still much to discuss."

"I think we must assume he does," Lezarius replied.

Luk stroked the bloodied hawk. "I will tend to her," he said, rising to his feet. "With care, she will live." He turned to Morvana. "Send a message to Rademacher that the Reverend Mother Clavis will join them with reinforcements. He is to hold his position."

"Of course, Reverend Father," she murmured.

Maria Karolo gave them all a cursory nod and swept from the chamber with her aide.

"I will walk with you, Luk," Lezarius said with a sigh. "Would that we were reunited for a happier occasion, but it is still wonderful to see you."

"And you, Lezarius." He smiled. "I am relieved to find you well again."

Alexei followed them out, pulling Misha aside as the knights from Jalghuth trailed the two pontifices down the corridor.

"Clavis looked grim," Mikhail said.

Alexei showed him a copy of the treaty. "It was a success, but the mages are besieging Saint Agnes. It's already begun, brother. I mean to find Patryk Spassov and Kasia Novak. I'll look for you later."

Mikhail nodded. "Stay on guard," he whispered. "Something doesn't feel right here."

Before Alexei could ask what he meant, Misha was jogging to catch up with Lezarius's honor guard. He'd taken half a step when a hand fell on his arm. She must have been lurking around the corner.

"Fra Bryce."

He looked into a pair of chilly green eyes, his heart sinking. "Bishop Zeigler."

"You owe me an explanation," she said.

"I know I do." Alexei glanced down the hall. "Can it wait?"

"No," she replied. "It can't. I saved your life. The least you can do is speak with me."

He'd known this was coming. "I suppose that's fair," he muttered. The corridor bustled with aides and secretaries. "Where do you want to talk?"

"Outside," she replied sharply.

He followed Morvana down the columned loggia and

through a side door from the palace. They set off along one of the lightly wooded pathways that wound through the Arx.

"Why did you leave without any word?" she asked tightly.

"Because I was protecting someone." He glanced at her. "I assume you found the bodies at the Danziger estate?"

"Bodies?"

"Jule and Hanne Danziger."

"We found nothing. I thought they'd fled."

"What about the servants?"

"Gone." She caught his eye, troubled. "What happened?"

He felt suddenly weary of the constant, endless suspicion. The Kvens had just signed a treaty of unity. If he believed in that, as he claimed, he had to give her the benefit of the doubt.

"The Danzigers were leaders of the Order," he said. "After I left you, I returned to the house. There were three women staying with them. And a priest. Friends of mine from Novostopol. The Danzigers were holding them hostage."

"Why?"

"It's not my secret to tell, Your Grace. But they had nothing to do with the Order. In fact, they were being hunted themselves. It's why they left Novostopol."

She looked annoyed, but nodded for him to continue.

"Did you see the half-human creatures in the laboratory?"

A grim nod. "*Ja.*"

"Jule Danziger was like that. A monster. He killed his aunt. Then he was killed in turn by one of the women."

"I still don't understand why you could not simply tell me this!"

"I'm sorry." He avoided her eyes. "But I didn't know how far the conspiracy went."

She stopped walking. "You thought I might be involved?"

Alexei nodded.

Morvana stared at him. "I am no follower of Balaur."

"I believe you," he said quickly. "How is Sofie Arnault?"

"Staying with the vestals. They dote on her, poor girl. We arrested the parents who were not at the laboratory. They admitted everything, including the name of the last child they planned to take." A grudging nod. "So you saved more than one, Bryce."

They walked in silence for a minute, passing the bronze Fountain of the Five Virtues. Coins winked from the shallow depths. Alexei wondered if he should toss one in for luck.

"Do you approve?" he asked. "Of Luk's decision?"

"After what I found in that laboratory? Yes." Morvana sighed. "I never expected to see this day. Open war again! But as he said, there is no choice."

Alexei waited for a pair of priests to pass them on the path. "I've wondered about something. Why didn't you send the hounds after me?"

She cast him a level look. "Hounds? I had other things to worry about, Bryce. You were a minor annoyance at that point."

"But you sent knights into the Morho."

"No, I did not."

"I saw them ride past hours after I left." He studied her face. As always, Morvana was hard to read. "Kommandant Rademacher tried to stop us on the road to Nantwich."

"Those were not my orders. I was busy rounding up the alchemists. We put their lair to the torch, but not before a thorough search. It took days. "

"So who did send them?"

She frowned. "I will ask the Reverend Father. Good day, Nuncio."

They'd reached a juncture in the pathway. Morvana gave him a neutral nod and strode off, long legs devouring the distance back to the palace. Alexei watched her go.

Well, he thought, that could have gone worse.

But he kept flashing back to the knights thundering past on Marksteeds, mere hours after they'd left Kvengard. Was

Morvana lying? She would have been well within her rights to send them. Why bother denying it?

It all circled back to his initial suspicion that someone else at the Arx was involved.

He shook his head and set off in search of anyone who could tell him where to find Kasia.

Chapter Twenty-Three

She pounded at the door for an hour straight. No one came.

Now Kasia regretted asking for a windowless chamber. But after her encounter with the winged monsters at the ruins, she'd felt safer that way. No one could creep inside while she slept.

At length, she used the Nine of Keys to open the liminal door again and prowled the empty stone corridors, searching for another way out. One that might take her into a different part of the Arx.

She found none.

Only a never-ending series of wide avenues, some with dry fountains at the intersections, others with vast plazas that held benches and statues and planters with arid dirt, as though flowers once bloomed there.

Stranger places, too. A lobby with patches of black mold growing on the wallpaper and an escalator so long it vanished into the dimness far above her head.

Even with her prodigious memory, Kasia was wary of exploring too deep into the secret city. Who knew how far it went? And what might be waiting there?

Yet she hoped she did encounter Jule Danziger again.

He'd caught her off guard, but she would be ready next time.

"And then I'll make sure you're properly dead," she muttered.

Exhaustion finally overtook her. She returned to her bedchamber and shook out the sheets, making sure there were no hidden stones. Then she curled to one side and sank into sleep.

———

THE GARDEN WAS sun-drenched at first, drowsy and sweet with the smell of new grass. She patrolled the flowerbeds with a pair of shears, pruning away any signs of rot. There seemed to be more than usual. A blight that turned the petals a sickly brown. It couldn't be allowed to spread.

Kasia snipped away every hint of the disease with ruthless efficiency. She filled a wheelbarrow with the offending stems and pushed it to a distant corner of the garden where the brambles grew thick. She threw everything into a mossy well. Then she wrestled a large stone over the edge to weigh the pile down. Kasia leaned over the edge, listening for a splash, but heard nothing.

The well was very deep.

By the time she finished, clouds darkened the sky. She brushed dirt from her hands and walked to one of her favorite places. A gazebo overlooking the pond. Kasia settled herself on the steps, watching a long-legged white bird hunt frogs in the marshy edges.

Rain pattered down, forming overlapping circles on the still water. It thickened to a downpour. She retreated beneath the roof and sat on a bench, listening to the steady drip. Rain would be good for the plants.

She wore a sleeveless sundress patterned in yellow flowers. It was soft, worn cotton and had large pockets to keep treasures in. She fished out the day's discoveries and set them on the bench. A smooth, oval stone with a line of white quartz. The feather from a barred owl. Two acorns. Half of a speckled blue shell from a finch's nest. Kasia stuck the acorns between her big and second toes. They fit perfectly.

A rustle of movement made her turn. A bent figure hobbled down one of the paths, aiming for her sanctuary. He leaned heavily on a staff. A hood concealed his face, but he walked with the stiff gait of an old man.

When he drew near, he threw the hood back, squinting at her through the rain.

"May I share your shelter?"

The voice was at odds with his appearance. Strong and commanding.

"You again," she said with a scowl.

He peered up at her through the hood. "I won't stay long. But it's raining very hard and my feet are weary."

Kasia studied him. His face was gaunt, the eyes shadowed with pain. She felt a stab of pity.

"Until it stops."

He smiled. "Thank you."

She swept up her treasures and let him share the bench.

"Ah, that is much better," he said. "How does your hunt go?"

He spoke as if they were continuing a conversation, though she couldn't recall it.

"Hunt?"

"For your friends."

Kasia blinked. "I found them. At a place called . . . ." She searched for the name, but it eluded her.

He laughed as if at some private joke. "The Lethe Club."

"Yes! That was it." She frowned. "There was loud music. I didn't like it."

"Do you know why they call it that?"

She shook her head.

"The Lethe is a river in the underworld. All who drink its waters experience total forgetfulness." He chuckled. "Some prefer oblivion to reality."

"But *I* remember."

"Because you are different."

A warning buzzed in her mind. "What is your name?"

"I never told you."

She rounded on him. "It is Balaur!"

He gazed out at the pond. "Very good. You are learning."

Kasia leapt to her feet. "What do you want of me?"

"Only to talk." He shrugged. "I am lonely."

"Go talk to someone else!"

His brow furrowed. "Why such animosity? I have never done you wrong."

"You murdered children!"

"I gave them eternal life."

She shook her head. "I saw them. You stole their innocence—"

"I restored it! They have been purified by the ley. Can you say they are not happy now? Never to experience sickness or hunger? To be one with the mystical force that flows on this planet. How can such a transformation be evil?" A gentle smile. "There are wonders you and I will never understand, but we needn't fear them."

"You twist everything."

He settled the staff between his knees. "Well, I promise you, I will not trouble them again. And I have no plans to interfere with any others. The Magnum Opus was not what I expected. Ah, well. We learn the greatest lessons from our failures, do we not?"

"I don't believe you."

"Believe what you wish." He rubbed the stumps of his fingers. "But I have helped you, Katarzynka."

"My name is Kasia."

"Whatever you prefer, it makes no difference to me." He

cocked his head. "Do you think you stumbled over that liminal door on your own?"

She crossed her arms.

"You don't remember our last discussion. I told you all about the undercity."

"More lies."

Yet a worm of doubt burrowed into her chest. She should be in complete command here, but he came and went as he chose. And she never remembered who he was until it was too late and he had tricked her into speaking with him.

"I told you other things, too," he said. "You are in danger, Kasia."

"From you!"

"Never from me," he said seriously. "I value you. Not for who I want you to be, but for who you *are*. You will say I do not know you, and that is true. But I know enough to see that you are too trusting. How did your friend know to paint that symbol on the card, hmmm? Why did she put it there unless she already knew about the Lethe Club?"

Kasia shook her head firmly. "No."

"How certain are you of Natalya Anderle? It would not be the first time someone close to you lied—"

"Don't you dare speak of Tessaria Foy to me!"

He recoiled at the fury in her voice. "Never mind. I understand the complexity of your feelings. Do you know, I never wanted to join the Church? But I was given no choice. My father was a cardinal. A severe man. He didn't beat me. That would violate their precious *Meliora*. But he insisted on strict propriety in all things.

"Even the slightest moral failing was an excuse for lengthy chastisement. Imagine how I felt when I discovered that I was the product of an illicit affair. With an Unmarked char." His lips pursed in distaste. "My mother was barren. She tolerated the affair and raised me as her own."

Kasia stared at him. A ruse to gain her sympathy? Yet his voice had the ring of truth.

"What happened to the char?"

"She was sent away. I don't know where. When I confronted my father, he forbade me to speak of it."

"How did you find out?"

"When I was twelve, I gained the ability to walk in the dreams of others. At first, I only spied on them for my own amusement. Truly, you would not believe what the most pious people get up to in dreams! But then I began to make mischief as boys will do. It came to the attention of the Pontifex of Bal Agnar. She summoned me before her. It is not a normal ability, you see. My father had concealed the truth of my birth even from her, but under duress, he confessed all. My views changed radically in that moment. I realized that he was nothing but a vile hypocrite.

"Yet who was punished?" A snort. "Not my father. The pontifex set me a penance caring for the dying. Bathing their putrid flesh. Spooning mush into trembling, toothless mouths." He shook his head in disgust. "She said it would teach me compassion. Well, I did learn a valuable lesson. This mortal coil is a prison, Kasia, with bars of flesh and bone in which the soul is left to bear witness to its own inevitable decay. Marks cannot save us from it. But alchemy! It promises another path. That was when I began to explore the forbidden texts. And to continue my dream-walking in greater secrecy.

Balaur sighed. "I am a half-blood, Kasia. That is my deepest shame. And greatest gift."

Kasia stared down at the fragments of blue shell at her feet. Her fingers had torn the pretty, fragile thing to pieces. "Why are you telling me all this?"

He gazed at her frankly. "Because you will not remember. And it unburdens me to speak of it with someone." His eyes sharpened. "There is another half-blood in the world. Newly arrived. I've seen the signs. We are very strong. Each with a unique ability to wield the ley. I would find this child."

"You just said you wouldn't hurt any more children!"

"Then help me, Kasia. There is another way." He waved his hand. "Look at these and tell me what they mean."

Seven keys floated in the air, each of a different size and shape. Silver and gold, bronze and tin. Mercury, iron and copper.

Beyond them, a gate with seven keyholes.

And beyond that a golden city, limned in fire by the rising sun—

"What do you see?" he demanded. "Where can I find them?"

Kasia waved her hand. The images vanished.

"I saw nothing," she said. "And I wouldn't tell you if I had."

His jaw knotted. "Why not?"

"Because you are evil."

"That is a relative concept. Is it evil to sever the hands of those who defy Church doctrine? Is it evil to shell an entire city to punish unbelievers?" His gaze swept her bare arms. "To test children for so-called deviancy and condemn those who fail to the margins of society before they've committed a single wrongful act?"

The last struck a nerve—as he'd intended—but she kept her voice calm. "You will not use me to further your own ambitions. So you might as well leave."

Anger flashed across his face. Then it smoothed out again. "What would *you* do with great power, Kasia? I could give that to you. The elixir of everlasting life—"

She laughed. "Is that what you've promised your follow-ers? The Magnum Opus failed, so now you will find a magical elixir! You chase illusions, Balaur."

"It is called the Amrita, silly girl. Sometimes the Aab-i-Hayat. And it exists! You will see—"

Kasia strode up to him. "Goodbye," she said.

Red ley coiled around his legs, binding him to the bench. "We have been down this path before. Many times. You cannot banish me." A smug smile. "I am the master and you are the pupil. Not even that. A mere fledgling—"

"No," she said icily. "I am the High Priestess!"

She seized his cloak. Balaur's eyes widened, the smile faltering, as she lifted him up and tossed him into the pond. The body had no substance. It vanished before it hit the water.

"I will not forget this time," Kasia vowed, fists clenching at her sides. "I will remember you. And I will remember how to make you go away!"

But the encounter was already slipping from her mind like grains of sand through splayed fingers.

Kasia growled in frustration. He had said things, shown her things, that were important. She gripped her skull as if she could somehow hold the knowledge inside by sheer force of will.

"*No!* I must remember! I must remember! I must—"

KASIA SAT WITH A GASP.

Sweat slicked her brow. The sheets lay on the floor. She must have kicked them off.

How long had she slept?

Thirst burned her throat. She staggered to the tiny bathroom and drank straight from the faucet. Then she tried the door from her chamber.

Still locked.

Kasia pressed her ear to the heavy oak.

Silence.

Gray had promised to send a char with food. But surely they would have come by now?

Her scalp prickled with sudden anxiety. What if everyone was already dead? What if the Order had overrun the Arx while she dozed and—

Stop it, she scolded herself. Don't think that way. There are hundreds of knights in the citadel. Thousands!

Yet she couldn't just sit there waiting for help to arrive.

There *was* a way out.

She would try it again.

Kasia went back to the bathroom and splashed water on her face. Then she dug out Tess's lipstick and painted her mouth, regarding her reflection in the mirror above the sink. She looked ghoulish with her tangle of black hair and dark-circled eyes.

"I *am* a ghoul," she whispered, baring her teeth. "A wraith."

Did Tess tell herself the same thing when she worked with the underground resistance in Bal Agnar? She must have seen horrors. Must have known they could come for her at any time of the day or night. The strength it would take not to run . . . . But Tessaria's faith kept her going.

Hypocrites. All of them.

Kasia frowned. The thought had come unbidden. It felt strange. Not her own.

She twisted the lipstick shut and tucked it in her pocket.

What would Tess do?

The answer was simple.

She would go back to the Lethe Club and finish that bastard.

Chapter Twenty-Four

With so much going on, Alexei expected Cardinal Gray to be with one of the delegations. But he wasn't with Clavis, nor was he in his office. Alexei fetched Alice from the kennels and they prowled through the grounds together. It took nearly two hours of searching, but Alexei finally found him in the basilica, kneeling before the altar. He waited for a moment, then sank down to join Gray in meditation, head bowed. He tried to still his mind, silently reciting the first sutra of the *Meliora*.

Nonviolence is one of the most consistent and reasonable doctrines ever taught to humanity. She who aggressively injures another fosters hatred, the root of all evil . . . .

"Fra Bryce," Gray whispered. "Er, I mean Nuncio. Do you need something?"

Alexei turned to find Clavis's aide staring at him.

"Yes. Where's Kasia?"

Gray looked awkward. "We thought it best if your friends stayed out of sight."

"Because of Karolo." The realization came as a relief.

He'd been worried when he saw no sign of any of them, but at least it wasn't because they were avoiding him.

"Yes," Gray said. "Happily, the talks were brief. I don't expect the delegation from Novostopol to remain for much longer now."

Wings fluttered overhead in the dim recesses of the vaulted ceiling.

"So where is she?"

Gray glanced around. A few other people knelt on the low benches, but none close by. "I suppose it's all right if you pay a visit now. The treaty has been signed." He pushed to his feet, wincing as his knees popped. "There are a million things to attend to. But it seemed right to take a moment in contemplation. Remind myself that there is always hope for a better future."

"I wasn't sure Luk would come on board," Alexei said.

"None of us were." He laughed. "But I think his instincts for self-preservation finally kicked in."

"And the Reverend Mother—"

"Has never lost a skirmish," Gray said. "She will return to us triumphant."

"Of course," Alexei said, though it did seem like a mighty coincidence.

If Clavis had a flaw, it was hubris—and a love of battle.

Yet all thoughts of strategy faded from his mind as they walked to the Villa of Saint Margrit. It was on the far side of the Arx, well away from the Pontifex's Palace. Alice had waited outside the basilica. Now she trotted at his heels, nearly invisible in the darkness. The hour was late, but Alexei couldn't wait until morning to see Kasia. His heart beat faster as they climbed the stairs to the second floor. If she was still angry, he would beg her forgiveness. Whatever it took—

"That's odd," Gray said, pausing in front of a door at the end of the hall.

Alexei realized that a bolt had been locked from the outside. It looked newly installed. His pulse turned instantly to a triphammer. He drew it and threw the door wide, fearing the worst.

The room was empty.

"Why the hell was she locked inside?" Alexei demanded.

"I have no idea." Gray had gone pasty. "She didn't object to keeping out of sight, but she wasn't a prisoner. You must believe me!"

Alexei moved into the room. Books on alchemy were piled everywhere, but there was no sign of her cards. He could still smell a trace of perfume in the air.

"She would have fought back," he muttered.

Alice sniffed around, but she didn't react as she would have if an alchemist had been inside. It was puzzling.

"It's my fault. She warned me," Gray said anxiously. "She kept insisting the Order was here, but I doubted her—"

Alice gave a sudden bark. She was staring at a blank section of wall. Alexei hurried over and examined it more closely.

"What is it, little sister?" he asked.

Alice barked again, standing on her hind legs to press her paws against the stone.

"Oh dear," Gray muttered.

Alexei rounded on him. "What?"

The cardinal took his glasses off, cleaning them nervously on his sleeve. "The Arx has liminal passages. I don't know them myself. They have fallen into disuse. But—" His eyes widened as Alexei gripped the front of his robes.

"Are you telling me you put her in a chamber with such a passage?" He could feel his Marks flaring, the rush of soothing blue ley, but it wasn't enough to quench his fury. "What were you thinking?"

"I didn't know it had one!" Gray squeaked. "They honeycomb the walls! She specifically requested this room for the lack of windows! I thought it was safe——"

"Saints." Alexei released him. "How do I open it?"

Gray backed up. "You must let me fetch some knights——"

"*How*," Alexei repeated firmly, "*do I open it?*"

"With liminal ley. That is all I know."

Alexei held out a hand. "Give me your blade."

Like all the clergy at Nantwich, Gray wore a sword across his back. He drew it from the sheath, handing it over hilt first.

"Thank you."

Alexei tore a glove off with his teeth and pressed his hand to the wall, delving through the surface to the thin layer of violet where blue mixed with red. A rectangle shimmered into view, dull and covered with a silvery mist. Alice gave a low growl.

"Where does it go?"

"Nowhere." Gray retreated another step at Alexei's expression. "It is a liminal space, Fra Bryce. A between-world." He scowled. "Kasia was explicitly ordered not to touch the ley by the Reverend Mother herself. It was a condition of her staying here. Clavis will not be pleased that she has violated her promise."

"What choice did she have? Someone locked her in!"

Gray's expression softened. "I am asking you to wait, Fra Bryce. This is rash——"

The rest of his words were lost as Alexei stepped through the doorway. With a growl, Alice dove through after him. He released the ley. The door closed behind him.

He stood in a blank white tunnel that extended in either direction.

"Which way, little sister?" he whispered.

After a moment's hesitation, she darted off. He laid Gray's sword flat across his palm, finding the balance. It was heavier at the hilt than he was used to, meaning it would slash quickly but with less power at the tip. He adjusted his grip a centimeter down the blade and followed the Markhound.

Stone walls gradually gave way to a bland pastel corridor that reminded him of the Batavia Institute. Then a cavernous white space with nothing but the wooden dock where a defendant sat to await their fate at trial. It was spotlight from above by some unseen light source.

"This place is seriously weird," he whispered to Alice.

She chuffed in agreement and trotted to the far side of the white chamber, where a white door sat flush with the wall. A tiny plaque said *Break Room/Staff Only*. He pushed the door and walked into a multi-level parking garage with slanted orange lines painted on the concrete and not a single car. His nerves sang as he followed her down through the sloping garage. Pillars stood at intervals, casting deep shadows. His footsteps echoed in the dark.

The endless stream of thoughts ceased. He was aware of every tiny sound. Aware of his surroundings only to the extent of watching for movement. The soldier who fought seven tours in the Void took over, for which Alexei was grateful. It spared him the agony of worrying about what might have happened to Kasia.

Down and down they went. Then, another stone corridor. Alice ran ahead. He found her sitting in front of a symbol he recognized.

Circle, square, triangle, circle. Crudely etched into the wall.

Adrenaline surged. Alexei opened a liminal doorway into a richly furnished antechamber. He crept on the balls of his feet down a diim hallway.

A card lay on the ground.

He picked it up.

The Jack of Wolves.

Hope and fear warred in his heart. Kasia was here. Most likely, the Order had her.

Alice ranged ahead, a silent wraith. He crossed an empty ballroom. Strobes flashed overhead, illuminating the hound's progress in jerky leaps.

Darkness and light, darkness and light.

Beyond, another hallway.

And beyond that, another room, this one with a long mirrored bar and red banquettes.

A woman was sitting at the bar, her back to the door. She wore a dress with black lace sleeves. Some instinct made her spin around, a card ready in her hand. Her eyes widened.

"Alexei?"

He ran forward, hardly daring to believe it. The sword clattered on the bar as he pulled her into an embrace, burying his face in her hair. Strong arms hugged him back. Finally, he pulled away and searched her face.

"I've dreamt of this moment often," he admitted. "But not like this. I thought they had you!"

"How on earth did you find me?"

He looked at Alice, who gave a happy bark. "She followed your scent."

He told Kasia about going to her room with Cardinal Gray and finding it bolted from the outside. "Do you know who did it?"

"No." Kasia frowned. "But the Order was here. I saw Jule Danziger. He's alive—or close enough it makes no difference."

"The nephew?"

She nodded. "Say you believe me. Please, I know what I saw—"

"Of course I believe you. Those children were dead, too. Now they're not." He glanced around. "What is this place?"

"It's called the Lethe Club. I stumbled over it by accident. When I came before, it was packed with people. Members of the Order, I'm sure of that." Frustration tightened her face. "But now they're gone."

"They let you go?"

"Not exactly. Jule would have stopped me. But I used the ley and he ran."

Kasia explained how she had returned to her room, found it locked, and searched for another way out.

"It's some kind of secret city within the city," she said. "A liminal space. It goes on and on. I have no idea how big it is."

"Gray knew. Why didn't Clavis tell you about it?"

"I'm nihilim. She doesn't trust me."

"That's ridiculous. And you're not!"

"Thank you. I agree. So do Natalya and Patryk. Have you seen them yet?"

"No, I just arrived a few hours ago." Alexei's gaze swept the thick shadows. "Are you sure none of the alchemists are here?"

"I've been sitting at the bar for an hour, hoping to lure them out." She shrugged. "No one's taken the bait. But there's more."

She tapped the bar. Four cards were laid out.

"The Hierophant," he said, squinting to read their titles in the dim light. "The Fool. The Tower of Destruction. The Star." He looked up at Kasia. "What do they mean?"

"The first two are Falke and Malach."

"I thought Falke was dead," Alexei said slowly.

"Well, he's not. I can say that with certainty. Cards are always inverted when they refer to someone who's dead."

"What about The Star?"

She shook her head. "Someone connected to the meteors. Another mage for certain. They're dangerous, obviously, yet I'm not sure they are *evil*. The Star is a symbol of hope." She swept the cards up. "I keep picking this same spread, over and over. It means something, Alexei." She reached for his hand. "Did you find your brother?"

"He's here with the delegation from Jalghuth. Lezarius named him captain of his guards."

Her face broke into a surprised smile. "So he is well? I'm so glad for you both!"

When Alexei didn't smile back, her grin faltered.

"What is it?"

"The Nightmark is no longer inverted. He seems his old self. Lezarius trusts him. But I see the signs, Kasia. The same as last time. He's slipping away."

Her face fell. "I'm so sorry."

"I thought maybe you could help him. Like you did with Spassov."

She nodded. "Of course I'll try. But I can't promise anything. It was different with Patryk. The dark ley was an alien thing inside him. This is a Mark. They're supposed to be indelible. Part of the psyche."

"I understand. But it can't hurt."

"Does he know what you intend?"

"Not yet," Alexei admitted.

She blew out a breath. "He'll need to be willing."

"I think he might be."

"And the children? Are they here, too?"

"They won't leave Jalghuth. But Misha brought them where they belong. They helped to defeat Balaur."

He quickly told her how the children had purified the ley. How Lezarius nearly died breaking the Void, but was returned to sanity. The discovery of Sinjali Lance's true purpose—to divide the ley into three currents that could be used by Marks, with the calming blue on the surface. Alexei had grown accustomed to this revelation, but he remembered his own amazement when he first learned that the division of the ley was not natural.

"So what is the ley in its pure form?" she wondered.

"I don't know," he admitted. "But it must come from somewhere—"

A flicker of light at the corner of his eye was the only

warning. A square of fiery abyssal ley opened in the floor like a portal to purgatory.

A leather-skinned creature leapt from the gap. Alexei's hacked at a sinewy arm. As he'd feared, the hilt-heavy sword failed to sever the limb, catching on the bone. He yanked it free, spinning away from outstretched talons as more swarmed through the gap.

Ley flashed in Kasia's hand. A jet of flames engulfed one of the alchemists. It rolled on the floor, howling. Alexei drove the sword into his attacker's midsection and kicked the thing free.

He heard Alice barking savagely. The next moments were a chaos of snapping jaws and inhuman shrieks. Gray's sword was lightning in his hands, blurring in short, vicious stabs. He feared the creatures would use the death ley, but perhaps they weren't strong enough.

At last, five alchemists lay dead or dying on the ground.

The doorway faded. Alice stood over it, snapping, until Alexei laid a hand on her flank. "Easy, little sister."

Kasia stared at the bodies. Her eyes were dark wells. "They come back," she whispered. "Stand aside."

Alexei grabbed Alice by the scruff and pulled her out of the way. Kasia drew a card from the suit of Flames, scouring the alchemical corpses until only stains of greasy ash remained.

"Gray promised to send knights after me," Alexei said. "They must be looking for us."

She stared at the spot where the liminal doorway had opened. "I want to know where that goes."

She had the trail now. He knew she wouldn't stop until she found the man who had killed Tessaria Foy.

"All right." Alexei hefted the sword. "Let's open it again."

They descended a tight spiral staircase that ended at a stone wall. Kasia used liminal ley to open another doorway. It led to a wide corridor with statues in niches. As they walked, she told him about the strange things she had seen. The classroom with its stopped clock, the hospital waiting room. He told her about the courtroom dock and the parking garage. They decided that some parts of the liminal city were ephemeral, fading in and out, while the stone corridors were the scaffolding holding it all together.

The section they found themselves in now was a maze of dead ends and blind alleys. Alexei was starting to fear they were lost when he heard a distant voice. Kasia shot him a look of excitement. He crouched down. *Sileo*, he mouthed to Alice.

She gave him a condescending look and slunk onward. After a few minutes, the corridor doglegged to a long balcony with a staircase at the far end. The light of many torches flickered against the ceiling. They crept forward on hands and knees, peering down between gaps in the stone balustrade.

An enormous chamber lay below, its edges lost to darkness. At least two hundred robed figures stood in a circle. Their cowls were pulled forward, concealing their faces, save for one. Jule Danziger stood in the center of the circle, blond hair gleaming in the candles that had been arranged into interlocking geometric figures on the floor. Circle, square, triangle, circle.

"They tell us all lives have the same worth," he declared. "They would make us equal with the common masses. The chars and halfwits! The blood of princes runs in our veins, but the Via Sancta would grind us to dust beneath its heel. The time has come to rise up. No one will defend our rights but us!"

Kasia stared down at Jule with loathing. Alexei shared her sentiment, though he couldn't help being impressed at the twisted logic. Apparently, a gated estate and manor house filled with servants translated to the Danzigers feeling oppressed.

"The Via Libertas offers the only true path to progress." Jule looked around. "We have all dreamt of Balaur. Seen his vision of a right and just world. You, my friends, are the patriotic standard-bearers. The few who kept the faith through years of persecution. But our long wait is almost over!

"Once the city has fallen and our position is secure, the true work must begin. It is not a task that can be accomplished in a single lifetime." Jule smiled. "But we will be beyond the grasping hand of death. Eternal rulers of the new order! This is the gift Balaur has promised. The one we have pledged our bodies and souls to achieve. Serve, and you will have wealth and power beyond imagining. A return to the glorious past when each man and woman knew their place. Peace derives from strength. Prosperity from obedience. These are lessons every child will learn."

He raised an arm. "All hail the Black Sun!"

Two hundred voices rose. "All hail the Black Sun! All hail the Black Sun!"

Alice's lips peeled back. The faintest growl rumbled in her chest. Alexei felt the vibration through his hand, which was resting on the hound's back. His fingers tightened in her fur. Alice shot him a guilty look.

The alchemists couldn't have heard it. Not above the chanting. There was no way—

Danziger's head whipped around. His gaze lifted to the balcony. Alexei slid back into the shadows, Kasia beside him. The voices faded to silence. Jule sniffed the air. Even from fifty meters away, Alexei felt the heat of his gaze.

"Come out, come out," he said softly, making a sharp gesture toward the staircase. "We won't hurt you, I promise." A toothy smile. "We're *civilized* here, Domina Novak."

Alexei grabbed Kasia's hand. They ran back the way they had come. The corridor was gone. A blank wall blocked their path. Alexei slapped his palm against the stone, pulling at the liminal ley. "Open, dammit," he hissed.

Feet pounded up the staircase. Hooded figures appeared at the end of the balcony. Alice started to lunge and Alexei just managed to catch the loose skin on her neck, dragging her back. There were too many. They would tear her apart.

"It isn't working," Kasia muttered. She had a card out, one of the Keys suit, but it failed to open the doorway.

"Having trouble?" Jule called out from below. "It's a shame you don't know these passages as well as I do. As you've just discovered, they can be sealed. There's no way out!"

The Order was nearly on them. Knives gleamed in the darkness. Cloth tore as their bodies shifted. Alice snapped and struggled, wild with bloodlust. The ley flowing from Kasia's card turned bright red. She was working abyssal power now. The stone bubbled. Ran like liquid fire. His own Marks flashed blue. His brain screamed an instinctive warning. *A mage! She's a mage!*

He silenced it with an effort. A moment later, the torrent broke through the barrier and carved a jagged hole in the stone. He saw a slice of night sky beyond. Smelled freshly mown grass.

When he looked back, one of the alchemists was standing in front of him. Her head tilted to the side, a swift, birdlike motion. Before Alexei's eyes, her lower jaw cracked and jutted outward, forming a distorted, hairless muzzle filled with tiny human teeth.

He pushed Kasia into the doorway and raised his sword, slashing at the hooded figures that crowded forward. He was almost through himself when Alice gave a violent twist. She slithered from his grasp and threw herself at the alchemist.

"No!" he screamed. "*Veni! Veni!*"

Kasia's hand gripped his arm, hauling him the rest of the way. The abyssal door closed. They'd come out through the rear wall of the Antiquarium, a brick structure at the north end of the plaza. Alexei gulped cool night air.

"I'm sorry!" Kasia looked stricken. "I couldn't hold the door!"

He pounded a fist on the wall. "Hold on, little sister!"

Alexei drew deep, delving straight to the churning red. His Marks fought the invasion of abyssal ley. Bile rose in his throat as he formed the image of a door. Willed it to open for him.

A shout came from behind. The ley slipped through his fingers. In an instant, they were surrounded by knights. Cardinal Gray strode up. Kasia ran to meet him, relief on her face.

"Lucas! The Order is here. Inside the Arx! You must—"

"Quiet," he snapped. "On your knees, both of you!"

Alexei raised the sword. "Just listen! An attack is planned. Let us show you—"

Gray held his palms up. "Calm yourself, Fra Bryce. Put the blade down and we'll talk." He glanced at Kasia. "I'm glad to see you returned to us, but this is still a very serious matter. The use of abyssal ley is forbidden within these walls. It is my duty to detain you both."

"You have to let me go back!" Alexei insisted. "My Markhound is on the other side of that wall! Along with about two hundred alchemists!"

Gray frowned. "If what you say is true, we'll go with you. But I must insist. Your cards, Kasia," he said firmly.

Her fingers tightened around the deck.

"Do what you want to me," she said. "But you must help Alice!"

"I swear it," Gray said, meeting her eye.

Kasia gave a forceful exhale through her nose. She surrendered her cards. Alexei watched Gray pocket the deck. The knights moved closer.

"The sword, Fra Bryce." He held out a gloved hand.

"No," Alexei said.

Kasia yelped as the knight behind her grabbed her hair, yanking her head back. A blade pressed to her throat.

"I'll ask again," Gray said. "Give me back my sword."

Alexei eyed the glow of lights in the palace. He could just make out the guards flanking the great bronze doors. They were too far away to aid him—but would they believe him anyway? Or would they follow Gray's orders? With Clavis gone, he was in charge.

Alexei tossed the blade aside with a curse.

"If you try to touch the ley, she dies, understand?" Wintry eyes turned to his knights. "Take the priest." The barest hint of a smile. "No need to be gentle."

Chapter Twenty-Five

The chain ran from a manacle around Kasia's left ankle to a thick eyebolt in the wall. It left her just enough slack to pace three steps in each direction.

No window. No door.

A liminal cell that existed between reality and shadow. Without the ley, she had no chance of escaping, so she passed the time thinking about Gray and how he had played her from the very beginning. All the names she'd given him that never came to anything.

Of course they hadn't.

Instead of investigating the Order, he'd *protected* them.

But he hadn't killed her. That meant she still had some use.

She had the queasy feeling she'd known it all along, and other things, too. Things she couldn't remember. Every time she tried, her head began to pound.

They'd beaten Alexei. For that, she would kill them. But it would require all her cunning to get out. She waited patiently, knowing they would come back after letting her stew in her own fear.

When the liminal doorway opened, Kasia was ready.

"Hello, Jule," she said.

No mask, no robe. Just a bespoke tweed suit, the jacket dangling from one finger. His wavy blond hair was neatly parted on the side, his cheeks smooth and ruddy with health. She caught a whiff of woody aftershave.

"Hello, Kasia." He stopped just beyond the chain's reach.

Behind him, the doorway shimmered.

"I suppose you're going to tell me resistance is futile." She smiled.

"Nothing so trite." He leaned back against the wall. "It's not my job to break you. That's for later."

"No? Then why have you come?"

"Merely to check on your welfare."

"I'm flattered."

"Do you want some water?"

"I am a bit thirsty."

He didn't move. Just peeled his gloves off and tucked them in the pocket of his trousers. He wore a heavy gold watch. Fine, light hairs gleamed on his wrist. They were the same color as his lashes. Whoever replicated him had done a masterful job.

"I hope you don't have pets, Jule. I don't think you'd do very well caring for them."

That made him smile. "I passed all the Probatio tests. Unlike you."

"Because you lied. Whereas I was honest."

"Fair enough. But I'm not a true sadist. Those are a rarer breed. I just don't give a shit."

"If you hurt Bryce, you'll get nothing from me. Ever."

He regarded her for a minute. Then he spun on his heel and walked out. A moment later, he returned with a cup of water.

"I'm going to set this down while you get back against the wall. Understood?"

"What do you think I'd do to you?"

"I have no idea."

Kasia laughed. She retreated against the wall. Jule set the cup down between them and backed away.

Her tongue was swollen with thirst, but she waited a moment before sauntering over and taking a drink. It was lukewarm, but she didn't taste anything besides water.

"How did you come back, Jule?"

Her eyes locked with his over the rim of the cup as she took another sip.

"I was never gone."

"Well, I'm gaining a new respect for alchemy. How's your aunt?"

"Oh, she's well," he replied carelessly. "May I smoke?"

"Go ahead."

Jule took out a silver case and withdrew a cigarette. He lit it with a match and drew deeply.

"Is she here?"

"Hanne is elsewhere." His eyes crawled over her. "So you're nihilim."

"That's right."

"But you can't use the ley without these." He took her deck from his pocket.

A taunt.

"I'll give you a reading if you like," she said.

Jule laughed. "I'll pass."

"You don't want to know what your future holds?"

"If I let you touch the cards, I can guess exactly what it will be."

"I don't know." She frowned. "You seem pretty hard to kill."

He exhaled a stream of smoke at the ceiling. "Well, I am. But it wasn't pleasant having my old body destroyed. I'd rather not repeat the experience."

"Did it hurt?"

"More than you can imagine." He said it lightly, but she sensed concealed anger.

Kasia's mood lifted. "How did you do it, Jule? How did you come back?"

Amusement glinted in his eyes. "I don't think I want to tell you that."

"Can everyone in the Order regenerate?"

The thought was horrifying.

"Only a few," he replied with a touch of arrogance. "The ones who are indispensable."

If he'd been smarter, he would have lied and said yes. But he couldn't resist putting himself above the rest.

"What makes *you* indispensable?" Kasia asked.

"Lots of things. Money. Power. Knowledge."

"The usual, in other words. How boring."

He didn't like that. His blond brows drew together. "You sound like Tessaria."

It took all her self-control not to lunge at him. But she knew his weakness now. Insecurity. Also boring, but typical of men like him. The only way they felt good about themselves was to lord it above others. It made him sloppy.

"She was given a chance, too," he continued. "She turned it down. And look where she ended up. Is that what you want, Kasia?"

Why bring up the woman he'd killed? Was he intentionally trying provoke her?

Or was it that, never having cared for anyone but himself, he truly didn't understand the depth of feeling one person could have for another?

"No," she said. "I want to live. More than anything."

Jule gazed at her seriously. "As do all creatures. But some are more fit than others. More deserving. It is not simply about *living*. It is about what one does with that gift." His eyes lingered on her hands, then moved slowly up to her face. "You could be great, Kasia. I felt it that night in the gardens. Felt your power when you were watching me in the woods."

Her skin crawled, but she held his hungry stare.

"You have no idea yet what he can offer you. But when the time comes, you will. And then we will see who you really are."

She swallowed, her throat dry again. "I'm intrigued."

The moment broke. Jule ground the cigarette butt beneath his heel. "I must go."

He turned to the door.

"Wait. I want to keep talking to you."

He exhaled a strangely shuddering breath. "Later," he said gruffly.

Jule stepped through the liminal door. It flickered and died.

She sank back against the wall, the smell of smoke hanging in the air.

Morvana watched from the window of her guest chamber as Clavis galloped into the portcullis, white cloak streaming, chain mail bright in the rising sun. A company of mounted knights rode behind her, flying the Crossed Keys of Nantwich and the Raven of Novostopol.

The bishop had a bad feeling about the incursion into the Morho, but Morvana understood the need to liberate the knights trapped inside the Fort of Saint Agnes. It was greater than a moral duty to save lives. If the forts fell, their supply lines would be disrupted and the mages would have a new line of control.

She laughed softly, with an edge of bitterness. "War! I have spend my life trying to prevent it and now here we are. A lesser evil, to be sure, but that is always the way. And where it leads—"

A knock came at the door. Morvana smoothed her dark blue robe and opened it a crack.

A tall man peered down at her. He had longish black hair pulled into a topknot and electric blue eyes. His tabard named him a knight of Jalghuth, yet she felt a jolt of recognition. Even with the beard, he looked too much like Alexei to be anyone but his brother.

"Your Grace," he said with a perfunctory bow. "I'm sorry to disturb you, but the matter is urgent."

"You are the older Bryce," she said in a cool tone. "Also a Beatus Laqueo, *ja?*"

Falke's special forces had been notorious in the guerrilla wars that followed the making of the Void. The Beatus Laqueo—whose name meant Holy Noose—represented everything Morvana loathed about Falke, the Saints preserve him. Alexei was carrying his brother's corax when he came to Kvengard. She had a sharp memory for detail—one did not become a nuncio at the age of thirty without paying attention to *everything*—and the name came to her immediately.

Mikhail Semyon Bryce. A captain, no less.

Her distaste must have showed, for he looked away, mouth tight.

"Not anymore. I serve Lezarius now."

A spark of fear kindled as she recalled the rest of Alexei's story. He'd told Luk a nihilim turned his brother's Marks. She cleared her throat. "I thought you were. . . ."

"Invertido?" he finished. "Also, not anymore."

"How can that be?"

"You know about the children? The Reborn?"

She gave a cautious nod.

"When Lezarius was restored, the same happened to me. I was with him at the time."

"Ah." She opened the door wider. "And what is it you want, Captain Bryce?"

A muscle feathered in his jaw. "My brother's gone missing."

"He has a habit of doing that," she said dryly.

"This is different. Please, I need your help."

She hesitated, not trusting this big knight with the intense stare. He might be *ex*-Invertido and *ex*-Laqueo. Or he might not. She nearly asked him to disrobe to prove it, but decided against it. If he was crazy, who knew how he might react?

"Why me?" she asked. "I'm just a guest here."

"Because you are the Kven bishop who holds my brother's Marks. I hoped you might care about him."

They regarded each other warily.

"Did you bring Markhounds?" Bryce asked. "We could try to track his scent."

"The packs are all with the knights in Kvengard. They will be marching for Nantwich, but it will be some time before they arrive. What about your brother's dog?"

"She is gone, too."

"I don't know what I can do," she said. "Are you certain he didn't just go off to be alone?"

"I'm certain." He paused. "Someone else is missing, too. You've seen what the Order is capable of. If he's in their hands, I fear the worst."

"You must tell Cardinal Gray. He will—"

"I already did. He denies that the Order even exists in Nantwich! But something is very wrong." A pause. "There's more you should know. If you'll agree to come with me, I'll explain everything."

"Where?" she demanded suspiciously.

"The Villa of Saint Margrit."

"Inside the Arx?"

"Yes."

She sighed. "Very well, Captain Bryce. I must admit, I misjudged your brother. If your claim is true, I will take it to the Reverend Father Luk. He will listen to me."

Bryce nodded, impatient, as she took a cloak from a peg on the wall and settled it across her shoulders. Morvana was tall for a woman, but he still loomed over her. She saw no signs of madness—unless he was adept at covering them up. Invertido could be cunning.

They left the palace. She was relieved to see that dozens of people were already up and about. If he deviated from their chosen destination, she would scream.

"You hunted the Order in Kvengard?" he asked, long legs devouring the ground.

Morvana hurried to keep up. "That's right."

"My brother spoke highly of you."

"Did he?" Morvana didn't believe that for an instant. Alexei had already admitted he didn't trust her.

"You didn't have to take his Marks." His gaze flicked over her. "He would have died. It was an act of charity."

"Anyone would do the same."

"Not anyone. You are bound together now."

She laughed uneasily. "I've given many Marks, Captain Bryce. The risk is only for those who receive them. As well you know."

"Then we must make sure you never come to harm," he said, slowing before a three-story building. The stucco facade had a whimsical mosaic made of pebbles and seashells. "Here we are."

"Here, what?"

His voice lowered. "I want you to meet Alexei's friends. They were in Kvengard. They know a great deal about the Order."

Ah. The mysterious people who Alexei claimed were held captive by the Danzigers.

"Why not bring them to me?" she said, trepidation mounting.

He looked around. "Because Maria Karolo would not be well pleased to know they're here."

Morvana had disliked the woman immediately upon meeting her. She herself had a reputation for coldness, but she wasn't really unfeeling. Just brisk and efficient. Emotion interfered with logical decisions. When Morvana's passions did flare, as they had when she saw the atrocities in the laboratory, her Marks did their work to soothe it away.

But Mario Karolo struck her as overly rigid. The sort of zealot who rose high through intimidation.

"The Reverend Mother Clavis gave them shelter here," Bryce explained. "But they're confined to their rooms until Karolo leaves."

Morvana considered this. It made sense. They could not be here without Clavis's sanction. And her curiosity was piqued now. If there were intrigues afoot, she had a duty to learn about them and make sure her own Reverend Father was safe.

"I give my word to keep silent," she said. "But if they have information, perhaps we should all go to Luk."

He nodded in relief. "Thank you."

"What are their names?" she asked, as they entered the building and climbed the stairs to the second floor.

"Natalya Anderle and Patryk Spassov. Fra Spassov was a priest with the Interfectorem. He served with Alexei."

They went down a corridor. Bryce rapped his knuckles on a door.

"It's me," he said.

The door swung open. Another big man waited across the threshold, older then Mikhail Bryce by a decade but still strong-looking. He had a shaved head and beaten, melancholy face. The strong odor of tobacco assaulted her nose. Brown eyes regarded her intently. A Raven Marked his neck, just visible over the cowl of his cassock.

"Your Grace," he said, stepping back.

Morvana entered. The room was messy, the bed unmade. An easel was propped in the corner. A young woman in her late twenties perched on the windowsill. She had bleach-blond hair and very white teeth against dark skin. She rose and nodded a greeting. She wore trousers and a beige turtleneck sweater.

"Your Grace."

Morvana heard the door close behind her. An instant later, a blade pressed to her throat.

"Not a sound," Bryce whispered in her ear.

She stiffened, then held herself perfectly still.

"Mikhail," the woman said, frowning. "That's not necessary."

"It is," he replied calmly.

Morvana's eyes flicked to the priest. He, too, looked unhappy. But he also eyed her with profound suspicion.

"Please," she said, appealing to the woman. "Don't let him hurt me."

The woman bit her lip. "I won't. Misha, put the fogging sword down!"

"After she talks."

"Talks about what? I don't know anything!"

His voice was a low hiss, raising the hairs on her nape. "My brother vanished after *you* met him! You were the last one seen with him. I know the Order was moving around the Arx in Kvengard. The Chapel of Saint Ydilia! Ring any bells?"

Morvana tried to remain calm. So he *was* a madman. "We searched those tunnels. We found nothing—"

"Bullshit!"

She swallowed hard against the edge of the blade.

"Stop," the priest growled. He took a step forward. "This isn't what we agreed, Misha."

The pressure didn't ease up, but he hadn't broken the skin. Not yet.

"I know about the Mark," she said. "All the Order have it. A circle inside a square, inside a triangle, inside a circle. Search me if you want. I am not Black Sun, you lunatics!"

Her back pressed tight against Bryce's chest. Morvana could feel his heart beating. Then, in one smooth motion, he withdrew the blade and stepped back.

"Prove it then," he said, voice cold.

She raised a hand to her neck. "Fine. I will show *her*." She turned to Natalya Anderle, who watched with wide eyes.

A rumbling laugh. "Oh, no. I'm not turning my back on you."

Bryce gestured with the dagger. Morvana held his stare. Then she tugged off her gloves and tossed them on the bed. She discarded her cloak and robe. Nantwich was a frigid city and she wore flannel leggings beneath. She sat on the bed and peeled them off, scowling.

She had six Marks. All were from a cardinal named Lindemann. Her first was the Running Wolf. Then a sailing ship for her restless nature, a badger for tenacity, a lone oak tree for solitude, three white poppies for peace, and a blindfolded woman holding the reins of a chariot drawn by a pair of shadowy Marksteeds. Of them all, she was most proud of the last. It signified a determination to see justice done without fear or favor.

Captain Bryce's gaze caught on the last. He studied the Marks with narrow eyes, each in turn, face thoughtful as if seeing something for the first time. As if he knew exactly what they meant, each and together.

It was unsettling.

At last, he looked away. "My sincere apologies, Your Grace."

There was no note of regret in his voice. Nor of fear that he had just forced a bishop to disrobe.

There was nothing at all.

She yanked the undershirt over her head. "Apologies? You're insane! All of you!"

"We're in the shit now," Natalya Anderle muttered.

Morvana popped her head through the neck of her robe. She ran a hand through her short hair, settling it into place.

"I told you the truth," Bryce said evenly, as if none of it had happened. "They were in Kvengard. The missing woman is named Kasia Novak. The Order wants her and—"

"Oh, enough," Morvana snapped. "If you had sought my help in the normal fashion, you would have gotten it. As things stand, I must report this incident to Cardinal Gray." She eyed his dagger with contempt. "Will you stab me, Captain? Throw my body in the river? Or will you let me leave?"

"Please, don't," Natalya said. "Tell, I mean. We've no right to ask, I know. But we're at wits end!"

Morvana scowled. "Have you tried calling his dog?"

"I have," the priest replied dourly. "She would die to defend him. Ah, damn." He turned away, wiping at the corner of his eye.

Morvana's Marks had already erased most of her anger. Now she felt a twinge of sympathy.

"How did you call her?"

The priest turned back, red-eyed. "Her name. What else?"

"You are not Kven, I see," she said dryly. "Luk made the hounds. We know a few tricks."

She drew a trickle of blue ley and pursed her lips. They all stared at her in puzzlement. The register was well above the range of human hearing. It took many years to perfect the whistle, but Morvana had grown up with Markhounds.

"If she's around, she'll come. Now, if you'll excuse me."

She stared at Bryce. The cords in his neck tightened, but he stepped aside. She had a hand on the doorknob when a whine made her turn back.

A shadow crouched in the corner.

"Saints," the priest whispered.

The dog's head hung low, one paw dangling limp. Her

muzzle swung towards Misha. She growled deep in her throat. He moved back, never taking his eyes from her.

"It's okay, baby." Natalya sank down, extending her hand.

The dog shivered. Another low, pathetic whine.

"It's okay, it's okay. You remember me, right?" Natalya crawled toward her. The hound lifted its head to sniff her hand. Its golden eyes were dazed and exhausted.

"She's hurt," Natalya said, voice tight. The priest hurried over, laying a gentle hand on her flank.

"Let me see," Morvana said.

She crouched down. An old scar crossed the dog's back leg, but fresh blood dripped from the paw. She had a dozen other wounds, some deep. They looked like they came from knives. Or claws.

"I will help her," Morvana said, rolling up her sleeves. She glanced back over her shoulder. "Make yourself useful, Captain Bryce. Fetch some water and clean linens."

He nodded quickly and backed out the door.

"Ah, this is bad," Patryk Spassov muttered.

The dog's name was Alice, Morvana recalled. In Kvengard, she and Alexei had been practically inseparable. When he wasn't working, he spent his time at the kennels. She knew because she hadn't trusted him, either.

The hound lay on her side now, flanks heaving. Who knew where she'd holed up to lick her wounds. But she must have used the last of her energy to answer the whistle.

Morvana drew again on the ley and laid her palms on Alice's ravaged side. The white of bone poked through one leg.

"I thought the ley couldn't heal," Spassov said.

"It cannot heal *us*," Morvana corrected. "But she is a creature of the ley. It is woven into her flesh and bone."

The door opened. Bryce set a jug of water on the floor. His other arm held a stack of clean sheets. He did not approach.

"The dog doesn't like you," Morvana remarked. "She is a good judge of character."

He winced at that but said nothing.

So he *does* feel, she thought. Still a dangerous man.

Morvana pushed Captain Bryce from her mind and focused on Alice, feeding ley into her blood and allowing the dog's unique physiology to heal itself. Natalya used the dagger to cut up a sheet and dampen the strips. Together, they wiped the blood from the hound's body.

"These wounds are recent," Morvana said. "She could not have lived long with them."

"Alexei went missing last night," Fra Spassov said.

"Where?"

"I'm not sure," Mikhail Bryce said. "He never returned to his rooms in the palace. He told me he was going to find his friends here. Last I saw of him, he was going off with you."

"We spoke briefly," Morvana replied. "I left him in the plaza. I have no idea where he went next."

"Well, I never saw him," Fra Spassov said.

"Nor did I," Natalya added.

Morvana stroked the hound. Her eyes had slipped shut, but her heartbeat felt steady. "The hound needs food. And rest."

"But you believe us now?" Spassov gazed at her earnestly. "Something attacked her."

Morvana nodded. "I will go to Luk."

"Your Grace."

She turned to Captain Bryce, who still hovered in the doorway.

"They are not to blame," he said. "I'll offer no defense if you decide to press charges. I ask only that you let me find my brother before you report this incident."

"I will think on it," she said. "In the meantime, I suggest you remain here while I make my own inquiries."

He bowed his head. "Thank you."

"Don't thank me yet," she said crisply. "I haven't made up my mind."

His blue eyes locked with hers. "You feel it don't you?" he said quietly. "The wrongness."

Morvana rose. "Stay out of trouble, Captain Bryce."

She felt his gaze on her back as she walked out the door.

Chapter Twenty-Six

Morvana found the Reverend Father on the balcony of his large guest quarters at the palace, gazing out at the sea. He looked even more tired than usual, but he smiled when he saw her and gestured for her to join him.

"Fra Bryce is missing," Morvana said. "But his Markhound just turned up. Gravely wounded."

Luk's gaze sharpened. "Did she die?"

"It was close, but I saved her."

His shoulders relaxed. "I am glad to hear it."

The Reverend Father had a great fondness for all his creations, but especially the hounds.

"The nature of her injuries troubles me," Morvana continued. "They appear to have been made by animals, but there are none in Nantwich large enough to overpower a Markhound. How could she have come by them?"

"What are you suggesting?"

"The alchemists can change their form."

"The Order of the Black Sun?" He frowned. "Clavis assured us they were gone."

"What if she's wrong, Reverend Father?"

He gripped the balustrade. "It is always possible. I will convey your concerns to Cardinal Gray."

"Thank you." She hesitated. "Before Fra Bryce vanished, he told me Rademacher had a warrant for his arrest. That knights were sent after him when he left Kvengard. Did you give the order, Reverend Father?"

"Naturally. It seemed only prudent. Did I neglect to tell you?"

"Yes," she muttered, stifling her annoyance.

He waved a hand. "I'm sorry, but there was so much going on. Bryce has diplomatic immunity now—not that I mean to detain him. What else did he say to you?"

"He thought there might be a connection between the alchemists and the clergy."

Luk sighed. "Not that again."

"The fact remains that he is missing. Until we solve this mystery, I fear for your safety, Reverend Father."

"Surely the palace is safe!"

"Fra Bryce disappeared from inside the Arx."

Luk's lips pursed. "Fra Bryce flits from city to city like a hummingbird, never landing for long. He claims loyalty to all, but I wonder if he truly believes in anything. For all we know, he is one of the Order himself."

"I'm sure that's not true, Reverend Father. He led me to them!"

"Exactly. His tale of stumbling over their laboratory is rather thin, if you ask me."

"I would agree, Reverend Father, if it weren't for the girl he rescued."

"Sofie Arnault?"

"Yes. You should have seen her cling to him. I cannot believe he had anything to do with it."

Luk nodded. "As I said, I will speak with Gray. But Bryce is no longer your concern, Morvana."

"I hold his Marks," she said quietly. "That gives me a moral obligation."

Luk's stern face softened. "I respect your devotion, but we have greater problems to worry about now." His gaze turned back to the horizon. "Have I made the right choice?"

That surprised her. Luk never second-guessed himself.

"I believe so, Reverend Father."

"Always I have rejected violence. But there comes a point when one must face the bitter truth. Sometimes accommodations must be made if the greater ideals are to be preserved." He gave a mirthless smile. "I sound like Falke now. He did his best, I suppose. But it wasn't enough. His hatred of the mages was too strong."

Morvana stared at him, puzzled. "I'm not sure I understand, Reverend Father."

"Never mind. The Wolves will march. At least I can count on their loyalty to me. The Via Sancta will endure." He nodded. "That much I can promise. But I take your warnings to heart. Stay with me for a while, Morvana. I feel better with your company."

"Of course, Reverend Father."

"It was good to see Lezarius. Did I ever tell you how we met?"

"I don't believe so."

"He came to Kvengard as a novice. It was back in the days when such exchanges were common. Bal Agnar and Bal Kirith were still part of the Curia and there were highways linking all the cities, with towns along the way. I met him in choir. He had a lovely singing voice. We grew to be fast friends. Lezarius loves animals, too."

The violet shadows lengthened as Luk spoke, bringing a chill to the air. They went inside and sat in chairs by the fire. He was usually a pragmatic sort, but the council seemed to have stirred up the ghosts of his past. He related stories of the days when he and

Lezarius were both young and the nihilim had not risen under the banners of Beleth and Balaur. She wondered if Luk was more ill than she realized. Did he view this treaty as his final legacy?

She listened with half an ear, watching the clock on the mantel. At last, she cleared her throat and interrupted his monologue. "I think you should speak with Cardinal Gray," she said firmly. "He needs to know that a member of the Jalghuth delegation is missing."

"Why don't you come with me?" Luk suggested.

Morvana hesitated. "I'm not feeling well. I think I will retire to my rooms."

He looked concerned. "I'm sorry, Morvana. Here I've been, yammering on. Of course, we must attend to this matter. I will inform you if I hear anything." Luk patted her hand. "But I have every confidence that Cardinal Gray will find him."

JULE DANZIGER NEVER RETURNED.

Kasia paced the cell, three steps in each direction before the chain ran out.

Not for the first time, she cursed her lack of Marks. The cards were powerful, but without them, she might as well be in the Void.

Patryk and Natalya might not even miss her yet. They were all supposed to stay in their rooms.

Or everyone she knew was already dead.

Kasia jerked the chain in frustration. What was happening? Would they leave her here forever?

She felt lightheaded from hunger. An empty, floating sensation that made it hard to focus. She found herself staring into space, adrift, and resumed the pacing.

Then, lines of shimmering ley. She could still see it, at least.

Cardinal Gray stepped through.

"If you had stayed in your room like I told you to, we could have avoided this," he said.

He looked the same, with his steel-rimmed glasses and boyish, homely face, but the mild manner was gone. His voice was pitiless, his brown eyes cold.

"Why didn't you just take my cards away?" she demanded.

"I thought you were obedient, Kasia. You hadn't touched the ley before. Why did you do it?"

"Because I knew something bad was going to happen."

"The cards told you?"

She nodded.

"I knew it would be tricky," he said, "keeping the truth from you. At first I doubted your abilities. But you kept singling out the wrong people."

"The right ones, you mean," she said bitterly.

"Fortunately, Clavis never knew about any of them." He chuckled. "She was so disappointed. Oh, she didn't show it, of course. But she'd expected greater things from you."

Rage sliced through her exhaustion. "So you had the Order waiting in the wings. And a few others inside the Arx, I imagine. But I cannot believe that every knight in this city follows Balaur! And you cannot kill them all!"

"We'll see. But it begins as we speak, Kasia. I wanted to tell you that. The hour has come and there is nothing you can do to stop it."

The cruel edge to his voice took her aback. "Why do you hate me? What have I ever done to you, Gray?"

His lips curled. "Do you know how many sleepless nights I've spent worrying about what you might discover? Fearing you would go directly to Clavis?"

"I should have," she muttered. "I was a fool not to! But I trusted you."

"A single word and all our plans might have crumbled to dust."

"Then why did you taunt me? Allow them to enter my rooms?"

His jaw set. "I didn't."

The realization struck. "Jule Danziger."

"He liked to play games with you. I told him it was dangerous! But he wouldn't listen."

"And he stands above you." Kasia eyed him with disdain. "You are nothing but Balaur's errand boy."

The cardinal's fists clenched as if he wanted to strike her.

Come closer, she thought. Just a little closer.

Gray mastered himself with an effort. "After tonight, he will see how worthy I am. None of it would be possible without *me*! While Jule drank and rutted like a pig at the Lethe Club, it was I who—" He bit off the words.

"Who what?"

When he didn't answer, she tried a new tack. "What made you abandon your faith, Lucas? Promises of wealth? Power?" Kasia eyed his purple robe. "Is your soul so cheap?"

"You don't understand anything," he replied, weary now. "I have not lost my faith. I do this for the Via Sancta."

She stared at him in disbelief. "It that a joke?"

"Our blood runs thin. We need the nihilim. The Marks are all that keep us from a return to the Dark Age. Without them, we will descend into savagery."

"I think you have already become the very thing you fear, Lucas."

He grimaced. "I vowed to keep you safe and I have. You may spend the next hours readying yourself for our new guests." A bleak smile. "They are not half as kind as I am."

Gray turned to leave. The manacle bit into her ankle as Kasia sprang like a cat, arm outstretched, yanking the chain taut.

Her fingers brushed the edge of his sleeve. Gray tore his arm away.

Then he was gone. The doorway vanished.

NIGHT FELL as Morvana crossed the Arx, heading for the Villa of Saint Margrit.

The deceit still stuck in her throat. It was the first lie she had ever told to the Pontifex. She still wasn't entirely sure why she'd pretended to be unwell. As Nuncio, her first duty was to Kvengard. Yet as she sat with Luk, listening to him ramble on, her worry for Alexei had only grown stronger.

It was the dog.

Alice's wounds reminded her too much of those vile creatures she'd found in the laboratory. The flesh had putrified, but the long talons remained. After checking each chamber twice, she'd ordered the place to be burned.

They had found several tunnels. One led to the shepherd's hut on the cliff where she met Alexei; another to Danziger Haus. A third ran all the way to the Arx and ended in the Chapel of Saint Ydilia.

The last disturbed her mightily.

Luk had forbidden her to conduct what he termed a "witch-hunt" of the clergy. He could not believe any of them were involved. Mostly likely, the Order was using it to spy.

But for what purpose? Their interest was in the children.

A chill wind tugged at her cloak. Morvana drew it tighter. She would check on the dog and ensure she was recovering. Luk had promised to raise the matter with Cardinal Gray. A search would be mounted. She resolved to make sure it was done before she went back to Kvengard. Morvana knew how to make a pest of herself.

She passed a group of knights patrolling the grounds and nodded respectfully. Priests and vestals moved along the pathways, some alone, others in twos and threes. The Arxes had stood for a thousand years. Islands of tranquility and faith, even when the world outside convulsed with madness. Yet it suddenly felt hopelessly fragile to her. As they all clung to a dream long dead without quite realizing it.

Why such dark thoughts? she reprimanded herself. Has Captain Bryce shaken your faith so easily?

He should not have been capable of doing what he did. A Marked knight! Threatening violence to a bishop! And without a flicker of regret.

She knew that many knights had gone over to their enemies. The Wards no longer suppressed the temptation of abyssal ley—or kept the nihilim out. But Lezarius seemed to trust him. And Morvana had liked the Pontifex of the Northern Curia. He was direct and to the point.

She'd said nothing to Luk about what happened. But she hoped Captain Bryce would not be there.

Morvana climbed the stairs and knocked on the door.

"It is Bishop Zeigler," she said. "I am alone."

The door opened. She looked up into a pair of ice-blue eyes.

"Your Grace," he said smoothly, stepping back.

She suppressed a shiver and entered the room. "How is the Markhound?"

Morvana couldn't help smiling as the dog limped over to her.

"Let me see that paw." Alice sank to her haunches and permitted Morvana to examine her. "You fed her, I see," she said approvingly.

"You wouldn't believe how much she ate," Natalya Anderle said, kneeling down to join them. "Misha raided the kitchens since we're not supposed to go out. Two roast chickens, a pound of raw beef, and some nasty sausage pudding."

"No chicken bones, I hope?" Morvana said, frowning.

Natalya glanced at the knight, who remained in the farthest corner of the room. "He pulled all the meat off for her."

"Good." She stroked the silky ears. "You look much better, Alice."

A sloppy tongue licked her cheek. Morvana wiped her face with a laugh.

"Thank you," Patryk Spassov said solemnly. "For the dog. But also for forgiving us the wrong we did you. I expected knights to show up and arrest us."

"I did not say I forgave you," she replied wryly. "I came here for Alice. And her master. But we will forget it for now."

The hound flopped down, chin resting on her paws. She heaved a deep canine sigh.

"She misses him," Captain Bryce said.

One of Alice's eyebrows cocked at the sound of his voice, but she seemed too depressed to growl.

"Is she well enough to track?" Natalya asked.

"I don't know. Let us ask her." Morvana leaned down. She imbued her voice with the power of the ley, whispering words only the hound could hear. At once, Alice pushed to her feet, ears perked. She gave a single bark.

"I think the answer is yes. But whatever happened to her left scars. She fears being abandoned."

"Never," Natalya said stoutly. "We will go with her."

"I thought you were confined to your rooms."

"It's dark out now. We'll be careful." She strode to the easel and opened a box. Morvana had assumed it held art supplies, but she unfurled a cloth and drew six short knives, tucking them into her boots and belt. Spassov was already pulling on his exorason and buckling a sword around his waist.

"Will she have me?"

They all turned. Captain Bryce stood at the door. His face was expressionless as he regarded the dog, but Morvana sensed his tension.

Natalya exchanged a quick look with the priest. "We need you, Misha," she said lightly. "So does your brother. Alice will have to, whether she likes it or not."

He gave a brief nod. "And Your Grace?"

She met his eyes. "I am Luk's nuncio. I cannot bring dishonor on him. If we are all found together, it would be awkward. But I will walk out with you."

The paths had emptied as they stepped out of the Villa. It was the dinner hour. Gray had planned a reception at the palace to celebrate the treaty, though Morvana had no appetite. Alice limped along, nose pressed to the ground.

Both Natalya and the priest wore cloaks with the hoods raised. A cursory inspection and they would pass for clergy. Captain Bryce was clearly with the Jalghuth contingent, which might draw attention, yet the grounds of the Arx were quiet.

Suddenly, Alice quivered as though a jolt of electricity had run through her body. She ran ahead with a halting gait, leaving a trail of phosphorescent paw prints behind her. Natalya and the priest hurried to follow.

"You should go now, Your Grace," Bryce said to her.

The tight leash he kept on himself was slipping. His gaze burned with eagerness.

"Well, I should," she said, exhaling a breath. "But I think I must see where she leads us first. Then I can fetch help." A firm nod. "Yes, that is what I shall do."

His lips formed the ghost of a smile. "Come, then."

She picked up the hem of her robe as they broke into a jog. The hound had ranged ahead, a faint shadow in the night. She paused for a moment, sniffing in a wide circle, then ran on, the others close behind.

Morvana glanced over her shoulder to make sure no one saw them. When she looked back, Bryce was the only one in view. The prints were fading rapidly.

"Wait for me!" Morvana cried.

To her surprise, Bryce did. They fell into step together, following the trail until it ended at the doors of a small chapel. He started to enter and she laid a hand on his arm.

"This is the equivalent of the Chapel of Saint Ydilia in Kvengard," she whispered, pulse racing.

A gloved hand fell to his sword hilt. "Stay behind me."

Morvana nodded as he opened the doors and strode inside. Candles burned in the niches, though they barely dispelled the enfolding dark. Fra Spassov and Natalya stood with Alice at the altar. The hound was whining and scratching at the wood.

Morvana felt a chill. "There must be a hidden—"

"Passage," Spassov finished. "I saw the one in Kvengard. There is another in Novostopol at the Iveron Chapel." He pressed a hidden lever and the stone altar slid aside. A gust of air guttered the candles.

Steel scraped from a scabbard. Bryce shouldered past her and peered into the recess. "Stairs."

Alice shrank away as he passed. Had he done her harm once? Yet Morvana had only seen him show the hound kindness.

"Captain Bryce!" Morvana called out.

He was already halfway down the winding stairs. A quick, impatient look back.

"We must fetch help! You cannot go down there alone!"

"Not alone," Fra Spassov said. "I'm going with him."

"Me, too," Natalya said, palming one of her knives.

Morvana shook her head. "Ah, I knew you were all insane."

She studied the knight from Jalghuth. His face was half in shadow and only one blue eye caught the light. But Captain Bryce had the look of a man who would not be dissuaded.

Blood would be shed. That much was certain. Morvana abhorred violence. What possible use could she be?

She looked down at Alice. Most people assumed the Markhounds had been bred to hunt nihilim, but this was not true. Their original purpose was simple companionship. They were fiercely loyal and gentle with small children. She used to tug their ears and try to ride them like ponies. Never had any of her dogs even growled. It saddened her that they had been used for war, with no choice in the matter.

Alice was a very intelligent, feeling animal. Morvana could see it in her eyes.

The hound gazed back at her as if to say, I am afraid too. But still I serve. For the ley, and for love of my master.

Morvana patted her head. Then she lifted her robes and followed them down into darkness.

Chapter Twenty-Seven

Awareness returned with a bucket of cold water to the face.

Alexei gasped. The darkness blurred, then drifted into focus.

Skulls leered down, anchored in place by shafts of bone. Long femurs and heart-shaped vertebrae. His cheek pressed against a stone floor. He must have been lying there for a while, hands bound behind his back, because his neck was a solid mass of pain.

A hand gripped his hair and dragged him up to sit.

"Where's Kasia?" he demanded hoarsely.

Five knights flanked Cardinal Lucas Gray. Torchlight reflected against round spectacles, hiding his eyes.

"Safe," he said. "Unlike you."

Alexei wiggled gloved fingers. White-hot needles lanced all the way to the shoulder. His wrists were tied so tightly the circulation was almost cut off. He breathed deeply through his nose, jaw clenching against the agony.

"The only reason you're not dead," Gray continued, "is because the cartomancer cares about you. You, Fra Bryce, are my leverage." He glanced around. "But I have no qualms about adding pieces of you to the catacombs if you misbehave." A quick, humorless smile. "Just the bits you won't need. An arm or leg, perhaps."

"I'll be good," Alexei said.

"Yes, you will." Gray consulted a pocket watch. "I believe you already know Balaur's Nuncio. A mage named Malach."

He tried to keep his face blank, but Gray gave a knowing laugh. "Clavis told me you two have a history. I suppose he'll want whatever's left of you after he arrives."

Heat flooded his chest. "Malach is coming here?"

"That's what I just said, isn't it?" Gray responded with a touch of impatience. "Now, did you tell anyone where you were going?"

The question gave him hope. Gray had conspirators within the Arx, but he still feared his plans being disrupted.

Alexei shook his head. It was the truth, but he knew Gray would be too paranoid to believe him.

The cardinal gestured to his knights. "Get the whole story. I'll return later."

Alexei braced himself as they came forward.

"Make sure he's still capable of speech when you're done," Gray called, footsteps receding. "I'm sure the Nuncio will want to interrogate him personally."

A gauntleted palm knocked Alexei's head back. Just a lazy cuff, but blood filled one eye.

"Let's start at the beginning, shall we?" the knight said crisply.

Alexei blinked. He was too slow to answer and the knight leaned hard on his shoulder. He bit back a scream.

"I went to her rooms, looking for her," he said through gritted teeth. "There was a doorway. I followed it."

"Just you?"

"Just me."

"Where did you go? Where was she?"

"A place called the Lethe Club. We already told you."

"How did you find it?"

"I . . . " He couldn't mention Alice. They might try to hunt her down.

Another cuff split his lip.

"I used the ley!"

"Bullshit." The gauntlet raised to strike him again.

"I have twenty Marks." The words came out mushy, through a mouthful of blood. He turned his head and spat. "I used them all to find her."

The fist lowered. "Twenty?" the knight echoed in disbelief.

"I was Beatus Laqueo. Seven tours in the Void."

"Rank?"

"Chaplain." He tried to focus over the ringing in his head. "But it was just to meet the quotas. I was a soldier like the rest."

"Special forces, eh? Let's see." The knight pulled a long blade from his belt and pressed the tip beneath Alexei's chin. A quick downward slash and his cassock fell open. The knight used the dagger to prod at his Marks. "Bloody hell, you're wall-to-wall, mate."

"Were you deployed?"

A quick nod. "Cavalry."

Alexei swallowed. "Why are you doing this? We're brothers—"

The tip of the knife dug in, drawing a thin line down his chest. "Not anymore." There wasn't a hint of mercy in his eyes. "They say that when a Mark is cut away, it grows back. I've always wondered if that was really true."

Alexei glanced at the others. They stood with hands resting on sword hilts, faces implacable.

"So I think you'd better start telling the truth," the knight said mildly. "Which one shall I start with, eh? The Raven on your neck? Or something bigger?"

Alexei's mouth went dry. "I'm telling you the truth—"

"No. You're not." The blade paused at his left nipple, just

below the Armored Wasp. "I like this one. Perhaps I'll dry it and put it in a frame."

A soft sound made him turn. Alexei strained to see around his mailed bulk.

"What the f—"

A meaty *thunk*. The knight's hands flew to his throat. He sagged against the wall, blood pouring through his fingers. Knobs of bone dug into Alexei's back as he used his feet to scramble away. Another knife was already flying from Natalya Anderle's hand. Swords rasped from scabbards.

Spassov stepped into the breach, ducking a slash. He crashed into one of the knights. They staggered down the dark passage.

A fierce bark sliced the mayhem. Alexei feared he'd imagined it until a pair of golden eyes resolved from the gloom. So that's how they'd found him. He was overjoyed to see the others, but he nearly broke down at the sight of his dog. He'd been so sure she was dead.

Half-healed wounds matted her coat as she limped over. A quick, sloppy kiss on his cheek. Then Alice took up a guard position in front of him, legs planted and head low, a warning growl in her throat.

The other three knights backed up to give themselves room as his brother stepped from the shadows. White teeth gleamed through his beard. "Protect the bishop," he said softly.

Natalya nodded, a knife ready in each hand.

The cut on Alexei's forehead still ran freely, drawing a red veil across his vision. Steel rang against steel. A meter away, he heard the quiet choking sounds of a man slowly bleeding out. The knight would die quicker if he withdrew Natalya's knife from his throat. Alexei wished he'd do it. End the suffering.

Sometimes, he heard the same sounds in meditation or at the edge of sleep, but he knew they weren't real. Just echoes from the past.

Time slipped by. Natalya bent to his side. "You're a fright, Alexei," she muttered, face tight as her eyes moved over him. "What did they do to you?"

"Just slapped me around some."

He winced as she started sawing through the bonds. An arm flopped free, numb and semi-useless, but he managed to wipe the blood from his eyes. The last of Gray's knights was crawling down the passage. Panting in fear at the echo of heavy footsteps behind him.

"Captain Bryce! Wait!"

Morvana Zeigler emerged from the darkness. His brother's words suddenly made sense. *Protect the bishop.*

"He is badly injured," she said. "Surely it is enough—"

"And what do we do with him, Your Grace?" Misha asked. "Spare him to tell the tale?"

He hefted the sword. A slash down his forearm dripped steadily, soaking the leather gauntlet.

"Glory to the Black Sun!" the knight cried in a cracked voice.

Misha chuckled. "I very much doubt it, *mate.*"

The man jerked like a pinned bug as the blade severed his spine. Another hard thrust and he stopped moving. Morvana shook her head and turned away. Misha wiped his sword on the knight's tabard, examining the blade with a critical eye.

"Forgive us, Your Grace, but it had to be done," Spassov said.

Alexei hadn't seen him return. He felt relieved that Patryk seemed unhurt, yet Alexei noticed the furtive glance he cast at Mikhail. His brother wore death like a mantle. Or a comfortable pair of slippers.

Alexei rose to his feet, rolling his aching shoulders. Patryk pulled him into an embrace.

"What is it with you and dungeons?" he asked, planting a kiss on the top of his head. "Some kind of fetish?"

"Ow," Alexei mumbled into his broad shoulder.

"Sorry." Patryk released him with a grimace. "You should have confessed everything."

"I tried. They weren't having it."

Misha tugged Alexei's gloves off and examined his hands, the touch surprisingly gentle. "I had worse when we trained for stress positions," he said. "Keep trying to flex your fingers. It'll hurt like hell in a minute, but it'll get the blood moving again."

The tone sounded sympathetic, but Alexei couldn't shake a suspicion that it was an act. It made him hate himself. Couldn't he feel a moment of gratitude? He'd be screaming his lungs out if they hadn't saved him.

"Where's Kasia?" Natalya asked. "We hoped she was with you."

"I don't know." He caught his brother's eye again. "Gray has her."

Misha nodded thoughtfully and adjusted his grip on the sword. "Then we find Gray."

Alexei almost warned his brother that Malach was coming, but the words stuck in his throat. He was afraid—no, terrified—of what would happen if the two of them came face to face again.

"You are bleeding yourself, Captain Bryce," Morvana said. She sounded angry. "Let me see."

Alexei expected Misha to shrug the injury off, but he held out his arm. She peeled the gauntlet down. The thick, scarred leather had taken the brunt of the blow, sparing his tendons but leaving a long, shallow cut from wrist to elbow.

Alexei stepped out of his soaked cassock. It was already slit down the front. "Use this."

Natalya retrieved her knives. She cut a wide strip of cloth and handed it to Morvana, who dressed the wound with a scowl. Alexei was still grappling with the fact that the bishop was here at all. She'd never liked him much and he was a far milder version of his brother. Mikhail embodied everything she despised—and she didn't even know about the Nightmark. In Kvengard, he'd led them to believe it was just a regular Sanctified Mark that Malach had flipped.

Alexei prayed she'd never find out.

"Thank you, Your Grace," Mikhail said absently. He was already looking down the tunnel. Anticipating an attack—or planning the next one.

Alexei braced a palm on the wall, drawing blue ley into his Marks. A wave of calm soothed the tangle of emotions. His mind cleared. "Gray said he'd return, but we can't wait. He's planning a coup."

Morvana's green eyes flashed. "A coup? I must warn Luk!"

"He has the Order behind him," Alexei said. "But I'm sure many of Clavis's knights remain loyal. No doubt the attack on the fort was a ruse to lure her away."

They started off through the catacombs, Misha taking up the rear. Alexei paused to pick up a fallen sword, forcing his fingers to close around the hilt. The hot prickling was a good sign. His body was waking up. Alice stuck close to his heels as he told them about following Kasia through the liminal tunnels. The discovery of the Order and Jule Danziger. Losing Alice when the doorway closed and running straight into Gray, who must have been waiting for them to emerge.

Natalya swore viciously at the part about Danziger. She dropped down to embrace the Markhound. "Don't worry, baby," she said. "We'll get the ones who did this to you."

Alice chuffed agreement, though Alexei sensed her fear. He had a sudden vision of knives in the dark. The rush of hatred made all his Marks flare at once. Blue light strobed in the darkness, then died, leaving calm in its wake.

"Are all the Order like this?" Morvana wondered. "The ones we arrested did not change their forms."

"Only some, I think," Alexei said.

"I'll take care of Danziger." Misha's voice drifted from behind.

"Not until we know where they've taken Kasia." Alexei stopped to walk beside his brother. "You must promise me!"

"I promise." He lowered his voice. "But if the bishop holds your Marks, we need to get her somewhere safe first. The woman will not touch a weapon. She's defenseless." He rubbed the back of his neck. "It's thanks to her we found you. I will not let her come to harm."

Was that guilt in his brother's voice? Alexei wondered uneasily how Morvana had gotten involved, but the whole story would have to wait.

"Take her to Lezarius," he said. "You can protect them both while I look for Gray. Nat and Spassov will back me up." A twinge of remorse. He'd argued for Lezarius to come here. "Your first loyalty must be to the Reverend Father of Jalghuth."

Mikhail was clearly torn, but he nodded. "I just wish we knew who to trust."

"Not Maria Karolo, that's for sure. We'll have to play it by ear."

Spassov slowed to wait for them. "Almost out," he said. "The Tomb of the Martyrs is ahead."

It was at that moment Alexei heard the first faint screams. He shared a quick look with his brother. They ran forward together, around a bend and up the narrow, twisting staircase he remembered from his last encounter with Kasia. Alexei burst through the exit first.

He never had nightmares for the simple reason that his Marks rendered him incapable of dreaming. But if he did, they might resemble the sight that awaited them.

A full moon floated above the basilica. People ran in every direction, pursued by loping silver dogs and other things he had no name for. Knights fought knights, steel singing. Mounted men galloped through the chaos, though Alexei had no idea whose side they were on. Bodies lay everywhere. The battle seemed hottest in front of the Pontifex's Palace where knots of guards clashed before the main doors. Then two dozen cloaked figures emerged, attacking from the rear. His heart sank as he understood that the palace had already fallen.

Knives flickered into Natalya's palms at the same instant Patryk brought his sword up. They edged together, back to back.

Alexei's gaze swept the scene, trying desperately to make sense of it. Who was winning? How many sides *were* there? He'd been in plenty of battles but none like this. Half the combatants weren't even human.

Alice made a sound somewhere between a bark and a whimper. Morvana muttered an oath in Kven.

"Looks like they started without us," Misha said dryly. "Get behind me, Your Grace."

A knight thundered toward the Tomb, hooves spewing clods of earth. His helm was down. Moonlight shone on the gold thread of his Crossed Keys tabard. Alexei's pulse quickened as he raised his broadsword. Mikhail parried a crushing downward blow that drove him to his knees. A hoof lashed out, sending him sprawling. The knight wheeled around and galloped back.

Time splintered into discrete ticks. He glimpsed a shaggy creature hurl itself at Patryk. The gleam of Natalya's knives. Morvana Zeigler sinking down, her pale hand clawing at the grass. The hollow drumbeat of the Marksteed bearing down. A shock through his arm as Alexei plunged his own sword into one of the white dogs as it leapt for his throat.

He yanked the blade free, chest heaving. Alice tore into the still-twitching body with savage growls. Somehow he was on the other side of the Tomb, though he didn't remember moving.

The world shrank to a narrow tunnel with his brother at the end of it. Misha slowly raised his head. Stared groggily up at his own death as the knight reined in above him, sword cutting a whistling swath through the air.

Then the mount screamed and reared. The man slid sideways, armor dragging him down with a crash. One foot was still hooked into the stirrup. His horse rolled its eyes, trembling all over, and galloped off, dragging the knight along.

Violet ley streamed from Morvana's sleeves as she rose to her feet. Alexei realized she had spooked the stallion.

Not so defenseless after all.

Misha drove the point of his sword into the ground and pushed himself up. The horse had kicked him in the head, but it must have been a glancing blow or he'd be out cold. Alexei hurried over for a closer look. His eyes looked glassy. The right pupil seemed a little larger than the left.

"I'm good," Misha slurred. "Really."

The fighting was already closing around them. Alexei knew his brother was concussed. How badly remained to be seen, but there was nothing he could do about it. Nothing but get his blade up and hope Misha did the same.

Steel clashed as he battered back an attack from a Raven knight. Alice dipped between the woman's legs, tripping her up. He wrenched her shield away and slammed the edge into her neck. When he spun back around, his brother was fending off two more. Misha's footwork was clumsy, but he managed to avoid being skewered until Alexei reached his side.

At every chance, he pressed a palm to the ground and filled his Marks with ley. It cleared the mind. Sharpened the reflexes. Blue light glimmered along the edge of his blade as he fought. Time seemed to stand still—or rush forward in jerky leaps.

Alice's snapping jaws kept the mounted riders at a distance, but it was a small reprieve. Liminal doors flashed open, disgorging things with scales and teeth and mindless bloodlust in their eyes. Volleys of arrows hissed down from slits in the buildings surrounding the plaza—though who was shooting at whom, Alexei couldn't say. Knights engaged in pitched skirmishes, some from different cities, others locked in battle with their own.

Natalya and Spassov were next to him at first, but the ebb and flow drew them farther apart. During a brief lull, Alexei realized he hadn't seen either of them in far too long. Only Mikhail remained, sword rising and falling, keeping a clear space around both him and Morvana Zeigler.

Later, he would forget whole hours of that night, yet recall inconsequential details with perfect clarity. A lone sandal tipped on its side with gum stuck to the sole. Reams of burning paper drifting down from a rooftop. Two riderless mounts galloping neck-in-neck down the Via Devana as though racing each other, inky tails streaming like banners.

Some of the traitors donned armbands emblazoned with the Black Sun against a red field. Others blended with the defenders until they saw their chance. Alexei learned this lesson when a soldier he had just saved turned on him. He would have died if his brother, who trusted no one, hadn't seen the woman draw a belt knife and try to plunge it into Alexei's back the instant he looked away.

The defenders regrouped at the portcullis, at least two hundred of them. They were killing anything unnatural that came within reach. So far, the gates were holding. Surely the knights at the outer walls of the city would come to their aid.

"We must try to reach the gates," Alexei panted.

They sheltered around the corner of a nondescript building no one seemed to care about. It sat halfway between the palace and the gates. The Antiquarium, according to a small plaque on one wall.

Misha gave a weary nod, getting his sword up as one of the white dogs sprang from the shadow of an archway. It snapped at the blade in its chest, refusing to die, until Alexei took its head off. Unlike the alchemical creations, the hounds were flesh and blood, though unlike anything he'd seen before. They had small pink eyes and coats like fresh snow.

He looked around for Alice and found her lying on her side, flanks heaving. Fear dried his throat as he ran his hands over her. She was covered in blood, but he found no fresh injuries.

"Go," he said to Misha. "I'll follow."

His brother's skin was ashen. He trembled with exhaustion. Yet he shook his head. "Not a chance, Alyosha."

"What is wrong with her?" Morvana crouched down. Alice stared with dull eyes, though her tail gave a thump when the bishop patted her head.

"I think she's just worn out," Alexei said.

"Then I will carry her." She lifted the Markhound in her arms.

The moon was on the other side of the Arx now, slivered behind the twin spires of the Apostolic Signatura. The two sides had pulled back to gather for a final contest. Gray's Order held the Pontifex's Palace and many of the other buildings, which flew Black Sun pennants alongside the Crossed Keys. Misshapen shadows slunk back and forth along the front lines before the palace. Sometimes they darted out and seized something in their teeth, dragging it back. Alexei was glad for the darkness.

"What about those liminal doors?" Morvana asked. "Could we open one into the palace ourselves? Try to rescue Luk and Lezarius, if they still live?"

Alexei had already considered it. "I don't know the passages well enough," he said. "They're a maze. We could end up anywhere. But the Order does know them. You can be sure they're guarding every entrance, liminal or otherwise."

Misha's head cocked. A moment later, Alexei heard it. A new sound, rising and falling in waves. The defenders at the gates were singing the anthem of Nantwich. The hair lifted on his arms as a chill wind carried their voices across three hundred meters of bloodied ground.

Freedom, freedom!
By the light and grace of the ley
We have held the virtues of this land
In lofty splendor,
And on its altars we once more vow
To die, rather than live as slaves.
Freedom, freedom!
The martial turmoil of yesterday
And the horrible clamour of war
Are silenced at last,
By sweet hymns of peace and unity.

Thirty years before, their fathers and mothers had done the same when Balaur's army camped outside the walls. The song was an answer to the twisted Via Libertas of the nihilim.

Half of Nantwich burned in the last stand that followed. To the south, Beleth's forces had surrounded Novostopol. If Lezarius hadn't made the Void, banishing the mages into the wilderness, Alexei would have grown up in an entirely different world.

Morvana joined in at the second chorus. Her voice was sweet and low. A moment later, Mikhail's baritone took up the harmony. He hummed his way through some of it, which frightened Alexei badly. Misha had taught him the words when they were little boys. They used to sing it all the time in their tree fort, pretending the squirrels rooting for acorns below were mages in disguise. There was no chance his brother had forgotten.

Alexei didn't blame the Nightmark. In Jalghuth, Misha often quoted lengthy passages of the *Meliora* to his knights without benefit of the book. He'd committed the whole thing to heart by the time he was nine.

It had to be the concussion. How his brother was even still standing, Alexei had no idea.

The last stanza was a bitter irony in light of their circumstances, but his heart lightened as he sang the words. A serenity that had nothing to do with his Marks. Alexei knew where he chose to die—alongside the defiant men and women at the gates.

The battle was as good as over. It wasn't a matter of numbers. The sides were more or less equally matched. But those of the Order who'd survived were wielding death ley. Alexei had seen dozens consumed by those reaching tendrils.

For the hundredth time, he wondered where the reinforcements were. What of the garrisons along the city walls? The knights patrolling the Morho? He couldn't believe they all followed Gray. From what he could tell, most of the Nants were loyal to Clavis.

The last words faded and the song began anew, drifting over in snatches.

"They did right to try to contain the enemy here," Misha said. "Worst case . . . I mean to say . . . ." He trailed off in obvious confusion.

Morvana touched his sleeve. "It's all right, Captain."

He blinked rapidly, pressing a hand over one eye. "Worst case, they can open the gates. At least there's a line of retreat."

"Then let us join them," she said, adjusting Alice in her arms.

For the first time in hours, Alexei noticed glints of gold in her short hair. The diamond stud in her nose and fine lines that touched the corners of her eyes. Dawn was breaking.

They picked their way through broken glass and bodies cushioned with arrows. Worse sights he'd grown numb to. The singing grew louder. Then Gray's forces launched into their own anthem. A discordant clamor of shouts and taunts and blood-curdling howls.

The white hounds trotted out to form a line across the plaza. Behind them, dozens of half-human beasts prowled. Then about a hundred cloaked figures and a scattering of armored knights.

Gray himself had yet to appear. No doubt hiding inside the palace, the coward.

The defenders were a mix of knights and clergy. When they saw the trio limping towards the gates, a few beckoned them on. Two broke from the crowd. One tall and slender, the other built like a balding sledgehammer. Covered in mud and blood, yet undeniably Patryk Spassov and Natalya Anderle. Tears stood in her eyes as she cupped Alexei's face.

"We'd given up hope," she said.

"Should have known better," Spassov grinned.

A ragged cry went up from the knights in the gatehouse. The chains of the portcullis winched upward. Alexei's heart lifted at the sight of hundreds of blue banners. A sea of them stretching back across the drawbridge beyond.

"That's what they were waiting for!" He grinned. "The Wolves from Kvengard!"

Misha clapped him on the shoulder. Morvana closed her eyes. *"Danke der ley,"* she murmured.

The first Kvens poured through before the portcullis was fully raised. A double column of knights in blue tabards followed by light cavalry and archers. The sun broke over the walls, shining on breastplates and pikes. The defenders let out a resounding cheer.

Not even the appearance of Kommandant Rademacher in the van could dampen Alexei's joy. The sound of marching feet and jangling harness filled the air. Rademacher rode out to the center of the plaza.

The white dogs were snapping and pawing at the ground. One streaked toward his horse. The animal whinnied nervously. Rademacher sawed at the reins and the mount quieted. His troops were fanning out, penning the defenders into the center of the plaza.

Alexei glanced up at the palace. A figure watched from one of the high balconies. Even at a distance, Alexei could make out the deep-set eyes and hollow cheeks of the Pontifex

Luk. The realization of what was happening struck him, but it was already too late.

Rademacher wheeled around, turning his back to their enemies.

"Throw down your swords," he shouted, "and you will be treated as prisoners of war with all the rights accorded under Curia law! Resist and you will be executed on the spot!"

There was a stunned silence. Then angry mutters swept the crowd. The defenders milled in confusion.

"Drop the portcullis!" someone shouted desperately.

The heavy iron grill was designed to slam down in an instant should the need arise. A struggle erupted at the gate-house. It was swiftly suppressed by the Kvens. The portcullis remained open. There seemed no end to Luk's army.

"On your knees!" Rademacher barked. "Hands in the air!"

Steel scraped on leather as the Kvens drew their swords. Arrows notched to bowstrings.

"Do it! Or I'll unleash the dogs on you!"

Outnumbered thirty to one, the defenders complied with grim faces. Alexei sank to his knees. So did Patryk and Natalya, who muttered vile oaths under her breath. Only Morvana and his brother remained standing. The bishop looked livid. She gently set Alice down and strode forward with clenched fists. Misha followed. Rademacher watched them approach with a stony expression.

"What is the meaning of this?" Morvana demanded. "Have you gone mad, Kommandant?" She turned in a slow circle, glaring at the Kvens. Some flinched away from her gaze. Most stared back impassively. "Do your vows mean nothing? We just signed a binding treaty with Nantwich! Our brothers and sisters in the Via Sancta! You would follow the orders of a traitor?"

"They are not my orders," Rademacher said with satisfaction. "It is the will of the Reverend Father Luk. *You* are the traitor."

Morvana followed his eyes to the balcony. The blood drained from her face. She shook her head in denial.

Maria Karolo had joined Luk at the balustrade. The sharp corner of her hair brushed a chilly half-smile.

"You are under arrest, Zeigler," Rademacher said. "Stripped of all offices and authority by order of the Reverend Father." He raised his voice. "The Nuncio is hereby excommunicated!" A nod at his men. "Take her into the Arx."

Misha raised his sword. "Touch her," he said loudly, "and it will be the last thing you do."

"No!" Morvana laid a hand on his arm. It was so quiet, Alexei heard her words clearly, though they were spoken for his brother. "You will not die for me, Captain. I will go."

"What will you do with Her Grace?" Misha demanded.

"That is for the Reverend Father to determine." Rademacher stared down from his horse. "My orders are merely to take her into custody." He smiled. "Come, Bryce. We know each other. Surely we can settle this without bloodshed."

Misha's lip curled in derision. "Without bloodshed?" He looked around. "You *are* mad."

"Enough!" A sharp gesture to his knights. "Detain them both."

A dozen men came forward. Alexei feared his brother would make a stand, but he threw the sword down. His eyes never left Rademacher's face as the knights dragged him away. Morvana strode for the palace with her back straight and head held high, her captors hurrying to keep her surrounded. Alexei sensed their unease. The bishop might be excommunicated, but she had been Luk's chief aide for years. None seemed eager to lay hands on her.

Rademacher hadn't seen Alexei yet, but he would at any moment. And it wasn't himself he feared for.

"Go," Alexei hissed. "Leave, little sister."

Alice's ears drooped. She wedged her tail between her legs, avoiding his eye.

The white hound at Rademacher's side sniffed the air. It caught her scent and barked aggressively. The others picked it up. They trotted across the plaza, muzzles frothing with saliva. A demonic chorus.

"Hide!" Alexei repeated fiercely. "Or I will die to protect you, understand?"

Alice tipped her snout up and bayed at the sky. The pack was coming now, lean hindquarters bunching and lengthening. Blood matted their jowls. The tiny pink eyes shone with anticipation.

"You can't save me if they tear you to pieces!" Alexei seized Alice's scruff and shook her hard. "Go away, damn you!"

Alice growled in fury and despair. She faded to smoke just as the alpha sprang. Its jaws snapped on air. The creature gave a whimper of surprise. Its head swung around, panting and snuffling the ground. Alexei kept perfectly still, on his knees, palms upraised. His heart thundered as the pack surrounded him, so close he could feel the chill radiating from their bodies, smell their coppery breath.

"Bloody Kven bastards!" someone shouted.

Rademacher's face darkened. He rode forward. "Who said that?"

The defenders kept their heads down. No one spoke.

A sharp whistle and the white hounds loped off.

Rademacher surveyed the prisoners. "You will march to Westfield Stadium in an orderly fashion. Cooperate and you will be treated well. Resist and you will learn how far my mercy extends."

Lances prodded them to their feet. A gap was opened in the Kven ranks. The skies were darkening. A thin rain began to fall as Alexei emerged from the portcullis.

"They had it all planned out," he muttered to Patryk, who walked beside him.

Spassov grimaced at the sky. "It's not over, eh? Maybe Clavis will come back. Kick their asses."

"Maybe." Alexei shivered as the rain thickened, soaking his shirt. He thought of what Gray had said. "But I'll tell you who else is coming, Patryk."

Chapter Twenty-Eight

Malach saw the smoke rising over Nantwich before they reached the walls. Scouts rode ahead, returning to jubilantly report that the city had fallen to the Kvens.

Our new allies, he thought, still stunned that Luk, of all people, had broken from the other Curiae.

He glanced at Falke. "Get your hood up, Severin."

The pontifex of Novostopol slumped in the saddle with a dazed expression. It lifted Malach's spirits.

They passed through the city gates, garrisoned by the Wolves now. The company numbered twenty mages, all young and handpicked by Malach for their level heads—and more importantly, their loyalty to *him.* Sydonie and Tristhus rode on either side, gaping at the tall buildings and broad boulevards. The Arx had spared no expense when it rebuilt after the war. Nantwich wasn't a large city, but the elegant baroque style rivaled Novostopol's oldest, wealthiest districts.

Shiny automobiles lined the curbs. Traffic lights flashed, though not a soul moved in the streets except for Kven soldiers on horseback. The patrols eyed their red cloaks warily, giving the mages a wide berth. Not for the first time, Malach wondered exactly what he'd gotten himself into.

He reminded himself that Nantwich was just a stepping stone. The ultimate goal was his own city. Not as it stood now —a looted husk occupied by Falke's Ravens—but a place of beauty and light.

The children had never seen a car that wasn't rusted out. Never peered into a single shop window. Most of the mages hadn't, either. When they entered a deserted commercial district, Syd leapt from the saddle and ran to a smashed plate glass window, sticking a hand through to fish out a beribboned sunhat and jam it on her head.

Malach reined up. "Make it quick, Syd."

"Okay, Cardinal!" A pair of huge sunglasses followed. She struck a pose, hand on hip. "How do I look?"

Whatever Sydonie did, Tristhus had to copy her. The younger boy slid from the saddle and ran to the shop.

"Watch the glass!" Malach called. Rachel squirmed in front of him.

"Want one, too," she whispered.

It was the first words she had spoken on the journey—to him, at least.

"Get a hat for Rachel," he called.

"Take whatever you want," Valdrian added with a dry laugh. "Spoils of war."

All the mages descended from Bal Kirith bloodlines—not Bal Agnar. Malach had made sure of that. They knew Syd and Trist and tolerated their antics with gruff indulgence. In turn, the children understood precisely how far they could go without earning a cuff, or worse. No one even attempted to supervise them except Malach, not that they listened to him.

Trithus found a silk top hat. It kept falling off, but he seemed determined to keep it. Syd picked out a man's derby with a feather in the band. She handed it to Malach, who set it on his daughter's head.

"Can you see?" he asked with a laugh.

She nodded, though he knew she couldn't. Malach's

laughter died as he gazed at the column of smoke drifting into the sky. Maybe it was better that way.

"Raise the banner," he told Valdrian.

His cousin galloped back to relay the command. The mage at their rear, a woman named Gammon, hoisted the Black Sun pennant just as a group of Kvens approached on horseback. Their leader flipped up his visor, revealing smooth pink cheeks and a thin, fussy mouth.

"Who are you?" Malach asked.

"Kommandant Rademacher." Cold eyes studied his crimson robe. "They're expecting you at the palace, mage."

"I am Balaur's Nuncio," Malach said. "What is the state of the city?"

"We are restoring order."

"Then why," he wondered, "is it burning?"

Rademacher scowled. "There was resistance in the Unmarked quarter. They are learning a lesson."

The Unmarked quarter. Malach thought of Nikola's flat in Ash Court. The families that lived jammed together in the tenements.

"Organize brigades to put out the flames," he snapped. "*Now.*"

Gloved hands tightened around the reins. "I follow the Reverend Father Luk's orders, mage," the kommandant replied tightly.

Malach stared at him until he looked away. He turned and repeated the order to Valdrian.

"If you encounter any knights, take them prisoner. They can be used as hostages. If they're mortally wounded, put them out of their misery. But civilians are to be treated gently, understand?"

Valdrian winked. "Got it, Nuncio."

Rademacher looked irritated, but didn't try to countermand the orders. Valdrian chose a dozen mages and galloped off toward the source of the smoke.

"If your hand is too heavy, the whole city will rise up against you," Malach said. "Hearts and minds. Do you understand nothing of strategy?"

"I understand that you appear when the fighting is done and we suffer all the casualties," Rademacher snapped, anger thickening his Kven accent. "But I will not hinder you, mage." He flung out an arm. "The Arx is that way."

Malach rode on, preoccupied with thoughts of their arrival. Falke had kept well back from the knights, face averted, but Luk would recognize him in an instant. Others, too.

When they reached the stone bridge spanning the Caerfax River, Malach sent Jessiel ahead to inform the knights in the gatehouse that he had arrived. A curtain wall enclosed the Arx —twice as high as the one at Bal Agnar—casting a long shadow across the placid river. Malach gazed up at the hundreds of Crossed Keys Wards etched into the battlements; all useless now. He spurred his mount forward.

In short order, the first portcullis was winched up. They rode through a tunnel and beneath a second portcullis into a bailey, which widened further to the vast green plaza that sat at the center of every Arx.

"Don't look," Malach whispered. "Just keep your eyes on the horse."

Of course, Rachel ignored this directive. She pushed the brim of the hat up. He could only make out her profile, but her mouth tightened as they rode along the edge of the plaza. The bodies had been removed, though the signs of battle were everywhere. Grass churned to red mud. Bits of clothing and the drone of flies.

Chars scrubbed blood from the steps of the rectangular palace fronting the plaza. Knights ran forward to take his bridle and attend to the other riders. A tall, slender man in a purple robe appeared at the doors. He trotted down the broad steps with a smile.

"I am Cardinal Lucas Gray," he said, peering at them through steel-rimmed spectacles. "We are pleased to welcome the delegation from Bal Agnar to our city."

"The Reverend Father Balaur accepts your hospitality," Malach replied. "It's been a long ride. I would like to see our rooms."

"Of course." His head bobbed. "You will have the east wing of the Pontifical Palace, Your Excellency."

Gray's eyes skipped over his companions. Did they catch for a moment on Falke? Malach wasn't sure. He handed Rachel down and slid from the saddle, legs aching.

"I hear your own Arx is far more impressive," Gray said, flashing a nervous smile. "Er, I mean from the outside, of course."

Both rebel cities had been looted down to the last bauble, but Bal Kirith at least retained a hint of its former grandeur. The Pontifex's Palace was made of astrum, which shone like cold fire beneath the moon and stars. The front was carved with vines and flowers that made it seem a part of the jungle.

"That is true," Malach agreed, studying the plain stone structure before him. "But our cities will be restored someday." He smiled. "And you will weep from the beauty of them."

Gray nodded uncertainly. He led them up the stairs and through a pair of bronze doors into a marble-floored antechamber. A small woman with straight black hair waited with hands clasped. She wore a ring of keys around her neck. Dark, tilted eyes met Malach's. She had a direct, no-nonsense gaze.

"This is the Mistress of Chars," Gray said. "She'll see you to your rooms. Once you've refreshed yourself, you may come to the main audience chamber." He bowed and retreated down one of the columned loggias.

"If you would follow me, Nuncio?" the Mistress of Chars asked.

Sydonie and Tristhus darted ahead, trailing grubby fingers along the ancient tapestries lining the walls. When Rachel yanked at his hand, he gave in and let her join them. Falke walked a few paces behind with his hood raised.

"We won't give you any trouble, Mistress," Malach said as they ascended a wide, curving staircase. "You have my word."

"I did not expect any," she replied in a polite tone, though her face was carved from granite.

"But I will need the keys to all the doors in this wing," he added.

"Of course. Your apartments are at the end of the corridor. They are the largest." She lifted the chain from her neck and unhooked a second ring of keys. Malach tucked it in his pocket.

"I brought my own manservant. There's no need to clean unless I request it."

"Should I send food?"

"Is there a common room?"

"The library."

"Bring it there." Malach gave a brief bow. "Thank you, Mistress."

She dropped a curtsy. "Excellency."

Malach watched her depart. The top of her head barely reached his shoulder, but she had more natural authority than Cardinal Gray—and didn't seem half as afraid of him.

"Take any rooms that strike your fancy," he told his cousins. "Syd and Trist, you can share."

The siblings had already flung open one of the doors. Sydonie ran to a huge four-poster bed and threw herself down. Tristhus galloped for the bathroom. Malach heard the faucets open full blast.

"There's water!" he shouted. "Cold *and* hot!"

"Don't forget to turn it off," Malach called.

"I won't!"

Syd rolled over until she fell off the bed. "Ow," she

muttered, bouncing back up again. Four strides and she was jumping up and down on the silk couch. Within seconds, it was covered with muddy bootprints.

"Come here, Rachel!" Trist shouted. "Come see the mirror!"

She darted off. Malach went into the bathroom and adjusted the water. Tristhus was making hideous faces at himself in the vanity.

"I want to stay here forever, Malach!" Syd cried.

"Take your shoes off. And someday, Bal Kirith will look like this. Even better."

She eyed him doubtfully.

"Shoes," he reminded her.

Syd rolled her eyes and tugged her boots off. "I want to stay *here.*"

"We'll see," he said. "Don't leave the east wing. I mean it, Syd."

"Okay!"

Her version of *we'll see.*

They eyed each other. "I *won't!*" she promised. "We'll all take baths and be ever so clean and pretty when you come back. I'll wash Rachel's hair!"

"Go easy on the knots." Malach closed the door behind him. Falke waited in the hall with a dour expression.

"Rachel needs me to look after her," he hissed.

Malach dropped his voice, though his kin had departed to find their own rooms. "I won't have you poisoning my child against me."

"I hardly need to. You're doing a masterful job of it yourself."

He ignored the jibe, gripping Falke's arm and guiding him down the corridor. Malach found his own apartments, then sought something close by that was unoccupied. A smaller room around the corner served nicely. The window looked down on a four-story drop. He pushed Falke inside.

"You might as well get used to it," Malach said. "This is your life now. Four walls and only regrets for company."

He slammed the door on Falke's glare and tried different keys until he found the right one. The lock clicked. Let the old bastard stew in his own juices. He'd get something to eat when Malach found the time.

He returned to his own apartments and splashed cold water on his face. Then he rooted through his saddlebags and changed into a fresh robe. By the time he found the library, the other mages were sprawled in leather chairs by a roaring fire. The Mistress had sent up roast fowl, bread and cheese, and a variety of pies, along with both wine and beer.

"Keep your wits," Malach warned. "I might need you."

Valdrian raised his glass with a wry grin. "Carpe noctem!" *Seize the night.*

Malach nodded to Caralexa and Jessiel. "Ready to put a little fear into our hosts?"

They rose to their feet. Jess tossed her chicken leg on the platter and wiped her hands on the tablecloth. Lexa shouldered her bow.

Malach grinned. "Let's go see Luk."

A PAIR of Wolf knights lounged outside the audience chamber. When they saw Malach's red robe, they snapped to attention and flung the doors wide.

"The Nuncio of Bal Agnar!" one cried.

Malach strode through the doors, Caralexa and Jessiel prowling at his heels.

Upwards of fifty people occupied the room. A dozen priests wearing cassocks embroidered with a sheaf of wheat stood along one wall. Kvens in blue tabards occupied the other. Six large white dogs sat at their feet. Malach tensed, but the dogs didn't bark.

Knots of men and women wearing armbands with the Black Sun gathered in the center of the chamber. They had the well-fed, permanently bored look of the very rich. People who had lived their entire lives with the certainty that every need would be attended to by someone else.

Malach had Marked many of their breed in Novostopol. No matter how much they had, there was always something else that lay just out of reach. Something only he could give them.

The crowd parted, whispering, as he approached a raised dais at the far end of the hall.

A cadaverous man sat on the pontifex's throne. Thin and bald with deep-set eyes. A sleeveless white robe revealed sinewy arms Marked with running wolves. To his right stood a middle-aged woman with chin-length brown hair. A bishop, her blue robe also marked with the sheaf of wheat. She watched Malach with narrow eyes.

Gray stood to Luk's left. The cardinal gave Malach a faltering smile.

"So you are Balaur's Nuncio?" Luk inclined his head. He had only a trace of the Kven accent.

"His regent," Malach corrected. "Which means you're sitting in my chair."

Gray visibly winced. There was a taut silence. The Wolf knights perked up. Luk regarded Malach without expression.

"The final disposition of Nantwich remains to be seen," he said. "In the interim—"

"You will not dishonor the alliance by pretending that you have already been named pontifex of this city," Malach interrupted. "Unless I am mistaken?" He looked around. "Perhaps we came to the wrong place. Is this Kvengard?"

A few members of the Order laughed. The rest watched him with measuring gazes. Then a tall blond man slipped from the crowd and climbed up to the dais. He whispered in

Luk's ear. The pontifex's jaw tightened, but he gave a brief nod.

"The seat is yours, Nuncio," he said. "Until your own Reverend Father arrives." The tone was mild, though Malach sensed an undercurrent of fury. "I have no designs on Nantwich. Which I imagine you well know."

"I know what I see," Malach replied, striding easily up to the dais. "But I appreciate your understanding." His gaze fell to the blond man's armband. "Symbols have power."

The man gave an oily smile. He'd averted a confrontation, but Malach instinctively disliked him.

Luk rose to his feet. Gray rushed forward to help him descend the dais. The bishop went with them. Malach settled himself into the throne and crossed his ankles. Caralexa and Jessiel took places to either side.

"Gray," he said. "Come here."

The cardinal swallowed and returned to the foot of the dais. "Any word on Clavis?"

"Not so far," he admitted. "Her force was ambushed, but they fought hard. She escaped."

"So she is still in the Morho. And what of Novostopol?"

The bishop lifted her pointy chin. "When I return, I will persuade them of the need to join this new alliance. The cardinals will see reason. They have no choice now—"

"Who are you?" Malach asked bluntly.

"Bishop Maria Karolo." She drew herself up. "Head of the Order of Saint Marcius."

"Well, Bishop Maria Karolo, I would not count on Novo dropping into our laps like a piece of overripe fruit. There are hardliners in the Arx who would happily die before making common cause with nihilim. Then we have the problem of the north. Where is Lezarius?"

"In custody."

"Bring him here."

A strange expression crossed Luk's face. He waved a finger. Two of the Wolf knights broke off and left the chamber.

Caralexa leaned over. "You should kill him!" she hissed. "He made the Void!"

"And he broke it," Malach replied. "I am curious to see him for myself."

She grunted. "Look at Luk. Is he about to faint?"

The Pontifex of Kvengard did look queasy. His face had gone the curdled hue of the eyeless slugs that dwelt under the leaf loam in the Morho Sarpanitum.

The knights returned, hauling an old man between them. He had kinky hair and light eyes that blazed from his dark face. He still wore the white robe of his office, though it was speckled with blood.

Malach leaned forward on the throne. So this was the Lion of the North. The architect of the mages' suffering. He looked strong for his age. Despite himself, Malach felt a reluctant admiration. He held his head high despite the hisses and catcalls from the Order.

Lezarius paid them no attention. Nor did he give Malach more than a cursory glance. His gaze fixed on Luk.

"It was *you*!" he cried, pointing a shaking finger. "*You* who changed my face!"

Luk flinched. "Balaur would have killed you. I showed you mercy."

"There were two figures on the Lance! I could never see them clearly. But I remember now!" He lunged at Luk. The knights restrained him. "Why? Why would you do such a thing?"

"The Praefator bloodlines run through the nihilim! If the Via Sancta is to be saved, we must pardon their crimes, as distasteful as we both find it."

Malach cocked a brow at Lexa. *Oh shit*, she mouthed back at him.

"We argued," Lezarius continued, his eyes distant. "Long

into the night. You urged me to release Balaur——"

"And you would not listen! You left us no choice." A mask of indifference slipped over Luk's face. "For the sake of our long friendship, I convinced him to turn your Marks and allow me to dispose of you. You were well-treated. You cannot deny it."

"Well-treated?" Lezarius echoed. "I won't bother to dignify that with a response." He raised a hand to his head. "Oh, what a fool I've been! You are the *only* one who could have done it! Use the ley to reknit my flesh, as you did with the hounds." A sudden calm came over him. "You are a monster, Luk. As bad as Balaur, if not worse. And your evil will return to you tenfold. Just as it says in the *Meliora*——"

"Get him out!" Luk thundered. "Out of my sight!"

The knights dragged Lezarius away, still cursing and struggling.

Malach listened to his furious cries fade down the corridor. Luk stood perfectly still, staring at nothing.

"Well," Malach said with a cheerful smile. "I think this audience is over. As regent, I intend to exercise my full authority over the governance of Nantwich until the Reverend Father Balaur arrives to finalize your agreement."

No one spoke. Mario Karolo eyed him with thinly disguised hostility. Luk seemed lost in his own dark thoughts.

Malach waved a hand. "You're all dismissed."

A slight milling around began.

"Now!" he snapped. "Out!"

Luk nodded at the Wolf knights. They formed a square around him as he left, leaning heavily on Maria Karolo. A few of the female members of the Order actually lifted their skirts to run.

"Not you, Gray." Malach beckoned with a finger. The cardinal scurried over. "Did you know all that?"

Gray shook his head. "It was enlightening, Nuncio."

"It was, indeed," he replied thoughtfully.

So Luk's treachery was not new. Balaur might have mentioned it before, but he'd told Malach almost nothing. Only that the Kvens had agreed to an alliance in exchange for infant mages. The same was promised to the Nants.

They were all desperate to renew their bloodlines. Desperate enough to snatch at any faint hope. Malach doubted Balaur would deliver on his promises. By the time they realized the truth, it would be too late. Idiots, he thought. If they had stood against us, they might have salvaged something in the end. They might even have won.

But the Via Sancta was shattered. Now it was a matter of squabbling over the pieces.

"See that Lezarius is kept safe," he told Gray. "Treat him well. But send a Markhawk north and tell whoever he left in charge that if they march, their pontifex will die. That should buy us some time."

Malach hopped down from the throne. He'd rather enjoyed the interlude, though he didn't give a fig whose bottom ultimately occupied the high seat. He turned to Lexa and Jess.

"Find Valdrian and tell him what you heard here. We'll meet in council later."

The women jogged from the chamber, Lexa's purple hair drawing a few stares. Only Lucas Gray remained. Malach wondered what he was getting out of the deal. Most likely he hoped to be named pontifex of Nantwich himself.

As if Balaur would ever give up the city once he was dug in here.

"Do you have the cartomancer in custody?"

"I do, Nuncio."

Malach gave a firm nod, feeling oddly nervous. "Then take me to her."

Chapter Twenty-Nine

Kasia was dozing when a flash of violet liminal light roused her. She lifted her head.

Gray again. And next to him, an attractive man of about thirty years with black hair curling behind his ears. Robes the color of fresh blood. He gazed at her intently.

"Leave us, Gray," he said. "Five minutes alone."

She remembered the voice, though it had been tight with anger the last time she heard it.

The Nant cardinal met her eyes briefly, then stepped back. The doorway faded.

Kasia rose to her feet, gut churning. But the cards had warned her he was coming. Again and again.

Why did the ley keep drawing them together? She wanted nothing to do with him. He was in league with the Order. Her own brother—

"What do you call yourself? Kasia or Katarzynka?"

She crushed the confusing tangle of emotions and adopted an attitude of nonchalance.

"I don't care. Call me what you like."

"Which one?" he persisted.

"Kasia."

Saints, but he did look like her. *Did he know?*

"How are you Unmarked?" he asked.

A weight eased from her chest. "I failed the tests."

"That's not what I mean. If you're a mage, you should have been Marked at birth."

She shrugged. "I don't know."

Malach leaned against the wall. "I didn't realize you were nihilim when we met."

"When you tried to strangle me, you mean?"

"I wasn't planning to kill you."

"You threatened to."

He didn't apologize. "Where do you come from?"

"I have no idea. I was adopted."

"Who found you?"

"My parents never told me."

His gaze lowered to the manacle around her ankle. A slight frown creased his brow.

"Why does Balaur want you? What do you know?" Malach's voice softened to a coaxing, seductive register. "Tell me and I'll get you out of here. Gray shouldn't have treated you like this."

Kasia smiled. "I do know a few things. You're here with Dmitry Falke, aren't you?"

His stunned expression was priceless. Malach opened his mouth and closed it again.

"I know Falke would never join you, so I can only assume you have him prisoner. Along with the mage who destroyed the Arx. A child?"

The blood drained from his face. "What *are* you?"

"You know what I am. A cartomancer who reads the past, the future, and everything in between." Her smile widened. "Do you want to know which card is yours, Malach?"

The barest nod.

"You are The Fool." She tilted her head. "But I don't

think you're stupid. So why don't we go somewhere more comfortable and talk about it? As you suggested."

A flat stare. He crossed his arms. "I'll get you out. But if you breathe a word of this, you'll be right back again."

"I understand."

He flexed his fingers. "I could use the ley to compel you."

"Like you did before," she said with a touch of bitterness.

"That was only a trickle. You've never experienced the most extreme degree of compulsion. It wipes the mind blank. There's nothing left but an all-consuming desire to please. But if you work with me, I'll see we both get what we want."

The threat unnerved her, but Kasia kept her voice calm. "What is it you think I want?"

"Your freedom, of course."

"I want a bit more than that," she replied. "But perhaps you *can* help me—"

She cut off as the doorway opened. Malach whipped around.

"Gray," he said sternly. "I will not have Domina Novak shackled like a criminal!"

"But my instructions—" he stammered.

"Are overridden. I will keep her in my custody."

"Of course, Nuncio." He fumbled the key from his robe and handed it over. "But she is dangerous. I warn you—"

Malach snatched the key. "I'll handle her."

In three strides, he was inside the bounds of the chain. Gray watched anxiously as Malach sank to one knee and unlocked the shackle. Red weals crossed the flesh beneath. Kasia flexed her ankle, then hobbled behind him to the door. She smiled at Gray as she passed. He shrank back.

"You see, Lucas? I'm perfectly civilized."

They passed through a series of liminal doors and emerged into a dim passage of the Arx. Malach dismissed Gray, who hurried off with a tight expression.

"I want my cards back," Kasia said.

"Not likely," Malach replied, steering her up a flight of stairs.

"I could tell you things."

"And work the ley."

"I promise I won't." She paused. "Is the city occupied?"

"By the Kvens. I just arrived from Bal Agnar."

"The *Kvens*?"

"Trust me, they'll come to regret it," he said dryly. "But they are the main force at the moment."

She felt cold. "What about all the delegations?"

Malach glanced at her. "Lezarius is locked up. Karolo has joined with Luk."

"That conniving bitch!"

"I don't doubt it. Do you know her?"

"She tried to arrest me," Kasia admitted. "Back in Novo."

"What for?"

"Killing the Reverend Mother Feizah."

Malach seemed to find this funny. Laughter rang through the empty corridor.

She shot him an annoyed look. "I know you didn't do it, either."

His mirth died. "Are you sure you're not a witch?"

"Karolo thought so." It was Kasia's turn to be amused. "But no, I am not a witch."

"You don't have the eyes," he muttered.

"What do eyes have to do with it?"

"Never mind." He guided her around a corner.

"I have friends here," Kasia said carefully. "I would know what became of them."

She felt reluctant to mention Natalya and Patryk. Alexei, most of all. Balaur might use them against her. But she had to know if they lived.

"I can look for them." Malach stopped, regarding her seriously. "A bargain, Kasia. If you keep my secrets."

"A bargain, mage," she replied, concealing her hatred.

"You say that as if you are not one of us."

"I'm not!" It came out more forcefully than she'd intended.

He eyed her askance. "I suppose you aren't. Though blood is blood."

She fell silent. They passed down a long corridor. Malach unlocked a door and Kasia stepped inside. A man in a drab tunic and baggy, patched trousers sat by the window. The light caught his silver hair, which stood up in tufts. He gazed at her in shock. "Domina Novak!"

How odd to stand before the man who had saved her life. And now here they all were again.

The Fool. The Hierophant. And The High Priestess, who was sometimes also The Mage.

No matter how often the deck was shuffled, it kept spitting out the same spread.

She held Falke's eyes, willing him to keep silent about who she was. He clearly hadn't told Malach the truth yet. Once they were alone, she would beg him to keep that silence forever.

"Reverend Father," she said, dropping a little curtsy.

"There's no need for that," Malach said brusquely. "His name is Severin. He's my servant."

Falke shot him a disgusted look.

None of it made sense. Why was Falke still alive? And pretending to be a servant?

"Who is The Star?" Kasia asked. "I've seen her in the cards."

Malach sank to the narrow bed, head dropping to his hands.

"Her name is Rachel," he said heavily. "She's my daughter."

Kasia stared at him, then at Falke. New layers of meaning came clear. She had a niece. One with terrifying powers.

"She's here?" Kasia asked, sweat beading the back of her neck.

Malach nodded. He glared at Falke. "This bastard stole her from me. He Marked her!"

Falke flushed.

Kasia remembered Alexei talking about Mark sickness. "Ah . . . so you took him to protect her?"

"I had no choice! If he dies, she dies. Until I find a way to remove it, I intend to keep him close." Malach's face clouded.

"But Balaur doesn't know," Kasia said slowly. "None of them do." She shook her head in wonder. "How on earth have you managed it?"

"People see what they expect to see," Malach replied. "Take away the ring, put him in servants' garb, and they're none the wiser." His gaze sharpened. "Did you tell anyone what you read in the cards? Gray, perhaps?"

Kasia hesitated. Would he kill her to keep her quiet?

"Answer the question."

"No, I didn't tell anyone."

He studied her. "I hope you're not lying to me."

The skin on her arms prickled. "If you let me do a reading, I could tell you more. I could—"

"There no way I'm giving you the ley, Kasia." He stood. "You'll stay here for now. What are the names of your friends?"

"Patryk Spassov and Natalya Anderle." Kasia described them.

"I'll do my best," Malach said. "But they're burning the dead to prevent disease. If your friends are among them . . . ."

Her stomach twisted. "There are two others."

A curt nod. "Who?"

"Alexei Bryce. And his brother, Mikhail Bryce."

Malach's face turned to stone. "The laqueos?"

"We had a bargain," she reminded him.

"I will ask," he said coldly, spinning on his heel.

"Wait!" she cried.

But Malach was gone.

She exhaled and turned to Falke. "How are you, Reverend Father?"

"Well enough. He hasn't severed me. Though the name he gave me was deliberate. A warning that he could at any time."

"Can't you use the ley to get us out of here?"

"I'm afraid to touch it. The taint of the Morho is strong." He clasped his gloved hands. "You wouldn't believe how many of my own knights were at Bal Agnar. It's madness!"

Kasia searched his face. "And this child, Rachel? Is she a monster like her father?"

"No, thank the Saints. Malach coerced her. But I fear for her safety. She was my hope for the future, Kasia." His jaw set. "*Appeasement.* That is their strategy!" He was talking about Luk and Karolo now. "They think they can reach an accommodation with Balaur that will spare their cities. What they fail to realize is that he *cannot* be appeased. His ambition is limitless. Once he's gained sufficient territory and power, he will turn on them and demand a complete surrender."

Kasia felt a chill. "The dragon devours itself. Then it devours the world," she said softly.

"Yes," Falke replied. "But I will not accept that outcome as inevitable. Some have been corrupted, but there are those of us who will fight to the bitter end." He paused. "Where is Tessaria Foy? She must have brought you here. Have you any word of her?"

Kasia laid her hand over his, throat tight. "Reverend Father, she is dead."

He stared at her, his body utterly still. Then, to Kasia's shock, his face crumpled. Falke began to weep, hoarse rasping sobs that seemed torn from the core of his being. Without thought, she drew him into her arms. The pontifex of Novostopol laid his cheek on her shoulder like a young boy.

His grief poured out and she realized that however deep his feelings for Tess, he also wept for the rest of them.

At last, he drew back. Falke wiped his eyes with the ragged hem of his sleeve. "I'm sorry," he said.

"Don't be. I still think of her every day. So she lives on, you see? In us."

He nodded, chest heaving with an unsteady breath. "She was the love of my life."

"And you were hers." Kasia paused. "She sent me to Clavis for a reason."

He looked up, gaze steely again, yet with that tenderness she'd seen when he bid her goodnight outside the Arx in Novostopol.

"I saw the sweven," Kasia said.

"Then you know all." He patted her hand. "I do not regret my choice. Not for either of you."

She couldn't believe it. "How can you say that?"

Falke held her gaze for a moment, then looked away. "I've done many things I am not proud of, Kasia. Ferran Massot, for instance. I should never have trusted him. You have my deepest apologies for that."

"Thank you," she said quietly.

"As for Malach, he was a child. I don't murder children. Not even if it had been Balaur himself."

Kasia found his reasoning to be flawed. One life balanced against so many! Balaur had grown into a man who murdered thousands, children included. The morally correct answer seemed clear—yet somehow she was wrong.

It was just the sort of test question she would have failed.

"How did Malach get into the Arx?"

"A char helped him. Rachel's mother. Her name is Nikola Thorn."

"I met her! The night I stayed with the vestals. She came into my room."

"No doubt she was under his influence even then. I don't know how, but she has learned lithomancy. Thorn is a witch."

"Saints!"

"They were going to take Rachel together, but she left him there. Malach forced Rachel to rain destruction down on the Arx so he could make his escape. You cannot imagine it, Kasia." Falke's eyes went blank for a moment. "I spent half my life in combat zones and I've never seen the like."

"She called down meteors?"

A brief nod. "But it wasn't the child's fault. There is good in her still. Perhaps in time she can turn him from this dark path." Falke eyed her speculatively. "You didn't tell him who you are."

"And I never will."

"Why?"

There were several plausible lies she might have given, but Kasia decided to be honest.

"Because he might show me kindness," she admitted. "And I don't want to soften towards him."

"But he also might give you more freedom——"

"No! Do not press me on this."

He sighed. "I understand. You want to reject him utterly. But he *is* your brother, Kasia. I have known Malach a long time. He can be surprising. Beleth raised him, but he is not like her. He lacks the coldness. I think that what he really wants is simple."

"And what is that?"

"To be loved."

Kasia laughed. "He is a nihilim."

"So were the Praefators. So are *you*. I've seen him with Rachel. He hasn't told her that he's her father. But he adores her. That much is obvious."

"He made her kill people!"

"Because he believed he had no other choice. He became

unhinged when he saw the Raven Mark. Perhaps under-standably."

Kasia stared in surprise. "You sound almost sympathetic."

"I am trying to be." Falke gazed at her seriously. "Because I believe Malach is our only chance of stopping Balaur now."

"Why not Rachel?"

"The girl has been used enough. He won't leave me alone with her, anyway. He fears I'd encourage her to use her power against him."

"Are you sure Balaur doesn't know about her?"

"He would never have allowed us to leave if he did."

"But how long can the ruse last?" Kasia wondered.

Something tickled the back of her mind. An old man in priestly robes.

There is another half-blood in the world. Newly arrived. I would find this child . . . .

She snatched at the memory, but it slipped through her fingers like smoke.

"Balaur has ways of knowing things," she said. "He entered my dreams in Kvengard."

Falke blanched. "What?"

Kasia told him about the stone she had found in her bed at the Danzigers' house and all that transpired after. Falke listened in horror when she told him about the Order of the Black Sun and their corruption of innocent children. His face grew even darker when he heard about the return of Jule Danziger. Tessaria's murderer.

"I thought you'd know everything," she said. "Coming from Bal Agnar."

"I did not. I'm not certain Malach does, either."

"Would he care?"

"Yes," Falke said thoughtfully. "I think he would."

"Then I will tell him myself."

Kasia drew her knees to her chest.

"You are hurt!" Falke exclaimed.

She glanced down at her ankle. "Just a bruise."

He clucked his tongue. "You should have said something." Falke disappeared into the bathroom, returning with a damp washcloth.

"Gray kept me manacled," she explained as he dabbed the chafed skin. "In a liminal space."

"The undercity," Falke murmured.

"You know about it!"

"Clavis told me."

"Perhaps she can use the passages to return."

"They don't extend beyond the Arx itself. If they did, Balaur wouldn't have needed the Kvens to take the city."

"So even if we got *inside*, we couldn't get *outside*," she said glumly.

"Correct."

"We could still try," she said. "You can use liminal ley. There might be a door—"

"No." He set the cloth aside. "I am . . . not safe."

"What do you mean?"

"There's too much anger in my heart. Too much sorrow." His lips twisted in a strange smile. "I have mage blood, too. It gives me the ability to bestow Marks. Some distant ancestor was nihilim. A great-grandparent, perhaps. The ability will die with me. I know because I have my own children and none of them inherited the traits."

Falke gazed out the dark, rain-streaked window. "I can touch abyssal ley, but I lack the strength to keep it from consuming me. As only a full mage can." He turned back to her. "As *you* can."

"I wouldn't touch it either," she said quickly.

"You already have, haven't you?"

His voice was gentle, without accusation, yet she still felt guilty.

"Only to save my own life or that of others," she admitted.

"I believe you. And you were able to let go of it again?"

"It wasn't easy. But yes."

"The liminal layer is very thin. The red beneath it surges. Well beyond anything I've ever sensed before. I cannot risk it, Kasia. I will not become like them!"

She touched his arm. "I understand. I feel the same."

A brisk knock came at the door, followed by the sound of the key. Malach stood in the doorway. He set a covered platter on the floor. "Food," he said. "And a clean gown. It's all I could find."

He dropped a bundle on the floor and closed it before Kasia could reply. The aroma of hot pastry made her ravenous.

"Have you eaten, Reverend Father?" she asked, tearing the lid off.

"You take it, Kasia. Malach has not starved me."

She stuffed herself with mince pies, washing them down with a bottle of cold beer. Falke watched her eat, refusing the repeated offers to share. He'd lost weight, but he didn't look as terrible as she would have expected. When the meal was gone, Kasia sat back with a contented sigh. Amazing what hot food and a view of the sky through an open window could accomplish. Not to mention company.

"How did you meet Tessaria?" she asked.

Falke ran the back of his hand along his silver-stubbled jaw, gaze distant. "I was thirty-six. Just returned from a campaign in the Morho. A bit drunk on my own success. She had a sharp tongue, as you might recall."

"I do."

"She looked me up and down and told me I needed a haircut before I met with the pontifex, and that she would give me one if I behaved."

Kasia gave him a mischievous grin. "I called it the inspection."

"She did it to you, too?"

"Every day." Kasia kept her tone light, though when she

was younger, she'd lived in fear of disappointing her guardian. "Tess taught me the importance of style. One should always have good taste, but also a bit of daring."

Falke cleared his throat. A minute passed before he spoke. "She had the kind of beauty to make a man's mouth dry. It never faded, not in all the years that came after. Needless to say, I agreed to the haircut." He smiled. "We became good friends after that. And eventually much more. She loved you like a daughter."

"If I hadn't found her . . . ." Kasia shook her head. "I don't know who I would be."

Falke gently took her hand. "You are proof that it's nurture, not nature, which counts the most. Sometimes I wish I had taken Malach, too. When he was still pliable." A sigh. "But the boy was already Marked with the Broken Chain of Bal Kirith. I didn't dare."

Kasia nearly asked him about their parents, but she feared what he might say.

"Reverend Father," she began, trying to formulate her thoughts before exhaustion won out.

"Better if you don't call me that here, Kasia."

"I won't call you Severin!"

"Dmitry, then."

She shook her head, bemused. "There's something I don't understand. But it's of the utmost importance. I hoped you might have the answer."

He gave an encouraging nod.

"The ley speaks to me through the cards. Not just people's secrets, but things yet to come. It is intelligent. Of that, I have no doubt. I have always believed it to be a force for good. Yet the ley permits unspeakable evil to exist in the world. How can that be?"

Falke gave a soft chuff of laughter. "The ultimate metaphysical question."

"But you are a . . . ." She lowered her voice to a whisper. "You are a pontifex! Surely you must know."

"I am a man, Kasia. And far greater intellects than mine have pondered the same with no clear answer. The ley interacts with our minds, *da*? It changes like a chameleon depending on who it touches, and for what purpose. So the real question, I think, is different."

She leaned forward.

"Which came first?" he asked, dark eyes gleaming. "The ley? Or us?"

She frowned. "Are you saying that *we* are the source?"

"The Masdaris say different. So do the witches. Every culture has its own explanation." He covered a yawn. "But I will say this. The ley is not always linear." He looped a finger. "Sometimes it works in spirals. Just when you think you are farthest from your goal, it leads you around a bend and what seemed impossible is waiting right in front of you."

She stared at him. "Have you ever considered taking up cartomancy?"

He laughed. "Your timing is excellent. I'm in rather desperate need of a second career."

Falke insisted that Kasia take the bed, rolling up in a blanket on the couch. She examined the other bundle Malach had left. It was the uniform of a char. Kasia didn't imagine herself to be better than the women who served at the Arx. But the day she failed the Curia's tests, she'd quietly vowed never to wear the color gray. Not ever.

She washed her own dress in the bathroom sink, took a hot shower, and swaddled herself in a sheet, hanging the dress to dry on one of the bedposts.

Sleep tried to claim her. She resisted, though her eyelids drooped. Not even the Garden felt safe anymore. Kasia sat at the window as dawn broke over Nantwich.

Was Alexei alive to see the new day? Natalya and Patryk?

There are those of us who will fight to the bitter end.

Yes, she thought. And I will stand among you.

MALACH TOSSED and turned in his bed that night.

The encounter with Kasia Novak had unnerved him. Could he really give her to Balaur? With all she knew? Beleth would quietly kill her and blame it on Gray, but Malach knew he couldn't do it. He lacked the stomach for such things now.

Kasia intrigued him. In some ways, she reminded him of Nikola. He couldn't tell what she was really thinking. He wanted her to give him a reading. Oh, so very much. But the cards were her Marks. Who knew what she would do with them?

Malach rolled over, resting his cheek on one arm. He would leave her locked up with Falke for now—and stay far away. The two of them could be hidden when Balaur came.

Leaving Nantwich wasn't an option. Not until the Ravens were gone from Bal Kirith.

He dressed shortly after dawn and summoned Gray to Clavis's study. Rain pelted the windows as Lucas took a seat across from the desk, smoothing his dark blue robes.

"I've prepared a public statement," Malach said. "You will transmit it over Arx Radio. I want it to come from you, Gray. A familiar voice will reassure them."

The cardinal nodded so vigorously the round spectacles slipped down his nose. He pushed them up with a gloved finger. "Certainly, Nuncio."

"You'll announce that the Reverend Mother Clavis is dead and they are free to mourn her. But the conflict is over. All parties have reached a peace accord. The Kvens are helping to restore order, but it's *not* an occupation. Nantwich is a free city."

Gray lifted a brow. "I'm not sure people will accept that

story," he said dryly, "considering that the streets are full of Kven patrols."

"It doesn't matter." Malach leaned across the desk. "You will still say the words. This is a propaganda war now. Give them the truth wholesale and they'll choke on it. No, we cut it into little bite-sized pieces and feed it to them a nibble at a time."

Gray nodded thoughtfully.

"Starving people are rebellious people. Everything must reopen in an orderly fashion. Crack down hard on any signs of hoarding. Citizens will report to their jobs. However, a curfew is in effect from nine in the evening until five in the morning. Cut the electricity at night, except for the Arx. Ration food, tobacco, toilet paper, alcohol and clothing." He consulted the list. "Shut the newspapers down for now. Announcements will be made over the radio twice a day."

It amused Malach no end that most of it was borrowed from Falke's tactical playbook *Fallout and Persuasion*, Volume Two.

"So, business as usual?" Gray asked, a hopeful note in his voice.

"Not entirely." Malach smiled. "In keeping with the ideals of the Via Libertas, the days of segregation are over."

A puzzled frown. "Segregation?"

"Of the Unmarked."

He'd expected Lucas to hate this part and he was not wrong.

"But they're deviants!" Gray protested.

"That is the will of the Reverend Father Balaur," Malach said, his voice cold now. "Do you take issue with it?"

In fact, Balaur had given no such instructions. But Malach trusted the Unmarked more than he did anyone else. He felt a strange kinship with them now that he couldn't touch the ley. Nothing, he told himself firmly, to do with Nikola.

Gray's mouth tightened. "What is it you propose?"

"First, discrimination against anyone without Marks will be severely punished."

"Punished how?"

"Don't specify just yet. Let their imaginations run wild. The chars who want to stay can stay. If they choose to pursue other positions outside the Arx, that's fine, too."

A curt nod.

"And you'll double everyone's pay starting today."

That caused a wince of genuine pain. "It's impossible," Gray spluttered. "You'll bankrupt the treasury!"

Malach glanced around at the lavish furnishings. "I doubt that. But if you need to raise funds, double taxes on the richest five percent."

"They're my most loyal supporters!"

"Then they should be willing to do as they're told." He handed Gray the handwritten address. "You'll take this to the station and make the announcement immediately. If you don't, I will hear of it and be most displeased." Malach tapped his fingers on the desk. Gray stared at his bare hand. Sweat beaded the bridge of his nose. He pushed his glasses up.

"Yes, Your Excellency."

"In the meantime, I want numbers on the Kvens. How many exactly and where they're stationed. Lines of command."

"That won't be easy—"

"I'm sure you'll manage. Moving on to the prisoners taken at the Arx. How many are there?"

"Several hundred."

"Where are they being held?'

"Westfield Stadium."

"Go over there and ask for these four."

Malach gave him the list of names. Gray looked it over. His eyes narrowed. "I'm sorry, Nuncio. I had Alexei Bryce in my custody. I meant to give him to you, but he killed my men and escaped. That was before we seized the Arx. I suppose it's possible he was captured again in the fighting."

"Find out."

"I know the other ones, too. Mikhail Bryce was the captain of Lezarius's guards. Patryk Spassov and Natalya Anderle are close associates of Kasia Novak."

He winked. "Exactly."

That ought to satisfy the man's curiosity. Let him believe Malach meant to use them as leverage.

"Ah, I see."

"Tell no one, Lucas. If you do find them, bring them back to the Arx. The regular cells, I suppose."

Gray nodded. "It will be done."

"How are the prisoners being treated?"

"Well," he replied quickly. "Kommandant Rademacher is in charge of them. He is a fair man."

Malach frowned. "I met him. He didn't make a good impression."

"Well, he follows Luk's orders, and Luk respects the rules of war. You can be sure no one is being unduly mistreated." A quizzical look. "Forgive me, but I'm surprised you're concerned for their welfare."

"Everything in this city is my concern, Lucas."

"Of course. Is there anything further, Your Excellency?"

"Not right now."

Gray departed. Malach leaned back in his chair, staring at the door. He'd kept his end of the bargain. He just hoped Kasia Novak did the same.

HE MET with the other mages, then spent the afternoon in Rachel's room with Sydonie and Tristhus, trying the keep the three children out of trouble. At his request, the Mistress of Chars brought lengths of fabric. Slippery silks and plush velvets. Heavy toile with pastoral scenes of castles and animals and people.

Two other women carried baskets piled high with needles and thread, satin ribbons and frothy spools of lace. They gave him shy smiles as they opened the baskets to whoops of delight.

"I heard the radio announcement this morning," the Mistress said. "Is it true?"

"Which part?" he asked dryly.

"You know which part, Nuncio."

"Then yes, it's true. And if Gray—or anyone else—fails to comply, I want you to report it to me immediately."

A brisk nod. "I'll do that."

"How many chars have stayed?"

"Most." She laughed. "You look surprised."

"I thought you'd all be eager to go."

Her dark eyes studied him. "Go where? We are no fools. The city is in chaos, whatever you claim." A small smile. "The salary increase was appreciated."

"I meant every word, Mistress. Make sure the others know they're free now."

"Free?" She chuckled. "I'll convey the message, Nuncio."

The women departed with a promise to bring lunch later. Malach permitted Sydonie to wield the scissors. They made themselves crude costumes and started arguing over which play they might perform. Malach vetoed the bloodiest scenarios, which earned a dark pout from Syd. When he left for five minutes to use the bathroom, she convinced Rachel that the delicate rose pattern of the sofa would be perfect to trim her cape. By the time he returned, huge swaths of fabric were shredded and they were throwing chunks of stuffing at each other.

"Mirabelle did it!" Sydonie said, brows drawing together. "I *told* her you'd get mad." She sighed and held up her arm, staring at the Mark of the evil red-haired doll.

"Oh, Mirabelle, you were very wicked! Tell him it's all your fault!"

The Mark did not speak. Syd scrunched her lips to the side. "I'm a very bad girl——"

Rachel started laughing. "She only talks when there's no grownups around!" Trist cried. "I've seen it! I *have*!"

Malach sent the siblings to their room. They'd ignore his command to stay there, but he needed a break. The rain had finally stopped and the skies were clear. Rachel sat on the window ledge, legs folded to her chest, staring up at the moon. It had been full when they crossed the Morho. He remembered her fixation when the horse topped a rise and it came into view between the mighty regnum trees. Her head craning to follow until they passed into the deep forest again and the silver orb disappeared.

"Would you like to see it better?" he asked.

She didn't answer him—she never did. Rachel only spoke to her cousins. But she let him take her hand and lead her up the winding stairs to the ramparts. A cool wind lifted his hair as they stepped outside. The electricity was off for curfew. Beyond the Arx, Nantwich was a sea of blackness except for a glowing ring in the distance he guessed might be the stadium. Rachel ran straight to the low wall, making his heart lurch, but she didn't look down like most people would.

She turned her face to the sky, eyes fever-bright.

Malach rested his arms on the wall. Everything was still damp. He wished he'd brought their cloaks, yet the fresh air was a balm. It held the scent of rain and a hint of the sea. Rachel started to hum. Her body swayed in a slow rhythm.

"Do you hear something?" he whispered.

She cast him a sharp look. He kept his mouth shut. After a while, the humming started again. So soft, he could barely hear it. A melancholy, ethereal tune. It made him feel empty and full at the same time. Tiny and too vast to comprehend.

Malach studied the stars. His child's display at the Arx had been an indiscriminate shell, blasting everything within its radius. But someday Rachel would master her power. Hone it to a dagger point. Perhaps she already had.

He watched for signs of movement above. A single chunk of rock, perhaps, whistling down at speeds that beggared the imagination. Aimed with precision at the very spot he stood in.

None came. The stars remained stationary. His daughter swayed and hummed to herself.

She was just listening to their music.

When the clouds returned and the skies broke open in a torrent again, he tugged her hand and they went back down. Malach gave her a hot bath and tucked her into bed.

"Goodnight," he said, pausing at the door.

Was that the barest nod? He turned away before she saw his smile and gently closed the door, locking it behind him.

Chapter Thirty

Steady winds bore the *Wayfarer* across the Parnassian Sea and around the continent's southwestern peninsula, past the high walls of Kvengard, and then north toward Nantwich. Three witches sat crosslegged at the bow—blond, cool Torvelle, quick-tempered Ashvi, and dreamy, quiet Gautami. Bethen, the teenaged novice who'd been raised to a full witch the morning they left Dur-Athaara, handed her sisters charged stones, disposing of those that were depleted.

Working air currents at scale expended vast amounts of ley. Nikola could scarcely imagine how many they'd already used up, though the hold was packed with gems and lumps of raw ore, coins and crystals, all stowed in iron-bound chests for which Heshima kept the master list.

Bethen caught Nikola's eye with a sunny smile. She gave a little wave, then quickly returned to her task as Ashvi snapped something inaudible.

Captain Aemlyn stood in the pilot house with her first mate, who shouted orders at seven deeply tanned, muscular women. Aemlyn and her crew were freebooters, sailing wherever the profits led them, but she seemed to have some loyalty to Dur-Athaara. Few captains were eager to go anywhere near the continent these days.

"The last time I was on this ship," Tashtemir remarked, "she had me chained in the hold."

Nikola cast him a wry look. "And I never got a refund for my one-way passage."

The captain's head turned, as if she knew they were talking about her. She wore a tight blue coat with two silver bars on the left shoulder, tall, polished boots, and a dagger at her hip.

"Perhaps they'll let you keep the kaldurite when they remove it from Malach," Tash said. "It does belong to you."

Nikola craned her neck. The Maid clung to the crow's nest far above, bare toes hooked into the rigging, hair streaming in the wind. The Mother and Crone were below in their cabin.

"I still cannot believe the Via Sancta is broken." Tash shook his head. "How many sides to this civil war now?"

Nikola counted on her fingers. "The mages and the Kvens. Allies now, but I can't see that holding for long. Jalghuth in the north. Novostopol, which occupies Bal Kirith but is still digging out from the starfall. Who am I missing? Oh yes, Clavis. Whereabouts unknown."

"Are you sure the intelligence is accurate?"

"Every witch with powers in divination confirmed it. What they *don't* know is how Malach fits into all this. Beyond the fact that he agreed to be Balaur's regent."

"The Cardinal is a cipher."

"Not really." Nikola leaned over the rail, watching the foaming seas slide past beneath. "He's protecting his daughter. That's all."

Tashtemir made a noncommittal sound.

"You don't think so?" she asked.

"I don't deny he loves you both, but his hatred for the Via Sancta runs deep. He would not weep to see it destroyed utterly." Tash gave her a sideways look. "Do you honestly believe he'll agree to return with you?"

Nikola sighed. "I don't know. But he's desperate to be rid of the kaldurite. I think he'd be open to a deal."

Tashtemir's voice lowered. "And you trust them to keep it?"

She glanced around. Both sailors and witches moved about the deck, but the flapping sails and rushing waves ought to drown out the conversation. "The Mahadeva never lies outright, but those women can be slippery," she admitted. "I think she sees things she's not telling the rest of us."

"Like?"

"What exactly she fears Malach might do. She speaks of disaster, but only in the vaguest terms."

"Maybe she doesn't know. In which case, the Alsakhan preserve us." He made a complex gesture, touching seven points on his chest.

The Masdari had started the journey in his skimpy Rahai —to the delight of Aemlyn's crew—but as the weather turned, they'd all donned long coats, and warm clothes beneath. Nikola had grown very fond of Tashtemir Kelevan over the last week. He had both wit and warmth, and a good heart, whatever crimes he may have committed in his homeland to earn himself exile.

He was an easy person to confide in. They'd talked a good deal, though he rarely mentioned the Masdar League. Perhaps it was too painful.

"The witches have Valmitra," she said. "The Via Sancta worships their Praefators. But I know little of your faith."

Tashtemir stroked his long mustaches. "What do you want to learn?"

"First off, what is this Alsakhan?"

"He is a dragon. Also called Al-jidhir. The Root, in Osterl-ish. He gives us the ley. It is the duty of the Imperator and the court to protect and serve him under the Covenant."

"Dragon, eh?" Nikola said. "That sounds a bit like the Great Serpent."

"They are one and the same," came the Crone's raspy voice behind her.

Nikola nearly jumped out of her skin. The ship crested a swell, rolling as it plowed down the back side. She offered a steadying hand and the Crone took it, her grip firm.

"Valmitra wears many guises," the Crone said. "You say *he*. We say *them*. But the Covenant you speak of is familiar."

"It's all new to me," Nikola remarked.

"Because the Via Sancta erased it from memory." The Crone's expression darkened. "They wish to forget the crimes of their ancestors."

Nikola waited, but the Crone said nothing more.

"That is why you dislike the aingeals?" she ventured.

"They are rebels." Her head swung toward Tashtemir. "But your people and mine have kept the faith."

He bowed. "It is as you say, Crone," Tashtemir murmured.

"Leave us, Masdari. I would speak with Nikola alone."

He swept another graceful bow, lower this time, and withdrew to the stern, saying something to the women coiling ropes that made them burst into laughter. Everyone liked him, except for Cairness, who didn't seem to like anyone.

"You wish to ask me something," the Crone said.

Nikola hesitated, but there was little point in hedging. "Will you keep your word and remove the kaldurite if he agrees to your terms?"

A dry chuckle. "It isn't his power we fear. The stone was merely to keep him docile while he was in Tenethe, though even that proved ineffectual."

"Docile is not a word I would choose to describe Malach," Nikola agreed.

The wrinkles on her brow deepened. "It is the child that concerns us more. *Her* power is not to be trifled with. She must be kept safe, yet her father has brought her into the eye of the storm."

"You left him no choice," Nikola snapped before she could think better of it.

The Crone ignored her tart tone. "The fact remains that she *must* be removed from the continent before it's too late. I don't deny that we misjudged the depth of his feeling for both of you, but that is water beneath the keel. You are the only one who might sway him now. He trusts you——"

"Trusts *me*?" She gave a hollow laugh, lowering her voice to a whisper. "You've left me in a very awkward position."

"Well, boo-hoo!" the Maid shouted from above, balling one hand into a fist and rubbing her eyes.

The Crone made a quelling gesture. "We have every confidence in you. The Masdari will accompany you to the Arx when we arrive."

"Just us two?" she asked hopefully.

"Paarjini and Heshima, as well."

Nikola stared in disbelief. "They're the ones who took him!"

"Nonetheless, they are the strongest and we shall not send you alone. Paarjini can track the kaldurite. Heshima will manage any trouble from the Kvens."

"But——"

"It is decided, Nikola Thorn." Her head tilted. "Now, your other question."

She turned away before the Crone saw her frustration. "I'm not sure——"

"You want to know how we became what we are."

Nikola blinked in surprise. "Yes," she admitted.

"And what it is like to be divided in three."

A slow nod.

"We were elected in a popular vote of all the Deir Fiuracha, but that much you already know. My predecessor died of natural causes. She was bitten by a yellow-ringed octopus while she swam in the sea. Their venom is deadly and swift. We were forty-two when we were chosen. About five decades ago."

"So you—the woman I see now—is the closest to your true age."

"Correct. Sometimes we think in tandem, but not always. We must reach consensus on important decisions. But the Crone remembers things the Maid does not because they haven't happened to her yet."

"That is . . . hard to comprehend," Nikola admitted.

She smiled, revealing pink gums and a scattering of strong white teeth. "The Maid keeps us all young at heart. Her enthusiasm for life remains undiluted. The child is preserved intact, just as the Crone's wisdom is untainted by childish impulses."

"And the Mother?"

Nikola sensed a new presence at her shoulder.

"I see both what was and what will come," she said.

"But how does it happen? The division?"

"That is a mystery no woman can know unless she is chosen," the Mother replied. She winked. "But now it is time for your gifts."

She produced a heavy pouch. Nikola tugged open the drawstrings, heart pounding. A rainbow of colors dazzled in the last rays of the setting sun. Moonstone and smoky quartz, obsidian, topaz and citrine. Bloodstone, white chalcedony, peridot and turquoise.

"Wait for me!" the Maid cried.

She scampered down from the rigging and pressed ten rings into Nikola's hand. "One for each finger," she said breathlessly, as Nikola laughed and slipped them on. She held her hands up to admire them. Aquamarine and amethyst, sapphire and moss agate, sunstone and azurite, rough ruby, golden beryl, tiger eye and jasper. Each was set in a different metal.

"Thank you! They're beautiful."

"And most importantly," the Crone said, "your namestone."

It hung from a new gold chain, identical to the one Heshima had torn from her neck. Nikola had sensed it in her pocket. The smoldering fire at the heart of the stone, cooling to protective blue and airy violet at the edges. She turned her back and the Crone clasped it around her neck. The serpent's eye settled into the notch of her collar bone. Nikola closed her eyes. A knot in her chest she'd hardly been aware of dissolved. She felt whole again.

"Never again will this be taken from you," the Mahadeva said in unison, voices raised for all to hear. "Not unless your body lies cold and dead."

Tears rose in Nikola's eyes as each of them kissed her in turn. "Welcome to the sisterhood of the Deir Fiuracha, Nikola Thorn."

Heshima, her old enemy, stepped forward with a broad smile. "Welcome, sister," she said, full lips brushing Nikola's cheek. Her gift was a brooch of projective stones: garnet, carnelian, cat's eye and aventurine.

One by one, each of the witches embraced her, bestowing their own gifts. An enormous diamond from Torvelle made her eyes widen—the witch had never been especially friendly. But Nikola accepted Bethen's plain coin with equal enthusiasm; copper brought healing, luck and protection.

Paarjini unwound the silver net from her hair and tied it atop Nikola's headscarf. "Silver for love," she said with a crooked grin. "And keepin' yer temper in check."

It was a receptive metal, ruled by the moon, in the class of the water elements. The net would resonate with the jade and turquoise, enhancing their power.

Even Cairness's usual scowl was gone. She nodded briskly and held up a small hand mirror, with pearls set in the handle. "Valmitra claims you," she said.

Nikola studied her reflection—the first she'd seen of herself in weeks. A thin line of reflective gray circled her dark irises. She touched the corner of her eye. The weight of the rings felt strange, though they all fit perfectly.

"I hope I live up to their expectations," she managed.

The Crone grunted. "So do we all."

And that was it. No oaths never to use manipulative magic. Not even a promise she wouldn't force again. Did they go by the honor system? Or was the Mahadeva deliberately leaving her the latitude to do whatever she must?

Nikola released a breath as they drifted away, leaving her alone at the rail. There were eighteen witches on the ship and more than a dozen crew. Solitude was in short demand. She felt grateful for the chance to think in peace.

A full witch now. It was what she wanted and she had no regrets. Her sisters could be heavy-handed, but she believed them to be a force for good in the world. They had treated Tashtemir kindly despite the fact that he'd aided Malach. They freed the Perditae slaves and gave them a new home. They opposed Balaur—although the blanket condemnation of the mages made her uneasy. She doubted the nihilim had ever heard of Valmitra, let alone that they descended from "rebels."

It was guilt that gnawed at her the most. She wasn't to blame for being summoned back, but she *had* wanted to leave the child behind. If she'd just continued quietly with her studies, none of it would have happened.

How will he react when he sees my eyes? After all that was done to him?

She'd pried the full story of Doctor Fithen from Paarjini. It was easily the most horrible tale she'd ever heard, yet Malach hadn't breathed a word of it. He probably wanted to forget.

Paarjini said Fithen had been banished to one of the outer

isles. If Nikola survived this trip, she intended to pay the doctor a visit.

She'd never prayed before, but *something* had given her the serpent's eye. Maybe it was listening.

Let him see reason, Valmitra. Or Alsakhan. Whichever you prefer. Let this war end. Somehow. Er . . . thy will be done.

She opened her eyes. Lightning flickered along the western horizon, where the swells of the open ocean stretched in an unbroken expanse. To the east, the rugged coast of the continent was a dark line in the distance. They were only a few hours from Nantwich now. Nikola raised her hood as the first drops pattered down.

It would be a wet night at the Arx.

Chapter Thirty-One

Alexei huddled in the rain, Natalya dozing on his shoulder. The two-day downpour had turned Westfield Stadium into a sodden mud pit. The skies had cleared once only, for about an hour, before the storm clouds returned. He sat back to back with Spassov, sharing the meager warmth. The three of them had managed to stay together during the chaotic processing of prisoners, but he had yet to find his brother.

About five hundred detainees filled the oval stadium. Alexei knew now what had happened to the knights on the walls. After opening the gates to the Kvens, they'd been swiftly overwhelmed and the survivors marched to the camp—if such a word could be used.

Despite Rademacher's promises, there was no shelter. Some of the prisoners were wounded, but Alexei saw no sign of medics. Nearby, a knight muttered with fever. His companions had wrapped him in their cloaks. Alexei doubted the man would last the night.

The only food he'd eaten in the last twenty-four hours was a heel of stale bread, tossed from horseback. There must be plumbing in the public restrooms, but no one was allowed to leave the field for any reason. Those who weren't injured had been forced to dig pit latrines, which were already overflowing. The stench made his eyes water.

Kvens rode up and down the perimeter, the white dogs loping at their heels. The hounds watched with small pink eyes. If a glove came off, the dogs erupted in howls, arrowing toward the source of the ley and savaging the culprit.

Nine bodies already hung from makeshift gallows in the goal zone.

At dusk, the Kvens cut off the bright arc lights—all the better to see if anyone's Marks flared. The riders carried pitch-soaked torches that hissed and sputtered in the rain.

Everyone was getting weak. The longer they waited to fight back, the worse the odds. But there were too many knights, well-armed, mounted and commanding packs of the dreaded dogs. He couldn't devise a plan that didn't end in another massacre.

His thoughts kept returning to Luk. Picking over every encounter he'd had with the Pontifex for some sign of his impending treachery. In Kvengard, he'd suspected Morvana, but Luk himself had been the connection between the Order of the Black Sun and the Arx. They'd been reporting to him all along.

In hindsight, it made a twisted sense. Luk had stayed neutral during the last conflict. He must have decided that throwing his lot in with Balaur was the only way to survive. Alexei had seen the power he wielded in Kvengard. Luk had been Pontifex for more than fifty years. His judgment was followed without question.

Yet Morvana wasn't part of it. So why did Luk bring her to Nantwich? Did he still have some brittle shell of a conscience that forbade him from killing his own nuncio? Or had she Marked too many Kvens to be disposed of?

"I watched a test match here eight years ago," Spassov said.

It was the first words either of them had spoken in hours. Alexei turned, catching Patryk's profile in the darkness.

"It was during an R&R leave. Bagwani hit a six in the last frame. Right into the bleachers. The whole stadium went wild." The corner of his mouth twitched. "The Kvens got their asses handed to them on a platter. They probably still hold a grudge."

"Was that the '72 Cup?"

"Yep. Final game. I traded one of my medals for the ticket."

Alexei tried to imagine it. The screaming crowd wearing the home team colors, green on yellow. Paper cups of overpriced beer spilling as they leapt to their feet. Five thousand voices chanting: *Bag-wan-ee! Bag-wan-ee!* The Kindu captain was so famous, he supposedly had a minor museum devoted just to him.

"Was it raining?" Alexei asked.

"No," Spassov replied wistfully. "The weather was perfect. Saints, I want a cigarette."

They both tensed as a pair of guards rode over, hooves splattering mud on the feverish knight. Alexei squinted against the sudden torchlight.

"Bryce!" A clipped order. "Come with us."

Natalya jerked awake. "You're not taking him!"

She started to rise and Alexei pulled her back down. He shot a hard look at Patryk, who was rolling his heavy shoulders in anticipation of a fight.

A fight they would lose.

Natalya caught his hand and squeezed it. Alexei forced a smile.

"Save my spot," he said, climbing to his feet.

"He's done nothing!" Spassov protested.

Two of the dogs trotted over, growling low in their throats. Alexei raised his hands.

"I'm coming," he said. "There's no problem."

One of the Kvens leaned down from the saddle and prodded him with a club. "Move!"

The nearest detainees watched with grim expressions. Knights and vestals sat shoulder to shoulder with bishops and cardinals. There were even a few gray-clad chars who'd fought the invaders with whatever lay at hand. They were all the same now.

"Stay strong!" someone shouted.

Alexei jogged between the the Kvens as they rode through the ranks of despondent prisoners. It felt good just to move. They passed through one of the gates into the tunnels beneath the bleachers. The knights handed him over to others. He was escorted down a long tunnel bearing the logos of the various teams that played at the stadium; past a dark, empty concession stand that still smelled of roasted peanuts and beer; then into a wood-paneled lift that led up to the skyboxes.

Kommandant Rademacher waited before a large glass window overlooking the stadium. The room had a bar and a dozen plush leather chairs. The carpet had been rolled up and set to one side. Misha was tied to one of the chairs, a gag stuffed into his mouth.

"Sit, Fra Bryce," Rademacher said, nodding at an empty chair.

Alexei sat. The knights took up positions behind him.

"So here we are, reunited at last!" Rademacher rubbed his hands.

"I know why you hate *me*." Alexei glanced at his brother. "But I thought you served together."

Misha looked alert and watchful. No new injuries. Whatever was happening here, it hadn't started yet.

The commandant's blue eyes twinkled. "Funny you mention it. We were just reminiscing about the old days. You might recall that I was embedded with Captain Bryce's unit for three months. It was quite an eye-opening tour."

Alexei stayed silent.

"I was supposed to discourage unsanctioned interrogation techniques. It was just after the Mornay Commission issued a very critical report on the Beatus Laqueo." Rademacher chuckled. "And they weren't wrong. But Captain Bryce could be very persuasive. To be fair, the nihilim were doing worse. So I decided to give him some latitude. Sublimin to induce waking nightmares, for example. Mock executions. Sensory deprivation. Everyone was doing it, were they not?"

"That was a long time ago."

"Not so long, really. I learned a great deal. Human beings are adaptable to a wide variety of environmental conditions. It is part of our evolution, *ja*? Extreme heat and cold. High and low altitude. In other words, we are tough. The mages even more so. But *your* unit made a scientific study of how to break the mind down. To penetrate those defenses and gain desired information."

His heels echoed as he walked to a table. It held a black metal box. Medium-sized.

"The creation of an extreme environment is the first step. One in which the subject has no control over their circumstances. Then a stimulus is introduced. Generally, something quite stressful. When the stimulus reaches a sufficient intensity, it has a dysfunctional impact on the subject's cognitive integrity."

A muscle fluttered in Alexei's eye. "You're quoting from the interrogation handbook."

"See?" He laid a hand on the box. "You don't need me to explain the details. You would have witnessed it firsthand yourself, *ja*? I say this so you know what's coming, Bryce."

Not a bluff. The kommandant looked almost eager.

"What do you think I can tell you?" Alexei wondered.

"Everything you know about Jalghuth's defenses." He glanced at Misha. "Or he will watch you suffer those same interrogation techniques. Watch as you slowly lose your ability to cope with the trauma." A click of the tongue. "The psychological damage from reaching such a point can be permanent."

Rademacher leaned back against the table, crossing his gleaming boots at the ankle. "Cardinal Gray just came to ask about you. I told him you were dead. Your bodies already burned. So you are both ghosts now, *ja*? I can do what I like."

Muffled sounds came through the gag. Rademacher flicked a finger and one of the Kvens yanked it out.

"You stupid prick," Misha said.

The kommandant's expression darkened.

"He doesn't know shit. I'm the one who designed the defenses." A chilling smile. "Do you want to know what we called you? The Radish. You come from the dirt of Wolftown and you turn red at the drop of a fucking visor."

The flush that crept up Rademacher's neck only seemed to enrage him further. "Be quiet——"

"You were nothing but a sad little voyeur. Did it turn you on? Get you hard?"

Misha's voice had an almost imperceptible slur. Two days before, he'd been kicked in the head by a *horse*. Rademacher obviously hadn't given him any medical care.

"You call yourselves knights, but everyone knows you Kvens are a bunch of pacifist pussies. I doubt you have the stomach for what it'll take to break my brother."

If one of his own knights had spoken so crudely, Misha would discipline them without hesitation. Besides which, they were all *supposed* to be pacifists. That was the bedrock of their faith.

"We shall see," Rademacher snarled. "Perhaps you'd like to go first, Captain Bryce?"

Misha yawned. "Wake me up when you're done."

The kommandant's Wolf Mark flared blue, then bloody red. "Gag them both," he snapped.

"He's lying, you idiot!" Alexei cried. "Trying to protect me——"

A heavy hand on his shoulder slammed him back into the chair. In seconds, he was bound and biting down on another rag.

"Such an ample menu to choose from." Rademacher snapped his fingers at an aide, who scurried off. "Ice baths. Simulated drowning. Sleep deprivation." A sigh. "The last one takes too long. And the others are . . . how would you say it? Ho-hum." He opened the box and took out a hypodermic needle. "No, I think we will start with a big dose of Sublimin and work our way from there."

Misha threw his head back and let out a deranged whoop. His eyes were chips of blue ice. "Let's get this party rolling!"

The kommandant's reflection swam in the glass as he prepped the needle. *Sublimin.* Rademacher planned to drill down to the bottom of the well, but he had no clue what was waiting for him in the dark.

Alexei wasn't sure he did either.

Chapter Thirty-Two

Who knew occupying a city could be so tedious?

Malach sat in his shirtsleeves, elbows propped on the enormous desk, trying to get a handle on the Arx's finances. Stacks of ledgers covered the floor. Everything from weapons in the armory to how many bags of flour were in the storerooms. He hoped to find records of the items looted from Bal Kirith, but all he'd done for the past six hours was drown in paperwork.

Malach chose a ledger from the pile and flipped it open, forcing his bleary eyes to focus. Gray had proved pliable, but he didn't trust Luk or Karolo. When Balaur arrived, Malach would present him with an accounting of the Arx's wealth. Not just the tangible objects—artwork, gold, priceless relics—but the vast real estate holdings, investments and shell companies. The Banco Barondesi was the Curia's financial arm. He'd have to go down to the main branch at some point and seize the records. Another item on his to-do list.

"Valdrian," he muttered.

There was no reply.

He glanced over. Valdrian sat on the carpet, rubbing his blond beard. The mage lifted his eyes. He strode over and dropped a yellowed newspaper clipping on the desk. A young woman in chainmail stood with one boot propped on a low wall. Next to her was an older man in plate armor, his helm raised. Malach recognized the location as Bal Kirith. It must have been taken shortly before the Cold Truce.

"What the fuck, Malach?" Valdrian said in a low voice.

The caption identified the first as the Reverend Mother Clavis. The second as Cardinal Dmitry Falke, Captain of the Knights of Saint Jule. The photograph was blurry, but not quite blurry enough.

"That's your servant," Valdrian snarled. "What the *fuck*? You've had Falke under our noses—"

"Keep your voice down," Malach hissed. He hustled to the door and closed it. "I can explain. Sit down."

Valdrian folded his arms.

"It's not a brief tale," Malach warned. "There's more than you know. Much more."

Valdrian shook his head, but perched on the edge of the desk. "This better be good."

Malach composed his racing thoughts. "It all started the night the Ravens took Bal Kirith. Well, before that really. With a char named Nikola Thorn. You know about the deal I made to stop the shelling?"

He nodded. "To give Falke a child."

"I tried. Many times. The women were willing, but all the pregnancies ended in miscarriages. Until I met Nikola. She didn't want my Mark. All she wanted was to leave the Via Sancta. She had this idea that she could make a new life for herself in Dur-Athaara. I promised to get her out if she gave me a child."

He told Valdrian about the doctor at the Batavia Institute who stumbled over the truth that Patient 9 was in fact the Pontifex Lezarius. How Malach broke into the Arx to learn the contents of the letter Massot had intended to give him.

"Falke was a step ahead. He waited for me with half a dozen knights." Malach glanced at the stump of Valdrian's left arm. "He tried to sever me. He would have done it, but the ley surged. It disabled the Wards. I barely got out of the Arx. I didn't kill Feizah. I've no idea who did. I found Nikola and we ran to Bal Kirith."

"You didn't kill Feizah?" Valdrian frowned.

"No, but I took the blame." He laughed. "I didn't even know she was dead! Not until much later. So I didn't expect Falke to hit back as hard as he did. Do you remember Tashtemir?"

"The Masdari? Of course."

"The two of us got out of Bal Kirith through the tunnels. Nikola had already run—"

"She knew the knights were coming?"

"No. She was running from *me*. I followed her to the coast. With Tash."

"Why?"

"She was carrying my child. And . . . I had feelings for her."

Valdrian looked skeptical. "You?"

"It is so impossible to believe?"

A shrug. "Go on."

"I found her there. I think we just missed each other, brother, because I ended up in chains on a ship with Perditae *you* had just sold to the smugglers."

"Get the fuck out," Valdrian said slowly, leaning forward.

"I'll describe them if you don't believe me. Woman with three kids. She had a streak of gray on the left side."

Valdrian stared at him in astonishment.

"We're not even up to the really crazy part. First off, the witches don't keep them for slaves. They remove the Marks and make them citizens of Dur-Athaara. So your conscience can rest easy," Malach added dryly.

Valdrian rubbed the back of his head. "That's, uh . . . good to know."

"I met the witch-queen. She's more powerful than you can imagine."

"But Cardinal . . . how did the witches take you?"

"Lithomancy." This was the worst part. "I need to know I can trust you."

A level look. "And I'm still waiting for you to explain about Falke."

"It's coming. But I need your word that you won't tell anyone the rest."

Valdrian sighed. "I'd be dead if not for you, Malach. I might kick your ass, but I'd never betray you."

Malach's hand probed his stomach. He couldn't feel the stone, but he never forgot it was there, not for a single instant. "The witches put kaldurite inside me. I can't touch the ley."

Whatever Valdrian had expected, that wasn't it. He blinked in surprise, swiftly followed by pity. "Shit."

"I tried to have the stone cut out, but that didn't go so well. So that's part of it. The other part is that the girl is my daughter. Falke's knights caught Nikola and brought her back to the Arx while I was held captive in Dur-Athaara." He paused. "Falke Marked her."

Understanding dawned. "Ah."

"I have to keep the bastard alive until I can deal with the Mark. If I gave him to Balaur, he'd be in pieces."

"But how did you get them both out of the Arx?"

"Nikola helped me. She escaped from Falke and fled to Dur-Athaara on her own."

"How?"

"She rowed."

"I see why you like this woman."

The knife in Malach's heart twisted. "Nikola learned lithomancy. She agreed to help me get my daughter back.

There's a thing called forcing. It uses the ley to move from one place to another, instantly. Nikola took me to the Arx. Right to Falke's bedroom."

Valdrian looked stunned.

"But Rachel . . . she didn't want to leave. Nikola panicked. She abandoned us at the Arx. That's when I learned what Rachel's power is. She made the starfall." He picked at a thread on his sleeve. "I told her that if she didn't do it, I'd kill Falke. She believes he's her father."

"Why haven't you told her the truth?"

"It's my choice."

"You must tell her, Malach."

"I will," he said wearily. "Someday. But do you understand now? If Balaur knew what she could do, he would use her. And she's *my* child! I will not have her made into a weapon."

Valdrian was silent for a long time. "This kaldurite stone. Where is it?"

"In my gut."

He glanced at the dagger in his belt. "I could give it a try—"

"No." Just the thought terrified him. "I've been down that path."

"You have to get rid of it."

"Once we have Bal Kirith back. I'll need a skilled surgeon. And you'll be standing behind them the whole time, making sure they do it right."

Valdrian studied him. "I'll keep your secret. But we must tell Jess and Lexa."

"No."

"What if something happens to you? Or to both of us? What will become of your daughter?" His good hand gripped Malach's shoulder. "We've been apart for too long, fighting our own battles. You say you want to rebuild Bal Kirith, but that requires trust. They'd cover for you if you came clean. But if you wait until they catch you in a lie, like I did, they'll be angry." Valdrian shook his head in wonder. "I can't believe no one's caught you yet, brother."

"Just them," Malach said. "No one else."

"Just them." He tossed the newspaper clipping in the fire. They watched it burn. "So you saw Dur-Athaara. What's it like?"

"A tropical paradise, brother," Malach replied with a straight face.

"Were you their slave?" A slow grin. "Did you wash the witch-queen's feet?"

"She has three incarnations, so happily no."

"Get the fuck out."

"First, they set me to work in a mine. That wasn't so bad. When I tried to escape, they moved me to a creche. I had to mind children—"

"Get," Valdrian crowed, "the fuck *out*!"

"—aged four to six." He assumed a modest expression. "I was good at it, actually."

"How is that possible?"

"It's common sense."

Valdrian eyed him sideways. "And they all survived the experience?"

"I even toilet trained one."

"Without threats of violence?"

He cast Valdrian an offended look. "What do you take me for?"

The mage chuckled. "Come now. I've known you for twenty years."

"Fair point," Malach conceded.

"I guess it bodes well for Rachel. Where is she?"

"With her cousins."

"The hell spawn?" His eyes widened. "Are you mad?"

"They're all I've got. They know who she is and they're nice to her. Mostly."

"You told Syd and Trist before you told me?"

"They figured it out. I had no choice."

"I always forget how smart those little vipers are."

Malach stood. "Speaking of which, I'd better look for them." He paused. "Would you talk to Jess and Lexa? I've been laughed at enough for one afternoon."

IT DIDN'T TAKE him long to find the children.

Malach was only a few steps outside the palace doors when a Kven knight ran up, breathing hard. "I was sent to bring you, Nuncio."

An icicle of fear stabbed his heart. "What is it? Speak!"

"Three of your kin, they are on the . . . ." He paused, searching for the word in Osterlish. Finally he pointed up at the palace and held his hand out flat, palm downward.

"Roof?" Malach asked.

"*Ja!*" The man nodded. "The roof of the Armory." He swallowed. "Dropping things on those who walk below. Only small things in the beginning." He held his fingers close together. "Now they throw big things."

"I'll handle it," Malach said tersely.

The man nodded. "I would not trouble you, but they will not come down. They make dreadful threats to Kommandant Fassbender when he goes up there—"

"Show me the way," Malach said.

The knight escorted him to the long stone Armory. A small crowd had gathered below, though they stood well back from the roof. As Malach approached, an object came flying over the edge. It smashed on the paving stones below. He picked up a shard of pottery and examined the rich blue glaze. Some priceless vase, no doubt.

"Hey!" he yelled.

Three small heads popped over the edge of the roof.

"Hello, Cardinal!" Sydonie yelled down with a smile.

"What the hell are you doing?"

"Teaching Rachel about gravity!"

He briefly closed his eyes. "Get down here this instant!"

A mutinous silence. He felt the Kvens staring.

"But we're doing science!"

Malach cupped his hands around his mouth. "Do you want to be locked in your rooms for the rest of the day?"

Three scowls.

"Then you'll do as I say!"

The heads vanished.

"Go about your business," Malach said in a loud voice.

The muttering crowd started to disperse. It did look like they were conducting experiments. He counted a tasseled pillow, four eggs, other nameless pieces of crockery, a dented can of tuna fish, six spoons, an empty shoebox, an expensive-looking fountain pen and the floppy hat Syd had taken from the shop when they first arrived. Malach picked the hat up and dusted it off. He waited for a few minutes. No further missiles were lobbed over the edge, but the children didn't appear.

"I'm coming up!" he yelled. "Do *not* throw anything!"

He glanced up at the edge of the roof, then swiftly crossed the impact zone, boot heels crunching on the shells. A clerk with thinning red hair hovered just inside the main doors.

"How do I get to the roof?" Malach asked.

The man gave a quick, frightened bow. "Just over here, Nuncio."

His accent marked him as a local. Offered the choice between collaborating with their new Kven masters or being handed over to Balaur as traitors when he arrived, most low-level functionaries in the Arx had opted for the former.

Malach climbed a winding flight of stairs. Loud wails greeted him as he stepped through the door to the roof.

Sydonie was sitting against the low wall, dirty face streaked with tears. She shut up the instant she saw him, though her chin trembled. Malach thought it was one of her dramatic performances until he saw the blood on her knee.

"She was running and fell down," Tristhus said. "We tried to do what you said!"

Rachel watched him with a neutral expression. The way you regarded a strange dog who might be friendly or who might just bite.

"Never mind." Malach crouched down. "Let me see."

"It's okay," Sydonie said with a little hiccup. "Just skinned it."

Malach gently brushed the scrape clean. The kneecap was already swelling. "Come on, we'll get it washed and bandaged." He stuck the floppy hat on her head.

"You're not mad?"

"I am, but I'll get you fixed up first."

She looked perplexed. Malach wondered if an adult had ever expressed concern over any of Syd's mishaps. *He* certainly hadn't. To be fair, he wasn't at Bal Kirith all that often. When he did visit, he'd viewed the children as a nuisance. Beleth's problem to deal with. And his aunt wasn't known for her maternal warmth.

Syd propped a hand on the wall and started hopping for the door. Tristhus took Rachel's hand and pulled her toward the stairs. She gazed up at her cousin worshipfully. That's how it always was. Kids took care of each other. It had been the same with him and Valdrian before they were old enough to go their separate ways.

Malach caught up to Sydonie, who limped along with a set expression, the hat jouncing up and down with each wobbly step.

Never show weakness. He'd learned that lesson, too.

"Come on, I'll give you a ride," he said.

"Huh?"

He bent over. "Hop on."

Her gaze narrowed as though expecting some trick.

"Just do it, Syd." He made his voice harder. "You'll take forever walking and I have things to do."

That was comprehensible. She flung her arms around his neck and climbed up to his back. Under the green cloak, the child must be thin as a reed. He barely felt her weight.

They hiked back to the palace together. As they approached the mages' wing, Syd laid her cheek on his shoulder. "Thanks, Malach," she mumbled sleepily.

He felt the hat slip off. "Sure, Syd."

Malach paused to pick it up. Once they reached her room, he bathed her knee in warm water and asked a char to bring ice wrapped in a towel.

"Keep it on there," he told her. "Ice makes a big difference if you do it right away."

Syd stared at him, fingers kneading the bundle against her knee. "What are you going to do to us? I mean for throwing shit?"

He glanced at Rachel, who was jumping up and down on the bed. "Language, Sydonie."

Trist burst out laughing, then cut off when Malach rounded on him. "I haven't decided yet. But you're both older. I want you to be a good influence on your cousin, not a bad one, understand?"

"Yes," Sydonie said quickly—too quickly. She gazed at him without guile. "We'll be very good from now on, Malach, I promise."

"You can begin by not lying to me."

Her eyes widened in outrage. "I'm not lying—"

"Enough." He glanced around the room. It looked like a dragon's lair. Jeweled chalices, stacks of oil paintings, gold effigies of the Church's martyrs, mounds of silver coins that winked in the lamplight. "If you make an effort, I might let you keep some of this."

"It's booty!" Syd protested. "Seized by the victors!"

"Which makes it Balaur's."

For the first time, Malach saw genuine fear in her eyes.

"We'll put it back," she said in a small voice.

"He won't know if you keep a few things." Malach pointed a finger at her. "And I won't tell him. But only if you find amusements that don't involve potentially killing people."

Syd licked her lips and shared a glance with her brother. "We can do that. But we get bored. There's nothing to do!"

"You could read books. There's about a dozen libraries."

She rolled her eyes.

"We don't know how," Trist admitted.

"You can't *read?*"

Beleth had taught Malach. Mainly, he suspected, so she could inflict her own writings on him. She must have run out of patience by the time his young cousins came along.

"It's no big deal," Sydonie burst out, her cheeks coloring. "Who gives a shit about . . . I mean, who cares about books?"

He shook his head. "We'll talk about it later. I can't teach you now, but you *will* learn. You're both smart. Rachel knows how."

Sydonie fell back on the bed, black hair snaking against the pillow. "She does?"

"Yes." Malach had an idea. One that might solve several problems at once, though it would set Beleth spinning in her grave. "I'll check on you in a while. Just ice that knee or you won't be running around for days."

He held out his hand to Rachel. She ignored it, but hopped down from the bed.

He passed the study. Valdrian had left, probably to find Jess and Lexa. He hoped he hadn't made a mistake in agreeing to tell them everything. He'd been sure he could trust Nikola, too. An error in judgment he would never repeat.

But Valdrian was right. The mages had to stick together. And it was a relief to bring them into his confidence.

Malach brought Rachel to a cozy sitting room with its own small library. The kids played in here sometimes and he noticed traces of jam on the carpet. At least, he hoped it was jam.

"Sit down," he said.

Rachel perched on the edge of a chair.

"I know Syd and Trist are your friends, but they don't always think before they do things. You're very young, but you need to understand that you mustn't always follow their lead. Today, for example. Someone could have gotten hurt."

She stared at him, utterly still.

Malach walked to the bookshelves that stretched from floor to ceiling. He drew out a slim volume and turned back to her. "You had your own *Meliora* at the Arx, didn't you? You must be a clever little girl to have learned your letters. I thought you might like to have another copy." He came over and held it out, heart pounding. "You could practice your reading again."

Malach couldn't quite believe he was offering her the foundational text of his sworn enemies. But what harm could it do? And it might be the one thing that proved his good intentions.

"I haven't read it myself," he admitted. "We never had a copy at Bal Kirith. But you could tell me about it." He smiled. "Who knows? Maybe I'll change my mind."

Rachel gazed at the book. Then she tore it from his hand and threw it to the floor.

"I hate you!" she shrieked. "I hate you, I hate you!"

Malach staggered back as she barreled into him, pounding tiny fists against his waist.

"You *made* me hurt people! You're a liar and I hate you!"

A dim memory stirred. A young boy beating his fists against a knight, bruising his knuckles on the plate armor, shaking with impotent rage. The thin cry of a baby in its cradle.

Run, boy!

Rachel paused for breath, face flushed and twisted. Her eye lit on the *Meliora*. It lay with the spine open on the floor. Rachel spat on it. Then she kicked it across the room.

"Go away!" she screamed. "Go away and leave me alone!"

Malach fled.

Chapter Thirty-Three

He locked the door with a trembling hand. Then he sank down, back pressed to the wood. Muffled sobs came through the door.

"If I could take it back," Malach said softly, "I would."

He'd replayed that night at the Arx in Novostopol a hundred times. The knights hacking through the door to Rachel's room. Nikola begging him to leave the child behind.

He rubbed his face and let out a long breath. Then he rose and went to a room a few corridors away. He sorted through the keys and found the right one. His hand was steady as he opened the door.

Falke dozed on the bed. Kasia Novak sat in a chair near the window. She leapt to her feet and he put a finger to his lips.

"Come with me," Malach whispered, glancing at Falke. He hadn't woken.

"Where?"

"We need to talk."

She eyed him with suspicion. "Has Balaur come?"

"I found your friends."

Her face lit up. Malach hardened his heart. "If you want

to know where they are, you'll give me a reading. That's all. No tricks."

A speculative look. "No tricks," she promised. "Gray has my cards—"

"And I took them from Gray." He glanced again at Falke. "Not here. Someplace private."

She gave a quick nod. Malach locked the door behind them and led her to Clavis's study. It was getting dark. He walked around and switched on the lamps.

"How does it work?" he asked.

"I can do a general reading. Or you can ask the ley a specific question." She eyed him shrewdly. "Do you have one?"

"Must I tell you what it is?"

Kasia hesitated. Then she shook her head. "You can keep it to yourself if you prefer."

He felt a surge of relief. Malach took the deck from a locked drawer of the desk. He'd already examined them. Seventy-eight cards divided into two groups. Fifty-six resembled normal playing cards. Suits corresponding with the Curiae—Flames, Wolves, Ravens and Keys. Aces through tens followed by face cards—Knight, Bishop, Cardinal, Pontifex.

The remaining cards were different. They looked like Marks, with titles painted in elegant gold lettering at the bottom. The Wheel. The Martyr. Death. The Lovers. The Fool. Twenty-two altogether.

Kasia stared at the deck, her gaze hungry.

"If anything unusual happens," he said, "anything at all, you'll be back in that liminal dungeon, understand me?"

She nodded.

"There's not a chance you'd make it out of the Arx. And I'll know if you try to use the ley against me."

Malach couldn't see it anymore, but his skin crawled when the power was used nearby. And Kasia had no idea he couldn't touch it himself.

"I won't," she said. "I swear."

He slid the cards across the desk. Kasia snatched them up. He watched her shuffle.

"Just hold the question in your mind," she said.

Malach nodded, leg jittering beneath the desk.

Will my daughter ever forgive me?

She fanned the deck face-down. He watched her closely. It could all be a fake. But she had known so much—

"Are you thinking of your question?" she asked.

"Yes."

Kasia closed her eyes. Her fingertips danced over the cards, pausing on some, then moving away again. Dark brows drew down in concentration. One by one, she drew five cards. Kasia opened her eyes and turned them over. The last was actually two stuck together. Malach studied the images.

"The Star," she said, touching each in turn. "The Emperor. The Serpent. The Twins. Those four stand alone." Her hand slid to the pair that had come from the deck as one. "The Sun. The Moon."

"What does it mean?"

She chewed her lip, frowning at the cards. "All Major Arcana. A significant spread. It does not speak of small events but large ones."

"The Star is Rachel," he said. "It looks like her."

"Yes. And the Emperor is Balaur. That much I know already."

Malach swore under his breath.

"You follow his orders," Kasia said with an angry edge. "You are his Nuncio."

"I do what I must."

"Listen to me, Malach." She leaned forward, intent. "Balaur has done things—"

"I'm not interested in his crimes!" he snapped. "Just finish the reading. What do the others mean?"

She drew a short, quick breath. When she spoke, her voice

was cool. "The Twins indicate a divided nature. That could speak to Rachel's Raven Mark and the conflict she feels between you and the Via Sancta, but I'm not certain of it." She tapped the last. "The Serpent is wisdom. Eternity and renewal, just as snakes shed their skin."

He stared at the card. The Serpent coiled around a tower. It had jet scales and the tower itself was black, so Malach could only tell one from the other by the light reflecting off the creature's skin. The hair on his nape stirred. Three woman stood holding hands at the base of the tower. One youthful, the second of middle years, the last bent and blind.

"Will I never be rid of them?" he muttered.

"Who?"

"Never mind. But you haven't answered my question yet."

She sat back, face pale. "The Sun and Moon together. That one is complex. The Moon is a card of illusion and deception. Something is not as it appears. The Sun is good fortune, joy and harmony. All coming together as it is meant to be. Clearly, they oppose each other." Her lips pinched in thought. "If the literal images are joined, we have twilight. Or dawn. One bringing darkness, the other light."

"So which is it?" he demanded.

"I cannot say."

"What else?"

She stared at the cards for a long time, eyes flicking between them. "There is deep-rooted hatred between the Serpent and the Emperor." She set the cards next to each other, almost touching. "Do you see how they stare at each other?"

Malach hadn't before. But the Serpent faced right, the Emperor left, and it did seem that their gazes locked in some silent struggle.

"Balaur seeks eternal life," Kasia said. "That is one obvious connection. Does this make any sense in regard to your question?"

"Fuck if I know," Malach said unhappily. "I was hoping for a simple yes or no. Not more riddles!"

"Well, the question does not have a simple answer," she replied. "It might help if you told me what it was——"

He swept the cards up. "Do it again."

Her jaw set. "First you'll tell me where my friends are."

He fumbled with the deck, smoothing it into a pile.

"Tell me!"

Malach couldn't meet her eyes. "I'm sorry, Kasia. They're dead."

A growl rose from her throat. She strode to the window and gripped the sill. Malach felt a stab of remorse. He'd never claimed they were alive, but he'd allowed her to have hope.

"Did you see the bodies?"

"No."

"Then how do you know?"

"The Kven captain in charge of the prisoners told Gray."

Kasia turned. "Kommandant Rademacher?"

Malach nodded.

"He's lying."

"Why would he lie?"

"Because he hates them. Alexei especially. We met him on the road to Nantwich. He wanted to arrest us, but Clavis's knights wouldn't let him."

Malach shook his head. "You have more enemies than I do."

"Where are the prisoners being held?"

"The sports stadium. Westfield."

"Go back. Search yourself!"

"Give me another reading."

Her mouth thinned. "After you find them."

Malach stood up, pocketing her cards. "I'll see what I can do. Not a word to Falke about any of this."

She stared at him. "How can you serve Balaur?"

"My reasons are my own. They're none of your concern."

"Did you know he's an alchemist?"

"Yes, I know. And I don't care!"

Malach thought she might say something else, but Kasia just strode past him to the door. They returned to the chamber in silence. Malach fished out the key.

"Thank you," he muttered. "I fear I expected too much."

Kasia looked grimly amused. "Now you will convince yourself that the cards mean nothing. Simply a random drawing. You will tell yourself that I made some lucky guesses before, but of course I cannot really foretell the future. It's a ridiculous notion."

He fitted the key into the lock. "I'm not sure what I believe anymore."

"But this sending from the ley *will* come to pass," Kasia continued. "If you took me into your confidence, I might know more."

He studied her. "And I think you know things you aren't telling me. If you want honesty, you can offer it in return."

She lifted her chin. "I tried to tell you. Balaur—"

"No," he interrupted harshly. "You have other secrets, cartomancer. Like who you really are!"

Kasia turned away, spots of color burning in her cheeks. "I have nothing to say to you, mage."

"Then we're done." Malach unlocked the door and pushed her inside.

———

THE INSTANT THE DOOR CLOSED, Kasia hurried over to Falke.

"What happened?" He searched her face, anxious. "I feared he'd given you to Balaur."

"Not yet. I gave him a reading." She drew a card from her sleeve with a flourish. "I palmed it when he looked away. We can use it to get out."

"And if he finds us gone?" He swept a hand through thick

silver hair. With the four-day beard, Falke was starting to resemble Father Caristia—though without the generous belly.

"Malach wasn't happy with what I told him." She chuckled. "I think he'll stew for a while."

"What did you see?"

"Rachel is involved. I'm sure she's what his question was about. But he wouldn't tell me what it was so it's hard to say." She peered out the window. The room looked down on a small cobbled courtyard, with a sliver of dark trees beyond. "The rain and dark will help hide us. We must leave right away."

Falke sat to pull his boots on. "Did you tell him about the Order?"

"I tried. He didn't want to hear it. But I know where the prisoners are being held. If we can get to the stadium and free them . . . well, it's too much to hope that we can take back the Arx, but at least we can all try to flee the city."

"And Rachel?"

Kasia gave him a level look. "If we try to take Malach's child again, I don't need the cards to foresee disaster. And he will certainly check on her before the night is over."

A reluctant nod. "There's still the matter of getting out of the Arx."

"It can be done. But I'll need a complete deck. Our first stop must be my old room at the Villa of Saint Margrit. There's a spare one hidden away. It has all the Major Arcana. Those are the most powerful cards, but I feared Malach might notice if I took one."

She went to the bathroom and changed into the char's uniform. For this, she could break her vow. It was tight in the bosom and a few inches too long, but it would serve.

When she emerged, Falke handed her the bundle of his cloak. "You take it, Kasia."

"What about you?"

"I'll be fine. It's just a little rain."

She wanted to argue, but she could see Falke was determined to be chivalrous. "Maybe we can find another at the Villa." Kasia pressed her ear to the door. "I'm sorry, but I'll need to use abyssal ley on the lock."

Falke held her gaze. "I trust you."

Clavis hadn't, but Kasia understood the difference between them now. Falke had loved Tess, and Tess loved *her*. She bound them together even in death. Perhaps more so now.

The Four of Keys flared red as she delved down, using only a thread of power and releasing the ley the instant she heard the tumblers click. Still, her hands shook a little from the taste of it.

Falke laid a hand on her shoulder. "Do you know how the mages beat us, Kasia? Before the Void?"

She shook her head, though she'd already guessed the answer.

"Compulsion. They would touch one knight and turn her against the others. Each one of us became a weapon in their hands. A single mage, if she was careful and clever, could wreak havoc on an entire company. *That* is why the Kvens fear them, though the nihilim are vastly outnumbered here." He swallowed. "You could do the same."

"Does compulsion work on the mages, too?"

"I don't know. I've never tried."

She nodded. "We will do what we must at the stadium. But first things first. I need that deck." Kasia eased the door open. The hall was empty.

"I know a route we can take," Falke whispered. "It will avoid the nihilim guarding the east wing."

"Do they know who you are?"

"Only a pair of hellacious orphans from Bal Kirith. Let us pray we don't encounter them."

They slipped out and crept down the corridor. One of the doors ahead stood wide open. Kasia stopped to listen. Three male voices, deep in conversation, none of them Malach. There was no way to pass without being seen.

Falke gestured for her to wait, then rapped on the open door. "Masters," he said, bowing low. "His Excellency sent us to ask if you wish for refreshments."

Gone was the deep voice used to barking commands. Falke sounded diffident and a touch frightened. He kept his eyes cast down. So did Kasia.

"Wine," one of them said. "Mulled, if they have any in the kitchens."

Kasia dropped a curtsy.

"Yes, masters," Falke said, backing out.

They shared a look and continued down the corridor. When the wine didn't arrive, the mages would wonder where they'd gone. Kasia judged they had about twenty minutes to get out of the palace before the alarm was raised.

Falke led her confidently through the maze of corridors. They encountered another pair of nihilim, women this time, but as before, Falke's status as Malach's servant and Kasia's gray dress made them beneath notice. At last, they reached a small stair leading down.

"Thank the Saints every building is laid out the same," Falke whispered as they descended. "I took this same stair many times in Novostopol when Feizah wished to see me in her private library. There should be a window at the bottom . . . ah, yes."

He stopped at the bottom of the stairs. A flash of lightning lit a narrow mullioned window. Falke patted his stomach with a rueful smile. "Two weeks ago, I'd never have managed it. But the rations at Bal Kirith left me in fighting form again."

Kasia used the balled-up cloak to shatter the glass in time with a roll of thunder, then knocked the shards from the sill. She squeezed through one side of the vertical wooden divider and dropped down to the damp earth below. Falke was wider in the shoulders. He got halfway through, huffing and puffing, and stuck like a cork in a bottle.

"Hurry!" she whispered.

Above the steady patter of rain, she heard the sound of feet crunching on gravel.

He twisted, red in the face, as they drew nearer. Kasia was about to push him back inside when cloth tore and he tumbled from the sill. They ran around the corner of the building just as a Kven patrol marched past along the pathway.

Kasia held her breath until they passed. They hadn't noticed the broken window.

"This way," she hissed, pointing.

They hugged the western flank of the palace, ducking low to pass the windows. If not for the foul weather, she felt sure they would have been seen, but it was raining buckets. Kasia shook out the cloak and put it on. She mapped out the next steps in her mind. Once they reached the end of the Pontifex's Palace, they'd have to cross the plaza to reach her room at the Villa. That would be the most dangerous part. With luck, they would be taken for chars running an errand.

They were nearly at the corner of the long stone building when Falke stopped beneath an overhang. After a moment, Kasia heard voices. The window above had been left slightly ajar.

Later, she would ponder that small oversight. Every other window they'd passed was shut tight against the storm. All that came after had depended on a single char forgetting to close it all the way.

Happenstance? Or the inscrutable will of the ley?

Kasia tugged at Falke's sleeve, impatient to continue. He made a sharp gesture.

"What are we to do with her?" a woman demanded.

"We've already discussed this." A deep male voice.

Kasia wondered if they were speaking of her.

"I don't understand why you brought her. She's disloyal!"

"Morvana Zeigler served me faithfully for ten years, the last six as my Nuncio."

Ah. Kasia's brows lifted. The man must be Luk. The first voice—dry and harsh—she already knew. Bishop Maria Karolo.

"Nonetheless—"

"I will not execute her in cold blood," Luk snapped. "I hold to the *Meliora*. As you must, too, Maria."

Kasia exchanged a look of disbelief with Falke.

"You should have left her in Kvengard," Karolo said.

"It would have looked suspicious if I arrived without her. Pretenses had to be maintained."

"I understand that, Reverend Father. But it does not help our cause to have dissent in the ranks. I fear some of your knights might listen to her. Can't she be persuaded?"

A long silence. "She took charge of the investigation into the children. I tried to leave it with the police, but she insisted. Their plight touched her greatly. I knew she wouldn't understand the necessity of the bargain. But the children were not —" A rumble of thunder drowned out of the rest of his words. "—are Reborn! Purified! It was a blessing."

"You don't fear undergoing the Magnum Opus, Reverend Father?" Karolo sounded uneasy.

"What is there to fear?" His voice faded, then grew strong again. Was he pacing? "Imagine it, Maria! When you are named Pontifex of the Eastern Curia, your reign will last for thousands of years. Together we can ensure stability. And the strictest interpretation of the *Meliora*, of course."

A gust of wind flapped Kasia's cloak. It smelled of roses. Lightning flickered again and she saw that they'd paused in front of a garden. The blossoms were all white or palest pink. No red.

As if banning a color had any effect on the ley itself.

"You will keep your promise?" Karolo asked.

"I will send troops to convince the cardinals in Novostopol. " A low chuckle. "Falke was the greatest obstacle, but he is dead."

"Perhaps the starfall *was* an act of the ley," Karolo said in pious tones. "Many died, but it disrupted Falke's regime. And a better one will rise from the ashes."

Kasia glanced at the pontifex. He shook his head in disgust.

"We must go," she whispered.

She turned from the window. Tall shadows closed in from every direction. Men on Marksteeds with glowing eyes. They'd blended with the night, perfectly silent until it was too late.

Within seconds they were surrounded. A rider reined up next to her. A hand yanked her hood back. She recognized its owner. One of the priests who had tried to kidnap her on the wharf in Novostopol. Her gaze flicked to the sheaf of wheat on his cloak, then back to his cold eyes. But he wasn't staring at her.

He was staring at Falke.

Kasia gripped the card in her pocket. The priest wore leather gloves and gauntlets. A thick cloak and boots. They thumped down with a splash as he swung from the saddle, landing next to her.

"Ley preserve me," he said in astonishment. "It's the Reverend—that is to say, it's him!"

Kasia rolled her head back, pretending to swoon. The priest reached out a steadying hand. Red light spilled from her sleeve as she sought the bare skin of his neck where a Raven poised mid-flight. He reared back, eyes widening. Her finger-tips were a centimeter from contact when an iron grip seized her wrist from behind, twisting it viciously. The boiling power in her blood vanished, leaving her with a residue of wordless fury.

"It's the cartomancer from Novo," one of his companions

hissed. She struggled and he jerked her arm up behind her back. Kasia bit back a cry of pain. "Search them both."

The card lay on the grass, beaded with rainwater. Three more burly priests dismounted. They gave the Four of Keys a wide berth, though it was useless without her touching it. She stood in the rain, shivering, as they took her cloak and patted her down. Falke was shoved to the ground. The Pontifex didn't bother complaining about his rough treatment, though he threw Kasia an apologetic look as they were dragged back inside the palace. Two Kven knights guarded a set of doors.

"Keep your mouths shut, *da?*" growled the priest Kasia had tried to compel. "We found these two lurking outside. I must tell the Reverend Father and the bishop."

The knights stood aside, eyeing the prisoners curiously. Kasia and Falke stood dripping in the hall while the priest ducked inside. She heard low voices. A moment later, he emerged. The priest had dark, expressive eyes and the kind of beard that started growing in an hour after he shaved. An attractive man—if he weren't a fanatic. He made a wry gesture of invitation.

"Come inside," he said. "Warm yourself by the fire."

As she turned to enter, Kasia glimpsed a flash of scarlet at the end of the corridor. Then it was gone. She followed Falke into a large library. A blaze roared in the hearth. The window, she noticed, was now firmly shut. Two chairs had been positioned near the flames. Neither occupant rose as they entered, though Maria Karolo leaned forward slightly, lips parted.

Kasia only knew Luk from a painting Tessaria kept in her home office. The artist had been kind. The Kven pontifex looked at death's door—a few steps into the lobby, actually—and Kasia realized that for all his talk of the *Meliora*, he'd struck the bargain with Balaur to save himself.

Falke had clearly deduced the same. He eyed Luk with contempt. "So you sold your ring for a cure. After all your self-righteous posturing, it seems you're more than willing to sacrifice thousands of lives to preserve your own. But you're a fool if you think—"

"Be silent!" Maria Karolo snapped. "What are you doing here? How did you get into the Arx?"

The priests fanned out, watching the exchange with guarded expressions.

Falke smiled coldly. "Wouldn't you like to know?"

Spots of color appeared in her cheeks. "Oh, you'll tell me." A quick glance at Kasia. "I'm not surprised your little pet is with you. But consorting with Unmarked murderers is the least of your crimes."

Falke's composure slipped. "*My* crimes?" he demanded. "I am the rightfully elected Pontifex of Novostopol!"

"Not for long," she replied with satisfaction. "Everyone believes you dead. I have no plans to disabuse them of the notion."

"The cardinals will never go along with you, Maria. When I return—"

"Enough," Luk said. "How did you come to be here?"

"Is your hold on the city slipping?" Falke asked softly. "Could it be that a force has marched from Bal Kirith, unbeknownst to you, and is at this very minute closing around the Arx?"

"He's bluffing." Karolo's gloved fingers picked at the arm of the chair.

"Of course he is," Luk agreed. "Yet the question remains."

"I'll convince him to talk," Karolo said, rising to her feet. "Hold the woman for me."

Two priests grabbed Kasia's arms. When Falke moved to intervene, he was clouted and shoved to his knees.

"I will not witness physical abuse," Luk said, thin lips drawing together in distaste.

"Then avert your eyes, Reverend Father," the bishop replied. She strode over to Kasia and grabbed a hank of hair.

A small, birdlike woman, yet stronger than she looked. Her sharp bob swayed as she leaned in.

"I looked for you for a long time," she hissed. "Where is Tessaria Foy?"

Kasia spit in her face. The bishop recoiled. "How dare you?" A hard yank of her scalp made Kasia's eyes water.

"Really, Maria," Luk said, though he made no move to stop her.

"Stop!" Falke cried. "I will tell you."

Karolo rounded on him, still gripping Kasia's hair.

Falke's jaw worked. He was clearly searching for some plausible explanation and coming up empty. Protecting Rachel, Kasia realized. If these two got hold of the child . . . . She suppressed a shudder.

"Mount a search of the grounds," Luk said. "Discreetly."

"I already gave the order," the stubbled priest replied. "If any others are here, we'll find them."

"No doubt the sorceress brought them both inside the walls." Karolo's gaze narrowed. "Or they are in league with the nihilim. Sent to spy on us."

Luk snorted. "Falke? I doubt it."

"Let's see if she's really Unmarked. I want her stripped, Fra Zaitsev."

He hesitated. "She tried to use the ley against me, Your Grace. But we took the card away. She hasn't tried it again since—"

"Did you not hear me?"

"Yes, Your Grace."

Kasia stared at the bishop. "I think *you're* the pervert," she said. "But that's often how it is, eh? Those who protest the loudest—"

Karolo slapped her. Kasia licked blood from her lip. "Like it rough, do you?" she asked.

The demented gleam in the bishop's eye confirmed the truth of this. Karolo gripped the collar of her gray dress and yanked. Buttons popped, bouncing across the carpet. The front fell open, exposing a skimpy camisole. The bishop clearly expected her to be humiliated and looked disappointed at the lack of a reaction.

Luk studied the rose and gold clouds painted on the ceiling. Falke spewed a torrent of impotent threats. The two priests restraining him wore the glazed looks of men who weren't quite sure how they'd ended up here, but were so used to doing what they were told that they couldn't conceive of any alternative.

Karolo was breathing hard now. "I'll ask again, are you in league with the mages?"

Kasia threw her head back. Laughter rang out. "Well, I don't know," she said at length. "Are you?

Chapter Thirty-Four

The *Wayfarer* dropped anchor just south of Nantwich's port. Forks of lightning gave glimpses of roiling clouds and a stony beach with steep cliffs beyond. The lights of the Arx glimmered at the top. About a league down the coast, the beam of a solitary lighthouse flashed on and off.

"Yer certain Balaur himself is not there?" Paarjini shouted over the wind. Without the silver net, her long brown hair whipped wildly in the salt-laden gale. "T'would be good to ken that beforehand."

The Maid shook her head, bouncing up and down on the deck.

"We do not sense his presence," the Mother replied.

"But he draws near," the Crone rasped. "We dare not wait for the storm to break. You must go tonight."

Two witches had cloaked the ship with illusion so it would blend with the waves, but Captain Aemlyn refused to enter the harbor. The danger of a collision with another vessel was too great. She'd chosen a sheltered cove for the landing party, but the seas were still rough and it was much worse now that the ship lay with sails furled and her beam to the waves, which rolled in broadside. Nikola braced on the pitching deck as four sailors prepared to swing a davit out over the rail. Despite the perils of forcing, she wished she just could magick herself inside the Arx.

Tashtemir clambered into the dinghy first, followed by Paarjini and Heshima. Nikola came last. The davit swung out and the crew winched them down. Heshima took the bench. She used an oar to push off from the ship, then started rowing. The waves rolling toward shore made it a swift journey. Nikola jumped out when the water was knee-deep and took the rope at the bow. Once everyone had disembarked, they dragged the dinghy well above the high tide line.

The beach was a narrow crescent of smooth rocks, girded by larger boulders to each side. Nikola studied the cliff face. It was riven with cracks and narrow ledges. She thought she saw a path to the top, though it would be a hairy ascent with the wind and rain.

"Come here," she called to Tashtemir, who was regarding the escarpment with a dubious expression.

"I hail from a flat land," he said. "The highest thing I've ever climbed is a ladder to fetch a bottle of Maroc from the upper rack of the Imperator's cellars. It gave me vertigo."

"Which is why I'll cast a spell of protection," Nikola replied. "And agility."

He grinned at her. "To be fair, I was already tipsy. Are these gifts permanent?"

She shook her head. "Nothing in lithomancy is permanent."

Nothing except my eyes, she thought.

"A pity." He made a flowery gesture that ended with a blown kiss. "But I accept with gratitude."

She fished a fragment of reddish yellow sard from her pouch, pressing the stone into his hand and using her will to draw out the ley and bind it around him. Red for courage, blue to bestow grace and balance, violet for luck. Tashtemir's eyes widened a little.

"I felt that," he muttered. "Let us hurry before I lose my nerve."

Paarjini was already halfway up the cliff, climbing like a monkey. Heshima moved more slowly, with cautious deliberation, gaze fixed above as she sought the next handhold.

"You go first," Nikola said. "I'll be right behind."

"And I will try not to fall upon you," Tashtemir promised, seizing the first handhold and starting up.

Tough, woody shrubs grew from some of the cracks. Tash tested each one before letting it take his weight. He followed the route Paarjini had blazed, sidling across cracks so narrow his heels hung over the edge. Nikola waited a moment, then followed. For a time, all was quiet as they each concentrated on navigating the slippery passage. By the time she looked up again, Paarjini had reached the top, leaning over to call down encouragement. Nikola herself didn't mind heights; she simply *chose* not to look down.

There was a bad moment when a loose stone gave beneath Tashtemir's boot, whizzing past her face. He clung to an outcropping, one leg dangling as the other scrambled for purchase, but he was already so near the top, Hashima and Paarjini managed to reach down and haul him the rest of the way. Nikola dragged herself over the rim a few seconds later, heart pounding.

"Lucky, eh?" Tashtemir whispered with a strangled laugh.

They were at the bottom of a high curtain wall, with only about two meters of ledge before the sheer drop to the beach. Paarjini signed that they should follow and set off along the wall, the others coming single file. It curved gently inland. At length, the space broadened out and they were able to walk two abreast. The wind tore at Nikola's cloak, but it eased as the wall moved away from the sea.

"I see the city gates," said Heshima, who had enhanced her night vision with lapis.

They paused to regroup and choose stones. "Don't forget

the Wolf Mark on the neck," Nikola reminded her sisters. "Just like the picture I drew for you. And blue cloaks, a few shades darker than the sea on a clear morning."

During her time as a char in Novo, she'd seen every city's Mark except for Jalghuth, which never sent clergy to visit.

Heshima nodded, fisting a chunk of antimony. Paarjini, as usual, was already three steps ahead. Tashtemir gave a clap of delight as the illusion shimmered into focus.

"Do ye fancy my beard?" Paarjini asked. Her voice had dropped an octave.

"How did you *do* that?" Nikola asked, deeply impressed. "The voice, I mean?"

"Throw in a bit o'bronze."

Nikola used the antimony backing on her sunstone ring to forge an illusion of a burly Kven knight with longish blond hair. She checked the greaves covering her shins and gauntlets on her hands. All looked in order. Then she drew a thread from the bronze bracelet Caelyn had given her, tied it around her vocal chords, and cleared her throat.

"How do I sound?"

Heshima nearly fell over at the foghorn croak.

"Maybe a wee bit too much," Paarjini said, holding her fingers a hair apart. She managed to keep a straight face, though her brown eyes brimmed with suppressed laughter.

Tashtemir clutched his chest. "I think I just—can you conjure a clean pair of trousers?"

"All right, all right," Nikola muttered sourly in her own voice. "I won't say anything. You two can deal with the sentries."

She let Heshima create Tashtemir's manacles and turn him into a Raven knight. A convincing illusion of a person was a tricky proposition, and maintaining it for any period of time even more so. The problem lay in the fact that a human face had hundreds of tiny muscular contractions to lend it expression. The area around the eyes was especially hard to mimic. People knew when they were looking at something a bit *wrong* and the emotional response was instinctive, intense revulsion.

It was worse if the illusion came very, very close but failed to pass muster. The effect was eerie. Uncanny, like an animated corpse. Heshima had demonstrated it to Nikola. How the eyes are never at rest, even when someone is quietly thinking. They dart around, the brows twitch, and since every muscle is interconnected, other parts of the face move, too. The precise way an eyelid folds against the skin, or how lips make contact with teeth when one smiles—a single off detail and the observing brain instantly picks up on it, whispering, *Oh, hell no.*

Only a very few witches had fully mastered this class of illusion. It made a destroyer battleship seem like child's play.

Heshima took a last look at the three of them. "Passable," she said with a frown. "The rain and dark will help."

All three Kven "knights" had pewter eyes—no spell could mask that—but hopefully no one would notice.

They threw their hoods up and approached the sentries at the gate. It was one of the smaller ones, with a sally port.

"Gutten avend!" Paarjini bellowed. "Wix haben einen gedankenen!"

Good evening! We have a prisoner!

It was the only Kven phrase she'd memorized. Nikola prayed they wouldn't detect her lilting Athaaran accent.

The knights in guardhouse called something down in Kven that seemed to demand a reply, but the spells of good fortune prevailed and the words were drowned out by a huge clap of thunder. The illusion of the Raven knight—Tashtemir —started to struggle. One of his captors clouted him.

A moment later, the sally port swung wide and a knight came out. He shouted something like "welk virma zend" but before he could finish the sentence, Heshima hit him with a spell of forgetfulness. Moonstone, Nikola thought, studying the flows, and a touch of pumice for the air element. The knight blinked in confusion and allowed Paarjini to lead him back through the gate.

The three men and a woman inside the guardhouse were quickly slammed with heavy sleep spells that should render them harmless for several hours. Paarjini released her own illusion and patted the cheek of the knight who'd come out. He gave her a quizzical smile.

"Wer vist du?" he wondered.

Who are you? Nikola guessed. Or maybe, *Who am I?*

"Ye, my wolfish friend, are goin' t' bed," she replied solemnly, as he slumped face-down at the table.

They all released the illusions. Tashtemir's was starting to slip anyway—the nose too long, the eyes like hard, shiny little marbles—rendering him solidly in the realm of "What on the ley's green earth *is* that thing?"

A quick check to make sure there were no more knights lurking about and they were on their way, hurrying through the pitch-black streets. "They must have cut the electricity," Nikola whispered to Tashtemir. "Nantwich is a modern city."

"Better for us," he replied, eying the dark windows. "Not so much for the Nants, though."

"I hope he hasn't been a bastard," she muttered.

"The Cardinal? Well, he does have the propensity for it. But I imagined his reign to be more like a giant party with the adults gone for the weekend."

Nikola laughed despite herself. "That sounds about right."

They avoided the Kven patrols on horseback, of which there were surprisingly few. The main force must be guarding the city walls and the Arx—where Malach would be, as well. Paarjini paused several times to confirm it with a spell to track the kaldurite.

Being one of the only structures with power, the Arx was not hard to find. They just followed the glow of lights. But getting through the portcullis was another matter. Too many knights, and the place was lit up like high noon. Their illusions would never pass.

"Invisibility it is," Paarjini said. "Ready your——"

"Cat's eye," Nikola said. "I know."

Her teeth gleamed in the dark. "Very good. We'll make a *laoch* of ye yet."

Nikola frowned. "I thought I already was."

"Yer a witch. Don't get too big for yer knickers——"

"Hssst!" Heshima made a slashing gesture. "A patrol's heading in."

Nikola focused instantly, pulling from the cat's eye in her pouch and bending the light into a reflective shield. "I got Tash!" she whispered, grabbing his arm.

Paarjini and Hashima faded to blurry blobs of shadow. True invisibility would violate natural law, but with a little improvisation you could get pretty close to the real thing. They sprinted to the portcullis just as the patrol rode through under the watchful gaze of a dozen Kven knights. The sharp teeth at the bottom caught a piece of her cloak as it descended and she wrenched it free. They were in a dank tunnel running below the Arx's massive outer wall.

Once the first portcullis slammed down with a heavy thud, a second iron grille lifted at the end of the tunnel. This time Nikola tried to be quicker, but she must have gotten too close to the Marksteed in the rear for it whinnied in alarm, jerking at the reins. The rider's helm turned. It was shaped like a wolf's head with a snarling muzzle. She froze, pressed so tightly to the Masdari she could feel his heart drumming, as the knight's gaze swept the tunnel through the visor. Then he dug his heels in and galloped ahead to catch up with the rest.

She couldn't see Hashima or Paarjini. She sprinted for the end of the tunnel, dragging Tash by the hand.

"We . . . won't . . . make it," he panted.

"Yes, we will!" She dragged him down with her and they rolled underneath just as the portcullis came down with a bone-jarring thud. Her shield vanished, but Nikola sensed another one drop down to cover them both an instant later.

"Valmitra's blood, ye like to cut it fine," whispered Paarjini's disembodied voice. A strong hand hauled Nikola to her feet. "Let's get out o' here."

The patrol was ahead now, across the bailey and trotting into the Arx proper. She startled at Heshima's whisper in her ear. "Do you feel it, Nikola?"

"Feel what?" she whispered back.

"Another citadel sitting beneath the first. Or . . . not beneath exactly. Alongside might be a better word. It's *big*. And strange."

"Is Malach there?" Paarjini demanded. "I can sense the kaldurite. He's close. That building, I think." A ghostly hand pointed across the plaza to a limestone rectangle with two wings that Nikola recognized as the Pontifex's Palace.

"Never mind." Heshima expelled a breath. "It's a quiet place. Not here nor there. As if it's *nowhere*."

The words unsettled her, but Nikola was already on edge. They were inside the Arx of a city occupied by their enemies. Rachel was here—the child she'd never wanted but who tugged at her nonetheless. Now she had to face the father, who believed she'd abandoned him.

Not for the first time. Not even for the second. She'd done nothing but run from him since the day they met.

She drew on a peridot for serenity and squared her shoulders. "Then let's go find Malach."

Chapter Thirty-Five

Malach leafed through a copy of *The Ninth Kingdom*, a tedious tome on morality penned by one of his distant Praefator ancestors. After two pages, he could hardly keep his eyes open. No wonder the volume looked pristine. Not even the zealots could hack through the impenetrable thickets of metaphor and bombast. He tossed it aside, rubbing his forehead.

The rest of the books he'd taken from the library were equally excruciating. Full of words like *heretofore* and *hegemony* and *elucidate*.

He needed something simple the children could use for lessons. Something that might hold their interest. Malach himself had cut his teeth on what, by any standard, would be considered graphic pornography. Beleth's twelve-volume *Philosophy of the Via Libertas* mingled dry lectures on the rights of the individual with long passages detailing sexual acrobatics of every variety. He'd spent most of his time devouring the latter. They were poorly written, but his aunt insisted on proper grammar and punctuation. He'd been able to spell *cunnilingus* by the age of six.

That was not what he had in mind for Syd and Trist.

Maybe he could start with newspapers. Short, punchy head-lines. Then Malach remembered he'd shut them all down.

A cookbook? The Mistress of Chars could be his ally. It would do the children good to learn their way around a kitchen. Syd would adore vomit soup—

"Malach!" Jessiel skidded into the room, face flushed. "Luk has Kasia Novak!"

He leapt to his feet, books scattering to the floor.

"Falke, too! Hurry!"

He yanked a crimson robe over his head and followed her into the hall. Malach didn't ask how it had happened. His heart was beating too fast for thought.

"Where?" he managed.

"West wing library. The one overlooking the rose gardens. I saw them both dragged inside."

"Get Valdrian. Go!"

Jess darted off. He pelted down the stairs and into the west wing. Two priests stood near the library doors. Malach heard raised voices beyond. One moved to block his way.

"Stand aside, please," he said.

"The bishop left orders not to be disturbed."

They were from Novostopol. Ravens on their necks, sheaves of wheat on their cassocks. Order of Saint Marcius. The ones who hated anything fun.

"Do you know who I am?" Malach asked.

"Balaur's Nuncio."

"Then get out of my fucking way."

They swapped a look. "I'm very sorry, Your Excellency, but we must ask you to return later. It's also the command of the Reverend Father Luk. They are in council."

Malach nodded with a sour expression. He half-turned away, then spun back and smashed an elbow into the priest's face. The man rocked against the door. Blood gushed from his nose. His companion shuffled back a step, whipping a knife from his sleeve. His eyes flicked to Malach's bare hands. He turned to run and skidded in the blood. Malach leapt after him. They tangled together on the ground. He pinned the man's wrist, prying at his gloved fingers.

He was so intent on the dagger, he didn't see the one with the broken nose stagger over. Malach took a kick to the ribs and another to his gut that nearly made him vomit.

Then he got the knife.

The fight ended shortly thereafter. Malach wiped blood from his eye. He stepped over the bodies and pushed the doors open. When he saw was what happening inside, a bubble of rage swelled in his chest.

Two priests held Kasia Novak by the arms. Maria Karolo had torn her dress wide open. The bishop's face was pink with excitement. The instant she saw him, her expression went blank. Like a child caught redhanded in some act of mischief.

"Let her go," Malach said, closing the doors behind him.

"This is Via Sancta business, Nuncio." Her head cocked, birdlike. "What have you done? Where are my men?"

"He has killed them, Maria," Luk said. "I think that much is obvious."

Falke lay facedown on the carpet, jowls mottled with fury. A priest knelt on his back. Another stood over him. Four altogether from the Order of Saint Marcius.

"Nor is he surprised to see our guests," Luk continued, "so that answers one question."

"Domina Novak is under my personal protection," Malach said, trying to rein his temper. "So is Falke. You will return them to me immediately or face the consequences."

Karolo looked to Luk. He sat by the fire, gaunt and heavy-lidded. "I don't think we will, Nuncio."

The title was uttered with open disdain. Malach knew the old pontifex hated him. The feeling was mutual. They'd avoided each other thus far, using Cardinal Gray as an intermediary, but a confrontation was inevitable. It might as well be now.

Kasia looked around with an interested gleam in her eye. A corner of her mouth quirked upward in a half smile, like someone who'd placed a wager and was eager to see how it turned out.

"Then we have a rather serious problem," Malach said, just as the doors burst open and his two cousins stepped inside. Valdrian quietly pressed the hilt of a short sword into his hand. Jessiel raised her crossbow.

Maria Karolo looked around, wild-eyed. Sweat matted the heavy curtain of bangs to her forehead in clumps. The contrast with her relaxed, half-naked prisoner would have made Malach laugh if he weren't so angry himself.

"You cannot have Falke," she ground out. "He is mine by rights!" Her voice rose to a screech. "A false pontifex!" She pushed Kasia away and scrambled over to Falke, fingers probing at his hands. "Where is the ring, Dmitry?" she panted. "Give it to me!"

Karolo yanked a stiletto from the boot of the priest kneeling on Falke's back. Time slowed as her arm lifted to plunge it down. Malach threw himself across the room, his only thought to stop her from killing the man he despised above all others. A swarm of wasps buzzed past his ear. Karolo spun to the side, a crossbow bolt jutting from her back. A second bolt took the priest in the throat.

Luk rose to his feet. He pulled his gloves off.

Malach knew he was a half blood like Rachel. Father of the ley-born—hounds, hawks and horses. And the white-coated dogs, which Malach liked even less than the others. His nape prickled as Luk gathered power. Their eyes locked. Malach adjusted his grip on the sword. The sounds of combat swelled around him.

He walked slowly up to the pontifex. A network of fine blue veins pulsed beneath chalky skin. The deep-set eyes regarded him warily.

"Karolo was disposable," Luk said, licking his lips. "I have no quarrel with you, regent. You may keep them both."

"It's too late for that."

"Why? You *need* us!" He swallowed. "We have a bargain!"

"With Balaur. Not with me."

He felt Kasia watching from the corner of his eye. She'd pulled Falke behind a heavy wooden table in the corner. A scream cut the air. It sounded like one of the priests.

"I'll tell you a secret." Malach leaned forward. "I didn't kill Feizah. I don't know who did. But I *do* have a reputation to maintain. One pontifex is as good as another."

Luk moved faster than he expected. An icy hand closed around Malach's forearm. Luk's palm was dry and papery, like fragile parchment. The gold ring dug into his flesh.

"Are you trying to turn me into something else?" Malach wondered. "Give me scales for skin? Hooves for feet?"

The grip tightened, a shiver scraped his spine, but the ley met an invisible wall. Luk's yellowed teeth ground together.

"You are a devil!" he gasped.

"Yes," Malach agreed. "I am."

He wrenched his arm free and swung the blade.

———

NIKOLA EYED the two dead priests in the corridor.

"Malach is beyond that door," Paarjini said.

Tashtemir tugged at his mustache. "The Cardinal does have a temper," he muttered.

"Who are they?" Heshima asked.

"Order of Saint Marcius," Nikola replied. "I wonder what they're doing here?"

"I don't like this," Paarjini said. "Perhaps you should have sent a message—"

"After what you did to him, he'd say no," Nikola replied.

"But he loves the child. He told me he believed she'd be safe in Dur-Athaara."

"She's yours, too," Heshima said. "You have rights to her."

"I'm not sure he'll see it that way," Nikola admitted. "Not anymore."

The witch's jaw set. "If only we could cast a spell over him. He'd be eating out of our hands."

"As well wish for the moon on a silver chain," Paarjini said impatiently. "We can't touch him and he knows it. We'll have to persuade him."

"Or we could just find the child and be done with it," Heshima suggested.

Nikola rounded on them both. "You heard what the Mahadeva said! If Rachel is taken from him against his will, he'll pull the world down around our ears to get her back. It would shift his path to the worst possible scenario. And I will not be part of betraying him again! If you try, I'll do everything I can to stop you."

The two women locked eyes. Nikola thumbed the agate on her ring, readying a protective spell. Tashtemir looked ready to run.

"She's right," Paarjini said at last. "I know it's tempting, but ye'll have to put that from yer mind, sister."

Hashima scowled and gave a brief nod. Nikola turned to the doors again. They'd come so far. She couldn't imagine trying to get inside the Arx a second time. Yet those dead priests didn't bode well.

She twisted her rings, buying a moment to think. She'd expected to find him in the audience chamber, lording it over his new subjects, or better yet alone in his rooms. But what if Malach was in trouble? The priests could have been assassins sent to kill him.

She couldn't leave without knowing.

"No threats," she said. "I'll do the talking."

Paarjini and Heshima nodded, though Tash looked like

he'd rather be anywhere else—even back at the Imperator's court. Nikola opened the door and stepped across the threshold.

Tall shelves of leather-bound books and a massive fireplace dominated one wall. Gilded standing lamps illuminated dark oil paintings and carved wooden furniture. She counted twelve people in the room.

Only five were still alive.

Malach stood over a long, very thin body in a white cassock, the top half of which was stained crimson. One foot wore a white satin slipper. The other rested in a spreading pool of blood. The gold ring on the third finger confirmed that it was a Pontifex. Running wolves along the bony arms named him Luk. His severed head had rolled a short distance away. The mouth gaped horribly.

In the center of the room lay a woman in the purple robes of a bishop. She'd fallen face-down, a crossbow bolt sticking from her back. Medium-length brown hair fanned across her shoulders. Her head was twisted to one side. Nikola glimpsed a Raven Mark. The rest of the dead were priests.

Was this massacre what the Mahadeva had foreseen? If so, they'd come too late.

Malach's head whipped around. He gripped a gore-streaked blade in both hands. The look in his eye chilled her to the bone.

Nikola held her palms out. "Easy. I'm just here to talk."

His expression froze. Then his gaze flicked past her shoulder. "That's why you brought the whole fucking coven?"

Heshima muttered something.

"Who are they?" a young woman demanded. She had a dark complexion and thick, curling hair that fell to the small of her back. She wore a red cloak and carried the crossbow that must have ended the bishop.

"Witches," her male companion said flatly, staring at

433

Nikola. "That's the one who gave me her horse. But she wasn't a witch then."

"My name is Nikola Thorn." She glanced at his missing hand. "I remember you. You're Valdrian."

She looked past Malach, trying to untangle what she'd just walked into. Because she knew the other two people, as well. Dmitry Falke and Kasia Novak. Both seemingly unharmed.

"You're not welcome here," Malach growled.

"Just hear me out," she said evenly. "We come with an offer of sanctuary. Whatever you've done, it doesn't matter."

"Sanctuary?" he echoed, his voice soft.

She nodded. "You and the child both—"

He tossed the bloody sword aside. "Get out. All of you."

Tashtemir stepped through the door. "Cardinal," he said hesitantly. "You should do as they say. It's for your own good."

Malach cast him a look of betrayal. "So you're their lapdog now?" He shook his head. "Well, I doubt they gave you a choice. But I've nothing to say to any of you. So piss off."

"Now listen, aingeal," Paarjini snapped. "We aim to speak with ye in a civilized manner."

"If you want an audience with the Nuncio of Bal Agnar," he said, "you'll ask for a formal invitation like everyone else. So scurry back to wherever you came from and I'll consider it."

He walked to a chair by the fire and sank down, hooking one leg over the arm.

Nikola bit back a surge of irritation. He had every right to be furious.

"This isn't what you want," she said. "Nor is it what's good for Rachel."

He tipped his head back and laughed. Heshima scowled.

"Somehow," Malach said, "I don't believe you have my best interests at heart."

"We offer you safety," Nikola persisted. "Only disaster will come from this course. The Mahadeva has seen it. You know her power of foretelling, Malach! Please, just listen—"

He sprang to his feet. "No, you listen! I would have gone back to Dur-Athaara, but you abandoned me. Left me to die! I will never forgive that."

"She didn't," Paarjini said in exasperation. "T'was a spell that summoned her."

Malach scowled. "I have no trust in anything you say. So be gone!"

"Not without the child," Heshima said. "Give her to us, Malach."

His gaze could have frozen marble. "No."

"She belongs to her mother just as much as she does to you."

"Her mother doesn't give a damn about her. Do you, Nikola?"

The words cut—as he'd intended. Malach shook his head in disgust when she didn't respond. "You're like all the rest. You just want to use her."

"I want to keep her safe," Nikola said quietly. "And you, as well—"

Malach recoiled as if she'd slapped him. "I would have done anything for you. Anything! But you—" He bit the words off, face going blank again. "We're done here. Go and don't come back."

"We've come a long way, aingeal. Let us help ye first," Paarjini said in a coaxing tone. "I'll remove the stone. I know ye want it gone."

"I told you *no!*"

The young mage lifted her crossbow. "You heard the regent. You're leaving now. On your feet or dragged out dead by the heels, your choice."

Heshima raised a hand. Before Nikola could stop her, the mage was blasted onto her rump. She skidded backwards along the carpet with a look of comical surprise.

Valdrian ran at them, a sharpened length of steel suddenly appearing from a hidden release along the leather gauntlet that covered his stump. Abyssal lay shimmered along the blade.

Paarjini delved into her pouch.

Nikola knew exactly what would happen next. Another bloodbath.

She slapped the stone from Paarjini's hand. Gripped the serpent's eye and formed a box around them. It came quick as thought now. The mage was seconds away when she forced the box with a clap of silent thunder.

The world blurred. She hit the beach on hands and knees, shaking with adrenaline. Beside her, Tashtemir retched violently. Curtains of rain swept the cove, drenching them all in an instant.

"Are ye mad?" Paarjini groaned. Somehow, the witch had kept her feet, though she looked green.

"Me?" Nikola demanded. "Or her?" She cast a baleful glance at Heshima, who brushed wet sand from her skirts, lips tight.

"Both of ye!" Paarjini rounded on Heshima. Vertigo made her stagger. "Gah, I feel like shite! What were ye thinking sister? We promised not to provoke him!"

"He was already provoked," Heshima said. "And I didn't fancy dying at the hands of aingeal dian. Bloodthirsty animals." She shot an exasperated look at Nikola. "But you still shouldn't have forced!"

"What choice did you leave me?" Nikola replied wearily. "If you'd killed his kin, any chance to reach him would be gone."

"You saw him! It's already gone." Her cool gaze flicked to the serpent's eye. "It's you who paid the biggest price, sister."

Paarjini slung an arm around Nikola's shoulders. "T'was an ill-timed entrance on our part. I'm not sure we wouldn't have joined the dead. Who were they?"

Nikola blinked rain from her eyes. "That was the Pontifex of Kvengard he beheaded."

"And the others?"

"The woman might have been Bishop Maria Karolo." Nikola had seen her at the Arx. A severe, unsmiling person who reported the tiniest infraction of the *Meliora*. The chars despised her.

"What about that pair in the corner?" Paarjini wondered.

"One was Dmitry Falke. The Pontifex of Novostopol. He's the one who took the child."

"And Malach let him live," Paarjini said thoughtfully. "Tha's interesting."

"The woman is named Kasia Novak." Nikola frowned. "I can't imagine what she was doing there. I met her once, a while back. She's the last person I expected to see in Nantwich."

"We should have stayed out of it," Paarjini muttered. "But the Mahadeva must know."

"Who gets to tell them?" Nikola asked wryly.

"Not I." Tashtemir wiped his mouth. "That was most unpleasant. I hope we're rowing back to the ship."

Nikola gripped her namestone. She'd only forced a short distance. A mere trickle of power. But it all added up, didn't it?

"I'll take the oars," she said. "I'm the one with the callouses anyway."

Chapter Thirty-Six

There was a flash of light. A roar of noise and stench of something burning.

In the first confused moments, Kasia thought the Arx was being shelled. She ducked and covered her head, instinct curling her body into a ball. When the ceiling didn't come down on top of her, she cautiously opened her eyes.

Valdrian lay on his back. The other mage ran to his side and cupped his face, murmuring faint words.

"Are you all right?"

Kasia turned to Falke, who pressed a hand to his forehead.

"I think so." Ley lines still shimmered in her vision. She blinked and they faded.

Only Malach seemed unaffected. He was on his feet, staring at the spot where Nikola Thorn had stood. All three witches were gone. So was the dark-haired man with a mustache who had accompanied them. The carpet was burnt to ash in a perfect square before the door.

"Malach," the young mage snapped.

No response.

"Cardinal!"

His head turned. When he saw Valdrian, he seemed to

wake from his trance. Malach hurried over. Valdrian was starting to stir. A thin line of blood ran from one nostril. He blotted it with a sleeve. "Was that *lightning*?" he croaked.

"They forced a box," Malach said.

Blank looks.

"They used a spell to fuck off," he muttered. "You're lucky you weren't any closer. Can you stand?"

Valdrian nodded. He touched his gauntlet and the blade retracted. Malach helped him to his feet.

"How did they get past the guards?" Valdrian wondered.

Malach didn't answer. He stood still for a minute, eyes clouded, as the two mages examined the charred cracks in the stone floor.

"Bloody hell," the woman murmured. "I wish I knew how to do that."

"Not a word of this," Malach said at last. His voice was distant. "Seal the chamber and make sure no one comes inside." He pointed a finger at Kasia and Falke. "You two, come with me."

There was no choice but to comply. Falke stared at Luk's body as they passed. He looked worried.

The room reeked of death and a sharp chemical smell that reminded Kasia of the swimming pool at her old secondary school. She'd quietly cheered when Luk died and had no regrets about Karolo or her disciples. However, it was obvious that Malach was nearing some sort of edge—and she really didn't want to know what waited on the other side.

"You have blood on your face," Kasia said.

He touched his cheek. Malach regarded the red stain on his fingers with detachment. Then he walked to the heavy velvet drapes and scrubbed it off.

"Where are we going?" she asked as he prodded them through the door and down the hall.

"Be quiet," he snarled.

She considered running for it, but dozens of Kven knights

strode through the corridors. They gave crisp salutes when they saw the Nuncio. Malach returned the greetings with a preoccupied nod, not breaking stride. Falke kept his head down. No one seemed to recognize him, but it was still a harrowing walk.

Saints, Kasia thought. What will the Kvens do when they discover their Pontifex is dead?

At last, they reached the long gallery that led to the east wing. Malach told a pair of green-cloaked mages lounging at the bronze doors not to allow any of the Kvens through.

"Kill them if you have to," he said. "But be quiet about it."

They were both young women, one fair-skinned, one dark, but Kasia was starting to recognize the nihilim bloodlines. The high cheekbones and classically proportioned features, as though they had been painted by the same artist. Someone with an eye for beauty. Yet their faces also had a hard, unyielding quality and Kasia didn't doubt that they'd carry out Malach's orders.

"What happened?" one asked.

"Luk is dead."

They exchanged a startled glance. "Cardinal—"

"Later," Malach snapped. "Just keep them out."

He strode on, one hand firmly around Kasia's arm. She used the other to hold her torn dress together at the front. The nihilim controlled the east wing. There must be only a few of them because the corridors and wide staircases were empty. Malach stopped at a door on the top floor and turned to Falke.

"Rachel must be protected." A pointed look. "Not only from Nikola, you understand?"

"I understand," Falke replied.

"Stay with her for now. I'll figure something out." Malach raised a hand to his head. It trembled slightly.

He's dangling by a thread, Kasia thought, her unease deepening.

Malach unlocked the door. A lamp burned next to a bed. Kasia glimpsed a small figure under the blankets. A stripe of black hair against the pillow. Falke slipped inside and sat in an armchair. He met Malach's eyes and nodded. Kasia sensed an unspoken agreement. A Cold Truce for the sake of the child. Then Falke turned away, face softening as he regarded Rachel.

He would die for her, Kasia realized. They both would.

Malach locked the door behind him. He leaned his forehead against the wood.

"Fuck," he whispered.

"What are you going to do with me?" Kasia asked.

His eyes were glassy as he turned to her. He stood upright and prodded her down the hall.

"Look," she said, fingers itching for the sharp edges of her deck. "I know you're angry. But thank you for intervening. You saved us both and I'm grateful."

Nothing.

"Maybe I should stay with Fa . . . er, Severin," she ventured. "I'm sure you have things to do. I don't want to be any more trouble."

He gave a hollow laugh and stopped in front of the chamber she'd shared with the pontifex. Kasia felt a wave of relief.

"Do you have another dress in there?" Malach asked, staring at a point beyond her head.

"Yes."

"Then put it on."

He waited in the doorway while she changed in the bathroom. It was the same one she'd worn to the Lethe Club when Alexei found her. The one she'd been virtually *living in* for days. Black and form-fitting in the bodice with long lace sleeves and loose, billowy skirts that brushed her feet. She'd loved it when she bought it at a boutique on Oxbridge Street. Now the slit up the thigh felt too revealing. She gripped it as she stepped out of the bathroom.

"I can stay here," she said with a friendly smile. "I don't have any more cards. There's no way I can—"

"No." He slowly looked her up and down. "You're coming with me."

"Where?" she asked, unsettled by his stare.

"Nowhere bad, I promise."

The words failed to reassure, but she followed him to a door just around the corner from Rachel's room. Malach unlocked it and gestured for her to go inside. Kasia hesitated.

"Please," he said quietly.

She stepped into a large, airy apartment overlooking the plaza. Frescoes adorned the high ceiling. Kasia's gaze flicked over carved wood paneling and ornate plasterwork. Doors led to a bedroom, study and bath. A breeze stirred long white curtains at the windows. It smelled of rain. She drew a slow, calming breath.

"Make yourself comfortable," Malach said, locking the door behind him.

Kasia eyed the sofa. Stuffing bulged from long slits in the damask silk.

"The kids did that," he muttered, grabbing a bottle from a walnut cabinet. Malach unscrewed the cap and took a long drink. He coughed, wiped his mouth, and drank again.

Kasia relaxed a little when he made no move to attack her. She sat on the ruined sofa and picked at the cotton wadding. Bits of ribbon were strewn across the floor.

"So," she said. "That was Rachel's mother?"

"In name only." Another long swig from the bottle. "Will you give me a reading?" Malach shook his head, cheeks flushed. "Never mind. I don't want to know."

He set the bottle on the windowsill. Then he pulled the crimson robe over his head. Kasia tensed, but he wore a linen shirt and trousers underneath. Malach tossed the robe aside and retrieved the bottle. His shirt was thin enough to see outlines on the skin beneath.

Every single one a Nightmark.

She had a sudden urge to examine them up close. To figure out what made him tick. The Fool was the most inscrutable of the Trumps. Zero in the Major Arcana. The lack of a fixed number made him rootless, a wanderer. Just look at him now, she thought with clinical interest, pacing up and down. Unable to keep still.

In a regular deck of playing cards, he was the Joker. Disrupting the game with a misdeal. But there was nothing funny about The Fool. It was the most powerful card in the deck. A transformative force that could create—or destroy.

"The Kvens will start to go mad," Malach said. "Very soon. Not all of them, but enough."

Kasia's fingers dug into the arm of the sofa. She cursed herself for forgetting. *That's* why Falke looked so worried. With everything else that happened, she hadn't made the connection.

Mark sickness. Just like Alexei had when Feizah died.

A chill swept her as she thought of all those knights inside the Arx. "Can't it be stopped?"

"By whom?" A dark chuckle. "There's no one left to take the Sanctified Marks. I certainly can't do it."

"What about Lezarius?"

"Burned out from breaking the Void. Gray told me."

"Falke—"

"Will never Mark anyone again. I swore that to myself." He tilted the bottle, savoring a long swallow. "And you know what?"

She eyed him, heart thumping.

"I don't give a shit."

Of course you don't, she thought bitterly. *You are the son of chaos.*

Malach sank down against the wall, the bottle between his knees. "Have you ever been in love?"

The question caught her off guard. "Yes."

"It's horrible," he said ruminatively.

Kasia cleared her throat. "Maybe the witches were telling the truth."

"Those women." He shook his head with a look of wonder. "They're a fucking force of nature. I'll give them that. But Kasia, they will bury you like an avalanche if you give them the chance." He raised the bottle in a grim salute. "Trust me, I know."

"I suppose you do," she said. "Are you sure you don't want a reading?"

"I'm sure."

It came out *mmm'shur.*

Malach was getting drunk.

"Want some?" He held out the bottle.

She crawled over and took a sip. It burned her throat, but the warm glow that followed loosened the knot of fear in her chest. Kasia handed the bottle back. Malach's fingers brushed hers as he took it and she thought of the night on the roof of her flat. The abyssal ley coursing from his palm as he gripped her throat. She snatched her hand back.

"Do you still have my cards?" she asked.

"Yep. Could you get some ice? Over there?"

She went to the cabinet and found a silver ice bucket like the ones they put in posh hotel rooms. She used tongs to drop the cubes into a crystal tumbler and brought it over. Malach filled the glass to the brim. He took a sip, crunching the ice between his teeth.

"I'm not a lush," he said seriously.

"Of course not." Kasia smiled.

"But I can see the attraction."

"It makes things better," she agreed. "Until the next morning."

He laughed loudly, though it was a trite remark.

"Do you have a family, Kasia?"

She stiffened. "Not really."

"But you didn't grow up in the Void."

"I told you. I was raised in Novostopol."

"What were they like?" He turned to her. "Your parents?"

"My adoptive parents? They were nice."

She certainly wasn't going to tell him about her mother kicking her out of the house.

"That's what I want for Rachel. A normal life. Whatever that means." He leaned over to set the glass on a low table and missed, spilling half the contents on the carpet before he managed to right it. "Oops."

"Maybe you should lie down," she suggested.

A slow smile. "With you?"

Her cheeks warmed. "No."

"Hmmm, too bad. Maybe for a minute." He moved away, stretching out on his back in the middle of the carpet. "Ah, you were right. It's lovely down here." His head turned. "Come try it."

Kasia crawled over, heart hammering. She could see the edge of her deck poking out of his pants pocket.

"I mustn't fall asleep," he mumbled.

"I won't let you," she promised.

"The Kvens . . . ."

"You said you didn't care."

"No, I do." He sighed heavily.

Blood thudded in her ears as Kasia eased the deck from his pocket. Malach gazed up at the ceiling, oblivious. His collar lay open at the neck, exposing the Broken Chain of Bal Kirith. An infinitely dangerous man. If she were smart, she would run to the door. He'd left the key in the lock. She might even make it out of the Arx now that she had her cards back.

But Malach was at her mercy. A chance that would never come again.

Kasia bit her lip. She had to be quick. The instant he sensed her using the ley, he'd fight back. The impaired state might make him even more violent.

She silently fanned the deck on the rug above his head. Malach was humming now. A wistful melody. She found The High Priestess, her namesake, and drew ley through the card. A deep dive all the way to the abyss. It flared red.

A hand came up and idly rubbed the back of his neck. Gooseflesh lifted on his arm, though he didn't seem to notice.

She recalled his words precisely. He'd threatened her in the cell, which meant it did work on nihilim.

You've never experienced the most extreme degree of compulsion. It wipes the mind blank. There's nothing left but an all-consuming desire to please.

Kasia focused it all on Malach, instinctively seeking the lizard core of his brain. The wheelhouse. She would force him to bring her to the stadium and release the prisoners before their Kven guards turned into howling lunatics.

The torrent of abyssal ley hit her in a rush of pleasure and fury and joy and sadness all tangled together—but the flow vanished the instant it touched him. She released the ley with a gasp. Malach seized her wrist and pulled her down to his chest. His head dipped up to kiss her. He tasted of whiskey.

She pulled back. He didn't hold on, just gazed up at her with hopeless eyes.

"Why don't you want me? I could make you feel so good—"

"Because," she spat, "you're my brother!"

The words spilled out, but she didn't regret them. It was past time for the truth.

"Games?" Malach murmured. "I like to play games." His lips curled in a drunken smile. "I'll be anyone you want. The filthier"—he hiccuped gently—"the better."

"I'm serious, you idiot!"

The grin faltered. He shook his head with a slight frown.

The hem of her skirts slid through his fingers as she walked away.

"Stay with me, Kasia," he murmured. "Don't go away——"

She grabbed the silver bucket of melting ice and stood over him. His eyes widened.

"What are you——"

Kasia dumped it on his face. Malach rolled to his side, gasping.

"You could just tell me to piss off!" he spluttered.

She crouched down so they were eye to eye. He brushed wet hair from his face with a glower.

"Listen to me closely, Malach. I'm your sister. Your blood sister."

He didn't look sober, but he was no longer quite as drunk. "She's dead," he hissed through clenched teeth. "Is this some scheme you cooked up with Falke?"

But he was staring now as if he saw her for the first time. The raven hair. The hazel eyes that were a perfect match of his own.

"You know I'm telling the truth," Kasia said.

He leaned forward, gaze narrow. "How is it even possible?"

"Falke couldn't bring himself to kill an infant. So he took me home with him."

A welter of emotions crossed Malach's face. He blinked and shook his head again, but she could see the denial draining away.

"I went back after the knights pulled out," he murmured. "Searched the rubble. You were gone, but I thought . . . Hell, I was only four years old. I just assumed . . ."

Kasia still clutched The High Priestess. His eye caught on the card in her hand, but he didn't try to take it back. "Why didn't you tell me before?" he demanded. "Why?"

She looked away. "Because I hated you. But you can't blame Falke for that! It was your own doing."

"Perhaps. But he knew you were alive all this time. All this time! And he allowed me to believe . . . ." Malach's chest heaved. "So Rachel was not the first child he stole. He is a fiend!"

He started to rise—probably to find Falke and beat the living daylights out of him. Kasia grabbed Malach's arm.

"Who are you to judge?" she snapped. "If he'd left me, I would have died!"

"Only because he'd killed our parents!" He kicked the ice bucket and sent it spinning across the room.

Pressure built in her chest like a violent storm. Kasia's voice rose. "And you serve a man who drowns children in the sea and then reanimates their bodies! The foulest magic I can conceive of, all so that he might live forever! Do not condemn Falke. At least he cared about my welfare!"

"What the fuck are you talking about?" Malach shouted back.

"Alchemy!" she hissed. "I saw it myself. I'll give you the sweven if you don't believe me!"

He recoiled at her fury. "It won't work."

"Why not?"

"The witches put a stone inside me. It blocks the ley." He rubbed his head. Glanced at the bottle but didn't pick it up.

"You were bluffing this whole time?" she asked in astonishment.

Malach didn't reply. His gaze had turned inward. Reassessing a great many things, she imagined. Kasia knew how he felt. Clavis had done the same thing to her.

"Saints," she muttered. "Well then, you'll just have to listen to me tell the whole story." She regarded him coolly. "And then I shall know what sort of man you are."

Malach nodded. His skin was ashen. "A bargain, Kasia. Just excuse me for a moment—"

He lurched to his feet. She waited while he ran to the bathroom and was noisily sick. She heard water running.

Malach returned in a dry shirt. He looked clammy, but his eyes were clear.

"Nine children," she said as he sat heavily on the sofa. "These are their names. I want you to remember them." She drew a deep breath. "Willem Danziger. Noach Beitz. Sofie Arnault. Eddi Haas. Ursula Fellbach. Wandy Keller. Isild Baumann. Karl Josef Zelig. Anna-Rose Laurent. The youngest was six years old."

Malach listened while she told him everything, sparing not a single excruciating detail. When she was done, he sat silent and staring at nothing.

"So," she said. "Will you still give me to Balaur?"

Malach's gaze lifted. "He is on his way to Nantwich. A messenger arrived this morning."

Sudden nausea stabbed her stomach. His features warped as if he sat behind a pane of thick, imperfect glass. The ley swirled in violent currents. Static noise buzzed inside her head.

Kasia gazed at the cards scattered across the carpet. The Fool lay in the center, his foot raised mid-stride and face tipped up to the sky, heedless of where he stepped. A little white dog nipped at his heel. A warning that he approached the edge of a wave-battered cliff, which represented either a blind leap of faith or plummet to disaster.

The rest of the deck lay helter-skelter around him. The Hierophant. The Empress. The Star and the Red King. The Moon and the Sun. The Knight of Storms. The Serpent and the Twins. Others, widening in a great spiral around The Fool.

Dozens of paths branched outward. Most led to ruin, a very few to salvation.

But they all started here. In this moment.

The vision faded. She heard the hiss of rain through the window. The slow clop of hooves in the plaza beyond.

The lines of Malach's face softened, as though some long struggle had finally ended.

"When Balaur gets here," he said, "I will kill him."

Kasia closed her eyes, tension ebbing from her shoulders. She sensed the threads of fate rearrange themselves. The Fool had surprised her—but that was his nature. The Wild Card.

"My weakness is also my advantage," Malach said. "He can't use the ley against me. And many of our cousins won't stand for this. They aren't all as the Via Sancta would have you believe, Kasia." A grim smile. "We might be mercenary, but we're not soulless. I'll speak to them."

"It won't be easy," she warned. "We must make certain he's really dead. Jule Danziger came back. I don't know how, but he did."

"What does Danziger look like?"

"Blond and blue-eyed. Arrogant."

A slow nod. "I think I know the one."

"I saw his body putrefy in Kvengard," Kasia said. "Now he's here."

She told him about the Lethe Club. "The Order of the Black Sun used the liminal passages when Gray staged his coup. That's how they took the Arx."

Malach swore. "I was hoping to hide Rachel there when Balaur came."

"No! It's the last place she'd be safe." Kasia chewed her lip. "But we can still use the passages to our advantage. Will Balaur stay in the pontifical apartments?"

"I assume so."

"When does he arrive?"

"Tonight, I'm afraid."

"Fog it. Is he coming with a whole army?"

"I don't think so. He believes Nantwich is secure and he can't afford to leave Bal Agnar undefended."

"All right. Then here's what we'll do."

She laid out her plan. Malach liked it. They spent the next

few minutes hashing out the details and refining certain aspects.

"You can hide Rachel and Falke in the Villa of Saint Margrit," Kasia said. "It's out of the way."

"There's still the problem of the Kvens, but I have a thought about that." He stood and found a decanter of water, drinking straight from the neck. "Trust me, you'll like it."

He opened a closet and took out a fresh robe but didn't put it on. Malach stood with his back to her. "My question to the ley," he said, "was whether Rachel would ever forgive me. It seems I must ask the same of you, Kasia."

He turned, kneading the robe in his hands. The tip of a long dagger touched one knuckle; the rest of the Mark was hidden in his sleeve. "I never meant to hurt you. But I didn't used to care much about anything."

"And having Rachel changed you?"

He shook his head. "Nikola changed me." A flash of pain crossed his face. He tugged the robe over his head. "I treated her poorly, too. Some lessons seem to return again and again. Maybe they'll sink in someday." He looked thoughtful. "But if we succeed in this, there might be hope for something different. I am weary of war, Kasia."

"We all are." A quick grin. She waved her hand mysteriously. "I foresee a new reading for The Fool. A change of fortune!"

Malach laughed. "That would be welcome," he said wryly.

Her smile died. "Once Balaur is dead, we will deal with his Order of the Black Sun. But Jule Danziger is *mine.*"

Their eyes locked in mutual understanding. For the first time, Kasia felt that another person saw what lay in the darkest recesses of her heart and passed no judgment.

"We'll burn the bodies and give the ashes to the wind." Malach's brows lowered. "Let's see them come back from *that.*"

Chapter Thirty-Seven

Morvana Zeigler held out a scrap of meat, coaxing the Markhound to take it. Alice stared at her glumly. She lay on the carpet, muzzle resting on her forepaws.

"I know," Morvana said. "You are depressed. But still you must eat."

She waved the meat under Alice's nose. The dog turned away with an annoyed chuff.

"Fine. Have it your way." She tossed the meat into a bowl of cold stew, brushing the flies away. Morvana had little appetite either. "At least your master has chosen the right side," she muttered. "Mine is a lackey of our enemies."

Luk had not come to see her, the coward, but he hadn't killed her yet. She supposed he would order it eventually. Perhaps after he transferred the Marks she'd given so many knights. Morvana Zeigler was one of the few clergy in Kvengard with the ability to bestow Marks anymore. Luk had admitted the truth to her a year before. That the ability was vanishing because it came from the nihilim and most of them were dead.

They'd kept her locked in a small chamber, too high to jump without cracking her skull. She scratched Alice behind the ears and earned a quick tail thump. At least they had each other for company. And she had been well-treated so far. Some of the Kven knights guarding the room had even looked at her with guilt in their eyes, though they ignored her pleas to revolt.

Supper was always brought at seven o'clock sharp, while the bells rang for Vespers, but no one had come. Morvana wondered if something had happened.

The sharp click of a key turning in the lock made her jump. Morvana made a quick shooing motion at the hound. She composed herself as Alice faded to shadow.

The door swung open, but it wasn't the Kvens. It was a nihilim. He wore deep crimson robes. His jaw was dark with stubble, his hair a bit wild.

"May I come in?" he asked.

She stared at him. "I am your prisoner. I think you can do what you like."

He stepped inside. A dark-haired woman with large, unsettling eyes followed.

"Bishop Zeigler?" she asked.

Morvana nodded warily. The mage closed the door.

"My name is Kasia Novak. A friend of Alexei Bryce. I believe you already know Malach."

She'd heard his name spoken by the knights. "Balaur's Nuncio."

The mage winced. "I didn't know what he had done in Kvengard." A glance at the woman. "But I do now. I serve him no longer."

"We need your help," Kasia said. "Balaur is coming here. He arrives at any moment. It is a chance to end him."

Morvana rose to her feet, hope warring with skepticism. "Truly?"

"But first you must know something. Luk is dead." The mage searched her face, gaze intent. "Did he Mark you?"

"Dead?" Despite all he'd done, she felt a wave of shock.

"Answer me," he repeated, an edge to his voice. *"Did he Mark you?"*

"No," she replied quickly. "I have five, all from cardinals. But he did Mark his knights."

"How many?"

"I . . . I don't know the exact number. But . . . hundreds."

"To ensure their loyalty, no doubt," Malach muttered. "How long before they go mad?"

Luk is dead. The words still bounced around her head. He'd been ill for as long as she could remember, but he never spoke of it. Everyone pretended his reign would last forever. She'd wondered what would happen when he was gone, but it seemed distant—

"How long?" the mage repeated.

She stood and paced to the narrow window. Covered her mouth with a hand, staring into the rainy dark. *Dead! Well, pull yourself together. And take what allies you can find.*

"It depends," she said. "The course is different in everyone. Sometimes it takes mere minutes. Sometimes hours or days."

"We must find a way to free the prisoners at the stadium," Malach said. "They would stand with us."

"Can't you order it?" Morvana asked. "You are still the regent."

He shook his head. "Not before Balaur arrives. He can't suspect anything is amiss. And I doubt the Kvens would heed me. But Rademacher might listen to you. You're still Luk's Nuncio."

She shook her head bitterly. "He knows I am excommunicated. If anything, he would throw me in with the other prisoners."

"Then it must look like a spontaneous uprising," Kasia said.

Morvana drew a deep breath. "What is it you want me to do?"

"I can give you two mages," Malach said.

She gave him a flat stare. "Three of us to liberate the entire stadium?"

"There are few I trust," he admitted. "I'd go myself, but Rademacher would resist. And there's little enough time as it is to lay our plans. Balaur is the first priority. If we fail with him, the rest hardly matters."

Morvana saw the truth of this. She had the glimmer of an idea. "There might be a way. Luk left several hundred of his knights camped in the Morho. They are not alone."

She pursed her lips and gave the silent whistle. Malach retreated a step as the Markhound materialized at her side. Alice gave a low snarl. Morvana tapped her shoulder.

"Cessa," she said sternly. A lip lifted, revealing a razored fang. Morvana stared at her, unblinking, until the Markhound looked away. She sank to her haunches and settled for a baleful stare.

"Alice!" Kasia cried.

The dog's head whipped around as if she hadn't noticed her before. She trotted over and sniffed Kasia's hand, tail waving.

"I can't believe it!" Kasia dropped down to embrace the hound. "I am so glad to see you, old friend." She gazed up at Morvana with new warmth. "If Alice trusts you, then I can be sure."

Morvana smiled. "I share your sentiments."

Malach seemed less certain. He pressed against the door, one hand gripping the knob. "What were you saying?" he asked faintly, gaze locked on the Markhound. "About the knights?"

"There are many dogs at the camp. Forged from all three layers of the ley acting in harmony. They cannot be corrupted like their masters." Her face darkened. "And I think they do not like these new creations of Luk."

"The white hounds," Malach said.

"Yes. I had not seen them before. Luk must have made them in secret."

"So his death doesn't affect them?" Kasia said in obvious disappointment.

"I'm afraid not. They are flesh and blood, independent, though woven with the ley."

"I have two other friends at the stadium," Kasia said. "Patryk Spassov and Natalya Anderle."

"I met them," Morvana said. "They thought I had something to do with your disappearance. And Alexei's." She cleared her throat. "After they realized I did not, we worked together to free him from a cell in the catacombs. When we emerged, the fighting was already hot. I lost them in the fray."

"But they were alive the last time you saw them?" Kasia asked.

Morvana nodded.

"Then I won't give up hope." She stood and clasped Morvana's hand. "You will help us?"

"Of course."

Malach cracked the door. Two young mages slipped inside. Brother and sister, from the looks of them. They wore green cloaks. Morvana could just make out the Broken Chain of Bal Kirith around their throats. The girl was taller, but she still couldn't be more than eleven.

"Sydonie," Malach said, introducing the girl. "And Tristhus."

"Hello," the girl said with a friendly smile. A bow hung over one shoulder.

The boy fingered a bone dagger. His face looked eerily like the winged cherubs cavorting in a fresco Morvana liked back at the basilica in Kvengard, except for the missing eyebrows.

"But they are so very young," Morvana said. "It will be dangerous—"

Malach laughed. "They grew up hunting and warring. Believe me, you couldn't have better companions."

Both looked pleased at this. Sydonie stroked the embroidered hem of Morvana's sleeve. "I like that," she said. "Can I have it?"

"I'll get you one just like it," Malach said.

"When?"

"As soon as you return."

"All right." She glanced at the hound. "Can I pet it?"

Alice snuffled in alarm. "Hell no," Malach exclaimed.

"But Mirabelle wants to!"

"Who is Mirabelle?" Morvana wondered, looking around.

"No one," Malach said, as the girl pulled her sleeve up and displayed a Mark of a doll with red apple cheeks and a sinister smile. The wide eyes sparkled with mischief.

"This is Mirabelle!" Sydonie said proudly. "She talks!"

Behind her back, Malach shook his head. *Not really*, he mouthed.

"She is very pretty," Morvana lied.

Sydonie beamed at her.

"I think you might be able to pet Alice. Let me ask her."

If Morvana's plan was to work, she had to make the hounds accept the children. Alice was an alpha. The rest of the pack would follow her lead. Morvana stroked her ears, whispering.

They are not your enemies. Not any more. Understand? They will help free your master, so you must be nice to them.

Alice gave a nervous yawn.

"Come here," Morvana said to Sydonie. "Slowly. No quick movements."

The girl's eyes shone with victory as she inched nearer.

"Are you sure about this?" Malach muttered.

"Quite sure," Morvana said. She guided the child's hand to Alice's flank. The Markhound's coat twitched as if a fly had landed there. She shivered but stood still, golden eyes staring at nothing, as Sydonie petted her. Then Tristhus crept forward. Chubby fingers closed around a nub of tail. The faintest rumble.

"Don't pull it," Morvana warned.

He nodded and ran his palm along her flank. Alice's lips peeled back from her teeth. Then, to Morvana's astonishment, she flopped down and rolled over. The children laughed in delight and rubbed her belly. The hound's eyes spun in the sockets, showing the whites all around. One of her legs started to judder.

"You found the magic spot," Morvana said.

"That's enough, eh?" Malach said nervously.

The children stepped back. Alice leapt to her feet and sat down in the corner, licking herself vigorously.

"When does Balaur get here?" Morvana asked.

"Tonight." They shared a look. "If you're successful, rally the prisoners and return to the Arx. One of us will come out and let you in."

"Understood."

The mage hoisted his crimson robe and pulled out a curved dagger from his belt. He offered it to her by the hilt. Morvana shook her head.

"I hold to the *Meliora*. I will not touch a weapon."

He looked puzzled.

"But I will try to call allies who act in concert with the ley. If they come to me, whatever happens . . . it is meant to be."

The mage shrugged and sheathed the dagger in his belt. "Protect the bishop," he instructed the children. "But be careful. No stupid heroics."

"Heroics?" Sydonie echoed, dark brows furrowing. "What does that mean?"

"Trying to be a hero. Sacrificing yourself for others."

The children eyed him, uncomprehending.

"Never mind," he said with a small grin.

"Just come back safe and sound," Kasia put in. "All of you."

458

She took off her own dark cloak and handed it to Morvana. "It's a stormy night. You'll want this."

"Where are the guards?" Morvana asked, settling it across her shoulders. She was much taller and it only reached her knees, but she was grateful for the covering.

"They weren't at their post when we arrived," Kasia replied. "I think it is already beginning."

Morvana nodded. "May Saint Isgarda, the Lighter of Lamps, show us the safe path."

The five of them slipped from the chamber and made their way down to a side door leading from the Pontifex's Palace. The children put their hoods up. Morvana followed suit.

"I misjudged you, Nuncio," she said to Malach. "Peace between our people has always been my greatest wish. I hope this is a new beginning for all of us."

He seemed startled but stammered a polite reply. Then the children were leading her across the rainy darkness of the plaza. Lights burned in the buildings, yet there was an unnatural stillness to the Arx. She saw only one of the usual patrols, eight Kvens on horseback. The children tugged her behind the marble statue as they galloped past.

A blond-bearded mage waited at one of the postern gates, concealed behind a dense stand of trees. It swing silently open. He briefly met her eyes and nodded. As he closed the gate behind them, she noticed that he was missing a hand, the stump covered with a scarred leather cap.

Severed.

Morvana felt a hot kernel of anger. Such barbarity! There was no place for it in a society that called itself civilized. It didn't matter what the mages had done. And this man was young. Too young to have been part of Balaur's decadent regime.

They are not all bad, she thought. *And we are not all good.*

But Balaur . . . Lezarius had spared him, thinking he did right. It had proved disastrous. She wouldn't quibble with whatever fate they had in store for the Beast of Bal Agnar—as long as it was permanent.

Thick darkness cloaked the cobbled streets of Nantwich. Curfew had taken effect and electrical service was suspended. Candles glimmered in windows, but that was all. They evaded the few patrols, ducking into alleys or doorways. She saw no signs of sickness, yet her skin crawled as she followed the children past the ornate limestone embassies and into the museum district.

Ley would be building in the blood of those Luk had Marked, unable to flow back out. And it was tainted here. She'd forgotten to account for that.

The Markhound was quiet but alert, her narrow muzzle swinging from side to side. Occasionally, she paused to sniff at the air, hackles lifting. Her master had worked for the Interfectorem. Alice would know the smell of madness.

"Will they be like the leeches?" Sydonie whispered.

They crouched behind a garbage bin in an alley, watching a group of knights ride past.

"What are leeches?" Morvana whispered back.

"Monsters," the girl replied.

"They try to eat you up," the boy said. "Sometimes they eat each other."

She realized they were speaking of Perditae.

"I hope not," she said. "But I do not know."

The children exchanged a look. "We'd better hurry up then," Sydonie said.

When they neared the city walls on the eastern side, Morvana gestured for the children to stop. The Kven encampment was somewhere on the other side. She'd never tried to call hounds from such a distance. And through pouring rain.

Morvana filled her lungs and whistled. Then she did it

twice more. Alice spun in a circle. She barked and Morvana shushed her with a scowl.

The children stood beneath an overhang, watching with dark eyes.

She'd been so sure the soldiers would bring the dogs. But what if Luk had ordered them not to? Her plan hinged on having at least a few. Sydonie and Tristhus might be brave, but she had no illusions that the two young mages would be enough for Rademacher and his knights.

"What's wrong?" Sydonie called. "Why won't they come?"

"I will try again," Morvana said.

She pursed her lips to whistle when Alice went on point, tail rigid. Her gait was stiff-legged, her head lowered in a challenge, as she moved to stand in front of Morvana.

To protect her.

Shadows moved in the night.

One or two at first. Then four, five . . . dozens.

They streamed down the avenue like liquid smoke, golden eyes luminous in the darkness. The asphalt glowed with overlapping paw prints in the ley. A rich, deep blue.

Alice trotted forward to meet them. She briefly touched noses with the leader, then aggressively sniffed his hindquarters. The hound stood still. He turned to give Alice a desultory sniff. She tolerated it for a moment, then snapped. He cringed away.

The pecking order established, Morvana peeled off a glove and gave them her own scent. They crowded around, black and tan bodies blurring with the downpour. At least three full packs.

Alice seemed torn between displaying the dignity that befitted an alpha and joy at finding brothers and sisters. A red tongue lolled as she trotted among them, offering some a playful pounce, others a stern glare. Before Morvana could speak the command, she sprinted to the children and ran two circles around them, then dropped to her haunches at Sydonie's feet.

A *very* intelligent dog.

The children had shown no sign of fear so far. But they froze as forty Markhounds bounded over to examine them. One dog conveyed its doubts with a snarl. Alice put a quick end to that, nipping its flank. The dog slunk away.

"How far is the stadium?" Morvana asked.

"Just there." Tristhus pointed. "About a kilometer."

Morvana gave another whistle. The hounds turned as one, eyes fixed on her.

Alice lifted her snout. She emitted a mournful howl.

In an instant, she was gone. The rest of the pack followed.

"Wait!" Morvana cried.

But all that remained were streaks of glowing ley in the puddles.

"He is alive," she whispered, a grin breaking across her face.

"Who?" Sydonie wondered.

"Alexei Bryce!" She lifted the hem of her robes and gave chase, the children just behind.

Chapter Thirty-Eight

Malach hung up the telephone. "He's through the city gates and approaching the Arx."

Kasia chewed a thumbnail. "What does Valdrian say?"

"The Kvens are starting to desert their posts. The ones still there are confused, but they're blaming the abyssal ley." He tucked a lock of dark hair behind one ear. "I have mages at the main gates to the Arx. All will appear normal when he arrives."

They stood in Clavis's wood-paneled library, which gave a clear view of the plaza and gates beyond. "The ones who are deserting," Kasia said. "I suppose they're roaming the city. Saints! You told people to stay inside?"

"I made a radio announcement. I kept it vague, but the curfew helps. No civilians will be on the streets."

"Still." Kasia felt sick. "They must be contained."

Malach nodded grimly. "Let us hope Bishop Zeigler is successful."

She tensed as headlights cut the darkness. A line of twelve black automobiles snaked through the grounds. She couldn't make out the plates in the driving rain, but then the lead car pulled to the curb and she saw the chrome Raven on the hood.

"Maria Karolo must have sent a convoy from Novo to pick him up."

Chars ran outside, unfurling black umbrellas. The rest of the cars braked in a line. Doors flung wide.

Kasia touched Malach's sleeve. "We must go."

He gave her a tight nod. They ran down a wide flight of stairs and through a pillared loggia to the main audience chamber. Jessiel and Caralexa stood to either side of the open doors. They gave taut nods and stepped aside.

The Order of the Black Sun had already assembled in anticipation of Balur's arrival. Cardinal Lucas Gray stood to the left of the Pontifex's seat, whey-faced behind his spectacles. He kept glancing around, obviously confused at the absence of his allies from Kvengard and Novostopol.

Poor Gray, Kasia thought without a trace of pity. *You have no clue, do you?*

"The Nuncio of Bal Agnar!" Jessiel bellowed.

Malach gripped Kasia's arm.

"Tighter," she urged.

He shot her a quick look of apology and clamped down, half-dragging her through the chamber to the other side of the throne from Gray. Kasia scowled and gave a little jerk. Malach glared back at her with loathing. "Behave yourself," he snapped.

Murmurs rippled across the chamber. Then a hush descended, so complete Kasia could hear the faint echo of footsteps along the loggia.

"The Reverend Father Balaur!" Jessiel shouted.

As one, the Order sank to their knees, including Gray. Only Kasia and Malach remained standing.

All was silent for a long minute. The footsteps grew louder.

First came a man and woman in crimson robes slitted up

the back to accommodate leathery wings. Dark ley pooled at their taloned feet. Twelve feral-looking creatures with the eyes of goats trailed behind. They wore jerkins and trousers stitched from hide. Macabre Nightmarks branded every visible inch of flesh. Short swords hung at their belts.

Malach had told her about the Perditae. Lost souls who scratched out an existence in the Morho Sarpanitum after the cities fell. From the nervous shifting among the Order, most had never seen one before. They brought a stench like meat left to spoil in the sun.

The advance guard took up positions surrounding the dais.

Then the Pontifex of Bal Agnar appeared, with a turbaned woman in a flowing black garment gliding three steps behind. He walked at a regal pace, smiling benevolently at his followers as he passed them. Kasia felt a jolt as their eyes met.

This was not the dying man Malach had described. He looked no older than fifty, smooth blond hair gleaming in the lamps. He wore a white satin robe that emphasized the ruddy vigor of his complexion.

For a moment, Kasia wondered if he had survived the Magnum Opus after all. But his eyes were blue, not the silvered mirrors of the albedo children. And there couldn't have been time for him to complete the transformation. Each stage of the process took forty days. It was a mere week since Malach had seen him bedridden in Bal Agnar.

As he neared the dais, Jule Danziger broke from the crowd. He sank down at Balaur's feet and kissed his hand. Balaur patted his head, as one might show affection to a faithful dog, and climbed the steps. He ignored Lucas Gray, turning to Kasia and Malach. The woman waited behind him, hands clasped loosely. Her large almond-shaped gave little away.

Kasia suddenly remembered standing at her bedroom

window that first night after they'd arrived in Kvengard. The smooth stone still beneath her palms as she watched the Masdari delegation emerge from Danziger Haus. The smell of Natalya's herbal shampoo as she leaned over Kasia's shoulder.

Marksteeds. They must be. Oh, it makes me dizzy to look at them . . . .

Kasia had been focused on the golden-eyed mounts, but she recalled every other detail. She felt sure this woman had been among the delegation. Kasia pulled her gaze away and stared sullenly at the ground.

"Reverend Father," Malach said. "We welcome you to Nantwich." A pause. "I believe you already know my sister."

She couldn't resist looking up. A flicker of surprise showed on Balaur's face.

He hadn't realized.

Kasia felt a powerful surge of satisfaction. Balaur was not all-seeing. He spun his webs, but soon he would be ensnared himself.

"Your sister?" he echoed.

She nodded, allowing her features to soften a fraction. "Clavis gave me a sweven revealing the secret."

"Falke stole her from the cradle," Malach said curtly. "The day my parents were killed."

"Ah." The blue eyes turned to Kasia. "And he denied you the ley. Your birthright."

She nodded again, lips tight.

Balaur's hand closed around her own. It was dry and warm, yet she felt as though she touched a clammy, dead thing. Kasia concealed her distaste as Balaur searched her face.

I am deeply conflicted, she thought, holding his gaze. *I am coming to hate the Via Sancta, but I am still unsure of you. Unsure where I belong. I am afraid, but part of me has always known I was different.*

It's why I'm Unmarked. Once, I felt shame for that. Now, I feel only resentment and confusion.

At that moment, she believed it all. For that was the secret of a convincing liar. The truth was what you made of it.

"Well, that is what the Curia does, my dear." He squeezed her hand once and let go. "You will share the sweven with me later. But know that you are safe. Your talents will be embraced, not stifled."

She swallowed hard. Gave a little nod.

His sharp gaze turned to Malach. "Where is Luk? Why does he not greet me himself?"

There was a pause.

"Luk plotted to seize Nantwich for himself," Malach replied. "He was in league with Maria Karolo."

A slight frown. "Truly?"

"They are both dead, Reverend Father. When I discovered it, I executed them on the spot."

Balaur stared at him in silence. Behind them, Kasia heard a dry rustle as one of the cardinals twitched its wings.

"His knights will go mad in time," Malach said casually. "If we give them Nightmarks, it might arrest the process." He shrugged. "Or we can just kill them all. I leave the choice to you, of course, Reverend Father."

One of the Perdite hissed, baring teeth that had been filed to points. Balaur waved a hand and silence fell again.

"This alters my plans considerably," he said. His cold gaze settled on Cardinal Gray, who visibly withered. "You knew nothing of this plot, Cardinal?"

"I didn't, I swear it, Reverend Father! The Nuncio only informed me a short while ago."

Malach leaned forward. "He denies it, Reverend Father," he whispered, "but I wonder. Gray was thick with them both."

Sweat trickled down Gray's forehead. "I am loyal!" he cried, thrusting out a trembling hand. "Look into my mind, you will see!"

Balaur smiled. "I'm sure you are, Lucas. But I have little need for you anymore. Surely, you can see the sense of that."

He shook his head. "You promised——"

"Nothing. You believed what you chose to believe." A slow, regretful shake of his blond head.

"It was I who found the cartomancer!" Gray said desperately.

"He mistreated me," Kasia said. "Kept me in chains." She lifted her skirt and displayed a bruised ankle.

Gray spun to her in a rage. "*You* are the liar!" He scrabbled across the dais and seized the hem of Balaur's white robe. "Don't listen to them, Reverend Father! They would turn you against me——"

Balaur kicked him away. "*They* are my kin. You are a sad little creature, Gray. Selling your services to the highest bidder. You already betrayed Clavis. It was only a matter of time before you betrayed me."

He flicked his finger. The woman cardinal stepped forward. Gray shied away as she seized him by the hair. He fought and cursed, but she held him effortlessly, face impassive. Kasia detected no hint of human feeling in her eyes.

Balaur's gaze swept the Order. Few managed to meet his stare. They were still on their knees, wearing their finest clothes and glittering jewels. Clearly they'd expected a celebratory reception. Perhaps with buckets of iced champagne and entertainments like those they'd enjoyed at the Lethe Club.

Instead, they were about to get an object lesson in choosing one's master more wisely.

"It is unfortunate," Balaur said, "that I am forced to make a demonstration of this man. I'm sure you all played your parts admirably. And you will be rewarded. But if any of you harbor ambitions beyond your station, take heed now."

Malach took Kasia's hand and pulled her a step back as tendrils of death ley coiled around Gray's jerking body. When it reached his throat and the thick veins turned black, his mouth working soundlessly, one of the women at the front of the crowd keeled over in a dead faint.

No one moved to help her.

Malach watched with tight lips, but he didn't turn away. Kasia didn't either. Balaur might have killed Gray eventually, but this was her doing. She'd been the one to suggest they incriminate him.

Only when the terrible, slow devouring was over did she look away, finding Jule Danziger at the foot of the dais. He studied Gray's withered corpse with a thoughtful expression. Their eyes met for a moment. Jule smiled, as though they shared some secret joke.

Kasia smiled back. *You're next*, she thought.

But Danziger stood higher than Gray in Balaur's regard. It would take more than a baseless accusation to ruin him. And she meant to kill him herself.

Once Tess would have reprimanded her for such vengeful thoughts, but surely she'd forgive them now.

Balaur strode to the great stone seat and sank down, resting his hands on the crossed keys carved into the arms. He'd clasped Kasia's hand with the right one. She frowned as she studied the left.

It was missing three fingers.

She had already known that. But how? Malach never told her, she felt sure of it.

The room tilted on its axis. Fragments of memory spun through her mind. An old man in priest's robes. She knew his voice well. A gravelly baritone. Balaur's was the same. He came to her Garden. Sometimes they spoke civilly, but it always ended in an argument.

Kasia's eyes narrowed. She'd thrown him into the pond—

"Are you well, my dear?"

She dragged herself back to the present. Balaur was studying her with an expression of concern.

"You look pale. The fault is mine. I should have disposed

of Gray more discreetly." He gestured to the Perditae. "Clear the audience chamber. See that these good people return safely to the Lethe Club until they are wanted."

The lines around his eyes and mouth looked deeper. The hand gripping the throne trembled slightly. Malach saw it, too. They shared a quick glance.

Balaur is not as hale as he would have us believe, Kasia thought. Yet she was shaken by the realization that he had been touching her dreams for months. What else had he gleaned? Not everything or he would have known about the sweven.

He can't read minds, she told herself firmly.

But he *did* spy on her Garden. The deepest realm of her unconscious, a place her rational mind was only dimly aware of. He might know other things. Things she didn't even admit to herself.

An awful thought.

Did I resist always? she wondered. Or were there times when I listened to his vile whispers? Saints, have my actions truly been my own?

She had to tell Malach. Had to consult the cards—

"I was hoping you could give me a reading," Balaur said as the Order scurried out, some on their knees all the way to the doors. Perditae stalked among them, deploying heavy boots to encourage those who didn't move fast enough. Balaur did nothing to discourage them. If anything, he looked amused.

Only Jule Danziger remained at the foot of the dais. He leaned back on his heels, blond hair perfectly combed, hands thrust into the pockets of his tailored suit. *Business casual,* she thought acidly, like one of the male models in the catalogues Natalya pored over for inspiration.

Kasia longed to set him on fire.

"A reading," she echoed.

Balaur made a tsking sound. "I assume Malach returned

your cards. Unlike the sanctimonious tyrants of the Curia, *I* would never deny them to you. You are free to say no, of course. But it would mean much to me."

She hesitated, then nodded. "I will do it."

He looked pleased, turning to Malach with a rueful expression. "Luk was dying anyway, you know. Pancreatic cancer. He fought it for years. Like most of us, he could not accept the inevitable. The dissolution of the body is painful to witness. More so for him, who had the gift of molding the ley like clay into new forms. His Markhounds, I mean. The hawks and so forth."

But Balaur's quick glance at Jule did not go unnoticed. So it was Luk who restored the bastard. Could there have been a spark of life inside that ruined body? Kasia suppressed a shudder of revulsion. If it *was* Luk who did it and he was dead now, he couldn't do it again.

"Such extraordinary power," Balaur mused. "Yet he lacked the courage to do the same for himself."

"How so?" Malach asked, gaze intent.

"The old body must die for the new one to be born, of course. Some have a sentimental attachment to the flesh, but it is the spirit that endures. Only the spirit. The rest is dumb matter. I told him that many times." A chuckle. "He thought the Magnum Opus would be his salvation. He feared the Nigredo, rightfully so, but in the end he saw no other choice and agreed to the bargain. As if I would allow one such as Luk to live forever! Can you imagine it? That joyless old skeleton spouting the *Meliora* for the next thousand years? No, we can do without him. Though it's a shame about his knights, they might have been useful." He cocked his head. "I presume anarchy reigns in the city?"

Balaur didn't sound bothered by this prospect.

"Not yet," Malach replied. "It's only been a few hours. Did you notice anything unusual during the drive?"

"Well, let's see. It was dark, so I can't be entirely sure, but I did glimpse several naked people. A few fistfights. Oh, and what appeared to be a mob. They were smashing store windows along Caerfax Road." Balaur smiled. "Just a bit of fun, I'm sure. Things will settle down." A shrug. "Or escalate. But we are safe within the walls of the Arx, are we not?"

"Perfectly," Malach assured him.

"Then let us retire to a more comfortable chamber." He shivered. "It's drafty in here."

All this time, the Masdari woman had stood without a single word or gesture, watching silently. Balaur held out a hand and she helped him rise from the throne.

"This is Jamila al-Jabban. My advisor. I would have her join us for the reading."

Kasia inclined her head.

"I am most eager to hear the foretelling," the Masdari said, her voice faintly accented.

"Malach, you must arrange for a supper to celebrate our success. We will discuss our plans for Bal Kirith."

He bowed. "I've already ordered the kitchens to prepare a feast in your honor."

"Excellent. Then you must see to the details while I speak with your sister."

Malach clearly didn't want to leave her, but he didn't dare refuse. "It will be ready in an hour, if that suits you."

"Perfectly. More than enough time, I'm sure."

Kasia led them to the upstairs library, the cardinals prowling a few paces behind. She hadn't expected Balaur would demand her services so quickly, but it worked well with her own plans.

Even better that he'd suggested it himself.

She knew Balaur didn't trust her. The cardinals were there for protection. But to give him a reading! Hopefully, the cards would show his impending demise. If not, at least she would have warning that their plans were doomed. Either way, she would tell him nothing but flattering lies.

Kasia suppressed a chuckle. *Such wonderful things I see for you, Reverend Father! Youth eternal! Puppies and rainbows! Enemies vanquished and all the world at your feet!*

Balaur settled into a chair by the hearth, Jamila al-Jabban at his side. Kasia dragged a small table over and sat down opposite them. She took the cards from her pocket. Balaur's gaze fixed on the deck. He licked his lips.

"Where do the cards come from?" he asked.

"A friend made them."

Kasia shuffled her cards. The reverse sides were black and gold. Each had a snake devouring its own tail with the phases of the moon in a circle around it and the four major suits in the corners—Flame, Keys, Raven, Wolf.

"Does that matter? Or can you do it with any cards?"

"Any cards. They serve as my Marks."

"Yes, of course." He tapped the table restlessly. "The Curia underestimated you. But blood will out, as they say."

She fanned the deck, ensuring the Ravens and Keys were on top, then closed her eyes and allowed her unconscious to guide her fingers. The ley felt oddly slippery. There one instant, gone the next. She chose five cards and turned them over.

Every single one was upside-down.

Kasia knew the cards were all facing the proper way before she drew. The ley did that sometimes, inverted them, but it was usually a single card. Not *all* of them.

Balaur squinted at the spread. "What does it mean?"

Kasia didn't reply right away. She'd expected Major Arcana or at least high clergy—Knight, Bishop, Cardinal, Pontifex. But they were all low pip cards. The two of Flames, four of Ravens, six of Keys and two of Wolves. She saw no connections at all. Just a random jumble. It was the first time in years that had happened.

"Sometimes the initial drawing is a prelude," she improvised. "It will become clear in the next I'm sure."

She examined the deck, confirming that all the cards were upright. Then she chose five more and flipped them over.

Low pips. Inverted.

A sudden movement near the window startled her. She rocked back in her chair. The leg caught on a fold of carpet. The seat tipped precariously. Kasia grabbed the edge of the table to steady herself, the cards sliding from her hand. In the corner of her eye, she saw a dark wing shake and furl itself again.

"That's quite a trick, my dear," Balaur said.

She stared down at the tower of cards on the carpet. Four tiers high, each triangular level supporting the next. The construction lasted only an instant before a breeze from the open window sent it tumbling down.

"You did that," she snapped.

Kasia felt furious. *Betrayed.* The cards were supposed to obey her, but they were misbehaving like impish children!

"Not I," Balaur said mildly. "Come now, why would I interfere? We both know how much I've desired this reading."

She bent down to retrieve the cards. He sounded sincere, though the man was clearly just as good a liar as she was. Was he toying with her? Or—and this struck her as plausible—was the ley around him too distorted, too twisted, to reveal the truth?

"I'm sorry," she said. "It isn't working."

She expected him to argue, but Balaur merely sighed. "Fair enough. I am weary from my journey anyway. The roads in the Morho are frightful. But I have other things I would show you later."

Curiosity sparked. "Like what?"

She leaned across the table. Balaur smiled—a warm, conspiratorial smile—and Kasia realized with dawning horror that she felt quite at ease in his presence. This conversation was just one of many they'd had in the past. His face, his voice, it was all so familiar.

But I resisted him in the end, she thought fiercely. I know I did. *Always.*

Saints let it be so.

"Books," he said. "I brought them with me from Bal Agnar. Some are in Masdari, but Jamila will translate for us. You might have some insights about the pictures."

"I would be very interested to see them," Kasia said, drawing back.

"I will rejoin you at supper then."

Balaur rose and took his leave on Jamila al-Jabban's arm, the cardinals stalking silently behind.

Kasia waited until she was sure they were gone. She stared down at the cards, still angry but unwilling to admit defeat.

"Does he suspect?" she whispered, plucking one out with an unsteady hand. "Will we succeed?"

Kasia turned it over.

Death grinned up at her.

The thirteenth card in the Major Arcana. Traditional decks put him astride a white horse, but Natalya was a rebel. This Grim Reaper danced on a mound of skulls. One skeletal hand gripped a half-moon sickle. He wore a suit of armor, visor raised. The empty sockets held tiny red embers.

"Huh," she muttered. "Good or bad?"

She knew better than to interpret any card literally. Green shoots poked up among the carnage, speaking to the promise of rejuvenation and new life. That was the usual meaning—a metaphorical death only. It might signify a change of careers or the end of a long relationship. Shedding an outdated perspective on life. Clients always recoiled when Death was drawn until she explained that it often betokened positive transformation.

But in this context, Kasia wondered—hoped—it meant exactly what it said.

Now, the wild dance . . . that was both change and stability. Bones endured after the flesh was gone, sometimes for millennia. The inner scaffolding of the human body laid bare, rendering everyone the same in the end.

"Mors vincit omnia," she whispered.

Death always wins.

Falke had said that to her in his study the night the Reverend Mother Feizah died. Kasia remembered the stockings she wore. The soft rasp of silk as she slid one from her leg. Falke had used it to knot a tourniquet above the stab wound in his thigh.

Malach is young and hungry, he'd said. *And I'm old and tired.*

The Fool and the Hierophant. Would they ever be free of each other?

Kasia studied the card, absorbing each grim detail, including the *XIII* cunningly etched on the skeleton's breast-plate. The card came just after The Serpent and just before The Twins. Every aspect of the Major Arcana was deliberate. The number was no accident.

Twelve months to a year. Twelve hours to a clock. In the orderly scheme of things, thirteen was an uninvited and unwelcome guest.

The Stranger.

Kasia touched the scythe, a deep furrow notching her forehead. Then she slipped the card back into the deck and hurried to find Malach.

Chapter Thirty-Nine

❧❀❧

The aromas of fresh bread and roasting meat wafted from the kitchens. Malach's stomach rumbled, though he had little appetite.

The Mistress of Chars stood just outside the doors, calling out rapid-fire instructions to the cooks and serving maids in gray who streamed past. "Make sure the wine is uncorked. Rosetto for the first course, then the Vechiny Száraz '42 and Nascetta '69 with dessert."

A breathless steward ran up. "We're low on napkins, Mistress."

Malach stepped aside for two women carrying covered tureens.

"Check the third linen closet in the south wing," she snapped. "Hurry!"

The young man rabbited off. She tucked a lock of glossy black hair behind her ear and consulted a list. Her skin tone was light brown, her features an appealing blend of Kindu and Novo. Malach wondered how she'd ended up here.

He approached with a bow. "Do you have a moment, Mistress?"

She turned to him with a harried look. "Nuncio. Of

course."

He drew her down the passage, away from the traffic headed for the dining hall.

"None of the chars have Marks, correct?" he said.

She eyed him with a touch of impatience. "That's correct, Nuncio."

"Which means you are unaffected by the taint of the ley."

"We cannot even see it," she said cautiously.

"And you remain loyal to Clavis?"

She stiffened. "Have I done something to displease you, Nuncio?"

"Not at all. In fact, I'm hoping the answer is yes."

She crossed her arms. "What are you after?"

Malach glanced along the passage. Chars hurried to and from the dining hall, but none were within earshot.

"Luk is dead," he said. "So is Maria Karolo."

The Mistress's eyes widened.

"We both know Balaur is a monster," he continued. "But I am not. Do you understand?"

She drew a sharp breath. "Yes."

"I plan to kill him. Will you help me?"

A startled blink. "Help you what exactly?"

Malach told her. The Mistress considered it in silence. He saw no fear in her eyes, just calculation. An intelligent woman running through different scenarios to assess the viability of the plan. He'd remembered what Nikola said about Unmarked. The Probatio labelled them sociopaths. Not a mental illness, but they shared certain traits. One was a willingness to take risks others would not.

The Curia had underestimated Nikola. Malach felt sure the other chars were equally resourceful. Either way, he knew she wouldn't betray him. All those years in Novostopol sniffing out candidates to take his Mark had honed his instincts for a person's character. Lucie Moss still carried a small painted icon of Clavis hidden in her stocking. He'd seen her take it out and kiss it through the crack of his door while she was in there cleaning. He'd retreated, then approached the door again with loud footsteps. By the time he entered, she was dusting and whistling a little tune. But there was a bulge at her ankle where she'd replaced it.

"What if the prisoners at the stadium aren't freed?" she asked at last. "What then?"

"I don't know," he replied. "We'll think of something. Assuming we aren't all dead."

She laughed. "At least you're honest, Nuncio."

"But if we succeed, you'll have your city back."

A hard look. "And you have no designs to seize power yourself?"

"How would I accomplish that, Mistress?" he asked. "The mages number barely two dozen. I have no army. But *you* do."

She nodded slowly. "That's true enough. Why this sudden change of heart?"

He held her skeptical gaze. "I learned things about Balaur that I could not stomach."

A sniff. "The Beast of Bal Agnar. And you expected different?"

"I lied to myself because he made promises to me. Whether he would actually keep them is immaterial now. I am a father, twice over, and I know the sort of world I want my children to live in. Men like Balaur have no part of it."

"I have children, too," she said. "Five of them." Her face softened. "They are devils, but I love them dearly." She gave a brisk nod. "We will play our part."

"The others will go along?"

"They despise the Kvens." Her face darkened. "They despise Balaur even more."

"Then stand ready." Malach turned to go.

"Nuncio?"

"Yes?"

She gazed at him for a moment. "The ley bless you."

"And you, Mistress." Malach spun on his heel and strode off, heading for the Villa of Saint Margit.

HE GAVE THE AGREED KNOCK, five short raps. Falke opened the door and stepped back.

Rachel stood at an easel, paintbrush in hand. She looked quite a bit taller and Malach wondered if the child had grown three inches in the last hour. Then he realized she was wearing shiny high-heeled boots about six sizes too big.

Kasia had suggested they use Natalya Anderle's old room to hide her. It was a mess, clothes strewn everywhere, but Rachel's eyes had lit up when she saw all the art supplies. So had Malach's. He knew how bored and cranky children got when they were confined.

The Villa was an ideal choice. Off in a distant corner of the grounds, nowhere near the barracks or the palace. No one else was staying there now. The front door had a stout lock for which Lucie Moss had given him the only key.

Malach studied Rachel's picture with a familiar ache of guilt. Little stick figures ran in every direction. Lightning sizzled down from a red sky. She'd drawn long yellow tails on the meteorites. Black for the shattered buildings of the Arx.

Rachel glanced over, but didn't acknowledge him.

"It's all in place," he said to Falke.

The old pontifex sat down on the edge of the bed. Malach lifted his robes and took out the dagger he'd offered to Morvana Zeigler. He flipped it around and held the hilt out to Falke.

"Take it," he said.

Falke's gaze fixed briefly on the white scar at Malach's wrist. Was that a hint of remorse for trying to sever him? If so, it would be the first Malach had ever seen.

Falke took the dagger and set it on a low table.

"You don't know a thing about kids, do you?" Malach muttered. He moved the dagger to the top of a high wardrobe. Out of Rachel's reach—even with the boots.

"I can't stay long," he said.

Falke clasped his hands together. "Malach," he said slowly. "I've been thinking. You might not come back." He glanced at Rachel. She was adding the blood now. Thick splotches of red on the stick figures, her mouth tight with concentration.

"Then take her out of here. Somewhere safe," Malach said. "Valdrian is at the postern gate. It's not far."

Falke looked startled. "That's not what I meant. But . . . you would entrust her to my care?"

"I already have, haven't I?" Malach snapped. He fished in his pocket and gave Falke the keys. "As much as it pains me, you're the best choice."

An uncertain nod, as if he'd expected this but still found it hard to reconcile. "Rachel," Falke said sharply.

She turned. "Yes, papa?"

"Come here."

She brushed a hand across her cheek, leaving a scarlet smear, and clomped over in her high-heeled boots.

Falke drew a deep breath. "I'm not your father, Rachel. *He* is."

Her features froze. Malach's heart thudded hard in his chest.

"The truth is that I stole you from him." Falke lifted his chin, voice firm. "I held your mother prisoner until she gave birth. Then I took you away from her. I believed it was best for you." A long pause. A muscle in his jaw twitched. "But that's not why I did it. I wanted you for the Church. So you might grow up and have children of your own to continue the Sanctified Marks."

Rachel twisted the paintbrush, picking at the bristles, tearing them out one by one, though her face was still blank.

"It is my fault that your father was forced to come and

take you as he did." Falke bowed his head. "I ask your forgiveness."

Not mine, Malach thought. But he didn't care. His breath caught as she turned to him.

"Is it true?"

Malach nodded.

Her lip trembled. "Why did you pretend?"

"I was afraid." He glanced at the painting. "Because of what I did to you."

Her face crumpled in confusion. He felt terribly sorry for her. Malach crouched down.

"I know you don't love me. But I *am* your father. And I will be a better man for you, Rachel. I promise. You mean everything to me. *Everything.*"

The paintbrush fell from red-stained fingers. She stared at him with brimming eyes. Then she flung herself into his arms, sobbing. Malach held her tight, burying his face in her hair. He heard Falke move away to the window. Everything faded. There was only the warm child pressed to his chest and an overwhelming grief mingled with happiness.

Malach let Rachel cry herself out, saying nothing more. The sobbing finally subsided to soft hiccups. Her small body went limp and he realized she had sought refuge in sleep. That was often the way.

His own eyes had dried by the time he carried her to the bed and lay her down, drawing the covers to her chin. She didn't stir when he kissed her forehead. One of the boots had fallen off. He slid the other from her foot, marveling at the perfect brown toes.

"Thank you," he said quietly.

Falke still stood at the window, staring out at the rain. He nodded without turning around.

Malach could think of nothing more to say. He waited in the corridor until he heard the key turn in the lock. Then he set off through driving rain for the Pontifex's Palace.

BALAUR RAISED his glass in a toast. "To the Black Sun!"

"To the Black Sun!" his dining companions echoed.

Malach took a small sip of wine. Only Kasia didn't lift her goblet. She was staring hard at Jule Danziger. He suppressed a smile. His sister was truly a gifted actress.

She hated Jule, of course. That much was real. It would have been suspicious if she didn't. But she struck just the right balance of uncertainty towards Balaur, casting him appraising glances from beneath her lashes as if she were weighing her options.

Balaur's weakness was that he believed what the Via Sancta said about the nihilim. He could not conceive of one of his own kin acting out of any impulse but self-interest. The string of victories had made him feel invincible. Why wouldn't she throw her lot in with him? Especially when Clavis had denied her the ley.

Jule Danziger met Kasia's glare with the satisfied smirk of a cat curled up on a sunny windowsill. He, too, thought he was untouchable.

Jamila al-Jabban sat at Balaur's right hand. She had not spoken once, but he occasionally leaned over to whisper in her ear. It was pierced with seven rings that glinted in the candle-light. Malach had the impression she was ill at ease. She picked at her food and barely touched her wine. Jamila was one who preferred to pull strings from the shadows, he thought. He wished he knew what they were plotting together.

Besides the mages, the rest of their table companions were all senior members of the Order of the Black Sun. Balaur's winged cardinals loomed like black specters behind his chair. Not even the Order cared to meet their soulless gaze.

"I have been thinking about the problem of the Kvens," Balaur said, twirling the glass between his fingers.

Conversation ceased.

"Most of them are at the stadium guarding the prisoners. A foolish waste of resources. What use do we have for prisoners?"

"None, certainly, Reverend Father," piped up a woman in a long, glittering gown.

He stared at her until she buried her face in her wine.

"Therefore, I issued an order for the prisoners to be disposed of. We might as well get some use out of the Kvens before they die."

Kasia's hand tightened around her goblet. "Can't we show mercy?"

Balaur gave her a kind smile. "The Kvens are beyond mercy now. As for the prisoners, you know little of warfare, my dear. I know it seems harsh, but we cannot have them making some pathetic attempt to take back the Arx, can we? No, it is cleaner this way. We will put the unpleasantness behind us and move forward. Nuncio, do you agree?"

"Seems sound to me," Malach said with a smile, forking a potato into his mouth.

"There, your own brother agrees with this plan. Do not trouble yourself, Kasia. It is the expedient solution."

She gave a reluctant nod.

Malach eyed her from the corner of his eye. He still couldn't quite believe it. He'd carried the burden his entire life; that he had run away and left her to die. Proof, he reflected, that he did care about someone other than himself, though he'd never recognized the emotion for what it was. *Guilt.*

Instead, it had manifested as hatred for Falke and the Via Sancta, which was easier to cope with. Shame had no solution. It simply ate away at you like a slow drip of water boring through stone. But hatred! One could *do* something with that.

He no longer knew what he truly believed. Only that the bastard sitting at the head of the table had to be put out of everyone's misery.

The Mistress of Chars was serving Balaur herself. She refilled his goblet and withdrew with a deep curtsy. Malach watched him lift the wine to his lips.

Would he taste the sleeping draught? If there was even a hint of bitterness . . . .

Balaur drank deeply and set the cup down. He wiped his mouth and turned to Jamila, saying something that made her smile.

Malach let out a long exhale.

He listened to the alchemists talking about the high positions they would hold in Nantwich, about Balaur's promise to send reinforcements from Bal Agnar to hold the city when the Kvens were dead. The idiots had no clue how demented Balaur's contingent of ex-knights were. They made the Wolves seem like tame little bunnies.

On his left, Valdrian drank and joked with Jessiel and Caralexa. Only those three knew what Malach planned. They'd agreed with him whole-heartedly. He expected the rest would, too, but it was too much of a risk to tell them ahead of time.

Besides the mages who had been assigned to guard duty, all were present. It was critical that none of them were missing from the dinner. None except for . . . .

"Where are your young cousins, Malach?" Balaur asked. "Sydonie and Tristhus? I hoped they would join us at table. Children are precious, indeed. They must be guided properly."

"Oh, they're somewhere," Malach said casually. "You know kids. Always getting into trouble."

There were a few polite titters.

Balaur frowned. "You must take a firmer hand with them, Malach."

"That's what my aunt used to say. I do try, Reverend Father." He slid a hand into his pocket. "I have a gift for you. I was waiting for the proper occasion."

Balaur arched a brow. "Well, what is it?"

Malach strode over, heart beating hard. He set it on the tablecloth.

"I took it from Bishop Karolo," he said.

Balaur picked it up and held it to the candlelight. He let out a startled laugh. "This is Dmitry Falke's ring!"

"It seems certain he is dead," Malach said.

"I still want my own back," Balaur said wryly, "but I will add this to the growing collection."

"You once told me symbols mean little, Reverend Father. Yet the Black Sun has given us all hope these many years. One day, you'll have all four rings to melt down and forge into something new. A crown with twelve jagged rays, perhaps." He bowed his head. "But I leave their disposition to you."

Balaur was silent and Malach wondered if he'd laid it on too thick. Then he felt a gnarled hand grasp his own.

"A fine sentiment, my son. The rest of you would do well to heed his example." He covered a yawn. "The hour grows late. By morning, we will have a fair amount of mopping up to do. The stadium would be an ideal location to give Night-marks to the populace, but it's better they're not wading through corpses, yes?" A chuckle as he turned to Danziger. "Jule, you'll see to that?"

"It would be my pleasure, Reverend Father," Jule said smoothly.

Everyone jumped to their feet as Balaur rose from the table. He paused in front of Kasia. Jamila al-Jabban and the winged cardinals hovered behind, their red robes gleaming like open wounds.

"We will speak more. I never had a chance to show you those books." Another yawn. "Ah, for the vigor of youth again. But it is past an old man's bedtime!"

She nodded, looking both eager and wary. "I await your summons."

Balaur patted her shoulder. "Sweet dreams, my dear."

Chapter Forty

"It's nearly time."

The knight from Nantwich turned. Rain coursed down his light brown skin, eyes gleaming in the darkness. "Once the signal goes around, we all take our gloves off and work the ley in concert," he whispered. "Who knows? Maybe we'll manage to call down lightning on those bastards."

Alexei nodded. Patryk and Natalya shared a quick look. She rocked on her toes, hardly able to contain her eagerness.

After two days of captivity with almost no food or water, they'd reached a collective decision to escape or die. No one needed persuading. Several dozen prisoners were already gone, taken by fever and festering wounds. At first, the Kvens had removed the bodies. But they no longer cared about even that semblance of human decency. A corpse lay not five meters away, open eyes staring into the rain.

Alexei had no idea if Misha was still alive. Rademacher had forced him to watch as they gave his brother a massive dose of Sublimin, then questioned him for hours. This produced nothing but rambling dissertations on the *Meliora*. In a fury, Rademacher had doubled the dosage.

The drug dissolved the barrier between the conscious and

unconscious mind. It's only approved use was to give Marks; interrogation was definitely off-label. Sublimin did work, though. Alexei had seen mages give up everything they knew under a much smaller quantity.

But Mikhail's mind was like the nesting dolls the war widows sold at Verskaya Square. Each layer showed a different face. Instead of breaking him, the second injection only made him lucid again.

"Fuck you, Radish," he said coldly. "Fuck your mother and fuck your sisters. Fuck Luk, twice over. Fuck your dog. If you have a wife, fuck her, too—"

That's when the physical torture began. Electric current through the soles of his feet.

Alexei had been about to tell them everything he knew, to hell with Jalghuth's defenses, when Misha caught his eye. Sweat plastered dark hair to his forehead. He looked ghastly.

Rademacher was fiddling with the car battery. They'd rigged it with wires that ran to a *clava*, a wand with a bronze tip and insulated rubber handle that delivered the current. Just the sight of it made Alexei's stomach clench. He'd never used one himself, but he suspected his brother might have.

Misha's torturer was a plump little woman with graying hair in a bun. Her back turned as she dumped a bucket of water over Misha's head. Wet skin conducted electricity better.

His brother spluttered and coughed. He blinked away the beads, gaze seeking out Alexei. Neither of the Kvens saw Misha wink at him. Alexei could still see that single blue eye. The twisted smile, exactly like the Mark on his chest.

Was he *enjoying* it?

Alexei had turned away, choking on bile through the gag. Rademacher grunted in disgust.

"Who is soft now?" he muttered. "Put him back in with the rest."

That was hours ago, but Alexei could still hear his brother's screams as they'd hauled him out.

Whispers crossed the camp like a soft breeze. One man or woman to the next, and the next. It would begin when the knight from Nantwich rose to his feet.

His name was Miles Rycroft.

Marked by Clavis herself. He claimed he felt fine. That meant the Reverend Mother was still alive somewhere in the Morho. Alexei believed it. He, too, wore Clavis's Mark. If they found her, she could lead the resistance. Rally the last loyal knights.

White hounds circled the perimeter, sometimes lunging to snap at a prisoner. Their Kven guards were dark silhouettes in the rain, riding up and down on shadowy Marksteeds. More manned the gates with swords and crossbows. But if they could just break through a single exit, a few might make it out. More than a few, Alexei hoped, though they were all weak.

Rycroft flexed his gloved fingers. "Virtus, veritas, lux," he muttered, thighs tensing to stand.

Blinding light. Alexei threw an arm across his face. In his exhausted delirium, his first thought was that they were all working the ley. The pure ley that Willem Danziger had spoken of.

Then Rycroft swore and he realized that it was the stadium arc lights.

The squalid scene burst into stark illumination. Hundreds of thin, muddy prisoners, cringing under the floodlights, and a company of Kvens riding out from one of the tunnels, Rademacher at their head. He galloped up and slid from the saddle.

"We grow bored," he declared. "It's time for some entertainment."

Two knights dismounted and dragged Alexei to his feet. Others used the dogs to clear a space in the midst of the prisoners. Rademacher's glittering gaze swept the prisoners.

"Saints, but you're a sorry bunch," he said. "Come now! Surely one of you has some spirit left."

His gaze skipped over Patryk Spassov, then bounced back. "You."

Rademacher pointed. Spassov got to his feet, expressionless.

The kommandant looked around at his knights. "We will have some sport," he said, rubbing his gloved hands together. "Fewer mouths to feed at the end, *ja?*"

Some of the men laughed, but others glanced at each other, uneasy. They were the same ones he'd seen distributing blankets to the eldest members of the clergy.

"Feed?" Spassov said slowly. "You've starved us, you son of a goat!"

Alexei expected the kommandant to erupt, but his good mood seemed unshakeable. "I sense discontent," he said. "Well, the victor will be rewarded with a hot dinner. How does that sound, eh?"

When neither of them reacted, he shrugged. "Or not. I don't really care." His voice hardened. "But you will give us sport or I will feed the others to the dogs, one by one, understand? Now, fight!" Spittle flew from his lips, though he still wore the rictus of a smile. "To the death!"

His rage was palpable, but the Wolf Mark on Rademacher's neck didn't change. Not a hint of ley, blue or otherwise. Alexei looked around at the Kvens. Most looked normal. But a few . . . he recognized the signs. The furtive, jerking glances.

Alexei started to laugh. It was all too perfect.

Rademacher watched him in astonishment. Even Patryk looked uneasy, as if he feared Alexei had finally snapped. But Spassov hadn't been through it himself.

"Are you seeing spiders yet?" Alexei wondered. "Crawling out of my mouth, perhaps?"

"This man is a lunatic," Rademacher declared. He looked around, a bit frantic now. "Someone else—"

"You don't know, do you?" He raised his voice so they'd all hear him over the driving rain. "Luk is dead!"

Rademacher bared his teeth. "Liar!"

"You're starting to feel it now, aren't you? The ley boiling in your blood. Trust me, it'll get worse." Alexei saw the flicker of doubt. The fear. It delighted him no end. "You were always vicious and cruel, kommandant. Congratulations! You're now clinically insane, too."

"Carry out the new orders!" Rademacher screamed. "Kill them! Kill them all!" He stumbled toward his horse.

Rycroft shot to his feet. "Now!" he yelled, tearing off a glove.

The dogs went mad. Screams sliced the night as they threw themselves at the prisoners. A ripple of panic coursed through the crowd. Everywhere, men and women rose on weary, trembling legs. They ran for the exits, pursued by knights on horseback. Shouted commands echoed around the perimeter.

Alexei reached Natalya just as a hound sank its jaws into her calf. Spassov threw his arms around its barrel chest. The dog twisted, fangs snapping shut a centimeter from his ear. Then Alexei had it by the head. He gazed into the flat pink eyes. A hard twist and the dog went limp.

"Can you walk?" he cried over the din.

There was no time to check the wound, though he could see her pant leg was bloodied.

Natalya winced, leaning heavily on Patryk. "I can stagger," she said through gritted teeth. "Go! Find your brother."

He hesitated. "Are you sure?"

"Yes." She tested the foot, then started off at a lumbering run, the bright lights trailing a long shadow behind her.

The floodlights. They were giving the archers perfect targets. Dozens of bodies sprawled on the ground with black-fletched arrows jutting from their backs and chests. Other prisoners writhed helplessly, hamstrung, as the mounted knights bore down on them. As Alexei feared, it was turning into a massacre.

"Get her out," Alexei said to Spassov. "I'll find you!"

Patryk wordlessly clasped his arm, then took off after Natalya.

Alexei sank to the muddy, torn-up turf. He yanked a glove off and drew ley deep into his Marks. Nineteen now. Would it be enough?

He poured all his desperate need into a single plea.

Blind them.

His Marks flared bright. The liminal rose up, riding a wave of turbulent abyssal ley. With an explosive shatter of glass, the arc lights blew out. Darkness descended.

Alexei was already on his feet, running for the tunnel they'd brought him through before. He tripped over a body and sprawled to the ground. Blood flooded his mouth. Adrenaline drove him to his feet again.

He caught a glimpse of Miles Rycroft, kicking a guard in the chest and taking his sword. A knot of soldiers swarmed over. Rycroft spun to face them and was swallowed from view.

The tunnel yawned before him.

As Alexei drew near, he heard new sounds in the darkness. Howls and snarls and frantic barking. He turned back to the darkened stadium. A single bulb, high above the bleachers, had survived the burst of ley. In its weak glow, he saw shadows darting among the mounted knights. One of the horses whinnied, then went down. The prisoners took advantage of the confusion to overwhelm the guards at one of the gates and swarm through. The white dogs were in a frenzy. They seemed to be battling invisible foes.

There was no time to watch the fight. He ran down the tunnel, then climbed the stairs two at a time. He burst into the skybox.

Rademacher was waiting with a crossbow. He aimed it at Alexei's chest.

Alexei raised his palms. Misha lay on the floor. A dirty rag was stuffed into his mouth. His hands were tied behind his back. They'd stripped his shirt off. Alexei flooded with relief when he saw his brother's chest still rose and fell.

"I knew you would come for him," Rademacher hissed. Madness glittered in his eyes. "But . . . you're not human! What is wrong with your face?"

Alexei watched him cautiously. "It's the sickness. You're starting to hallucinate."

"No! You're a . . . monster." He licked his lips. "You want to kill me. To eat me like the Perditae. You are one of them. You served in the Void too long. It has taken you—"

"Listen to me." He took a step forward. "You are not well, Kommandant."

Whether Rademacher had *ever* been entirely sane was questionable. Now, the man had taken a swan dive off the cliff. The poison would kill him in time.

But not soon enough.

Rademacher tilted his head as though listening. He muttered to himself in Kven. Alexei caught most of it.

"*Ja*, I see it now. They are *all* Perditae. And I must stop them. I am the only one who can."

Calm settled over his features as he adjusted the sights. Alexei tensed as Rademacher's finger tightened on the release mechanism.

A blurred streak erupted from the shadows, hitting the kommandant square in the chest. The bolt whizzed past Alexei's shoulder. Rademacher tumbled backwards. He gave a keening scream as Alice sank her jaws into his throat. She tore savagely, head swinging from side to side. His heels drummed for a minute, then fell still.

Alexei sank down, tears dampening his eyes. "I am well, little sister." He buried his fingers in her coat. "Never have I been so happy to see you." He eyed her gory muzzle. "Just don't lick me, eh?"

She barked and ran to Rademacher, sniffing. Then she lifted her leg and peed on his corpse.

Alexei thought of the vile collar the kommandant had tried to force around her neck when they met him on the road. Clearly, Alice hadn't forgotten either.

Alexei tore the gag from his brother's mouth. His flesh felt cold, the pulse weak. Alexei took a bloody knife from the table and sliced through Misha's bonds. Then he pulled his own shirt off and grappled with his brother's limp body, pulling his arms through the sleeves. It was a tight fit, but it would keep him warm.

And Alexei knew his brother wouldn't want anyone seeing him like this.

Alice sat on her haunches, eyeing them both warily. She didn't like Mikhail, but her master had chastened her often enough about showing it.

He was doing up the last buttons when she barked again, sharply, head whipping to the door. He grabbed the crossbow, which he'd kept close at hand.

"Your Grace," he said in surprise.

"She found you. Thank the Saints."

Morvana Zeigler strode into the skybox. Her cool gaze lit on Rademacher. "I am not sorry to see him gone. It seems we came just in time." She moved to Alexei's side and knelt down. "Captain Bryce saved my life. Perhaps just to save yours, but I am still grateful. How can I help him?"

Mikhail's eyes opened at the sound of her voice. The pupils were hugely dilated. They must have given him more Sublimin. Bloodshot eyes found her face. He smiled faintly, then slipped away again.

"We must carry him," Alexei said. "What's happening out there?"

She glanced though the dark plate glass window. "I brought three packs of true Markhounds. They killed most of the others, though no doubt a few escaped. But the tide has turned in the stadium, at least. The guards fled."

"How did you get out of the Arx?"

"The Nuncio released me. He was with a woman. Kasia Novak."

Alexei's gut flipped. "She's unharmed?"

"Perfectly." She looked thoughtful. "The mage changed his mind when he learned about what had been done to the children. They mean to kill Balaur."

Alexei frowned. That didn't sound like Malach. "And you believed him?"

"Yes," she said simply. "Balaur is coming to the Arx this very night. They sent me to rally whatever resistance I could."

"Then we must go now!" He turned back to his brother, wondering how on earth he could bring Misha along. Alexei had broken a sweat just trying to get a shirt on him.

"If you agree, I will stay here with him," Morvana said. "I think he cannot be moved. Even if he were not such a big man."

"They tortured him with electricity. Drugged him, too."

Her light brows knit together. "Saints," she murmured. "It is a wonder he's alive."

"My brother is stronger than you can imagine." Alexei pressed the crossbow into her hand. "Keep this. In case any of the guards show up. Or the white dogs."

She stared at it for a moment. Then her fingers tightened around the grip. "I will defend us both," she said heavily.

"Do you want Alice? I could make her stay."

She cast a wry glance at the Markhound, who pressed tight against Alexei's thigh. "I'm not so sure of that, Fra Bryce. I doubt she will let you out of her sight again. No, we will be fine. There are other hounds about."

Alexei started for the door.

"And Bryce?"

He turned back.

"I came with two mage children. Dark-haired with green cloaks." She shook her head with a grin. "They are hellions. I saw them fight knights twice their size and win. Try to find them. They will aid you."

Alexei only nodded, beyond surprise at this point. The game board he knew had been upended. The Kvens were going mad. Clavis's chief aide was allied with the Order of the Black Sun and the mages were now his friends. If the bishop who held his Marks wasn't sitting right in front of him, he'd wonder if *he* were the one losing his mind.

"Thank you, Bishop Zeigler."

She gave a tense smile. "It is Morvana, *ja?*"

Chapter Forty-One

Alexei jogged behind Alice, breath coming in sharp bursts. He was frozen to the bone and soaking wet. In the dark, storm-wracked night, it was hard to tell friend from foe. Sometimes he saw Kven knights loping through the streets like packs of wild dogs, attacking anything that moved. Because of the curfew, that invariably meant other Kven knights.

Sometimes he saw lone, shadowy figures that might have been his fellow prisoners.

Or not.

He feared to approach, hoping that Alice would pick up a familiar scent and lead him to Patryk and Natalya. But the mass insanity gripping the city seemed to muddle her senses. The hound warned him with low growls when sick knights came near, though she often paused to spin in circles, snapping at her own tail.

"I kn . . . know how you f-f-feel," he whispered through chattering teeth. "It's b-b-bloody chaos."

He couldn't make it much farther without something to block the cutting wind. Alexei was more than willing to break a store window, but the area was all residential. The Unmarked district, judging by the rundown brick towers and cracked sidewalks. He passed an empty, trash-strewn lot. Someone had painted WOLVES SOD OFF! in meter-high letters on the wooden fence.

Then he spotted a single candle burning in the second floor of a house down the block. It had a tiny front yard, with a rusted tricycle lying on its side in the weeds. Alexei staggered to the front door and pounded with a fist. No answer. He tried the knocker.

"Hello?" he shouted, squinting up into the icy rain. "Please, if someone's in there . . . ." A deep shiver ran through him. "I'm a priest from Novostopol! Held prisoner at the stadium." His lips could barely form the words. "I'm f-f-frozen."

Alexei rested his forehead against the door.

No answer.

He could hardly blame them. He must look like another lunatic, half-naked and wild-eyed. Alexei didn't regret giving his shirt to Mikhail. His brother needed it more than he did. And it kept Morvana from seeing the grotesque image on his brother's chest. No one could know about that. Not until they fixed it.

But Saints, he'd never been so cold.

He was turning away when the bolt shot. A young woman opened the door a crack. She stared at him with a frightened expression, at the Marks covering his bare torso, then thrust a coat through the gap.

"I'm sorry," she said quickly. "I can't let you in. My children . . . ."

He gazed at her dumbly.

"Well, go on! Take it!"

Alexei took the coat. He opened his mouth to thank her but the door was already closing, the bolt sliding shut. The coat was gray wool with a thick collar, like the kind sailors wore. His fingers were too clumsy to manage the buttons so he pulled it tight and jammed his hands in the pockets.

He felt something inside the left one. Alexei drew out a pair of half-moon spectacles in tortoiseshell frames.

He regarded the glasses, brows cocked in puzzlement. In the pouring rain, with death and madness all around, they looked like an alien artifact. Something from another world where people sat by the hearth, a pot of tea at one elbow and a clock on the mantle ticking away the idle hours.

He carefully set the glasses on the doormat.

Then he put his head down and continued on.

Bodies littered the roundabout at Sherwood Park. All Kvens. He picked up a sword. Eyed the heavy Wolf cloaks, but decided not to take one. It could get him killed if he was mistaken for one of them.

It wasn't long after that Alice gave an excited bark. She arrowed ahead. Alexei followed her glowing paw prints into the park. He saw Natalya waving her arms. Spassov's bulk next to her, his stubbled face split in a wide grin. They were with dozens of the Nants, including Miles Rycroft, but also men and women in gray. Unmarked who'd come out of their homes to make a stand with the knights.

They embraced, clapping shoulders and laughing. Rycroft had dried blood on his face, but he was still standing.

"Did you see the other Markhounds?" he said, eying Alice fondly. "They saved our bacon. It was a bloody miracle!"

"Rademacher is dead," Alexei said. "I found my brother. He's with Bishop Zeigler."

He briefly related what Morvana had told him.

"Thank the Saints Kasia is alive," Natalya said slowly. "But Balaur is coming here? And she means to kill him?"

"I have faith in her," he said. "But they'll need our help. We must get to the Arx."

Rycroft nodded and called together the motley band. "Oi!" he shouted. "We're taking back the Arx! Who's coming with us?"

Fifty voices raised in a shout. Most of them had swords taken from the Kvens. A few wielded homemade weapons.

They assembled and started for the Arx when two green-cloaked children ran up. A boy and a girl, dark-haired. One carried a bow, the other a long dagger.

Nihilim.

For the first time in his life, Alexei felt no instinctive revulsion. They were just kids. Dangerous, certainly, but not the monsters he'd been led to believe.

The girl gave Miles Rycroft a crisp salute. They seemed to be enjoying themselves. "We saw cars," she said. "Loads of them. They just went inside the Arx."

"Balaur," Alexei muttered.

"There's a big company of Kvens, too," her brother put in. "They were headed that way." He pointed back toward the stadium.

Alexei cursed. "How many?"

"About three hundred."

Natalya eyed him with sympathy. "I say we continue to the Arx."

Rycroft nodded. "I'm truly sorry about your brother, but we have to take this chance. We go back there, we'll die. Stick with the original plan and we might make the difference."

He knew they were right, but the choice still sickened him.

"Whatever you decide," Patryk said, "I'm with you, Alyosha."

He looked back at the stadium. He knew what Misha would tell him to do.

"The Arx it is," he said.

MIKHAIL SEMYON BRYCE MUTTERED INCOHERENTLY, lost in some dark delirium. Morvana peeled a glove off and laid a hand on his brow. His forehead was hot and dry.

"Try to be quiet, Captain," she whispered.

He gave no sign of hearing.

Rain drummed against the plate glass window overlooking the stadium. Nothing moved in the dark, muddy field below. She wondered how Alexei was faring. How they were all faring.

Bryce's lips were parched with thirst. She searched the room. There was an empty bucket and four glass water bottles, also empty. Morvana put them in the bucket and went to the door, holding the crossbow in her other hand. The corridor was quiet, but also very dark.

She crept along, listening for the sound of footsteps. The prisoners who had survived would not linger here. She had never taken a human or animal life, and fervently hoped she never would, but if she did run into one of the guards, she resolved to shoot them. If she didn't, they would kill Mikhail Bryce and probably her, as well.

The guards would not live much longer anyway.

She told herself this, but she hoped she would have the courage when the time came. She still didn't understand how so many of her compatriots could have followed Luk in his madness. It disturbed her greatly.

We have not come as far as I believed, she thought. Not nearly as far.

She stumbled over something soft and nearly screamed when she saw the white fur and lolling red tongue. But the hound was dead. She stepped over it, still shaking, and found a bathroom at the end of the hall. When she turned the tap, cold water came out. She drank deeply, then filled the water bottles and put them in the bucket, filling that halfway. It felt much heavier carrying it back.

The captain was where she'd left him, sweating now. She lifted his head and poured a little water into his mouth. At first, it trickled through his beard. But then he swallowed. She gave him some more. He coughed. His eyes opened.

"You are safe now," she said.

"Where is . . . my brother?" he rasped.

"Gone to liberate the Arx." She let his head fall back and found a rag. She dipped it in the bucket and wiped his brow. "Do you want more water?"

His skin looked ashen. "Just . . . talk to me."

"About what?"

His eyes closed. "Anything."

"Yes. All right."

Talk? She cast about for something to say to this man with whom she had nothing in common. "Er, you came from Jalghuth? Light and law. That is my favorite motto. I always thought I was born in the wrong city."

Was that a faint smile?

"I have great admiration for Lezarius. He tried his best. I think you follow a good man now. The best of them all." She gazed down at him. "I am so sorry for what Rademacher did to you. It is beyond imagination."

"I . . . asked for it."

She frowned. "No, that is . . . that makes no sense."

His pupils were huge. Sublimin, she realized uneasily.

"You don't know the things I've done," he whispered.

"Yes, well, it is in the past now, *ja*? Do not tax yourself, Captain. Better you sleep. I will watch over you."

He nodded. "Water?"

She gave him some more water. "When I was a girl, my grandmother used to tell a story about three novice priests who decided to run away. They stole a raft and leapt aboard, paddling for all they were worth. Yet they could not seem to make any progress across the river.

"Paddle harder! the first one urged his fellows. Throw your backs into it! So they did, until the sweat poured down into their faces and their muscles ached from exertion."

Morvana paused to sip from one of the bottles. "No, said the second, you are doing it wrong. That is the problem! He showed them the proper way and they gathered their strength, digging in with their poles." She shrugged. "Nothing. Finally, a vestal came along. She watched them for a while, laughing to herself. What is so funny, the third priest demanded? Well, she replied, your technique is very good, and you are all strong men. But you have neglected to untie the raft!"

She mopped the captain's forehead. Saints, but he felt hot.

"You Kvens . . . like your moral lessons," he said without opening his eyes.

"Ah, but do you understand that one, hmmm?"

Bryce said nothing for a very long time. She thought he had passed out again.

"What if it is not a rope . . . but a chain and padlock? For which they have lost the key?"

She thought for a moment. "Then you jump off and swim for it."

His eyes opened. He looked saner now. "Your Grace, I—"

"Hssst!" she slapped a hand over his mouth. The bright blue eyes went wide. She pointed to the window and slowly withdrew her hand. Morvana crept over and looked down.

Hundreds of riders filled the stadium below. They wore blue Wolf cloaks. She scrambled back, heart pounding.

"We must hide," she whispered.

But where? They would surely search the entire stadium. The bathroom? Maybe if they locked themselves in a stall . . . Morvana knew it was hopeless, but she could think of nothing else. She'd expected a lone guard or two, not a whole company.

She was a tall, strong woman, but when she tried to lift Captain Bryce, her back nearly gave out.

"I can walk," he insisted.

"Don't be ridiculous. Your feet . . . . No, I will drag you."

She gripped him under the shoulders and started hauling him to the door. How long would it take them to reach the sky boxes? Two minutes? Less?

"Run," he snapped, trying to push her away. "Go!"

Morvana ignored his protests. His dark hair pressed to her cheek as she inched his bulk across the carpet and she had a moment to notice how silky it was when the rest of him was so rough—and to berate herself for utter foolishness—before the door flew open and four armored Kvens strode inside the room.

Morvana dove for the crossbow. She snatched it up and stood over the captain.

"Touch him and I will shoot you!" she said in Kven, amazed at how strong her voice sounded when she was quaking inside.

The knights exchanged a startled look and raised their palms. "What is wrong, Nuncio?" one asked. "We've had no word for days."

Morvana blinked. "Who is your Kommandant?"

"Goldmann, Your Grace."

She breathed a sigh of relief. They were the company who had been camped in the Morho. "Fetch him at once."

The knight ran off. She lowered the crossbow, but watched the others warily. "Who among you were Marked by Luk?"

Two women and a man remained. They all shook their heads. A minute later, Kommandant Goldmann hurried up. He was a smallish man, renowned for his quick intellect and kind spirit. When he swept a formal bow, Morvana nearly wept in thankfulness that not all of her compatriots had gone insane.

"We followed the hounds from camp, Your Grace," Goldmann said. "I do not understand what has happened. My orders were to wait for the council to conclude."

"Luk told you nothing else?"

"Nothing, Your Grace."

It all came clear in a flash. Luk was hedging his bets. If the assault failed, he intended to retreat with the troops in the Morho and blame it all on rogue elements. The ones he

Marked himself would be perceived as the most loyal. The ones he hand-picked to serve in the occupation. Which meant there was a good chance that none of the Kvens at the stadium now were suffering from the sickness.

But what would Goldmann do when she told him the truth?

"This man needs medical care," she said. "There must be an infirmary here."

The kommandant nodded. "It is on the ground floor. We already searched it."

"Then I will explain the situation on the way."

She didn't know how much Bryce understood of this exchange. Very little, judging by the worried look on his face.

"They are here to help," she said in Osterlish. "Will you allow them to move you?"

He nodded in surprise.

"What happened to this man?" Goldmann asked. His gaze lit on the car battery and hideous contraption attached to it. He swallowed hard.

"Rademacher tortured him," she replied. "And that is the least of it."

The kommandant looked shocked. So did his knights.

"Just wait until you hear the rest," she said.

Bryce was carried to the infirmary. It was rudimentary, intended only for minor injuries, but the company had a medic. Morvana left her tending to the captain and had a long talk with Kommandant Goldmann. By the time she was done, he looked like a man who has just been told that his sweet, doting grandfather is actually a mass murderer. He stared into space, his Marks flaring blue. But he did not attempt to deny it. He'd already seen ample evidence in the stadium that she spoke truth.

"*Ja*, I know," she said. "I felt the same."

Goldmann looked at her with hollow eyes. "This is not

what we stand for," he said angrily. "Luk has brought shame on all of us. We will follow you, Nuncio!"

She decided not to quibble over the title. "Are you sure the rest will feel the same?"

He gave her a level stare. "They follow my orders, Your Grace. And I follow yours."

She gripped his hand. "Then help to liberate this city!"

NIKOLA PACED UP and down the small cabin. Paarjini sat cross-legged on one of the built-in bunks, watching her. A lantern illuminated the planes of her dark-tanned face and chestnut hair caught up in a silver circlet. They'd changed from their soaked clothes, which hung drying on pegs.

"Would ye stop that?" Paarjini muttered. "Yer making me dizzy and the seas are rough enough already."

Nikola peered out the porthole. The lights of the Arx gleamed atop the cliff. "Something's wrong."

She could feel the shift in her stones. The receptive gems were very weak, but those with projective qualities—the ones that held red ley—simmered like soup pots at a high boil.

"A pontifex is dead," Paarjini said. "I reckon it's the Kvens." She blew out a breath. "A whole city goin' mad."

"Maybe." She rubbed her arms. "But what if it's more than that?"

"There's naught we can do about it."

"Then why did we come all this way?"

The witch sighed. "Ye heard the Mahadeva. We poked a wasps' nest. 'Tis lucky we weren't stung."

The Mahadeva had been angry that Nikola forced again, but more so at Heshima for attacking first. Only Tashtemir had escaped the tongue-lashing that followed. The witch-queen had retreated into her cabin to cast the stones again. That was hours ago.

"I'm going to speak with her," Nikola said.

"Want me to come?"

"No, I've gotten you in enough trouble."

Paarjini's gray eyes studied her. "I feel it, too," she admitted. "If I had a lick of talent for foretelling, I'd try to cast myself. Cairness could do it, but—"

"Cairness won't," Nikola finished with a sigh. "She hates Malach even more now."

"Old school, she is," Paarjini agreed. "Go then. I'll be here if ye want me."

"Thank you," Nikola said. "For everything."

Paarjini had taken her side when she told the tale of what happened in the library.

"Ah well. I suppose the bloodthirsty aingeal's grown on me." She smiled. "And ye, as well, Nikola Thorn. But watch yer step. The Mahadeva's in a fine feckle."

Captain Aemlyn had given her own quarters to the Mahadeva. Nikola groped her way along the heaving passageway to the large cabin at the stern. She rapped her knuckles on the hatch.

After a moment, it swung wide.

The Crone sat at a round table, the Mother across from her. A cloth had been spread across the table, with lines dividing it into four quadrants, each of a different color. Numbers and symbols formed the border. The Crone was tapping her fingers against the cloth with a scowl. The Maid sprawled on her belly, playing with a pile of stones on the carpet. She beckoned at Nikola to enter.

"You wish to know if the disaster we foresaw has already come to pass," she said, arranging the stones in a circle. "If we arrived too late."

Nikola nodded.

"It has not," the Mother said—yet she looked troubled. "The threads of Malach's fate shifted. Luk's death is a mere ripple in the cross-currents."

Nikola approached them, bracing a palm against the bulkhead as the deck gave a slow, stomach-churning roll. "The death of a pontifex is a *ripple?*"

"Luk played his part," the Maid carelessly. "What became of him after mattered little." Pewter eyes fixed on the stones as she sat up and started to juggle them.

"The world is a better place for it," the Mother said, "so put the Kven from your mind."

"Put him from my mind," Nikola muttered. "I just saw his headless corpse lying at Malach's feet!"

"An unpleasant sight no doubt," the Crone said impatiently. "But heed us now! The aingeal has chosen a new path. *That* is the turbulence we see." Her face was grim. "Malach will try to kill Balaur."

Nikola blinked. "Isn't that good?"

"It changes some things. Not others." She flattened her hands on the cloth. "This is called the Crossroads' Shadow. It was invented by a witch named Crowther a very long time ago. The system is useful in predicting a chain of events."

The Crone shook her head. "But it is impossible to get a clear reading. The ley is muddy this night."

Lightning flashed through the large square windows at the stern. Beyond the natural harbor, the seas were dark and foaming.

"Please," Nikola said. "If Balaur is here, it is a chance to stop him for good!"

"What is it you would have us do?" the Mother asked.

"Cast the stones again."

"We have tried a dozen times. They will fall the same as always—"

"You don't know that."

"Fine." The Crone snapped her fingers. The Maid scooped up the stones and poured them into the dicing cup. With a flick of her bony wrist, the Crone threw the stones across the cloth. They were not the usual sparkly gems, but smooth pebbles with painted glyphs.

Threads of power coiled outward like wisps of violet smoke, branching and branching again. They touched the numbers and symbols at the border. Nikola could make no sense of the pattern—foretelling was not her talent—but the Mother gave a soft gasp. The Crone sat without expression.

"Must it be so?" the Maid asked softly.

"The ley has spoken," the Crone said.

"But—"

The Mother made a quelling gesture. The Maid fell silent. "We are sorry, but it is too late to intervene now."

The pity in her voice made Nikola go cold. "Will Malach die?"

The Crone studied the pattern. "What will be, must be."

"What does that mean?" Her heart pounded. "Will you do nothing?"

"There is nothing we *can* do. Not yet."

Heat surged to her face. "So we came to Nantwich to sit idle on the ship while Balaur kills them all?"

The Mother eyed her wearily. "Leave us, Nikola. There is still much to decipher here."

"No! You can't just—"

She shrank back as the three women rounded on her, namestones blazing with light.

"Get out!" they screamed in unison.

A force pushed Nikola backward into the door. She scrambled for the knob and twisted it, tumbling into the narrow corridor. It slammed shut of its own accord.

She stood there for a moment, livid and trembling.

Think! What exactly did they say?

The Mahadeva Sahevis didn't lie outright, but she had a history of withholding the full truth.

Chosen a new path.

What will be, must be.

Too late to intervene.

It all amounted to nothing. Hashima said divination was simply a reading of what might be—not always what will be.

Yet the Maid's sorrow didn't seem feigned. Something bad was about to happen. Nikola could feel it.

Balaur. The bogeyman of her childhood. They said he sat on a throne of human bones and had mindless servants to do his bidding. Poor souls with no other desire than to follow his orders, however horrible. There were a hundred tales surrounding the pontifex of Bal Agnar. Most made Beleth's worst crimes pale in comparison.

Malach will try to kill Balaur. The Mother hadn't hedged on that part. It was the word "try" that worried Nikola the most.

If Balaur survived an attempt on his life—one by his own Nuncio—he'd be enraged.

"I will not run from this," Nikola muttered. "Not again."

Forcing was out. But she could still use regular witchcraft. She checked her stones. Half were used up from her last trip into the Arx, but she had enough left for what needed to be done. She'd paid attention when Paarjini tracked the kaldurite. She thought she could manage the spell herself.

She climbed the ladder to the deck. The sailors on watch were snug inside the pilothouse. In the heavy rain, they wouldn't see her unless she came too close. She stripped her clothes off and bundled them in her cloak. The *Wayfarer* rode up a swell, sinking into the next trough. She didn't relish swimming through the storm, but the combers were all headed for the beach.

Nikola waited for the next wave to come, timing her jump from the bow. Chill water closed over her head. She bobbed up, took her bearings, and started stroking for the shore.

Chapter Forty-Two

The broad stone corridors seemed endless. Malach strode at Kasia's side as she led him confidently through the maze.

"How did you learn this place so quickly?" he asked.

She shrugged. "I remember things after seeing them once. I don't try, it just happens." A quick glance. "It's something I was meaning to ask you about. I wondered if all nihilim have the ability."

"Not that I know of," he said.

"It's strange, isn't it?"

"Your memory?"

"My mind." She tapped her forehead. "I failed their tests, you know. The Curia says my moral compass is defective. But it seems fine to me."

He thought of Nikola. She, too, had failed. Once he'd trusted her, but she'd shown her true colors. Or maybe it was just *him* she cared nothing for.

"I think the real purpose of the tests is to create an underclass," he said. "People they can pay less and force to take the jobs no one else wants."

Kasia was silent for a while. "I felt sorry for Nikola Thorn when I first met her as a char. It could so easily have been me in her place. But I knew we were alike even then. Not just Unmarked, I mean." A frown. "She had power in her. I sensed it."

"I don't want to speak of Nikola," Malach said.

"All right. But you're not done with her yet. Or she with you."

The words cut him. Unwillingly, he stopped walking. "You saw this?"

"The first time was when Natalya made my new deck." She swallowed, obviously thinking of her friend. "The Major Arcana has twenty-two cards, laid out in a very specific order. They represent the basic archetypes and will never change, no matter what happens in a person's life. When one of these cards appears, we must pay close attention. I'd been so focused on the readings, I hadn't thought of the deck as a whole, in proper order. But looking at the sketches, I had a revelation."

She fanned the cards. "I already explained that you're The Fool. That's zero. Then comes The Mage and The High Priestess. I'm both." She regarded him seriously. "Brother and sister. Next is the Empress. I knew that I would meet her someday. That I might have already without knowing it. And I had. That night at the Arx in Novo when she came to my room."

Malach nodded. It was the same night he'd crossed the Wards.

"Just a chance encounter. But it wasn't, not really. It was the beginning of something more. When I saw Nikola again earlier, I knew she was The Empress." She held up the card.

It showed a dark-skinned woman holding a scepter, the other hand clutching a falcon to her breast. She reclined in an open field. Vines heavy with white flowers tangled around her bare feet. A lazy smile curled her full lips.

"That's her," Malach said hoarsely. "The silver tooth . . . ."

"Natalya is gifted," Kasia said. "The ley guided her hand when she painted that, Malach. They'd never met."

His gaze met hers. The hair on his neck lifted.

Kasia slipped the card back into the deck and drew another. A stern man in purple robes sat on a throne, arms upraised.

"Falke," Malach said immediately.

"The Hierophant. Keeper of dogma and tradition. He's the fifth trump. Do you see how she touches both of you? The Empress is a very strong archetype. A force to be reckoned with."

"I don't deny that," he muttered wryly. "But did you see what part she will play?"

Or how she truly feels about *me*? he thought, though he didn't voice the question.

Kasia tilted her head. "I'm afraid not. But I can tell you that she values love over power. That is an essential aspect of her nature. Her authority comes from the heart not the head, and is all the greater for it."

Malach blinked in surprise as Kasia took his hand. "I don't know what passed between you," she said. "I only suggest you don't judge her so harshly. The Empress might act impulsively at times, but there is no cruelty in her. I think she would be an ally if you allowed it." A pointed look. "And we can use more of those."

He exhaled and nodded. "So Falke is the fifth. And The Empress the third. Who is the fourth?"

"The Emperor. The Red King." Her face darkened as she drew the card. "Balaur."

Malach studied it. A deep hood shadowed his face, leaving only bloodless lips. Arcane symbols were painted in the four corners of the card. He held a ring of keys in one white hand, a sword in the other, also engraved with strange runes.

"What do they mean?" Malach asked, tearing his gaze

from the blank face. It dizzied him to look at it, as though he gazed into a bottomless chasm.

"I'm not sure," Kasia admitted.

"But your friend painted it!"

"And she was ill for a day afterwards. I directed many of the cards, but not that one."

"You should have left it out," he muttered. "Put it away."

She gathered the cards and slid them into her pocket.

"Then the deck wouldn't work," Kasia said simply. "All the Major Arcana must be represented for it to have balance."

"What if you tore it up?"

"It's just wax cardstock, Malach."

He forced a smile. "Right."

"The power comes from the ley. But *that* I can wield against him."

They resumed walking. Sweat dampened his palms. The plan would work. It had to. And if he died in the attempt . . . . Malach had no regrets. He didn't know the children Balaur stole from their homes, but when he thought of them he saw the faces of his little ones in Dur-Athaara. Of his own daughter.

Had the Mahadeva known? Malach was certain he would have made the same choice whether or not he'd worked at the creche, but the experience *had* changed him. He could still remember the perfect trust in their eyes that he would show them kindness and care. No one had ever looked at him like that before.

That parents would drown their own children . . . it stoked a rage even hotter than he'd felt for the Via Sancta. The Broken Chain of Bal Kirith stood for freedom, not barbarism.

Beleth was dead. Soon Balaur would be, too. The old guard, all gone. The mages who had grown up in the Void, as he did, would realize that they needed to build, not destroy.

A lovely dream if he could pull it off.

Kasia touched his sleeve, drawing him to a halt. She pressed a finger to her lips.

They were nearing a junction. She gestured to indicate that their destination was near. Malach crept forward on the balls of his feet and paused a meter from the corner, listening.

It was quiet for a minute. Then, a rustle of movement. A quick, rasping breath.

He glanced back to find Kasia approaching in stocking feet, shoes dangling from one hand.

Malach sniffed the air. Perditae. A pair at least. The creatures' ripe odor masked his own, but he knew how to get their attention.

Very slowly, Malach eased a sword from the scabbard at his hip. He drew the edge along the fleshy ball of his thumb, squeezing the cut so drops of blood pattered to the stone floor.

A snuffling grunt came from around the corner.

Stay back, he mouthed.

Malach had been both hunter and prey in the Void. A solitary Perditae posed little danger, but get a pack on your trail . . . . He'd once spent two days up a regnum tree before Dantarion happened along with a group of their kin and rescued him.

Some Perditae could smell human blood five kilometers away. They were strong and fast, but not very smart.

Boots pounded on stone. The stench grew thicker. He gripped the hilt with both hands.

When the first one rounded the corner, he was ready. Malach drove the blade between its ribs, yanked it free, and slit the creature's throat. Almost before it hit the ground, two more were on top of him. He ducked a dagger and pivoted away, parrying a downward blow from a thick cudgel. Malach lashed out with a boot, kicking the creature backwards.

When they saw Kasia, the Perditae howled. She stared back, gaze flinty, just the way Jessiel or Caralexa would have. A tall, muscular female lunged, lips wet with saliva. Kasia had a card ready in her hand, but only as a last resort. They'd already agreed that she should avoid using the ley in case Balaur somehow sensed it.

Malach let the monster pass him by, then thrust the blade between its shoulder blades. The third was two steps from Kasia when he crashed into it from the side. They hit the wall. A hand gripped his throat, lifting him up. Malach stabbed it twice in the chest. The creature dropped him. Kasia pulled him away from its death throes.

She hadn't even flinched.

Definitely his sister.

Malach caught his breath. He wiped the blade on one of the leather jerkins. "I guess we're in the right place."

Kasia studied the bodies with a frown. "Abyssal ley did that?" she asked. "Changed them?"

He nodded. "Partly. But their Marks came from mages who died in the war. The Void delayed the symptoms, kept it from killing them, but whenever the ley surged, they became what you see here. It's another form of Mark sickness."

"That's horrible," Kasia said, pity in her face.

Malach was so used to Perditae, he'd stopped thinking of them as human. But the memory of Tashtemir healing an injured girl in a village reminded him that not all were the same. Hundreds of them lived peacefully in Dur-Athaara. It was Balaur's fault that the jungle had grown corrupted.

But not just his. It was Beleth's fault, too.

As he stared at the pathetic creatures he'd just massacred, Malach faced a truth he had always known, deep down, but refused to accept. Beleth hadn't saved him out of compassion or love. She'd wanted a weapon against the Via Sancta. He'd been groomed for that purpose, and that purpose only.

She'd forgotten the central tenet of the Via Libertas.

Free will.

Tempting, that sublime wrath. That glorious thirst for vengeance against those who had cast the nihilim into the

Void. But it was just another form of bondage, he saw that now.

Malach followed Kasia around the corner. She stopped before a blank stone wall.

"This is it," she said. "I used one of Natalya's charcoals so I'd be certain. See?"

She pointed to a faint smudge near the bottom of the wall. It looked like all the others—but this one had a liminal doorway that led straight into Clavis's bedchamber where Balaur slept.

Thanks to the Order, Balaur was well aware of the liminal passages. That's why he'd posted the Perditae outside.

The winged cardinals were guarding the main doors to the bedchamber. Malach had already confirmed that before they entered the secret city. They were more dangerous by far, but Kasia claimed they *could* be killed.

"Cut off the head," Malach whispered, "and the body follows. Falke said that. Once their god is destroyed, the Order will scatter like fleas from a dead rat."

Kasia's face was calm. "I will burn him to ash. If his foul creations *are* inside—"

"Their power cannot touch me," Malach finished.

He hoped it was so.

She drew a card from the suit of Flames. Malach's own adrenaline was pumping now, readying his muscles to spring. He raised the sword.

Stone faded to dark mist as the doorway opened before them.

He rushed through, Kasia at his heels. The chamber was large but sparely furnished. A lamp burned on a bedside table. The bed itself was unoccupied.

Balaur sat in an armchair by the window. Rachel squirmed in his lap.

"Malach!" she cried.

He was vaguely aware of a sudden heat against his skin

that died as quickly as it came. Some part of him understood that Kasia struggled to contain an explosive gout of fire. But all he could see was Rachel's terrified face. The arms covered in arcane symbols that hugged her small body tight.

He dropped the sword.

"You neglected to tell me about your daughter," Balaur said. "She's a delightful child."

"Please," he whispered. "Don't hurt her."

Balaur stroked Rachel's cheek with a scarred nub. "I fear my new Nuncio has played me false. But now we've found each other, haven't we? I promise to take very good care of her, Malach. Such a powerful little girl. Why, with her, I won't even need an army."

"*Give her back.*" Kasia's voice rang with icy authority.

Balaur's lip curled. "Did you take me for a fool? I pried the truth from your own mind! You betrayed them both!"

"Liar! I told you nothing!" Yet her face had gone pale.

"I come and go in your Garden as I please. Your dreams are an open book to me." His gaze turned to Malach. "But you . . . I knew the instant we met that something was amiss. All your cousins I drew to me in their dreams, but yours were veiled behind a wall, with not a single chink in the defenses. So I made enquiries." Balaur laughed. "The witches unmanned you. You let them put kaldurite in your belly.

"I only made you my nuncio because you were toothless. You would hold the throne for me, but had no ability to keep it for yourself." A flicker of fury contorted his face. "But that is not all of your deceit. Not all of it! You had this child with you at Bal Agnar. You hid her from me!"

He squeezed Rachel tight, eliciting a soft cry. "Just as your cousin did with her own whelp. I scoured the Morho for them yet she eludes me still. No matter. I have the stronger of the two. And when I find Dantarion, she will regret her defiance."

Balaur bared his teeth. "Now you mean to murder me in

my sleep! But your plans have failed. So let us test this stone, Nuncio. Truly, I am curious about its properties."

He beckoned to the dim recesses of the chamber. The cardinals drifted into the circle of lamplight. Their forms were indistinct, as though the shadows clung to their deep red cloaks. One dragged Falke in its gloved hand, bloody and beaten.

"I'm sorry," he mumbled through swollen lips. "I fought them with all I had. Saints, forgive me."

A ribbon of darkness unfurled, coiling around Malach's foot.

He was intimately familiar with pain.

The dull, bone-scraping pain of the Wards. The sharp sting of Dr. Fithen's scalpel.

But those things paled in comparison to the agony that sank its claws into him now. His fingers dug furrows in the carpet. His life spilled out, draining away into nothingness.

He dimly saw Kasia raise a card. Then she was gone, swallowed up by a square of darkness. It looked like one of the vertical shafts at the Pit, a black well leading down and down.

The hole sealed itself, and he was alone with his agony.

Chapter Forty-Three

A flicker of violet light at her feet was the only warning. The trapdoor opened an instant later and Kasia fell straight through it. She landed badly, twisting her ankle.

Wind tore at her hair. Rain soaked her dress.

She gasped and rolled to one side, teeth gritted. Through tears of pain, she saw dark waves in the distance and a landscape of tiled roofs.

The liminal door had opened atop a parapet of the Pontifex's Palace. A low, crenellated stone wall enclosed the ramparts. Her stomach churned when she saw the drop beyond. She'd been a hair's breadth from falling to the bailey below.

Kasia pushed sodden hair from her face, peering through the downpour. Oh saints, Malach! And his poor daughter. *My niece.*

She had curly hair like Natalya. A beautiful little girl with her father's bold nose and sturdy build.

Balaur had known they were coming. Known everything.

Her fists balled in helpless anger. She should have killed him when she had the chance. He'd been so close when they were in the library, right across the table.

But there was no time for regrets. She could flog herself later. Someone had brought her here.

And Kasia knew who it was.

"Danziger!" she screamed. "Show yourself!"

No answer came.

Kasia tested her foot. Needling pain shot up her leg. She probed the ankle. Tender, but not broken. She hopped to the wall, leaning against it. She'd held onto her cards with a death grip when the trapdoor opened. The edges of the deck bit into her palm as she scanned the narrow walkway.

"Come get me, you coward!" she yelled. "Or are you scared?"

She inched along, every reflex taut. Square towers anchored the corners of the palace. They would have stairs leading down. She made for the closest one, trying to conceal the limp, her free hand braced against the rain-slick stone. The roof looked empty. But she sensed a watchful presence.

The deck in her hand reassured her. Seventy-eight weapons, each capable of bringing pain like he'd never known—

Kasia reared back as a dark form vaulted over the parapet in front of her. Nails scored her arm, wrenching the cards away. A vicious backhand blow and she was flying through the air. Stone rushed up to meet her. Kasia's ears buzzed. She lay there stunned, tasting the hot copper of her own blood.

She blearily lifted her head. Jule stood over her. Rain coursed down his face. High cheekbones. A square jaw. Sea-blue eyes. Yet the elegant suit fit him wrong, the shoulders tearing at the seams. And his hands . . . .

"I never wanted to kill you. Why do you fight us, Kasia?"

She scrabbled backwards. Jule advanced, the cards gripped in one hairy fist.

"You have no place with them. Look how they've treated you! Balaur offers power beyond your wildest dreams!" His eyes blazed. "Life eternal. Never to bow to anyone save for him!"

Kasia spat blood. "Do you really believe he'll keep his promises?" she said scornfully. "Look what he did to Gray!"

"*Gray.*" Jule shook his head. "He was undeserving. But we're different, you and I. Balaur knows it."

He could have finished me already, she thought. Why hasn't he?

"Let me go," she said. "You don't have to do this."

Blood poured from the deep scratches along her arm. She pressed her other hand to the wounds, trying to staunch the flow.

"And where would you run to next, Kasia? We will always find you. Once you've let him in, you can't close the door again—"

"I didn't *let* him. You did, with that damned stone!"

"It makes no difference now. He knows your secrets. Your hiding places. This stubborn resistance, it just prolongs the inevitable. He will come to you again and again, and one day you will see the truth in his words. You will give yourself willingly."

It echoed her own fears too closely.

"Shut up!" Kasia snapped. "If you mean to kill me, just do it!"

"You're angry because you know I'm right. There's no escaping destiny, Kasia. And ours is glorious! The world at our feet!"

The rampart pressed against her back. Kasia stared at him defiantly.

"Nothing you have will ever be enough, Jule. That is your nature. To covet more and more."

He laughed. "Perhaps. But I still choose the winning side. And he *will* win. With that half-blood child, no one can stand against him. Your brother is dead by now. And this city will follow him into the grave."

She eyed him with disgust. "So you mean to destroy everything? What will be left to rule?"

"Not everything. There is a task yet to complete. Then we will possess the ley itself and all the power of creation that stems from it." His voice trembled with hunger. "I speak of godhead, Kasia! A new race! Will you be master or slave?"

A gust of icy wind lifted her hair. "If what you say is true, then there will only be one master, Jule. And you will be in chains like the rest of us!"

His mouth twisted. "So be it."

A hand reached for her throat. The long nails dug into her flesh as he lifted her up until her feet dangled above the ground.

"I offered you a final chance."

Kasia gasped for air as his grip tightened. Her gaze fell on the cards in his other hand. Too far to reach.

"The long night awaits with no chance of salvation." He shook her like a rag doll. "And the Black Sun will rise whether you are there to see it or not. Your name will be forgotten, while I live on—"

Her groping fingers found his wrist. It was covered in thick reddish fur like the pelt of a fox. Black motes danced before her eyes as she *pulled*, reaching for the ley through his flesh. Jule's eyes widened as blue light flared from the cards. He flinched and dropped her. The cards scattered in the wind. Kasia's hand shot out. She caught the edge of one as it blew past.

For Tessaria, she thought, pressing it to his heart. Chill radiance bathed Jule's face.

"No!" he cried.

The light burned white-hot. She saw the outline of his skull, the hollows of his eye sockets.

Kasia gave Jule a mighty shove. He toppled back against the parapet, arms wheeling. One caught her sleeve as he fell, slamming her into the stone wall, his weight dragging her down. She dug her knees in, frantically prying at his fingers. Bone snapped. Jule shrieked.

Then he was gone, plummeting into darkness.

MALACH FOUGHT to hands and knees. He crawled toward his daughter, forcing trembling limbs to obey. Tears stood in her eyes. She looked out the window, mouth tight and chin tilted to the heavens. When she looked back, he saw the question on her face.

Malach coughed weakly and shook his head.

Her power was too vast. Too terrible. She would destroy the city to save him, kill thousands of innocents, but he would never ask that of her again.

"And so you crawl like a worm at the end," Balaur said. "It suits you, Malach."

His heart grew heavy in his chest, each beat slower than the last. Rachel struggled madly, but couldn't escape Balaur's grip.

"Your mother was a whore, you know," Balaur said.

Malach lifted his head.

"Don't . . . you dare speak of . . . Nikola," he rasped.

"I wasn't talking to the girl. I was talking to *you*." Balaur peered down at him. "She told me you were mine. You and your sister both. I thought the infant was dead, but at least you held some promise." A sigh. "It seems that both of my children are a disappointment." He chucked Rachel under the chin. "But not you, little one. I will mold you into a true nihilim."

"More lies," Malach rasped.

"Rachel has my blood running through her veins. Diluted by the char, true, but that gives her the half-blood power." Balaur peered down at him with mild interest. "You should be dead. The kaldurite is having a mild deterrent effect. But not enough to save you. Only to prolong the agony——"

Balaur roared in pain as Rachel sank her teeth into his arm. His face contorted in rage.

"You little beast!" He shook her hard. Malach managed to curl a hand around Balaur's foot. Balaur kicked him away.

A terrible scream from behind. Malach sank to the carpet. And in that place, at the threshold of death, he glimpsed the ley again. Saw Dmitry Falke's Raven Mark erupt with crimson light.

The Pontifex of Novostopol drew himself up. Malach realized that he'd never been broken, not even close. He was their greatest general. The most feared man in the Eastern Curia. And while he might despise abyssal ley, he had the power to wield it.

The cardinals stumbled back under the sudden onslaught. The black tendrils that snared Malach's body shrank away, sizzling, like cobwebs touched by flame. His body was still ice cold, but the remorseless devouring of his soul ceased.

The red ley was *life* in its purest, most unrestrained form. Chaotic, evolutionary, dangerous. It poured from Falke in throbbing bursts like an open vein.

"Run!" he screamed at Rachel. "Run, child!"

Malach shook his head, past and present blurring together.

Run, boy! Run!

Dark wings unfurled. One buffeted Falke, knocking him aside.

Balaur's eyes were swirling blue holes. The runes along his arms lit up. Rachel bit him again, a frenzied mouse fighting the hawk's clutches. His lips pulled back in a silent snarl.

Malach's hand closed around the sword he'd dropped. He lifted it an inch, muscles quivering. It felt like cast iron.

The cardinals were gathering to strike back. Smoke drifted from their robes where abyssal ley warred with whatever foul substance they were made of. But they held black swords that repelled the lamplight. Ley flowed from Falke's palms as the swords lifted in unison.

"No!" Balaur shouted.

The door burst open. A tall, gaunt figure loomed in the frame. It wore white robes, drenched in blood. It had no head.

The cardinals paused, swords raised. Balaur blinked in astonishment.

Then the arms rose—each Marked with a running Wolf—and Malach realized that Luk was carrying his own head around. The eyes gleamed with fury. The mouth lolled open.

"Nice try, motherfucker," the pontifex said.

It looked like someone working a hand puppet. The jaws opened and closed with each syllable, but the rubbery lips didn't quite match the words.

I am losing my mind, Malach thought, as Luk hurled his head at Balaur.

The world turned to flame. A bone-chilling screech came from the cardinals. One thrashed on the ground. Its frenzied flapping only made the inferno worse. The death ley coiling around him vanished. So did Headless Luk.

Nikola stood there, radiant and terrible.

The second cardinal sprang for the window. Her hand rose. Another gout of fire burst from her palm.

Balaur roared as Rachel broke free. Malach gripped his sword with both hands. Somehow, he gained his feet. The sudden fear in Balaur's face gave him strength.

"Wait!" he screamed. "You cannot kill me! I am your—"

Malach swung the blade with everything he had. Balaur's head flew across the chamber, rolling to a stop at Falke's feet. The mouth was open, the eyes glazed, but Malach thought he saw malevolent light in them still.

"Burn him!" Malach shouted.

One of the cardinals was already charred to ash. The other reeled across the chamber, beating at its flaming robes.

"Move!" Nikola snapped at Falke.

He stumbled out of the way as she shot another jet of flame at Balaur's gaping head. The hair caught. The skin peeled away in blackening strips. Yet the body in the chair still twitched, scarred fingers jerking spasmodically.

Nikola strode past, mouth twisted in revulsion. She clutched a huge diamond. The white robe erupted. Malach crawled to Rachel and swept her into his arms. She clung to him, sobbing. Through a curtain of fire, he watched Balaur's robe turn to ash. The Marks beneath caught and those strange runes were consumed, one by one. The whole chair was burning now. The heavy curtains were alight where the cardinal slumped lifeless against them.

Acrid smoke filled his lungs. Nikola slung an arm beneath his shoulders and helped him rise, Rachel between them.

"You came back," he said, coughing weakly.

Nikola met his eyes. "Of course I did."

Valdrian and Jess stood in the doorway, blades red with the blood of more Perditae guards outside the chamber. They surveyed the scene with grim approval.

"Let it burn," Malach said wearily, as Falke limped over.

Together, they walked out and shut the door.

Chapter Forty-Four

Kasia limped down the winding stairs from the tower. She searched the rain-swept bailey below the parapet.

Jule Danziger wasn't there.

"You've got to be *kidding* me," she muttered.

The wind had strewn her cards far and wide. She spotted one under a bush and went to retrieve it, keeping a sharp eye on the skies above. He must have shifted into something else. Maybe something with wings.

Kasia snatched the card up just as a strong gust nearly blew it away again.

The Lovers.

The woman had long dark hair. The man's face was in shadow, but she knew it was Alexei. A Mark of two flaming towers was etched on his back.

Kasia turned to the gates. Lights burned in the guard-house. Morvana had left hours ago, but she saw no sign of the prisoners from the stadium. Was the ley telling her to go there herself? In her current mood, she'd have no trouble unleashing a tidal wave of abyssal ley against the Kvens.

But her ankle throbbed with each step. And Malach had

been left alone with Balaur. Saints, the child! They needed her, too.

She stood for a moment, torn. Go back to the palace or—

Her nose wrinkled. The wind carried a faint stench. Rotting meat and spoiled milk. Kasia turned.

If she hadn't been standing downwind, they would have caught her. The six Perditae made no sound as they crept across the slick cobblestones. Rain coursed down pale arms stitched with Marks out of nightmare. They gripped short swords in their hands. Their eyes were slitted horizontally like goats, shining yellow in the darkness.

"Come closer," she said with a smile, pulling abyssal ley through the card. "That's it. Come on."

The leader sniffed the air. Blood still dripped down her arm where Jule's claws had raked her. They fanned out in a semicircle, slowing.

The creatures were not like the alchemists. Would the red ley even slow them down? Their Marks fed on it.

Kasia backed toward the portcullis, teeth gritting against the pain in her ankle. The leader sniffed again and grunted, making a hand signal to the others. They moved with a loping gait, slightly bent over as though they were more accustomed to moving on all fours. One darted forward. She raised the card, releasing the red and pulling on the blue instead. It flared brightly. The Perditae flinched and shuffled back.

But they were closing in. From the ravenous way they eyed her, the creatures would not give up easily.

More grunts and hand signals. Two spread out to flank her and come up from behind.

She was almost at the guardhouse.

Kasia held onto the blue ley, sweeping the card before her like a blade. They didn't like it, yet it didn't seem to harm them—and they were starting to realize it. She could never manage so many at once if they decided to rush her. Kasia turned and staggered for the gatehouse. The action seemed to trip a wire of predatory bloodlust for the Perditae howled in unison and gave chase.

She hit the door and pounded on it. There was no answer from within. Kasia ducked a slashing blade. Hands grabbed at her dress. She somehow jerked free and slithered away. The portcullis was to her left. Four Perditae blocked the way back across the bailey. The nearest one snapped its teeth. She jerked back and her bad foot hit a patch of mud. She slipped and hit the ground hard. Instinct made her pull on the liminal ley. The ley of chance and luck.

No shimmering violet doorway opened for her, but a real one did. Two Kvens spilled out of the gatehouse. They looked around wildly, blinking in the rain. Mindless with hunger now, the Perditae attacked the warm bodies in front of them. Kasia scrambled to her feet. She hopped away from the melee as more guards stumbled out. They were all waxen and sweating, without helms. One wore nothing at all. He stood with eyes shut tight and face tipped to the heavens, drinking in the rain with parched lips.

Well, she thought. Now I've gone and done it.

A knight stared at her with an expression of horrified disgust. He shouted something in Kven and charged, catching her around the waist and slamming her into the portcullis. One hand gripped her throat while the other pried the card from her fingers.

"Monstros," he growled. "Abscheulich!"

He seemed to look right through her, blue eyes wide and terrified. Kasia struggled to break free. He pinned her against the iron lattice. Then the man's eyes rolled back in his head. He slumped to the ground. The Mistress of Chars stood there with a heavy rolling pin in her hand.

"We must get to the winch!" she shouted.

Kasia looked around. Women in gray were running from the palace, mops and brooms in their hands. Some of the Kvens milled in confusion. Others made a stand, but the women were fighting for home and freedom. They picked up swords from those who'd fallen, wielding them clumsily but with fierce determination.

"You are hurt," the Mistress exclaimed, eyeing her bloody arm.

"It's not too bad. Let's go!"

Kasia gripped her shoulder as they pushed against the tide, reaching the gatehouse. A Kven stood at the first winch, muttering to himself. Lucie Moss marched up and prodded him in the chest with the rolling pin. He slunk off, gaze darting around as if he followed the progress of a buzzing fly. Together, they cranked the winch that operated the pulleys. The first portcullis lifted.

Kasia limped back to the door. More Kvens had arrived in the bailey, these on horseback. Not all looked mad and she saw a char fall to one of their blades.

"We must hurry!" she called to Lucie. "They're coming from across the Arx!"

The battle spilled into the open tunnel. Judging from the screams, the Kvens were trapping their foes against the second portcullis.

The found the second winch and started to crank. It jammed after two turns.

"One, two . . . *three!*" Lucie cried.

They threw their backs into it, but the winch wouldn't budge. Kasia examined the mechanism. There must be a kink in the chain somewhere, though she couldn't see it. The chains disappeared into a hole in the wall.

"Hold it!" she screamed at Lucie Moss and another char who had joined them. The women nodded grimly, muscles straining as they gripped the great cog of the winch.

Kasia went back outside. Through the chaos, she saw her card lying half-covered with mud. She dodged a Kven on horseback who nearly trampled it and snatched up the card.

Through the blackness of the tunnel, she saw faces pressed against the iron grille.

From the other side.

It had lifted just enough for some of them to wiggle through. Her heart lifted.

She delved into the rich torrent of abyssal ley running at her feet. Poured all her fury into an urgent command. The heavy chains set into grooves on either side of the portcullis trembled. The kink loosened.

"Now!" she cried.

Lucie and the other woman leaned hard on the winch. The portcullis rose all the way. The Kvens inside the tunnel wheeled around and tried to retreat. They were swiftly overwhelmed. Riderless horses galloped from the tunnel, fleeing back into the Arx. The prisoners from the stadium forced their way through into the bailey.

Kasia stood in their midst, ragged, cheering people streaming past on either side, searching each face as it passed. Where were they? Her smile faltered. Where—

Her gaze fixed on a man in a gray coat, his arm slung around a young woman who walked with a limp. A tall, broad-shouldered priest strode at their side.

Kasia ran forward, laughing and crying at the same time.

Alexei looked up. Their eyes met. Stark relief painted his face. Natalya gave a hoot. The next moments were a crush of bodies as they all embraced each other. Alexei lifted her off her feet, his arms tight around her. He finally let go and saw her arm. "You're bleeding!"

"Never mind that. Where's Misha?"

"I had to leave him at the stadium. He was hurt."

"Badly?"

"He'll make it. He's with Morvana Zeigler."

Yet he didn't look as happy as she thought he'd be. "So she came!"

"With Markhounds." He looked around and pointed at

two short figures in green cloaks. One was unleashing a flurry of arrows at the fleeing Kvens. The other fought with a long dagger. "And them. Malach's cousins."

"Sydonie and Tristhus," Kasia said.

"And your plan?" Natalya gazed at her intently. "It worked?"

"I don't know." She briefly explained what had happened. "We must get to the palace."

"I'll find Rycroft," Patryk said. He hefted a sword from one of the fallen Kvens in the tunnel. "Looks like they're already storming the main entrance."

"I'll go with you," Natalya said. She embraced Kasia again, tears standing in her eyes. "Girl, never thought I'd see you again." Her gaze fixed over Kasia's shoulder. "Oh, shit."

A company of armored Kvens trotted through the portcullis. They just kept coming and coming. Two hundred at least, riding in good order, lances set at precisely the same angle.

Lucie Moss ran from the gatehouse and stepped into their path.

She'd picked up her rolling pin. Now she shook it at their kommandant, who rode in the van.

"Go home!" she said in ringing tones. "Your Reverend Father is dead!"

Alexei and Patryk ran to stand behind her, their faces grim. Kasia put her arm around Natalya. Clinging together, they managed to limp over.

The kommandant reined up and slid from the saddle.

He was a small man, not much bigger than Lucie Moss. To Kasia's surprise, he bowed before the char. When he rose, his face was lined with sorrow.

"My name is Goldmann, Mistress. We ask permission to enter the Arx and contain the traitors who followed Luk. We were sent by Bishop Morvana Zeigler, Supreme Servant of the

Ley, Living Exemplar of the Five Virtues, and Protector of Kvengard."

Kasia inhaled sharply. Those were the titles given to a pontifex.

Lucie Moss regarded him. "None of you were Marked by Luk?"

"Not one, Mistress. We knew nothing of what transpired here. He left us in the Morho. We follow Her Grace now."

Kasia turned to the palace. Smoke poured from a window on the upper story. She broke away from the group and headed for the plaza as fast as her twisted ankle allowed. Alexei caught up to her in four strides.

"That's the Pontifex's bedchamber!" she said, pulse thudding hard.

The crowd gathered before the palace parted as an old man came leaping down the wide stairs. He gave a cackle of laughter, dancing a little jig in the puddles that soaked the ground.

Kasia frowned. His face was different, but she knew this man. The wiry graying hair against a nut-brown complexion. And the white robes. Could it be?

"He is dead!" Lezarius cried, waving his arms. "Balaur is dead at the hands of his Nuncio!"

———

A DRIZZLY DAWN broke over Nantwich the next morning. A joint force of Kvens and Nants hunted the last of Luk's mad knights, aided by packs of Markhounds. Most had reached the stage where they simply lay in the streets, shivering. Kommandant Goldmann took charge of the last, bearing them out to the camp in the Morho where they were given cots and blankets and last rites.

Despite the evils they had done, no one objected to this display of compassion. It was in keeping with the *Meliora*.

People huddled around their radios, following instructions from the Arx to stay inside. Telephone service had been restored, but the curfew remained in effect.

That was the state of the city proper. The one of shops and pubs and schools, and doors with knobs you opened with a twist of the hand.

In the liminal city, the undercity, another search was taking place, also led by the hounds.

It ended at the Lethe Club.

There, the Order of the Black Sun in Nantwich lay in final sleep. Some reclined on velvet couches, dressed in their finest, crystal goblets clutched in stiff fingers. Others were found in rows on the crimson carpet, eyes wide and staring, lips crusted black where the poison had touched.

Kasia prowled through the rooms, Alexei moving silently at her side, blade in hand.

She paused to examine each face, then moved on with a small shake of the head.

More than two hundred altogether. Jule Danziger was not among them.

"Cowards," Miles Rycroft said when they found him in the antechamber. "They took the easy way out."

A dozen knights were moving through the rooms with cans of kerosene, dousing the bodies.

"Not too easy, I hope," Alexei muttered, though whatever they'd swallowed had left their expressions serene. No doubt it was laced with a heavy narcotic. He almost wished he believed in hell.

But that was a place, he thought darkly, reserved for the living.

"I can't believe that bastard got away again," Kasia said, jaw tight.

"Where can he possibly go?" Alexei replied. "If he fled into the Morho, he won't last long."

"I'm not so sure of that. I think he'd be right at home in the jungle."

Her gaze fell on a large man with short white-blond hair who lay entangled with an older woman in a glittering cocktail dress. "That was the Danzigers' gardener."

Her pupils dilated. Alexei actually saw it happen. A dark blossoming of rage.

"Hanne is out there, too. Jule told me."

Kasia strode over and knelt down. She grabbed the man's lapels, shaking him. Rigor mortis had already passed and the body flopped limply, head rolling. "Where are they?" she snapped. "Where are your masters?"

Rycroft blinked in surprise. Alexei dropped to one knee. "Kasia! He's dead. Please. Stop."

A tendril of hair shook loose. She blew it from her face. "Fucker," she growled, shoving the body away.

He caught Rycroft's eye. They listened to the staccato rhythm of heels stalking away.

"I don't blame her," Rycroft said. "Go on. We'll burn the lot."

ALEXEI CAUGHT up with Kasia halfway down the broad stone corridor. She'd sunk to the ground, face buried in Alice's coat. The dog sat on her haunches, tongue lolling.

He'd done the same many times when he wanted nothing but wordless companionship.

"I can hear her heart beating," Kasia said softly. "So fast."

"Twice as fast as ours. That's why she's so warm."

She rubbed the deep chest and sat up, leaning back against the wall. "It won't be over for me until Danziger is dead."

"I know."

Kasia turned to him. "Is that how you feel about Malach?"

"I never wanted him dead."

But it was a lie. Alexei wanted him dead *before* he'd Marked his brother. Now their lives were entwined.

"But you hate him."

"Do you really want to do this now?"

She shook her head. "No. Never mind. I want to feel the sun on my face. That's what I want."

He smiled. "Then let's give it to you."

It was still overcast when they emerged through the liminal door by the bailey, but when Alexei spotted Natalya and Spassov at the archery butts, he steered Kasia in their direction, careful of her wounded arm. A night packed in ice had reduced the swelling on her ankle, but how she managed in those shoes, he had no idea.

"I don't think I can stand Natalya's brazen cheerfulness right now," she muttered.

"No," he said. "It's exactly what you need. Not to be alone. Because you aren't, Kasia."

Her face softened as she looked at him. "I know that."

"Then let's see what those miscreants are up to."

The bandage bulging underneath Natalya's faux snakeskin leggings didn't seem to hinder her stance. A slender arm blurred as she drew a knife from her belt and hurled it at the target.

Spassov jammed the cigarette between his lips and applauded. "Better than a blind woman with palsy, I'll grant you that."

"Oh, please." She stalked to the target and withdrew the blade. It had struck a hair left of center. "You can barely get your piss in the bog."

Spassov laughed. "But I always remember to put the seat back down."

"What a catch." Natalya scrutinized the target. "If only you knew how to crochet, I'd marry you myself."

"I knit," Spassov said. "Does that count?"

A second knife blurred towards the target. This time it hit dead center. Natalya crowed and drew another knife. She turned to Spassov with a thoughtful expression. "Do you really knit? I could introduce you to my grandmother. You might be a little old for her, but—"

The banter broke off as she spotted Kasia and Alexei. Natalya hobbled up and hugged them both. "Just in time," she said in a low, serious voice. "Spassov was saying the crudest things about Babushka Galya—"

"The one who died nine years ago?" Kasia wondered.

"Ooooh, you liar," Spassov said, ambling over. "Promises, promises." He studied Kasia's face and sobered up. "What is it?"

"The Order are all dead. Mass suicide."

A puzzled look. "And that's not good *because* . . .?"

"Jule Danziger wasn't among the corpses."

"Shit," Natalya muttered. Her knuckles went white around the blade.

"They're burning the bodies," Alexei said. "Any happy news to share?"

"Nothing on Clavis yet," Spassov said. "But Morvana has the Kvens well in hand. The ones not Marked by Luk were just following his orders." He scrubbed a hand across his shorn scalp. "Just soldiers, you know? Poor bastards. They've been sent back to Kvengard. From what I hear, most seemed glad for it."

Natalya sheathed the blade in her belt. She glanced at Kasia. "Here's an interesting development. Guess who's patrolling six of the districts?"

"Tell me," Kasia replied with a faint smile.

"Militias of Unmarked. They put up the fiercest resistance, you know. And they can't use the ley so they're untouched by the abyssal taint." A wry laugh. "They've gone from being the least trusted to the *only* ones people can trust. Shit's gonna change. Not just here, I hope. Everywhere."

"There's still the problem of Bal Agnar," Spassov remarked, lighting another cigarette.

"Really, Patryk?" Alexei muttered, snatching it away and grinding it under his boot heel. "How about you breathe actual air for a few minutes?"

"I'm making up for lost time," he grumbled.

"In what? Your quest for lung cancer?"

"That's what I said." Natalya shot him a look.

Outnumbered, Spassov hunched his shoulders. "As I was *saying*, the war isn't over."

"No, but we made a good start," Natalya replied. "I plan to return to Novo once the roads are open. What about you?"

He shrugged. "I hear Archbishop Kireyev died in the starfall. I guess I'll be getting a new boss now."

Natalya snorted. "After what Karolo did, I imagine Falke will be planning a major shake-up when he returns to the Arx."

"What's left of it," Alexei said.

Kasia had told them the truth. That it was Malach's daughter who caused the damage.

Alexei wasn't sure who to blame for the disaster. He knew all too well how deceitful and conniving Falke could be. He'd failed to learn his lesson with Dr. Ferran Massot. Stealing children was despicable, regardless of who the parents happened to be.

If it had been anyone else who'd dropped on the Arx like a hammer to take back his daughter. . . well, Alexei would have felt some degree of sympathy.

But he still loathed Malach with every fiber of his being. One good deed didn't erase the ocean of wrongs he'd committed. He knew Kasia didn't see it quite that way. They'd avoided the issue so far, but it lodged between them like a sharp stone.

"I know you're not coming back," Spassov said to Alexei. "Kasia?"

She shook her head. "I don't know. I want to plan a proper memorial for Tess. But whether or not I'd stay afterwards. . . I'm not sure. It depends on a lot of things."

She didn't look at him, but Alexei knew she was thinking of Mikhail.

He'd been moved to the infirmary at the Arx. The doctors said he'd be walking again in a week or so. Alexei had left him playing chess with Lezarius, who spent most of his time at Misha's bedside. The two of them enjoyed a warmth and closeness Alexei envied.

It made sense. They'd been through various hells together and survived. Lezarius understood his brother in ways Alexei never could. His faith was unflagging.

It made Alexei feel guilty for the dark fears that plagued him.

But he didn't trust Mikhail. Especially not after what he'd seen at the stadium.

Was it his own hatred for Malach bleeding through? Or was he right? Would his brother slowly get worse and worse, until one day Alexei no longer recognized him? Just like last time?

Mikhail refused to discuss it anymore. He was obviously weary of Alexei's constant concern—one reason he preferred the company of Lezarius, who acted like the Nightmark didn't even exist.

Which led to the conclusion Alexei had resisted for so many years.

Was it time to walk away?

It's what his father always told him to do. *Begged* him to do.

Just pretend his brother was dead and get on with life.

It was tempting. But then the memories would flood him.

The whispered conversations under a blanket late at night when their mother was dying and their father could hardly bear to be in the room with her for more than five minutes. After the lights went out, Alexei would sneak into his brother's room. Misha would tell him what she ate that day and the jokes she cracked. He always acted like she was getting better, even though they both knew deep down she wouldn't.

Misha had been the one who administered the complicated regimen of pills. Fed her and sat with her. He read books, mostly legal thrillers. Alexei's most vivid recollections from that time were of tiptoeing past the sickroom door and hearing his brother's voice. Funny how the cadence of a person reading aloud is immediately discernible from someone just talking. The measured tone of the words. The lack of hesitation.

Sometimes he would sit outside and listen through the crack. He didn't follow much of the plots, but he liked to listen anyway. It buried the seed of terror in his heart. The knowledge that everything around him was slowly disintegrating and there was nothing at all he could do to stop it.

She smoked to the bitter end. Every now and then, a long pause would come as Misha lit a cigarette for her. The crisp *snick* of a lighter snapping shut still made Alexei think of his mother, the carpet under his bare feet, and the sweet smell of tobacco drifting through the crack.

Mikhail had watched the cancer eat her up, piece by piece, without a word of blame or self-pity. When she finally died, he never walled her memory away like their father did. He spoke of her often, telling the old stories again and again so his younger brother didn't forget.

Misha was ten when she was first diagnosed. Twelve when she passed.

Alexei, who turned nine the day after his mother's funeral, already worshipped the ground his brother walked on. But those two years taught him something about love. About sticking around when no one else wants to. Not closing your eyes to ugliness and pain. Mikhail had borne the brunt of it alone, but he made Alexei feel like he was there, too, a part of caring for her, when in reality he'd only seen her for half an hour or so a day.

The final irony was that everyone seemed to view Alexei as their mother's favorite. The one who took after her the most. A mind that couldn't stop running the angles. Top of his law school class.

Just like your mother, they said.

But he knew it was Mikhail who'd inherited her generosity of spirit.

When his brother grew older, he transferred that ferocious loyalty to the Church. And look where it had gotten him. If their situations were reversed, Alexei knew what Misha would do.

He watched Natalya hurl several knives in quick succession. Dimly heard raucous cheers as they hit the target in a tight cluster.

No, walking away was not an option.

Alexei listened to Patryk and Natalya's good-natured teasing with half an ear. He could feel the undertow of the past tugging at his feet. Feel the water rising in a black tide. The sutras preached mindfulness and sometimes it worked. On good days, he found a measure of quiet in meditation. But those occasions had grown rare of late. It was as if a spring ratcheted tight inside him, unspooling worries in a never-ending thread. He wished he could just break the mechanism. Smash it with a hammer like Kasia had smashed Balaur's charred skull—

A warm hand closed around his. "Care to walk with me?" she asked.

He blinked, surprised to see it was late afternoon already. "Yes."

They waved a goodbye. Natalya had talked Spassov into

standing sideways in front of the target with an unlit cigarette in his mouth.

"Now that's trust," Kasia remarked.

"They're peas in a pod," Alexei said. "I think Spassov found his female half."

She cast him a surmising glance. "Something going on there? I never thought so. And we've spent the last four months together."

"Not like that. But they take nothing seriously. And everything. If that makes any sense."

"Perfect sense."

They both paused to watch Natalya wind up. Spassov squeezed his eyes shut. "Watch the naughty bits," he said between clenched teeth.

Natalya smiled. "They don't stick out that much. Trust me, you're safe."

The knife hissed through the air. It neatly snapped the cigarette in half. Patryk sagged against the target, clutching his chest.

"Never again," he vowed.

"Once more."

"No—"

"I'll buy you a pack at the commissary."

"Still no."

"And a pint."

"Two pints?"

Alexei turned to Kasia as the negotiations grew more heated. "Where are we going?" he asked.

A playful look. "Oh, I don't know. Did you sleep last night?"

"Like the dead," he said with a slow grin.

That much was true. By the time he'd seen Mikhail carried into the infirmary, his needle was deep in the red. He'd dragged a chair to his brother's bedside and propped it against the wall. Alexei preferred to sleep in chairs anyway. It was the best rest he'd gotten in weeks.

"Would you like to see my new room?"

He pretended to think about it. "Any skulls?"

"Not one."

"Then yes. Saints, yes."

There actually *was* a cure for maudlin moods, he reflected, as they hurried through a fresh drizzle. Clearly, Kasia was of like mind. Her new rooms were one of the guest houses at the Arx. A tiny cottage near the kennels. He wondered if Alice had gone there. She'd disappeared after a cursory sniff of Natalya's boots.

There was a large, handsome hound from Kvengard with a notched ear he'd seen her running with on several occasions. Now he wondered what he'd do with a litter of Markpups. They chewed anything that hit the floor.

This minor concern evaporated when they got inside and closed the door. He itched to pull her into his arms, but her expression was serious as she peeled off her short jacket and sat down on the fold-out bed. "Come here, Bryce."

Alexei approached and sat down next to her.

"I just want to be clear," Kasia said, her brows furrowing. "It's a peculiar situation we find ourselves in. You already know all the knotty details, so I won't rehash them. But I think that since we've already managed to overcome a number of obstacles, we should persevere."

He suppressed a smile. "I agree."

She drew a deep breath. "Good. I have given it much thought. We are supremely unsuitable for each other in some ways, but most are no fault of our own. They should therefore be dismissed from consideration." Her chin lifted. "In the ways that matter, we are very compatible."

He couldn't help tweaking her. "What are those?"

Kasia opened her mouth, then closed it again. She reached into her pocket. He knew she gripped the cards. Was she about to give him a reading? If so, by all the Saints and Martyrs, let it be one that pleased her.

"I love you," she said, searching his face. "The thought of losing you again makes me deeply unhappy. So I hope we can work together to—"

The rest was lost as he leaned in and kissed her, dizzy with joy. "I love you, too, Kasia Novak," he whispered in her ear. "More than life itself."

She laughed at his tickling breath. "Stop!"

"So yes, we should work most diligently to overcome—"

The words died as Kasia stood and hoisted the dress over her head. Alexei drank in the lines of her body. The slight crease where stockings met silken skin.

"Most diligently," she muttered, sinking down in his lap. "Without rest—"

"If it kills the both of us," he finished, tumbling back to the bed.

Kasia covered him in kisses and for a time, the world melted away as they energetically strove to reconcile their differences. The shadows were lengthening when she rolled to her side to face him, dark hair fanned across his chest.

"I'll help your brother if I can," she said. "But he must be willing."

"What about Malach? Are you sure he can't remove the Mark?"

"I'll ask him. If he can't, I'll try myself." Her gaze turned inward. "The ley works differently with cards. It interacts with basic archetypes. Most of the time these archetypes never change, but on very rare occasions they do. Your brother used to be The Mage, inverted. It represented what Malach had done to him. But after he saved Lezarius, he became the Knight of Storms. A one-eyed card revealing his dual nature."

She frowned in thought. "If I could somehow change his archetype again, it might affect the Nightmark. Remove it or render it harmless. But I've never attempted such a thing. I'm not sure it's possible."

"But it did change once."

"The ley changed it. Not I."

"No one knows about the Mark. Only Spassov and Natalya. Lezarius, of course." He paused. "And your brother."

He was getting used to saying it now.

"He's still sleeping it off," she said. "The death ley nearly finished him."

Alexei made a noncommittal noise.

"I know you hate him. I would too, if I were you."

"But you don't." The words were out before he could rethink them.

"I won't lie. I certainly don't love him like a sibling, but I no longer feel hatred. More of a neutral sensation. I . . . I'm sorry."

"Don't be." He frowned. "It's not my business how you feel. And my grudges are not yours."

"But they are, aren't they? If I love you?"

"It doesn't have to work like that," he said gently. "Unless you plan on donning a red robe and moving to Bal Kirith, I can live with whatever choice you make."

"No chance of that." She waved a hand mysteriously. "I am Katarzynka, cartomancer and fortune-teller extraordinaire. A fancy cape might be in order, but no clerical garments for me, thank you."

"Hmmmm. Can you tell me what I'll be doing in thirty seconds?" he wondered, stroking her thigh.

"The path is clear!" She laughed. He liked the breathless edge to it. "But oh . . . I did not foresee *that*, though the ley commands you to continue . . . ."

Chapter Forty-Five

Malach slept like the dead.

He woke in a soft bed, morning sun streaming through the windows. Not his own apartments. These had peacocks painted on the walls. Rachel curled up next to him. One thumb was tucked into her mouth. The tiny Raven was half-hidden by her shoulder, but he could see the tip of a beak, the sweep of a wing.

He shifted and her eyes opened. She gazed at him with that solemn expression she had. He feared to say anything. Then she smiled. "You woke up."

He touched her strip of curly hair. "It's tangled."

"Will you fix it?"

"Yes." He pulled her to his chest, felt the small heart beating against his own. "I'll fix everything."

He felt weak as tap water, but he was alive. The kaldurite had saved him after all.

"Have you seen Nikola?" he asked.

"She brought me. I waited, but you didn't wake up. Guess I fell asleep, too."

"You weren't hurt?"

She was quiet for a long time. "The pontifex tried to Mark me. He got mad when it didn't work."

Malach pulled back to study her face. "What happened?"

She touched the Raven. "It wouldn't let the red ley come inside."

A vise around his chest loosened. "I'm glad."

"Is he dead?"

"I think so."

"I want to go home now," Rachel said softly.

Home. The word was supposed to conjure feelings of safety. Belonging and small comforts. Malach had never known any of those things, but he wanted them all for her.

"Do you mean Novostopol?"

She shook her head with a puzzled frown. "I don't know where it is."

"Do you . . . do you wish I had never come to the Arx? I wouldn't blame you if you did."

She was silent again. "You came because you loved me?"

"Yes." His voice was hoarse. "More than anything."

"Then I'm glad. But I don't want to hurt anybody else."

"Never again," he vowed. "I only want you to be happy."

"It would make me happy to stay with Syd and Trist." Rachel looked up at him. "Can I?"

"Of course. We will all live together at Bal Kirith. I'll make it beautiful for you, Rachel."

"Will Nikola Thorn come, too?"

Malach hesitated. "I don't know. I'll ask her. I hope she does."

A frank look. "She is my mother?"

"Yes."

"Does she love me, too?"

"Without a doubt. She came back to save us, didn't she?" How to explain without hurting her? "But Nikola is a witch. That's not a bad thing. It makes her very powerful. But it comes with responsibilities."

"Where do witches live?"

"A place called Dur-Athaara. We'll visit someday, together. There are children I'd like you to meet."

"Brothers and sisters?" she asked hopefully.

"Not by blood. But I still care for them very much."

She seemed to accept this. "Will they like me?"

"They'll adore you. I'll tell you about them."

He prattled on about Ealish and Roseen, Lonan and Inry and Cristory. Rachel had been kept apart from other young children at the Arx and she listened intently. Talking about them made Malach realize how much he missed them all, but it wasn't the same soul-devouring ache he'd felt when he'd thought about Rachel before he found her. Did their parents ever regret giving them up?

And what did Nikola feel when she looked at their daughter? Some selfish part of him hoped she did feel anguish. It might bind her to him. Bind her to them both.

"You have a lot of Marks," Rachel said, eyeing his bare chest.

"You could have more someday, if you want them. I leave the choice to you."

Malach turned at a knock on the door. It cracked open and Nikola stuck her head through. She smiled, but there was a distance in it. "You're awake."

Rachel looked at her warily. Malach gave her a quick hug and set her on her feet.

"Can I go play now?" she asked.

"Where?"

She shrugged. "Around."

The fear was instantaneous and crushing. He shook his head, trying to keep the panic from his voice. "It's not safe, Rachel. You must stay with me."

"But I'm bored! I want my cousins!"

"I'll play a game with you," he said quickly. "Let me just speak to Nikola first, okay?"

She gave him a mutinous look and ran out to the balcony. He had a vision of her broken body on the flagstones below.

"No climbing!" Malach shouted after her.

"I won't!"

He dragged his eyes to Nikola, though they kept flicking back to the balcony.

"Is the Arx secure?" he asked.

"Searched top to bottom." A pointed look. "And everywhere in between. How do you feel?"

"Terrible." He grinned. "But it'll pass. Tell me everything."

He hoped she might come over to the bed, but Nikola sank into a chair. She wore one of those complicated witch dresses, the kind that wrapped down one arm, leaving the other bare. The serpent's eye nestled at the juncture of her collarbone. She looked thin.

Also more beautiful than any woman had a right to be.

"What about Falke?" Malach chewed a thumbnail, then thought of Rachel's thumb-sucking and forced himself to stop. "Will he try to take her back?"

Nikola gave him a level look. "After what just happened to her? Falke knows it would make him a monster."

"He never cared about that before."

"Yes, he did. But he managed to justify it to himself." She paused. "I spoke with Kasia. She told me you're her brother. That Falke spared her life."

"For his own ends."

"That's not the point. She's alive. It must be strange."

Malach laced his hands behind his head. "Strange barely scratches the surface."

Her silver tooth flashed. "I bet you're glad now I made you promise not to kill her."

He scowled. "I wasn't going to."

"Sure you weren't." She held up a hand at his irritated expression. "Well, I like her. We both oversaw the disposal of Balaur's remains. She seemed to think he might come back."

"Balaur was an alchemist. He knew all kinds of crazy shit. Where are his ashes?"

"We scrubbed the room down with buckets of lye. A few bones were left. Kasia smashed them to dust. Then we scrubbed everything again and dumped the buckets in the sea. The bastard is gone, Malach."

"Good."

"I searched Rachel for Marks. Just in case."

He wanted to be angry. The child had been through enough. But he knew it had to be done.

"There were none. I mean, no new ones."

"What about Falke?"

Nikola tilted her head. "Are you asking if I examined the Pontifex of Novostopol's naked body? Because the answer is no."

"Someone has to," Malach muttered. "He was in Balaur's custody."

"You can tell him to strip down yourself."

"I will. What about the rest of Balaur's entourage?"

"The Perditae? All dead."

A sudden realization hit him. Malach sat up. It made his head spin. "The Masdari woman!"

"Was caught trying to flee. They have her in custody."

"Who's *they*?"

"The Arx is under the control of the Nants again. And a legion of Kvens who follow Bishop Morvana Zeigler. You slept for a full day."

Malach considered this. "Where do I stand, Nikola?"

"I suppose that's to be determined. But you're not a prisoner." A pause. "You'll have to meet with them."

"All I want is Bal Kirith." His lips thinned. "And Falke had better give it to me."

She was silent for a minute, twisting the rings on her

fingers. "I told you the truth, Malach. I didn't abandon you at the Arx. The witches summoned me back." Brown eyes flashed. "And they were royally pissed. They took my name-stone and threw me in a hole for a week."

"I'm sorry."

"You should be."

He looked away. "If you had chosen any other moment to arrive unannounced, I might have listened. But your timing was poor, to say the least."

"I know," she conceded. "From what I hear about Luk, you did everyone a favor."

Malach wondered if Paarjini's offer had been real. He still didn't trust them, but he was desperate to get the ley back—and a spell was by far the easiest way to do it.

"I want the kaldurite gone, Nikola. Do you know I don't even dream anymore? It's like a barren place in my head. A black hole."

"I will ask the Mahadeva."

"She's here?"

"Her ship is still anchored offshore, but I have no idea if she's pleased with me or intends to flay me alive. I came back without her authorization."

"You defied her?" he asked in surprise.

Nikola nodded. "She saw something in the stones, Malach. She wouldn't tell me what it was, but I feared it was your death. She said your path had changed, but it made no differ-ence. She refused to intervene. So I used a spell to trace the kaldurite." A smile touched her lips. "Did you like my illusion?"

"Headless Luk?" He grinned back. "It was a nice touch. You had *me* fooled."

"I figured it would buy a few seconds of distraction."

She fell silent. Malach gathered his courage. There was so much he needed to say to her. "Nikola—"

"I will go speak to the Mahadeva." She stood up. "She owes it to you to remove the stone."

"Thank you. But I won't go out to that ship. Not a chance, you understand?"

She didn't seem surprised. "You want them to come to you?"

"A humble request. Do you think she'd agree?"

"Maybe. I think the Mahadeva wants to see you very much. Not to drag you back. But you're . . . important to her. She knows she handled you badly."

"They must come in secret. I can make arrangements." He found a pen and paper in the bedside table. Malach scribbled a number. "This goes to the main switchboard of the Arx. If you call, they'll put it through to me."

Nikola took the paper. Their fingers brushed.

"And I'm truly sorry," he said, holding her eyes. "Sorry I doubted you—"

"That's the funny thing." There was sadness in her voice. "Because I never doubted you, Malach."

She was gone before he could respond.

Malach stared at the door. Nikola's eyes had changed. A full witch now.

It wasn't the drab gray they'd forced her to wear as a char. The irises were a bright, metallic hue like polished steel. It suited her.

He turned to the balcony, unnerved by the sudden silence. He couldn't see his daughter.

"Rachel?" he called, pulse thumping.

A moment of unbridled terror. Then she galloped into the room.

She was at the far end, he realized. A blind spot.

"I saw pigeons! Will you play with me now?"

He cast about for something that didn't require standing up. A dim memory stirred of his own father. He must have been very young, only three or so. Kasia had not yet been born. A patchwork quilt and the steady drip of rain at an open window. The humid, *alive* smell of the jungle.

"I know a game," he said. "It's called Counterpane. Are you ready?"

She nodded eagerly. He patted the bed. "Come up here."

Malach shook out the blanket, then drew it up over his knees and folded it into hills and valleys. He patted his bent knees. "These are the mountains. That's the town down there. And the lake. Do you see it?"

She nodded and walked her fingers up his leg to the top of his knee.

"Who's that?" he asked.

"An explorer. She just planted a flag. She's also the pontifex."

"Ah. That means she gets to name everything. What shall we call the mountain?"

Rachel thought for a moment. "Skytop."

"Good one." He walked his fingers up her chubby arm.

Rachel giggled. "That tickles."

Malach dug into her armpit. "What's inside this dark cave? I think there might be treasure—"

She wheezed, breathless. "No treasure in there—"

"I can feel it." He frowned seriously and found her ribs. "Gold bullion. The dragon must have stashed it . . . ."

He trailed off as her young cousins crowded through the door. Syd leapt on his chest, knocking him back to the bed. She planted a moist kiss on his forehead.

"We freed the prisoners! Will you give us Marks now? Really vicious ones?"

He fended her off, laughing. "Yes. Now go away."

Syd interpreted this as an invitation to start jumping on the bed.

"No!" Rachel wailed. "You're ruining Counterpane!"

Syd kept jumping. Rachel was winding up for another

howl when Tristhus tugged her from the bed. "Round and round!" he yelled.

The children clung to each other, spinning until they finally collapsed to the floor with peals of laughter.

"Let's play mages and leeches," Syd suggested, knocking over the lamp on her way down from the bed.

"Wait!" Malach grabbed her arm. "Where?"

"Just outside." She tried to pull her arm away. "In the hall!"

He licked his lips, torn between the desire for some peace and a deep reluctance to let them out of his sight.

Rachel stared at him pleadingly. "Please, Malach. Please let us!"

He couldn't keep his daughter confined forever. She'd end up hating him again. And Nikola had promised that the Arx was secure.

"Okay, but—"

They darted away before he could reel off the long list of stipulations. Malach swore under his breath.

"Stay inside the palace!" he yelled as they scampered out the door in a swirl of green cloaks. "Will they listen?" he muttered. "Probably not. Which means I need to get it together."

He made his way to the door on watery legs and clung to the frame until a rosy-cheeked char bustled past.

"Might I trouble someone for hot bathwater?" he asked. "And food?"

"Oh! Yes, er . . . ." She seemed uncertain of his proper title.

He was no longer Nuncio. Nor was he a civilian.

"Cardinal Malach," he said with a benevolent smile.

He would give not a centimeter of ground. If Falke was pontifex again then Malach was a senior member of the Church-in-exile and they would do well to remember it.

She bobbed a curtsy. "Yes, Your Eminence."

He limped back to bed, already scheming for whatever advantage he could extract in the negotiations to come. For if he indulged in thoughts of Nikola Thorn, Malach knew he would surely end up getting blind drunk again.

THE MISTRESS OF CHARS herself returned with two helpers. They carried trays of hot bread and poached eggs, apple tarts and garlicky greens.

"Cardinal!" she said with a beaming smile. "You look awful."

"Thank you, Mistress." He managed a bow. "And you are as radiant as ever."

She chuckled. "I will see a tub is brought." She cast a stern look at the helpers. "Make sure the towels are warm. And light a fire in the hearth."

Malach watched them do her bidding. "Has nothing changed?"

"What do you mean?"

"I mean this division between Marked and Unmarked."

She gave him a small smile. "Not overnight, Cardinal. Those in power never cede it willingly. But we are organizing. There will be a union of chars. If they fail to meet our demands, we will go on strike. See how they like washing their own robes." She shrugged. "Perhaps other Unmarked will follow our lead."

He regarded her with admiration. "They should make you Pontifex."

"Not while the Reverend Mother still lives," she replied with a frown. "She will return."

"Is there no word?"

"Nothing," she admitted. "A conclave elected Cardinal Gerrault as the voice of the Western Curia for now."

"Gerrault, eh? Was she held at the stadium?"

The Mistress nodded.

"She won't like me much, then."

"They blame the Kvens. I think you will find her a decent woman." She plumped the pillows. "I suggested that the mage wing of the palace be left alone until you woke. No knights, no clergy. That is how we manage visiting delegations from the other cities. Gerrault agreed."

"Thank you."

She sniffed. "I posted chars at the entrances to ensure you were not disturbed. We will see she keeps her word. Now eat, Cardinal." She patted his cheek. "You are skin and bone."

Malach was devouring a forkful of eggs when Valdrian arrived with Jessiel and Caralexa. It gladdened his heart to see them. Lexa had put something in her narrow strip of lilac hair to make it stand straight up. It looked like the crest of an exotic bird.

"We must leave while they still allow it," she said after they'd exchanged greetings. "Are you fit to ride?"

"How many of us are left?"

"A dozen," Valdrian replied, glancing uneasily at the door. "Some departed for Bal Agnar to carry the news. They were not stopped."

"But you stayed?"

She exchanged a look with Jess. "We follow you, Malach. There is no choice now."

"Who do you think Balaur left in charge?"

"One of his old cronies, no doubt. But others will come to you once they learn Balaur is dead."

Malach nodded. "That's our bargaining power. Falke might concede Bal Kirith if we agree to a truce."

"And if he doesn't?"

"He will."

In truth, Malach was uncertain. But it was his last hope.

"How can we trust them?" Jess wondered. "They're still our enemies!"

"I know. But the alternative is an unending conflict. And I trust those knights who defected to Balaur even less than I trust Falke. You saw the camp. They're practically Perditae! They'll be eating each other in another month, if they aren't already."

Jessiel gave a grudging nod. The others did, too.

"Balaur was an evil creature," Malach continued. "I think he did corrupt the ley in the Morho. But now that he's gone, it will eventually return to normal. We have a chance to build something new! Not the Via Sancta but our own vision of freedom."

Caralexa laughed. "What do you call this utopia, Malach?"

He thought for a moment. "The Via Aperta."

"The Open Road?" Valdrian muttered. "Well, sign me up. But the matter needs to be resolved." He rubbed the stump of his severed hand. "They could turn on us at any moment."

"We aren't defenseless," Jessiel said. "But I agree with Valdrian. I wish to be gone. If not to Bal Kirith, then into the Morho. The forest will shelter us until we can gather the rest of our kin."

Malach promised to arrange a meeting, but he felt exhausted.

"Have you seen my daughter?"

Valdrian nodded. "Digging in the flowerbeds."

"Where?"

He pointed to the window. The three children were squatting in the dirt. Rachel looked up and gave a merry wave. Black earth caked her fingernails.

"What are you doing?" Malach called down.

"Looking for moles!"

"*They're* the moles," Jess muttered, peering at the wreckage of the garden below.

Rachel was in her own little world, methodically uprooting plants and clawing through the dirt. The older pair argued about the rules of some game they'd invented. It went on and on, haggling over every conceivable eventuality. The game itself was beside the point. What mattered was the *rules*.

Kids, he'd noticed, were obsessed with the notion of fairness. It didn't matter if they were nihilim or human. Nothing drove them crazier than some perceived injustice. At the creche, he'd spent the majority of his time settling disputes that usually started with a wail of *"No fair!"*

Then you grew up and realized the whole system was rigged.

"Go down and keep an eye on them, will you?" he asked Jess.

She arched a brow. "Why?"

It was a miracle any of them had survived to adulthood.

"Because I'm asking you to."

She sighed. "You go, Lexa."

"Why me?"

"You're good with kids."

She laughed. "We both know *that's* not true."

"I'll do it," Valdrian offered.

Their heads swiveled his way. "What?" He shrugged. "I like them."

"Great." Jessiel bounded to the door. "I'm hungry."

"I'm not," Caralexa said.

"So? Come with me. There's cake left. And wine."

"Don't feel like it."

Malach closed his eyes. Yes, it was better that Valdrian watched the children.

And speaking of fairness, if he didn't get rid of the kaldurite so he could give them the promised Marks, there would be a horrific tantrum, swiftly followed by retaliation. Just the thought made him want to go back to bed.

"I'm taking my bath now," Malach announced.

"I'll scrub your back," Lexa said, waggling her eyebrows.

He gave her a wan smile. "I doubt I'd be up to your standards."

"I'll lower them." She grinned. "Substantially."

"Not today."

Or ever.

Malach realized with a frisson of horror that he felt no attraction for her. Or any other woman. His drunken pass at Kasia was nothing but a pathetic attempt to distract himself from Nikola—who clearly had no plans for him herself.

Which left his prospects looking dim indeed.

Caralexa covered a yawn. "Okay." She frowned. "You know, I am a little hungry."

Malach extracted a promise from Valdrian to keep the children in view at all times. After they left, he sank into the hot bath and soaked for a while. Then he crawled naked into bed and promptly fell asleep. The sun was setting when he woke. He ate the last apple tart and washed it down with a glass of water.

He needed to organize a meeting with Falke. Negotiate terms.

Malach wandered out to the balcony, eyes still gritty. He stretched and was rewarded with a satisfying crack from his left shoulder. Then he looked down, hoping to catch a glimpse of his daughter.

A crowd packed the bailey below. Women in gray stood next to priests and knights in Crossed Keys tabards. They all stared up at him. One of the knights drew his sword and waved it in the air.

A mob aiming to lynch Balaur's former regent?

"*Shit,*" he mouthed.

Malach wondered if they'd let him get dressed first. He was scanning the grounds for a hastily erected gallows when a roar went up. It echoed against the walls of the palace. The cheering rose to a fevered pitch. A few people tossed flowers at him.

Malach plucked a daisy from the balustrade and tucked it behind his ear. He gave the crowd a hesitant wave, glad the wall reached his waist.

"Rumors spread that you killed both Luk and Balaur," an amused voice said behind him. "They wanted to see the mage who did it for themselves."

He whipped around. The door stood wide. Kasia perched on the edge of the bed, ankles crossed. She wore a high-necked dress with dagged sleeves and heels that could put someone's eye out.

"You might have warned me," he muttered. "You could also turn your back."

He didn't like the way she studied his Marks. As if she *saw* things. Malach came inside and hastily wrapped a damp towel around his hips.

"We're kin," Kasia said without embarrassment.

"True enough." He thought of his cousin Dantarion. "But it's still. . . ."

"Improper?" She laughed. "Saints, is that a blush?"

He scowled to cover his confusion. "No."

He would never tell her what Balaur had said about their mother. Lies, for certain. A final twist of the knife. He just hoped Rachel hadn't been listening.

"I came to tell you you're wanted," Kasia said.

"By whom?"

She ticked them off on her fingers. "Falke. Lezarius. Morvana Zeigler. Some cardinal or other."

So they were already planning their strategy.

"Gerrault?"

She nodded. "That's the one."

"Where's my robe?"

"Burned."

"Then I'll need a new one."

She tossed a bundle at him. He shook out a plain brown cassock. Malach eyed it with disdain. "I'm not wearing this."

"It's all I could find," she said blandly.

"I want red." He cast it aside. "Something the color of fresh blood."

Kasia regarded him. "Are you so eager to provoke them, Malach?"

"Its not a provocation. Merely a statement."

She examined her nails. Somehow, the woman had found time to paint them purple.

"Check my old apartments," he pressed. "I know I have a spare robe."

"Do I look like an errand girl? Get it yourself."

"Fine. Where is this meeting?"

"The library where we waited for Balaur." Her face softened. "I will tell you this, Malach. There's no love lost between Falke and Lezarius. They stare at each other like strange cats in a sack. And Morvana Zeigler is a principled woman. She will support you if you can manage not to mortally offend her."

He nodded slowly. "I'll try."

"I have no interest in seeing more people die pointlessly. Do what you can to avert bloodshed."

"That's my intention. Will you be there?"

She smiled. "I wasn't invited."

"Do you want to come?"

"I don't belong there." A heel tapped restlessly against the carpet. "Malach?"

"Yes?"

"If you didn't have the kaldurite, could you remove Mikhail Bryce's Nightmark?"

"No. It can't be undone." He hesitated. "Not by me."

She leaned forward. "Who then?"

He'd meant to keep the idea to himself, but the desperate look in her eyes got to him.

"You can't say anything. Not until I know if they'll do it."

"I promise," Kasia said quickly.

"The witches can remove Marks. I don't know how, but they can. I intend to ask the Mahadeva Sahevis, she's their queen, to remove Rachel's."

"Does your daughter want that?"

"I haven't asked her yet. But I will."

"Would they do it for Mikhail?"

"He's here?"

"He came with Lezarius. It's affected him badly, Malach." Her expression turned grim. Accusing. "Does that happen to everyone you've Marked?"

"Not all. It just loosens inhibitions. But if he's someone who suffered from a conflict in the mind, perhaps one that was deeply hidden, it might cause . . . fractures. Everyone is different, Kasia."

"Do this for me. Please."

"Why do you care about Mikhail Bryce?"

She was silent.

"Ah. The brother."

"Don't," she snapped.

"I suppose I shouldn't judge your poor choices." He laughed bitterly. "I share the same affliction."

Kasia seemed on the verge of a tart reply but stopped herself. "Will you do it?"

"Nikola went to meet with the delegation from Dur-Athaara. If they agree to come, I'll ask." He gave her a pointed look. "But not a word beforehand."

She nodded reluctantly. "I've agreed to examine the Mark myself. There might be something I can do."

Malach finger-combed his hair in the mirror above the dressing table. No time for a shave, but he wouldn't ask for a delay. Best to get it over with.

Kasia stood. "Good luck, Malach."

He caught her eye in the mirror. "You think I'll need it?"

She laughed and walked out the door.

Chapter Forty-Six

Malach crept through the palace in his towel, gaze fixed straight ahead. His old rooms were just as he'd left them. A bottle on the floor. Whiskey fumes lingering in the air. The smell made his stomach twist.

He dressed and made his way to the third-floor library. A pair of wooden-faced knights stood outside. They parted to let him pass, staring straight ahead.

A fire crackled in the grate. A large round table sat in the center of the room. Dmitry Falke occupied a chair facing the door, sporting an impressive black eye. His palms lay flat on the table. The gold pontifical ring shone on the third finger of his right hand. Malach imagined him on hands and knees sifting through Balaur's ashes for it.

Their eyes locked. *Oh, yes,* Malach thought with relish. Plenty of bad blood still. He would have felt disappointed if it had been otherwise.

On the opposite side was the Pontifex of Jalghuth. White-haired and dark-skinned, older then Falke but more youthful in a way Malach couldn't quite fix. It was the eyes, he decided. Clear green and undulled by Falke's weary cynicism.

Bishop Morvana Zeigler sat between them. She had classic

Kven looks, blond and fair. A small diamond glinted from a piercing in her nose. She was half the age of the two men but had a presence that commanded equal attention.

The fourth chair was occupied by an elderly woman in purple who must be Cardinal Gerrault from Nantwich. Owlish eyes peered at him through thick glasses. She had steel gray hair in a fringe.

The fifth chair held Lucie Moss, the Mistress of Chars. She gave Malach a quick wink.

Bishop Zeigler rose to her feet and gestured to an empty seat between Lezarius and the cardinal. "Thank you for coming," she said. "I will chair this council, if that is agreeable."

"It is," Malach said, sitting down.

She peered at a piece of paper, then pushed it aside. "Let us skip over the agenda items of no relevance to you and move directly to the question of how to proceed." She eyed him frankly. "Where is your allegiance now, Malach?"

"Not to us, I can promise you that," Falke muttered.

"Us?" Lezarius echoed. "There is no *us*, Dmitry."

Zeigler cleared her throat. "Perhaps we should let the cardinal answer."

Lezarius fell silent. Falke stared sullenly out the window.

"My allegiance," Malach replied, "is to my people. Which is why I demand that Falke's knights withdraw from Bal Kirith immediately."

The pontifex's heavy-lidded gaze swung his way. "You are in no position to demand anything."

"I think he is," Lucie Moss said, leaning forward. "He killed your worst enemy, didn't he? Rousted the Kvens?" A quick glance at Zeigler. "The bad ones, I mean. No offense, Your Grace."

"None taken. What do you you say, Lezarius?"

The Pontifex of Jalguth eyed Malach coldly. "You Marked someone dear to me. Mikhail Bryce. I would be more inclined to grant concessions if you rectified the matter."

"It can't be removed." Malach glanced at Falke. "Just as my daughter cannot be rid of the Raven he gave her."

"That was to protect her," Falke said.

"At least Bryce consented to it," Malach shot back. "We struck a bargain. One of a voluntary nature. When he tried to kill me, I turned the Mark in self-defense. Don't you remember?"

Falke flushed and fell silent. He knew what role he'd played. Falke was as much to blame as Malach—more so even. But the others didn't seem to notice his discomfort.

"The Mark is no longer inverted," Lezarius said. "But Mikhail wishes to be rid of it."

"I propose that we set the matter of both Marks aside for the purposes of this council," Malach said. "There might be a way to appease all parties, but I'm not at liberty to discuss it here."

"When?" Lezarius demanded.

"Tomorrow," Malach said. "I promise."

The pontifex gave him a hard look, then nodded. "Tomorrow," he agreed. "As to the disposition of Bal Kirith, I would support a return to mage control under certain conditions."

Malach folded his hands. This was the meat of it. "What are they?"

Lezarius held up a finger. "No slavery."

"Done," Malach said immediately.

"No indentured servitude."

"Agreed."

"No child labor. No forced conscription into military service. Freedom of movement for all citizens. A code of civil rights and rule of law."

"Who devises the code? We will not be a satellite state of the Via Sancta."

"This is ridiculous," Falke muttered. "They will sink into anarchy within days—"

"Reverend Father," Bishop Zeigler said in her clipped accent. "You agreed to be bound by the decision reached by this council. I would ask that you refrain from interruptions with no substantive value to the negotiations."

Falke's eyes narrowed. Malach suppressed a grin.

"Would you prefer that the mages return to Bal Agnar and take up arms against us?" Lezarius asked quietly. "What of all your talk about the Last War, Dmitry? Or are you so hungry for retribution that you would throw the rest of your knights into the meat grinder?"

Falke drew a deep breath. To Malach's amazement, he looked chastened. "No, I do not want that," he said. "And I am willing to concede the city if acceptable terms are reached."

A knot between Malach's shoulders he'd been unaware of loosened. "Then let us put it all in writing. I have no objection to the points raised by Lezarius. But here are *my* terms. No military presence within a hundred kilometers of the city. Free trade with the Curia. We will need supplies to rebuild. Engineers and equipment to restore the power grid. A return of the objects looted from the Arx—"

"Can you prove the provenance?" Falke asked shrewdly.

"You know what you took," Malach replied. "And Beleth kept extensive lists. If you haven't destroyed them, they provide a good starting point."

The cardinal from Nantwich spoke up. "I have always felt uneasy about the plundering," she said, pushing horn-rimmed spectacles up on her long nose. "The Praefators would not have approved. There are many priceless artifacts in our museums that belong to the mages. Here in the Arx, as well. If it would bring peace, I think they should be given back."

"I second that," Lucie Moss said. "And the chars know where they are."

Falke drummed gloved fingers on the table. "The relics were merely taken for safekeeping," he said. "Please record my objection to the terms *loot* and *plunder*."

"Duly noted," Morvana said dryly.

Lezarius cocked a shaggy white brow. "Jalghuth stole nothing, but I support a full inventory of ill-gotten gains by the other cities."

It was an odd thing to find the man who'd made the Void taking Malach's side, but when Lezarius was joined by Bishop Ziegler and the two Nants, Falke sourly agreed to it.

The astronomical value of the looted items made Malach's dream seem possible. Artwork, gold, tapestries, furnishings. With luck, the museums might buy some of it. Then he could use the money to get the city up and running again.

The question of Bal Agnar was complex. Malach argued that the knights there were the Curia's problem. They composed the majority of the force in the city. With Balaur dead, it was unclear what they might do. Everyone's fear was that they'd end up with hundreds of crazed Perditae roaming the Morho.

"All I can do is offer a beacon of stability to the younger mages," Malach said, addressing Falke. "You never understood the differences among us, but there's a whole generation who grew up in the Void. Stateless and fending for themselves. They've never known safety and they're hardened for it. But they are not their parents. They sold Perditae to the witches because it was the only currency they had, but they follow the Via Libertas in name only. Most barely know what it stood for, nor do they care. They just want a roof over their heads and food in their bellies."

"How will you draw them out?" Bishop Zeigler wondered.

"I'll send two of my cousins. They would be welcomed into the Arx. Obviously, they will say nothing of *who* killed Balaur, only that he is dead. Those who wish to leave can depart the city for Bal Kirith." Malach leaned back. "Then you can shell the living shit out of it if you want. I don't care. Just let me get my people out first."

Falke gazed into the middle distance, a thoughtful expression on his face. No doubt planning his next campaign. Even the mild-mannered cardinal from Nantwich was nodding. But Bishop Zeigler and Lezarius looked alarmed.

"I cannot approve wholesale slaughter," Zeigler said firmly.

"Nor I," Lezarius said.

"Of course," Falke said smoothly. "But as the mage said, that is a question for the Curia to decide among ourselves. I have no objection to an emissary as long as I'm informed when the evacuation is complete."

"Done," Malach said.

By the time he inked the final treaty, he was bleary with exhaustion. But he thought his cousins would be pleased with the outcome.

"There is one last matter to discuss," he said.

Zeigler frowned. "We have already signed, Cardinal."

"It's not to do with the treaty." He looked at Falke. "Someone must examine your Marks."

"What? Is this some kind of joke?"

"Not at all. You were alone with Balaur for an untold amount of time. Luk managed to revive a member of the Order of the Black Sun who was most definitely deceased. From what I understand, it involved extraction of the consciousness from the body. If it can be taken out, it can be put back in. To someone else, perhaps."

Outrage mottled Falke's features. "This is ridiculous!"

Malach turned to Morvana Zeigler. "Am I correct?"

"Yes." A glance at Lezarius. "You have seen the children."

He nodded. "They are a force for good. But some occupy bodies that have no pulse. So I cannot comment on the boundaries of alchemical magic."

"Magic!" Falke threw his hands up. "You're all mad."

Zeigler's brows lowered. "So you refuse?"

"Malach was in the room, too," Falke protested. "In fact, it was he who was touched by the dark ley."

"And I am more than willing to bare all." He smiled. "I'll show you mine if you show me yours."

"How do you know," Falke said tightly, "that Marks are involved? I thought we speak of alchemy."

"I don't know. And I could be wrong. But the Order all had them. We would be remiss not to look, don't you think?"

There was a lengthy pause. Lucie Moss and Cardinal Gerrault stared at them both with new apprehension.

"Not in front of him," Falke said, gaze flicking to Lezarius. "Or the ladies."

"Just you and me," Malach said cheerfully. "Right now."

"Fine. Let us put this absurdity to rest."

Morvana shuffled her papers together and stood. The others rose as well.

"We will wait in the hall," she said. "Is ten minutes adequate?"

A surly nod from Falke.

"And if one of them is not who they claim to be?" Lucie Moss wondered. "What then?"

"You'll hear a kerfuffle," Malach replied. "Feel free to storm the chamber with armed knights."

"Er, yes," Zeigler said. "I will take precautions for that eventuality."

She strode from the room with brisk Kven efficiency, followed by Lezarius and the others.

Malach and Falke faced each other across the table.

"You know I'm not Balaur," Falke said. "The very notion is ludicrous."

Malach stood and tugged the robe over his head. He started on the buttons of his trousers.

"I mean to go through with it," he said. "Though I'm sure

the sight will scar me for life."

He sat down again to kick his boots off. Falke rose and shed his own garment. Purple, since pontifical robes didn't exactly grow on trees. He wore silk boxer shorts beneath, also purple.

In short order, they were both naked. Malach squinted at the Marks on Falke's chest and thighs.

"By the devil, you're hairy," he said. "What is that? A milkmaid?"

"A Praefator," Falke responded stonily. He pointed. "What's *that*? Some dominatrix?"

"The Lady of Masks."

Falke laughed. "You've named them?"

"You don't name yours?"

His gaze slid to Malach's thigh. "No, I go by number. Saints, your mind is twisted. What is that creature?"

Malach glanced down. "The Red Warden." He turned around. "Summoning the Storm. That's just above my spectacular ass." He flexed his cheeks for emphasis. "Today for Tomorrow, right shoulder blade. Dark Mirror, lower back. Tiger in a Cage—"

An exasperated sigh. "They're all demented! How could I possibly tell if Balaur gave you one?"

"Hmmm. I suppose you can't." He strode a brief circle around Falke. "Yours are all boring enough."

Falke snatched his robe from the back of the chair. "Are we done?"

"Socks," Malach said, staring at his feet.

Falke briefly closed his eyes. He peeled his black socks off, revealing bony ankles that were bare of Marks.

"You're pretty fit for an old rook," Malach said as they got dressed. "I won't deny it."

Falke made no reply. He slammed the door on the way out.

Malach grinned. This day just kept getting better.

Chapter Forty-Seven

Nikola tossed scraps of bread to the family of ducks paddling past the *Wayfarer*. Four little yellow ducklings followed the parents, bobbing like toy boats on the ripples. The ship had moved from its hidden cove to the harbor, where it sat at anchor in the shallows.

She looked over as Heshima joined her at the rail.

"They're coming up," the witch said.

For the last day, since Nikola had returned bearing the news of Balaur's death, the Mahadeva Sahevis had retired in contemplation, refusing food or drink. They'd said nothing about her disobedience in going to the Arx alone. She had the strong feeling they had known it would happen and done nothing to prevent it. That her actions were part of the divination, not in defiance of it.

Nikola still didn't understand what exactly they had foreseen. How the ley interacted with free will remained a mystery. But the stones had settled down and Nikola felt hopeful that the meeting to come would open a door for better relations between Dur-Athaara and the continent.

"Will you return with us?" Heshima asked. "After it is done?"

Nikola met her eye. "I am *laoch* now," she said. "My loyalty is to the sisterhood of the Deir Fiuracha."

Heshima smiled. "I am glad."

She hadn't told Malach yet, but she sensed he already knew. It wasn't an easy decision. She still loved him—madly, passionately. But no matter how hard she tried, she couldn't picture herself living at Bal Kirith. The Mahadeva had said they were not meant for each other. If he took Rachel back to the creche . . . . But no, Malach would never want that now. Not when he had his own city to rebuild.

She was glad for him, but it was still a bitter pill.

Nikola pushed her heartache aside as the Maid scampered up and leaned over the rail. The Mother was not far behind, supporting the Crone on one arm. The three of them stood in silence for a moment, gazing at the harbor. A breeze caught the Crone's long white hair, lifting it from her shoulders. They wore simple gowns of forest green, embroidered at the hems in silver thread.

"It is a beautiful morning," the Maid said, tipping her head back to the sun.

Something in her voice made Nikola frown. "Are you well, Mother?"

"We are well," she replied. "We will remove the Mark and the kaldurite. It is Valmitra's will."

"I still don't like the idea of you entering the Arx," Heshima said. "The Via Sancta—"

"Is an enemy no longer, sister," the Crone replied. "This must be done. The aingeal will not come to us, so we will go to him. It is time we meet the child ourselves."

"At least allow us to escort you," Heshima said. "I would bring Torvelle and Bethen. She has made much progress on the journey."

Torvelle nodded approval. Bethen flushed and gave a shy smile.

"Yer not goin' without me," Paarjini said.

"Very well," the Crone said. "You four and Nikola, of course."

Cairness had been listening with her usual expression of irritation. "Bethen? She has no experience—"

"You are needed here," the Crone said firmly. "It is decided."

Nikola turned away to cover a scowl. She tugged Heshima aside. "Really?" she demanded. "After you assaulted his kin?"

"Only when they were about to assault *us*," Heshima replied. "But I will only use lithomancy again in defense of the Mahadeva. You have my word. So if you truly believe his intentions are honorable, you have nothing to fear from me." She glanced at Cairness and arched a brow. "Unless you prefer *her*? Because if I do not go, she will surely be named in my place."

It was no secret how much Cairness hated the "aingeals." Bringing her would spell certain disaster.

"Fine," she muttered. "But remember your oath. I cannot imagine he'd be so stupid as to provoke you. Not when he needs the Mahadeva so badly." Nikola sighed. "Of course, it is Malach we're talking about. He's not always a master of diplomacy."

"'Tis not him that concerns me," Paarjini said, wandering over. "The girl is more fearsome by far."

"She's just a kid," Nikola said. "She barely knows what she's doing."

"And tha's what concerns me," Paarjini murmured.

They all shut up as the Mahadeva beckoned them over. The three women were holding each other's hands. Spring, summer, autumn. Crescent moon, full moon, dark moon. Nikola read the rhythm of the seasons in their faces, the movement of the tides in their bodies.

A cloud covered the sun. The wind had a bitter edge. She pulled her cloak tighter, remembering the coils of a great serpent. The hissed command.

Free me, daughter.

Then the moment passed. The sun came out again, silvering their irises like polished scales.

"It has been more than three thousand years since a Mahadeva Sahevis stepped foot on the soil of the continent," the Crone said.

"We are the first," said the Mother.

The ducks reappeared at that moment, quacking just below. Hoping for more bread, no doubt. The Maid laughed in delight, darting off to follow their slow progress alongside the bow. She whispered something to herself, so soft only Nikola heard it. But the words would come back to her much later as the *Wayfarer* set sail from Nantwich harbor.

The Maid said, *"And the last."*

"I MET DANTARION, YOU KNOW."

Malach had just popped a grape into his mouth. He coughed violently. It shot past Lezarius's ear and landed on the carpet. Rachel crawled over and polished it on a sleeve. She held it up.

"You dropped your grape."

Malach smiled, slipping it into his pocket when she wasn't looking. How had he forgotten? It seemed so long ago now, but he'd been at Bal Kirith when a messenger arrived with the news that Lezarius was in Dantarion's custody.

"Er . . . how was that?" he asked, leaning forward to light Lezarius's cigarette with a taper.

They sat in matching wing chairs before the fireplace in Malach's room, a black telephone on the table between them.

Lezarius exhaled a stream of smoke. He looked pensive. "Very unpleasant at first."

Malach turned to his daughter, who was building a fort

with the couch cushions. "There's more pillows in the linen closet down the hall. And a sheet you can use for the roof."

"Okay!" She darted out the door.

"Did my cousin torture you?" Malach asked. "If so, I apologize."

"Only if you call debating her convoluted logic torture," Lezarius replied. "No, she laid not a finger on me." His face darkened. "In fact, she saved me from Falke's knights. They had my death warrant."

"Because you were Invertido."

"Falke feared I would break the Void in my madness. He sent priests to kill me at the Batavia Institute, too." Lezarius gestured with the cigarette. "That's where I picked up this bad habit. If not for Mikhail Bryce, they would have succeeded."

"I will do what I can for Bryce," Malach said. "You have my word."

A log shifted in the fire, sending a burst of embers up the chimney. The weather had turned overnight. Dead leaves skittered past the window and a fierce autumn wind bent the trees in the plaza.

"As for Dantarion," Lezarius continued, "we travelled north through the Void together to Jalghuth. She told me she carried your child." Lezarius shook his head. "But that was later. I didn't know she was pregnant when I pulled her from Lake Khotang. The ice was thinner than we realized."

"You rescued her?" Malach frowned. "But wasn't she your captor?"

Lazarius pinched the cigarette Novo-style between thumb and forefinger, drawing deeply. "I could hear her pounding from beneath the ice. It was terrible. How could I do nothing?" A slight smile. "And I knew it would confound her if I saved her life. Both mother and child survived the icy dip." A sharp look. "But you knew this already."

"The witch-queen told me I had two children in the world.

But even if she hadn't, I would never believe Dante was dead until I saw her body myself."

"She is fierce," Lezarius agreed. "And independent. She lost her taste for Balaur quickly and fled Jalghuth."

"Do you know where she went?"

"No." He looked up from the flames and met Malach's eye. "But she did something selfless before she went. She found the Reborn children and saved them from Yann Danziger. They cannot be killed except for . . . ." Lezarius trailed off. "Never mind. But that is part of the reason I support your return to Bal Kirith. Dantarion surprised me. I didn't think she had the capacity for pity. Or mercy."

"Nor did I," Malach muttered.

Rachel staggered into the room with two more pillows, dragging a huge quilt behind her. She started working on the fort again.

"No candles," Malach said sternly.

"But it's dark in there!"

"Then make a flap."

She scowled but set the candle down.

The Pontifex stretched his feet to the fire. "It's a peculiar thing, Malach. I do not miss the ley. Nor do I feel any different now that my Marks are useless. I wonder if we need them at all."

Malach stared at him. "But they're the foundation of your faith!"

"So men like Falke would say. Yet when one reads the *Meliora*, Marks are not even mentioned. The essence of the Via Sancta is simple. Try to do good. That is all." He chuckled. "Thousands of words have been written on the subject. Millions! But those four suffice. Marks are nothing but a shortcut. Worse, a panacea. They lull us into thinking we needn't do the hard work of examining our own actions."

A noise of disgust. "And look at where we are now. I spent the afternoon trying to talk the Pontifex of Novostopol out of shelling his own troops! All because their minds are sick. And why are their minds sick?"

"Sanctified Marks?" Malach ventured.

"Precisely!" He waved a hand. "Well, yours are different. They suppress nothing."

Malach had not told Lezarius that he, too was severed from the ley. "They make me feel powerful," he confessed. "But it's more than that. Like a drug. A really, *really* good one." Just saying the words made his heart beat faster. "You don't miss the power you wielded? Over the ley itself?"

"It always scared me, to be honest. I am a half-blood like your daughter." He gazed fondly at Rachel. She was humming to herself, utterly absorbed. "Our power can be a terrible thing," he said in a low voice pitched for Malach's ears only. "You must protect her from it as long as you can. And protect others—"

The telephone rang, a strident buzz. Malach pounced on it. "Hello?"

The line crackled. "Malach?"

"It's me. Where are you?"

"Um, in a public call box at the harbor. Next to Poppy's Fish & Chips."

He jotted it down. "Okay, I'm sending a car. How many witches?"

"Don't be alarmed. Me and four others." A soft laugh. "Plus the holy trinity."

"Two cars then. Sit tight. They'll be there in fifteen minutes."

"Do we have time for chips?"

He smiled. "They're open?"

"Yeah. There's already a line."

"Then get on it."

He heard muffled talk in the background. The screech of a gull. "Okay, bye."

Nikola hung up. Malach dialed another number and

handed the phone to Lezarius. He pressed it to his ear, squinting as though that would help him hear better.

"Is this the car pool?" he inquired loudly. A pause. "This is the Pontifex of Jalghuth speaking. I need two automobiles. Yes, with drivers."

Malach handed him the paper.

"The pickup location is Poppy's Fish & Chips. Uh-huh. The names of the visitors?"

Malach shook his head.

"That's confidential. But they have my personal guarantee. They are to be brought to the Arx through the Gate of Saint George. I will greet them myself." He looked at Malach. "How many visitors?"

Eight, Malach mouthed.

More than he'd bargained for, but the Mahadeva Sahevis would hardly turn up without an entourage.

"Eight," Lezarius said. "All women . . . Ah, yes, the *Invicta 72* model sounds fine." He made a confused face at Malach, who shrugged. "Thank you. Oh, and you can call this number when they arrive."

Lezarius hung up. "They're coming," he said with child-like glee. "Witches!"

"Don't get your hopes up," Malach warned. "They might say no. And my daughter gets precedence."

The pontifex looked thoughtful. "I hope their Mahadeva will speak with me. After your business is concluded, of course. This animosity between Dur-Athara and the continent has never made sense. Perhaps we can end more than one old feud, eh?"

Against his will, Malach had grown to like Lezarius. He seemed genuinely well-intentioned. They'd spoken at length after the council. Lezarius claimed he'd made the Void not to punish the mages, as Malach had always believed, but to avoid wholesale slaughter. He'd strongly opposed the shelling and subsequent occupations.

For his part, Malach explained that he only inverted Mikhail Bryce's Mark when the man tried to kill him. He'd thought he was being merciful. Had Beleth gotten her hands on Bryce, the result would have been far uglier.

Their mutual loathing of Falke cemented the new friendship.

Malach stood and paced to the window.

He'd watched Falke send letters with his pontifical seal to the Arx in Novostopol and his commanders in Bal Kirith. His cousins were pleased at the withdrawal, but they still didn't trust Falke—understandably. All were eager to put the walls of Nantwich behind them.

Malach went to the fort and sank to all fours. Rachel was sitting inside with her knees drawn to her chest. She'd obviously been listening to the telephone conversation. He looked her in the eye. "Are you ready to see your mother again?"

She nodded.

"She is coming with the witch-queen. Don't let them intimidate you. The Crone is not really blind. You'll like the Maid, though she pinches sometimes. The Mother is the nicest of the bunch, but never forget it is one woman you speak to." He searched her face. "Are you sure this is what you want?"

Another nod, firmer this time.

"Good. Now I will tell you the truth that Falke withheld from you. There is danger in sanctified Marks. If the one who gives them dies, his or her Marked will die also."

"Like the Kvens?" she asked shrewdly.

"Like the Kvens," he agreed.

"Why didn't you tell me before?"

"Because I wanted to know your heart first."

"So you wouldn't really have killed Falke? The night you took me away?"

How quick she was. "No, I wouldn't have."

She frowned. "You lied to me."

There was no denying it. "Yes."

"Will you kill him once it's gone?"

"No. That I swear to you."

Rachel bit her lip.

"But Falke is not young," Malach said gently. "One day, he will die of old age. Long before your time, Rachel. And I could not bear to lose you. So you understand now. The Raven is more than a symbol. It ties your lives together. I want you to be free."

"I understand." She touched the Raven on her neck. "Can I still use the ley after it's gone?"

He shook his head. "Not unless you choose to take my Mark someday."

And no one else's, he thought fiercely.

Relief crossed her features. "Then no one could make me hurt people."

He felt a stab of guilt. "That won't happen again. But yes, without a Mark, you cannot touch the ley at all."

"I like talking to the sky." She sounded philosophical. "But I worry about what I might do by accident. This is better."

"Then we are agreed."

She crawled out. He stood and took her hand with a laugh. "If all goes well, you will lose the ley and I will gain it again."

She gazed up at him. "Use it wisely, Malach."

Chapter Forty-Eight

An hour later, Malach and Rachel walked together through an adjoining door into the sitting room he had chosen for the occasion. It was neither the grandest nor the smallest in the palace. Just a comfortable chamber with a few books and old, lived-in furnishings, but it had a nice view of the sea and was warmed by the afternoon sun.

Nikola stood by the window. She caught both their eyes and smiled. The Mahadeva occupied a couch, the Crone on one end, the Mother on the other, and the Maid between, legs swinging. Four other witches stood against the wall. Malach recognized Heshima and Paarjini, who gave him a saucy grin. The third was tall and cool, the last very young. She stared at Rachel with wide eyes.

"Mahadeva," he said with a bow. "Thank you for agreeing to come."

"Malach." The Mother smiled at him. "We are pleased to see you well." Her gaze drifted to Rachel. "And this is your daughter."

Rachel curtsied as he'd told her to.

"I imagine you want the stone removed first," the Mother said.

The temptation to be rid of the kaldurite immediately was strong, but if anything happened, he didn't want them using the power against him. He'd rather live with the stone than lose the chance to free his daughter.

"First the Mark," he said stiffly.

She arched a brow. "All right." The Mother held out a hand. "Come here, child. Let us see it."

Rachel clutched his hand. She shot him an anxious look.

"It's all right," Malach said. "We'll go together."

They walked to the Mahadeva, sweat gluing their palms together. The Maid skulked over, leaning in close to examine the Mark.

"She is so young," the Crone said after a moment. "It should be a simple matter to disentangle it from her mind."

She extended a gnarled hand. Rachel shied away. The white cauls seemed to frighten her.

"I cannot remove it without touching you, child," she said gently. "Do you cede this Mark of your own free will?"

A quick, determined nod.

"That is the only thing that matters. Come, it will take but a moment."

Rachel cast Malach a quick look. She dropped his hand and stepped closer, allowing the Crone to rest a hand on her shoulder. Rings glittered on every finger. Gold and silver, tin and copper, each with a different gemstone.

"Yes, I feel it," the Crone said with a toothless smile—the first Malach had ever seen on that stern, regal face. "Now I will use the ley to draw it out."

Rachel's eyes tightened. Malach studied the Raven on her neck. Would it disappear gradually or all in an instant? The Crone gave nothing away, so he cast a sneaky glance at the Mother. Her face was serene, focused. Malach's eyes flicked to the Maid.

Her mouth was a hard slash. The hands at her sides knotted into fists. He felt a touch of worry. The others were practiced at hiding their emotions, but the Maid wore hers plainly. Was the Mark giving them trouble?

Rachel moaned, a low animal sound. Beads of sweat trickled from her hairline.

"What's happening?" Malach demanded.

None of them answered. He turned to Nikola. "What are they doing?"

She shook her head, brows knitting in a frown.

Rachel went rigid. Her eyes rolled in the sockets. "No," she croaked.

"Stop!" Malach said. "Can't you see it isn't working?"

The Crone's hand gripped Rachel's shoulder tight. His daughter's fingers twitched spasmodically. She gazed into those blind eyes with an expression of horror. He reached for the Mahadeva and felt strong hands on his shirt, jerking him back.

"This wasn't what you agreed!" Nikola said heatedly. "Let him go!"

Paarjini and Heshima released him but stood to block his path.

"Mother," he growled, appealing to the one who always had the kindest heart. "I trusted you!"

"We are trying to save her, Malach," the Mother replied calmly, never taking her gaze from Rachel. "Your daughter is here, but she is not alone."

The hair on his neck stood up. "No," he muttered. "No, no, no."

The Crone gasped. Her fingers dug furrows in the tender flesh of Rachel's shoulder. "He fights back."

He.

Malach felt sick. It couldn't be. He would have known—

"They're hurting me!" Rachel screamed. "Make it stop! *Please*, daddy!"

How he had longed to hear that word on her lips.

Always, she called him Malach.

Falke had been *papa*.

His panicked eyes found Nikola, but she simply gazed at their child with stunned disbelief.

"Let her go!" he cried. "You're wrong!"

"Balaur is a parasite." The Maid's cheeks glowed pink with anger. "He feeds on her, but she is still alive."

"Daddy!" A sob of anguish. "Help me!"

The Maid and Mother swept forward. Six hands seized Rachel's arms, jeweled rings winking in the light. She let out a wail that gouged Malach to his marrow.

"What are they doing to her, Nikola?" he asked brokenly. "What are they doing?"

"You are bound now," the Crone said. "You cannot escape us again."

Rachel's struggles ceased. Her head turned through a slow arc, staring at each incarnation of the Mahadeva Sahevis in turn. Her small chest swelled.

"*LET ME GO!*" she shrieked.

Rachel's voice. But the bottomless rage that twisted her features into a monstrous mask?

Malach stepped back, gripped by a sudden, paralyzing cold.

No.

This was not his daughter.

"WILL you let her examine it, brother?"

Misha eyed him wearily. "For what purpose?"

"She healed Spassov with the ley once. If there's even a chance, we must try."

"What does it involve?"

"A reading with her cards first."

He stared at the ceiling. "If it makes you happy, go ahead."

Alexei fetched Kasia from the corridor. She came inside and sat down on the edge of the bed. "Hey there," she said easily.

Misha eyed the cards in her hand. "You use the ley?"

"Uh-huh."

He smiled. "Lezarius was wrong about you."

"How's that?"

"He said you were harmless."

She laughed. "No, he said I was an innocent. They are two different things, I think."

Misha nodded slowly. "Do you want to see it?"

"Yes." There was no pity in her voice, which Misha seemed grateful for. He untied the hospital gown and spread it open across his chest. When she failed to gasp or react in any way, his shoulders relaxed.

"It's quite beautiful," she said with a frown. "I did not expect that."

Beautiful? Alexei covered his own vigorous disagreement.

"But all Marks are beautiful in their way," she continued. "It's a shame it troubles you so. Let us see what it means, eh? That is a good place to start." She chewed her lip. "Normally, I choose the cards. But I think I'll let you do it."

"Okay."

His brother did not believe, Alexei knew, or he wouldn't be so cavalier at having his deepest secrets exposed.

Kasia fanned the deck across the bed, face down. "Choose four," she said.

He reached for the cards and she touched his wrist. "Eyes closed."

Misha seemed to be suppressing a grin. He dutifully closed his eyes and drew four cards.

"Interesting," she said.

His brother opened his eyes. He'd laid them crosswise, each neatly atop the next.

"The path spread," she said, eyes sparkling. "Did you mean to do that?"

He frowned. "No."

"Hmmm. Let us see what they are. Turn over the first. . . Ah, The Wheel. This sets your destiny. Next? The Pole Star. A journey north, perhaps. But also that a guiding light is coming to you."

Mikhail turned over the third card. Two serpents wrapped around the bole of a tree, one red, one blue.

"Temperance," she said. "Seeking balance between the light and dark inside us. Now, the last?"

His brother drew a sharp breath as the card was revealed. Kasia seemed not to notice.

"The Chariot of Justice," she declared. "Seventh of the trumps. You know, in my old deck—the one that was destroyed by fire in the Morho—it was called the Sword of Justice. Both cards mean essentially the same thing. A devotion to truth. But Natalya made this one different. Interesting choice, *da*?"

Mikhail stared at her. "Who made this?"

"Like I said, Natalya Anderle."

Alexei sensed some undercurrent to the conversation that he wasn't privy to.

"That looks exactly like one of Bishop Zeigler's Marks," Misha said.

He touched the chariot, tracing the outline of the blind-folded woman who held the reins. She had a tiny gem in her nose, just like Morvana.

"Wait. How do you know that?" Alexei asked slowly.

Morvana's only visible Mark was the Wolf on her neck. Not even Alexei, who had known her for months, had any clue what the others were. Unlike many of the Kvens, she was always covered head to toe.

A flush rose to his brother's cheeks. "She showed them to me. Under duress."

"*What?*"

Kasia swept the cards up. "I think you know what it all means, Mikhail."

He turned to her with a look of desperation. "No, I don't!"

"It seems very clear to me. But I will let you consider it yourself." She shot Alexei a quelling look. "Now, with your permission, I will touch the Nightmark and see what can be done with it."

Misha looked too stunned to argue. He gave a brief, disconsolate nod.

She drew a glove off and laid her hand flat on his chest, the other gripping a card. There was a long, pulsing flash of blue, darkening to purple. Mikhail winced and she quickly withdrew her hand.

"I'm sorry," she said. "It is as I expected. This is not an alien thing. It is part of you. It cannot be simply torn away. I don't know what would be left, but I would never attempt it."

To Alexei's surprise, Misha patted her hand. "Thank you for trying," he said quietly. "My hopes were not high, so you haven't dashed them."

"Heed the message from the ley," she said. "The more you fight, the harder it will be for you."

His brother's face went blank. "I'll do as I must," he said.

Kasia did not look satisfied with this response, but she didn't press him.

Misha said he was tired and they left him pretending to read a book, though Alexei could see he was just staring at the page.

"Does Bishop Zeigler know about the Nightmark?" Kasia asked, when they were out in the hall.

Alexei shook his head.

"Why not?"

"It's not that I'm ashamed of him. I just don't want anyone to treat him differently, you know?"

"I understand. That's how I always felt about being Unmarked. It's viewed as a stain on the character." Her lips thinned. "Unfairly."

He rubbed his forehead, swallowing the bitterness. "Every time I think there's a chance, it falls apart. I don't know what to do, Kasia."

She hugged him, rubbing his back. He felt his muscles relax. Not for the first time, he wondered at his good luck in finding this woman. Her patience with him seemed boundless. Yet he didn't want to drag her down.

"It's my responsibility," he said heavily, holding her close. "I'll think of something. You have enough to deal with."

Kasia was quiet for a minute. "I'm not supposed to tell you this, but there's another way."

Alexei pulled back, searching her face. "What?"

"Promise you'll do as I say."

"I promise," he said instantly.

She looked around the infirmary. "Malach said the witches can remove Marks. He's asking them to get rid of Rachel's. The Raven Falke gave her. He promised to ask for Mikhail too. I'm so sorry I didn't tell you before. Malach made me swear! He was afraid of messing it up. The witches can be touchy." She blew out a breath. "This is the first solemn oath I've ever broken, Bryce."

He grinned, hardly daring to believe it. But she would never joke about such a thing. "They *remove* Marks?"

"With lithomancy. They do it with the Perditae. Which makes sense. I can't imagine they'd let them run around free if they had Nightmarks, right?"

Alexei cupped her face and kissed her.

"You're not mad?" she asked breathlessly when he finally let her go.

"I'm not mad. Saints! You already asked him to do it and he said yes!"

"The witches haven't said yes."

"Why wouldn't they?"

"No, I'm sure they will. They're here now. Listen, I'll go ask again. But you must wait outside."

"Of course. Where are they?"

"A room in the west wing." She bit her lip. "You can come, just stay out of sight until I've confirmed it. Then we can bring Misha. Or they can go to him. Whichever they prefer."

He nodded, still dumbstruck at this swift reversal from despair to hope. He cautioned himself not to count on it, but this felt different. The first evidence that a cure was real. Witches! He'd never even thought of it. But from what Kasia had told him about Nikola Thorn, they could do things with the ley he'd never dreamt of.

They hurried across the plaza and into the palace. Both were known to the guards and entered without challenge. He barely saw his surroundings, following Kasia as she made her way through the labyrinthine building. Once Mikhail was well, they would both be free to follow their hearts. The Reborn would surely be willing to have his brother return to Jalghuth. His heart brimmed with happiness. Lezarius was the pontifex Misha deserved. Pure of heart and trustworthy—unlike Dmitry Falke. If Kasia wanted to go back to Novostopol, he would gladly follow her.

Wherever she went, he would be at her side.

He was so caught up in his fantasies, it took him a moment to realize she had stopped dead, a worried frown on her face. Then he heard raised voices behind the door. A child's furious shriek—but with a horrible deeper timbre beneath. He'd never heard anything quite like it.

Kasia tried the knob.

Locked.

Something heavy thudded, like furniture toppling. More muffled yelling.

They exchanged a startled look. Alexei tore a glove off.

Then all hell broke loose inside.

Chapter Forty-Nine

It all happened in a heartbeat.

Rachel wrested free of the Mahadeva's grip. She crouched down. Nikola had the odd thought that the child meant to tie her shoe, but then she saw the flash of a knife. Three quick stabs. The Maid collapsed without a sound. Malach sank to his knees, cradling her in his arms.

Heshima lunged at Rachel, but Nikola got there first. She twisted the child's arm behind her back. A squeal of pain. The dagger clattered to the ground.

"She didn't do it!" Malach shouted. His shirt was soaked with the Maid's blood. "Don't hurt her, Nikola! Don't!"

"Let go of me, you *filthy char*," Rachel growled, jerking impotently at Nikola's grip.

"Shut up!" Nikola snarled back.

Across the chamber, the Mother helped the Crone to a chair. Weak, Nikola thought. They are growing weaker . . . .

"Get back from her," Heshima snapped. Ley blazed from the stone in her palm. "I will drive him out, but you must let go!"

Nikola stared down at the writhing child in her grasp.

"Don't hurt her!" Malach screamed, a raw plea in his face. "Please!"

"It won't hurt *her*," Heshima replied. "It's a spell of protection!" Black eyes fixed on Nikola. "But if you are touching her, you might be the next vessel when he is evicted."

Rachel gave no sign of hearing. She kicked and spat like a cornered animal.

"But how——" Nikola began.

"I can save her! Just let go!"

Malach made a grab at Heshima's hem. "Don't do it, Nikola! They'll kill her! You *know* they will!"

Nikola's eyes flicked among them. "Mahadeva! What should I do?"

The Mother's eyes were hooded, her expression one of resignation.

"Let her go," the Mother said.

Nikola nodded, breath coming in sharp pants. Malach thrust out a bloody hand. "No!"

She shoved the child away.

"A wise choice," Heshima said, fingers springing open.

The blast wave sent Nikola flying clear across the room. She struck the stone sill of a window and bounced to the floor, tasting blood. Through a haze, she saw Rachel run to Heshima. Saw Paarjini raise a hand and get knocked backwards by a burst of projective magic from Torvelle.

Light flared from the Crone's sapphire namestone, but Heshima countered the attack with a protective spell. Torvelle used a garnet to slam the Mother against the floor and pin her down.

"Hurry, Bethen," Heshima snapped at the newly minted witch.

Bethen swallowed hard and ran to join her sisters.

A string of vile curses ran through Nikola's mind, but there was no time to dwell on their treachery.

Heshima's bracelets were lighting up. Antimony and iron,

gold and brass—all projective metals. She wore them on her right wrist. Copper and lodestone—both receptive—flared at the same time on her left.

Force gathered as a box took shape around the three witches and the possessed child. Nikola rolled to a half-sitting position and dumped her pouch on the floor. Her rings were already depleted from the trips into the Arx. So were most of the projective stones. But she still had a lump of silvery black hematite. Fire element, and projective, but it also held grounding properties.

"You're not going anywhere, bitches," she mumbled.

She tried to still her mind, but her head felt swathed in wool. She had no clue what would happen if a box was disrupted. Perhaps it would create a singularity that vaporized the entire planet.

At that moment, she didn't care.

Shimmering lines of ley formed a cage around the four of them. Paarjini staggered to her feet. She unleashed a stream of bluish fire. Heshima's eyes tightened as she fought to repel it.

Malach still held the Maid in his arms, but his eyes were locked on Rachel. Horror and fury mingled on his face as the child yanked at Heshima's dress. "Hurry," she growled. "Get us out, you fool!"

Paarjini threw the sunstone away, depleted. She reached for her own namestone, a massive chunk of fool's gold set in iron and tin.

"Get out of the way!" Nikola shouted, as her own sundering spell took shape.

Paarjini glanced over her shoulder just as Bethen hit her with another spell. It tore the jeweled pin from her hair and sent her slamming into a wall of books with a sickening crunch. They spilled from the shelves, half burying her limp body.

Nikola locked eyes with Heshima. The box was fully

formed now, stretching across nearly a third of the chamber. Everything within its confines would be yanked to whatever destination they had in mind. Torvelle's icy calm contrasted with Bethen, who pressed a queasy hand to her stomach. Rachel bounced on her toes in eager anticipation.

Nikola raised her hand. The hematite blazed with power just as Malach leapt to his feet and lunged for his daughter. There was no time to scream a warning. He was almost at the razor-sharp border of the box when the door to the room shuddered in its frame. Another blow and the lock splintered. The door crashed open.

A priest stumbled into the chamber. Dark, short hair, youngish. Malach collided with him mid-step. They both went tumbling to the floor.

Nikola's grounding spell shot over their heads and struck Heshima's box.

Spiderwebs of power lanced across the cube. It wobbled and lost its shape, like the instant before a giant soap bubble pops.

Malach wrestled free of the priest's cassock.

He has no idea what's happening, Nikola realized, as the ley lines swept over him.

With an angry, crackling thump she felt through the soles of her feet, the cube snapped back into place. Heshima smiled. She didn't notice the flaw in its construction. The weakness where Nikola's attack had struck. An instant later, the box split apart.

Torvelle was standing at the juncture. She screamed as it severed a hand and part of a leg. Bethen gave a high-pitched shriek and scrambled to press against Heshima, who looked utterly shocked.

The second box was smaller. It closed around Malach and the priest, who was trying to gain his feet. Judging by the wild look in his eye, he *did* see the bars of power coursing around them both.

Pulsing brighter and brighter.

Nikola threw an arm up. Light burst through skin and tissue. She saw her own radial bone. Two overlapping claps of silent thunder, sensed only as a deep vibration in her chest. The windows exploded. Air rushed to fill the sudden vacuum. The ferrous stink of melted stone saturated her nostrils.

"Nikola Thorn?"

She blinked, an afterimage of the boxes still shimmering in the air. Her head turned blindly as hands pulled her to her feet.

"It's Kasia Novak," a low, shaken voice said. "Are you all right?"

Her face swam into focus. Nikola nodded. "Mother?" she cried. "Crone?"

"We are here," their voices replied in unison. "But not for much longer. Come quickly!"

Nikola staggered past melted stone and charred wood. Past the body of the Maid, who lay with one arm flung wide, the other folded across her chest.

Everyone else was gone except for Paarjini, who stirred weakly.

The Crone sat in a chair just beyond the line of destruction. The Mother slumped between her legs, head resting on the Crone's bony knee. She reached out a hand. Nikola clasped her fingers.

"We saw this," the Crone rasped. "Our own end, though not the rest."

She felt a surge of helpless anger. "Then why come here?"

"It was Valmitra's will."

"Was it their will that my daughter by taken by Balaur?" Nikola demanded. "And that the man I love be killed?"

"Malach is not dead. Nor is the one who went with him."

"Thank the Saints," Kasia said quietly but with intense emotion. "Thank the Saints."

"But where have they gone?"

The Mother's eyes slipped shut. Her chest rose and fell in shallow breaths. Only the Crone still held her head high. The eldest and strongest. "The Great Serpent stirs at last," she whispered.

The Mother's fingers squeezed Nikola's hand, though her eyes remained closed.

"We could not stop Balaur, but *you* will," the Crone said. "You must go after the child. Save her . . . ."

A rustle made Nikola turn. Paarjini gazed at the Mahadeva with damp eyes. "I've failed ye," she said miserably.

"Don't be foolish. If *we* did not know the sisters were corrupted, how could you? They used unnatural magic to hide their intentions from the ley." Her lips thinned. "But it will rebound upon them tenfold."

"I still canna believe it," Paarjini muttered. "I will flay Heshima's hide in strips for this! It is she who guided the others, you can be sure o'that—"

"*Listen.*" An impatient hiss. "You must go after them. But no forcing! It is too dangerous."

"Where have they gone?" Nikola asked.

"Promise me first."

She eyed what remained of Torvelle, stomach churning. "I won't force again."

"Nor will I," Paarjini said.

The Crone's breath rattled in her chest. Nikola feared it was her last, but then she raised her chin. "I cast a spell to wall Balaur away from the child. She sleeps and he cannot touch her dreams. Nor can he leave her vessel of his own volition."

"How do we drive him out?" Nikola asked. "Can it be done?"

A slow nod. "I believe so, but you will have to find the way." Her blind gaze moved past Nikola's shoulder. "The cartomancer will help. She must go with you."

Kasia Novak sank to one knee before the Crone. Her face was full of awe.

"I have seen you in the stones," the Crone said.

"And I have seen you in the cards," Kasia replied. "You are the Serpent."

A quick shake of her head. "I serve the Serpent. That is all. You have seen the city?"

Kasia nodded. "Yes, but——"

"Find it and you will find Balaur. You will do . . . what must be done."

"Are Malach and Alexei with him?"

"They . . . have taken another path." A faint smile. "I did not see that, either. Valmitra . . . always did have a sense of humor." The Crone gripped a ruby at her throat. The light within it flickered. "But they are both a part of it. The ley brought them where they need to be. Bah! I should have . . . ."

The light in the stone faded.

"Please, don't go!" Nikola clutched the Mother's limp hand. "We need you!"

The Crone's head fell back, lips slightly parted. Sounds drifted into the silence. The twitter of birds nesting on the narrow ledge beyond the window. The distant purr of a car engine. The murmur of voices passing along the pathway, rising to shouts as they found the broken glass from the windows.

Paarjini leaned forward and touched the Mahadeva's namestone. "Rest in the coils of Valmitra," she said hoarsely.

Nikola disengaged her fingers. She braced a palm against her eyelids, pushing back the hot flood of grief. There would be time for that later. Wherever Balaur had gone, he was far ahead of them now and there wasn't a moment to waste. She turned to Kasia.

"What city?" she asked. "Where have they gone?"

"Balaur showed it to me in a dream. I only caught a glimpse, but I'm afraid I haven't a clue where it is." She eyed

Nikola. "I gather that Balaur is not dead. But what did she mean, he was *walled away?*"

Nikola stared at the melted stone. "Balaur took the body of my child."

Kasia covered her mouth. She stood and paced to the window. "The Twins," she muttered. "The Emperor and the Star. It was all in the reading I gave to Malach! I'm so sorry. I should have seen this."

"We were betrayed," Nikola said. "The other witches used lithomancy to escape with her. They were in league with Balaur."

"And that flash of light?"

"They cast a powerful spell," Paarjini put in. "Malach and the other man—Alexei—were caught in the backwash."

"It's my fault," Nikola said heavily. "I broke the box in two."

"And ye saved 'em," Paarjini said firmly. "Had they been in that box with Heshima, ye can be sure she would've killed 'em both as soon as they got where they were goin'."

The door burst open. Valdrian stepped inside. The sword at his belt swept from its sheath. Paarjini reached for her pouch, but Nikola laid a hand on her arm.

"This is not our doing, Valdrian," she said calmly. "Please, let me explain."

"Where is he?"

She quickly recounted everything that had happened. His hard gaze swept the room, lingering on the witch-queen and the damage from the forcing. He swore under his breath. "I believe you," he said at last, sheathing the blade. "So Malach could be anywhere?"

"Yes," she said with a sudden realization. "But we can still find him with the kaldurite. It was never removed!"

Valdrian nodded. "Do it."

She sorted through the remaining stones and used a piece of chalcedony. The strong receptive quality would pick up echoes of Paarjini's spell. Every witch left a signature from her own mind when she used magic. It was as distinctive as their voice.

"Yer a quick study," Paarjini said with approval. "Ye only saw me do it once."

"I paid attention," Nikola said dryly. She closed her eyes and *listened.*

At first there was nothing. Fear gripped her. What if he was dead after all? But then she detected a faint resonance.

"He is to the south," she said after a long moment.

"Novostopol?" Valdrian wondered. "Or Kvengard?"

"Farther. The trail is very faint."

Paarjini frowned. "Wha's farther south than that?"

"The Masdar League!" Kasia said. "Balaur has ties with the emiratis. There was a woman with him. Jamila al-Jabban—"

"Who was taken into custody," Nikola finished grimly. "Let us pray she has not escaped, too."

"I'll find Lezarius," Kasia said. "We cannot keep this secret now."

"And I must return to the ship," Paarjini said. "The other sisters must be told—"

A small woman in gray whom Nikola recognized from her ring of keys as the Mistress of Chars stuck her head through the door. She gasped when she saw the scorch marks. Half the carpet was gone, along with every stick of furniture that had been standing on it. One armchair was sliced in half, the edges still smoldering.

Kasia hurried forward. "Mistress, you must fetch the Reverend Father Lezarius."

She drew a breath, recovering her composure. "I will, Domina Novak." She glanced at the bodies. "Do you need a physician?"

"It's too late for that. Just Lezarius."

A quick nod. "There is a woman at the gates of the Arx

demanding to see the delegation from Dur-Athaara. A captain named Aemyln. She's with Tashtemir Kelevan."

Nikola and Paarjini shared a look. "Thank you, Mistress," Nikola said. "Bring her in."

Valdrian paced up and down, rubbing the leather cap of his stump. "How did Balaur manage it?" he wondered. "Alchemy?"

"It must be," Kasia replied. "Balaur said the old body must die for the new one to be born. I think he allowed Malach to kill him. His plans were already laid."

"I saw Marks on his body when it burned," Nikola said. "But not regular ones. Runes. He worked some vile magic in that chamber."

Valdrian was silent, his expression angry and brooding. "I cannot believe I ever followed him," he said at last. "But I didn't know about his designs. None of us did."

"What will you do now?" Nikola asked.

"I don't know. I must discuss this with my cousins." He turned to her. "What will *you* do?"

"Go after them," she said without hesitation.

Valdrian met her gaze. "Malach wanted peace. It almost seemed possible." A glance at Paarjini. "Why would Balaur go to the Masdar League, witch?"

"That's wha' we aim to find out, aingeal," she replied.

He nodded. Then he swept his red cloak off and offered it to her. "For your queen."

Paarjini looked surprised. She gave him a sad smile. "I do not think she would mind. She did not hate yer kind as some do."

Valdrian helped them lay the three bodies together on the carpet. They covered the Mahadeva in his cloak, pulling it to her chins. They waited in silence after that, each lost in their own dark thoughts.

Captain Aemlyn arrived with Tashtemir and Lezarius. The two men stood in the doorway with grim faces as she dropped to one knee next to the Mahadeva, head bowed. Her uniform was torn and bloodied. At length, she lifted reddened eyes. "Who did this?"

"Balaur," Paarjini replied. "In the guise of a child."

The captain rose to her feet. "About an hour after you left, three of your sisters tried to take control of my vessel." Paarjini's glower deepened as she recited the names. Nikola didn't know any of them well.

"Cairness and Ashvi fought back and prevailed," the captain said. A quick, approving glance at Tashtemir. "It was thanks to him we had warning. The rebels are dead. And two of my crew as well."

Paarjini's face darkened. "I am shamed, captain."

Aemlyn made a weary gesture. "You are not to blame. We feared . . . ." Her gaze rested on the three faces, smooth now in death. "Well, it has already come to pass."

"Tell the sisters that Heshima and Bethen betrayed us. Torvelle, as well, but she is dead. They have gone to the Masdar League."

Aemlyn arched a brow. "The League?" she repeated, eyes narrowing.

"Will ye take us there? It was the Mahadeva's command, but I would go regardless."

"The *Wayfarer* is known in those parts. I could get us through customs without raising any alarms." Aemlyn let out a slow breath. "I will aid you in your quest for vengeance, Paarjini an dàrna."

An dàrna meant *second* in Athaaran. Nikola realized that Paarjini was next in line until a new Mahadeva Sahevis was chosen.

"Thank ye, Aemlyn," Paarjini said, gripping her forearm. "We must sail tonight. They have a head start on us."

Kasia Novak had been quietly speaking with Lezarius. Now he stepped forward, green eyes alert. "The Masdari woman remains in custody. I will have her brought to the audience chamber." His kind face was lined with sorrow. "I am very sorry, Domina Thorn. I hope we can all be allies in the next course of action."

At first, Paarjini had eyed the pontifex with wariness, but she seemed reassured by his sincerity and gentle demeanor. "Let us question her then." She turned to Aemlyn. "Go to the ship and tell my sisters what happened here. Get whatever provisions ye need for the journey."

"I will assist with that," the Mistress of Chars said. She beckoned to Captain Aemlyn and the two of them left, speaking quietly.

"I must find Jessiel and Caralexa," Valdrian said. "We'll join you at the audience chamber."

Lezarius moved aside as he strode past. Nikola did not expect Kasia to know the pontifex of Jalghuth, but she approached him with a funny little smile.

"How is your cat, Reverend Father?" she asked.

"Greylight is well," he replied. "In Jalghuth with the children."

Kasia's voice sank to a whisper, but Nikola still heard it. "I cannot believe you carried that shoebox through the Void."

"She outgrew it swiftly. I kept her in my shirt. But do you know, she played a very important role in the events to come."

"Really? Tell me."

Nikola watched them walk into the hallway together.

"What are they on about?" Paarjini wondered.

"I don't know." Nikola's fists knotted. "Heshima! Why would she do it, Paarjini? Why?"

"I canna say," Paarjini replied. "But I do remember that she wanted to take the child when we first came. I think if I had not been there, ye might've found a knife in yer back."

"The Mahadeva said they used unnatural magic to hide their intentions."

"Aye. There are spells to muddle the ley. 'Tis akin to forcing."

"Could we summon Heshima back? Like you did to me?"

"Nine sisters are needed for such a spell. And she will have taken precautions against it. Charms of protection."

"Damn."

"We can track Malach, though he's no longer with 'em so I dinna know what good that'll do. I think we must pry the truth from this Masdari." She looked at Tashtemir, who stood by the window. "Southerner!" she called. "Will ye come with us to the audience chamber? Perhaps ye can catch her in a lie. Ye might even know her."

"I will come," he replied. "Ah, the poor Cardinal. He can't get a break, can he?"

"What happened on the ship, Tash?" Nikola asked.

She was surprised that Cairness was one of the good ones. Nikola would have put her at the top of the list of potential villains.

"It was luck, really. I was in my cabin composing a poem and couldn't think of a rhyme for *fruitless*. So I went up for some fresh air and stumbled over a body. I shouted for help and then all Gedannah broke loose."

"Can ye think of any reason Balaur would go t' yer homeland?"

He shook his head. "By the Root, I cannot, Paarjini. But I know next to nothing about the man."

"Fair enough." She turned to Nikola. "Who else do ye reckon'll be there?"

"Dmitry Falke, for certain. Cardinal Gerrault. She's running Nantwich now. Others, I suppose."

"Falke is the one who held ye prisoner and stole yer child?"

Nikola nodded.

"I'd hoped not to have dealings with the Via Sancta," Paarjini said heavily. "But we have no choice. Do ye trust any of 'em?"

"No," Nikola replied.

"Nor do I, sister. What about Kasia Novak?"

"Yes. The Mahadeva did."

"I liked her, too. She's a cartomancer, eh?"

"And Malach's sister."

Paarjini scratched her head. "What about Valdrian?"

"He helped us. So yes, I think I trust him."

"I knew him at Bal Kirith," Tashtemir put in. "He never gave me trouble. And he's loyal to Malach."

A slow nod. "Do ye ken where this audience chamber is?"

"Every Arx is the same," Nikola replied. "I know where it is."

Chapter Fifty

Cardinal Gerrault sat in the high seat, spectacles glinting in the torchlight. The two pontifices flanked her, Falke on the left, Lezarius on the right. A regal woman with short blond hair whom Nikola presumed was Bishop Morvana Zeigler stood two steps down, representing the Kvens.

Kasia Novak waited with Valdrian, Jessiel and Caralexa at the foot of the dais. She met Nikola's gaze with a slight nod.

Gerrault stood. "I have not formally welcomed the representatives from Dur-Athaara," she said in a gravelly voice. "First, let me express my deepest condolences for the loss of your queen. It was a vile deed and it shames me that it occurred within these walls." A slight pause. "If I had been aware she was here, I would have provided proper security. But we are pleased to welcome you and hope that our differences can be set aside."

After a moment's hesitation, Paarjini dipped her head. "I hope so, too," she muttered.

There was an awkward pause.

"Er, thank you, Reverend Mother," Nikola said. "The events that occurred were disastrous for all of us. I myself am formerly a citizen of the Via Sancta." Her gaze fell on Falke, who stared back, expressionless. "Unmarked. Perhaps you know that already."

Gerrault gave a slow nod. "I do, Nikola Thorn."

"Good. It's out of the way, then."

The cardinal seemed to cover a smile. "I take it you are a witch now and will be treated as such. I must say, it is extraordinary that you are here. This could well be the first time in a thousand years that our people have spoken face to face. Despite the circumstances, it is a momentous occasion." Her gaze turned to Tashtemir. "You are Masdari."

He swept a low, elegant bow. "Tashtemir Keleven, Reverend Mother."

"Ye can call me Paarjini," Paarjini said, looking around. "Where's the prisoner?"

"On the way from her cell," Gerrault replied. "I thought we'd question her in here. It's an intimidating chamber, eh? Let her sweat a little."

Nikola decided she liked this woman. "May we approach?"

"Certainly." Gerrault pushed her glasses up her nose and waved them both forward. "I confess, I'm not clear on what happened." Her voice lowered in sympathy. "But Falke tells me you are the mother of this child that Balaur . . . . " She cleared her throat. "Well, I'm very sorry."

Nikola smoothed her face. Her feelings for Rachel were such a tangle, she hardly dared to touch them. "Thank you."

Paarjini explained the concept of forcing in simple terms, omitting the bit about it fraying the seams of the known universe.

"Our sisters violated every rule when they aided Balaur's escape and they will be sorely punished when we find them," she said.

"Did you not do the same thing yourself?" Falke asked Nikola in a chilly tone. "On several occasions—"

"I had no choice." She stared at him with equal hostility. "As you well know."

"Still, Domina Thorn—"

"Let us stay focused," Kasia interrupted with a hard look at Falke. To Nikola's surprise, he flushed and closed his mouth. "The facts are these. Balaur has stolen Rachel's body, but that is not what he truly wants."

All eyes turned her way. "How do you know this?" the Kven bishop asked.

"He entered my dreams and spoke to me."

There was a shocked silence.

"He covered his tracks," Kasia said. "I didn't realize it for a long time. But I remember now. Everything." She smiled grimly. "He made a mistake in tipping his hand, but he is arrogant."

"So what *does* he want?" Falke wondered. "Surely he has returned to Bal Agnar. His forces are in the midst of a war for dominion over the continent! He can't just abandon them."

"That's what he would have you believe. But he doesn't really care what happens to Bal Agnar. Not until he achieves his true goal. To gain immortality. It's his driving obsession." She looked at Nikola. "Your daughter is powerful, but she cannot give him that. He is merely using her. A means to an end."

"He tried to achieve this with the children in Kvengard," Morvana said. "Using alchemy."

"Yes," Kasia agreed. "But he realized that the Magnum Opus will not work on him. His soul is too corrupted. He admitted that his experiment was a failure."

"The Reborn are in Jalghuth now," Lezarius said. "Where they belong."

"I'm glad. But Balaur has not given up. He mentioned something called the Amrita. Also the Aab-i-Hayat."

"That's Masdari," Tashtemir said. "It means the Elixir of Life."

"That's exactly what he called it," Kasia said. "What do you know of it?"

"Nothing. I only gave you the translation." Yet Tash looked uneasy. Nikola resolved to pump him for information later.

"This is silly," Falke said with a note of impatience. "There's no such thing."

Kasia turned to him. "It doesn't matter. What matters is that Balaur believes in it. If we wish to catch him, we must follow in his footsteps. He showed me other things. A city. He wanted to know how to find it. I tell you, he has gone after—"

She cut off as the audience chamber doors swung open and six knights entered. A bedraggled prisoner walked between them, her arms and legs in irons.

They quickly resumed their places. Cardinal Gerrault sat down in the throne with a severe expression. "Jamila al-Jabban," she said. "You stand accused of treason and conspiracy. Accessory to murder and a host of other crimes."

Nikola eyed the prisoner curiously. She was young, no more than mid-twenties. Strong brows and a bold nose. Possibly pretty, though it was impossible to tell. Her black hair was a tangle. Deep shadows ringed her eyes. She gazed up at the dais with visibly shaking hands. Then she fell to her knees, prostrating herself on the floor as much as the chains would admit.

"Please," she whispered into the stone. "I humbly beg pardon. I am an insect, unfit to look upon your magnificence. But if you spare me the torture chamber, I will tell all." A quiet sob. "The Alsakhan has cursed me. It matters not anymore."

Nikola couldn't tell if she was faking. Kasia eyed her coldly, but the others looked alarmed. Bishop Zeigler took a half step toward her before stopping herself. Lezarius stroked his chin with a troubled frown.

"Bring her to her feet," Gerrault told the knights.

They hauled Jamila up. She sagged between them, lank wisps of hair veiling her face.

"No one will torture you," Gerrault said. "That is not our way."

The prisoner looked doubtful. Nikola shared a look with Paarjini. She gave a sour shrug.

"But you *will* speak. If I am satisfied with your answers, I will consider clemency."

Jamila clasped her hands together. She looked on the verge of sinking to her knees again, but the knights held her up. "Thank you, Reverend Mother. Oh, thank you. I know a good deal!"

"I am not the Reverend Mother," Gerrault corrected. "You may address me as Your Eminence."

She licked chapped lips. "You will find me useful, I promise, Your Eminence."

"Bring her some water," Bishop Zeigler said.

One of the knights ran off.

Nikola leaned over to Tashtemir, pitching her voice low. "Do you recognize her?"

He shook his head.

"How did you come to be in Balaur's service?" Gerrault asked.

"I am not in his service, Your Eminence."

"Then whose?"

"A noble family of Luba, Your Eminence."

The Cardinal turned to Tashtemir. "Refresh my memory, Domine Kelevan. Where is Luba?"

"The southernmost of the emirates," he replied.

Gerrault steepled her fingers, turning again to the prisoner. "Go on."

"My mistress is the khedive, Your Eminence. Her name is Tawfiq al-Mirza, Your Eminence."

Gerrault sighed. "On second thought, let us dispense with the honorific, else this interrogation will last the night."

They all waited as the knight returned with a cup of water and a full jug. Jamila al-Jabbar snatched the cup and drank. Her voice was clearer when she resumed.

"Two years ago, one of my mistress's trade caravans was caught in a sandstorm on the way back from Paravai. A very bad one that lasted two days and nights. When it cleared, the hilt of a blade was sticking up from the dune where they had made camp. The winds must have uncovered it."

She clutched her dusty black robes, kneading the fabric. "There was no rust on the blade, though it must have laid hidden in the desert for a long time. A *very* long time. They brought it back." A nervous swallow. "The sword had runes. My mistress summoned her *Sahir* to read them."

"Her advisor," Tashtemir said quietly. "They are learned men. Mystics."

Jamila bobbed her head. "After some study, he told her what it was. The fabled sword of Gavriel."

Paarjini drew a sharp breath. Nikola turned to her, but the witch made a quelling motion, her eyes locked on the Masdari woman.

"I have seen the blade myself. I think this is true." She shook her head, frightened. "It has power in it. The day after it came, the man who had carried it fell ill. He died that afternoon. I think . . . I think the sword did not want to be found."

Nikola had a dim memory of her dream in the hole. *A sword of great power.* Goosebumps prickled her arms.

"Who is this Gavriel?" Gerrault asked.

Jamila's gaze flicked to Paarjini. She hung her head and said nothing.

"Speak!" Gerrault snapped.

"He was the aingeal who cut off his own mother's head," Paarjini said in a low, angry voice. "The rebel who founded your Via Sancta!"

Falke stiffened. "That is a lie!"

"'Tis the truth," Paarjini retorted. "Whether ye like or not!"

Falke had gone red. He opened his mouth when Gerrault rose to her feet, voice ringing against the vaulted ceiling.

"Let us remember why we are gathered here," she said sternly. "It is not to squabble over the past, but to learn where Balaur has gone, and why. Else there might be no future for any of us!"

Falke subsided, visibly gathering himself. Paarjini drew a deep breath.

"She has the right of it. I apologize. I ken yer beliefs are different from mine. But ye asked who Gavriel was and I told ye. In our lore, he is the aingeal who defied the Great Serpent, and that is the use for which he forged his blade. Valmitra dinna die from the blow, but it severed the aingeals from her gifts so they could no longer touch the ley. Which is why," she added, not looking at Falke, "yer kind invented Marks. Tha' is the story I was taught as a girl."

"It is the story I was taught, too," Tashtemir said slowly. "Or a version of it. The witches are the Alsakhan's children and so are my people. Three races in the beginning. But only two kept the faith."

Valdrian cleared his throat. "I have heard the name Gavriel. It was used as an ancient curse. But I never knew who he was."

Jessiel and Caralexa eyed each other. "The same," Caralexa muttered. "My ma said the tale goes back two thousand years at least. But she called Gavriel a hero. Said he did it for freedom."

Paarjini scowled, saying nothing.

"Setting our *cultural differences* aside," Gerrault said, "what does the blade mean to Balaur?" She stared down at the prisoner. "Are you claiming it grants eternal life?"

Jamila al-Jabban shook her head. "No, Your Eminence. The *Sahir* said it was but the first sign. Proof that the Alsakhan had blessed my mistress with good fortune." Dirty fingers picked at the sleeve of her dress. "Luba has many debts. We are the smallest and weakest of the emiratis, surrounded on all sides by far more powerful neighbors."

"Is that correct, Domine Kelevan?" Gerrault asked.

"I have not been home for several years," he replied, "but I cannot imagine the situation has changed much. The khedives of Luba rely on a network of alliances to preserve their territory, and it shifts as often as the sands. Their position has always been precarious."

Jamila nodded agreement. "My mistress has expensive tastes," she said with a touch of bitterness. "The treasury is nearly empty. But the *Sahir* said there are great riches to be had by whoever finds the City of Dawn."

Tashtemir gave a shocked laugh. "She cannot mean to *loot* the seat of the Alsakhan?"

Jamila looked like she wanted to shrink into the floor. "She did not use the word, but I am sure it is her intention. She has convinced herself it is the solution to all her problems."

"How did she come to be involved with Balaur?" Gerrault demanded.

"He came to her dreams. They communed in this way for the last year or so. When he escaped Jalghuth, he bade her to send someone to guide him and cement their alliance. It was always his intention to go to the League. But he . . . ." She licked her lips. "He said he had business to attend to in Nantwich first. He did not confide in me what it was. I was merely a messenger."

Nikola doubted this, but she kept her peace.

"They struck a bargain. My mistress would get the gold and jewels. Balaur would get the Aab-i-Hayat."

"The Elixir of Life," Lezarius said quietly.

"And where is this city?" Gerrault asked.

"That is the difficulty," Jamila replied. "The precise location is unknown. I think my mistress knows more, but she would not tell one such as me. Nor did she tell Balaur. She did not trust him not to go without her. He pressed me hard, but I could not tell him what I do not know, Your Eminence."

"So they have gone to Luba?"

A quick nod. "That was the plan. The khedive was awaiting his arrival."

"Did she know he has witches with him?" Paarjini asked.

"He said he had allies."

"And why did he let ye live, Jamila al-Jabban? I find it strange he'd abandon one who knew so much."

She flinched under Paarjini's skeptical glare. "It was not his intention to leave me," she said, staring at the ground. "He wanted you to remove the Raven Mark from the child. He hoped you would not realize the truth. Then he planned to take me with him."

Paarjini snorted. "Ye have an answer for everything, don't ye?"

"It is the truth, mistress."

"Can you describe the blade?" Lezarius asked.

"I can do better," Jamila said, casting a fearful look at Paarjini. "I can draw the runes for you."

"Fetch a paper and pen," Morvana told the knights.

"I have seen this city in a vision," Kasia said. "And in the cards, as well. The Sun and Moon together, representing dawn. All of it was in the last reading I gave to Malach—including a warning that Balaur would take his daughter, though I was too thick to understand at the time." She sounded angry. "I believe her."

"And the Elixir of Life?" Falke demanded. "Can that possibly be real, too?"

"Perhaps not, but if there's even a remote chance . . . ." Her face might have been set in stone. "Balaur cannot be allowed near it, Reverend Father."

No one disagreed with that sentiment.

One of the knights returned with a pad and pencil. Jamila

sat cross-legged on the floor, resting the pad on her knee. The scratch of the nib was the only sound for a minute. Then she held up the drawing.

"To the best of my memory, this is what I saw engraved upon the edge of the blade."

They looked like meaningless stick figures to Nikola, but Lezarius hurried down from the dais. He was spry for a man in his late seventies. He took the pad from Jamila and studied it briefly. When he looked up, his expression was grave.

"I saw similar runes in a chamber deep beneath Sinjali's Lance just before I came here. It had been sealed—possibly since the Lance's construction. The Reborn said they were very old. Some kind of warding charm. The children could not decipher them, but I am certain these are identical."

"You see?" Jamila said eagerly. "I tell you the truth!"

His shaggy brows drew down. "Do you know what they say?"

"They are in the tongue of the aingeals. Only the *Sahir* can read it."

"Valdrian?" Nikola prompted.

He strode over to Lezarius and glanced at the pad. "They mean nothing to me."

"Nor I," Paarjini said. "But if ye have seen them at Jalghuth, it lends credence to her tale."

Jamila clasped her hands together, rising to her knees. "I throw myself upon your mercy! I am but the khedive's servant. Hardly better than a slave! She would whip me until I was dead if she knew I had revealed her secrets." She turned to Tashtemir. "Tell them!"

He gazed at her with a guarded expression. "Not all khedives are so harsh, but a few do treat their servants like chattel. I don't know this Tawfiq al-Mirza."

He said a few words to her in Masdari. She replied in the same tongue, then switched back to Osterlish.

"Let me stay here!" Tears ran down Jamila's cheeks, cutting trails in the dirt. "Grant me asylum. Please, I beg you!"

Gerrault turned to the others. "Do you have any more questions at present?"

"I do." Kasia stepped forward. "I saw you leaving the Danzigers' manor house in Kvengard. You were with the delegation from the Imperator."

Jamila looked shocked. She licked her lips. "Well, yes, that is true."

"Does the Imperator know about this plot?"

"No! It was merely a ruse to get me to the continent without raising suspicions. That night, I met with Jule Danziger in private. He said he was Balaur's agent. I was supposed to go to Jalghuth with him, but something happened. He missed our next appointment."

"Because he was dead," Kasia said coldly.

Jamila flinched. "I do not know about that. But he did come to me eventually, at the embassy in Kvengard. He said the plans had changed and he would take me to Bal Agnar." She shuddered. "I did not like it there and was glad to leave again. That is all I know! I swear!"

"Does anyone have further questions for her?" Gerrault asked.

"Not for now," Paarjini muttered.

No one else spoke up.

"Take Jamila al-Jabban back to her cell," Gerrault instructed the knights. "See she is fed and give her a bucket to wash with."

They saluted and escorted the Masdari from the chamber. Gerrault slid her spectacles off and polished them on the sleeve of her robe.

"Well," she said at length, "what do you make of all *that*?"

Chapter Fifty-One

"I believe they've gone south to the Masdar League," Paarjini said. "And I intend to hunt down the sisters who conspired with Balaur. As for the rest of it, I canna say."

"Jamila's accent is Luban," Tashtemir put in. "Educated enough to be a high-ranking servant. The rings in her ear confirm that rank. And the beads sewn into the hem of her gown."

"What of the city?" Gerrault asked.

He seemed deeply reluctant to speak, eyes darting across the high ceiling of the chamber.

"Tell us what you know, Masdari," commanded Falke's deep, peremptory voice.

"He is a guest here, not our prisoner," Morvana protested. "It is for him to decide."

Tashtemir swallowed and seemed to reach a decision. "I heard it mentioned at the Imperator's court once or twice, but only in whispers. There is a city in the desert where the Alsakhan resides. It can only be found by the anointed. The eunuch priests. They guard their secrets closely, so I can tell you little else. Only that it is supposedly a place of wealth beyond imagining."

"Which is no doubt why they keep it secret," Falke said dryly. "Every mercenary adventurer would seek it out."

"Just so," Tashtemir said. "But also because it is a holy place. The city's true name is forbidden to be spoken. I doubt very much that this khedive can easily find it, which should buy us some time."

"Us?" Nikola dropped her voice. "I assumed you would stay behind, Tash."

He was in exile and very much on the Imperator's bad side. If he'd preferred to live at Bal Kirith with Beleth in residence . . . well, that said volumes about the punishment he faced at home.

"Do any of you speak Masdari?" he asked loudly, looking around. "Can you identify the different tribes from their dress and manner of speech? Are you familiar with the six hundred and fourteen rules of etiquette that govern daily life in the League? The routes of the caravans and what it costs to hire one?"

No one spoke.

"We are a proud people, and great believers in formality." A wry look at Paarjini. "Forgive me, but you wouldn't last ten minutes without giving insult. And if you offend the wrong person, you will swiftly find yourselves in the Imperator's dungeons."

"Which is exactly where you'll be if you go back," Nikola hissed.

Tashtemir pretended not to hear.

"I was hoping' ye would ask." Paarjini grinned. "I accept the offer with gratitude."

"I will go with you, as well," Kasia said. "I know how Balaur's mind works. Perhaps my cards can help us find him."

Nikola knew she would. The Mahadeva had foreseen it. But the next volunteer surprised her.

"As we will," Valdrian added. "If you agree."

Paarjini stiffened. Nikola shot her a hard look. "We need them," she said under her breath.

"Will ye follow my orders?"

"Until we reach the Masdar League, yes," Valdrian replied. "But if we decide to hunt Malach on our own after that, you cannot stop us."

Paarjini considered this. "Fair enough. Ye may come."

Falke leaned over and whispered something to Cardinal Gerrault. She nodded.

"I intend to keep my word," he said. "Bal Kirith is yours. So is our aid in rebuilding it."

Nikola was surprised at that, but Valdrian only nodded. "Then we'll send a dozen mages there, as planned. But I won't abandon Malach. Nor will my two cousins. The three of us will go south."

Gerrault rose to her feet. "The Via Sancta has a strong interest in the outcome of this endeavor."

Here it comes, Nikola thought.

"We will send a token force with you," Gerrault said. "Two knights from Nantwich. I wish it could be more, but we have suffered great losses. Our priority must be to find the Reverend Mother Clavis."

"You may have two from Jalghuth," Lezarius said.

"The Eastern Curia should be represented," Falke said with a frown.

"Might I suggest Fra Patryk Spassov?" Kasia suggested. "If he agrees."

"He accompanied you from Novostopol?"

"He did. And proved himself a fiercely loyal companion."

Paarjini's head swung like a cornered badger. "Hold on now. I dinna say yes!"

A silence fell. Gerrault looked at her solemnly. "I was a girl when Nantwich fell to Balaur. His victory was brief, but we had a taste of his rule and that was more than enough. Thirty years ago, we were saved by Lezarius, but it is clear now that the Void only postponed an inevitable confrontation."

She paused, looking thoughtful. "It must be done the right way this time. With all of us united against him." A nod at Paarjini. "The witches." Her gaze lit on Valdrian and his cousins. "The mages." A quick glance at Kasia. "Marked and Unmarked. Our numbers are small, but there is power in this alliance. It is a thing never done before."

Nikola remembered the Mahadeva's words when she gave her foretelling.

The three nations broken must be made whole again.

A wave of sorrow broke over her. They had lost a very wise woman that day. A hot stone of hatred lodged in her heart. Of all Balaur's crimes, that one had cost them the most.

"It is a thing I would never have imagined even one hour ago," Paarjini admitted. "But perhaps yer right. I'll take yer knights on one condition. Give us the prisoner. I have a strong feelin' there's more she's not sayin'. But I'll have it out of her on the journey."

Gerrault turned to Falke and Lezarius. "What say you, Reverend Fathers?"

"I have no objection," Falke said.

"Nor do I," Lezarius said, frowning slightly to be in agreement with Falke.

"Then Jamila al-Jabban is yours," Gerrault said.

Running feet echoed in the corridor. A knight conferred briefly with those at the doors, then trotted into the chamber. He was so agitated, he barely acknowledged the two pontifices.

"What is it?" Gerrault demanded.

"An emissary has arrived from Bal Agnar, Your Eminence!"

"Indeed?" Gerrault kept her tone mild, but her gloved hand tightened on the arm of the throne.

"A mage. She claims to have news of the Reverend Mother Clavis, but will say nothing more."

The cardinal's expression hardened. "Bring her in."

He retreated at a run.

"Well, it cannot be from Balaur," Falke said. "The messenger would have departed the city a full day ago."

"Could they already know what has happened?" Morvana wondered.

"Balaur walks in dreams," Valdrian said, eyeing the door. "They know."

A moment later, Dantarion strode into the chamber, flanked by four knights. Her hair was tied back in an auburn ponytail, her boots muddy from travel. She wore a green cloak and crimson doublet beneath. Malach's cousin.

She must have borne his child, but it was nowhere in evidence. She looked the same as Nikola remembered, young and fresh-faced, like a first-year student at the Lyceum. Her cool gaze swept the assembled company. It caught for a moment on Nikola, then moved on to Valdrian, Jessiel and Caralexa. They stared back, expressionless.

"That's far enough," one of her escorts said when she was fifteen meters from the dais.

Dantarion stopped. "Lezarius," she said with a feral smile. "You look different. But I know you nonetheless."

He inclined his head. "Who sent you?"

"The Reverend Mother, of course." Her grin widened. "Beleth."

"She is in Novostopol," Falke said slowly.

"Not anymore. The starfall broke her prison and killed the guards, but she was spared." Dantarion cast a pious glance at the ground. "It was the will of the ley."

Nikola thought of her last afternoon in Novostopol, just before Captain Komenko let her go—at Falke's orders, apparently. Beleth confessing her sins before a rapt crowd. Nikola had pitied her then, but it was the way you pitied a large, toothy predator behind bars at the zoo. You might feel bad for its state of captivity, but that didn't mean you wanted it roaming loose in your flat. A small shiver ran down her spine. Beleth, alive and in Bal Agnar.

She must be *pissed*.

"More like luck," Gerrault said crisply. "What is it you want?"

"A parley." Dantarion opened her gloved hand—no doubt a condition of entering the audience chamber—and tossed a small, shiny object to the foot of the dais. It bounced on the stairs and rolled to a stop. "Guess who we found?"

Morvana picked it up, then passed it to Gerrault, who studied it for a moment, jaw tight.

"That is Clavis's ring, if you require proof," Dantarion said. "You already know she lives or all those she Marked would be screaming in their death throes. But we're willing to offer an exchange." Green eyes glittered with amusement. "The terms are quite reasonable."

"I'm listening," Gerrault said, cupping the ring in her hand.

"The Reverend Mother seeks a return to the Cold Truce. Balaur is gone from the continent. Personally, I do not care what happens to him, nor does the Reverend Mother. We wish only to be left in peace." Her icy regard settled on Falke. "Once justice has been served."

"What are the terms?" Falke asked dryly.

"We will return Clavis and what's left of her knights. Withdraw from the Morho and occupy only the cities that are rightfully ours. Leave us alone and we leave you alone." A finger rose, pointing to Falke. "All Beleth wants is his right hand."

Gerrault stood. "Is this a joke?"

"Not at all. I think the terms are more than fair. But they are not negotiable. He took her hand. She will have one in return. Just one. He may keep the other."

"This is outrageous," Gerrault snapped. "Beleth is insane—"

"Then we will send you Clavis's hands. Followed by her feet and lastly, her head. That is the offer. Take it or leave it."

Lezarius muttered angrily. Morvana looked appalled. But Falke wore a thoughtful expression.

"Where would this exchange take place?" he asked.

"You cannot be seriously considering—" Gerrault began.

"I want to hear her out."

Dantarion inclined her head. "A wise decision. We would meet in the Morho."

Lezarius stepped forward. "Then I choose the location for this parley. We will not walk into a trap."

The others looked shocked at his swift acceptance. Falke merely nodded with a grim expression.

"Beleth expected as much," Dantarion said. "Where do you propose?"

"The shore of Lake Khotang," Lezarius said. "It lies between Nantwich and Bal Agnar."

Dantarion considered it. "The southern shore. We will not parley in the shadow of Jalghuth."

Lezarius frowned. "Very well."

"I agree," Falke said.

"Reverend Fathers," Gerrault said firmly. "I vote against this course."

"It is my decision." Falke turned back to Dantarion. "We will need a week to get there. I want assurances that Clavis will not be mistreated."

"She is in fair condition—at the moment. But if you do not appear . . . ."

"I'll be there. With an escort, of course."

"No Raven knights. If Novostopol marches north, the deal is off."

"How about Kvens?"

A grudging nod. "That is acceptable."

Morvana shot Falke a dark look, which he ignored.

Dantarion eyed the other mages. "Where is Malach?"

"He would not approve of this, Dantarion," Jessiel said.

"And that is not an answer."

"He is gone," she said carefully. "But he had his own plans for peace with the Curia. If you pursue this, you put all of them at risk."

"Is he dead?"

"No, but—"

"Then let him convince Beleth himself. Until then, I follow her orders." Her gaze fell to Valdrian's stump. "I thought you of all people would see the equity in this proposal."

A muscle fluttered at the corner of his eye. "Beleth was severed?"

"It should not have been done," Morvana muttered.

"Yet it was," Dantarion said softly. "And it cannot be taken back."

Valdrian spun on his heel and stalked from the chamber, leaving through a side door. After a moment, Jessiel and Caralexa followed.

"Let them think on what you have done," Dantarion said. "They will see the sense in Beleth's solution." Her gaze narrowed as she noticed Paarjini's eyes for the first time. A hand fell to her hip, instinctively reaching for a blade that had already been taken. "Since when," she asked slowly, "does the Via Sancta consort with *witches*?"

"Times are changin', aingeal," Paarjini replied with a chilly smile.

"If I see a single one of you bitches at Lake Khotang—"

"Ye won't. 'Tis none of our business."

"It had better not be."

There was a tense silence.

"Do you want food or drink before you return to Bal Agnar?" Gerrault asked sourly.

Dantarion dragged her gaze away from Paarjini. "No, I'll

fend for myself." She swept a sardonic bow. "I'll bring your answer to the Reverend Mother without delay. One week." She looked at Falke. "If it had been me, I'd ask for both hands. So count yourself fortunate."

She spun on her heel and marched from the chamber, the knights surrounding her in a box. The instant her footsteps had faded, Falke chuckled.

"Beleth *is* insane," he said. "And that is to our great advantage. All she had to do was stay inside the walls of Bal Agnar. We've broken our teeth against the city for months. But her thirst for vengeance will lure her out."

Lezarius slumped against the throne and shared a look with Falke. "I did not think she would agree to Lake Khotang, Dmitry. She doesn't know."

"Know what?" Morvana asked, color rising to her cheeks. "I still dislike this very much! We will be outnumbered ten to one!"

"The Reborn children have cleansed the ley there," Lezarius said. "It runs pure and clean. There is a chance that the knights who follow Beleth will come to their senses. The blue is very strong at Jalghuth." He cleared his throat. "I will consult with the captain of my guard, Mikhail Bryce. He knows the terrain well."

"Bryce served under me for years," Falke said. "He is a fine strategist. I welcome his advice."

"But won't Beleth realize the ley is different?" Kasia wondered.

"The mages cannot work the blue at all. She might not—" Morvana cut off as Caralexa jogged back into the chamber.

"Valdrian is upset," she said tightly. "Understandably so. But we will not throw Bal Kirith away over this."

"The severing was done by knights in the field," Falke said quietly. "Not at my orders. But I take full responsibility."

"Two of us will accompany you to Lake Khotang," Jessiel

said. "Give the mages who show up a choice to cease this fight and go to Bal Kirith instead."

"What about Beleth?"

"She would try to rule us just as Balaur did. We have no loyalty to her. She is old wine in a new bottle. But do you agree to spare the others if Beleth is dead?"

"You have my solemn promise," Morvana said with a quick glance at Falke. "The Kvens follow *my* orders."

"And mine," Lezarius added quickly. "I have no desire to see more bloodshed."

"What about Dantarion?" Falke asked. "Is she representative of the sentiment among the mages?"

"Beleth is her mother," Jessiel said.

Lezarius nodded. "She told me as much. I know you think she is ruthless, and she is. But I would not be standing here if she hadn't saved the children. Perhaps I can speak with her alone when we reach Lake Khotang. Appeal to her better nature."

Jessiel looked doubtful—and Nikola shared her opinion—but his words seemed to reassure the mage that every attempt would be made to minimize casualties. Assuming they weren't massacred themselves. It still struck Nikola as a risky plan.

"I will not abandon Clavis," Falke said. "Beleth knows that. I am sure she has her own plans, but she is the last figurehead of the old Via Libertas. Once she's gone, a lasting peace is more than possible." He turned to Paarjini. "Assuming you are successful in killing Balaur."

"Aye. And he is already far ahead of us. If the ship is resupplied, we will sail right away. So those of ye who mean to come better pack yer things and get down to the docks." Paarjini nodded at Gerrault, Morvana and the two pontifices. "Good luck to ye in the north."

"And to you in the south," Gerrault said seriously. "What of your queen?"

"We'll be takin' her with us," Paarjini said.

"Ah, of course. I'll order transports to the docks for everyone. Please, allow us to help in any way we can."

"Thank ye," Paarjini said. She turned to Nikola, speaking softly. "We'll bring her home eventually. In the meantime, I'll cast a spell of preservation on the bodies."

Nikola nodded, her eyes tight. They left the four leaders of the Via Sancta conferring with each other over Beleth, though Nikola's thoughts were already ranging ahead to the Masdar League and what she would do to Hashima when she got hold of her. And Bethen! All her sunny smiles took on a sinister aspect now.

The girl had been trained by Cairness. Nikola resolved to keep a close eye on the plump, ill-tempered witch. Tashtemir said she'd fought back against the mutiny aboard the *Wayfarer*, but what if it was all a clever ruse to plant a spy in their midst?

She trusted Tash. He hadn't even wanted to come back to the continent. Now he was risking his life to go home again. And Nikola couldn't bring herself to suspect Paarjini. But as for everyone else . . . She'd have to be very, very careful.

Kasia caught up with the three of them at the door to the audience chamber. "I would bring my friend Natalya Anderle, as well, if you agree."

Paarjini barked a mirthless laugh. "Why not? The more, the merrier. I dinna expect half of Nantwich to board my vessel, but it seems we will lack not for company."

"There's a dog, too."

She waved a hand, not breaking step. "As long as it's tame."

"She is. Sort of." Kasia's hand shot out, drawing Paarjini to a halt. "I have a favor to ask. A big one."

"What now?" Paarjini demanded impatiently.

"I heard you can remove Marks. Alexei's brother has one he needs to be rid of. It's . . . it's killing him. A Nightmark given by Malach—"

Paarjini's voice softened. "I'm sorry, but I canna help ye."

Kasia's face fell. "Why not?"

"The erasure of Marks is a gift given only to the Mahadeva. Perhaps the next ones can do it. But 'tis not within my power."

Kasia looked away, clearly disappointed. "I had to ask."

"Best round up yer friends and join us on the *Wayfarer*. I ken the Mahadeva said yer important, but I don't care to wait for stragglers."

"We'll be there," Kasia promised.

Chapter Fifty-Two

Kasia returned to the audience chamber and looked around for the Kven bishop. Morvana stood on the steps of the dais, speaking with Falke. He beckoned her over.

"We were just talking about the old days," he said. "You're both too young to remember."

"I've read the histories," Morvana said.

"Books." Falke chuckled, though there was little humor in it. "When Tessaria left for Bal Agnar in '49, she confessed to me that she was afraid. More afraid than she had ever been. The war had not yet begun, you see, but we all knew it was close. You cannot imagine the terror in that city. Everyone dreaded the knock on the door. The police wagon pulling up in the dead of night. She said she didn't know if we would win, but that wasn't why she fought."

Falke drew a breath, holding Kasia's gaze. "She said she fought because they were fascists. That is the only reason she needed. If you understand what they are, then there is no other choice. Even if you *know* you're going to lose, you fight anyway."

"We won't lose," Kasia said.

Falke nodded. "I hope not. Give my regards to Natalya Anderle. Keep her safe."

Falke had given Natalya her dragon Mark.

"I will," Kasia promised.

He looked like he might say more, but Morvana Zeigler was standing there. Falke settled for a brusque nod and strode off to catch up with Bishop Gerrault.

"May I have a word, Your Grace?" Kasia asked.

Morvana Zeigler nodded. "Certainly."

"It seems Mikhail Bryce will be going north for this parley," Kasia said.

"Naturally. Lezarius holds him in high esteem. Why?"

The bishop didn't know about Mikhail's Nightmark. Kasia chose her words carefully.

"It would mean a great deal to Alexei if you kept an eye on him."

Morvana frowned. "He is healing. I think he'll be fit to ride by the time we depart."

"It is not his body that suffers."

"I know he was Invertido," the bishop replied slowly. "But I thought the Mark was restored."

"It was. But Alexei feared . . . echoes remain. That he might try to harm himself." *Or others.*

The bishop looked alarmed. "What is it you want me to do?"

"Just be kind to him." Kasia paused. "I gave him a reading this morning. I saw you in the cards, Your Grace."

Her brows drew together. "What?"

"You are the Chariot of Justice," Kasia said. "You stand for truth, fairness, the rule of law. These ideals are a bedrock part of your nature."

She took out her deck and found the card. Morvana studied it. When she looked up, her face was taut. "This is my Mark."

"The deck was made months before you came here,"

Kasia said. "By a woman who had never met you. It is the ley who named you, Bishop Zeigler."

Morvana shook her head in wonder. "I heard that you used it in this way, but I . . . ." She flushed slightly. "I did not entirely believe it."

"Understandable. But I've learned the hard way that when the Major Arcana are involved, we must listen. And the message is that you are important to Mikhail in some way. I know you have other responsibilities, but Alexei used to look after him and he's gone now. I have no one else to ask. Just be a friend to him."

"But how can he be fit for this journey if he is unstable?"

"Lezarius would never leave him behind. They, too, are bound together."

Morvana turned as a group of Kven knights approached. "I must go," she said. "There is much to do. But I promise to try my best."

"Thank you, Your Grace."

"Peace be upon you," Morvana said, striding away to greet her knights.

Kasia felt guilty keeping the Nightmark a secret, but she felt sure he didn't pose a danger to the bishop. Morvana Zeigler might be able to reach him—or at least slow the Mark's progress. She represented the faith that Mikhail was losing. There was something pure about her. As much as Kasia had grown fond of Falke, he had the ability to ratio-nalize almost anything in service of the Curia. But Bishop Zeigler had refused to carry any weapon when she went to the stadium, which Kasia thought very brave.

She set off for the Villa of Saint Margrit hoping to find Patryk and Natalya. She hadn't seen either of them since breakfast, which felt like a hundred years ago. To her frustra-tion, neither was there.

Obviously, they had no idea what had happened. They

could have gone anywhere. And she feared that Paarjini would keep her vow not to wait for stragglers.

After a moment's consideration, she used a Key card to jimmy the locks and rummage through her friends' belongings. Spassov would want his carton of *Encore* cigarettes, reading glasses and case, dirty books, and a spare cassock. She shoved it all into a bag.

Natalya had a ludicrous quantity of clothes, shoes and accessories, most of them living on the floor. Kasia chose only a few practical items, including charcoals, paper and pencils so Natalya wouldn't moan the whole way. When she was done, she sat on the bulging suitcase and flipped the latches. Natalya carried her knives everywhere and Kasia didn't bother hunting for them.

She lugged everything to the guest house by the kennels. Kasia quickly packed a small bag for herself. Her gaze landed on the book Alexei had loaned her, sitting on a table with the other texts on alchemy she'd dug up from the archives. *Der Cherubinischer Wandersmann* by Angelus Silesius. She leafed to the last page, studying the image that Alexei said had haunted him since the first time he saw it.

It was the same picture Balaur had shown her.

A city of golden minarets. Around the edges, a sun and moon and seven keys, each of a different shape and size.

Die Stadt der Morgenröte. The City of Dawn.

"I'll find you, Bryce," she said quietly, her chest tight. "If I must search for the rest of my life."

Kasia wrapped the book in a nightgown and carefully stowed it in her valise. She was tempted to do a reading, but decided to wait until she was on board the ship. When she went outside, she found a car waiting. The young tousle-headed priest behind the wheel helped her load all three cases in the trunk.

"It's not all mine," she explained. "I need to find two more people. Can you wait just a minute while I run over to the kennels?"

"Cheers." He slid behind the wheel and turned the heat up.

Kasia found the hound lying under a tree while half a dozen others bounded around the yard. Kasia knew Alice right away from her size and the scar along her haunch. As usual, the hound didn't notice her until she crouched down and held out a hand.

Alice gave a desultory sniff, but didn't lift her head.

"I am going to find Alexei," Kasia said. "Big brother."

A pointy ear twitched. Her tail thumped, once.

"I think he would want me to take you, Alice, even though it will be dangerous. We must go on a ship. I suppose you came on one from Jalghuth, so maybe you don't mind the sea. I hope to find your master. He is lost, you see."

The hound didn't speak Osterlish and showed no sign of interest. Her eyes went dull again.

Kasia rooted through her cards and found The Knight. She filled it with blue ley and held it out.

Alice jumped to her feet as if goosed. She barked once, loudly. The other dogs stopped playing to watch.

"Yes!" Kasia laughed. "Him!" She stood up and held the hound's intelligent gaze. What was it Alexei used to say? "*Veni.*"

Alice understood the Old Tongue command for *come*. She trotted at Kasia's heels and leapt into the waiting car, sticking her snout out the window. Kasia looked around the Arx. It was vast. Where could they be? Seized by a sudden inspiration, she popped the trunk and wrestled with the overstuffed suitcases until she found one of Spassov's black socks. She held it out to Alice, who eyed her quizzically.

"What's the Old Tongue word for hunt?" she asked the priest.

He scratched his chestnut mop. "Present imperative?"

"I guess so."

"Er, *venari*, I think."

Alice seemed to grasp what she wanted, for she jumped out again and sniffed around, then arrowed off for the gates. Kasia leapt into the passenger seat and buckled her seatbelt.

"Follow that Markhound!" she cried.

The priest gunned the engine. They sped up to the gates, slowing for the first portcullis, the tunnel, the second portcullis, and the bridge over the Caerfax River that led into the city. Traffic was light and he managed to keep the glowing blue paw prints in view, though Alice was already far ahead.

The trail led down to the docks. Kasia was starting to wonder if Natalya had some psychic ability she was unaware of when she spotted Alice sitting outside a tavern. A creaking, weather-beaten sign declared it to be The Cat & Custard. The priest put the car in park, letting the engine idle as she got out.

Kasia peered through the grimy window. They were playing darts. A pitcher of beer sat on the table, next to an ashtray with a burning cigarette and a half-empty bottle of Androniki vodka, rimed with frost. Natalya threw her head back and cackled. She wound up and threw a bull's eye while Spassov watched with a long-suffering scowl.

Kasia knocked on the glass. They turned with identical expressions of surprise. Spassov took a swallow of beer and ambled to the door, Natalya at his heels.

"She cheats," he said.

"It's called talent, you motherless ox," Nashka said, slinging an arm around his waist. She seemed a bit unsteady on her feet. All for the better, Kasia thought evilly.

"I suppose you're celebrating," she said with a smile.

"Damn straight," Natalya agreed. "Come join us!"

"What would you say to a nice holiday? In warmer climes?"

"The beach?" Natalya looked down with a frown. She

wore a stretchy minidress and clunky, battered boots. "Forgot my bathing costume though, didn't I?"

"Don't worry, I packed it for you."

Spassov, the professional alcoholic, eyed her suspiciously. "Where are we going, Kasia?"

"Your chips are up!" the barmaid called. "Extra vinegar!"

"Grease," Natalya muttered. "Yes."

Alice trotted over, tail wagging. She gnawed at the scar on her haunch, then lifted her muzzle and gave a mournful howl. Patryk met Kasia's eye with new sobriety.

"Oh, no," he whispered.

"Finish your ciggie." She patted his cheek and turned to the barmaid. "They'll take those chips to go."

———

IT HAD BEEN a long time since Morvana Zeigler felt like she had a firm grasp on events—any grasp at all, really—and she didn't like it.

She'd always run her office like a tightly wound clock. All her aides knew their tasks and carried them out to her satisfaction or she had them reassigned elsewhere. She was not without compassion, but she believed in efficiency and details. Planning and foresight.

Now Kvengard was rudderless. The knights treated her like some sort of pontifex-in-waiting, which was ridiculous. She was only twenty-nine! Somehow, she'd promised to escort Dmitry Falke north through the Morho to meet one of the worst people in modern history, who commanded legions of deranged soldiers and planned to chop Falke's hand off.

Madness.

What she *should* do is return to Kvengard and try to sort this mess out. But then, she thought, Clavis would die. And it will be my fault.

She strode along the pathway, muttering to herself, barely

aware of the curious glances from a group of passing vestals. If all that were not enough, Kasia Novak had entrusted her with a former Beatus Laqueo who was, apparently, suicidal. Alexei's brother.

Poor Alexei.

It was all a great deal to process. She only knew the ley through Marks, but the witches did extraordinary things with lithomancy, things she'd never even dreamt of.

And cartomancy—not just a party trick after all. Seeing herself gripping the reins of the Chariot of Justice had sent a chill down her spine.

The ley *knew* her.

Morvana's steps slowed at the infirmary. She asked the duty nurse which room was Captain Bryce's and was given a number on the second floor. She went upstairs and felt relieved when she heard Lezarius's voice through the open door. At least she would not be the one to break the news to him.

Morvana stood for a moment in the hall. She didn't want them to think she was eavesdropping. She was about to leave and come back another time when Lezarius emerged.

"Morvana," he said in surprise. "I did not expect to see you here."

"How is he?"

"Worried, of course. He is eager to be out of bed."

"What do the doctors say?"

"Another day or two and he will be walking."

"That's good."

"Well, it's kind of you to come. All his friends are gone."

She smiled, feeling awkward. "I will say hello . . . unless you think he prefers to be alone?"

"He might prefer it, but I doubt it would be good for him." Lezarius smiled, though she saw concern in his eyes. "I will return later."

The elderly pontifex made his way down the stairs.

Morvana eyed the open door, then released a sigh and approached. Mikhail Bryce lay in bed wearing a dark blue hospital gown. Light bandages covered his feet. He was staring out the window, but his head turned as he sensed her presence.

"Captain," she said. "I hope I'm not disturbing you."

He half rose from the bed and she held out a hand. "Please, don't get up."

He sank back against the pillows with a frown. "Why are you here, Your Grace?"

"I'm very sorry about your brother."

Blue eyes sparked in sudden anger. "He's not dead!"

"I didn't say he was," she replied evenly. "I'm sure they will find him and bring him back to you."

The glare softened. "I apologize, Your Grace," he muttered. "You had nothing to do with it."

She studied him for a moment. "You needn't use the honorific, Captain Bryce. Morvana will do."

"That is not appropriate. You are a Kven bishop."

"I am an excommunicant."

He scowled. "By order of a dead pontifex who betrayed everything the Via Sancta stands for."

"Fair enough. But Luk *was* pontifex at the time. Under Section Four of Curia law—"

"You sound like my brother." The ghost of a smile played at the corner of his mouth.

"We are much alike," she conceded. "I enjoyed working with him. He has a logical mind."

"Overly, sometimes."

"How can one be too logical?"

"One can be logical and still refuse to face reality."

"I'm afraid you've lost me, Captain Bryce."

He looked away. "If you are to be Morvana, than I am Mikhail."

She smiled. "Did Lezarius tell you I would be bringing a company of knights north with you?"

"He did." The lines at the corners of his eyes crinkled. "You see? I am not the only one who still deems you a bishop. The Kvens agree."

"They are desperate for someone to follow."

"I think they could do worse, Your—" He cleared his throat. "Morvana."

The way he pronounced her name, with a thick Osterlish accent that swallowed the vowels and slightly rolled the *R*, warmed her. It was an unwelcome development.

"I don't wish to keep you," he said. "I'm sure you have other duties."

The perfect excuse to take her leave. She did have other duties—a hundred of them. Messages needed to be sent to the clergy in Kvengard she hoped were loyal. She had to meet with Cardinal Gerrault about supplies. The list was endless.

But he looked pathetic lying there with his bandaged feet and she had promised Kasia to make an effort.

"I have time for a game," she said, eyeing the chess board. "If you'd like to play."

He frowned and she thought he'd refuse the offer. But then Bryce cocked his head, a challenge in his gaze. "Do I dare pit my own meager intellect against that logical mind of yours?"

"Not so meager, I think," she said. "But be warned. My pacifism does not extend to the board. I am merciless."

He laughed and started to arrange the pieces. "I hope you are." He palmed two priests, one of each color, and held his gloved fists out. Morvana tapped the left. He opened his hand.

"Black," she muttered. "Then you will have the advantage of the first move."

His face relaxed as he lined up his priests, adjusting each one just so. The forts, knights and bishops came next, followed by the cardinal and the pontifex. The pontifex was the weakest piece, the cardinal the most terrifying, capable of sweeping across the board in any direction.

She wondered what his opening gambit would be. Much could be read about a person in the style they played. When Bryce slide his f2 priest two squares forward, she knew she was dealing with an aggressive player and one not averse to risk. She defended with a priest to d5, and the game slid into a reverse Gottschalk pattern. The slaughter that ensued nearly ended in a draw, but she finally managed to corner his pontifex between her last remaining knight and bishop. Mikhail tipped the piece over with a wry smile.

"Well played. I saw that coming six moves ago but was powerless to stop it."

"Only six? I planned it from the start."

"No, you didn't. Or you would have used the Vorokov defense at your nineteenth move."

She snorted. "Again?"

He looked like he wanted to. But then his gaze slid down to her right thigh. The Chariot of Justice. Covered now, but he stared for a moment as though he saw the Mark through her robe. Mikhail shook his head.

"Thank you for visiting," he said stiffly. "But I should rest."

"Of course." She stood. "I will come again before we leave for the north."

He looked alarmed. "There's no need for that."

She studied him. "Do you remember the story I told you at the stadium?"

"I'm afraid not."

A lie. She could see it in his eyes.

"It isn't the suffering but the cause that makes the martyr," she said.

His gaze flickered. "Sutra sixty, line four."

"Yes. What is *your* cause, I wonder? And is it worth it?" She patted his gloved hand. "I will stop in tomorrow, Captain. Give you a chance for revenge."

Despite himself, his mouth quirked. "I thought forgiveness was one of the five virtues, Your Grace."

"Oh, it is. The most important of all, in fact." She laughed, feeling unaccountably light of heart. "But we are only human, *ja?*"

THE *WAYFARER* OCCUPIED a slip at the long pier where the ferries docked. The air smelled of fried fish and coffee and engine oil and the salty tang of the harbor.

The Mahadeva, Valmitra grant her eternal rest, was stowed in the hold, her three bodies wrapped in white linen and wound with charms to keep the flesh from decaying until she could be given a proper funeral in Dur-Athaara. Assuming they made it back.

Nikola had sat with them for a while, thoughts drifting. She kept going over the terrible events in that room. It *wasn't* Rachel, she knew that, but the image of her own daughter wielding the knife was hard to forget.

She wondered what she could have done differently. If there was any way it could have been prevented, or if the Mahadeva was right it was part of Valmitra's grand plan.

She kept remembering the Maid's words as she left the ship, knowing she went to her death.

It's a beautiful day.

Nikola hoped she would have that same courage herself when the time came.

If even half of what Jamila al-Jabban said was true, they faced a formidable enemy in the khedive of Luba. Two witches and six knights were belowdecks guarding the prisoner, who had been hauled aboard sobbing and kicking up an awful fuss. When she realized where they were taking her, Jamila had begged them to slit her throat or simply throw her overboard in her chains. She'd only quieted down when Ashvi threatened to deliver her to her mistress naked and stuffed into a sack.

Neither Cairness nor Ashvi had been pleased to see any of the foreigners, but Paarjini was in charge and they'd angrily acquiesced—both still red-eyed from their queen's murder.

Now Nikola stood at the stern with Tashtemir and Paarjini as a long black Curia car pulled up, disgorging three people and one Markhound.

"It's Kasia Novak," she said, watching the group unload bags from the trunk. "I haven't met the other two."

One was a burly, balding priest of about forty. He juggled a suitcase in one hand and a bag of chips in the other, with a cigarette dangling from the corner of his mouth. A skinny woman with big blonde hair and sunglasses dragged another suitcase behind her, this one on wheels. Her skin was as dark as Nikola's, so the hair must be a bleach job. A dragon Mark wound around one arm.

The sunglasses made it hard to gauge her expression, but she seemed to be looking around in confusion. Kasia took her arm and guided her to the gangplank. The dog faded in and out like flitting sun shadows. Nikola wondered how Markhounds felt about witches. And if lithomancy would even work on the creature, should it turn out to be hostile.

"They're the last," Paarjini said with a brisk nod. She looked relieved to be underway.

Captain Aemlyn gave an order and the crew leapt to prepare the ship for departure. The *Wayfarer* had three masts with triangular sails. In short order, they were hoisted and bellying with a fresh breeze. The mooring ropes had just been tossed to the dock when two small figures in green cloaks came hurtling down the pier.

"Nikola, Nikola!" the taller one cried, waving a hand. A bow bounced on her back.

Tashtemir muttered an oath in Masdari.

"Who is it now?" Paarjini asked with an edge of exasperation.

"The kids," Nikola said.

The gap to the pier was widening. Another few seconds and they'd be left behind. Better that way, she told herself. This mission was too dangerous.

They were too dangerous.

Syd drew close enough to see the streaks of dried tears down her cheeks. They had nothing but the ragged clothes on their backs. Where would they go? The Morho Sarpanitum?

Nikola sighed and caught the captain's eye with a nod.

"Come on, then!" Aemlyn bellowed, waving.

Sydonie grabbed her brother's hand and leapt, landing in a hard sprawl on the deck. Nikola hurried over.

"Are you all right, honey?" she asked, crouching down.

Syd gave her a gap-toothed wince. "Yeah. I hurt my knee a couple days ago. Then one of the Wolf knights kicked me at the stadium." Her lips trembled. She grabbed Nikola's hand. "Everyone left us behind!"

"We know what happened to Rachel," Tristhus said, scowling.

"She's our *cousin*." Syd's expression darkened. "Mirabelle says she'll make Balaur pay!"

"Mirabelle?"

Sydonie pulled her sleeve up, showing Nikola the Mark of a creepy red-haired doll with one squinting eye. "Please let us come along. We got nowhere to go."

"And we want to help Cardinal Malach," Trist put in. "He's our favorite."

The boy stared past Nikola's shoulder. She turned and saw Valdrian, relief on his handsome face.

"I looked everywhere for you two!" he exclaimed, tugging at his blond beard. "Where were you hiding?"

"Nowhere," Trist mumbled with a shifty sideways glance.

"We have to tell," Syd said firmly, reaching into her cloak.

"We searched Jamila's room just in case the grown-ups missed anything important." A snort. "Of course they *did*. We found this sewn into her pillow."

She showed Nikola a small figurine of a fox with enormous ears.

"A *fenak*," Tashtemir said. "They live in the desert."

"Carved from black amber," Nikola said thoughtfully. "A charm against nightmares."

"Well, we know Jamila isn't stupid," said Kasia Novak, striding up to join them. She looked down at the children with a smile. "I'm pleased to see you again."

They eyed her with a touch of awe. "You're the cartomancer," Syd muttered.

"That's right." Kasia reached out and closed the girl's fingers around the figurine. "Keep this with you, child. You'll need it to block Balaur from your dreams."

A solemn nod. "I will."

"You can also return my carnelian bracelet," Nikola added.

Syd eyed her innocently. "What?"

"The one you just took." She held out a hand. "Give it up, or I'll use magic to shake you upside down until it falls out."

Syd fished in her pocket and handed over the bracelet. "I just meant to *borrow* it——"

"Right," Nikola said dryly. "Why don't you both get settled in the cabin with Caralexa and Valdrian?"

He gave Nikola an amused smile.

"Thank you, Nikola!" Syd hugged her tight, planting a sticky kiss on her chin.

"You're welcome. But you must behave yourselves."

Sweet, merry laughter. "We promise! Mirabelle says she will, too!"

Nikola counted her jewelry again as Valdrian led the children to the ladder heading belowdecks. Kasia trailed along behind, gathering her two friends.

"Let's see if I have this straight," Tashtemir said, leaning on his elbows over the rail. "Kasia is Malach's sister."

Nikola nodded.

"And she asked you to remove Malach's Mark from the brother of the priest who got—" He splayed his fingers and made a fizzing noise.

"Zapped to who knows where?" Nikola nodded. "Right again."

"Did ye know about any o' that business before?" Paarjini wondered.

"No, but . . . ." Nikola frowned. "Ohhh."

Tashtemir arched a brow.

"I think I understand why the Mahadeva said the Great Serpent has a sense of humor."

"Eh?" Paarjini grunted.

"Well, wherever Malach went, him and that priest were in the same box. So they're together."

"I don't ken ye."

Nikola gave a queasy laugh. "I'll have to ask Kasia for the whole story, but I imagine they don't get along very well."

The *Wayfarer* slid past the harbor mouth. The lights of Nantwich dwindled behind. Paarjini stared at the southern horizon, one hand fingering the lump of fool's gold at her neck.

"I'd say tha's the least o' their problems," she said softly, "wouldn't you?"

Chapter Fifty-Three

"Nikola!"

Alexei groaned. He rolled over and spat out a mouthful of grit. The movement made his stomach clench. He spent the next minute dry-heaving. The air was an open forge.

"*Nikola!*"

Reddish sand and deep blue sky swam into focus. A dark silhouette stood atop a dune, hands cupped to its mouth, bellowing.

"NIKOLA!"

The shouting was like a hatchet to his skull, cleaving it in half.

"Please stop," Alexei whispered.

"Nikola! Paarjini!"

A slew of curses.

There was nobody around to hear.

Nobody at all.

The last thing he remembered, he was breaking down a door.

It was at the Pontifex's Palace. Yes—the Arx in Nantwich. Kasia was with him.

What happened after that splintered into muddled fragments. Two groups of women were inside the room. Some old, some young. Vast amounts of ley focused into high-pressure jets bounced around. He'd felt a sickening sensation of weightlessness. Blinding light and a terrible noise. Then a headlong slide down a dune.

He pushed himself up. The silhouette turned, backlit by the sun. Blurring movement and it was on top of him. A fist caught his jaw, knocking him flat again.

"Motherfucker!" Malach screamed. "This is *your* fault!"

Instinct kicked in. He brought his knee up, driving it between Malach's spread legs. The mage toppled, curling into a ball. Alexei grabbed his hair and slammed his head against the sand. He would have kept going, but the movement made him want to vomit again. He collapsed next to Malach, who gave a weak kick. The mage's bare hand was too close for comfort, but Alexei lacked the energy to crawl away.

"Touch me again and you're dead," he said, closing his eyes.

Malach coughed. He said something that sounded like "gaaarrrr."

Neither of them moved for a long time. The sun blasted down overhead like the glaring eye of a vengeful god. It was very quiet.

Malach was the first to get up. Alexei tensed, but he just brushed sand from his face and staggered away.

"Where are you going?" Alexei called, rolling to one side.

No answer.

"Hey! Where are we?"

Malach glanced back. "Fuck if I know."

Alexei felt a thin layer of surface ley flowing westward toward the sinking sun. Barren desert stretched to the horizon. He scrambled to the top of the dune. There was an armchair on the other side, silk brocade with a pattern of crossed keys, and a square of carpet, scorched at the edges. A hand with jeweled rings rested on the carpet. The stump was cauterized.

He stared at that for a minute.

"I'm dreaming," Alexei muttered.

But he never dreamed. And everything hurt—too vividly. His right temple thumped like a bass drum. Nausea came and went in waves. Looking at the hand didn't help.

"Wait," he croaked, sliding down the dune after Malach.

The mage did not wait. He seemed to blame Alexei for their predicament. But Malach knew more than he was admitting. He seemed angry, but not completely disoriented.

The witches did this to us, Alexei realized. But why? And where were they?

He looked around at the endless, rippling ocean of sand. There were no deserts in the Via Sancta.

For an awful moment, Alexei wondered if he was actually in the skybox at Westfield Stadium, pumped full of Sublimin and living his worst nightmare while Rademacher drank beer and laughed.

But that made no sense either. His worst nightmare would be set in the Morho Sarpanitum, not this wasteland.

Malach dwindled to a speck on the horizon. The stars came out. Alexei didn't recognize any of the constellations. At last, he lay down and fell into an exhausted sleep.

He did not dream.

MALACH WALKED THROUGH THE NIGHT, hoping to find something, anything, but there was nothing.

Just more sand.

It could only be one of the emiratis. The witches had forced a box with his daughter inside. For some reason, it hadn't worked as planned. He and the laqueus had been dragged along and dumped somewhere else.

But he would find them.

Malach couldn't think about Rachel for more than two

seconds before his brain kicked the door shut and locked up the horror lurking behind it. It was unbearable, in the literal sense. If he dwelled on what had been done to his daughter, the rage and grief would bring him to his knees. It felt like an animal digging razor claws into his chest. Shredding him open.

No, he would focus on finding civilization and making a plan. The Mahadeva had said she contained the *thing* inside Rachel. She'd tried to save her.

The Maid had died in his arms. The one he liked best.

He pressed a hand to his forehead, eyes hot. Malach firmly closed the door. *I won't think about that now. Not just yet.*

He wished he knew more about the Masdar League. All those years with Tashtemir and he'd never thought to ask questions. Not that Tash was eager to talk about his homeland. The southerner had his own locked doors.

By midday, Malach started to worry. If he didn't find water soon, he'd be done for. The League occupied a continent that was smaller than the Via Sancta and bigger than Dur-Athaara, but he had no other sense of scale. The desert might be a thousand kilometers wide. Five thousand. He had no idea.

Then he crested a dune and saw something other than another dune. He saw a faint line of blue smoke. Malach made for it with renewed vigor. He crawled to the top of a hill. Down at the bottom was a circle of covered wagons and long-necked animals sitting in the sand. There was a fire going, though he didn't see any people. He was downwind. The aroma of roasting meat would have made his mouth water if he had any spit left.

He watched for a minute, pretending to be smart and get a handle on them first, but he knew he would go down there even if they turned out to be slavers. He didn't care if they put him in chains as long they gave him water and a ride out.

But first he had to get rid of his shirt. It was stiff with the

Maid's blood. They'd think he was some kind of maniac. He buried it deep in the sand and scrubbed his chest.

Then he half-hiked, half-slid down the dune. The beasts followed his progress with mild interest. They had lumpy backs and long curly eyelashes. He walked up to one of the wagons and knocked on the door. It was made of fine-grained *bokang* wood, lacquered to a gleaming finish, with words painted in cursive script he couldn't read.

It was opened by the most extraordinarily beautiful person Malach had ever seen. Long, blue-black hair. Eyes like onyx, fine high cheekbones and a delicate, chiseled jaw. Flawless skin of an olive hue. They wore an embroidered silk robe, also very beautiful, belted at the waist. He couldn't decide if they were a man or a woman, but it seemed to make little difference.

"Ehlah," he croaked, which was the only word he knew in the southern tongue. *Hello.*

The almond eyes widened in surprise. They turned their head to someone in the wagon. A fluid stream of Masdari issued forth. The voice was on the deep side and Malach decided he was male.

"Ehlah, ehlah." The vision stepped back, gesturing for him to enter.

Definitely a man, he decided, though slight of build. The robe was open in a deep vee, revealing the flat planes of his chest. A silver chain hung around his neck, with a single yellowed claw.

Malach climbed the steps. The reprieve from the scorching heat nearly made him weep.

There were two others in the wagon, reclining on silken pillows. One wore only a pair of loose trousers. His head was shaved. Just a boy. The other was a woman, dark-skinned and full-lipped, wearing a sheer gown. Malach's eyes moved downward. Or perhaps not a woman in every respect.

The first one moved gracefully to a pitcher and poured

him a cup of water. He pressed it into Malach's hands with a smile, nodding.

The water gushed down his throat, releasing cramped muscles. His head cleared a little. Malach emptied the cup. The man refilled it. He drank again and held it out. Another stream of Masdari. Malach shook his head. The man pantomimed getting sick and made a gesture that he should wait a little bit. He pressed a hand to his chest. "Hassan," he said.

Even his voice was exquisite, clear and of a pleasing timbre somewhere in the middle of high and low.

Malach nodded and repeated the gesture. "Malach."

The boy gave him a shy smile. "Ameer," he said.

The third one looked him up and down with faint amusement. "Koko," she said.

They conferred among themselves for a minute, obviously confounded at how he had come into their midst. There was no way to pantomime being forced in a lithomantic box from the Via Sancta so Malach merely smiled and nodded when they glanced at him.

The cushioned lounge area must double as sleeping quarters. The rest of the space was devoted to chests and boxes and racks of clothing. He pointed to a vanity table with a mirror and bench, raising his brows in a question. Hassan nodded, shooing his hands to please, sit down.

Malach sat. He studied himself in the mirror. Unshaven, burnt by the sun, filthy, drenched in salt sweat. He felt like a wild animal who had barged into some lovely garden party. Cosmetics covered the vanity, pots of umber and vermilion, soft rose and shimmery bronze. Stands held wigs of various lengths and textures. His saviors were all so pretty, he could scarcely imagine what they looked like in full makeup. Only Koko wore any at the moment, a touch of coral lipstick and shadow that made her dark eyes even larger.

Hassan touched Malach's arm. He pointed to his stomach. "Jawan?"

"Very jawan," Malach agreed.

They stepped out of the wagon. He instantly broke out in a sweat again. It was obvious why they stayed inside. But people were emerging from the other wagons now and erecting an open-sided cloth pavilion. Three were big and bearded, with curved daggers at their waists. Hired guards, no doubt. The other four wore elegant silk robes like Hassan. All eyed him curiously.

Hassan went over and explained things. Malach could imagine what he was saying. *I don't know, this unkempt foreigner just appeared among us, we'd better feed him something.*

He thought of the laqueus. The priest did have a name— Alexei Bryce. Whom Kasia was apparently in love with. What would he tell his sister when he saw her again?

Malach eyed the skewers of roasting meat, then climbed to the top of the hill, shading his eyes. Nothing to the east. Nothing to the west. To the south . . . a tiny speck.

Stumbling along in the wrong direction.

Malach watched for a minute. Bryce had stabbed him in Novostopol. He'd probably do it again given half a chance. If he hadn't barged into the chamber, Rachel might be safe in his arms right now.

Of course, she wasn't really Rachel, was she?

Malach slammed the door.

He went back down and approached Hassan, pointing at the dune. Hassan frowned. Malach mimed walking with his fingers and pointed again. Hassan gave an apologetic shrug.

"Does anyone speak Osterlish?" he asked, looking around.

A young man in his early twenties drifted forward. The only fair one, with blue eyes and improbably pale skin. He wore a big straw hat and kept the rest of himself well covered up.

"A little," he said in a thick Kven accent.

Malach blinked in surprise. "You come from the continent?"

A nod. "When I have thirteen years. On a boat."

The Kvens traded with the League, Malach remembered. It was the only city in the Curia that had diplomatic relations with the Golden Imperator's court.

"My companion, he is lost." Malach pointed. "Over there. Not far." He shaded his eyes again. "I see him. Not far."

"*Ja!*" The boy nodded. He turned and spoke rapidly in Masdari.

Thus it came to pass that twenty minutes later, Malach slid down from a camel and poked the laqueus with the toe of his boot. "Get up," he said.

Alexei Bryce raised his head. He looked so bad, Malach almost felt sorry for him.

"Or stay here," he said. "But they tell me it's a long walk out. Like a week."

Alexei got up. He made it four steps before he fainted again, but one of the guards had come along to make sure Malach didn't steal the camel. Together, they draped him between two humps and walked back to camp.

The sun finally drowned behind the dunes in a blaze of orange. Alexei was stripped and wrapped in wet towels and tucked into one of the wagons after deliriously accepting a few mouthfuls of water. Malach figured he'd make it. The bastard was fairly tough.

The rest of them gathered around the fire in folding canvas chairs. Hassan gave him a white *thawb*, which was a loose ankle-length tunic that buttoned down the front. It felt cool and soft against his burned skin.

The Kven, he learned, was called Karl, though that was just his given name. He went by Katy Wulf when he performed. Koko was always Koko. Hassan was also Sultana, the Bride of Azzabad, and Karl said she was the most celebrated singer in all of the emiratis.

The others gave their names, but he was too tired to remember them.

Malach devoured two skewers of meat and a sweet, creamy custard with rice and raisins. Bottles of wine were uncorked. He was still dehydrated so he stuck with plain water. Everyone was kind to him, even the guards. They laughed a lot and were very expressive with their hands and bodies, in the Masdari fashion.

Speaking in broken Osterlish, Karl conveyed that men who were also women, or women who were also men, were considered divine in the League, blessed of the Alsakhan, and feted wherever they went. This group were mainly singers and dancers, though Koko also recited poetry. They were on their way to Paravai for the celebrations surrounding the transfer of power from one Imperator to the next, which involved two weeks of parties and parades and street festivals. It was a long journey to the capital, at least a month, and they planned to stop in various cities and towns along the way.

Malach knew there was no hostility toward mages in the League—Tash had told him as much—so he opened the *thawb* and formally pointed to his Marks by way of explaining who he was. Koko swept over in a rustle of diaphanous fabric, oohing and ahhing over each one with dramatic flair. She especially liked the Lady of Masks.

Hassan declared Tiger in a Cage to be his favorite. Ameer was enamored of the two-headed snake Malach had named Today for Tomorrow. Much debate and teasing ensued, though he didn't understand half of it.

Koko cupped his chin and turned his face this way and that, examining him critically. She had a gentle touch. It felt pleasant, like having someone comb your hair. There was more rapid talk in Masdari, and more laughter.

"She says you are not half bad under all that . . . hmmm, fur?" Karl said.

"I'll shave it off if you have a razor." He mimed scraping a blade down his cheek.

Karl laughed. "Yes, we have that." He touched his own face. "Must be very smooth for the stage, *ja?*"

Malach caught Hassan's eye. He sprawled in one of the chairs, loose-limbed and relaxed, surveying his brood with the serene gaze of a merchant prince whose fleet always enjoys fair weather. A cup of wine dangled from slender fingers, though he hadn't drunk much.

"Will you take us with you?" Malach asked. "I'll do any work you need. Anything."

Karl translated. Hassan smiled and made a reply. The others all nodded.

"He says the word for *guest* and *stranger* is the same in this land," Karl said. "You are both welcome for as long as you wish to stay, Malach."

"How do you say thank you?"

"Shalam tak."

"Shalam tak," Malach repeated. "But I mean it. I don't mind earning my keep."

Karl frowned.

"Doing work," he explained.

"*Ja*, maybe," Karl said, though Malach had the sense it was just to make him stop asking.

It was cozy with the wagons circled around and the fire crackling and the low murmur of voices. Malach pondered his luck in stumbling across the caravan. If not for that thin line of smoke, he would have ended up a pile of bleached bones. And his daughter—

Malach kicked the door shut. But he knew they would ask and he decided to tell the truth—or part of it at least.

"How do you come here?" Karl asked, looking around at the emptiness on all sides, "to this place?"

"Witches," Malach said. "Very bad witches."

"Charbaz!" he exclaimed, choking on his wine.

Hassan leaned forward, dark brows drawing together.

"Charbaz?"

The others looked both appalled and sympathetic.

"Charbaz," Malach echoed with an exaggerated grimace, relieved to find they disliked witches as much as he did.

Koko drew her gown more tightly around herself, crossing her arms. She said something with great emphasis.

"We will hide you," Karl said. "If they come."

"Shalam tak," Malach said.

Hassan looked troubled, but he nodded agreement.

"Jamila al-Jabban," Malach said. "Do you know this name?"

The company looked at each other and shook their heads.

"What does she look like?" Karl asked.

Malach described her. When he mentioned the seven silver rings in her ear, Karl perked up. "Left or right?" he asked.

"Right."

"Ah! She is the servant of a khedive. The inner household. What color are the beads on her *abbaz*? Her cloak?"

Malach thought for a moment. "Blue and white."

"Those are the colors of Luba. Is this Jamila a friend of yours?"

After a moment, Malach nodded. "Yes. Will you pass through Luba?"

"In ten days or so, if we are not slowed by a storm."

Malach's heart beat quicker. He had a starting point. A place to begin the hunt.

Hassan finished his wine and rose to his feet. The others followed suit. Malach hardly knew them, yet he felt strangely protective. The odds were long that Hashima would come walking up in the middle of nowhere, but the witches must be in the Masdar League. He didn't want to bring suffering down on these nice people. Once they reached Luba, he would make his own way from there.

One of the guards kicked out the embers of the fire. He

expected to be handed a blanket, but Koko took his hand and led him to one of the wagons. She pointed to the script on the side, then to herself. He smiled and traced it with a finger. That's what her name looked like in Masdari. It was more elegant than Osterlish, sinuous and curving.

Her wagon was smaller than the rest, but she seemed to have it to herself. Thick carpets covered the floor. She threw the shutters open and cool air spilled inside. She lit a candle and pointed to the stack of cushions, then sat down at a tiny table and began to rub cream into her face. Malach lay back and laced his hands behind his head. There were show posters on the walls, and framed portraits of Koko looking fabulous. Lots of books, too. She recited poetry, he remembered.

He didn't realize she was wearing a wig until she took it off. She had short, wiry hair underneath. It was matted from the hairpiece and she fluffed it with her fingers.

"You're still pretty," Malach said.

She couldn't have understood, but she smiled anyway.

Koko blew out the candle and lay down next him. She smelled of vanilla. He hoped he wasn't too offensive. If water hadn't been at a premium, he would have bathed. But that would have to wait for the next village.

"Tab marwak," she said sleepily, plumping her pillow.

"Tab marwak," he repeated. "Good night!"

Koko giggled. "Good night," she whispered, making the words sound hopelessly exotic.

He heard wagon doors slamming outside, a snatch of song and burst of laughter. Then silence. Malach closed his eyes. Within seconds, he slid into oblivion.

Hours later, when the moon was just a silver sickle above the horizon, he stirred in his sleep. One hand crept to his belly, where the kaldurite burned with sudden fierce cold. A frown creased his brow. Then it grew smooth again.

Thwarted, the Dreamer skulked on.

There were many others to visit this night.

Afterword

The fourth and final book in the Nightmarked series, **City of Dawn**, comes out in May 2023. You can find links to all retailers at www.katrossbooks.com.

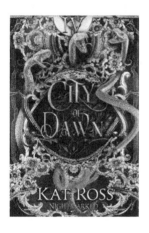

Sign up for my newsletter so you don't miss new releases, as well as a free book and exclusive sales and discounts!

Glossary of People, Places & Things

Alexei Vladimir Bryce. A priest with the Interfectorem and former knight of Saint Jule. Suffers from severe insomnia. Marks include the Two Towers, the Maiden and the Armored Wasp. Enjoyed a successful law career before joining the Beatus Laqueo.

Alice. A Markhound and loyal friend to Alexei. Has a scar on her haunch from Beleth and harbors a special hatred for nihilim.

Arx. The inner citadels of the Via Sancta, they're akin to small cities and sit atop deep, churning pools of ley power. The Arxes in the two rebel cities were largely spared by the Curia's bombing campaigns, but they've fallen into ruin.

Bal Agnar. Situated in the northern reaches of the Morho Sarpanitum, amid the foothills of the Torquemite Range, called the Sundar Kush in Jalghuth, the city was abandoned after Balaur's defeat. Emblem is the Black Sun, a circle with twelve jagged rays.

Bal Kirith. Twin city to Bal Agnar, located in the central Morho on the Ascalon River. Its emblem is a Broken Chain symbolizing free will, although slavery and abuses were rampant. Before the war, the city was controlled by a small, vicious oligarchy with the blessing of the Church, led by Beleth.

Beatus Laqueo. A specialized Order of the Knights of Saint Jule whose name means *Holy Noose* in the old tongue. Notorious for using extreme tactics against the mages. Motto is Foras admonitio. *Without warning.*

Beleth. Malach's aunt and the former pontifex of Bal Kirith. Fond of wigs, powder and decadent parties, she's spent the last three decades writing books of poetry and philosophy that are banned throughout the Curia, as well as a manifesto on the *Via Libertas*, a counter ideology to the Via Sancta that embraces the Shadow Side as inevitable and argues for the rule of the strongest. Despite Beleth's eccentricities, she's cunning and formidable with a sword. Dotes on Malach, whom she raised as her own.

Balaur. The former pontifex of Bal Agnar. His symbol is the Black Sun. Believed dead since the war, he still has secret followers in every city. His Tarot card is The Emperor.

Cairness. A witch of Dur-Athaara, very hostile to the mages.

Cartomancy. Divination using cards. Kasia uses it to foretell the future with oracle decks made by her best friend, Natalya Anderle. In Novostopol, it's fairly lighthearted entertainment, often done at parties, but also for certain wealthy men and women who are devotees of the occult.

Casimir Kireyev. The archbishop of Novostopol, head of the Office of the General Directorate. Widely believed to be the Pontifex's spymaster. Gnomelike and bespectacled, he is one of the most feared men in the Church.

Clavis. The Pontifex of the Eastern Curia in Nantwich. The youngest ever to wear the ring, Clavis's special powers encompass doors, boundaries, and crossroads. A keeper of knowledge and technology from the past.

Corax. The word for *raven* in the old tongue. Symbolizes Fate's Messenger, a bridge between the material and spiritual realms. In common parlance, coraxes are copper coins given to knights in the field and used to identify bodies burned or mutilated beyond recognition. One side is engraved with the owner's name, while the other side indicates the Order within the Curia.

Dantarion. A bishop of Bal Kirith, she is Malach's cousin and daughter of Beleth. Also the mother of Malach's second child.

Dark Age (second). A cataclysmic period a thousand years before in which the world devolved into violent anarchy. Led to the founding of the Via Sancta and the abolition of most technology.

Dmitry Falke. The Pontifex of Novostopol, his card is The Hierophant. A keeper of dogma and tradition, but also ruthless in his quest to save the Via Sancta. He led the Curia to victory against the Nightmages and defeated Balaur in single combat, severing three of his fingers. Balaur's signet ring is now encased in a glass paperweight on Falke's desk.

Dur-Athaara. Capital city of the island of Tenethe, part of the witches' realm across the sea in the far east.

Feizah. The former Pontifex of the Eastern Curia in Novostopol, she was killed by Mikhail Bryce when he was Invertido.

Ferran Massot. The chief doctor at the Batavia Institute. Marked by Malach. Conducted illicit experiments on his patients, in the course of which he discovered Patient 9's true identity as Lezarius.

Interfectorem. The Order tasked with hunting and detaining Invertido. Emblem is an inverted trident. The name means *murder* in the old tongue.

Invertido. Unfortunates whose Marks suddenly reverse, causing insanity. Symptoms include narcissism, paranoia, lack of remorse and severely impaired empathy. A genetic component is suspected as it often runs in families, although the condition can be deliberately inflicted using abyssal ley. Generally believed to be incurable.

Jalghuth. The capital of the Northern Curia, it's located in the far north. Surrounded by glacial fields with hundreds of stelae to repel nihilim. Its emblem is the Blue Flame. Motto is Lux et lex, *Light and law.*

Jamila al-Jabban. A Masdari advisor of Balaur, claims to be a servant of the khedive of Luba.

Kasia Novak. A cartomancer with a rare ability to work the ley through her tarot deck. Classified as a sociopath by the Curia, although she adheres to her own moral code and doesn't always act selfishly. Her cards are both The Mage and The High Priestess.

Kvengard. The capital of the Southern Curia, it sits on a rocky, windswept peninsula between the Northern and Southern Oceans. Emblem is the Wolf, often depicted running in profile.

Ley. Psychoactive power that upwells from the core of the planet. Neither good nor evil, it's altered by interaction with the mind. Divided into three currents that correspond with the layers of consciousness: surface (blue), liminal (violet) and abyssal (red). These opposing currents flow in counterpoint to each other. The ley itself can become corrupted when thousands of people behave in selfish, wicked ways.

Lezarius. The Pontifex of the Northern Curia in Jalghuth. Also called Lezarius the Righteous. Creator of the Void and the stelae. A geographer by training.

Liberation Day. A holiday commemorating the surrender of the mage cities and the end of the civil war, marked with parades and celebrations in the streets.

Light-bringers. Also, **lucifers** and **aingeal dian**. What nihilim were called before Beleth and Balaur led their fellow clergy to disgrace and excommunication from the Via Sancta, they are a species distinct from humans, although the differences all involve the structures of the brain. Light-bringers learned to use the ley and offered refuge to those fleeing the Second Dark Age.

Lithomancy. Divination/magic using gems and minerals. Practiced by the witches in Dur-Athaara. Kaldurite, for example, absorbs the ley and prevents it from being used against you.

Lucas Gray. Chief aide to Clavis and a cardinal of Nantwich.

Luk. The Pontifex of the Southern Curia in Kvengard. His unique talent is wielding the ley as an evolutionary force. Luk created the Markhounds and the shadow mounts used by Kven knights.

Mage trap. Four interconnected Wards that form a box with no ley power inside the boundary. Can only be activated by someone with Holy Marks. During the war, it was one of the few effective defenses against the nihilim.

Mahadeva Sahevis. The witch-queen of Dur-Athaara. Has a triple aspect of Mother, Maid and Crone.

Malach. A mage of Bal Kirith. His card is The Fool, the most powerful of the Major Arcana.

Maria Karolo. A bishop at the Arx in Novostopol and head of the Order of Saint Marcius, which enforces the *Meliora*.

Markhounds. Creatures of the ley, bred to detect specific Marks. Invaluable during the war to hunt nihilim in the ruins. Now the hounds are mainly used by the Interfectorem because they sense it when someone's Marks invert and start to howl.

Marks. Intricate pictures on the skin bestowed by someone with mage blood. Civil Marks suppress anger, greed and aggression and enhance creative talents. They primarily use surface ley. Holy Marks are only given to the clergy. They can use the deeper liminal ley and twist chance. However, if the person who bestowed the Mark dies, it causes a sickness that begins with hallucinations and is invariably fatal.

Masdar League. A federation of kingdoms to the south of the continent, it is composed of seven Emiratis and ruled by the Golden Imperator, who serves a seven-year term. The name means the League of the Source.

Meliora. The foundational text of the Via Sancta. Written by the Praefators, it has forty-four sutras dealing with the human condition. Its title means "for the pursuit of the better." The *Meliora* argues that form of government is irrelevant and the root of all evil is violence against Nature and ourselves. Technology is a false panacea that creates social disharmony. According to the *Meliora*, the Church itself will eventually become obsolete when society reaches a state of utopia.

Mikhail Semyon Bryce. Alexei's older brother. A former captain of the Beatus Laqueo, he spent four years at the Batavia Institute. Marked by Malach. His card is the Knight of Storms.

Morho Sarpanitum. The primeval jungle at the heart of the continent.

Morvana Zeigler. A Kven bishop who takes on Alexei's Marks. Luk's Nuncio in Novostopol. Her card is The Chariot of Justice.

Nantwich. The capital of the Western Curia, it sits on the shore of the Mare Borealis. Emblem is Crossed Keys.

Natalya Anderle. A free-spirited artist and unrepentant rake. Kasia's best friend, she teaches herself to throw Tessaria's knives.

Nightmage. Also called **Nihilim**. A somewhat derogatory term to describe light-bringers after their fall from grace. They wear blood-red robes and maintain a church in exile called the *Via Libertas* that espouses a version of extreme free will. In Bal Kirith, they have human servants who've been promised wealth and status when the mages regain power. Motto is Mox nox: *Soon, nightfall.*

Nightmark. A Mark bestowed by a mage, distinguished from the Civil and Holy Marks given by the Curia in both form and function. First practiced by Beleth and Balaur, it allows the Marked to tap abyssal ley and to twist chance in their favor more directly and violently. In return, they are beholden to the mage. Nightmarks morally corrupt over time and the images are much darker in tone than regular Marks.

Novostopol. Capital of the Eastern Curia. Humid, warm and rainy. A port city, it sits amid two branches of the Montmoray where the river empties into the Southern Ocean. Despite the dreary climate, Novostopol is a lively place, with bustling cafes and nightlife. Thanks to the system of Civil Marks, crime is virtually nonexistent.

Office of the General Directorate. The most powerful organ of the Curia, headed in Novostopol by Archbishop Kireyev. Ostensibly, it oversees the other offices and reports directly to the Pontifex. Has a vast intelligence network and used to run covert operations in the mage cities. Emblem is the Golden Bough.

Oprichniki. A regular force of civilian gendarmes in Novostopol. Uniform is a yellow rain jacket and stylish cap. They carry only batons.

Order of the Black Sun. Human followers of Balaur who have awaited his return. Most bear an alchemical Mark of a small circle inside a triangle, inside a square, inside a larger circle.

Order of Saint Marcius. Tasked with enforcing adherence to the philosophy laid out in the *Meliora*, in particular, the tight restrictions on technology. Emblem is a sheaf of wheat.

Oto Valek. An orderly at the Batavia Institute. On the payroll of Archbishop Kireyev and the OGD, Oto is a shady mercenary—and a bad penny who just keeps turning up.

Paarjini. A witch of the *laoch*, the Guardians who protect Dur-Athaara. She captured Malach.

Patryk Spassov. A priest of Novostopol, Alexei's former partner at the Interfectorem and good friend to Kasia and Natalya.

Perditum (pl., perditae). Feral humans who live in the Void. Once residents of Bal Agnar and Bal Kirith, they were warped by the psychic degradation of the ley before Lezarius created the grid. Some are more intelligent than others, but all succumb to bloodlust when the ley floods. Smart enough to fear and avoid Nightmages (whom they recognize by scent), but anyone else is fair game. Also called leeches.

Praefators. Founders of the Via Sancta, they were visionaries who discovered how to use the ley through Marks. The name means *wizard* in the old tongue. Most now comprise the canon of Saints, but due to the tumultuous upheavals of the Second Dark Age, little is known about the first Praetators beyond their names. It is assumed they were all light-bringers.

Praesidia ex Divina Sanguis. Protectors of the Divine Blood, in the old tongue. Founded by Cardinal Falke, this secret Order strives to ensure the continuation of lucifer bloodlines in service to the Via Sancta. Motto is Hoc ego defendam. *This I will protect.*

Probatio. The office of the Curia that administers morality tests. Emblem is a trident, indicating all three layers of mind.

Rachel. Malach and Nikola's daughter, she has the ability to work celestial magic. Her card is The Star.

Reborn. Also called *The Wandering Cherubim*. The children from Kvengard who survived Balaur's alchemical Magnum Opus. They live at Sinjali's Lance and have a deep connection to the ley. The Reborn are immortal and have the ability to read minds, although they are incapable of doing harm to any living creature.

Saviors' Eve. The night before Den Spasitelya (Saviors' Day), a holiday commemorating the building of the Arxes. It has a grimmer theme, with young people donning masks and costumes evoking the evils of the Second Dark Age.

Sinjali's Lance. A focal point of the ley in Jalghuth.

Sweven. A memory, vision or fantasy shared directly with another person through the ley, as if they're experiencing it firsthand.

Stelae. Also called **wardstones**. Pillars engraved with Wards to repel nihilim. Found in the Void at the junctures of the ley lines. Most stelae are emblazoned with an emblem of the Curia (Raven, Crossed Keys, Flame, or Wolf, depending on the location) and a pithy maxim such as *Ad altiora tendo* (I strive toward higher things), *Fiat iustitia et pereat mundus* (Let justice be done though the world shall perish) and Vincit qui se vincit (He conquers who conquers himself).

Sublimin. A psychotropic drug used to bestow or transfer Marks, it temporarily dissolves the barrier between the conscious and unconscious.

Sydonie. A young Nightmage at Bal Kirith, sister to Tristhus.

Tabularium. A vast archive, it's one of the few buildings in the Arx to have electricity. The Tabularium holds files on every citizen of Novostopol, as well as a separate register for members of the clergy. An even larger Tabularium exists in Nantwich, with records dating back to the Second Dark Age.

Tashtemir Kelavan. A veterinarian who serves as the only doctor at Bal Kirith. Tashtemir was forced to flee the Masdar League when he offended the Golden Imperator, who put a bounty on his head.

Tessaria Foy. A retired Vestal and godmother of Kasia Novak. Close to Cardinal Falke and Archbishop Kireyev. In her mid-seventies, Tess was an elegant and enigmatic figure. Murdered by Jule Danziger.

Tristhus. A young Nightmage, brother to Sydonie, whose lead he follows without question.

Unmarked. Individuals who fail the morality tests administered by the Probatio and are denied Marks. The lowest caste of society, they live by the charity of the Curia since few will employ them. All the chars at the Arx are Unmarked, as proclaimed by their gray uniforms. Unmarked comprise about one percent of the population. In Novostopol, they're relegated to a slum district called Ash Court.

Valdrian. A mage of Bal Kirith, he wears a spring-loaded blade on the stump of his hand (which was severed by knights when he was just a teenager). Cousin to **Jessiel** and **Caralexa**.

Valmitra. The three-headed serpent goddess worshipped by the witches. They believe she coils around the core of the planet and her breath is the ley. Called the *Alsakhan* in the Masdar League.

Via Sancta. The Blessed Way. A social, scientific and spiritual experiment to improve humanity. Teaches non-violence and beauty in all things.

The Void. Also called the **Black Zone**. The region where the ley has been banished. Encompasses the cities of Bal Agnar and Bal Kirith and most of the Morho Sarpanitum.

Wards. Symbols imbued with emotional power that concentrate the ley for a specific purpose. Some repel nihilim, others force the ley from a particular area (see mage trap). A surge can cause them to short for minutes to days, but they self-repair. Most use surface ley and thus glow bright blue. Activated by touch.

Acknowledgments

Thanks as always to Laura Pilli and Leonie Henderson, my first and best readers; to Carol Edholm, whose sharp eye caught a slew of errors that nearly snuck through; and to Mom, for everything.

About the Author

Kat Ross worked as a journalist at the United Nations for ten years before happily falling back into what she likes best: making stuff up. She's the author of the Nightmarked series, the Lingua Magika trilogy, the Fourth Element and Fourth Talisman fantasy series, the Gaslamp Gothic mysteries, and the dystopian thriller *Some Fine Day*. She loves myths, monsters and doomsday scenarios.

www.katrossbooks.com
kat@katrossbooks.com

facebook.com/KatRossAuthor

instagram.com/katross2014

bookbub.com/authors/kat-ross

pinterest.com/katrosswriter

Also by Kat Ross

Made in the USA
Monee, IL
03 September 2022

13134182R10402